Ciresi, Rita.

Pink slip.

$21.95

DATE			

Pink *Slip*

Pink *Slip*

Rita Ciresi

Delacorte Press

Published by
Delacorte Press
Bantam Doubleday Dell Publishing Group, Inc.
1540 Broadway
New York, New York 10036

Chapter One was published in a slightly different form in *Quarterly West*.

The trademark Delacorte Press® is registered in the U.S. Patent and Trademark Office.

Library of Congress Cataloging in Publication Data

Ciresi, Rita.
    Pink slip / by Rita Ciresi.
        p.   cm.
    ISBN 0-385-32362-X
    1. Italian Americans—New York (State)—Fiction.   I. Title.
PS3553.I7P5   1999
813′ .54—dc21   98-21130
                                                CIP

Manufactured in the United States of America
Published simultaneously in Canada

January 1999

10 9 8 7 6 5 4 3 2 1

BVG

for Celeste

Acknowledgments

I wish to thank the Collins C. Diboll Foundation, the Pirate's Alley Faulkner Society, the Ragdale Foundation, the University of South Florida, and the Virginia Commission on the Arts for their generous financial support, and Kathleen Jayes and Geri Thoma for their suggestions on the manuscript.

My deepest thanks to my husband, Jeff Lipkes, for his editorial advice and encouragement.

Pink *Slip*

O love, love, love!
Love is like a dizziness;
It winna let a poor body
Gang about his biziness!

—JAMES HOGG

Chapter One

I Know You Are, But What Am I?

1985

On my twenty-fifth birthday, my mother gave me a man.

This was unusual. I hadn't received a gift from Mama since my father had a massive coronary four years before. After Daddy's death, Mama claimed I didn't appreciate her last birthday gifts (the turquoise nylon briefs and the plastic Pagliacci shower cap), nor did I carry the tote bag she had ordered after sending in sixteen blue stickers off the Chiquita bananas—so that would be the end of any largesse from her social-security check, thank you very much.

I started to protest, then thought better of it. "Fine by me," I told Mama. Because the tote bag showed a dancing twelve-inch Carmen Miranda banana shaking a pair of maracas to this message: JUST PUT ONE IN YOUR MOUTH. I needed those kinds of gifts like I needed the kind of whopper crotch infection I got after wearing those polyester birthday briefs Mama surely had picked out of a Railroad Salvage Store bin labeled: CHOO-CHOO CHEAPO ASKS SHOPPERS—CAN YOU BEAT THIS PRICE? FIVE FOR A BUCK! Mama must have been having trouble with her bifocals that day, because not a single one of the five briefs was the right size. Either that, or she didn't like how skinny I was getting and hoped I would eat enough to fill out first a size six, then a size seven, and then three size eights.

Twenty-five was a big birthday for me—if only to put twenty-four behind me. On the cusp of my quarter-of-a-century anniversary on earth, I found in my kitchen cabinet a monstrous rodent chewing himself blue in the face on a Brillo pad, causing me to bag Brooklyn and my grunt job in publishing and move out to the 'burbs—Ossining, to be exact, where I had landed an assistant-manager position in the Editorial division of Boorman Pharmaceuticals, whose corporate headquarters squatted like a behemoth battleship in the middle of the lush Hudson River Valley. The job—or rather, the seemingly hefty paycheck attached to it—permitted me to rent an apartment with a closet and a real bathroom sink. I bought my first car—a silver Toyota Corolla—and wondered, as I drove it back to Con-

necticut to show it off to my mother and sister, if I would get free samples
of drugs.

It was unusually hot for May, and my T-shirt was soaked through by
the time I made it to New Haven. The only way I could afford the car was
to have the dealer strip it of the power brakes, the power steering, the floor
mats, the cassette player—and, unfortunately, the air-conditioning.

"You want me to remove the engine too?" the salesman asked.

"You can keep that in," I said, as I signed on the bottom line. After he
asked me, too pointedly, if I'd like to take a ride up to Hyde Park in his
fully air-conditioned Celica, I told him, "Sorry, I need to stay home and
clean out my vegetable crisper." I honked my horn long and loud when I
left the lot. Cocky men like that gave me the creeps—yet sometimes they
had their uses. In my brief but wanton sexual career in the city, I prided
myself on having whipped more than a few hopeless characters into datable shape—or at the very least I had pulled the plug on one sheepskin-
lined water bed and trained its owner not to wear black shoes with tan
pants, and vice versa. But the quest for a tolerable Friday-night escort was
slow going. A girl could easily get discouraged. She also could get desperate. I posted the car salesman's business card on my freezer door, underneath a magnet that said MONEY STINKS, BUT BOY DO I LOVE THE SMELL! just as a
reminder of that.

At home I found my older sister, Carol, parked on my mother's red
plaid couch. Why Carol ever had gotten married was beyond me. She
moved only two blocks away and visited Mama every afternoon. Her husband's name was Alfonso. Everyone called him Al. His middle name was
Dante. Carol didn't even think this was funny. Al Dante was the ultimate
in *guido*: He used to work for our father's cement business before Daddy
died and the company went under. Al drove a gold Cutlass with a jacked-
up rear. Al said, "Whazzadoin' now?" whenever he got annoyed at Carol—
which was practically every time she opened her mouth—and every Friday
night he took his bowling bag down to the Ten Pin. Once Carol begged me
to come along to watch, and I actually saw Al make the sign of the cross
before he sent the big black ball barreling down the alley. "Fuggin' A!" he
hollered when the Holy Mother granted him a strike.

But Al loved Carol, in a way no man yet had loved me. I knew it from
the way he came up behind her and licked—like a kitten lapping at a bowl
of milk—the back of her neck as she washed the dinner dishes. And Carol
loved Al, in a way I had yet to love any man—I knew it from the way she
squawked, "Get outta here," and jumped so hard that dish soap flew like
joyous Spumante bubbles over the faucet and dishwater dripped from the
sink.

Sometimes I envied what my sister and her husband had together: a closeness that allowed them to sit in silence after dinner, Al crushing walnuts with my father's old pewter nutcracker and Carol using a silver dentistlike implement to pick out the meat, saving the particularly good-looking nuts to pop into Al's mouth. Other times I thought that what Carol and Al had between them was nothing more than what my own parents had possessed: a beat-up car, a chipped front porch, and a worn shag carpet. Like my mother, Carol wore an apron every day. Like my father, Al never dressed up except to go to a wedding or funeral. On such occasions Al would not let Carol wear high heels, because then she would be taller than he was. "Why don't you just tell Al to go blow?" I asked once, and Carol said, "Oh, for God's sake, Lisa, until you get married yourself, you just won't get it. You don't get it." Then she sighed as she bent over the creaking wicker laundry basket and sorted Al's underwear into one pile and hers into another. His and hers. His and hers. I watched her, horrified. If that was marriage, I thought, those two could have it.

The back door of my mother's house usually was locked against murderers, burglars, and aunts who wanted to borrow (without asking) my mother's prized no-stick lasagne pan. But the early advent of summer apparently had melted down Mama's caution. I let myself in through the screen door.

On the couch, Carol dropped her knitting needles and clutched the double skein of white yarn in her lap. "Lisa, you scared me. I lost count of my purls. Besides, you could have been a rapist!"

"Why don't you lock the door if you're so scared of that?" I asked.

"Because it's ninety degrees outside!"

"Tell me about it," I said, wiping my face on my wet T-shirt. "How can you knit in this heat?"

Carol resumed clacking her teal-green needles together. "I just got these new number nines," she said. "And this great white yarn for half price—" Then she brayed up the stairs, "Ma. Maaaaa! The working girl is here!"

There was a thud—my mother's feet hitting the ground as she rolled out of bed from her afternoon nap—and then the dull sound of something being dragged along the bare wooden floor. My mother came downstairs the way things usually got done in my family, *culo avanti*—or in regular English, *bass ackwards*. On each step Mama bumped a long brown box that reminded me of the cardboard coffin my cousin Dodici and I used to fashion out of the container that held our five-foot artificial Christmas tree.

Dodie and I were strange kids. We liked to play funeral.

"What's that?" Carol asked.

"For the birthday girl," Mama said. After making a real production out of dragging the box downstairs, Mama hoisted it up so easily I suspected there was nothing but tissue paper inside. She motioned me to sit down on the couch and put the box in front of my feet. Carol made annoyed clucking sounds as she gathered up her white yarn and looked so enviously at the box I could tell she hadn't a clue about the contents. The sheer size of the box seemed to promise that whatever was inside would make up for all those past bad gifts and prove that Mama was a real mother.

Then I remembered how the words *real mother* always were used as an insult in junior high.

YOUR UNIQUE SECURITY PRODUCT HAS ARRIVED! the outside of the box announced in green letters. With the sewing scissors Carol reluctantly offered me, I slit the tape. When I turned down the flaps, a man mannequin—dressed in a white V-neck T-shirt—solemnly gazed back at me. He was naked from the waist down. On his head he wore a navy Yankees cap exactly like the one that had belonged to my father.

"It's a dead man," Carol said. "In Daddy's baseball cap!"

"It's not a real *uomo*," Mama said. "Not a real man."

"I can tell that, Mother," I said, as I checked his groin and found only two white buttons—big as cream doughnuts—that connected his limp cloth legs to his more substantial body.

"You put him in the car," Mama said. "Next to you. While you're driving. So people don't think you're alone."

I reached into the box, uncertain how I should retrieve the man from his resting place—by the waist or the legs or the arms. Finally I grabbed his head—which was covered, beneath the Yankees cap, with very nonthreatening reddish hair—and pulled him into my lap, where I discovered (from the soft, lamenting fart sounds he made) that the top half of his body was fashioned from vinyl and full of hot air. He wore an ID tag around his neck that gave his name and dimensions: *SECURITY MAN is a life-size simulated male who appears to be six feet tall and weigh 175 pounds. When not watching over your well-being, he easily deflates and stores in his own optional tote bag.* I riffled through the tissue paper left in the box, but apparently the tote bag was a luxury Mama had not indulged in. A repair patch, however, was included.

"You like him?" Mama asked.

"I've never dated a redhead," I said.

"Or any man in a baseball cap," Carol added.

"Where's his pants?" I asked.

"Nobody sees him from the waist down if you're driving," Mama said. "What if I get pulled over by a cop?"

"He's supposed to scare away strangers," Mama insisted.

In one of our rare sisterly moments—usually inspired by our mutual amusement at Mama—Carol and I looked at one another and cracked up laughing. I thrust Security Man into her lap like a beanbag and then she tossed him back. He was the guy nobody wanted to dance with, the one you loathed to sit down next to at dinner, the one to whom you confided you were considering joining a convent, so Saturday night was—sorry, Charlie!—totally out of the question.

Security Man looked up at me. He had a smooth face and impassive brown eyes, like one of the crash dummies used to test seat belts or demonstrate CPR. I had the insane urge to slit his lips with Carol's scissors and thrust my juicy tongue into his dry mouth.

After Carol asked Mama, "Why'd you waste your money on that useless piece of *wuss*?" my mother wrinkled up her nose, not because she disapproved of the word *wuss,* but because it was yet another Americanism she didn't understand. Mama defended herself by saying she had heard— from Auntie Beppina—that in Ossining there was a maximum-security prison—with a Chinese name—right in my own backyard.

"Sing Sing guys are all locked up," I said.

"Even if they did get out," Carol said, "I doubt they'd go for women."

Mama narrowed her eyes. "Every time I turn around you're telling me there's more of that funny stuff in the world," she said. "I don't believe it."

That's exactly what she said—*Holy Mary Mother of God, non posso crederci*—when she found out, six years ago, that my cousin and best friend Dodici was gay. It was Holy Week. We were all in the kitchen making lasagne—Carol chopping a dozen hard-boiled eggs, me slicing the meatballs, and Mama stirring the sauce and the noodles—when the phone rang. We knew it was Auntie Beppina the moment the conversation degenerated into a lot of spitty Sicilian that neither Carol nor I could follow. We figured Auntie Beppina and Mama were talking about something gross, like piles or boils or some great-aunt's carbuncles, until Mama hung up and returned to the kitchen, gesturing with both hands back toward the phone.

"Auntie Beppina . . . she calls . . . from the emergency room . . . she goes to me . . . she says . . . *Madonna,* Dodie's a *uomo.*"

Carol let out a gleeful bleat. "*Homo,*" she corrected Mama, at the same time I told my mother, "You don't take people to the emergency room for that!"

Mama pressed her lips together. "It's Zio Gianni—on the table at

Saint Raphael's—he got so mad at Dodie, he lost his breath and had a heart attack."

"Whoa, Ma," I said. "Backtrack."

Mama gestured to the phone again. "Auntie Beppina . . . she says Dodie comes home today for Easter—from that school—with the name that sounds like a dog, I always forget—"

"Duke, Ma," I said.

"—and what's he got on him? In his ear? An earring in his ear. Auntie Beppina, she don't say nothing. Zio Gianni, when he gets home, it's the first thing he notices. And he goes to Dodie, *What you got in your ear?* and Auntie Beppina, she tries to save Dodie, she tries to tell Zio it's something to do with a fraternity, but Gianni, *madonna mi,* you know what a temper he has, he tells Dodie to get that earring out of his ear or get the—" Mama paused. "You know Gianni, he used the F word."

Carol and I let out mock gasps, which seemed to convince Mama that we were appropriately shocked. She lowered her voice to imitate Zio Gianni. *Get that earring out of your ear or get the F out of this house,* he says—and Auntie Beppina said he got so mad he didn't even give Dodie a chance to make the choice, he just reached over to rip out the earring. Dodie started bleeding—"

My stomach sunk. Carol let out a nervous laugh, which showed she still held a grudge against Dodie—and me—for making a scene at her wedding by slow-dancing, complete with lunges and dips, to "Strangers in the Night." She probably was still pissed that I rebuffed her efforts to throw me the bouquet. "Stand in the back," she had whispered, "on the right, and I'll wing it right toward you. But what's the matter with you, giving me that face, don't you want to catch it? It's not like it's cheating, it's not like it's a sin, and even if it is, just go confess."

To keep the peace I had stood where Carol told me, but when that ballistic missile of lilies of the valley and baby's breath came careening toward me, I dodged it, an act that my mother observed and frequently commented upon for at least two years afterward. Dodie also created another minor scandal that same afternoon, by remaining seated in front of his plateful of melting spumoni and soggy wedding cake and ignoring the pleas of the obnoxious deejay (*All eligible bachelors are called up to the dance floor!*) to catch the garter. My mother also noted his refusal but had not commented upon that.

"The blood!" Mama repeated. "The blood, Beppina says, squirted from his ear—"

"Ugh!" Carol said. "It's like van Gogh. Or J. Paul Getty the Third."

"And now Zio Gianni's on the new heart machine at Saint Raphael's—that's gonna cost a few bucks," Mama said.

"What happened to Dodie?" I asked.

"He got the F out," Mama said.

She sighed. She went over to the stove, and I knew the repetitive motion of stirring the sauce would calm her down. I went back to slicing meatballs. Carol finished chopping the eggs and started cubing the mozzarella.

"I can't believe it," Mama murmured. *"Non posso crederci—"*

"What are you, blind, Ma?" I asked. "This is common knowledge."

Mama stopped stirring. "You knew about him?" she asked. "Why didn't you say nothing? You could have told Auntie Beppina. She could have stopped him—"

"Get with it, Ma," I said. "You can't stop people from being who they are."

"Especially when they're the original three-dollar bill," Carol added.

This reference seemed to confuse Mama, who never dealt with money beyond the ten Alexander Hamiltons our dad gave her every Friday so she could buy groceries and pay the bills on Saturday. After Daddy died, Mama always went to a male teller at the bank—claiming the women weren't good at math and were more likely to make a mistake—and told him to give her the same amount (*Ten tens, I want,* she kept saying, *one hundred altogether that makes*) from her social-security check. Then she wondered why the amount that once had lasted her only a week wouldn't cover expenses for an entire month. Only after Carol and I had used a calendar *and* a calculator to illustrate to her this complex problem could Mama finally fathom it.

"You girls," Mama muttered. "Half the time I don't *capisce* what you're saying."

Carol looked at Mama and enunciated very clearly, "Dodie's been gay—*omosessuale*—since the day he was born."

"But that was the same day Lisa was born!" Mama said, and Carol and I looked at one another with disgust. Here once again came the reminder that on the cusp of the 1960s, some strange chemical must have floated through the New Haven water supply—an aphrodisiac that overtook even the grimmest of adults (like our parents) and made them rut like rodents. In 1959 Carol and Dodie's brother Jocko were born a week apart, and eleven months later Dodie and I appeared on the scene. Dodie was born eight hours ahead of me. He was delivered by the same doctor—who jokingly christened us Romulus and Remus—and he slept right next to me in his own fiberglass crib. We looked so much alike, my mother often told me, that everyone assumed we were twins. The only way the nurses could tell us apart was by looking at the sign posted on Dodie's crib that announced in Magic Marker: CIRCUMCISED.

Of course, they also could—and did—check our plastic hospital bracelets, so tiny there was hardly room to sport our preposterously long names. I've never really minded my Italian name—Elisabetta Diodetto—because it was bent into the very American *Lisa* once I started school, and Lisa it had been ever since. But Dodie had a cursed name that came from being the unfortunate twelfth grandchild on my dad's side. Had I arrived just eight hours earlier, Dodie would have been *numero tredici*—number thirteen—and his parents, just like mine, would have been far too superstitious to use that name. Dodici then could have been given a normal Italian name—Vitti or Weegie or Chickie or Chi-Chi.

Carol popped a cube of mozzarella in her mouth. *"Ascolti,"* she said to Mama. "I'm going to explain it one more time: Dodie was born tootie, and Lisa wasn't."

"But Auntie Beppina says he just turned that way," Mama said, as if Dodie were a loaf of bread that had suddenly gone stale. She kept stirring the sauce and murmuring to herself the whole time Carol and I chopped the mozzarella and the meatballs and then took turns grating the parmesan, a one-pound chunk that made our arms ache just to look at it. "We've never had a *finocchio* on my side of the family. . . . Of course, Dodie had that infection when he was a baby . . . he caught the mumps, you girls didn't . . . he used to bang his brains against the side of the crib until he fell asleep, maybe it did something weird to his head. . . ."

"Lisa did that too," Carol said.

"I did not!" I said.

"I remember," Carol insisted.

"So you wet the bed," I said.

Mama went on. "Dodie never wet the bed . . . he was a good boy . . . but so short . . ."

"Ma, name me a Sicilian man over six feet tall," Carol said.

Mama kept on murmuring as she took the flat lasagne noodles out of the boiling water with a pair of tongs and draped them over clean kitchen towels on the back of two chairs. "I told Beppina, she should have given him an American name, a name everybody could pronounce. . . . I told her, she never should have let him play that xylophone . . . she never should have let him go to that school—*chi sa* what they do in South Carolina—"

"Ma," I said. "That school is called Duke University. That school is in *North* Carolina, and they gave Dodie a huge scholarship to go there—get it through your head."

Nothing seemed to penetrate Mama. She continued mumbling to herself, like a praying woman or some psycho shuffling down the chips and dips aisle in the Stop & Shop. "She said it was a diamond earring: does that mean he's engaged to another boy? They say . . . they say times are changing . . . I don't know . . . I've never really thought about it . . . I don't know anybody like that. But do you suppose? Those men who work at the Pier One store? I had a feeling, I had a feeling when Dodie was born, it was a full moon . . . he came out *culo* first. . . ."

Carol pointed at me. "Lisa came out bass ackwards too."

My mother looked at me suspiciously. "Dodie always liked you, Lisa."

"They're still friends," Carol said. "Dodie's been writing her. I know. I've seen the mail when it drops through the slot."

"Mannaggia," Mama said, the alarm in her voice enough to indicate she thought I could catch homosexuality through the U.S. Postal Service. "You two write! What does he say in his letters? Does he say? How he got the way he got?"

"How did you get the way you are?" I asked Mama, and she stepped back a little as the sauce began to boil and spit. She turned down the burner.

The lenses of Mama's eyeglasses clouded over with steam when she dumped the boiling water from the noodles into the sink. "They say God made everyone," she said. "Even Son of Sam."

"Oh, for Christ's sake!" I said.

The arrest of serial killer David Berkowitz—who claimed he heard the voice of God through his parents' dog, and the God-Dog told him his duty in life was to pop off women—had been all over the papers that year. And Mama, who had the bad grammatical habit of letting articles drop from her speech—*You got moneys to pay for that? You need fruits from the store?*—kept wondering how Son of Sam could come from that religious group she always prefaced with the definite article, which belied her fear and respect: *The Jews. You don't think of the Jewish boys being mass murderers,* she'd said. *Aren't they supposed to be nicer than that?*

I got up from the table in disgust when Mama, who just wouldn't let it go, finally said, "Maybe Dodie could become a priest . . ." and I pounded up the stairs so loudly I almost didn't catch her saying, "Ah, me, ah, me. I'm his *comare.* He'll always be my godson. I guess I gotta love him."

The lasagne that Easter tasted dry as hate. Mama had forgotten to put down a layer of sauce first, and she was so distracted by this newsflash on Dodie that she left the mozzarella off the entire third layer. For months afterward she kept asking me, "How did you know about Dodie? He must have told you," until I figured out the repetition of the question indicated Mama's own worst fears about me. Because Dodie was *this way,* I had to be *that,* a fear practically confirmed when I transferred from Albertus Magnus College in New Haven to Sarah Lawrence in my junior year, and my parents insisted on driving me into Bronxville to drop me off, following me into the dorm while I unpacked, where my father expressed his keen disappointment that there was no view of Yankee Stadium from my room window, and my mother, gazing down at the quad, told me, "I thought you said this was a girls' school."

"It used to be a girls' school," I told her.

"Hmm," my mother said. "What do you call *that*?"

I went over to the window and gazed down on a group of girls butched out in buzz cuts and work boots. "Dykes," I told my mother, and resumed unpacking, leaving my father to translate into Italian—in far more detail than was necessary—this concept so foreign to my mother.

Mama gasped. "That's no way to have the children," she said, looking hard at me, and I knew she was remembering Dodie and thinking, *Takes one to know one.* I shrugged. How could I tell her I had already let more than a dozen boys fork me by the time I was eighteen? How could I tell her I knew about Dodie as early as when we were both eleven years old? On a sweltering summer day at Lighthouse Beach, we cousins had amused our-selves for over an hour with chicken fights—Carol riding on top of Jocko's shoulders, and me on Dodie's. As Carol and I pushed and shoved at one another to see who would get toppled first into the water, sometimes I would look down and see—when there wasn't too much seaweed in the harbor—that Jocko got a hard-on whenever Carol straddled him. No mat-ter how hard I squeezed his head in the vise of my thighs—so repeatedly he had to have known what I was doing—I never provoked the same response in Dodie.

Sometimes I found it convenient to blame Dodie for this sad fact: Although I loved Proust and Chekhov, the Brontë sisters and Beethoven, Verdi and Brahms, and even Mahler and Wagner, although I dreamed of someday writing a novel that would pull on its audience as wrenchingly as a Puccini aria or resound as gloriously as Bach's most magnificent choral music—deep inside of me still burned the soul of a stupid and simple girl, who wanted nothing more out of life than to induce in every man she met a good hard boner.

• • •

After Carol and I tossed Security Man back and forth between us, finally parking him in our father's old La-Z-Boy and even leaning him back on the footrest to make sure he was comfortable, Mama went into the backyard with a tin bucket to see if the lawn had sprouted any dandelion greens she could fix in a salad for supper.

Carol and I stayed inside, contemplating Security Man's strange anatomy. "Who'd be scared of that wimpy thing?" Carol asked, as she picked up her knitting again. "He looks like some gag gift Margaret should have gotten for her bachelorette party."

The previous week our cousin Margaret had thrown herself a stagette party at the Elks Club. Assuming it would be a reverse version of the stag parties our dad had routinely attended when we were young—which probably involved a lot of cigar smoke and blue movies and G-strings dangling over empty shot glasses—I had not attended.

"So how was that stag-ette?" I asked Carol.

"Oh, Margaret went all out," Carol said. "She hired these Chippendale wanna-bes—"

I squinched up my face. "That's disgusting," I said. Then I asked, "What was it like?"

Carol gave a low, moronic laugh. "You know. They wear bikini underwear and those little bow ties like Playboy bunnies. They're nothing but muscle and washboard abs. I mean, there's absolutely no hair whatsoever on their chests, so they must shave 'em."

"Do they have hairy legs?"

"Who the hell looks at a man's legs?"

"I do."

"You're weird. You've always been weird," Carol said, clacking her number-nine needles, and I remembered that time she got boiling mad at me when I made a joke about Al Dante's firm noodle, and she said, *You probably want men to do perverted things to you, like suck on your big toes and pee in your mouth,* and I said, *Yeah, preferably when we're both riding around on a Toro lawn mower.*

"Well, what do you look at?" I asked.

"I'm a married woman," Carol said.

"So what do you look at?" I repeated.

She shrugged. "Their face and their ass."

"So how was their face and their ass?"

"I don't know. I was so drunk, I kept watching their crotch. I'm sure they stuffed 'em with zucchini, no man could be so big."

"How gross," I said.

"Mmm," Carol said. "They're all muscled and oiled and you get to hoot at them—"

"That's reverse sexism."

"Fuck it. It was fun. You shoulda been there. You've never seen such tight bums. One of them did the limbo under a broomstick. Mama stuck a five-spot in his thong bikini."

"Jesus!" I said, and looked over at Security Man, as if I half-expected him to give me a wink.

"She took off her glasses first," Carol said.

I clucked my tongue. "Chippendales are probably all gay."

"Go on," Carol said, wrapping her yarn around the needle. "Then why do they dance for women?"

"It's a paycheck."

"One of them *did* look like he had on eyeliner," Carol said. After a sly pause she added, "Why don't you ask your kissing cousin?"

I slit my eyes at her. "He's not my *kissing* cousin," I said. "He's my regular cousin. Yours too." I got up and released the lever of the La-Z-Boy. Security Man fell forward and bounced back, like a whiplash victim. I steadied his head. Remembering how rude Carol always had been toward me and Dodie, my sisterly feelings took a nosedive and disappeared completely the moment Carol said, "Auntie Beppina says sometimes you spend weekends with Dodie. What do you two do together anyway? Go antiquing?"

"He's my friend."

"He's a queen."

"No fucking duh," I said. "Why do you have to make such a big deal out of it?"

"I'm not making a big deal out of it. I really don't care what Dodie does with—well, whatever."

"*Who*ever."

"You should tell him to be careful." Carol clacked her needles. "I mean, that gay cancer thing—"

"It's not gay cancer. It has a name—"

"—is scary. Auntie Beppina's about to go bonkers worrying about it. She's afraid he's going to get what Great-Zio Oozie had."

Daddy's Uncle Oozie, toward the end of his life, was covered with strange spots that we kids, who had watched one too many a catechism movie, took for leprosy. Our parents must have made the same mistake, because we were not allowed to go within six feet of Oozie's wheelchair. Twenty years later *The New York Times* taught me that his ravaged skin was not the result of a Biblical plague, but just a disease called KS that struck old Italian and Jewish guys and had moved, mysteriously, over to gay men.

"Just because Oozie looked like a leper doesn't mean you have to treat Dodie like one," I said.

"I'm not saying treat him like a leper. I'm saying keep your distance."

"Give me one good reason."

Carol didn't answer right away. She was concentrating on her purls. Finally she pursed her lips. "Lisa, somebody needs to tell you this."

I waited.

"Really tell you. For your own good."

I waited some more.

"You're twenty-five," Carol said. "Twenty-*five*. You'll never meet no-body hanging around Dodie."

"*Anybody*," I corrected her. "Meet *anybody*. And what does one have to do with the other?"

"Do I gotta spell it out to you?"

"You'd probably spell it wrong."

Carol clicked her knitting needles. "The word is *fag hag*."

"That's two words," I said, pulling Security Man up and hugging his limp self to my body.

"My, aren't we such a good editor. No wonder we've gotten such a fancy promotion to the la-de-da Hudson River Valley."

I paused. I stared, hard, at the cellulite busting out beneath the hem of Carol's shorts. Then I said slowly, "You have fat thighs."

Instead of stabbing me with her number nines, Carol actually smiled. "Wait 'til I stand up and you get a load of my stomach." She laughed. "Oh, Lisa! Finally. I'm pregnant. Look at your face! Isn't it great?"

I sucked in my breath; it tasted acrid as cough medicine. For seven years Carol had been married to Al Dante, and so far nothing—to use my mother's phrase—*had ever come of it*. I knew Al was not the kind of man who would let his wife use birth control. I knew Carol desperately wanted to—in her words—*give him a baby*. I had seen her eyes cloud up with tears during Christmas mass when they read the story of the birth of Jesus; I had seen her light the votives in front of the statue of Saint Jude tucked in the back alcove of the church. So I had felt sorry for her, she who seemed bitter and barren as Rachel, who envied her sister and—as the Bible put it—*said unto Jacob, Give me children, or else I die*. But now my pity gave way to unfounded envy, and the note of triumph in Carol's voice made me want to come back at her with some adolescent retort such as *So you want a medal or a chest to pin it on?* or *I know you are, but what am I?* And all I

could do was stare at the stiff little knitting that hung from her needles—
was it booties or a cap or a sweater for her baby?—and feel old and all
alone.

"Congratulations," I said.

"I knew you'd be happy for me."

"Sure. I'm thrilled. Really, Carol, I'm really thrilled."

"It's a boy," Carol said. "We saw the penis. On the ultrasound. We
want you to be his godmother."

"Sure," I said. But then I panicked, knowing I would have to go back
to Confession before I took on this task, knowing I would have to hold the
baby in my arms over the font and hypocritically repeat after the priest,
"We renounce the devil and all his works. . . ."

"Who's going to be the godfather?" I asked.

Carol shrugged. She said Al would pick the *compare*. Clacking her
needles, she added, "Unless, of course, you get married in the next few
months—"

"Don't hold your breath," I said. Although I wanted to turn around
right then and drive back to New York, I made a valiant effort to let out
some distinctly female gurgles of joy and ask my sister the usual questions
about whether she felt nauseated in the morning and when was the due
date. Carol was going to deliver at the end of summer.

"God, you're really far along," I said. "Why didn't you tell me?"

"I was afraid I'd jinx it."

My college anthropology classes had taught me fascination and
respect for the superstitions of Australian aborigines and African
bushwomen. But the superstitions of my own family—perhaps because
they had seeped into my own bones and could not be shaken out—still
managed to annoy me. Carol's fear was irrational, but I understood it all
the same.

After I had knocked on the wood of the doorjamb—and my sister
lowered her head, where I was afraid she was putting in a quick prayer to
the Virgin—Carol set down her knitting needles, stood up, and lifted her
shirt to show me her distended stomach.

"Didn't you used to have an innie belly button?" I asked.

"It's an outie now."

"Oh, my God," I said. "Look. It's moving."

"Do you want to feel it? Go on, feel it."

I held my palm against her hard, fish-white stomach and felt a few
liquidy ripples.

"He's a swimmer," Carol said.

"He'll like the beach," I said, my hand perceptibly rising with the gentle lull of the baby's waves. Then a thud—a punch or a kick—got me right in the palm. "My God, Carol, there's a riot going on!"

"A swimmer *and* a boxer."

"Doesn't that hurt?"

"Nah—it's just like Daddy's birthday whacks. Harmless stuff."

But my father's birthday whacks had hurt me more than anyone ever suspected. Although he was an angry man—just like his brother Gianni— Daddy never did more than threaten Carol and me with his open palm and utter between clenched teeth the phrase *if you two weren't girls!* to let us know point-blank that if we had been born boys it would have been his delight to land a few good cracks across our sassy faces on a regular basis. Because fathers weren't supposed to hit daughters, Daddy saved his corporal punishment for his infamous birthday whacks—one smack on the rear for every year on earth. For as far back as I could remember, Birthday Whacks were doled out with prolonged ceremony before the blowing out of candles and the cutting of chocolate cake. Daddy put a halt to whacks when Carol turned twelve and I turned eleven, and in a decade-long display of emotional stinginess that rivaled Mama's skinflintedness, he never touched either of us again.

Although I knew from reading the *Village Voice* personal ads that plenty of women liked to be spanked, I wasn't one of them. On my twenty-fifth birthday I stood there in my father's house longing for someplace else to call home and for some other man to touch me in a much more loving way. Depressed, I dragged Security Man out to my new car—which no one had yet admired—and parked him in the passenger seat, where he looked like a Middlesex Mental Hospital patient ready to be driven home from a lobotomy. I strapped him in with the safety belt to keep him upright.

After a while Mama came out from behind the garage with her bucket. Two dark circles stained the armpits of her muumuu; her apron ties were hanging loose, and she was sweating so hard her glasses kept falling down her nose and she kept pushing them back up.

"So, your sister tell you the good news?" she asked.

I nodded.

"She said she'd tell you today for your birthday. But don't say nothing more. Don't jinx it. I got a feeling it's a boy—"

"They *know* it's a boy, Mama. They had an ultrasound."

"Bah. I don't trust the X rays."

"They saw between its legs."

"He wants the boy so bad, that Al, he mighta imagined it."

"What if it turns out a girl?" I asked.

"Nobody's going to send it back—"

"That's generous," I started to say, but my mother overrode me by adding, "—so long as it's healthy. That's all we can ask for in life, for good health and the bills to get paid."

What about all the rest? I wanted to ask her. Didn't my mother ever want anything more out of life beyond not having to worry about how she would pay for her next bottle of aspirin? But if I asked her, *What about love?* she'd probably reply, *What about it?* and if I said, *What about happiness?* she'd say, *Somebody's unhappy? Tell me who and I'll say a prayer.*

My mother stopped by the side of my Toyota. "You got yourself a nice car here."

"I'm making more money at this new job. If you need anything—"

She shook her head. "I got the social security. But you won't get none if you don't get married—"

"I'll get what *I* paid into it," I said. "*I* pay into social security, and I don't need a husband to do it for me—"

"You don't?" Mama asked, and when I opened my mouth to try to explain the system to Mama—she who had never earned a paycheck in her life—she said, "What does it matter where it comes from? Save your money for the day that rains."

Mama peered into the front seat at Security Man, nodding with approval. "He looks good in there," she said, and pulled one of the first few dandelion greens, clotted with dirt, from the bucket. "Real. He looks real enough to sink his teeth into one of these *cicoria.* But you're right. He needs the pants. I still got a pair of Pop's that he ordered from the *Parade* magazine; they never fit him anyway. This guy here can have 'em."

"How much did you pay for this man?" I asked her.

"Sixty-five."

I pressed my lips together. "You got ripped."

"What do you mean, ripped?"

This was where a real mother would pause, where a real mother would say, *He's worth a million bucks—every penny and more—if he keeps my most precious daughter from harm.*

Instead, my mother said, "He looked just like Perry Como. I couldn't resist."

Chapter Two

Deep-Six

On the following Saturday—just for kicks—I strapped Security Man in the passenger seat. As I gunned my Toyota down to the Ossining train station, I practiced on my partner the *bon vivant* conversational skills I had tried to master in the city but never quite perfected. I cracked a few lame jokes and even posed a couple of philosophical questions (*Why is man mortal? Better yet: Why can't woman relate to him?*), but I elicited nothing more than a stock masculine silence. No matter. Another man soon would arrive to take Security's place; Dodie was coming from the city to visit me.

When I got to the depot, I found I had misread the nine-point type inside the paper pamphlet that recorded the comings and goings of the Hudson Line. In my eagerness to pick up Dodie, I had looked at the Monday–Friday schedule instead of Saturday's and had twenty minutes to kill before his train arrived.

I wandered into the station and eyed the vending machines. After a long debate on the pleasures and evils of Milky Ways versus M&Ms, I bit my lip, pinched my side, and moved away to avoid temptation. There were only two things in life I felt I could control: getting fat and getting pregnant. I didn't want to be either. But for a long time I'd been thinking it would just be easier to have a sex-change operation than to make a lifetime career out of dodging calories and sperm. Men certainly didn't seem to hold their breath as they stepped upon a bathroom scale and waited for the dial to settle on a disappointingly high number. No man I ever knew had slumped morosely over a copy of *Cosmopolitan* in the lobby of an abortion clinic, dreading the appearance of a white-uniformed nurse with a clipboard, who would call out his name as callously as bakery clerks called out the next number. Men—or at least the kind of men I went with—got off easy.

These thoughts depressed me, and I went back outside to let the sun lift my spirits. Although suburbia already seemed too dull to sustain me forever, it was a relief to sit outdoors on the wooden bench and stare at the empty tracks without fearing that some nut would creep from behind a pillar and push me into the path of an oncoming train. It felt good to loosen the death grip on my purse and to let my keys jingle idly from my hands. My outfit—Reeboks and denim cutoffs and a man's T-shirt—hardly would have won any big-city fashion awards, but it felt comfortable. No longer was I an urban animal. I was what my mother called a *human bean* again.

Dodie alone knew how I had paid my dues in the city; without him, I'd never have survived Manhattan for as long (or as short) as I did. Although we had the same GPA in high school, Dodie (because he was a boy) was allowed to skip a grade, and then (because he wanted to save money—Dodie always had a good head for money) he charged through Duke in three years instead of four. By the time I transferred as a junior to Sarah Lawrence, Dodie already was working for Price Waterhouse, and by then the gap between our experiences seemed enormous. His New Haven had been my New Haven, but his New York was not my New York. I arrived in Bronxville green as a Bartlett pear. I had never eaten a pistachio. Dodie was the one who held the wrinkled red nut out to me for the first time and said, "Go ahead, Lise. It won't kill you." It was Dodie who told me that the phrase *Catholic taste* could be applied to more than just those of us who had suffered through years of catechism and CYO, and Dodie who taught me that jazz was considered cool and that Jaco Pastorius was not a thirteenth-century mystic, but a famous electric-bass player. It was Dodie who trained me not to order a brandy Alexander in the heat of July or a screwdriver in the middle of winter—who, in fact, taught me it was best to avoid these kinds of cocktails altogether. Dodie weaned me away from baby-girl drinks and put me on more-effective substances, such as gin and bourbon. He provided me with dope far smoother than New Haven nickel-bag pot and with the kind of drugs floating around freely in those days: coke and ludes and poppers and once, even, a shot of smack that left me so deluded I lost track of two whole days. But that seemed light-years ago; we had both since regained our fear of intravenous needles.

Dodie taught me how to dress. I arrived at "Sally Larry" (a school known for the gender-impaired) wedded to the Annie Hall look—a man's 15½ dress shirt dyed purple, a loosely knotted knit tie, baggy olive carpenter pants, pink leg warmers, rubbery green army boots, and on top of everything, a black velvet fedora perched jauntily on my bobbed head. On Dodie's first visit to my dorm room, he took one look at me and asked, "Are we questioning our sexual identity here?"

"What do you mean?" I asked.

"Well, Jesus, Lise—you're all butched out with no place to go. Just get a load of yourself in the mirror."

But there wasn't any mirror. My roommate had taken it down, first thing, after plopping her duffel bag on the other twin bed and loudly announcing she was a feminist.

Dodie dragged me down to Canal Jean in the Village, where we spent hours going back and forth to the coed dressing rooms, Dodie's cute eyes shining and winking at me above the latticed doors as we tried on black jackets and black T-shirts and black jeans, which we modeled for one another—obviously not so much for the color, but for the cut. And so—banished were my gauze shirts *sans* bra, the peasant broomstick skirts, and the cuffed Lees. I went into Canal Jean looking like Diane Keaton and came out looking like a dominatrix.

Dodie faux-Manhattanized me, and Sarah Lawrence did the rest of the trick. I put down Albert Camus and picked up Jean Genet. I dropped *schifato!* and *vafanculo!* from my vocabulary, and for a few months I even went by my full name—Elisabetta—when I realized some people actually thought it was chic to be Italian—European Italian, that is. I smoked French cigarettes and didn't even blink when my roommate offered to shave my pubic hair. "No thanks," I said. "I'd rather hang on to it."

But much as I liked New York—the museums and the concerts and the bookstores—I never felt at home there. After the dorms in Bronxville I had to move out to my one-room dump in Brooklyn, which was all I could afford on my piddly publishing salary. Only after three stubborn years of sleeping on a mildewed mattress on the floor could I admit to myself that the subway in summer smelled worse than steerage and that all the culture in the world could not make up for the fact that I was living worse than my own mother and father did when they first crossed over to America. So my mother wore a threadbare apron every day in New Haven—how far had I really progressed wearing a black leather skirt (which I could not afford to have cleaned) in a bigger but meaner city? I thought I was living the literary life, but I had not fulfilled the promise I had made to myself on my first visit to New York, when I had pressed my naive thumb inside the ridge of one of the black columns at Scribner's bookstore (as if it were a holy relic that would inspire me to devote myself to the Great God of Language) and swore that someday I would write something wonderful that would be printed on twenty-pound vellum and packaged in cloth binding (with a striking cover, of course), something that made people cry or laugh, a story that pressed on their chest so hard it made them hear their own heartbeat, if only for half a second. Publishing made me sick of words, and when I discovered that every manuscript, no matter how frivolous or serious its subject matter, would be treated as a commodity—just like a slotted spoon, a disposable cigarette lighter, a diamond engagement

ring, or a plastic figurine of a saint—I had pitched the scribbled musings
and daily journals I scrupulously kept at Sarah Lawrence. Of my two-year
career as a poet there, the only opus I now could even recall was a poem
with a run-in title. It began:

Fist-fucked by grief . . .

This choice line was followed by a dramatic, breathless dash à la
Emily Dickinson.

Thank God I could not remember the rest.

So I initially embraced Ossining, with its sleepy main street lined
with one brick bank and tiny post office and family bakery (all closed on
Sunday) that I could visit without feeling like I had to don a costume
designed either to make me blend in with the crowd or turn people's
heads. Although I kept all my black clothes in the closet (figuring they
might come in handy when I finally hunkered down to write my novel on
1980s corporate life), for my job at Boorman Pharmaceuticals I pulled on
sheer pantyhose and navy pumps every morning. I even painted my nails
on Sunday evening—not emerald green or raisin black, but a pale, discreet
color that made no political statement beyond the fact that I valued good
grooming. In Ossining, I told myself, I would pursue a healthier lifestyle—
eat more cruciferous vegetables and get a few girlfriends instead of hanging out with just men. Every time I went out with a guy, I told myself, I
would put in my diaphragm. So far I had stuck to my promise, at least in
regards to the girls and the vegetables. On my first day at Boorman, I
lunched with a group with my coworkers from Editorial—all women—in
the company cafeteria, which had a nifty salad bar. I liked the combination
of crisp spinach leaves, bright green peas, and chopped hard-boiled eggs.
The conversation, however, was less than fascinating.

"Are you married?" asked a woman whose chunky engagement and
wedding rings glinted beneath the fluorescent lights as she dug into her
baked potato covered with chili.

I held out my bare left hand next to her diamonds—or what on closer
inspection proved to be cubic zirconium.

"Oh," she said, and went on to complain about her own husband.

"You're *lucky* you've never been married," said the obvious divorcée to
my left, who then took up her knife and fork and lit into a crouton with a
fury that sent her Caesar dressing flying in all directions, including right
onto the sleeve of my new cream-color silk blouse. Some of the other
women at the table—who had heard and reheard the divorcée's bitter tales
of complaint—cut her off by filling me in on the rules for taking coffee
breaks and the benefits of the new dental-insurance package. I nodded and
smiled and wondered if I was the only person at the table who liked read-

ing Dostoyevsky. Then I remembered that *I* didn't like reading Dostoyev-sky. *Crime and Punishment* made me feel suicidal, and *The Brothers Karamazov* brought out the pugilist in me. *One more pious word out of Alyosha,* I thought as I plowed my way through that novel, *and I'm going to sock this Christian wimp right in the nose.*

I ate my salad and thought, *Like it or not, these are Boorman's women, so learn to live with it, Lisa—at least they'll laugh at your large stock of dumb-guy jokes.* I forked a big piece of spinach and surreptitiously scoped out the men in the cafeteria. The guys in R&D—with their white lab coats and dorky rubber-soled shoes—seemed smart but distant (a feature I would come to value after I discovered three-quarters of them smelled of *eau de* formaldehyde). After someone finally asked me if I had a boy-friend—to which I replied, "Not at the moment"—I was informed that most of the lab scientists were unavailable. "They all get married in gradu-ate school," I was told, "and their wives stay home and take care of their kids." I also was told that the sales reps and account executives—married and single—were a bunch of on-the-make pigs, and the management—well, nobody even dreamed of management. From what little I had seen on my two interviews, I already had the top dogs pegged: these were men who drove German and Italian cars, who dressed in subtle shirts and suits from Barney's, and who had photographs on their desks of toddlers and wives whose youthful skin and thin hips and bleached-blond hair made it clear that every executive in the company was on his second or third marriage, and that their spouses regularly visited plastic surgeons, manicurists, hair salons, and tanning beds.

The field did not look promising. It looked even worse in the after-noon when my new boss, Karen, who was four months pregnant but al-ready looked close to eight, marched me around Boorman's corporate headquarters and laboratory, introducing me to what seemed like hun-dreds of people.

Among the more memorable persons I encountered were the superi-ors who oversaw the Editorial division. The senior vice-president for Research and Development, Dr. Peggy Schoenbarger, was a great steel-haired Teutonic wonder of a woman, who looked just as suited to wearing a Wagnerian helmet with horns as she did to directing the production of more-effective over-the-counter enemas. The diplomas on her wall an-nounced she had a doctorate in biochemistry from Rutgers and a master's in management from Penn State. Her smarts frightened me. As we were introduced, I wished I wore glasses.

"Greetings," Dr. Peggy Schoenbarger said, giving me a firm hand-shake, and I was so taken aback I merely repeated, "Yes, *greetings.*"

"Lisa's been hired to make sure we put all our commas in the right place," Karen explained.

"Very fine," Peggy said. "We can all use help with that."

"Please feel free to call me if you should have a question about grammar usage," I said, immediately questioning whether my use of the subjunctive in that sentence had been correct.

"I'll do that," she said, and I inwardly cringed, knowing I would spend the weekend curled up with nothing more romantic than *The Chicago Manual of Style* just to bone up on usage of the verb *to be*. I also knew I would get paranoid the moment she called and I answered the phone with a normal *hello,* because she'd say, "Is this Ms. Diodetto?" and I'd be hard-pressed to give her a grammatically correct answer, because I didn't know which one was kosher: "This is her" or "This is she" or "This is I," and I'd do something dumb like blurt out, "It's me, yes, it's me!"

Karen actually congratulated me on that fiasco. "You played that just right, Lisa," she whispered. "Dr. Schoenbarger writes a lot of important correspondence, and now she's sure to call you for advice. She'll like you even more if you're a golfer—"

"A golfer!"

"Her dream is to play at Saint Andrews in Scotland. Once she gets to know you—but she has to be really *fond* of you to do it—she might even invite you out on the green. I heard she once thought of turning pro and going on tour."

"I don't doubt it," I said, and added to my homework looking up the definition of *birdie* and the origin of the term *links*.

After that, Karen led me to the door of yet another spacious, plush-carpeted corner office. This deluxe model also had a wonderful view of the cascading fountain on the front lawn, which rolled on lusher than the eighteenth green before it reached, beyond a windbreak of poplars, the main road. Dr. Peggy Schoenbarger's immediate underling, the vice-president for new-product development, was a much younger—and shorter—man with black hair, who wore the kind of intellectual wire-rimmed glasses I had just wished I wore to impress Dr. Peg. He sat at a conference table beneath a Thomas Eakins print of a rower, obviously about to confer with a group of other white-shirted, red-tied corporate clones. Karen suggested we return later, but his secretary said the meeting hadn't gotten started yet.

She buzzed the VP on the intercom—although one good hoot through the door would have sufficed to catch his attention—and we were sent in. As Karen introduced us, I felt a brief second of kinship with Mr. Eben Strauss, perhaps because we both clearly were the only two folks in

the room who had to spell our names—slowly and distinctly—every time
we used the phone to book a restaurant reservation or make a doctor's
appointment. For half a second he gave me the impression that he, too,
acknowledged this kinship, for when he rose from the table to greet me,
his dark eyes—darker than anyone else's I had met so far at Boorman—
blinked as if in recognition.

"Welcome on board," he said as he shook my hand, and my warm
feelings toward him went down faster than the *Titanic*. *What is this,* I felt
like asking, *the Good Ship Lollipop?* If so, he had just made it clear that he
was the captain and I was the third mate, or even just the lowly hand who
got tossed a mop without even a verbal command to swab down the poop
deck.

This hearty, one-of-the-boys corporate lingo—*get on board, be a team
player, take the initiative, prioritize,* and that most loathsome of phrases,
let's touch base in the morning—made me seasick. I smiled queasily, told
him I was very pleased to make his acquaintance, and tried hard not to
stare at his diamond-patterned tie, which could only be described by one
word: *ugly.*

"Where are you from originally?" he asked.

"New Haven."

"I've heard of that," he said, and that's when I saw—over his shoulder—that the framed degrees on his wall were from Cornell and Harvard. I
wondered how well his ivy aura sat with public-school Peggy.

He gestured to the other men at the table and apologized for not
having a chance to talk more. Later, he certainly hoped we would have
that opportunity. But for now he had this meeting. If we would excuse
him—

"Certainly," Karen said crisply, and took me by the arm where that
blasted Caesar dressing had spotted the silk. I saw Mr. Eben Strauss look,
too long, at my sleeve.

After we left his office, Karen told me that Eben Strauss was a decent
man. I tried hard not to yawn. "If you have to work under a man," Karen
told me, "he's the man to do it under." She also told me that Eben Strauss
was the only guy in the corporation willing—or even capable—of working
for a woman senior vice-president. From this I surmised either that Dr.
Peggy Schoenbarger was a bitch on wheels or that the rest of the male
crew at Boorman were a bunch of chauvinists.

As Karen and I continued down the hall to meet yet another man in a
navy suit, she was quick to point out that she alone was my supervisor, and
even though *the chain of command* eventually led back to the big guns, she
would act just like those poplars outside their windows: as a buffer or

windbreak. Besides, Karen told me, Dr. Schoenbarger and Mr. Strauss were the perfect bosses—she was so busy overseeing research for new drugs and he was always jetting around the country supervising the production and marketing end of it. "They trust us to get the jobs done," Karen said, "and we do it."

"But why is Editorial under Research and Development?" I asked Karen, kicking myself for not examining the organizational chart before I accepted the position. "Wouldn't it make more sense for us to be under Communications?"

"We were there for a while," Karen said. "But it didn't work out."

"Why not?"

She looked up and down the hall. Lowering her voice—people always seemed to be lowering their voice at Boorman, as if the walls were bugged—she told me with pride that while Communications was the brawn of Boorman, Research and Development was the brains. "Communications just didn't understand the scientific end of our work," she said. "A lot of our editing jobs are highly technical and require the utmost discipline and accuracy." Lowering her voice still further, she said, "A single mistake can result in tremendous loss of life."

I gave her a grave nod and thought, *My, someone does need to feel self-important this afternoon.*

"Dr. Schoenbarger and Mr. Strauss hold us to very high standards," she said, adding in a whisper that Communications could be considered *very loosey-goosey.* Once I had the chance to interact with *some of those characters in advertising,* I would see exactly what she meant.

Little did she know how desperately I wanted to find out—not only because Communications probably held the key to any romantic interest I would find at Boorman, but also because the really good jobs came out of that department. As a newcomer, I was assigned the dullest stuff: proofreading patient-information manuals, revising label copy, drafting routine correspondence, and once even editing the CEO's barf-inducing Rotary Club speech. As senior editor, Karen took care of Boorman's glitzier promotional material, which came out under the aegis of Communications: the advertisements destined to appear on the glossy pages of *RN* and *Lancet* and *JAMA,* and the four-color corporate brochures that showed, on the cover, grains of wheat and multicolored pills and white-coated scientists in face masks contemplating beakers full of urine-color liquid.

Yet Karen was bound, sooner or later, for a maternity leave. Knowing I did not want to spend the rest of my days at Boorman proofreading again and again the phrase CARCINOGENESIS, MUTAGENESIS, AND IMPAIRMENT OF FERTILITY, I made sure I was nice to her—which in the end didn't prove hard.

Although she seemed a little too proud of her degree in French literature from Bryn Mawr—and too eager to introduce me to others as a "Sarah Lawrence graduate"—she gave me a lot of responsibility and tons of praise for catching a couple of my coworkers on some proofreading mistakes. She was the only one in Editorial who stopped to examine the old photo of me and Carol and Mama and Daddy posing in front of church after Easter mass (1968), which I had felt compelled to put on my desk after realizing it was practically de rigueur at Boorman to demonstrate warm feelings toward your family. "Isn't this sweet," she said. "But why aren't your parents smiling?"

I didn't bother to explain. Instead, the next time I went into her office, I reciprocated by admiring the canned studio portrait Karen displayed of her own engineer husband, who looked handsome enough even though he was posed in front of a navy blue velvet backdrop and the photographer clearly had touched up his teeth.

The artwork Karen had up in her office (representations of snowy New England villages and covered bridges) appalled me, and I hated the way her briefcase and number-two pencils and even one of her Shetland sweaters were monogrammed (as if she were some Alzheimer's patient in danger of forgetting her name). She also prefaced all of her gossip—and she had a lot of it—with the statement "I don't want to spread rumors, but . . ." Yet I had to make friends with someone, and I knew it was more prudent to find that friend further up a notch on the organizational chart than to pal around with the secretary. Of all the women I worked with, Karen had the most in common with me. She alone did not regard her cuticles as an interesting source of conversation. She alone was known to read a good nineteenth-century novel while she ate a too-wholesome bagged lunch at her desk during break. She liked Jane Austen and Henry James and Balzac, and we shared a penchant for the Brontës, although I liked Emily best and she preferred Charlotte (to my mind, for all the wrong reasons). Karen seemed taken aback when I described *Jane Eyre* as "hot" and very grave indeed when I said I always rooted for Jane to run off with Mr. Rochester to France and become his mistress.

"But if she ran off with him, then we would lose the great moral dilemma of the heroine," she said.

"We also would lose the proselytizing of her cousin," I said, because the passages full of Saint John Rivers's moralizing thrilled me about as much as the chapters on agriculture in *Anna Karenina*: that is to say, not one bit.

"Saint John does get a bit tedious, doesn't he," Karen admitted. "But he's a necessary part of the plot. Jane has to reconsider her relationship to

God and come into financial independence. And Mr. Rochester's pride has to be taken down a peg before they can have an equal union in the end."

I shrugged. "Of course, I'm not married," I said, "and of course, Brontë's not a true realist, but I don't think an equal union is possible in this life."

"Well," said Karen, "maybe not." She sighed. "I'll wait to see how many diapers my husband changes."

"Let me know," I said, and we both laughed. The next day she hinted a few times she might like to introduce me to one of her husband's cousins, and after I kept declining, she finally said, "Just as well. He's almost forty."

"Balding?" I asked.

"No, but he *does* have thick glasses and I know you're Catholic. I mean: He's been married before."

"I don't do divorced men," I said.

Karen gave me a tense smile and lowered her voice to a confidential whisper. "You know, Lisa, I probably shouldn't say this, but the word *do* sometimes has sexual connotations."

"Oh," I said. "Thanks for telling me. I was completely unaware of that." I glanced at the clock. "So, you think I should skip *doing* my scheduled lunch with Dr. Schoenbarger?"

"You have another appointment with Dr. Schoenbarger?" Karen's forehead furrowed. "She's really taken a shine to you, Lisa."

Karen looked worried. But she had no reason to be. The stuffy corporate culture of Boorman clearly didn't hold much promise in the way of *any* kind of romance—lesbian (should I be so inclined) or straight. To widen my chances of meeting men, I joined a health club and found out, to my dismay, that Friday nights the gym would be populated by me and (as Dodie would put it) *every single gee-gee* (short for gay guy) *who missed the ferry to Fire Island.* I sat down at the rowing machine, grabbed the bar that was supposed to simulate an oar, and got to work on my muscles, which already were starting to firm up. The free weights tempted me, but I avoided them with the same kind of care I passed by the Milky Ways and M&Ms. I had inherited my mother's shorter legs and worse, my father's upper-body build, which made me look so masculine in a turtleneck I could have supplied the inspiration for a new men's cologne called *Sturdy Sicilian Shoulders.* Ringing in my ears was the echo of Dodie's comment— *all butched out with no place to go.* I was determined not to bulk up my upper body beyond giving my tits—a satisfying 36C—a little lift.

• • •

With a whistle and slow, monotonous chug, the train pulled into the station. As I stood up from the bench I spotted Dodie's essential weekend outfit—black jeans and a deep blue denim shirt—through the grimy window by the door. When he came down the steps, his black leather tote bag (which I hoped contained at least one joint) slung over his shoulder, I thought again about how lucky Dodie was. In the great lottery of looks, he had pulled a winning ticket, at least among the Sicilian subset. Dodie and I both had a smooth, fair complexion, and by some odd genetic fluke we also got brown hair that became slightly brassy in the summertime, not the black hair that thickly covered our parents' heads. Yet unlike me, Dodie got what we all thought of as a more *Northern* face: a clean chin and chiseled cheekbones. And so he was better-looking than I was. What's worse, he was prettier, and that pissed me off.

I greeted him with a kiss. "God, I've missed you."

Dodie hugged me. "Hey, the train really does go beneath Sing Sing."

"Forget the train," I said. "Come on, check out my new car."

"Japanese, I hope."

"*Sayonara,* Galaxy Five Hundred," I said, dismissing with one swoop the car model that both Dodie's parents and mine had sworn by, even though it had lived up to Ford's nickname of *Fix Or Repair Daily.* As we walked along the platform I realized my pride in my Corolla made me too akin for comfort to my father, who often fondly reported the glow he felt when he purchased his first—*used*—Model T.

The parking lot wasn't crowded. When we got over to my Toyota, Dodie gave me an appreciative smile. After a moment I saw he had eyes not for my new wheels, but for the inflatable man in the passenger seat.

Dodie slung his leather bag onto the closed trunk of the car. "Unlock the door," he said. I took out my key and opened the passenger side. Like a cop, Dodie reached in and yanked Security Man out by the scruff of his neck, held him up, and evaluated him. After just a brief week on Planet Earth, Security Man suddenly seemed slightly shriveled, less hardy, and less full of himself.

"He looks like he needs a good blow job," Dodie said.

"All yours," I said, pushing up Security Man's T-shirt and pointing to the spigot on his plastic belly.

"I've sworn off strangers," Dodie said. "But if you'd like to take a turn, I wouldn't mind experiencing a little vicarious pleasure—"

"I'm cleaning up my act, remember?"

"This I gotta see."

"You'll see it," I said glumly, and helped Dodie stuff Security Man—who wasn't cooperating—into the backseat.

We got into the Toyota. As I backed out of the parking space, I spotted in the rearview mirror a country-club couple with silvery hair loading their Hartmann luggage into their Jag. They turned and stared at our strange threesome as we went on our way.

"I won't ask where you picked this man up," Dodie said on the drive back. "But—can I guess?—your mother approves."

"I forgot to thank her," I said, suddenly remembering. Maybe Mama was right. Maybe I didn't deserve any gifts.

"Isn't that your father's old Yankees cap?"

"And his pants," I said.

"So now you've finally found him: the man who looks like dear old Dad—"

"He doesn't look like my dad or anyone else we're related to."

"What's his name?" Dodie asked. "Rex?"

"Frankie?" I suggested. "Vinnie?"

"Nah. You just said he doesn't look like any relative of ours."

"He looks Bohunk," I said. "With that red hair."

Dodie snapped his fingers. "That's it—Red Rover, Red Rover."

"Oh, won't you come over?"

We laughed, and Dodie looked out the window. "My God," he said, with all the wonder and stupidity of someone who had lived too long in the city. "What are those green things out there?"

"They're called trees."

"Oh." Dodie put his hand over his chest. "No wonder I feel asthmatic." Then he turned around and looked long and hard into the backseat. "Lise?"

"What?"

"Can I play the bitchy fag for half a second?"

"Don't let me cramp your style."

"He's a bad dresser," Dodie said. "Dump him."

I put on the brakes. We pulled over to the side of the road, and like a couple of Mafiosi getting rid of the guy who betrayed the family honor, we deep-sixed him into the ditch.

Dodie had the playful smile and sly hands of a magician. When we got back to my place, he didn't pull any mind-benders out of his black bag, but he did conjure forth a housewarming present and a belated birthday gift: a pound of chocolate raspberry coffee beans and a pair of bone-china mugs in blue and white porcelain etched with gold, in a process I knew from one of my art-history courses was called "clobbering." Remembering my manners this time—and still feeling slightly giddy and guilty about ditching Security Man in such a dramatic way—I warmly thanked Dodie and gave him his belated birthday present (a copy of Updike's tribute to suburban adultery, *Couples*). Then I led him around my apartment so he could admire everything I had lacked during my dark, miserable years in Brooklyn. Dodie was effusive in his praise of the amenities most Americans, except for those who lived in shacks in the Tennessee hills and in the two-by-four studios of major cities, took for granted: a bathtub big enough to lie down in, a pulsating shower head, a double kitchen sink, a stove with four functioning burners, kitchen cabinets free of rodents and water bugs and roaches, gray industrial carpeting, a real foam couch from the Door Store, and a place to hang your coat at the end of the day.

"Wow," Dodie said. "Great closet." For even though Dodie had a very plum studio in a high-rise on the edge of the Financial District—with a window that gave out onto the street and a white chaise longue from Roche-Bobois and even a doorman who smoked Virginia Slims all day beneath the ripped canopy—he had only one cramped closet in which to hang his extensive wardrobe. In Brooklyn I had owned a wooden clothes tree that tipped over when too many hangers were placed on the pegs.

"I owe all of this to you," I told him.

"Nah."

"Come on. Really. I mean, I feel almost guilty. I can never pay you back."

"So shut up and give me your monthly payment. You're behind a couple of days, you know."

I got out my purse and wrote Dodie a hefty check. Dodie worked off Wall Street as an investment counselor, specializing in finding smaller or newer companies worth entering *on the ground floor*. His client list was long and included a few Broadway actors, two tenors from the Met, a Pulitzer prize–winning author, two department-store magnates, and a host of little old ladies who wore mink stoles in the summertime and stank of Estée Lauder perfume on a year-round basis. And then, of course, there was me. From the day I got my first job in publishing, Dodie insisted I send him at least twenty-five bucks a week out of my meager paycheck. He handled my money. Sometimes he passed on to me the Christmas gifts he got from the little old ladies—which came in lacquered turquoise Tiffany bags—and shared with me the comp tickets to the Metropolitan Opera and the Philharmonic. We had our own social lives, to be sure, but every now and then we both welcomed having a pressureless date.

After I showed off my apartment, I took Dodie on a leisurely drive around Ossining and past Boorman's corporate headquarters with its well-manicured lawns and ostentatious fountain.

"Let's go in," Dodie said.

"Will you behave?"

"But of course."

I doubted it. But I wanted to show off my new office, and I figured since it was Saturday the chances of us bumping into anyone in my department were extremely slim. Only four or five cars were in the staff lot behind my building. The best-looking was a tan BMW in the area reserved for top management. Next to it was parked a less pretentious silver Audi.

Neither Dodie nor I had a real thing for cars. Still, we walked close enough to check out these luxury vehicles, and Dodie commented, "Now these are wheels, Lise."

"Nice," I agreed.

At the back entrance we had to sign in with the armed security guard—a Dominican guy named Gussie who had a gut fatter than my father's, but a much better disposition and a sweeter smile. Gussie glanced down at the clipboard after I scribbled *L. and D. Diodetto.*

"Miss Lisa," Gussie scolded, "I didn't know you were married."

"My cousin."

"Then there's still hope for me?"

I laughed and introduced Dodie, who shook Gussie's hand too quickly. Armed men made him nervous, and he had mentioned to me—more than once—that he could not understand the strange phenomenon of people dressing up in their bedrooms as traffic cops, Cossacks, Israeli commandos, Gestapo guards, and even Roman centurions. *I know sex is sometimes about power,* he'd said, *but does this have to be illustrated in costume? How do people keep a straight face?*

As we rounded the corner and started down the first long carpeted corridor, Dodie whispered, "Why was that guard flirting with you?"

"He's bored. And I'm beautiful."

"He's old," Dodie said. "And you're not."

"The man is harmless."

"A harmless man with a gun?"

"He's not going to use it on me. He's supposed to shoot folks who stuff too many aspirin-substitute samples down their shirt. Now stop acting like my mother"—Dodie's look of horror was a joy to behold—"and get ready for the grand tour."

I took Dodie around to my office the long way, past the art shop, the financial office, the lavish boardrooms, and the chief administrative officer's suite. As we rounded the corner that led to the ramp to the lab, I heard the faint sound of music—an aria—that reminded me of cold winter afternoons back in Brooklyn, when I would bag the trash and iron clothes and sweep the bugs off my floor to the sad sounds of the Metropolitan Opera Saturday broadcast.

Dodie's ears perked up. "Do I detect a *paesano* on the premises?"

"Shh," I said, for I was sure the music came from Dr. Peggy Schoenbarger's office, although it did sound more like Puccini than Wagner. I told Dodie I hadn't yet perused our internal phone directory, but so far I seemed to be the token Sicilian at Boorman, with the possible exception of a certain Tony Russo in maintenance, who had posted an index card on the cafeteria bulletin board announcing no problem was too large or too small for the man whose weekend pseudonym was MR. FIX IT!

Dodie wasn't listening. His head was cocked toward the music. "What is that song, Lise? I know that song; it's from *Gianni Schicchi*—"

I also listened. *"O mio bambino caro?"*

Dodie gave me a playful shove. "It's *mio babbino caro*—my darling daddy, not my darling baby."

I shrugged. I didn't like being thought uncultured, but the truth was I had never seen a performance of *Gianni Schicchi*—I only knew the aria from my *Great Opera Highlights* tape.

The fluid, swelling music pleased me as much as an unexpected gift—it seemed so out of whack with the straight and narrow corridors of Boorman. We listened until the end of the aria, then stopped to peer into the cafeteria and the well-appointed employee lounge.

"You done good, Lise," Dodie said.

"I owe you this one too," I said—for Dodie had urged me to get out of the city and helped me research my prospects in the Fortune 500. He told me how to find Boorman's annual report in the public library and got me an MCAT study guide so I could memorize enough medical terminology to ace Boorman's stiff editing exam.

"I now can spell—and define—*contraindication* and *retrovirus*," I told Dodie.

"Not bad for the girl who got a C in freshman biology."

"And now I spell them, and define them, in a private office," I added, as I ushered him back into Editorial. I was proud of my bright, clean office in the back wing, where my sparkling white-laminate work station was wiped and dusted every evening and my wastebasket was emptied every single day. Every morning I marveled at how and why I ever had worked in a cubicle at a steel desk whose rusted drawers would not pull out and which I would have been loath to open anyway for fear of what I would find there. For three years in publishing I had faced, every morning, a stack of yellow and blue and white boxes containing pounds of the written word. All day long—as water bugs marched across the frayed carpet and an occasional mouse made a straight trajectory from under one pile of manuscripts in the corner into the other—I opened the boxes and logged them in, answered phones, and made copies. After six months of having only the privilege of typing my own fatuous, high-minded reader's reports, I had begun to edit, and after I displayed my talent for ripping into particularly dense prose, I always was given the "weightier" manuscripts. My dreary job seemed to have nothing to do with the end product—the beautiful books with neat, colorful spines, the glitzy covers that shined like molten wax, and the full-page ads in *The New York Times Book Review* and *Publishers Weekly*.

"I'm never editing somebody else's shit manuscript again," I told Dodie. "I'm writing my own. And I'm done with wearing black."

"Covers up the dirt," Dodie said, "but after a while it grows boring, doesn't it?" Out of the corner of his eye, he checked me out. "You look different already, Lise. Tighter. Healthier."

"I'm working out. Every day. At a gym. If you're a good boy, I'll let you feel up my biceps after dinner."

"I can hardly wait," Dodie said in a distinctly unenthusiastic voice. He turned toward my desk. "Is that Big Blue or a Wang?"

"Pardon me?"

"Your word processor."

"It's a computer. I was terrified of it at first. It's like something out of *1984*—it's hooked up to some kind of Big Brother-like eyeball—"

"That's called a *mainframe*."

"Whatever. It makes me nervous. Tons of records are stored on it, and there's even this program on it called All-in-1, where you can check who's working on their computer at any given time and send them messages."

Dodie examined my unwieldy dot-matrix printer, which shook the windowpanes whenever I ran off one of my word-processing files. He had been working on a computer for over a year now and was not impressed.

Dodie sat down and recommended I ask for another desk chair—with arms—to make it clear I was not just a glorified secretary at Boorman. Then he picked up the photo of my family I had felt compelled to post on my desk. "You don't look half-bad in an Easter bonnet."

"Thanks."

"Even Carol looks cute in this picture."

"And my mother?"

Dodie didn't deign to comment on my mother's stern posture and stony face. "Your father was good-looking, in his own way. You ever miss him?"

"Why should I?"

"You cried a lot at his funeral."

I shrugged. Although Dodie would have been the first to understand, it still hurt to admit my tears had been for the love my father and I did not have between us. I cried for what I had wanted, not for what I had lost.

"He never paid attention to me," I told Dodie. "He never even talked to me."

"He never talked to anyone," Dodie said. "Not even my dad."

Dodie's parents—Zio Gianni and Auntie Beppina—lived two doors down from us. Although our mothers visited back and forth, our fathers (who were brothers) never said boo to one another. I always had the feeling my dad was jealous of Zio Gianni for having Jocko and Dodie while he got stuck with a pair of girls. To add to his misery, Beppina went on to have three more boys after Dodie—younger brothers Dodie hadn't spoken to in years—while my mother had only miscarriages.

"Do you suppose your mother—?" Dodie asked. "You know, misses him?"

I shrugged again. I didn't know why the fact that there was no love lost between my parents should still bother me. But it did. Mama and Daddy were famous for trading insults *sotto voce*—as if the barbs didn't count if they were delivered under the dramatic illusion that the offended party couldn't hear. I never once saw them hold hands or kiss. They never even said each other's names. They were simply "you" to each other's face, and behind each other's back, "Pops" or "The Mama"—or plenty of other names much worse.

Yet Mama remained faithful to his memory. She swept the autumn leaves off Daddy's grave, and she always spent a long time haggling with the owner of the garden store where she bought the geraniums she planted every spring in front of his headstone, claiming, "Pops would have wanted the best for the least." Whenever we sat down to dinner now, she made it a big point to remind Al Dante, "Here, you sit in Pops's old chair. You sit here; this is what he would have liked."

I did not ask Dodie if he missed his own father—whom he hadn't talked to since the famous earring incident, which had left a thin white stripe of a scar on his lobe that I always was tempted to reach out and touch, as if the pressure of my finger could heal it.

"You want to see my boss's office?"

"Actually, I need to see the can."

"Too much coffee on the train?" I asked, because Dodie had already used the bathroom twice at my place.

"Actually, bad Mexican food last night."

I took Dodie into Karen's office, where I knew she kept in her bottom file drawer some over-the-counter remedy for diarrhea and indigestion. I poured him a Dixie cup full of the pink liquid. Dodie swallowed it, then poured himself another. "Your boss is going to come up short the next time Montezuma strikes," he said.

"She can't have this anymore," I said, tucking the bottle back where I found it. "She's pregnant."

"You didn't tell me that."

"Why do you think I took the job?"

"Oh. Lise. You're smarter than I thought." Dodie looked around the large office with admiration in his eyes, then shook his head at Karen's New England snowy scenes and her monogrammed pencil cup and the stained-glass sun-catcher in the shape of the letter *K*.

"She's nice," I said. "I swear it."

"Still, you'd better redecorate."

After that I walked him down the hallway to the men's room, which was across from the employee lounge. I moved a discreet twenty feet or so down the corridor to the window, where I gazed out on the flower beds— purple hyacinths and yellow tulips and jonquils tinged light blue that reminded me of the lilies that graced the altar on the day of the Resurrection. I moved in closer to the glass, wishing I could hear the soothing sound of Boorman's showcase fountain.

What I heard—in its place—was the thunk of a vending machine from inside the employee lounge. I heard the snap and fizz of a soda can and turned, expecting to see Dodie surface from the lounge with some Canada Dry to ease his upset stomach. Instead, a man in a white shirt and chinos rounded the doorway. He stopped in his tracks. Either I startled Mr. Eben Strauss—whom I hardly recognized *sans* ugly tie—or he was embarrassed to be seen drinking a generic brand of root beer, which announced on the side OLD TIME FIZZ!

"Working overtime already?" he asked.

Here was the perfect opportunity to score a few points with management. "I just had a few things to clear up on my desk," I said.

"I have the same dilemma."

"I'm done now."

"I wish I could say the same."

We stood there awkwardly for a moment.

"So that was you, then, listening to the Puccini?" I asked. "That was pretty. I mean, beautiful. I stopped to listen . . ."

My voice trailed away. He made me nervous, the way he was staring and holding the soda can too far away from his body, as if he were scared he would spill it all over his own white shirt. He really looked good in that shirt, never mind those chinos—both of which were so neatly pressed he clearly had donned them straight from the dry cleaner's bag. Maybe he wanted to avoid yet another trip to the cleaner's. He certainly didn't need to worry about tripping and spraying fizz on my highly unprofessional out- fit: a pair of cutoffs and a man's white V-neck T-shirt that Dodie pro- claimed was the equivalent of a neon sign that said GUINEA. The ethnic theme was further reinforced by the blue miraculous medal hanging con- spicuously on a silver chain between my breasts.

"If you're leaving," Mr. Strauss said, "I'll walk you to the door."

"That's quite all right—"

"I'd be happy to walk you—"

"I don't need to be walked—"

"You should be careful here after hours. There's only one security guard."

Behind him, loud and sudden as a sonic boom, came the flush of a toilet. Mr. Strauss turned and frowned at the men's room door.

I felt myself blush. "I brought along a bodyguard."

"I see. Well, in that case, I'll let you get back to—" He frowned again at my bare knees. "It's a beautiful day. Enjoy the sunshine."

He and his root beer disappeared down the hall. I bit my lip and looked to confirm, once again, that I had knock-knees, an offense I consid- ered second only to being bowlegged.

When Dodie came out of the men's room, he glanced up and down the hallway, tucked in his chin, pushed out his belly, and put his hand to his crotch to dramatically yank at the tab of his fly—all in imitation of my father and his own dad, who were notorious for the conspicuous way they adjusted themselves after they came out of any bathroom, public or private.

"Cut it out," I whispered. "Somebody might see you—"

"Nobody's here—"

"My boss just went by."

Dodie's eyebrow went up. "Little Miss Currier and Ives?" he whis- pered.

"No, a bigger gun," I said. "A guy."

"Was he the one listening to opera?"

"I'm not sure. But he definitely was drinking a root beer. Do you want a ginger ale for your stomach?"

"Nah. Head for the nearest grocery store. I hear the eggplant calling me. Let's do *parmigiana* for dinner."

We bid good-bye to Gussie and headed back to the Toyota, rolling down the windows to let in whatever moving air there was to be had on such a warm day. After we got on the road, Dodie said, "Now for the real scoop. Dare I ask about the man situation in this drug company of yours?"

After the lecture he once had given me on the glass ceiling, I hardly wanted to admit to Dodie I now moved in pink-collar country, where Tupperware and Sarah Coventry get-togethers lurked on every horizon and where I already had offended my coworkers by politely declining invitations to purchase iced-tea pitchers, five-quart casseroles with hermetically sealed lids, and hideous tricolor jewelry made out of silver, bronze, and gold, as if the designer were undergoing major PMS and couldn't decide which metal to work with that day. I tried to sound upbeat as I asked Dodie, "Couldn't you tell—just from the interior-decorating scheme—that everybody in my division keeps extra tampons in their desk drawer?"

"Oh! Didn't I tell you to check out whether there were any guys in your department?"

"But, Dodie, my boss is pregnant, I'm next in line for her position—"

"Still! You've got to learn how to play with the guys. The guys are where the power is at."

"Don't I know it," I said. "Boorman's totally good-old-boy. There's only one woman in top management, and she's built like a Valkyrie."

"Is she in the loop? One of the boys?"

"She's definitely not one of the girls," I said. Dr. Peggy Schoenbarger's standard uniform—a staunch gray double-breasted blazer and polyester blouse with a floppy rabbit-eared bow—as good as announced her as a lesbian. During my first week at work I had seen her scoping out my skirt in the hall, and what at first I took to be a sexual overture I quickly realized was disapprobation. She clearly thought women should flex, but not show, their muscles. I half-expected her to take out a yardstick and measure my hem, then whack me over the rear with the long end of the stick.

The Doctor certainly was a formidable creature. But the way she withheld emotion reminded me of my own mother, and up close and personal—or at least one on one—she had proved herself to be less of a hard-ass than I first imagined. I had since revised my initial impression of her as a Wagnerian entity incarnate (or at least as a dead ringer for the first female governor of Connecticut—a woman my relatives delighted in criticizing because she looked like a man but sported a first name, Ella, that meant *she* in Italian). Peggy now looked to me like one of my favorite childhood authors, Beatrix Potter, standing in the doorway of her cottage in a frumpy blouse and tweed skirt that only an English countrywoman would think to wear. Why Peggy reminded me of Potter, I couldn't quite say—for I was sure she wouldn't have approved of Potter's stories in which glum frogs and mischievous kittens and errant bunnies raided the cabbage patch and trashed dollhouses and never even dreamed of apologizing for their irrational behavior, never mind mending their criminal ways.

"You gotta meet this woman sometime," I told Dodie. "I swear she looks like something out of *Ring of the Nibelungs*. And she plays golf!"

"Hopefully you won't cross swords—or clubs—with this Brunhilda of the Bunkers."

"Actually, she sort of oversees my department."

"En garde."

"What for? She's been nice to me. And I don't care if she's a dyke."

"But, Lise, you're so girly-girl—"

"I am not—"

"—and this is not looked upon kindly by the lesbian element."

"Oh," I said. "Yeah. *The lesbian element.* Tell me, are they as intolerant as that other group we all know and love, the *practicing homosexuals*?"

Dodie put his hand over a fake lariat and tried—not too successfully—to imitate the voice of our cowboy president. "Any of those subversives we can lasso here?"

I looked over my shoulder to change lanes. "If they are, they're mothball material."

"Any datable straights?"

"I haven't totally scoped it out yet."

"This I find hard to believe."

I sighed. I thought about root beer. "There's nobody. So far. So forget it. Anything good going on in your life?"

"Yeah. Right. Everybody's so paranoid. I should join the priesthood."

"Maybe you should just get gay-married to somebody."

"Like who?"

I personally would have cast a very strong vote for Dodie's last boyfriend, George, who was a chef with the James Beard Foundation. George was half-Asian, and I would have killed for that boy's long glossy hair—kept back in a ponytail that Dodie, who thought it was too fem, kept threatening to cut off with his pizza scissors. Last year Dodie as good as announced he and George had serious intentions when he invited me three weeks in advance for a Friday soiree. George had volunteered to

make dinner. Although I was curious, I hadn't looked forward to the evening. I didn't much like meeting Dodie's partners. I knew it was wrong, but
I got jealous: Dodie's relationships with men always seemed better than
my relationships with men, and it wasn't just because his partners were
better-looking and better-dressed than mine. It was because they seemed
to share with Dodie what I so far had lacked in all my encounters with
guys: genuine friendship.

But I found I really liked George. He made us a spectacular dinner
and even divulged his secret recipe for the delicious spinach soup (which
tasted horrible when I later tried to make it). During the cheese course,
however, when the subject came up about Prince Charles's latest rumored
infidelity, I got the feeling that George and Dodie did not share the same
definition of the word *commitment*. That hunch seemed more than confirmed during dessert—an utterly heavenly tiramisù coated with powdered
chocolate—when I felt someone's stockinged foot grazing mine beneath
the table and then the light pressure of toes on my lower leg. I was drunk
enough to endure it—and then drunk enough to begin enjoying it—before
I finally came to my senses and excused myself to use the bathroom, where
I threw cold water on my face, only to come out looking—in Dodie's
words—paler than a ghost. "I think I had too much to drink," I said, and
made motions to beat a hasty retreat to the subway, over Dodie's strenuous
objections that I stick around awhile: George hadn't even fired up the
Gaggia for cappuccino, never mind there was more than enough marijuana in Dodie's cookie jar to stuff a bong the size of my mother's spaghetti
pot.

"Really, really," I said. "I have to go."

That was when George and Dodie looked at each other and started
shaking with laughter.

"Listen, Lise," Dodie said, "George thought he had my gam under
the table."

I bit my lip. "I shave my legs!"

"So what? We both have jeans on."

"Sorry, Lisa," George kept saying. "Really sorry. When you got up to
use the bathroom, I found I couldn't have made a worse mistake."

Although I also laughed—and eventually stuck around for both the
cappuccino and the marijuana—that whole episode sufficiently pissed me
off so that I greeted only with sympathetic silence the news Dodie delivered in a hoarse, broken voice two months later, that he and George had
parted ways. "I'm really sorry," I finally told Dodie—and I was. But mixed
with disappointment was a selfish relief. There's nothing worse than having to hear about your best friend's love affair when you have no informa-

tion to impart about your own. Besides, Dodie's relationship with George inspired in me an unhealthy envy. Nobody ever had played footsie with me beneath a table. Nobody ever kissed my hair or affectionately slapped me on the rump with an Irish linen tea towel, as George did to Dodie while I stood watching the milk froth into a stainless-steel pitcher.

"You should have married George," I told Dodie.

"George should have married *me*. Damn him. And damn you too, Lise—"

"Me!"

"Just out of curiosity, how long did you let him play footsie with you before you took your leg away?"

I certainly hoped George hadn't clocked me. "I thought it was your foot, Dodie."

"Nice try, Lise. But I don't believe that for a second."

"Shut up and let me concentrate on driving, will you?"

"When you stop trying to steal my boyfriends. Where are we going anyway? This looks really rural."

The two-lane country road looked more than rural to me—in fact, it looked like lost. But I didn't want to admit I'd been so busy talking I had gotten totally turned around. Already, with Dodie, I had the reputation of being a crazy woman driver—due more to my caution than my wildness behind the wheel. Maybe it was just another expression of my need to rebel against authority, but I did have a bad habit of braking at green lights and screeching to dead halts right beneath the yellows, so I either had to back up—which was against the law—or inch forward through the intersection, also an illegal maneuver.

As I went left at the next big intersection, I hoped Dodie wouldn't notice I was about to head back the same way we came. "You know," I said, "you've never totally 'fessed up what happened between you and George."

"I told you," Dodie said, keeping his head turned out the car window. "He wasn't faithful. And toward the end it got weird."

"But what's weird? Everything's weird."

"It wasn't just one thing. It was all sorts of little things." Dodie continued gazing out the window. "Besides, he wanted me to say unoriginal things to him. In bed."

I bit my lip, not eager to admit my own verbal repertoire was limited to *oh God, that feels so good* and the highly redundant *fuck me, fuck me, oh God, fuck me*, which actually had led one of my partners to reply, "What the hell do you think I'm doing, brushing your teeth?"

"Bed is hardly the place for original dialogue," I said.

"Yes, but I don't care to utter lines out of a B porn movie."

"Such as?"

"Well. My God. Put yourself in my shoes." Dodie gave me a nervous laugh. "He wanted me to call him a dirty fucking whore."

"George? Sweet George?"

"Stop spitting on the steering wheel, Lisa—it's unsanitary."

"Please tell me you're kidding."

"How I wish I were."

We kept on driving. Although I felt curiosity gnawing at me like a cough in my throat, I waited until we finally found our way back to the main road and were parked in the grocery-store lot before I asked, "So did you?"

"What?"

"Call George a dirty fucking whore?"

"I loved him," Dodie said, and I didn't know which was stronger: the sadness I felt that I never had experienced such emotion, or my wonder that if this was what constituted love, then why did I still want so desperately to seek it out?

Back at my apartment, Dodie sliced the *melanzana*—a deep ripe purple, which sported a brown fool's cap on the end—and I dredged it in salt and egg and flour. Eggplant always smoked in the pan, no matter how low the flame, so I disconnected the battery on the smoke detector, over Dodie's junior-fire-marshal–like protests that such doings were not safe.

As we took turns standing over the spitting, hissing pan with a pair of silver tongs, Dodie and I bemoaned our boy-craziness, which I insisted we shared because we were born on the same day.

"There's something to be said for the stars," Dodie agreed. "Personally, I find it easier to blame my mother."

"How about your father?"

Dodie nudged my arm. "How about blaming *you*, Lise?"

I snorted. Dodie always claimed his own love of boys dated back to Halloween of 1966, a dark and thundery afternoon on which Jocko and Carol took turns scaring the pants off us by reading aloud from a thick library volume of ghost tales. The last story they read that day concerned a boy named Reuben ("That's a Jewish name," Jocko added, as if this made the story even scarier). For some reason Reuben was frightened of the closet in his room, and he made the mistake of revealing his fear to his older brother, who carried Reuben kicking and yelling to the closet. Reuben got locked in, and after less than a minute, his screaming suddenly ceased. The closet went silent. Reuben had disappeared. "He entered the fifth dimension," Carol and Jocko cried in unison, as they dragged Dodie and me across the bedroom and locked us both into the closet. Dodie and I had screamed and stomped our feet until we heard Auntie Beppina burst into the bedroom demanding to know what was going on. "Dodie showed Lisa his peenie," Jocko answered, "so me and Carol locked them in the closet."

That afternoon Dodie got turned over Auntie Beppina's knee and spanked with the very volume of ghost tales that had inspired the whole episode. The spanking obviously had left a deep impression. "That's when I knew," Dodie told me, as he pulled another slice of eggplant out of the popping oil. "I have you to thank, Lise. That's when I thought to myself, 'Why would I ever want to show my penis to Lisa, or any other girl, for that matter?' "

I began to layer the fried eggplant slices with sauce and slices of mozzarella in a white Corning casserole dish. I told Dodie, "And that's when I started to sense—after my mother told me, *Don't you ever, ever let a boy show you his thing!*—that one of my biggest concerns in life was going to be convincing boys to show me."

But by junior high school I had gathered plenty of evidence that most boys didn't need convincing. *Boys of the male species* (as Dodie called heterosexual adolescents) took whatever they wanted, whenever they wanted it, and the rest of the world could spin out of orbit for all they cared. *Boys will be boys!* was one of the few American idioms our parents memorized correctly and obviously valued—for our boy cousins (with the exception of Dodie) ran wild, smoking and drinking and knocking girls up before they settled down to their jobs with Midas Muffler or the Southern New England Telephone Company. And girls—true girls—were like my sister, Carol, who liked to bake and tat and knit and buy domestic items for the Lane cedar hope chests we each were given when we turned sixteen. I never put anything in mine. When Mama made a deposit of half a dozen steak knives purchased with Betty Crocker coupons or a place setting of willowware dishes that came free with fifty dollars' worth of groceries, I gave mine up to Carol, who gladly accepted double the trousseau, as if she anticipated marrying twins.

Later I regretted having done that—not because I wanted to recover the cheap contents of that hope chest, but because my image of Carol having two husbands had fueled my first sexual fantasy, which I'd never been able to shake. The scenario was quite simple: Two clonelike men took me, one at a time. After the first twin had done a good number on me that brought me halfway to the top, I snapped my fingers and the second stepped up to finish the trick. I was sixteen when I first pictured this, and almost ten years later I found myself still clutching upon the image when the going got rough and I needed some extra help to round the corner into climax.

Sometimes I was ashamed of myself for thinking of such things—and wondered, did other women? But who in the world could I ask—my mother? Carol? Karen? Dr. Schoenbarger? And how would I phrase such a question? *Excuse me, but do you gals have these sick-turkey kind of fantasies too?* No point in pursuing this line of inquiry when I already knew what sad tale it told: that my body had become separate from my heart, that the way I wanted men in my fantasies—as perpetually firm, pulsing pistons whose only function was to satisfy my desire—lacked feeling and romance and had little to do with what the Bible called the greatest of human emotions, love.

Or was that charity?

"Dodie," I said. "Sometimes I worry about myself. I have these strange fantasies—"

"Alt!" Dodie said. "Stop right there, please."

"But why do I think such weird things?"

"I told you, Lisa, you'd better start writing that novel of yours, or you're going to end up in jail."

I shrugged. In a fit of boredom last weekend, I *had* started writing it, but what I hoped would develop into a witty parlor-comedy look at corporate life—Noel Coward goes to IBM—had quickly degenerated into a pornographic version of day-to-day life at Boorman Pharmaceuticals. I hadn't gotten more than eight pages into it and already there was copious screwing on the boardroom table, a little lesbian intrigue in the basement ladies' room, and a ludicrous culinary oral-sex orgy behind the cafeteria counter that involved a four-quart crock of sauerkraut and a barrel of dill pickles toppling to the tile floor. My tentative title was *Stop It Some More*. This nomer, more than anything in the thin plot, made me fear for my sanity, and I was saved only by the knowledge that any publishing house interested in my manuscript would immediately change the title, claiming I needed to *better convey the novel's concept,* or it would end up on the shredder or the remainder table after less than two months on the market.

"Do you think I'm a nymphomaniac?" I asked Dodie. "And don't say the way to cure a nymphomaniac is to—"

So Dodie said it: *"Marry her!"* He laughed, rinsed out a sponge from the sink, and started attacking the grease on top of the stove. "You *do* operate more like a man than a woman."

This much was true: I liked to swear, tell dirty jokes, have sex so hard it hurt, and even conk right out to sleep afterward, a habit that might have caused me shame had any of my partners hung around or woken up long enough to notice. My face must have expressed discontent, for Dodie was quick to assure me that operating like a man was more compliment than insult.

"Why shouldn't women go out and get what they want?" he asked. "Guys do it on a daily basis."

I dumped a too-big spoonful of sauce on top of the last layer of eggplant. "Do you think I'm a feminist, then?"

"Would a real feminist ask that?"

"That's what I mean."

Dodie thought about it for a moment. "Can a feminist be Machiavellian?"

"You got me," I told Dodie, too embarrassed to admit I had never read the second-most famous of Italian authors after Dante.

Dodie swiped the fool's cap from the eggplant out of the trash and put it on my head. "I dub thee the feminist prince."

I took the cap off. "I refuse the title."

"Well, why do you need a permanent title, Lise? Why can't you be a nympho one minute and a feminist the next?"

"They're not compatible."

"Oh, what's compatible inside any human being? You have a heart and a head. And a soul. And a pretty good body."

As if to confirm—or protest—this, my stomach let out a leonine growl.

"Just be Lisa," Dodie suggested.

"I'm not sure I like her."

"Learn to," Dodie said. "Or nobody else will."

At the table we talked until the wine bottle was empty. Then we cleaned up. Or rather, Dodie went to town on my kitchen, chiding me for the rust stains in my sink and making me put every single fork and spoon and pot and pan away. No air-drying for him. Afterward, we settled on the couch just like some old married couple, trading sections of the newspaper and commenting on absurd things we came across in the *Times*.

"An entire village went blind from staring at the sun because they thought they'd see a vision of the Virgin Mary."

"A new operation on the horizon will permit men to elongate their penis."

"The gorilla in the San Diego Zoo has undergone another enema."

"The Japanese are getting taller."

"And more women get depressed than men."

After reading about the traffic problems in Hyannisport, Dodie intoned in a dark, dire voice, "The Kennedys. Which one of these mindless millionaire micks would you shoot, maim, or drown first? Fat Teddy? Booze-Hound Ethel? Sargent Shriver?"

"Isn't he an in-law?" I asked. "He's got to be an in-law; he doesn't have those horsey teeth—"

"Jackie Oh-So-Moronic? Princess Caroline? Dumb-Dumb John-John?"

"Have you ever noticed how he always manages to have his shirt off when he gets photographed?" I asked.

Dodie snorted. "Beats looking at Bonny Prince Charles's skinny gams under a kilt."

"Hey, that reminds me." I put down the Arts page and told Dodie, "Margaret hired Chippendales to dance at her stag-ette party."

Dodie lowered the Metro section just enough to show me his forehead. "Behold my quizzical eyebrows," he said.

"I didn't go. Carol told me about it."

"Oh. Carol. She probably got the hots so bad for those hunks she rode Al Dante like a horse for days after."

I laughed, far too loudly, considering Carol was my own dear sister. Trying not to make it a leading question, I asked Dodie, "What do you think about Chippendales?"

"I guess it's a job. Like any other."

"Most jobs require you to keep your clothes on."

"Oh, yeah. I forgot about that."

"Would you strip for money?" I asked Dodie.

"How much money?"

I didn't answer. I went back to the newspaper and tried to read a review of a ponderous tome I had edited the previous year on the benefits of having more women in the work force. But I couldn't concentrate. Curiosity was killing me, and finally I asked Dodie point-blank, "Do you think Chippendale dancers are straight or gay?"

Dodie dropped the newspaper to his lap. "Why do you think I'd know? Or that there's even one right answer?"

"Don't get your huff up," I said. "I mean, I was talking about it with Carol—"

"Sounds like a real intelligent conversation—"

"—and we got to wondering. I don't think there's anything wrong in wondering. You ask me questions about being straight all the time; why can't I ask you questions back?"

"Because I've told you a million times. It's like that book we used to stare at when we were kids."

Illusioni was one of the few books in our grandparents' house. When we got bored we pulled it down off the shelf and stared at its black-and-white optical illusions and the captions in Italian:

Ragazza o vecchia?

Vuoto o pieno?

Mario lei o . . .

Young girl or old woman?

Empty or full?

Is Mario reading his book or . . .

Mario's eyes flickered from his book to a sexually indeterminate figure in the distance. Perhaps it was just a bad drawing. But that one page in *Illusioni* seemed to contend that often gender was a grand deception.

"Carol never clued in, did she, about that drawing of darling Mario?" Dodie sighed. "Your sister's always been so dense about sex."

"She's more on target than my mother."

"Who *isn't* more on target than your mother?"

"*Your* mother," I told Dodie, and he thought about it for a moment before he reluctantly agreed. Dodie said that trying to tell Auntie Beppina about homosexuality was like trying to teach a kid about how much money there was in the world. She couldn't even begin to fathom it.

"Well, we watched *Davey and Goliath* and didn't realize it was Christian," I said. "We didn't get that Dr. Seuss had a moral."

"We were kids," Dodie said. "We lacked a context. What excuse do our mothers have?"

"They're Italian," I reminded him.

"I forgot about that," Dodie said. "Yet we love them all the same."

Speak for yourself, I felt like telling Dodie. But I didn't. Even though Dodie had been on the outs for years with Uncle Gianni, he remained close to Auntie Beppina. They called each other frequently and she visited him every once in a while in the city—although she never once went to his apartment. Claiming he liked kitsch, Dodie took her to Radio City Music Hall and rode the ferry to the Statue of Liberty. My mother never visited me, nor did I invite her to do so.

"Mama probably still thinks I'm a lesbian," I said.

"Hmm," said Dodie. "This afternoon you did leap rather vigorously to the defense of gals in combat boots—"

"I don't have a thing for boots," I said. "I like feminine women. I admire images of the female form, I like to look at nudes, I mean—"

Dodie nodded encouragingly. "Go ahead, Lise. Spit it out."

I bit my lip. "Sometimes I get aroused by lingerie ads."

"Do tell."

I shrugged. "I don't know. It's weird. I used to think it meant some-thing. Then I thought it was just a sort of fantasy—you know, you get hot because you project yourself onto the woman in the picture. All of a sud-den you're the one with the pouty lips and the big tits and the come-hither look in your eyes."

"And on the other side of the magazine page is a man?"

"Well. Yeah. Sure. You know, some equally hot-looking guy." Then I added, "I don't think there's anything wrong with it. Everybody's supposed to be bi, to a certain extent."

"Maybe."

We had run over this ground before, but I decided to run over it again. "Are you sure you never look at women?"

"For Christ's sake, I'm not blind," Dodie said. "I mean, I notice when they're dressed well or when they're fat or ugly or have mongo bazooms—"

"But you never find them sexy?"

"Sometimes. If they're in a fencing outfit, say, and they have on those vests that squeeze it all in, and a hood over their head, and that leash on their butt that pulls tight when they stick out their rears and they lunge forward—"

"Get serious!"

"I'm completely serious. I like a woman with a sword. And pregnant women, maybe. I don't know why. I just have this urge to feel up their stomachs. It seems so soft—"

"It's hard," I said. "The stomach gets hard, Dodie."

He looked disappointed. "Another optical illusion."

I tried to make my voice sound casual. "Hey, by the way, Carol's preg-o."

"No shit!" Dodie said. "Why didn't you tell me before?"

"I forgot about it."

Dodie looked at me sorrowfully. Then he lay facedown on the floor in a position of complete penitence. Claiming his spine was out of line, he commanded me, "Get over here, girl, and walk the kinks out of my back."

Chapter Three

The Story of My Abortion

Dodie was the only person on the planet—besides the Hispanic receptionist at the clinic, who was the first person in years to pronounce my name right; the doctor, who held the vacuum tube as if he were cleaning out the backseat of his car; the assisting nurse, who yawned so wide I could see the silver fillings on her molars; and the priest at Saint Patrick's to whom I eventually confessed—who could hazard a good guess why my sister's pregnancy bothered me and why I fled the city for the suburbs.

In Brooklyn, I'd had an abortion.

I hadn't meant to tell Dodie—nor the priest. But confession seemed embedded in my nature. Just as high-school boys undoubtedly inscribed on the bathroom walls: *If you want a good time, call Lisa D.*, my family and friends could have scribbled: *If you want an honest answer, just ask Lisa.* Lisa did not know the value of a secret. Lisa liked to tell it like it was—especially when *the way it was* wasn't pretty.

Back in January—probably right around the time that one of Al Dante's millions of sperm finally penetrated one of Carol's eggs—I proved myself a truly schizophrenic Gemini by dating two guys at once (the single guy on the weekend, and the married one on Wednesday nights). I didn't even realize I was *in the family way* until one afternoon when I was on the phone, superlong-distance, with an Israeli author who had written a turgid memoir about Nazi-hunting in Chile and Argentina. He had spent the last month ogling tits on a French nudist beach, which meant his corrected manuscript was six weeks overdue.

As I hung on the phone with the Nazi hunter, trying to enforce a second deadline I knew he never would meet, I looked down at my desk calendar. The number 26 stared back at me. I pulled my chair closer to the desk, but its rusty wheels got stuck in the dustball-ridden carpet and I almost fell off my seat. *Hey*, I thought, *wait a minute.* I put the author on hold, yanked open my desk drawer, pulled out my appointment book, and gazed down at the cute row of X's I always used to mark the arrival and departure of "my friend" (another one of my mother's stupid euphemisms), which suddenly resembled the shorthand used by teenage girls to sign their letters with love: XXXOOO.

My lunch—a tahini-and-bean-sprout pita—came back into my throat, and I practically blew my cookies all over my calendar. Math never had been my best subject. I kept recounting, trying to deny that each time the sum came to an ominous thirty-three—thirty-three days instead of the usual twenty-seven, which meant six days overdue, and that meant only one thing. I dropped my calendar and picked up the phone to reconnect with the author, but ended up cutting him off because I didn't push the button down all the way.

I buzzed him back and got into a tightwire-taut discussion that ended with him asking me over and over in his heavy accent, "Who is the name of your supervisor, young lady? Tell me the name of your supervisor, young lady!"

I told him. This time he hung up on me. The next quarter of an hour was tense. From a neighboring cubicle I heard an editorial assistant put through a long-distance call—*"Collect,"* she kept calling, "the guy's livid, he's calling *collect* from Tel Aviv!"—to the editor-in-chief. We all hated the editor-in-chief. Although his Puritan blood surely was unsullied by a single Squanto-like corpuscle, those of us low on the totem pole had secretly nicknamed him He Big Chief and sometimes even whispered *"How!"* after he pompously paraded by our desks (not in feathers and war paint, but gray Armani).

From my cubicle I could hear He Big Chief whining and cajoling, and the more he whined and cajoled, the more the editorial assistants looked covetously at my dented metal desk and IBM Selectric with the space bar that was known to stick. Then He Big Chief strode over to my desk with all the confidence that came with the knowledge that his daddy owned three-quarters of the company. "Why can't you get along with people, Lisa?"

"Reasonable people?" I asked.

"Let me give you a name," he said, and supplied the Nazi-hunter's poetic handle—which sounded like the title of an ancient Hebrew text or the name of a forlorn, dusty desert.

"The guy has a tad of a temper," I said.

So did He Big Chief, who went into one of his infamous, unwarranted rages. He wanted that book bound and on the shelves! Klaus Barbie was in the news, and maybe—just maybe—he could get the author on *MacNeil/Lehrer* when the Butcher of Lyon came to trial—maybe even *Nightline* if the asshole got convicted!

Because I needed my job—and because the mere thought of Barbie made me want to throw up—I quickly assured He Big Chief that I would write the Nazi hunter a letter expressing my unbridled enthusiasm for his manuscript, and once I got the pages in my hands I would take them home and slave over them every night.

That promise was the first of many self-imposed punishments that came out of my realization: *Holy Mary, mother of God, I'm pregnant.*

I knew what I had to do. Later that week I did it. After it was over, I dragged myself home from the clinic. My purse never felt so heavy on my shoulder, even though I had just emptied it of three hundred and fifty dollars in cash—an amount I dared to carry on the subway only because I did not want to write a check. The kind of God I believed in, however, didn't need a paper trail to find me. Although I thought of myself as a cheerfully lapsed Catholic, when I returned from the clinic I felt I had done something deeply wrong, and I was terrified of divine retribution. I hadn't been to church in years, not counting the obligatory Christmas and Easter masses I attended when I went home to visit Mama, but I still believed enough doctrine to feel that I had committed the most grievous sin on earth. At the clinic I had been put under the haze of twilight sleep, and in that fog I felt I heard the voice of the fetus crying from limbo, or the Dumpster—or a tin bucket—wherever its soul and unformed body went.

How I wished the father—whoever he was—could have heard that voice too. But I didn't feel as if I could tell either of the two men the news that I carried inside me the beginnings of a boy or girl who someday might address him as *Daddy.* My weekend partner couldn't be taken seriously beyond his competent lovemaking techniques. Although he was pushing thirty, he went by the childish (and faux British) name of Davey and was a PacMan fanatic. He also was best friends with one of my coworkers, and telling him I was off to the Emma Goldman Clinic would have been the equivalent of getting out a bullhorn and announcing to the entire office I was a killer of unborn children. The married man, Brian, was a shameless bar pickup who I continued to see mainly because he represented a good hot meal once a week (delivered by hotel room service). I knew more about his wife than I did about him, or at least about how his spouse refused to please him in bed. How could I even think of having the child of a man whose constant refrain was, *Oh yes, my wife would never do this; oh yes, my wife would never do this?* The minute the doctor stopped the sucking of the pump and pulled out the tube, I knew I'd never see either Davey or Brian again.

As I stood in front of my apartment door fumbling with my key ring, I heard a voice inside, and in my drug-induced delirium I thought a pair of guys were burglarizing my apartment. Then I remembered the answering machine. I quickly turned the bolts of all three locks and lunged for the phone.

It was Dodie, chiding me for calling in sick to work—accusing me of staying home to watch *Days of Our Lives*—and for missing my monthly payment to him—that little wad of cash I always sent for him to invest any way he saw fit.

"I don't have it," I said.

Dodie clucked his tongue. "I told you to stay out of the pool hall."

"I wasn't in the pool hall. I was in the abortion clinic."

The phone went silent. Realizing I hadn't even bolted the door behind me, I cradled the phone against my shoulder, walked over, and sadly turned the locks one by one. I sat down on my director's chair—the only piece of furniture I had in the entire apartment besides a double mattress on the floor, two TV trays that served as impromptu dinner tables, a rickety clothes tree rescued from the side of the curb, which I meant to paint white but never did, and two cardboard chests of drawers with blue plastic handles that usually fell off when you pulled them.

"Are you all alone now?" Dodie asked.

"Take an educated guess."

"I'll come over when I get off work. In the meantime, don't do anything stupid."

"I think I've already done it."

Dodie hesitated. "You can't take it back now."

"Don't I know it," I said, and burst into tears.

Dodie showed up at eight-thirty. I pulled myself off my bed, where I had spent the last four hours curled up, alternately dreaming and weeping, relieved that at least my mattress wasn't the place where I had conceived the only baby I probably ever would have. Or not have. Otherwise I couldn't have put my head down on the foam and fallen asleep.

When I opened the door, the apartment was flooded with the smell of Chinese takeout. Dodie came in cradling a paper bag in his arm, which he put down in what passed for my kitchen: a gas stove with only one functional burner, a mini-refrigerator with a freezing unit chock-full of ice, and a small cabinet, all jammed in what probably used to be a walk-in closet. I crawled back into bed, and Dodie sat down next to me in the director's chair, his face grim and serious.

"Don't look at me that way," I said.

"What way?"

"You know. So disapproving."

"I'm not sitting in judgment on you, Lise."

I didn't believe him. For a short, painful moment—as the radiator clicked and then hissed on—I was intensely aware that Dodie was a man, and although he was a man who didn't love women, his gender irritated me. He never would know how far my stomach dropped when I counted up to thirty-three. He never would be forced to make the kind of decision I just had made. For the first time in my life I envied Dodie's sexuality, simply because he could not get pregnant, nor would he ever get somebody else—to use another of my mother's garbled idioms—*in the trouble.* Then I remembered he could only—*only!*—get AIDS.

"Why don't you understand?" I asked him.

"But I do. What else could you have done?"

"That's what I keep telling myself. What else could I have done? I mean, I was careful. I had my diaphragm in. It just didn't work, it didn't work. . . . Why couldn't it have happened to Carol? Why did I get pregnant without even trying or wanting, and she tries and wants, but can't?"

I reached for my box of Kleenex, conveniently parked right by my pillow. Dodie's sad face functioned as a mirror for me: I knew I looked like hell, absolutely wild and scary, with my hair every which way, my clothes all rumpled, and my face bloated.

Dodie leaned his elbows on the shaky arms of the director's chair. "How much did it cost?"

"Three fifty." I grabbed a Kleenex and blew my nose. "Did you know you could put an abortion on a Visa?"

"Did you?"

I shook my head. "Cash on the nail."

Dodie looked around my apartment, his eyes lingering on the cardboard chest of drawers and the monstrous gray radiator, then finally settling on one of the many long cracks that splintered the ceiling. "You're going to be strapped. You already *are* strapped. You'd better think about getting out of New York, Lise. You can't live like this forever."

"How'm I gonna live, then?"

"Like a decent human being."

"I don't have it in me to be decent now."

"Who's talking morals? I'm talking finances."

"How much do I have saved?"

"Oh, no. I'm not going to let you touch that."

"It's my money."

"You agreed, way back when, not to touch it. I won't let you touch it." He stared hard at me. "Get a good haircut and get another job."

"All right. God. I can't help my hair. I've tried everything, even mayonnaise."

"George claimed sesame oil was good."

"Why do I need *grease* when already I look like Al Pacino from the back? When it's wet or oily it's even worse—totally Sinatra, and I don't mean Nancy either." I blew my nose again. "God. I'm going nuts. I'm editing this terrible manuscript at work."

"Another shit book on discovering the child within?"

"No, this is a new one. I'm the Nazi expert now. This is a collection of Holocaust memories."

"How cheerful," Dodie said. "Why don't they give it to somebody Jewish? Don't you have any Jews in your office?"

"There's only one. She edits the Mafia books—"

"And who does the books on how to talk to your dog and have atomic sex while drinking espresso and eating chili peppers all at the same time? That nice gee-gee I met?"

"No, he does the books on wedding etiquette."

"How disgusting," Dodie said. "Come on, Lise. Get out of publishing."

"But what else am I going to do?" I fixed my pillow, trying unsuccessfully to plump up its battered feathers before I put my head back down on it. I stared at the ceiling. "This manuscript I'm working on is really getting to me. It's making me sick to look at it. I keep staring at the pages and trying to concentrate on the words, but I get so wrapped up in the stories, and then I have to go back and read the page all over again, and it's all so crazy and weird and I start thinking how could stuff like that ever happen?"

"The word is *evil*," Dodie said.

I blew my nose. I had just edited three hundred and fifty pages of evil, and I still had another two hundred and twenty-five to go. I focused on the flaking paint on the ceiling. "In this manuscript—you know, the one I'm working on—there's this story about a guy who watched a Gestapo guard throw his pregnant wife down on the camp ground and stomp on her stomach until the baby came out. Then he stuck a Luger up her crotch and pulled the trigger—"

"Stop it," Dodie said. "Don't tell me that stuff."

"I can't stop thinking about it," I said. "I mean, the guy's still alive, he has to go to work every morning and pick out green beans with almonds at the grocery store and write checks to cover his electric bill, and how does he do it?"

"Did he say? In the manuscript?"

"He said he hated to go to sleep because he was afraid to dream about it. And then he said, 'I just wanted to survive, that's all I wanted, just to hang on to my own life.' "

"God. What for?" Dodie bit his lip. "I'd throw myself against the fence." He rose and went into the kitchen. "Which do you want," he called out, "the wonton or the hot-and-sour?"

"I'm not hungry."

"You've got to eat something. I'm not leaving until you put something in your stomach."

How could I put anything in me, considering what had just been taken out? But to please Dodie, I had a little of the wonton broth. Dodie went after the hot-and-sour, then cleaned out the entire pint of pork fried rice. He crunched on the fried noodles with such obvious relish that I had to give in and have a few myself, even though I didn't want to leave crumbs on the bed sheet.

"Fortune-cookie time," Dodie said at the end.

I shook my head. I didn't feel I deserved good fortune—and since when did those neat little slips of paper folded inside the hard cookies ever tell you anything negative?

Dodie cracked the first cookie and unscrolled the paper. "The tree on the top of the mountain feels the most wind," he said. He had to grit his teeth to open the cellophane bag of the second cookie, and the cookie itself was so hard it splintered into pieces before he pulled the slip out. He read it and crumpled it.

"No," I said. "Show it to me." I reached up and pried it from his fist.

A child is as good as its parent.

I recrumpled it and fell back on the mattress, crying again. Dodie sighed. He got out my broom and swept up the fortune-cookie crumbs, then cleaned up in the kitchen in a futile attempt to stave off the cockroaches. He used my phone to rearrange his plans ("It's my cousin, she's in bad shape, no really, I can't, I just can't, she's a mess, here, listen to her crying, go ahead, crank it up, Lise, for the benefit of those who won't believe me!"). I cranked it up. Dodie got off the phone, dimmed the lamp, and sat next to me on the mattress. He lit up a joint and we smoked it. It grew later and later, and still Dodie sat over me.

I drifted off. The next thing I knew the digital clock clicked onto 1:00. I heard Dodie testing the top door lock. His wallet thudded onto the canvas seat of the director's chair. His keys clanked on top. These were the sounds I liked to hear from men, the sounds I actually preferred to their voices (unless, of course, they were whispering my name in my ear). Shoes dropping to the floor. The slide of a tie along a collar. The softness of buttons being undone. The clack of the belt. The promising metal rip of a zipper.

"Move over," Dodie said.

I already had rolled completely against the wall, but it was only a double mattress, and when Dodie climbed under the quilt and sheet, I could feel the brush of his leg against mine. I sensed that Dodie had kept on his T-shirt and shorts, but I was fully clothed, in my sweat suit and socks and even a hairband to keep my dirty curls off my face.

Many times, over the years, Dodie and I had slept in the same room. But we never had shared a bed. The situation felt uneasy until Dodie finally hung a name on it. "This is *weird*," he whispered.

"I know," I said.

"I've never slept with a girl before. I've never even slept with an *Italian* before."

Because I still felt the marijuana running through me, I snorted and burst into giggles, making the mattress quiver. I kicked him under the covers. He nudged me back.

"I stopped sleeping with guinea guys when I left New Haven," I said. *Sleep,* however, was a misnomer, for none of these boys had done me in a position in which it was physically possible to catch forty winks afterward.

"You certainly did your share of them," Dodie said.

"I know, Mr. Mathematician. I, too, can count."

Dodie hesitated. "Why do you do this to yourself?"

"Do what?"

"You know. Sleep around."

"Like you never did?"

"In my case, there *was* a selection process involved."

"I'm choosy too," I said. "I draw the line at men who spit."

"Like your father?"

"Yeah," I said. My father had been known for chewing the ends of his White Owl cigars and spewing them—with admirable skill—from the cracked steps on our back porch ten feet away into my mother's tomato garden. When she yelled at him, he claimed the chewed tobacco made good fertilizer.

My stomach felt hollow as I thought of the gruff relationship my mother and father had with one another and the coldness that had seeped into every corner of my parents' house, so that it still felt like winter far beyond my birthday every May.

Dodie must have been thinking the same about his own parents, because without a word spoken, he took my hand and squeezed it. We lay there quietly in the dark for a long time, listening to the doors opening and closing in the echo of the hall and the intermittent sound of sirens. Just before I fell asleep, Dodie's voice—distant, almost disembodied—murmured, "Man, I used to get down on my knees and pray my mother was not my mother and my father not my father. I used to *pray.*"

A week later I stood in line at Saint Patrick's for confession. My heart thumped as I went into the prayer box and knelt in the corner. I heard the priest mumbling to the person on the other side, and just as I was about to bolt, the screen slid back, and I stared into the space reserved for the priest. I knew I wasn't supposed to look directly at him, nor was he supposed to turn his eyes on me. Yet I peeked long enough to discover the priest was young—surely no more than thirty. I took this as a sign he would be more forgiving.

"Father," I whispered, "I've forgotten the words."

He asked if I wanted to repeat them after him, and so I did, up until the phrase *and these are my sins.*

Then I told him why I was there.

"This is a very serious offense against God," he finally said. "Are you married?"

"No."

"The father?"

"I don't know who it was."

"It sounds as if you have other things you need to confess."

"Where should I start?" I asked. "I mean, I could confess my whole life. I could say I'm sorry for being a human being—"

"God doesn't want you to do that."

"Well, what does God want us to do?" I asked, too loudly.

He lowered his voice as a reminder that I should do the same. "God wants us to live our faith."

"I guess I don't have faith."

"You do or you wouldn't be here."

"I'm confused."

"You obviously don't keep the sacraments. Go to church. Make frequent confessions and take Communion. And pray."

I think I made a face, which I was afraid he saw—for he, too, was disobeying the rules and looking out of the corner of his eye at me.

"Isn't there anything more than that?" I asked.

"Don't live for yourself. God gave you life. He didn't give you life so you could take it away from others—"

"I can't fix it now. I can't take it back—"

"Are you sorry for this? Or just sorry you've gotten caught?"

"Both," I said. Then I added, "Look, I'm holding up the line outside."

"This isn't a department store," the priest said. "I'm still waiting to hear the rest of your confession."

"I'm not sure I'm sorry for anything else."

"Then I can't grant you absolution."

Well, what the hell? I thought, before I opened my mouth and let it all spill out. My attention to detail—the very thing that made me a good editor—also made me a thorough storyteller. I told him about my dirty dozen back in New Haven and all the guys—there had been a lot of guys—in New York. I also told him I slept with Dodie. Even though we hadn't done anything more than hold each other that night, we woke up to find a spot of blood—rusty as a flaking barbed-wire fence—on the sheet between us.

"That's called incest," the priest said.

"But we didn't do anything—"

"Did you want to"—his voice tightened—"*do* something?"

"I don't know. Maybe. Probably. How am I supposed to put a stop to my imagination? Why did God give me such an imagination if he didn't want me to use it?"

The priest told me that God may have granted me imagination, but the devil himself made fine use of it.

I couldn't argue with that.

"Put your imagination to work for God," he told me, and granted me absolution. A minute later I was on my knees in one of the side pews, reciting my penance, which the priest made me promise to say every evening until I felt confident I could lead a better, purer life.

"Every evening," the priest said. "Will you do that for me?"

Anything for you, I almost said—because I already had formed a foolish crush on him. As I mumbled my Hail Marys, I thought about how I wanted to step through the screen that separated us and have the priest wrap me up in his robes and tell me, *There, there, Lise, I love you more than God Himself.*

Was there any greater sin than this? Fantasizing about embracing—or boinking—a priest? Wouldn't this be one of the crimes we studied in catechism—one of the sins that *cried out for vengeance?* What were they again? Murder. Sodomy (*What's that?* someone asked Sister Matthew, and she said it was *ill treatment of other men*). Taking advantage of the poor? Depriving the worker of his wages? Lusting after people who already had pledged their lives to other human beings or to Christ?

As I got up from the pew I remembered how easy it all had seemed back in the days of catechism, marching into the confessional and admitting I had told a few lies and said an occasional *shit* or *damn*. Then I had slipped up to the altar and recited my three Hail Marys and two Our Fathers, leaving the church feeling utterly free and pure, as if the pressing weight of the cross itself had been lifted off my shoulders.

Yet this time it hadn't worked. I felt no better when I came out of Saint Patrick's than when I went in. This time I would have to forgive myself, but I didn't feel capable of making that leap. Maybe I didn't want to. Maybe this was my version of the self-punishment I used to witness in the dorms at Sarah Lawrence: the neurotic girls who cut fine lines on their forearms with razors, who gave themselves nightly enemas, or who sat in front of the bathroom mirror with a pair of tweezers, yanking hair after hair out of the front of their scalps until they resembled the women in medieval portraits whose high foreheads shone as bright as the polished hood on my brother-in-law's car.

Yes, I punished myself. Then God Himself took a turn. After I finished editing the Nazi hunter's memoirs, I had to proofread yet another killer manuscript: a collection of interviews with the children of survivors, in which they described the trauma of growing up with parents who had looked the worst kind of evil right in the face. The stories both the children and the parents told sickened me, and every night when I went to bed and said my penance I tried hard not to question why I was praying to a God who permitted such things to happen.

One night in the middle of the Act of Contrition, I heard a dry scratching sound coming from the kitchen. I listened. The scritch-scratch sounded like the static on a radio speaker, as if at any moment a voice might come in. But the senseless, untranslatable noise continued. I rose from the mattress, failing to close off my communion with God—as we were taught to do—with a *good* sign of the cross ("Touch your forehead and your breastbone and each shoulder as if you're proud to carry the cross like Jesus," Sister Joseph said).

I sneaked into the kitchen, threw on the light, and pulled open the kitchen cabinet. There was a flash of wild eyes, and bare teeth, and black claws, and then the rat dropped the Brillo pad, and I screamed and closed the cabinet. Back in the living room, I took all three volumes of Proust off the floor beside my mattress and then stacked them against the cabinet door.

A month later I landed up in Ossining, away from the scene of my crime, away from the rat and the half-finished second-generation survivor manuscript. I wished I could have left myself—the rotten side of myself—behind too.

Instead, I took her along for the ride to Boorman, and my evil twin threatened to break out right when Karen's uterus slipped and she had to take to bed to save her baby.

Chapter Four

There's a Man in the Picture

As if she were the grammar-school nurse about to deliver the infamous "little talk" about the facts of life, Dr. Peggy Schoenbarger herded the editorial staff into the break room, where she announced that Karen would be out of commission for the next four weeks, and perhaps indefinitely. The tight-lipped way Peggy eked out the words *placenta previa* made it sound as if Karen had contracted crabs or cooties. Her stern look seemed the prelude to her hosing down the rest of us in Editorial with a can of pesticide that would render us all infertile and thus ineligible to take any future maternity leaves.

"This situation is very regrettable," Peggy said. "I'm sure we all feel for Karen. However, we have deadlines. Important deadlines. Deadlines that Karen also wants you to meet."

I was sure deadlines were the furthest thing from Karen's mind. But as if to demonstrate that she and Karen spoke with one voice, Peggy held up her legal pad, where she had recorded careful notes of her conversation with the unfortunate mother-to-be. "Karen wants to remind you that the newsletter is due at the printer next week. The employee-benefits manual needs to be turned around by the end of the month. And there's the new spinal block."

Since *coming on board,* it seemed as if I had heard of nothing but this fabulous injection, which had just cleared the final FDA hurdle and was about to be released onto the market with as much fanfare as a cure for cancer.

"Karen has taken tremendous responsibility for the spinal-block project. Who will volunteer to take her place?"

Summer was up and running. July and August reservations had been made at the Jersey shore. I was the only one in Editorial—other than Karen—who didn't bolt the moment her digital clock slid onto 5:00. It was no surprise my hand was the first—and the only—one in the air.

Peggy's curt nod showed she admired any young woman—such as me (or was that *I?*)—who had nothing better to do with her free time than *give her all to Boorman.* "Very fine, Ms. Diodetto. Mr. Strauss said if you didn't volunteer for the spinal block, to go ahead and give it to you anyway."

I shifted the position of my rump—which suddenly felt sore and uncomfortable—in my chair. I noticed that several of my coworkers smirked at the very idea of Mr. Strauss—or, rather, the good Doctor herself—administering an anesthetic into my gluteus maximus.

Peggy cleared her throat. "Mr. Strauss really should be here having this conversation with you—"

More smiles, as we all thought of Mr. Strauss giving us a frank talk about placental abruption.

"—but he's out of town and will call you with the details. You can work out the overtime with Human Resources."

Dr. Schoenbarger then gave us a speech about the need to keep up standards in Karen's absence. She said she was a busy woman and so was Mr. Strauss (here she provoked an audible snicker). "Neither one of us has much time to keep our eyes on you," she said. "We trust you to run a tight ship here and conduct yourselves like professionals."

We gave her our solemn word we would do just that. Then the moment she left the break room, we sent the secretary out to Dunkin' Donuts and fired up Mr. Coffee.

A half hour later (our eyes on the glass door to make sure Peggy didn't swing back to deliver a few more words on the dangers of employing women of childbearing age), we reconvened over mocha java and two dozen glazed and frosted crullers. We did a lot of tut-tutting over Karen and her baby before the married women predictably began to swap stories of failed pregnancies and gruesome labors and deliveries. Another single woman thankfully cut them off by asking, "Are you nuts, Lisa?"

"How so?" I asked, washing down a mouthful of cream puff with black coffee.

"Doctor Peggy is such an I-don't-know-what. You need to have your *head* examined, volunteering to work closer with her."

"What's the big deal?" I asked. "Karen gets along with her all right."

"She's a roaring bitch."

"And Mr. Strauss is no dream boss either," someone else added.

"He seems nice enough," I ventured.

"Compared to the Doctor."

"He's worse than she is."

"So fussy."

"A perfectionist."

"Totally uptight."

"You don't do something once for him, you do it five times."

"At least he says please."

"The Doctor never says please."

Giddy on sugar and caffeine, I let down my guard. "That's true," I said. "When I first met her, the Doctor said, *Greetings.*"

They burst into laughter. "Do it again, Lisa."

"*Greetings,*" I repeated in Peggy's low voice, and with that single word I established myself as one of the girls.

Their advice then flew fast and thick:

"Listen, Lisa, we didn't want to tell you since you were in so good with Karen, but the further you stay away from the big guys, the better."

"That's not true. When you're putting together the newsletter, interview the CEO at every chance you get."

"Watch out for those guys in the ad room."

"Wear short skirts when you go in there."

"And definitely wear a pantsuit when you have a meeting with Peggy—"

"—Mr. Strauss might like that too—"

"Go on. You think he's—"

"He isn't married."

"So what?"

"Well, it's just a feeling; don't you sometimes have that *feeling*?"

Opinion seemed divided on the subject, but I wasn't able to hear the full extent of the debate, because my office phone was ringing. It was Karen.

"I just stepped away from my desk," I said, carefully enunciating my words to disguise the sound of the last bite of doughnut going down my throat. "How are you?"

Karen was upset from her encounter with Peggy and anxious about her ability to still supervise us from her bed. She asked me to take out a pencil so she could give me a long list of tasks to accomplish. If I felt uncomfortable about using her misfortune to muscle in, prematurely, on her position—and I did—she took my guilt away by saying, "Thank God you're there, Lisa—otherwise the work wouldn't get done half as well and Dr. Schoenbarger would get even more bent out of shape."

"What did she say to you?" I asked.

"It was more what she *didn't* say. She only once said she was sorry. Mr. Strauss sent me flowers—I mean, and he's even out of town—but she did nothing but grill me about my medical condition for half an hour."

"Maybe she has a scientific interest in your condition."

"Maybe she's got a grudge against me because I'm pregnant." Karen paused. "I probably shouldn't be telling you this—I don't want to spread rumors, but . . ."

I rolled my eyes and waited.

Karen lowered her voice as if she were in the office right next to me instead of five miles away on the phone. "Well. Lisa. Dr. Schoenbarger *lives with another woman*—"

No! I felt like answering. *I'm shocked beyond belief.*

"I'm very sorry to hear that," I said, holding the phone away from my ear and sticking my tongue out at Karen through the receiver.

"—and I happen to know—from a friend who volunteers at Catholic Charities—that she and this woman friend of hers have been trying to adopt a child from Central America." Karen raised her voice back up again. "I'm sorry. I just can't imagine Dr. Schoenbarger a mother. She doesn't have a maternal bone in her body."

"I wouldn't totally agree with that," I said. "Sometimes she treats me—and even Mr. Strauss—like a kid."

Peggy Schoenbarger's motherly instincts first came to my attention when she silently conveyed her disapproval of my wardrobe and were further confirmed when she took me up on my offer of help with her correspondence. As we sat at her conference table hashing out the wording of some form letters, I decided she was less interested in chastising me than in gently converting me—if not over to true feminism (whatever that was) then at least over to below-knee-length skirts. Her inordinate interest in how I was *getting along at Boorman* seemed to signal that she was ready to take me under her wing—a position that Mr. Strauss also curiously seemed to hold, as was illustrated when he strode right into her office and got stopped (by one of her forbidding looks) halfway across the carpet.

"I thought you were out. Excuse me for interrupting." He pointed to her desk. "May I pick up something here—"

"Yes, you may," Peggy told him. He went over to the desk, ignoring me completely. I wasn't wearing the recommended pantsuit for my meeting with Peggy, and the way I sat—sideways at the table—probably displayed too much of my legs for his prudish taste.

"He *does* know how to knock," Dr. Schoenbarger told me.

"You have me well trained, Peg," he said.

"Now I'll have to get to work on some others. Who shall remain nameless." She shuffled the papers in front of her and made a few vague comments about the need to promote more women within the ranks of Boorman. "What were your grades in science, Ms. Diodetto?" she asked, perhaps hoping she could send me back to night school to produce the next Madame Curie.

"Must I admit to them?" I asked, trying hard not to look at a certain section of Eben Strauss's anatomy—i.e., his admirable butt—as he leaned slightly over a pile of file folders.

"Very well. Grammar is a science too. Now, about this letter: Isn't there any more enlightened way to open than *Dear Sir or Madam*?"

"It's antiquated," I said, "but that's still the accepted way."

"Does a woman—of your generation—like being called *Madam*?"

"Well. No. It makes me feel like I'm in a brothel."

Some of the gray hair on her forehead stiffened, and I rushed in to say, "But I guess most men don't mind that opening. The *Sir* part, at least."

"Do they, Eben?" Peggy asked.

"Pardon me?" he said, although I was quite sure he'd been listening—and even smiled when I said *brothel*.

"Mind *Dear Sir* as the opening of a letter?"

"Why don't you try *To Whom It May Concern*?"

"That's very cold—"

"It's not a love letter, I take it?"

"—to the point of being rude."

"But it's gender nonspecific, if that's what you're looking for."

"What are *you* looking for?" she asked him impatiently—because he *was* taking an awfully long time to find what he needed on her remarkably clean desk.

He held up a red file folder and smiled. "Did you ask Ms. Diodetto if golf is her game?"

"All in due time."

Then they both turned and gave me the once-over, as if trying to assess how fine a figure I would cut on the golf course—and I sat there like a living specimen of the kind of woman who infinitely preferred heels to cleats.

After I related an (edited) version of that scene to Karen, she admitted, "Dr. Schoenbarger and Mr. Strauss *do* have a tight relationship. Personally, I think it's a very *odd* relationship."

I waited for her to breathlessly confide in me, *I don't want to spread rumors, but . . . Dr. Schoenbarger gave birth to Mr. Strauss through artificial insemination long before the process was even invented!*

"Maybe she always wanted to have a son," Karen said. "And I *am* sorry she couldn't get that girl to adopt from Central America. But I didn't ask for this to happen to me. I fully expected to work up to the ninth month—" Karen started to cry. "Oh, Lisa! Can you bring me my Rolodex on your way home from work?"

"Give me your address," I said, "and I'll even bring you some leftover doughnuts."

"Doughnuts?" Karen asked, her voice fraught with dismay.

I got off the phone in a hurry.

Right after this I got a call from the printer. Then yet a third call came, from Cleveland: Mr. Eben Strauss, his voice half drowned out by the bustle of a crowd and airline gates being announced.

"Your line has been busy," he said. "I'm in a hurry, but I want you to call Karen—"

"I just spoke to Karen."

"Oh. How is she? This is unfortunate. She really wanted this baby."

"She hasn't lost it."

"But to be confined to bed—like an invalid—" He cleared his throat. "I hope you won't mind calling her back and asking her, please, where she is with the spec sheets and the brochures on the spinal block."

"I'm already on the spec sheets—"

"Could you speak up? I can hardly—"

My voice always sounded rude when I raised it. "I'm already doing them," I loudly said, and added, "sir."

"And the ads? We'll need the ads. I'm concerned about the ads—"

"Relax," I said. "Trust me."

My comment—clearly inappropriate from his point of view—was greeted with a silence so long I heard this complete announcement in the background: *Final call for Flight 4298 to Peoria. All ticketed passengers should now be on board.* I wished I were on that plane, with a big stiff drink in my hand. I wished I didn't have such problems, all the time, with authority.

I charged back in to set the situation right. "What I meant to say was, I hope you'll trust me to take care of it."

After he coolly assured me that was his plan, I hung up the phone, unable to determine whether I was more pissed at myself for calling him *sir* or for telling him to chill out and relax.

Two days later Karen's ob/gyn ordered her onto complete bed rest for the remainder of her pregnancy, and although I didn't get her title or her office, I got all her responsibilities—plus a substantial raise, which took some of the sting out of picking up her work load and helping to cover for the women on vacation. During the two weeks that followed, I stayed late to take care of the spec sheets and the physician-information brochures and the ads for that spinal-block project and sometimes didn't get to the gym until 8:00 P.M.—mainly because I didn't have a computer at home, and I was determined to type up the few scribbled notes I'd made on *Stop It Some More.* When I returned to my apartment, I flopped my sweaty body onto the couch and cracked open a bag of popcorn and my latest library book—that is, until my extracurricular activities took on a more interesting light. Then my whole life seemed to revolve around not letting anyone suspect my social scene had changed for the better.

Although I dropped a few coy hints to Dodie (who also had taken up with a mysterious partner), I couldn't talk about my new romantic interest to anyone, beyond casually alluding to his existence in the Bloomingdale's dressing room when a helpful saleswoman wanted to know if I was updating my wardrobe because of a career change. I nodded. "There's also a man in the picture," I said, looking over my shoulder into the three-way mirror to check out the panty-line situation on the skirt.

She congratulated me on achieving success at both work and play, little suspecting that if I didn't handle myself just right, I'd lose at both of them. I knew the rules. Karen had forewarned me of the rules: that those in my lowly position should not mix with management, except through occasional phone calls to the higher-ups to confirm some tidbit of news that was going to run in our internal house organ, a sickeningly upbeat monthly newsletter I edited called *The Grapevine,* in which we reported births, weddings, new policies on smoking and trash collection, who won the local quilting contest, which VP got another wood and brass plaque from the Rotary Club, and the standing of our corporate baseball, basketball, and bowling leagues.

On my computer I had written a hilarious (at least to my mind) send-up of the text of this newsletter, which I had the bad judgment to share with a few other girls in the office. Instead of *The Grapevine,* my banner read *Face Crime!* My articles reported that the CEO was parked in a drying-out facility, the staff social worker was arrested for pedophilia, the head of the chemical plant was a confirmed dope addict, and our trustworthy custodians made up for their lousy salaries by filching number-two pencils and ludes from the lab. My headlines proclaimed: DRUG ABUSE RAMPANT IN THE INNER CIRCLE and SECRETARIES QUERY TOP EXECS: WHY DO OUR DRINKING FOUNTAINS TASTE LIKE BONG WATER?

Needless to say, I did not share this choice document with Karen, whom I visited at her home from time to time and with whom I kept up the most professional of demeanors—knowing, of course, that her good recommendation was crucial to my moving my stapler and paper-clip holder into her office for good. After it became clear that this move was in the cards, I rued ever having composed *Face Crime!*, because I was afraid my coworkers, jealous of my power, would use this lapse of judgment to sabotage me.

But I had a way of handing the enemy more than enough ammunition to blast me out of the water. Why else did I become Boorman's equivalent of a high-school hussy, who could have been framed by one of the very second-coming headlines I had so delighted in composing on my computer: EDITOR SEDUCES RELUCTANT VEEP!

I fell in love—the only way to do it, madly—with a man I was careful to describe to Karen as a *stuffed shirt*.

His name was Eben Strauss.

Strauss and I got off to a rocky start. He was out of town when I first began work on the spinal-block material, and we communicated mostly through pink while-you-were-out messages: *3:00 P.M. Mr. Strauss. Wants to know where you're at with the JAMA ad, leave message with his secretary. 11:15. Mr. Strauss. Call printer and up number of brochures by 3,000.* When he came back to the office, he visited Editorial—unannounced—to inspect our project log. More than once I had to leap up from my chair and plant myself in front of my noisy dot-matrix printer, where the latest draft of *Stop It Some More* was pounding hot off the press. Plenty of Boorman's literature referred—in frank detail—to male and female body parts, but I was sure he'd think something was amiss if his eyes fixed upon a manuscript containing the words *luscious tush* and *stiff, saluting prick*.

I couldn't fathom why Karen ever described him as a laid-back boss, until I guessed he probably was watching us closely at her request. Still, he didn't have to treat us like toddlers in imminent danger of falling into the deep end of the pool. I blamed myself, in part, for his compulsion to play camp lifeguard. *Trust me* was a phrase that usually came out of the most untrustworthy of mouths, and clearly recognizing that, he seemed to single me out as the one who needed the closest supervision. Maybe because he knew I had my eye on Karen's office, he kept his eye on me. Or at least he *seemed* to have his eye on me. When he wasn't carefully phrasing his orders over the phone—our conversations were rushed when they weren't punctuated by uncomfortable, half-second silences—he left polite commands on my computer using the All-in-1 messaging system.

Tired of his close supervision, I told the secretary, "He can't leave town often enough." My heart sank when I saw his car was in the parking lot. He owned the Audi, not the Beemer. I couldn't help noticing he also owned—in spite of that one wretched tie—a good wardrobe, which was more than I could have vouched for most of the male specimens at Boorman. Sometimes when I passed him in the hall coming or going to the vending machines (where I found, to my dismay, I had regained my own childish taste for root beer), I remembered the Saturday I had bumped into him in the hall. He hadn't looked half-bad in his shirtsleeves.

Too bad his demeanor was less than appealing. One evening as I signed out at 7:00 P.M.—remarking to Gussie that I wanted to be taken out for a round of margaritas when this blasted project was finally over—Gussie smiled and said, "Here comes your shadow; maybe he can take you."

I turned. The least likely candidate for a wild night out on the town approached: Eben Strauss, with a look on his face equivalent to the frown the dental hygienist always gave me when I admitted I never flossed.

"Miss Lisa's here late again," Gussie told him.

"So I see."

"She's in here every weekend."

"So am I."

"You're working her to death, Mr. Strauss."

"Am I?" he asked me.

"At last count I was still breathing," I said, handing him the clipboard.

"I'm glad to hear it," he said, scrawling his signature and dropping the pen back to the clipboard. He practically lunged to hold the door open for me, which forced me to edge by him so closely I brushed against the tweed of his jacket.

The sun hung low in the sky beyond the lab. He walked next to me, in an awkward silence that he finally broke with, "We appreciate the long hours you're putting in."

"No problem."

"Once this project pushes through, you can get back to your family."

"My family lives in Connecticut."

"But your husband—"

"I don't have a husband," I said.

He looked embarrassed. I couldn't for the life of me figure out where he had gotten that cockamamy idea, until I remembered the Saturday I took Dodie on a tour of Boorman. He must have seen my signature—*L. and D. Diodetto*—on Gussie's clipboard when he himself signed out. Still, plenty of times he'd gotten close enough to see that my left hand was bare of everything but paper cuts.

"You have a brother, then," he said.

"I don't have a brother."

The confusion on his face was so interesting, I didn't bother telling him it was my cousin who'd been temporarily incapacitated by diarrhea in the men's room. *Let him think whatever he wants,* I thought, and no doubt he did, because he dismissed me by saying, "I must have you mixed up with someone else. Have a good evening."

He waited for me to pull my car out first so his Audi could escort me, at a respectful distance, down the long winding driveway that led to the street. "Did I ask for a chaperon?" I muttered to myself, tempted to pump my brake so he'd have to stop short. I feared he would follow me to make sure I didn't stop at the nearest cantina. But in my rearview mirror I saw that after I turned left, he turned right—probably back toward that rural area where I had gotten lost driving around with Dodie. I also lived to the right, but my gym was in the opposite direction.

Sure that Karen had put him on my trail, I ventured to comment the next time I spoke to her: "Mr. Strauss is always *supervising* me."

"Maybe Dr. Schoenbarger told him to."

"I never thought of that."

"He always left me alone, but I'd been working there for four years before we moved under him. After you prove you can do a good job, he'll probably ease up."

As far as I was concerned, that couldn't happen fast enough, and I marked on my calendar—with a sickening smiley face—the day we would meet with the bigwigs in Communications and Marketing to discuss sending off the spinal block onto the market.

My mouth felt dry as I entered Boorman's executive boardroom for that much-anticipated meeting. The long table reminded me of the bowed galleys of slave ships in catechism movies. As I took my place at one of the plush, wheeled chairs along the side, I feared that in the background would rise the monotonous sound of a drum, and I would have to start rowing. After all the long, horny hours I had spent in the gym, I probably could have outrowed all the Ivy Leaguers at the table, some of whom probably actually had sculled down the Housatonic or Charles Rivers. But I wasn't at this meeting to exhibit my newly acquired athletic prowess. I had been invited to present the boards I had drawn up with the designers and the typesetters, which showed the final form of the information manual that would be included in every new package of the spinal block before it got distributed to operating rooms across the country.

By then I was used to the whole corporate dog-and-pony show, and I played along as if my life depended on it. I knew that for this presentation I was supposed to wear a navy suit and a bold but not too strangely colored silk blouse and thick gold earrings that spoke of my confidence and power. I knew I was supposed to mingle beforehand in the conference room and drink just enough coffee to wire me, but not enough to swell my bladder. I knew I was not supposed to yawn when I sat down, or look at my watch for the next one to two hours. I knew I was supposed to shut up when the boss man—for it was always a man at Boorman, with the exception of Peggy—assumed his seat at the head of the table, and that the ensuing silence meant the meeting had started.

Eben Strauss commanded attention not by rapping his coffee cup on the table, nor by tapping his silver pen on his leather portfolio, but by staring impassively to signal his impatience with the few guys still joking around at the end of the table. Since this was my first meeting with the men (and two women) of marketing, Mr. Strauss asked me to stand and introduce myself.

The wheel of my chair latched onto my neighbor's, and we had a slight tussle before I raised myself up and said, "Lisa Diodetto. Thank you for asking me, Mr. Strauss."

"Strauss," he said, and I remained standing, positive I had said his name right, so why was he repeating it back to me? "You can call me Strauss."

"I just did," I said, which for some reason provoked a round of laughter.

"He goes by his last name," one of the original jokers at the other end of the room told me. "Nobody calls him by his first name except Peg."

Thanks for telling me, I felt like saying—angry because Strauss had made Karen and me call him Mister when all the rest of these guys called him by his last name.

There followed some mild heckling of the man everyone claimed didn't look like an Eben, or a Bennie, or even a Ben. Someone—although I later found out it was a division manager—even made so bold as to say, "What was your mother thinking of, Strauss, when you were born?"

"I imagine she was sedated," Strauss replied.

"Strauss is so polite he probably didn't even cry when he came out."

"He probably shook the doctor's hand."

"He probably held the door open for the nurse."

"He probably had a thousand-word vocabulary."

"He probably said, *Yes, yes, all this fuss is all very well, but could we please get down to business?*"

Laughter. A few mild-mannered hoots. Strauss looked down at the table—and smiled. The teasing was clear evidence that they all liked and even respected him—if they didn't, they would have been sweet as pie to him to his face, saving their nastier numbers to perform behind his back.

Strauss cleared his throat and told me I could sit down—thus calling further attention to the fact that I was ass enough to still be standing. We *got down to business.* The meeting was a blasting bore; it went on—in common office parlance—like the orgasm of a thirty-five-year-old woman, i.e., *forever.* I made my presentation—and was thanked by Strauss for my brevity—then spent the last half hour with my legs crossed against the evil effects of the coffee. When our business finally was transacted in exactly twice the amount of time really needed to move through the agenda, I bolted from my chair and hightailed it down the hall to the ladies' room, where I audibly sighed as I emptied my aching bladder.

While I was washing my hands, I examined myself in the mirror. Something seemed off. Of course, my skin had that sick PMS look, and a light dusting of office lint covered my lapel. I looked closer. Then my hand flew up to the side of my head. I looked down to the floor and ran back to the stall. I was missing an earring. It was either in the hallway, or back in the boardroom, or—a worse scenario yet—lying crushed in the parking lot. I had just given a major presentation looking like a lopsided talking head. I pulled off the other earring and put it into my pocket. I had to return to the meeting room to retrieve my boards, and I carefully retraced my path on the hall carpet, trying not to give off signs of panic. But I was frantic. The earrings (bold clips that I bought at Bloomie's when I got the job) were eighteen-carat gold and cost me half a week's salary. I couldn't afford to replace them.

The meeting room was dark and empty. The wastebasket was stuffed with squished styrofoam cups; a lone yellow pencil lay on the table. I flicked on the lights and scanned the floor by the easel where my boards were still propped. Then I yanked out the chair I had sat in during the meeting and dived under the table to fetch my big clip, which lay on the carpet, dull and innocuous as an oyster on the bottom of the ocean floor.

Half a second later a pair of men's shoes—nice-looking cordovan loafers, with the kind of high gloss that seemed to announce they were Italian—entered through the glass door. The loafers came around the side of the room, then stopped when I reached forward to grab my earring and my head knocked—loudly—against the top of the table.

Tears came to my eyes. *"Fanculo,"* I blurted out.

Pause. Then a voice said, "I haven't heard that word in years."

My face heated up. I continued crouching on the floor. "I guess you're not a Scorsese fan, then," I told the disembodied voice, which I

didn't immediately recognize, for it had a touch of Brooklyn in its formation of *word* and *years*.

"I saw *Mean Streets*," the voice said, and I bumped my head again as
I crawled backward out from the table, and emerged, wild-haired, to con-
front the man who did not want to go by Eben or Ben, and whom I now
knew had clearly *wukked hod, all dese years*, to get rid of his Brooklyn
accent.

He blinked at me.

"Did you like it?" I asked. "The movie, I mean?"

"No," Strauss said. "Too violent."

His gaze—too insistent—disconcerted me. I held out the prize in my
palm and said, "I lost my earring."

He continued staring. "I think you've lost both."

I shook my head and pulled the spare out of my pocket. "I pulled this
one off in the john—"

The word *john* clearly made him uneasy and made me realize that in
spite of my efforts to the contrary, I was turning out to be a clone of my
mother, at least in terms of vocabulary.

"I mean, I looked in the mirror—in the bathroom—and saw the other
one—the first one—the one under the table—was missing—"

He nodded. "Lucky you noticed. I left something behind too." He
went over to the head of the table and retrieved his leather portfolio from
the floor, where he had placed it when the tons of written material circulating at the table began to come his way.

After shoving both the earrings into my pocket, I went over to the
easel. Strauss was looking at my feet—probably checking out my shoes. I
didn't mind that my Via Spigas gave his loafers some competition. But
then I sneaked a peek down at myself and realized that my lunge under the
table had caused my navy stockings to bunch at the ankles.

How do girls who grew up poor dress rich? By donning a Tahari suit
over underwear riddled with holes. By wearing Via Spiga pumps that cost a
hundred dollars a pop with fifty-nine-cent grocery-store-label panty hose
underneath.

Between the panty hose and the *fanculo*—never mind the reference
to the *john*—Strauss had my number now. His disapproval seemed as
palpable as the stagnant air in the meeting room, suffocatingly still after
having the door closed for the past two hours. Why else would he be
watching me so intently as I took down the boards? His silence unnerved
me and seemed to say, *Young lady, your behavior need serious adjusting*.

"Here, let me help you with those," he said.

"It's just cardboard," I told him. Then I remembered he was a vice-president, the boards were unwieldy, and I had a long walk back to the art shop.

"You can carry this," he said, giving me his portfolio, which seemed a fair trade, at least until I got it in my hands and realized it weighed more than the boards themselves did.

He turned left—instead of right—after asking where we were going, which prolonged even further the long trek back to the art shop. He thanked me again for all the hard work I had done in Karen's absence and asked me to refresh his memory: exactly how long had I *been with Boorman?*

"Since the end of spring."

"You haven't had much of a summer, then."

"Nor have you," I said. "When will you take vacation?"

"I rarely take vacation."

The thought made me crazy, that I would have to suffer through the rest of beach season with this veep making sure I dotted my i's and put a healthy loop on my p's and q's. "How long have you *been on board?*" I asked him.

Strauss recently celebrated his fifth anniversary. "Karen and I came in together," he said. "Of course, we didn't really get to know one another until just recently."

"That's right," I said. "She said our division used to be with Communications."

"That's right. The search is on for a new VP in that area."

I wondered what crime the last one had committed. He probably came in two under par while playing Dr. Schoenbarger in golf. "Boorman doesn't seem to have a lot of turnover among the management," I said.

"We're all happy to be here."

Speak for yourself, I felt like telling him. For we had just passed by the window, and I saw, once again, that it was a great day for the beach. "Well," I said in a too-hearty voice, "*I'm* certainly glad I made the move here."

"Where were you before?"

"In publishing."

"That's right. Karen told me when we were introduced."

"Actually, I don't think she did."

"Funny. I was sure she told me then."

"Funny. I'm sure not. You were in a meeting—"

"I'm always in a meeting."

"And you stood up from the table and said, '*Welcome on board*'—"

"Are you sure?"

"—and you had on a red tie—" I said, leaving out the word *ugly*.

"I hope you'll forgive me," he said.

"For the tie? Or for saying *welcome on board*?"

He frowned. Obviously he didn't think either one was a crime. "No, for forgetting."

We had reached a set of glass doors, and I held one open for him. He didn't like that. Or maybe it bothered him that when he went through the door first—reaching back to hold it open for me—the two-inch heels on my pumps brought our eyes practically even. But if he minded that, how could he take working for Doctor Peggy, who at worst could be called Amazonian, and at best, statuesque?

"I hope you don't mind me carrying these boards back," he said.

"Why should I mind?"

"You seem to object."

"I don't object." And then I had the guts—or the *brazen coglioni*, as Dodie might say—to add, "Dr. Schoenbarger, however, might call you on the carpet for it."

He smiled. "She knows—and forgives—my bad habits."

"That's nice," I said, although I doubted the Doctor would approve of him carrying a couple of three-pound pieces of cardboard for a girl who regularly lifted weights. The truth was, his portfolio was four or five times heavier than those boards and threatened to bust my right bicep. "What do you have in here?" I asked. "The Gutenberg Bible?"

Then I blushed, because I remembered he was Jewish, which meant I had just committed what was getting to be the great sin of the 1980s—being *culturally insensitive*—until I remembered Jews read the Bible too, although they were subjected only to what I thought of as the "Hollywood half"—full of Universal Studio-like floods and fires and earthquakes and big-busted women writhing over golden calves and being turned into pillars of salt.

Bible references apparently didn't make him too nervous. He gazed down at the thick portfolio and told me it was all the paperwork that circulated during the meeting and copies of the legal documents that would clear the spinal block for the market.

"This is a good drug," he said.

"Are there bad ones?" I asked, forgetting my audience. Luckily he missed—or pretended to miss—the gist of this remark as well, because he made reference to a current, well-known lawsuit against one of our rival companies over an antidepressant that had bizarre side effects—reportedly causing patients to hallucinate and kill themselves.

"That's a bad one," he said, "and someone's going to pay for it."

Strauss left the boards in the art shop; I handed over his legal documents. We said *good-bye, nice to have spoken with you.* When Strauss extended his hand, it felt warm to the touch, probably because he had gripped, a little too tightly, the top of the thick art boards to keep from dropping them.

I returned to my office. During the next hour at my desk, I sank into the kind of depression worth medicating. The spinal-block project was over and done with, and I nursed a letdown similar to the kind I felt after my birthday or Christmas or the end of a semester—that feeling of *what now?* and *so what?* I gazed outside. It was summer—mating season—the time I seemed programmed to begin an affair. Then I'd walk away, when the leaves started to fall, without much regret. Now my days loomed before me—dull and uneventful. That night I would leave at five o'clock and go back home to what? Another exciting evening of rearranging the bras in my underwear drawer, plucking the foil gum wrappers and used Kleenexes out of my messy purse, or balancing my checkbook (just to make the task more interesting) in the nude? A thrilling session in hot pursuit of stray eyebrows and chin whiskers with the only male companion in my life, a trusty metal implement known as Tweezerman? There was always my corporate novel to work on. Although I had reworked the first two chapters of *Stop It Some More*—toning down the emphasis on sex and cultivating a hot romantic interest between the art-shop director, an aspiring cartoonist named Donna Dilano, and the chief financial officer, a stern taskmaster and ex-member of the Yale rowing team known as Thomas Akins—I realized how stymied I felt by lack of material. What did I really know about the inner workings of a corporation? I needed a juicy subplot to catch the reader's interest.

As if in answer to a prayer, my computer buzzed. I turned to my keyboard and logged on to All-in-1 without even checking to see who sent the message.

My Italian is rusty. Does your last name mean what I think it means?
The top of the screen identified the sender as *Strauss, E.*

My radar had been down so long, it had gone completely awry. I no longer knew how to read the signals—faint and cautious as they had been—and the message surprised me. *Oh,* I thought. *So that's why he walked me to the art shop.*

A real feminist, I suspected, would have been offended. I was horny and intrigued. Strauss, E. was hitting on me. Or at least I hoped he was hitting on me, as boldly as he knew how. Discretion, of course, was necessary in the halls of Boorman. His, I thought, had been brilliant to the point of literary—or at least it called to mind the sexy, silent disapproval ex-

pressed by my favorite romantic hero, the haughty Mr. Darcy, toward the
high-spirited Miss Elizabeth Bennet in *Pride and Prejudice.*

Strauss, E. was not Mr. Fitzwilliam Darcy. I was sure he never went
hunting with the hounds nor drank anything stronger than root beer, never
mind an occasional polite sherry. He'd look like Mickey Mouse in white
gloves. But for that matter, I'd look like something out of junior-high-
school drama class in a tulle gown and ringlets. After a half hour of being
cooped up in one of Austen's parlors, you'd have to scrape me off the
ceiling.

We are who we are. And here, sad to say, was who I was back then—a
girl whose idea of thinking things through went like this: Hey, I've never
been in an Audi before. I wonder if it has leather seats. I thought: Great
shoes, nice shine, and even though he's obviously worn them at least once,
I bet they still smell good enough to eat. Then I thought: God, he's older
than I am, but not by much if he has only five years at Boorman. He also
wasn't much taller than I was. But I didn't have a thing for height. Having
grown up surrounded by short men, I was conditioned to finding anything
over six feet utterly gratuitous.

I considered Strauss some more. He was too polite. Too cautious. He
struck me as the kind of man who probably would not stop to watch a
juggler on the street. He probably *did* shake the doctor's hand when he
was born. He probably kissed his own mother on the cheek. But he clearly
had a deeply suppressed wilder streak (or at least the need to rebel against
the strong hand of Peggy) if he was willing to put out a feeler in my
direction. During the meeting he showed he did have a sense of humor—
or at the very least, a penchant for being teased, if only by those over
whom he held the power to shut up. And he had a corner office. With a
view of the fountain. With books on his shelves. And his own secretary,
who probably acted more professional than the so-called "professional
staff." Surely she refrained from making personal phone calls on company
time and forbore to peddle Tupperware, Avon, and Sarah Coventry jewelry
to her coworkers. She called him *Mr. Strauss* and he probably never corrected her (although it took him long enough to correct me). Strauss sat at
a huge desk made of real cherry, not laminated wood products. He did not
keep his bag lunch and his running shoes—and stinky balled-up tube
socks—in the bottom drawer of his file cabinet, nor did he write with pens
that exploded blue ink all over his starched cuffs. His expense account was
probably larger than my annual salary.

He was interesting, no doubt about it. But would a company yes-man
(who I suspected would never dare cop a feel unless it was written into the
annual strategic plan) really risk so much to show his interest in me? I

placed my fingertips on my keyboard—knowing the low electric current coursing through my body had nothing at all to do with the hum emanating from the computer—and I tried to determine how to answer, besides asking him if he was still kicking himself for taking only two semesters' worth of Italian in college or inquiring if he had a side interest in the theory of names. Composing the reply was tricky. Because if a man in his position had to move forward slowly, inch by inch, a woman—in my position—would have to stick her neck out a bit more. Meet him slightly more than halfway, or else he might retreat.

I typed out the three simple letters that spelled *Yes,* followed by a rough translation of my last name into English: *God said.*

But since that alone didn't seem adequate to provoke another response, I dared to add, *Why don't you go by your first name?*

I hit the return and waited.

I clocked him. A minute passed, then two, then three, before he indirectly answered, *My parents call me Ibby. But you might not want to tell anyone else that.*

It's our secret, I typed, and hit RETURN.

The phone rang half a minute later. I smiled. *Gotcha,* I thought, before I picked up the receiver.

Chapter Five

All Business

His voice was all business when he asked if he could take me out to lunch as a way of offering his thanks for my hard work.

"I don't eat lunch," I told him.

He paused. "Do you eat dinner?"

"I eat dinner," I said, and realizing I had him backed in the corner, I said, "*When* should we eat dinner?"

"I don't suppose you're free on Friday?"

"I have a date," I said (strategic pause), "with a rowing machine. At my gym. But you probably make better conversation."

He gave me one of those split-second silences that made me nervous. For a moment I felt a twinge of longing for the man I was about to stand up—the little guy called the Pacer, who rode his own scull across the display screen of the rowing machine, shouting into his megaphone, *Row, row, row that boat!* to which I always silently replied, *Up your rectum and then some, bub,* before I gritted my teeth and stepped up the speed. Since the start of summer, the Pacer and I had formed a very intimate relationship. He knew my strokes. He knew how to make me grunt and groan and sweat, and he always kept me coming back for more.

Strauss could only promise to *give it his best shot.* When I gave him my address—after he asked if I didn't mind *being picked up,* a question I greeted with my own amused form of silence—he said, "I thought you lived in the opposite direction."

"What gave you that impression?"

"That night I followed you out."

"That's the way to my gym," I said. "I go to the gym every night."

"Do you jog?"

"I lift weights."

He got off the phone quickly.

For the next two days I alternately dreaded and looked forward to our dinner. I knew he would take me someplace dignified and quiet. I knew I would have to watch how much I drank and keep my elbows off the table for fear of knocking onto the floor three-quarters of the silverware laid out before me like heavy artillery. Above all I knew I would have to avoid bad-mouthing anyone at work or the company in general and put a lid on my famous dumb-guy jokes, which routinely sent the editorial staff into peals of laughter (example: *What's the diff between a woman and a computer? A computer can take a five-inch floppy!*).

On Friday night Strauss showed up at my apartment wearing a coat and tie and stayed in the doorway while I fetched my purse. He held open the door of the Audi and looked the other way when I slid into the leather passenger seat. The seat belts automatically slipped forward when he closed his door. I jumped when he hit the power locks.

"Sorry," he said. "Next time I'll give you warning." He adjusted his rearview mirror. "Are you buckled in?"

"Your car just did it for me."

"That's the shoulder. You need the lap. It's a little bit hidden. Really reach back."

I groped. "Let me find it."

"Take your time."

"We could be here all night."

"My father set the record last time he visited. It took him close to five minutes."

"How old is your father?"

"He has a few years on you."

"I guess I win runner-up," I said when I finally found the end of the belt and snapped it. Although I didn't mind the thought of Strauss leaning over me, the last thing I wanted him to do was buckle me in like a geriatric patient or a squirmy, ill-behaved kid.

On the way to the restaurant—and it was a long drive—I found out Strauss's father was *in the carpet business.* He grew up in Brooklyn—in what he vaguely defined as a "not-so-nice neighborhood"—and his parents now lived in Park Slope. He went to Cornell to lose his accent, and Harvard Business School to unlearn everything he had been taught at Cornell. He worked for another drug company outside of Princeton before he came to Ossining.

"What exactly do you do all day at Boorman?" I asked him.

"Is your bullshit detector down?"

"That's how you'll know I'm dead."

"Well. I go to meetings. A lot of meetings—"

"My sympathies," I said, for based on my limited experience I already knew that meetings at Boorman were about as productive as complaining about the weather. "How did you wind up at Boorman?"

"I was recruited. By Peg."

"You must like a challenge."

I provoked one of his infamous frowns. "You seem to get along very well with her."

"Oh, I do. I do."

"She's in a difficult position, you know. But we probably shouldn't talk shop. Should we agree not to talk shop?" Strauss asked, with a neutrality that seemed to imply, *with particular emphasis on avoiding certain problematic personalities who wouldn't approve of our meeting outside the office, unless it was at a power lunch overlooking the eighteenth green.*

"Fine by me," I said. Although I regretted losing the opportunity to grill him about life at the top, the last thing I wanted was the ghost of Peggy riding in the backseat. That was enough to kill any romantic prospect for the evening.

We fell silent. To avoid keeping my eye on the speedometer (Strauss, surprisingly, drove faster than I ever dared), I looked out the window at the darkening sky and thought Peggy would make a great Mother Superior. Schoenbarger was a German name though—and what little I knew of Germans beyond the usual foul association was that they brewed great beer and manufactured swell cars, but few of them shared my faith. Yet Karen had said Peggy was trying to adopt a girl through Catholic Charities. Maybe her live-in lover was an ex-nun. The thought amused me, and I filed it away as raw material for the novel. The more I wrote on *Stop It Some More,* the guiltier I felt—but not guilty enough to put the brakes on my runaway imagination.

At the Italian restaurant in Dobbs Ferry there wasn't a red-checked tablecloth or a bowl of waxed fruit in sight. The maître d' didn't shout, *You back again?* nor did the bartender holler, *What's your poison, paesan?* The booths were black leather—not vinyl—and the candles hardly dripped. The menu was in both Italian and English, and there wasn't a single meatball on it, never mind any mention of *puttanesca.*

I perused the list of entrees for so long that Strauss must have thought I had trouble deciding. "They do a good veal chop," he suggested.

"I don't eat meat on Fridays," I said, not having the vaguest idea why I told this blatant lie. Maybe I thought it would make me seem more interesting, or I felt like being perverse. Maybe I just wanted to watch his reaction.

He apologized, as if he were sorry he wasn't Catholic too. Then he said he hoped I wouldn't think him blasphemous—in his own way?—for ordering the shrimp *fra diavolo.*

"Have what you want," I told him, and I was pleased when he looked down at the menu and made his first unguarded remark of the evening: that keeping kosher seemed to have been invented for the sole purpose of keeping women in the kitchen.

"Does your mother?" I asked.

"No, but she's in the kitchen most of the time anyway."

"So is mine," I said.

"Your mother doesn't work, then, either?"

"Strauss," I said, "my mother beats throw rugs—with a big wooden spoon—over the back porch railing to get the dust out."

He smiled. "My mother waxes the kitchen floor on her hands and knees."

"Beats vacuuming the ceiling. Really. I kid you not. My mother vacuums the ceiling."

We looked at one another, instant understanding in our eyes. Then we both hid, once again, behind our menus. He decided to skip the *fra diavolo*—perhaps because of the garlic factor. He got the chicken breast stuffed with fontina and artichoke hearts, and I ordered the *salmone* dressed with asparagus and lemon, hoping it wouldn't skid off the table when I first cut into it, like that blasted piece of tough prime rib that ended up in my lap during my sister's wedding reception. My mother had descended on me with a white napkin and a gallon of club soda, which only spread the stain even farther on that hideous yellow maid-of-honor dress that made me look about as svelte as a melting pound of butter.

"Wine?" Strauss asked and I said, "Just a glass," although I wanted to knock myself out of the sheer awkwardness of eating and conversing with a man I hardly even knew, in such a formal setting, for which I had dressed all wrong—in a velour skirt that (thank God) was black, but in a white blouse, which made me look like I should have been waiting on tables instead of being served. Or maybe I looked even worse: like I ought to get up and dance around the restaurant with a bottle of Chianti balanced on my head.

I knocked over the salt shaker when I handed back the menu.

"*Al lupo*," Strauss said. Although it could have been just another Italian phrase (like *vafanculo*) that he picked up during his childhood in Brooklyn, I was surprised he knew this shortened version of *good luck*.

"So how many semesters of Italian *did* you take in college?" I asked him.

"Just four. But didn't I tell you my father's from Italy?" He seemed amused by the confused look on my face. "Mind, I didn't say he was Italian."

"Oh," I said. "I get it." Because I had read my Levi, my Bassani, and my Ginzburg, and I knew there were Italian Jews, although I had never met one in my life.

"But your last name is—well, your father must have grown up in the north, right?" When he nodded, I said, "My parents are from outside Palermo."

"Sicily is very beautiful."

"I've never been. You actually have?"

"In college. On an archeology dig, of all things."

"What'd you find?"

"A couple of bones. A bad sunburn. And a short-lived girlfriend."

More on that chick later, I thought. "I'd like to go. But it's so expensive. Besides, I'm a little afraid of the language barrier."

"I thought you spoke."

"Just a bit."

"Can you say *costs too much*?"

"After watching my mother haggle for years?"

"And *stop, thief*?"

I laughed.

"I shouldn't have said that," he said. "I've offended you."

"Do it some more."

He blinked. I blushed. Then we both took another—long—sip of water. He asked if my parents ever had gone back.

"They always talked like they hated it," I said.

"That's natural. If they had it hard?"

"They had it hard."

"And you got to hear all about it?"

"You sound as if you might have heard some of the same stories."

"Actually, my father doesn't talk about it."

"Men of that generation don't seem to have much of a voice," I said. "Unless it's raised."

After the wine came, Strauss admitted that his father, at least, never raised his voice, but sometimes played the ventriloquist. He said that for as far back as he could remember, on those rare occasions that his family went to a restaurant, his father—*whom I dearly love, don't get me wrong*—always told the waiter what his mother wanted, as if his mother were a deaf-mute who could not communicate her own desire for the steak or the halibut.

I said my father—*whom I dearly did* not *love*—did the same damn thing when he was alive.

Strauss offered his condolences.

"It was a long time ago," I said.

"But you should have told me. I never would have gone on about my father. I'm sorry."

I shrugged. Because for a very brief moment—just long enough for the candles to flicker when the air conditioner hummed on overhead—I felt complete and utter shame. I was sorry, and yet I *wasn't* sorry, my father was dead. And I wanted to ask Strauss, as if he could provide the answer: *You know, if I never loved him, then why did I want him to love me?*

We sat there in awkward silence. Then Strauss asked me if I had a large family.

"Can you beat this—thirty-four first cousins on my father's side, and twenty-one on my mother's?"

He didn't even ask if that was a joke. "I can't begin to compete," he said. "I suppose you have to attend a lot of weddings?"

"And funerals."

Strauss sat back in the booth and adjusted his shirt cuff. "I've heard tell you have a mouth," he said, smiling slightly to indicate he'd made his inquiries about the office.

"And a sister," I told him. "Just one sister."

"Are you close?"

"Are you kidding?"

Strauss also had a sister, with whom he admitted he once had *a rocky relationship*. However, now they got along fine. They had made their peace. She was married to an accountant and lived in Bergen County.

"And your parents are pleased with this," I said.

"Not exactly."

"What's the issue?"

"They objected to her marriage."

"Oh."

"It's not what you think. She married a Jew—"

"This is a problem?"

"He's very religious—"

"This is a problem?" I repeated.

"He's a bit of a fanatic—" Strauss said, still idly adjusting his shirt cuff.

"I'm about to play editor here."

"Grammar's never been my strong point."

"You can never be a *bit* of a fanatic—" Then my eyes widened. I remembered how I once took the subway farther inland than anyone in her right mind should dare to go and could hardly believe the fur-hatted, forelocked customers who got on at Crown Heights. "Oh, my God," I said. "He's a Lubavitcher!"

"Not that extreme—"

"A Jew for Jesus?" I said, in a voice almost as insistent as the full-page ads these Messiah proselytizers often ran in *The New York Times*. Those ads always sent Dodie over the edge. For in spite of belonging to an oppressed category himself, Dodie had a wide streak of intolerance in him, and he reacted to Jews for Jesus the same way he got his back up at bisexuals. He rattled the newspaper and chastised them, "Please: Make up your mind!"

Strauss shook his head. He told me his brother-in-law was not Hasidic, not even Orthodox, but Conservative—very Conservative. "You look mixed up," he said. "Should I explain?"

"Please."

"On the most basic level—this is a gross oversimplification, of course—Conservative Jews obsess about what they eat and have a lot of kids."

"Sounds Italian," I said. Which still did not explain why Strauss's father would object to having this fellow in the family. "So how many kids does she have?"

"A boy and two twins. I mean, a set of twins. Three all together." Strauss looked flustered for a moment, then added, "Of course, she's lucky to have any at all."

Quite matter-of-factly, he informed me his sister suffered from fertility problems, which she finally overcame by using a drug manufactured by our very own mother company, Boorman Pharmaceuticals. After she had her first child she was photographed and quoted in a four-color glossy ad for the drug that ran in *JAMA*.

"I don't think my parents approved of the publicity," Strauss said. "But now they do nothing but dote on the grandchildren. The oldest one can talk now, and he says things like, 'You know what, Uncle Ibby? Your birthday is the day when you were born.'"

"The kid's a genius."

"So my parents think," Strauss said, smiling.

I smiled back, in a way I hoped illustrated the meaning of the adverb *warmly*. Because all of a sudden I found myself liking him. *Really* liking him.

The waiter brought our salads. After the first glass of wine—and the tenth time he called me *Lisar* (clear evidence that not all of Brooklyn had been pounded out of him)—I didn't have the heart to suggest he might want to drop the superfluous *r* on the end of my name, so I told him, "People close to me call me *Lise.*"

He wanted to know what *Lise* did on the weekends.

"You probably play golf," I said.

"Badly."

"Isn't that the core curriculum at Harvard Business School—how to distinguish between a wood and an iron?"

He took the gibe well. "Yes, and to get your degree at Cornell you stand in front of the dean while he holds up two screwdrivers. If you can't identify the Phillips, you get to graduate."

"Which one has the four prongs?" I asked.

"You forget I graduated."

"*Summa?*"

"*Magna.* And you?"

"Just *cum.*" But I didn't give the *U* enough resonance and the word sounded slightly obscene when it came out. So I quickly added, "But I bombed biology. Don't tell—" I was saved from uttering Peg's name by the arrival of the bread.

He returned to his original topic. "You must do things on the weekends with your girlfriends." He took a sip of wine and added, "Or maybe I should say boyfriends?"

I wanted to laugh at the 1950s ring to his vocabulary. "If you're still trying to identify my bodyguard that Saturday you saw me in the office—"

"I've tried not to give it too much thought—"

"It was my cousin. I'm close to my cousin. Of course, he's gay."

The minute the words were out of my mouth, I felt as if I had betrayed Dodie, by doing exactly what he didn't want me to do: identify him first and foremost, just like Auntie Beppina, by where he did or did not plug it.

Strauss answered only with a nod and then by adding that he hoped I didn't mind him saying this? he really didn't believe in making generalizations, but—?

"Spit it out," I told him.

—but he supposed, from what little I had told him, that this was rather taboo in my family, just as it would be in his?

"You got it," I said.

I didn't go on to embellish my relationship with my cousin. I didn't tell Strauss that Dodie was the only person in my family I could talk to about anything more significant than the tide patterns in New Haven Harbor and the results of the Connecticut Lottery. I did not say that when I left his apartment, Dodie handed me a long rectangular pan and asked if I could manage to get it home on the train without getting mugged for the treasure within—a dozen beautifully rolled vegetable enchiladas. I didn't tell him that Dodie gave me a bowl full of black beans and a container full of five-alarm salsa that he assured me must be consumed only on the weekends, in the privacy of my own home, or he would not be held responsible for the consequences. I didn't say Dodie made the best pot brownies this side of the Mississippi, and baby, did they send me flying. I did not tell Strauss that Dodie was the only man—indeed, the only person on the planet—I knew who had read *all* of Proust and who liked to discuss the motives of the characters and compare the relative merits of the focused *Albertine Disparue* with the broad scope of *Cities of the Plain.* I didn't tell Strauss that my cousin directed where I invested my very limited amount of extra money, so that over the years I had accumulated much more than I ever would bumbling around in the world of mutual funds and stocks and bonds all by myself or by letting it sit in a savings account, where it would collect a measly two-and-one-half percent.

Instead, over my Friday fish dinner, I played Peter and betrayed my cousin once more by giving Strauss a mildly ugly reading of my relationship to Dodie, an interpretation not without a grain of truth: that I liked to invite Dodie to dinner because he cleaned up so well afterward—better and cheaper than a maid, the price being only a little bit of scolding about what a slob I was. I left out the best part of this story: that the last time Dodie went on a cleaning rampage he went so far as to invade my bathroom and come back with my toothbrush, which he sprinkled with Comet and used to polish the filthy, water-stained spigots. When I protested, Dodie said, "You're supposed to change your toothbrush every six months anyway. Relax, Garlic Breath. I'll get you a new Oral-B in the morning."

After a blast of cappuccino and a few spoonfuls of Strauss's *zabaglione,* which I felt obliged to eat rather than admit that eggs sometimes upset my sensitive tummy, Strauss took me home. In the parking lot, I didn't grab him by the lapels and say, "Let's get upstairs and read my tarot cards!" but I did invite him in for a highly redundant round of coffee, which I actually felt forced to make once we were in the kitchen, until he said, "You know, I really shouldn't have any more; I'll never get to sleep." I was just about to take this as a cue to slip into the bathroom and discreetly address the birth-control situation, when Strauss squelched my desire by examining the stuff I had posted on my refrigerator, which I had forgotten to hide in my haste to scrub out the bathtub and change the sheets, pegging him as the kind of guy who expected to spend the entire night.

God, why didn't I remember to take that shit down before he could find out I clipped coupons for Jergens soap and belonged to the Hanes panty-hose club at Macy's? Why didn't I toss that coupon from the Toyota dealership that announced YOU NEED A LUBE RIGHT NOW! Why didn't I hide that grainy photograph that showed Dodie and me singing into a microphone at a Little Italy coffee bar on La Festa di San Gennaro? After smoking a big stiff joint and throwing back three shots of grappa each, Dodie and I had belted out "Bella Ciao" to a ragged accordion accompaniment and then thunderous cheers. This performance had felt radically different from the time we stood as fifth-graders on the front steps of the Hartford capitol two weeks before election day and sang, *"Buon giorno, mio caro,"* to a group of dark-suited state senators, who felt obliged to show their appreciation of Italian-American culture with a polite round of Protestant applause.

"That's a horrible old photo," I said, when Strauss kept peering at it.

"I have to say, red eyes don't become you, Lisar. Is this your cousin?"

"That's my one-time drug buddy," I blurted out, kicking myself a moment later for not blaming my pot-red eyes on the camera's flash.

When Strauss remarked, a little too neutrally, "You don't strike me as the type who does—I mean *did*—drugs," I knew I had better put a lid on a large part of my history with Dodie.

I also suddenly remembered I was standing in the kitchen with one of six vice-presidents of my company, which had a clearly articulated substance-abuse policy. Before I was hired I had to sign an oath that I did not abuse drugs, including alcohol, and sign consent for an FBI background check. I had blithely put my pen to the document, curling the last *a* and *o* in my names with a flourish, as if to express my good fortune in never having been arrested. Three hours later I was in Dodie's apartment, quarked out on ludes, my head hanging off the mattress so when Dodie came out of the kitchen in his *I'll Be Grateful When They're Dead* T-shirt, he not only looked upside down, but double. "May I have this dance?" Dodie had asked the two obscene-looking squash we earlier had selected at the Korean grocer's. He bowed to the first squash and then waltzed with it for a few moments before dumping it for his next partner.

"Whatever happened to George?" I asked Dodie in a slow-motion voice. "You've never told me why you broke up with George."

"He played bridge. And he sang in a barbershop quartet—"

"But he had such great hair."

"Don't ever date a man who cooks for his own mother," Dodie told me. "Don't even *talk* to a man who *talks* to his mother."

But I hadn't heeded Dodie's warning. There I stood in my own kitchen, with exactly that kind of dutiful man. I doubted Eben Strauss had ever waltzed with a root vegetable. I was sure he called his mother every Sunday morning.

I told Strauss, "There's a rumor circulating at work—"

"There's always a rumor circulating at work—"

"—that we all might have to undergo random drug testing."

"Everyone in the lab has to undergo a weekly urine screening. That's policy."

"The question is, will we all have to pee into a Dixie cup on Monday morning?"

"If the spirit moves you, please feel free. Unless you're afraid you won't pass—"

"That picture was taken in college," I said.

Strauss finally gave me a smile. "I was young once. Too."

"I'm twenty-five."

"I'm thirty-six," he said. "Does that surprise you?"

"Not at all," I said, holding back an astounded gasp. "And you've never been married before?"

"No," he said. "Have you?"

"Good God, no," I said. And when I asked, "Do I *look* like it?" he peered over my shoulder at the doorway and said, "Is there a living room back there?"

I invited him into it. I sat on the couch and slipped off my Pappagallos. He sat on the chair and leaned back all the way. He asked me about my former stint in publishing, and when he found out I used to live in Brooklyn, he got all nostalgic and started talking about the bridge and Prospect Park, until I told him about the two-ton rat I found chowing down on a Brillo pad in my grungy apartment, and he assured me New York had become a jungle, there was crime everywhere, the filth now overshadowed the fun and the glamour, and he stopped just short of uttering what my uncles always used to say when I went home for Christmas: *The Big Apple is no place for a nice-a-girl like you!*

We conversed about the revitalization of downtown Ossining and the ominous presence of Sing Sing, and then, after breaking our own established rule and wandering onto shop talk, we ended up squatting on the very subject we both had been trying to avoid all evening.

"Peg thinks very highly of your work," Strauss said.

"She never says so."

"She's not one for superfluous words."

"So I noticed."

"You think she's difficult to please, don't you?"

Over dinner—after his self-effacing comments about his performance on the green—Strauss had admitted it was Peggy who had helped
him hone his golf game. I thought that showed a fair amount of compassion on her part. I imagined she had taught him how to keep his eye on the
ball, but I doubted she had showed him how to be wicked with a driver—
or whatever that club was called that packed the most punch.

"I think Peggy's a hard-ass," I said, "with a heart."

"That's a good read on her."

But I wanted a better one. Something about Peggy intrigued me.
"Why doesn't she ever give out compliments?"

"She's of the school that thinks people will fall flat on their face if
you pat them on the back."

"So how am I supposed to know how I'm doing?"

"You can take it from me. I'll tell you."

"Will you? How will you? By giving me more work?"

"So you've sniffed out my strategy."

"It took a while. But I think I'm on to you."

There was a silence. I'd gone too far—either that, or the wine was
wearing off for both of us, leading me to add, "Then again, maybe not."

The wall next to the couch vibrated for a moment. Downstairs, my
neighbor had turned on the plumbing. Strauss hesitated before he said, "I
hope I haven't given you the wrong impression by asking you to dinner."

"Not at all."

"Some people might . . . misinterpret the gesture."

"Of course." Because all the fun of the evening seemed to be rapidly
slipping away, I said, "I don't think there's anything wrong with being
friends outside of the office."

"Nor do I."

"But I know—just like you said—some people might have other opinions."

He paused. I was about to ask him if he'd like to hear my opinion,
when my voice was stolen away by the digital clock on the side of the
couch, which clicked as it slipped forward onto 11:48. We both looked at
it, and as if he feared his Audi was about to turn into a pumpkin, he
cleared his throat, glanced at his watch to confirm my clock was right, and
said perhaps this discussion was best reserved for another time. He had
enjoyed the evening. It was late and he needed his rest—"No," he insisted,
holding up his hands as he rose from his chair, "don't protest, I'm an old
man, I remember the dollar movie and carbon paper—"

"I remember carbon paper," I said, and the utter banality of this
remark hung in the air like a bad smell that just wouldn't go away.

Flabbergasted used to be my favorite word when I was in fourth grade. Suddenly I was back at nine years old, astounded by Strauss's quick turnaround from flirtatiousness to all business. Strauss held out his hand toward me like I was a German shepherd about to perform some canine trick. I took his hand. He actually shook mine, then practically assured me I didn't have to play guide dog by saying, "I can find my way out."

"I've got manners," I told him. "I'll escort you to the door."

But at the door I discovered that the double locks meant to keep strange men out could effectively detain, for just a crucial moment, another more desirable man within. In my haste to get Strauss inside my apartment, I had left off the safety chain, but I couldn't remember if I had turned the lock on the doorknob, which functioned as backup to the dead bolt. It turned into the seat-belt scenario all over again, only this time I didn't dare say, *Now we really could be here all night.*

"I'm very sorry," I said.

"No, you're very impatient. Take your time."

"I am taking it," I said. "That's the problem. I can't remember which one I locked, if either—"

"You should always lock your doors."

"Were you on the safety patrol in elementary school?"

"My mother wouldn't let me. She thought it was dangerous to stand out in the street."

"Oh," I said. "So did mine. Did she also make you hang up the phone when you heard thunder?"

Strauss reached around me and met my fingers on the doorknob. "May I kiss you?" he asked.

A non sequitur had never sounded so good. "Yes, you may."

Strauss gently pulled me toward him, just long enough so I got a whiff of soap on his neck and felt against my blouse the nap of wool on his jacket. The kiss was soft—just a brush of his rough cheek against my hair.

"Good night," he said, and left in such haste I wondered if he didn't think I was a Roman candle or some other explosive device marked LIGHT FUSE AND GET AWAY.

Chapter Six

That's the Way I Like It

In the morning—at an hour that bordered on the afternoon—I had to pop myself out of groggyland with two cups of Cuban coffee before I was ready to make my run for the *Times* and a cheese-filled Danish dribbled with frosting. On my way out the door, I tripped and skidded on something. *"Fanculo,"* I said again—this was getting to be a reflex—before I looked down at a long white box parked on the mat. I carried it back inside and set it down on my kitchen counter. For the second time since turning twenty-five, I had received an unexpected gift. Yet this package looked more promising than the coffin that held Security Man. The vanilla-colored bow neatly tied around the box reminded me of the elaborate taffeta ribbons that topped my childhood Easter baskets, and the green cellophane inside practically led me to expect a flock of marshmallow chicks clucking over a nest of solid chocolate eggs. But I had seen enough forties movies to know what the box really contained. Inside were a dozen yellow roses and a small white envelope.

The card read only *Ibby*.

"Wow," I said. No man had ever sent me flowers before. Were they an apology for not sticking around the previous night, an expression of regret for what he probably saw as the sheer brazenness of asking me out, or counsel to the receiver that he believed in the traditional interpretation of the color yellow: patience?

What did the message matter? The frog had come a courtin'.

The how-to-care-for-your-flowers instruction card, tucked beneath a cushion of baby's breath, told me to clip the stems first. With the ragged kitchen shears I usually reserved to cut pizza, I hacked two inches off the stems. The hard green rods went flying all over the floor, and I pricked myself on a thorn. Then I dumped the rest of the Minute Maid left in the refrigerator (the juice was beginning to turn anyway) and broke open the top of the carton. I filled it with water and dumped in the packet of white preservative powder before I stuffed in the roses and the baby's breath.

A geisha girl or a Southern belle, skilled in the art of flower arrange-

ment, would have howled at the mess I made. Despite their dubious container, the flowers still looked velvety-smooth and perfectly formed, and
when I tentatively lowered my nose toward them (afraid of more thorns), I
caught a subtle whiff of what my apartment was going to smell like in
three or four hours. I counted the blooms, all the way up to twelve in
Italian, pausing for a moment on the last number: *dodici.*

I collected my purse and keys, reluctant to leave the flowers on their
own, as if they might rise and dance a waltz to Tchaikovsky in my absence.
Then I remembered: Last night I assured Strauss I had manners. Now
came my chance to prove it.

The Ossining phone book—one-tenth the size of the Brooklyn White
Pages—awaited me by the kitchen extension. *Strauss, Eben* lived somewhere called Crickle Wood Road. While the phone chirped, I memorized
the number and the address. He picked it up on the third ring, and all the
warmth in his voice indicated he had been expecting me. I wondered how
long he'd been sitting there.

"*Grazie,*" I said.

"*Prego.*"

"I don't even own a vase."

"I would get one if I were you."

I sucked on my injured finger. "I just woke up," I said.

He paused, and I imagined him looking with disapproval at his
watch, the one with the black crocodile band and the burnished gold face I
had tried not to stare at last evening, dying to know if it was a Rolex.

"It's eleven-thirty," he said.

"I couldn't go to sleep."

"Why was that?"

"I was thinking."

"I also did some thinking," he said.

"Would you like to share your thoughts?"

"I hope you'll give me a chance. Next weekend."

"Not this afternoon?"

"I've already committed to being Ibby for the rest of the weekend."

"A shame," I said. "Don't slip on the floor wax."

"And don't you spend the rest of the weekend beating the throw rugs
with a wooden spoon."

"Actually, I plan to vacuum the ceiling."

Strauss's voice sounded censorious when he promised to *connect* on
Monday. "Of course, we'll be at the office. I wish I didn't have to say
this—"

"But you don't," I assured him. "I totally *capisce.*"

I made my run to the grocery store. I drank too much coffee, perused the *Times,* and then spent the rest of the afternoon in the gym trying to work off my cheese Danish. Unlike Friday nights, the gym on Saturday afternoons always was populated with the Westchester exec set who needed to sweat off all the martinis and London broil they had consumed during the week. It made me feel good (or at least more powerful) to know I could outstroke those highly salaried guys on the rowing machine any day—thanks mostly to my response to the Pacer, who as usual continued to bark and goad and chastise me through his little dildo-shaped megaphone, spurring me on to great heights and making me feel I missed my calling to be a gondolier on the Grand Canal.

Even though I stretched for ten minutes after my workout, my muscles already hinted they planned to burn later that evening. In the locker room I stood under the hot pounding shower, actually saying "oooh" and "aaah" as the heat hit my back. The dressing area remained empty when I got out, and in the mirror I watched my body, too closely, as I wrapped myself in my towel. I thought about Strauss's body. I remembered the warmth of his hand when he shook mine. I pictured him taking off his watch and dropping it onto the nightstand beside my bed. I saw his glasses folded next to the watch. I imagined his thighs against mine and felt the pressure of his entire body on mine.

For a second I actually considered it—going back into the shower stall, pulling the curtain, leaning my body against the water-beaded tile, and making love to myself with a corner of my wet towel (because the roses Strauss sent me rendered my usual finger useless for this sort of activity by necessitating a Band-Aid).

Then I thought, *Whoa, gal. You are seriously losing it. Whack off in a public bathroom and you could get carted away.* If I got arrested, then not only would I not have Strauss—or any other man—I also would lose my club membership and thus my best substitute for sex, which was to work myself to death on those stupid machines until every muscle in my body ached and I felt myself pulsing from my shoulders down to my feet. I would turn into the kind of exhibitionist I once cautioned Dodie about. The one time Dodie and I went to a Manhattan gym, I noticed he was being checked out in the mirror by some of the Fire Island gang. After we got off the Exercycles and decided to clean up and hit a movie, I left Dodie outside the men's locker room with this mock warning: "I want you out here in five minutes."

Dodie raised his eyebrow at me. "A lot can happen in five minutes. The whole world can change in just one—"

"*Cinque minuti,* pal."

"I'm a big boy, Lise."

"That's what I'm afraid of."

How Dodie had laughed! For he claimed—just to get on my nerves—that my biggest fantasy in life was to discover just how well (or how measly) he was endowed, a charge I vigorously denied, although I have to admit that the more he talked along these lines, the more my curiosity was piqued. Like me, Dodie was a verbal exhibitionist. But over the past couple of years he had been more talk than action. In any case, he had enough sense not to monkey around with somebody else—or his towel or his own finger—in a place as public as a health-club locker room.

Back at home, I ate a bagel and cream cheese for dinner and took out my notebook and pen. I decided the juicy subplot in *Stop It Some More* would be an internal rather than external scandal—a seemingly mild-mannered senior vice-president for Research and Development would plow his way through the secretarial forces before being brought to his knees by a feisty young feminist determined to force his Don Juanism to a tragic end. I wasn't sure how I'd get these steamy scenes to mesh with the chapters that dealt with Donna Dilano and the broad-shouldered ex-rower Thomas Akins, because I had sanitized their romance so squeaky clean I now feared those hard-written pages were destined to become only toilet paper. After a couple of hours of scribbling, I despaired. Why should the Casanova have all the fun? Why couldn't Donna have some torrid activity in her life? But if I didn't find a focus—or at least a consistent tone—I'd never get beyond the third chapter. I wanted realism, but my pen kept bleeding potboiler. And my muscles ached. I got out my trusty tube of Ben Gay and slathered the numbing cream all over my thighs and calves. As I was washing my hands in the kitchen, the phone rang.

"What's new?" Carol asked, in a voice crazed by boredom.

"Nothing," I said, gazing at my roses. A lie had never given me such pleasure.

"I keep waiting," Carol said. "My whole life seems like nothing but waiting."

I stroked one of the yellow petals. "So does mine."

"I swear this baby is never going to get here. When is this baby getting here?"

"You don't want it to be premature, do you?"

"I want it to stop making me fat. Lisa, I'm so fat."

"You're not fat. You're pregnant. And I'm sure you're beautiful," I said, even though I was sure Carol wasn't. The figures of pregnant women—exaggerated to cartoon proportions—may have pleased Dodie, but they frightened me. I knew the condition was temporary, and I knew it all went toward a good cause—the perpetuation of mankind, which was woman's sad fate to carry out—but still, I couldn't imagine myself swelling to the circumference of a Broadmouth trash can, then struggling for months afterward just to make it back into a pair of jeans two sizes bigger than what I wore before. Carol's complaints hardly inspired me in that general direction.

"My butt looks like ground round," Carol said. "My boobs feel like bowling balls—"

"I bet Al can hardly keep his hands off you then—"

"Lisa! Would you listen to me! I'm never going to lose this weight."

"How much have you put on?"

"Twenty-five pounds."

I refrained from bleating back an astonished *Twenty-five pounds!* and eked out, "Oh, that's nothing. At least one-third of that is baby—"

"Pretty soon I'm going to weigh more than Al, and then I won't even fit into his clothes."

"Mama still has some of Daddy's."

"What the hell is she hanging on to those for?" Carol said. "He's not coming back from the dead." Then she launched into a long bitch against all the busybody women in our family who kept telling her what not to eat and what not to do, as if her pregnant body had become public property. I punctuated Carol's tirade against Mama and Auntie Beppina with so many *mm-hmms* and *uh-huhs* that Carol finally stopped and said, "You're not listening."

"Au contraire. It's fascinating. Please proceed."

"Well, what's so fascinating about your life? What are you really up to these days besides working?"

"Playing."

"With who?"

"With *whom?"*

"Like I give a shit about grammar?"

"Obviously not."

"Still seeing Dodie all the time?"

"No," I said, my finger hovering above the phone button as I flirted with the idea of hanging up.

Carol's voice rose in expectation. "You're seeing someone else then?"

I hesitated. Although the joy in my sister's voice came from what I considered an extremely limited, if not warped, world view, it was joy nonetheless. It had been so long since anybody in my family had been happy for me about anything. I could have told her there was someone promising in my life. But something perverse inside led me to ask, "Carol, have you ever wanted to rape a man?"

"Lisa, you are totally sick and I am pregnant!"

"Don't pregnancy hormones put you into sexual overdrive?"

"They make me want to eat and sleep."

"But do they give you—you know, like, erotic dreams?"

"Well," Carol said, in a cunning whisper. "Don't tell Al."

"Never."

Then Carol admitted to a one-time nocturnal assault on the star of *Saturday Night Fever*.

"How boring," I said.

"It was not! It was very exciting!"

"But John Travolta is a clear stand-in for Al."

"Al wouldn't be caught dead in platform shoes. He thinks they're fruity and the Bee Gees are too."

Personally, my opinion on the Brothers Gibb was that they looked like Little Lord Fauntleroy in triplicate thirty years later; Dodie called the entire group *fey in the worst of ways* and proof that lightning could strike more than once in the same family. Carol had chosen "How Deep Is Your Love" for the theme song of her wedding, over Al's loud protests that he did not want to take his first dance as a married man to the crooning of a man named Robin. But Carol insisted and so Al danced it. Or shuffled it. Or rocked back and forth to it.

It was a cute memory, I had to admit.

On Monday morning, I *greeted* the secretary, then dived into my office to avoid the crowd in the break room. Now that Karen was on leave, the Editorial staff spent a lot of time fussing over Mr. Coffee, trading stories about picnics and baseball games and movies and visits to their in-laws, and eating up corporate gossip with the same amount of relish that we all scarfed down the vanilla-frosted sheet cakes brought in to celebrate our colleagues' birthdays. That gossip once had amused me. Now fearing I would become the brunt of it, I vowed never to introduce another interesting factoid into the rumor mill again.

I squirreled myself away in my office for so long that the other girls surely thought I had major PMS, a conjecture probably confirmed when caffeine withdrawal started to pound a regular tom-tom in my head. I

grabbed my porcelain cup that said INSTANT HUMAN: JUST ADD COFFEE and ran
to the break room, where of course I found that someone had left only the
dregs in the decanter, forcing me to fire up a new pot.

"Shit," I said, loud enough to be heard down the hall. Right at that
moment everyone in Editorial suddenly seemed to crave a good strong cup
of joe, and pretty soon the break room was full of women. "Greetings, Lisa.
We haven't heard about *your* weekend yet."

"I did my laundry," I said, and no one asked me out to lunch.

Noon found me sitting at my desk like a seventh-grader too scared to
enter the cafeteria all by herself, so I slung my purse over my shoulder and
went out to the parking lot to make a fast-food run, where I had the bad
fortune to view Strauss and two other hotshots in suits piling into a car in
the VIP parking lot, probably on their way to a very extended lunch at one
of the nearby restaurants. I suspected I would not bump into them at the
local Pizza Hut. Strauss nodded at me, and I gave him a weak smile and a
halfhearted wave—minus the Band-Aid, which fell off my forefinger during my morning editing session.

The timing couldn't have been worse. Human Resources—a name I
thought made people sound like toxic waste products—had called that
morning and asked if someone in Editorial could review ASAP the sexual-
harassment policy that Boorman's legal counsel was hoping to put into
place by autumn. I accepted the job. The document was full of lawyerese
and went on for more than twenty single-spaced pages. My eyes latched
onto the words *involuntary attentions* and *mutual* and *consensual.* As I
penciled in my marginal notes—*subject/object is unclear, language is am-
biguous*—I told myself, *This doesn't have squat to do with me.* So why did
my stomach nag at me, the way it had ached and churned after I first let a
boy finger me and then ran to *The Baltimore Catechism* to see if I could
excuse my bad behavior by convincing myself the action wasn't included in
the phrase *impure acts?*

I considered leaving this job off the project log. But in the end I
recorded it and watched Strauss blink when he came down to my office to
review the log on Friday.

"Peg put you on that job?" he asked me quietly.

"I edited for grammar," I said, "not content."

Without further comment, he signed off on it.

        Strauss and I began doing something I thought existed only
back in the days of drive-ins and Levittown: *dating.* Which meant I waited
for him to call, and when I heard his voice on the other end of the line—

sometimes from Crickle Wood, but more often than not from Providence or Atlanta or Charlotte—my heart did a bellywhopper. No topic was too mundane for those phone conversations—even the pervasive fragrance of popcorn in the New Orleans airport and my futile attempt to time my stir-fry vegetables just right—although the subject of Boorman, for the most part, remained off-limits. When I put down the receiver, I went straight to my refrigerator, opened the door and stared at all the food I shouldn't eat, and thought about Strauss's outdated way of treating women. The flowers, the tie and coat at dinner, the fingers placed very lightly on my wrist, and that soft, brushing kiss all signaled that he valued that stuff my mother always warned me to demand: respect. But she warned me far too late. By then it was a useless, unobtainable commodity, for I no longer respected myself.

The blinder Strauss seemed to my past—the wanton chapters, at least—the more I wanted to hide it. I metamorphosed from one kind of woman into another. Or maybe I just stopped thinking of myself as a girl. In any case, I quit shopping the Juniors' department and marched straight to the Misses'. I redid my weekend wardrobe. Gone were the leotards and the tank tops and the bitchin' black jumpsuit that made me look like a paratrooper. I bought clothes for which the manufacturers provided extra buttons: khaki pants and button-down shirts and even a white broadcloth blouse, which I wore underneath a new jumper on our fourth date. "You look nice," Strauss said when he came to fetch me, and I thought, *okay, moving right along here.* But never had I gone at such a snail's pace.

We always drove at least twenty miles out of town before we began our date. On the bright Sunday afternoon we visited West Point, Strauss wore a pair of tortoiseshell prescription sunglasses that made me want to jump him. As he carefully inspected the foldout map of the grounds we picked up at the visitors' information center, I speculated whether he always took his glasses off before he moved in for the kill, or if he had ever been so swept away he left them on through the entire act.

"Do you want to see all the chapels?" he asked.

"How many are there?"

"Three. One is Catholic."

"I'd rather scope out the cadets."

From behind the light-brown lenses of his sunglasses, Strauss looked at me impassively, and I had the bad feeling he was thinking that my strip Vuarnets didn't exactly match my excessively prim chintz jumper, with the empire waist that might have given some people the mistaken impression I was pregnant. He quoted from the brochure: "The cadets are on review September through November and March through May only."

"I guess I'm stuck looking at you, then."

"There are worse fates, I hope."

"Could you put that map down?" I asked him. "For half a second?"

I pushed my sunglasses up on my head. Still he did not take the hint. Although the days had been getting hotter and hotter, I had yet to see him in short sleeves—or shorts—but the rolled-up cuffs of his cotton sleeves revealed wiry muscles and the promise of more black body hair than I previously had imagined. I reached out and touched one of his cuffs.

He smiled. "You seem to like my shirt."

"I do."

"And the person inside?"

"He also has his attractions. And please don't tell me *that's useful information.*"

"That's useful information," he said, and I was about to groan when he looked around the lawn to see if we had an audience. Determining the coast was clear, he leaned over the unfolded map and silenced me with a kiss.

"Will that keep you quiet for a while?" he asked.

"How long do I have to wait for the next one?"

He shook out the map and tried to refold it along the original creases.

"It's not origami," I said. "Just fold it any old way."

"There's a proper way to do it. Have patience."

"I am patient. I am very patient."

"You'll forgive me if I wouldn't call that one of your strong points," he said, as he finally collapsed the map. He put it in his shirt pocket, and when I continued looking at him expectantly, he gave in and put his arm around my shoulder, drawing my head against his chest.

For years I had wondered how Dodie had kept himself from putting his arm around his lovers in public—at least above Fourteenth Street— and now I finally knew the truth of what he answered: *But, sweetheart, that's actually a little side benefit of homophobia—it's so much sexier not being able to touch someone. The word* wrong *is a powerful aphrodisiac. Swallow it sometime, and you'll see what I mean.*

"It's hard seeing you at work," I told Strauss as we walked along, "and not being able to say anything. But the secrecy is kind of fun."

"I hate to admit it. But it is."

"Do you suppose anyone notices?" I asked, although I had given this plenty of thought and had come to the conclusion that if I couldn't tell if he was hitting on me, how could anyone else pick up on it?

"What's to notice? I only come down to your office once a week now.

I never call you into mine." He thought about it for a moment. "I saw you in Peg's office the other day."

"You should have stuck your head in and offered us *greetings*."

Strauss lightly pinched my sleeve. "What did she want?"

"I thought we weren't supposed to talk shop."

"It's an innocent question. Don't answer if you like."

"I'm working on more form letters for her."

"Is she still quibbling about *Dear Sir or Madam*?"

"So you *were* listening that day."

"Guilty."

"And you were looking at my legs."

"I was not."

"I was looking at your—"

"Lisar, please. Just hold the line a little. That's all I ask."

I shrugged, but not enough to throw off his embrace. "I've been thinking," he said. "If Peg asks you to do anything that involves the two of us, tell her your work load is heavy and ask if she can assign it to someone else."

"But what if it's a really good job?"

"I don't care. I'd like your word that you'll do that." After a pause, he said, "I'm looking out for you, you know."

"I can look out for myself. But I'm touched. And you have my word."

"And now you have my thanks, and let's drop the subject." We kept walking. Half a minute later he broke his own rule. "That was a wickedly good imitation of Peg. Say it again."

"Greetings."

He laughed.

"I've been practicing," I said.

"I'd hate to see how you imitate me."

"I don't want to imitate you," I said, which wasn't entirely true, because the root-beer-swilling philanderer in *Stop It Some More* had lately been blinking and pushing up his glasses far too much for even my own comfort. But I hadn't told Strauss I was working on a novel, hardly eager to answer his first probable question about the whole endeavor: "So, Lisar, what's it about?"

The grounds of West Point were dotted with tourists and what appeared to be a group of retirees doing an Elderhostel. By the time we did the circuit of the reservoir and the chapels and the museum that displayed Napoleon's sword and the baton used by Goering to usher millions to their death, I imagined that everyone who looked at us—for I knew we were

giving off that sickeningly saccharine glow of budding lovers—realized I
was putty in Strauss's hands. He called the shots—no matter how gently,
and no matter if they always were phrased as questions. He was the one
who asked, "Ready to roll?" and "What do you feel like for dinner?" and
who asked, "May I see you inside?" when he dropped me off, late, very
late, and told me he could only stay a few moments because—he hadn't
wanted to mention it before and ruin the day—he had to go home and
pack. The next day he was off to Cincinnati and Des Moines and a couple
of other cities no one in their right mind ever elected to visit.

"I'll miss you," I said.

We stood in the cramped entry of my apartment, and when I stepped
forward to meet him, my foot grazed a blue-and-white golf umbrella I
forgot to put away after the last hard rain. I stumbled back against the
door. The knob on the end of the safety chain—which wasn't fastened—
dug into my shoulder blade. Strauss held me a long time. We began to kiss,
softly at first, and then harder, until he reached down and clumsily unbuttoned the top two—then the top three—buttons on my jumper, and I knew
he was annoyed when he realized he had to do the same on my blouse if he
wanted to get inside.

How good it felt—his fingers fumbling on the broadcloth, his breath
and then his tongue in my ear as he finally made enough progress to slip
his hand in my blouse to caress me. Echoing Donna Dilano's inane words
to Thomas Akins, I whispered, "Don't stop, oh, don't stop kissing me—"

Why didn't I just keep my mouth shut, instead of giving him *bright
idears*? He immediately pulled away, brought together the two sides of my
blouse, and set me away from the door. "I'm leaving now," he said.

"Call me?"

"Every night."

He left me half-buttoned and totally frustrated. I had never longed
for a guy so badly before in my life, and what made me feel even more
helpless was not being able to thoroughly discuss it, not even with Dodie.

"How's Mr. Mystery?" Dodie asked when he called.

"Stop calling him Mr. Mystery."

"But Lise—what should I call him? Who is he? A Mafioso?"

"Right."

"A tae kwon do instructor? No, don't tell me—you're running a po-
etry workshop at Sing Sing. The guy's a convict. You recite bombastic lyrics
at one another from the opposite side of jail bars. You are doomed never to
touch—"

I was afraid the last was true. "Dodie, please. I haven't even gone to
bed with this guy—"

"Maybe you better send him in my direction."

"No way. You degenerate. I feel the vibes. The vibes are there—"

"So what's the holdup? Have you put on weight or something?"

"Nah."

"He's met your mother?"

"Dodie!"

"Maybe he wants you to meet *his* mother—"

"God forbid."

"Can you check his prostate?"

"How?"

"God, did you go to college or what?" Dodie laughed. "I can't wait to meet him."

"You're not meeting him."

"Then you're not meeting mine."

"Fine," I said, although I was curious who Dodie was seeing. Deep inside, I hoped he had gotten back together with George and was just holding back the joyous news as another form of having fun with me. But I didn't want to say George's name until Dodie said it to me first. I don't know why I thought that might jinx their relationship, but I did.

Strauss was gone five days. There were a couple of phone calls from airports and prolonged late-night conversations from Marriotts and Ramada Inns. On the last night before he was due to come back we ran out of news to discuss, and when Strauss said, "I miss you more than I thought I would," I told him, "Describe the hotel room."

"It's just a regular room."

"Tell me what it's like," I said.

"You know. Clean. Empty."

"Is the bed hard or soft?"

"Hard," he said.

I cradled the phone in my ear, as if to bring the breathlessness of that word right into the room with me. I started to say, "That's the way I like it—" when Strauss cut me off.

"Lise," he said. "I— Look. We need to have a long talk. I'm struggling with this. You work under me."

I let that statement hang in the air. For I had found that sometimes Strauss was just as disconcerted by what I didn't say as by the pointed suggestions I let fly out of my mouth. Sure enough, my silence got to him. He asked if he could pick me up—at my apartment—the next day on his way back from the airport. He said he found it difficult to talk about *sticky issues* on the phone, that he wanted to talk to me face to face about the *moral dimensions* of our relationship. I wanted to tell him, *I have a great idear, dear: Let's not let morals get in the way of our romantic life,* but I also let this go unsaid and was glad of it: because the point was completely moot the next day when he picked me up and took me back for the first time to his place, where, without even unloading the luggage from the car, he fucked me on his living-room carpet in front of the fireplace, stopping only long enough to hastily shove a big cotton floor pillow beneath my tush after he asked me if I *was protected.*

Oh, it *had* been a long time. Far too long! I'd like to think I sang like Callas when he penetrated me, but I'm sure I moaned like a cow, and kept groaning so loud that if I were back in my flat in Brooklyn, I would have scared off not only the roaches, but even that enormous rat in my kitchen cabinet.

Afterward we rolled off the pillow and he turned it over—wet side down—and put it beneath our heads. Then he took off his glasses and slid them onto the coffee table. He reached around me and unhooked my bra, which he had pulled down but not removed all the way. I pulled his head close to mine and whispered, "Now we *really* need to have that talk."

He gave me a gentle swat on the rump. "I didn't mean for that to happen."

"I did."

"So soon, I meant. I didn't mean for it to happen so soon."

"You can't take it back now."

"I wouldn't dream of it," Strauss said. "In fact, I'm already dreaming of a repeat performance."

"When?"

"Give me a little downtime."

"Then give me a little something to drink."

"Red or white?"

"White," I said, slightly annoyed that Strauss didn't remember what I'd already told him: Red wine always gave me a headache. "But don't go just yet," I told him, stretching my thigh over his to lock him in a moment more. I kissed the crinkly part of his eyes—which became even more crinkly when he smiled. He smelled like a combination of hotel deodorant soap and the stale smoke of airports. It pleased me.

Strauss's skin was slightly paler than mine, with a yellow undertone that seemed more pronounced against the plush pile of the cream-colored rug. "Is this your father's carpet?"

"How did you guess?"

I ran my hand over the pile. "It's nice carpet. Soft. Good for fuck-ing—"

He smiled. "You make a lot of noise," he said. I took this as criticism until he pulled my head near his and quietly added, "I like that. I really like that."

My sense of triumph was completely out of proportion to the compli-ment—especially considering that I later saw him surreptitiously wiggling his finger in his right ear, as if to gauge whether I had damaged his hear-ing.

When Strauss got up, he covered me with a cotton throw that had been draped over the armchair—just for this purpose, or was it there because his mother got chilly when she visited? The blanket did not smell like Strauss, nor like anything or anyone else for that matter. It was proba-bly just a decorative piece. As I smoothed the fringed edges I remembered a conversation Dodie and I had in which we determined that *the blanket issue* was probably the only definitive difference between men and women, beyond the obvious genital issue, of course. "No man—straight or gay— sits on the couch with an afghan tucked around his tootsies," Dodie had said. "And women—all women—always do."

While Strauss was in the kitchen—a long galley that looked gleaming white from my position on the floor—I propped my head on the pillow and checked out the place. The inside of the condo was sparsely furnished with a leather sofa and a more inviting dark-brown armchair. Next to the fireplace—covered with a black screen and bricked with pale Umbrian tiles—lay more of the big creamy cotton pillows identical to the one be-neath my head. One of the blurrier Degas racehorse prints hung on the wall, and over by the dining area—which consisted only of a glass table and four bentwood chairs—hung an odd photograph of a gargoyle who rudely stuck out his tongue. There was no TV, at least downstairs, which I considered a good sign, but there didn't seem to be any books around other than a stack of magazines on the coffee table and some week-old *Wall Street Journal*s. We hadn't talked very much about books—the one time we did, I found out, to my dismay, that Strauss had never read anything by Chekhov—and suddenly I was afraid Strauss read Washington-based power novels, or worse, mysteries. But there was still the upstairs to ex-plore. For a single guy, Strauss had a lot of space.

When we drove in, I noticed the condo was in the far back corner of the complex—and on the end, which undoubtedly added something to the price tag. But who wouldn't want to shell out big bucks—if he had it—for this swell unit? The entire back wall of the sunken living room was glass, and the view gave out onto a creek big enough to accommodate sporting little creatures like otters and beavers. On the other side was a thicket of trees that looked like it might be home to even more friendly woodland creatures along the lines of Squirrel Nutkin and Mrs. Tittlemouse.

"Are there deer in those woods?" I called out to Strauss.

"And skunks too."

"Has Peggy ever visited?"

"Once or twice—why do you ask?"

"She reminds me of Beatrix Potter. You know, the little animals in the forest that always get into mischief—Peter Rabbit, Tom Kitten, Jemima Puddle-Duck?"

"I read one called *Pigling Bland* to my nephew. Of course, it had to pass the censor first."

"Is that your brother-in-law?"

"None other."

"What's he looking for?"

"Any character who has a larger-than-average nose."

"That rules out *Pinocchio,* I guess."

There was a pause, then Strauss said, "Can you hear me smiling from out there?"

"I'd rather hear you laugh. You don't laugh enough."

"But I can't laugh at that. It drives me crazy, the way he finds anti-Semitism in everything from Shylock to Scrooge McDuck—"

"Who's Scrooge McDuck?"

"The old one with the glasses. I think he's supposed to be the grand-father of those triplet ducks—Huey, Dewey, and Louie—or Pee-uwie, I forget their names now—"

"But his beak is no bigger than mine—is it?"

The laugh I finally elicited from Strauss was loud enough to be heard above the clinking and clanking he created as he rummaged through his silverware drawer. I knew I was a prime candidate for a schnoz job. Still, a little argument on his part would have been polite.

I heard the drawer close. "What I'm trying to tell you," Strauss called out, "is that he finds it everywhere. He would find it in you, and he defi-nitely finds it in me."

"In you! Is he crazy? It's not like you're marching around on Yom Kippur with a Yasser Arafat dish towel on your head."

"But I'm not Jewish enough."

"But what does that mean?"

The squeaking sound of a corkscrew came from the kitchen. The cork must have been stubborn; Strauss seemed to be talking through slightly gritted teeth. "It means I told him once there are better ways to serve God than to go looking for hatred in every nook and cranny on earth."

"What'd he say to that?"

"He argued with me and I argued back until my mother said, 'Please, this headache I have,' and my father said, 'Did you hear her, your mother has a headache,' and then we both shut up."

"Your house sounds—a little—like my house."

"I'm sure there are similarities."

The cork popped.

Strauss came back with a bottle and two goblets. He had not covered himself up—in spite of his insistence or his ill-founded belief that I wanted and needed to. I tried not to stare at him—I had a shy side too—but I looked long enough to confirm his body was just like his philosophy in life: moderation in all things. When he set the bottle and the glasses down on the carpet and got us a few more pillows so we could make a nest together, I told him, "You look good without a tie on."

"So do you."

He sat beside me and I adjusted the afghan to cover us both. "This is definitely a man's place," I said. "You could open the front door and immediately know that a guy lived here. It just has that aura."

"Of something lacking?"

"Not really. It just isn't done up. You know how women always try to do up a place."

"Like yours," he said, probably remembering the pictures on the fridge and the lace on my coffee table and the set of clay figures on the bookcase. He had never gone to the back of my apartment, not even to use the bathroom (where I was guilty of keeping scented soaps in a china dish on the back of the toilet) or to peek into my bedroom, which was utterly froufrou in a way I was ashamed to like, because it seemed so adolescent and unsophisticated to have matching crocheted dust ruffles and pillow shams—even if they were pure white—and a cut-glass lamp by the side of my bed.

"How long have you lived here?" I asked Strauss.

"Four years. I waited a year to buy. I wanted to make sure I was happy at Boorman."

"Are you?"

"If you're asking me if I want to spend the rest of my life waiting for my luggage to come off the belt at JFK—"

"That's one way to guarantee an extremely long life."

"—the answer is no. I wish I were home more often."

Even when he was in Ossining, Strauss went into the office early and sometimes did not leave until after I had already worked out and showered at the gym. Although I couldn't quite figure out what he did all day, he certainly put in the hours.

"Why do you work so hard?" I asked him.

"I'm my father's son," he said. "You know how that is?"

"Can't say that I do."

"I mean, I've inherited a competitive streak. I can't settle for the B. I always want the A. But why do you say you don't get it? You clearly want the A too."

My lust for the highest grade wasn't inherited. My need to ace my classes and be the best editor in the office had nothing to do with my father, unless it was a reaction toward his own complacency. Daddy had worked like a dog, but he had never even dreamed of moving beyond—or even of expanding—his business. His feet—but not his heart—had been stuck in his own cement. The kind of work ethic he had passed on to me was valuable, but I felt it also had engendered something servile in me. I never felt comfortable asking the secretary to type something for me. I cleaned Mr. Coffee and the microwave, chucked the rotten leftovers out of Editorial's refrigerator, and even dusted my desk the night before the janitor was scheduled to do it.

"Everyone at your level at Boorman seems totally married to their jobs," I said. "There's more to life than who has the biggest mound of paper clips."

"You're smarter than I am," Strauss said, "if you've figured that out before you turned thirty. I just clued in to that last year." Strauss poured me some wine—a souvenir from a recent trip to California he had taken with some business-school buddies. The vacation was fun, Strauss said, but there were some awkward moments. He never had much in common with those guys, outside of the hard work they all went through to get through the program. After graduation they all had gone their separate ways—making fortunes and marriages that made *The New York Times*. Now, on the lam from their wives and kids, they drank too much and told locker-room jokes and kept talking about how they wanted to quit their executive-level jobs and open a coffee bar in Madison, Wisconsin, or Burlington, Vermont, or retire up to the Maine woods and make furniture out of logs they had cut down themselves.

"These are guys who can't even drive a straight nail, never mind fix a cup of Sanka," Strauss said. "And all of a sudden they want to be gourmet chefs or lumberjacks."

"Is that what you call midlife crisis?" I asked. "Have you had yours yet?"

"It's not part of my game plan."

I let that one go without comment.

Strauss was the first man I'd ever been with who used the word *priorities* while he was naked. He told me lately his had been changing. Last winter his plane had landed at LaGuardia in the middle of a sleet storm, and the roads were slicked with a sheet of ice. He had considered staying with his parents in Park Slope, but he needed some papers in his office and decided to chance the drive back. "I was coming up 9A through Yonkers when I went into a skid," he said. "I practically sideswiped the guardrail. And then, after I sat there for a moment—thank God nobody was coming behind me—I righted the car and kept going. I don't know why I didn't pull over. It just seemed so important to make it home. But then when I got here, there were all these rooms in front of me, and they had never seemed so empty—so quiet I could hear the ice cracking on the creek outside the window. I just kept moving from room to room, and there seemed too many places to sit down, and none of them seemed comfortable."

He asked me if I understood. When I said *yes,* he seemed to know instinctively that I really meant *no.*

"Maybe you're too young," he said.

"I'm really not that young."

"But you don't remember when JFK was called Idlewild." Strauss poured us both more wine. "What I meant to say is that when I came home I questioned who would care if I crashed the car and killed myself?"

"Your mom and dad, of course."

"My parents aren't going to be alive forever."

"I would miss you. I *did* miss you, Strauss. I turn on the TV every night when you go away, to see if your plane has crashed."

"Lisar. I'm very touched." He smiled. "My mother—and Peg—do the same thing."

"Peg!"

"She can be a worrywart. She's a very nervous traveler. She suffers from motion sickness. She can't sit backward in a stretch limousine. When we take trips together, I have to remind her to take her Dramamine."

"Oh, don't tell me these things. Tell me something else."

"This?" He set my glass down on the carpet and kissed me so long and delicately his tongue seemed to push the taste of the wine around in my mouth.

"Yes, that. And *that*. Mmm. Give me some more of *that*."

As I wrapped my arms around him, I wished the weather were unusual. I wished for rain splattering on the skylight, or maybe—even though it was summer—for some of that snow and sleet that almost killed Strauss on the highway last winter, just so we could hear the wind howling and the ice creaking in the eaves. But it was a rather ordinary late afternoon, the sky beginning to go gray as we embraced. The second time felt slower and sweeter and Strauss had plenty of opportunity to prove his persistence. I was a long time coming and felt compelled to apologize afterward. As if to prove that *Sorry* was my middle name, I chose that moment to knock my wine onto the carpet and reveal my lowly upbringing by using my cast-off blouse to soak it up.

"Good thing it's white wine," I said. "Or your father's carpet would be ruined."

"I doubt he'd mind. Considering the cause."

"Aren't your parents prudes?"

"About sex? No, not at all. They want me to be happy."

"Come on. No way."

"Why is that so hard to understand?"

"Because I'm a girl."

"And what did your parents want for their girl?"

"To keep quiet," I said. "Not to make trouble."

"Yes, but beyond that."

"There is no *beyond that* in my family."

Up until then I had tried—hard—not to play my violin and to make my childhood seem like a fun joke. But there it sat, for just a moment, noticeable as the wine on the carpet: all my resentment toward my family, the way they had failed me—and the way, I supposed, I had failed them.

I wondered how Strauss had let down his own parents. "You never wanted to go into business with your father?" I asked, imagining a storefront in Brooklyn, bolt after bolt of remnants stacked to the high ceiling, a counter where customers could sit and flip through swatches.

"He has someone under him who will buy out the business when he retires."

"He's never pressured you?"

"I wouldn't go that far." He shrugged. "I find it hard to get excited about carpet."

"But you're excited about drugs?"

"Drugs—good drugs—can really help people," he said.

"Carpet can keep old people from breaking their hips."

Strauss smiled. "I like the thought, at least, of helping other people. I tried premed. But it was no good. The dissection got to me."

"You couldn't stand digging into that poor formaldehyded kitty on the table?"

"It was a pig. I knew if I couldn't take that, I'd never make it up to the cadavers."

"You're too nice to be a doctor," I said. "Doctors are callous."

"Not all of them."

"Oh. Don't tell me. You have an uncle—"

"All my relatives are in business."

"So are mine," I assured him, although I didn't mention that among these establishments were a tuxedo-rental outfit, a shoemaker's shop, two liquor stores, a newsstand even my mother seemed aware was a cover for a numbers-running operation, and a storefront labeled FAST CASH NOW FOR YOUR CAR TITLE.

"My mother almost hit the roof when I told her I took a job with a drug company," I told Strauss. "Get my relatives together on a Sunday and they'll abuse everyone in the medical profession. For hours they'll complain about the cost of their high-blood-pressure medicines and hemorrhoid pads. They think Boorman makes its buck off people's misery."

Strauss launched into a Kiwanis Club speech that made me want to groan. "As companies go, Boorman has very high ideals. And pharmaceuticals can really help people. I mean, I wish you could have seen my sister before and after she got pregnant. The change was so radical. It turned her life around."

I didn't know Strauss's sister, but already I questioned whether I would like this fertility goddess of Bergen County, who only had to pop a Boorman pill, open her legs to her religious-fanatic husband, and a cornucopia of children came flying forth. On a surreptitious visit to the advertising back files, I had looked up the ad that featured her and the drug that assured her success. She was lit from below, in that fuzzy Hallmark card kind of glow found on Mother's Day cards. She sat in a rocking chair, and her head was bent toward her swaddled baby, yet I could tell—just from looking at her long, glossy, kinky hair and thin, ballet-dancer features— that if Strauss had gotten the brains in the family, she sure had gotten the looks. She was beautiful in a way I'd never be. And the baby—no words, I thought, could ever adequately describe the beauty of a newborn baby. Already I knew my eyes would grow wet when Carol let me hold Al Dante Junior for the first time. Probably the only thing that would stop me from full-fledged crying would be Carol's inevitable smug remark: "I hope you'll have children too, someday, Lisa. Because now you see how wonderful it is." That would not be the appropriate moment, I knew, to remind Carol how bitterly she had complained to me about her bowling-ball boobs. But I knew I'd be tempted.

The tears that came to my eyes as I gazed at Strauss's sister in the ad also fortunately were stopped by the text below: *In six years, there will be piano and ballet lessons . . . in sixteen years, boys will come knocking at the front door. . . .*

Oh, Christ, what a barf, I thought, pushing the ad back into the folder and slamming the file drawer shut with a bang. My desire to poke fun at the whole thing was further satisfied when I remembered Strauss mentioned having a nephew, not a niece. His sister's oldest child—the baby in the picture—was not a girl, but a boy. I wondered how she felt about having his sex changed for the purposes of promoting this fertility drug. Maybe this was the basis for Strauss's parents' objection to the ad, which apparently had run for two years in all the medical journals and probably accounted, at least partly, for the drug's whopping success.

"How old is your sister?" I asked Strauss.

"Thirty-one."

"And she has three kids!"

"This surprises you, who has fifty-plus cousins?"

Oh, why had I ever told him about those fifty-plus cousins? It just seemed to confirm the stereotype that all Catholic girls had to do was look at a guy and they would squirt out kids faster than sinners spit out frogs in those weird Hieronymus Bosch paintings.

"My sister probably wouldn't have had kids at all if my brother-in-law hadn't been so dogged about it," Strauss said. "I can understand wanting to have children, but he turned it into a crusade—a *children-are-the-best-revenge* sort of thing. He put so much pressure on her, it was painful to watch."

"Why didn't you say anything?"

"As I was reminded by my mother—more than once—it wasn't my marriage."

We were both quiet for a moment. Finally I said, "My sister had trouble getting pregnant too."

"Why didn't you tell me you had nieces and nephews?"

"I don't. Carol's expecting at the end of summer."

"That's nice news. You'll like being an aunt."

I shrugged. "I get kind of bored by Chutes and Ladders."

"Uncle Wiggly is much worse," Strauss said.

"I don't know about that. Some of the names of the characters are fun at least: Skeezicks. Dr. Possum. And the Bad Pipsisewah."

"I see you've played fairly recently."

"All those younger cousins," I assured him.

"Is your mother excited? About your sister's baby?"

"Believe me, she's beside herself. It's going to be a boy. She always wanted a boy. So did my father."

"How old were you when your father died?"

"Twenty-one. He was fifty-nine. Why? How old is your father?"

"Seventy-eight."

There followed a big pause, while I did what constituted (for me) complicated math in my head. "Wow," I said. "He had you kind of late too."

"It was his second marriage."

"Oh," I said. "Like the execs at Boorman?"

"Not quite."

I did more math in my head. "Your mother must be more than a little younger than your father."

"There's a difference in age, yes."

"How *much* of a difference in age?"

"Fifteen years."

Now it was my turn to refrain from saying, *That's useful information.* "Got any stepbrothers or stepsisters?" I asked.

"No."

"So who'd your father marry the first time around?"

"That's a long story."

"We have all night."

"I'll save it," Strauss said, with a finality that I knew was meant to close the subject.

We drank three-quarters of the bottle, and Strauss brought us a plate of peanut butter and crackers that served as our dinner. As we finished up, I told him, "You keep your place really neat."

"Actually, just the opposite."

"You?" I asked. "A slob? Your desk at work is always clear."

"I have a secretary. And here, a cleaning woman. I mostly live upstairs. I'm afraid you'll have to see it now."

"It's almost dark."

"Yes, but it gets very sunny, very fast, in the morning."

"Is that an invitation?"

"Of course you'll spend the night," Strauss said, as he got up and pulled on his trousers, leading me to think of how my mother and aunts always made fun of bossy men: *Hmmph! They think they're God, but they still have to put their pants on one leg at a time!* "I mean, you will spend the night, won't you? I want you to."

"I want to too," I said. All of a sudden I craved nothing more than to watch him do the ordinary things that made him look so much more approachable than he ever was at the office, such as buttoning his wrinkled shirt and buckling his belt.

Strauss said he would bring me something *to slip on* before he showed me the bedroom, as if I wouldn't dream of walking naked upstairs with him. But what he brought me from the front-hall closet made me despair: a starched shirt still in its dry-cleaner bag.

I gave him a look that showed him he was hopeless. "Get me something that's been worn. By you. Preferably a few times."

"You're sure?"

I nodded. He went upstairs and I heard him rooting around in his closet or drawers and I knew he had a lot of stinky laundry to choose from. This was confirmed when I followed him up the curved stairwell wearing the denim shirt he brought back for me. He was a disgusting housekeeper. In the room at the top of the stairs, a low bed was covered with wrinkled white sheets and a pile of laundry. The floor was littered with socks and tennis shoes, a pile of receipts and unopened mail sat on the chest of drawers, and in the corner leaned a baseball bat, the hardball kind my father gave me when I went off to college, for the purpose of fending off boys and other intruders and which I seriously thought of using on the rat I found below my kitchen sink before I slammed the cabinet door shut and boxed him in with all three volumes of *Remembrance of Things Past*. I wondered if Strauss also got his for free at Yankee Stadium on Bat Day.

The only thing that announced the room didn't belong to a sloppy seventeen-year-old boy was the size of the bed (queen) and the skylight that topped the slanted ceiling.

"Highly commodious," I said.

"I'll change the sheets."

"Don't bother."

"I insist. For you."

"When was the last time you changed them—for your last girlfriend?"

He told me there hadn't been anyone else. *In quite some time.* I wondered how he defined *some time*. Then I realized he was waiting, and I took my cue and told him he was the first person I'd been out with since moving to Ossining.

"But there was someone else back in New York?"

"Why do you ask?"

"I had a feeling you were running away from someone."

"Well," I said, "there *was* that rat in my kitchen cabinet."

Strauss actually started to whistle as he went into the closet to get some clean sheets—and another pillow, for I suddenly noticed there was only one on his bed. His relief both flattered and bothered me. What would he have done if I told him about those guys back in New York and then something very telling about the nature of those relationships: I might have called it *sleeping with* men—but the first time I ever did it and took a snooze afterward I was twenty-one. In spite of my extensive sexual experience—what some might call pure promiscuity—I never before had helped a man make a bed.

The task pleased me. Strauss stripped the old sheets and blankets, and then—as if he were bent on playing the doofus in one of my dumb-guy jokes that split the sides of my office colleagues—he stupidly deposited the bundle of poorly folded clean sheets down on the mattress. I smiled and moved them onto the floor. The sheets were soft but thick—two hundred fifty threads per inch, I was sure of it.

"These are nice," I said. "Did your mother pick them out?"

He tossed a pillow at me. I caught it and threw it back. Then he started to put the fitted sheet down backward, and I said, "I can see you didn't pass Bedmaking 101 at Harvard," and he said, "Cornell. I learned to make my own bed at Cornell," and we gave each other shy smiles and said, "After you," "No, after *you*," before we both pulled the fitted sheet at the same time and practically ripped it in two as we tried to hook the elastic over our respective sides of the mattress.

"We may just end up sleeping on the carpet," he said.

We smoothed the flat sheet and made sure there was equal overhang on each side of the bed. As he rescued the cotton bedspread from the floor, I asked, "Are you a blanket hog?"

"No," he said. "But I have to warn you, I can get a little restless at night."

"Do you kick?"

He shook his head. "Insomnia."

"Will you wake me up too?"

"Of course not," he said. As if I were a kid he planned to tuck in for forty winks, he said, "I want you to have a good night's sleep."

We straightened the covers and stuffed the soft feather pillows into their cases. I wondered why this simple activity made me feel so buoyant. Strauss seemed to like it too. His voice was happier than I'd ever heard it when he asked, "Which side do you want? . . . Which pillow do you want?" and he might have been offering me gold and diamonds for all the joy I felt as I chose a down pillow from among the two he had and selected the side closest to the bathroom just in case I had to get up during the night. Then Strauss played the Jewish mother and brought me a flashlight so I wouldn't trip and break my ankle in the dark. He asked me if I liked cereal for breakfast—because quite frankly that was probably all he had in the kitchen cabinet.

"I can handle cereal," I said, "as long as you don't tell me your dreams over the breakfast table."

"I wouldn't think of boring you."

"Unless it's a really good one. About a tidal wave or something."

"I promise to keep mum on the subject."

Strauss brought more wine upstairs. As the room grew darker and the shadows of the furniture were cast on the walls from the faint illumination that came in through the skylight, we sat up in bed, spending just as much time talking as we did keeping silent. Then we lay down and I kept my arms around him and he kept his arms around me, which set a record. I definitely had never held anyone for so long before, and I wasn't moved to let him go until he asked me, hesitantly—not to spoil the mood or any-thing—but downstairs . . . when I said I was protected . . . was I on the pill?

"Not right now."

"Then—?"

His thorough inquiry compelled me to admit I was at that very mo-ment wearing an arc-spring diaphragm manufactured by Boorman's rival. Then I remembered that Boorman didn't manufacture contraceptives and that of course the barrier method was good for only one go-around, after which you needed another shot of spermicide, which I had been stupid enough to leave at home. If Strauss was aware of that fact, he didn't call me on it.

Strauss would have been appalled if he knew how careless I had been about birth control when I first started messing around with boys. I could still shock myself by thinking of it. It was a wonder no one called me *Mommy* by the time I was fifteen. During my teenage years I relied on dubious behaviors—known as finger-fucking, dry-humping, or pulling out—until I got my driver's license and made the hair-raising drive over the Quinnipiac Bridge to the downtown Rexall, where I purchased shots of foam that I hid like a small mound of tampons in my locked jewelry box. Until then I had functioned under the illusion that not wanting children was enough to protect you from getting them, just as children think that not wanting to die is a guarantee of immortality.

At sixteen all that turned around. After Dodie got that scholarship to Duke, I set my sights even harder on college, and although I hardly cleaned up my act, I made sure I was protected, because a baby would bar me from the university gates. But after all the years that I'd been scrupulous about birth control (whether it worked or not), that evening I found my recklessness had come back to haunt me. I still hadn't learned my lesson. For there I was, suddenly worried—hoping, and bound to even do some praying later that night—that I did not get pregnant again.

For a moment I remembered the abortion—the cold shivery feeling that tingled up from my toes as I got down off the examination table and shed the paper gown, crumpling it into a tight hard ball before I shoved it into the wastebasket—and I immediately shut out the memory, resolving never to share it with Strauss. He would never understand. It would not do to tell him I played roulette before and lost at it, especially after he said he was ashamed he hadn't brought up this subject earlier, because he cared about me—cared *for* me—and he wouldn't want anything to happen that we would regret—for my sake.

His tenderness touched me, until he dispelled it one second later with this businesslike command: "I want you to go on the pill."

"We're not in the office," I reminded him. "We're in bed."

"I know we're in bed."

"So why are you acting like commander-in-chief of my ovaries?"

"What did I say?"

"It was *how* you said it. Just rephrase it, okay, and add a question mark?"

"I mean, will you go on the pill, Lisar, please, so we can be together—if you want to be together—and not have to worry about this?"

"Much better," I said. "But the pill makes me dizzy."

"How long has it been since you've tried it?"

"Back in college."

"They have lower doses of estrogen now. But I don't want you to take it if it makes you sick."

"Actually it just makes me fat."

"You don't need to be concerned about your weight."

"I'm not," I lied. "But I guess—if this sort of thing is going to be a regular occurrence?"

"It will be if you want it to be."

"I do. So I *could* try it again."

"Only if you want to."

"I'll call a doctor on Monday morning."

"I'll pay for it, of course."

The mention of money embarrassed me, and to brush it off I said, "Why don't you just swipe me some samples from the lab?"

Even in the dark I could feel him frowning. "Just a joke," I said, and put my fingers over his lips before he could offer to make a midnight run to the drugstore and start lecturing me about how we had better, for both our sakes, continue to keep our relationship a secret from everyone at work—as if I might be tempted to put it in the headline of *The Grapevine*.

When I took my finger off his lips, he said, "Boorman doesn't do the pill, and you and I had better have that serious talk in the morning."

His voice saddened me. "I know," I said. "I'll be ready."

We kissed each other good night. I tossed around, trying to find my groove in that strange mattress, and trying to forget I'd been careless with myself yet again. Then I, too, fell asleep. For the first time since I went to Confession and got my penance from the priest—on the one night I really could have used God's help—I forgot to say my prayers.

The skylight may have aided romance at night, but in the morning it served only to illuminate the creases on my face—or at least, the crinkles on Strauss's face as he continued to sleep, which were a good indication I had a few of my own. I hightailed it to the bathroom, splashed supercold water on my cheeks, swished a dab of Crest around in my mouth, and quietly returned to my original position. *Oh God*, I thought, *I'm in bed with my boss*. And my boss was stretching the muscles of his legs. He popped a knee joint. He opened his eyes, smiled, and gave me a boardroom greeting: "Good morning."

"I heard you walking around last night," I told him, for in the dark hours I felt the bed jolt. This was followed by a loud sigh. A few minutes later a light shone faintly at the bottom of the stairs. "Jet lag?"

"I warned you. I'm restless. Sometimes I can't sleep."

"I have sleeping pills. At home, I mean." Then I added, "They're prescription. I got them from a doctor."

"You don't take them regularly, do you?"

I shook my head. The night before he all but wrote me an Rx for the pill. But he clearly had some odd concerns about other medications. I wondered if his dad, like Dodie's, had an alcohol problem, or if his mother couldn't get through the afternoon without Valium. I wondered if Strauss had been sick at some point in his life, with a kind of slow, lingering illness that later made him place a premium on good health.

In high school I had a bad case of mono. My mother told everyone it was the flu, until it went on so long she had to confess I had the kissing disease, which she equated with VD. I spent four months lying in bed, thinking about how horrible it would be to have a terminal illness that kept you strapped to the mattress, waiting only to die. Outside my window the sky grew grayer by the day, the maple tree dropped leaves, and then snow fell on the empty bird's nest left high in its bare branches. Downstairs my mother made baked ziti and eggplant parmigiana and fried peppers and roasted potatoes. I slept and ate, slept and ate—ten extra pounds' worth, to be exact, which stuck on my butt for years afterward—and the world went on without me. While lying in that bed, I valued my health above anything else. But the moment I got up, I continued my crusade to ruin it—the drugs, the sex, and some wild dieting.

Since turning sixteen, I had gone up and down the scale, sliding back and forth between 101 and my sworn limit of 125. I never let myself break that number—which was the weight my sister Carol always talked about wanting to be, but never achieved. No matter how many pounds I shed, however, I still felt fat, because I had a chubby face. I'd never get rid of those cheeks that Dodie once described as *eminently squeezable—plumper than my mother's ravioli*. I didn't want eminently squeezable cheeks. I wanted cheek*bones,* the kind that God had given Dodie but not me. If there was one thing I liked about Strauss (among many), it was the way he reminded me that I could afford to cut loose with food on a more regular basis. If there was one thing I didn't like about my coworkers—and I had come to hold plenty of petty grievances—it was the bitchy way they urged me to feed my face: "You can stand that extra doughnut, Lisa. Lisa, have some more of this cake before we do the whole thing in. Lisa, this last piece of chocolate has your name on it. Better your hips than mine, girl!"

I was reminded of how lean my body was—at least in comparison to my chubby face—when Strauss offered me first crack at the shower. The entire wall above the vanity was mirrored, making it impossible to avoid looking at myself unless I kept my eyes down to inspect the pale tile floor. Strauss's bathroom sparkled far brighter than mine—thanks to his cleaning lady (who obviously steered clear of his bedroom) and to the brand-new tub and brass fixtures. Somehow this represented to me the heights of wealth—to own a bathroom that did not require you to get down on your hands and knees with an old toothbrush and an SOS pad to scrub the mold from the grout. The shower head was adjustable. I turned it so the water pounded hard. Strauss's soap was blue as a built-in swimming pool, and even though it was harsher and more drying than my usual Camay, I liked scrubbing myself with it because it made me smell like him. I toweled off and returned to the bedroom, where I reluctantly put on my clothes from the day before—all except my wrinkled, wine-stained blouse, which I replaced with Strauss's shirt. My reflection in the mirror over the chest of drawers seemed far from flattering. Funny. I liked *wearing* Strauss's shirt. But I didn't like the way I *looked* in it. He wore a 15 neck, and the 32 sleeves were too long on me.

I rolled up the cuffs. While he was in the bathroom, I wandered around the bedroom, touching things—old airline tickets and restaurant receipts he had yet to turn in for reimbursement for company travel, the baseball bat in the corner and the soft leather glove on the floor. I had forgotten he sometimes subbed on Boorman's Friday night company league, precluded from having a regular spot on the roster because of his travel. I wondered what position he played. I hoped he wore a jock strap.

His closet door was halfway open. I slid the door back on the track and stared at the long row of shirts in the blue dry-cleaner bags. I touched the elbows on one of his jackets and smoothed my finger along the leather of one of his belts. On the end of the rack hung the tie Strauss had been wearing that first day I met him, when he stood up from the table and said, "Welcome on board." The tie had red diamonds on a black background, which reminded me of a deck of cards, or a harlequin. I hated it. I snatched it off the rack, folded it into quarters, crept downstairs, and tucked it into the zippered compartment of my purse, where I usually stashed my tampons and a lucky penny. Then I tried to translate the shame I felt for swiping his tie into something mystical. *She Big Chief* had just performed some powerful magic, akin to stealing a bit of a man's soul or speaking an Indian's secret name.

Voodoo always had pleased me. And although I professed to loathe them—and swore I'd never practice them myself—feminine methods of control and deceit (such as were reported by Carol) also held my interest, if only for their anthropological value. "The first thing you do when you get married," Carol told me, "is march in there and toss the absolute worst clothes from his closet, and then when he asks where they are, you say, *Sorry, I needed more rags to wax the dining-room floor.*" To my mind—considering Al's current wardrobe—Carol could have found several other floors that needed to be polished. But every woman knew her limits.

For a moment I thought it was my duty to stay downstairs and start the coffee. Then I wondered how long Strauss would be in the shower and how much I could find out about him while he was obliviously scrubbing his scalp with antidandruff treatment.

What exactly was I looking for? Proof that he was not as swift a catch as I was starting to think? And what would that proof consist of—a Yankees baseball cap? A neatly stacked pyramid of imported-beer cans that announced he was a quality drinker? A Marilyn Monroe calendar? A toilet covered with sheepskin? Ballpark franks and boily-bag rice in the freezer, snack-packs of vanilla pudding in the refrigerator, and in the cabinet, powdered mashed-potato mix, half a dozen Kraft macaroni and cheese boxes next to several cans of Campbell's cream of mushroom soup—the bachelor's best friend? Evidence that he belonged to a college fraternity? A wool ski mask that might belong to a serial killer or a sexual pervert? A complete lack of books in the house, or worse (since I knew firsthand the kind of absurd shit that routinely got published), glossy, full-color coffee-table editions titled *Maine's Covered Bridges* and *Famous Outhouses of the Wild, Wild West* (hawked on the back cover with this pithy line: *Jesse James did his business here!*)?

I went back upstairs and wandered into the room at the back of the condo. It was set up as a study and proved what Strauss said the night before—that he lived mainly upstairs. Here were all the books (a lot of them), his stereo, and the records and tapes, arranged in alphabetical order. Strauss had too much baroque—the Bach section seemed to go on forever. At the end of the alphabet, I found a Herb Alpert record that Carol and I also owned (*A Taste of Honey*) and *Greatest Hits of Petula Clark*. Ha! To think that I hid from him my Rodgers and Hammerstein tapes and my copy of *Opera Without Words,* for fear he would think me a Philistine. Back they go, I thought, into a prominent place on my stereo shelf.

Along the front wall Strauss had a long white table littered with statements from companies like Scudder and Merrill Lynch and Fidelity and corporations whose price-earning ratios Dodie no doubt was familiar with to the T. There were white envelopes with the tops slit open from the American Cancer Society and the Juvenile Diabetes Foundation and the Simon Wiesenthal Center. A corkboard right above his phone—I tried not to judge this as adolescent—was dotted with multicolored pushpins and four photographs, all in black and white.

The first picture showed a middle-aged couple and a serious little boy standing in front of a stone fountain; the woman held a tightly wrapped bundle in her arms. I peered closely at it. The boy was Strauss—young Eben, with an expression that seemed to politely request of the photographer, *Please hurry, for I am being massively drenched by the spray from this antique but powerful fountain.* The bundle with no face must have been Eben's soon-to-be-beautiful sister. The couple, whom I took at first to be

Strauss's grandparents, probably were his mother and father. Dressed in their fifties best—a suit and tie for Strauss's dad, and a below-the-knee lace dress for his mom—they smiled for the camera. Strauss's mom had a thin, pale face. His dad was a big bear of a man, with coarse features and huge hands—so ugly it was positively sexy.

The other three photographs were of children. *Smiling* children. Smiling *dark-skinned* children. These head shots bewildered me, until I connected them back to the envelopes from the charities. I bit my lip. Strauss was a foster dad. He sponsored Third World children. Every month he sent money so these children could have beans and wheat and straw hats for their heads and a chance to attend the one-room mud school-house. In return, he got these dolled-up photographs. He got notes, per-haps twice a year, like the one posted beneath the first photo of a young girl in tight braids wearing what looked suspiciously like a Catholic-school plaid jumper. *Dear Mr. Struss, I like the shoes and I read the books. I am your Angie.*

The note depressed me—for it brought home the sad truth that pov-erty was the worst epidemic, seeping through the pores of the planet like groundwater ran through the earth. The note also made me feel ashamed—for in the city, I had walked by the homeless people slumped in Grand Central, and I always slipped my measly fistful of change into the red Salvation Army bucket without looking in the eyes of the thin, white-haired lady ringing the bell or the wrinkled old black guy playing the trumpet. Charity was one of the theological virtues that so far had escaped me. But I admired it. As much as Dodie and I liked to laugh at the saints, tortured on wheels and splayed with arrows and skinned alive—we drew the line at Mother Teresa jokes. We knew somebody had to mind the poor, and those who couldn't look suffering right in the face had better find their own guilty way to help the saints among us to do it.

So there was Strauss's guilt, tacked right up there on the corkboard—his mother, his father, his sister, and his foster children. And it seemed to tell me *Lisar, Lisar. Do not chide this man for neglecting his Chekhov and for playing golf. Compassion is the highest form of imagination.*

On top of the high bookshelf Strauss actually had some college texts—an earlier edition of the economics text I struggled with at Albertus Magnus, and then, surprisingly, Dante and Machiavelli and even some novels by Moravia and Lampedusa. Below this—even more of a surprise—sat the books that, judging from their yellowed pages and hopelessly out-dated prices on the back, must have consumed him after he quit premed at Cornell: his Kierkegaard and Nietzsche and Hume and Spinoza, the *Bha-gavad-Gita* and Confucius's *Analects*. Beneath this stood a row of history books—medieval and Renaissance and even some art history—and below were three rows of books that at first I thought were about World War II battles—but when I looked closer, I saw every single one had to do with the Holocaust.

For some reason this bothered me. I was about to turn away when I spotted, on the end, the melodramatic title of the very book I had been proofreading when I left publishing: *The Cursed Generation: Children of Holocaust Survivors Speak.* Since I left the company before I could even finish the manuscript, I never had seen the book in its final form, although I could have guessed they'd market it in a bloodred dust jacket with black lettering meant to evoke the colors of the Nazi flag.

You want to know why I left publishing? I'd once told Strauss. *Because I got sick of the way they tried to sell books by putting either an Irish setter or a swastika on the cover.*

How had he answered?

I remembered he pushed up his glasses.

I remembered he changed the subject.

I stared at the red-and-black spine of the book, and then I remembered more and more—in fact, a strange wave of déjà vu overtook me. I remembered: Italy. Park Slope. Carpet. Cornell. A sister. A father who was fifteen years older than his mother. A second marriage. His mother . . .

The shower, on the other side of the wall, continued running. As Strauss soaped his feet or scrubbed his neck or got up a good lather on his scalp, I grabbed the book off the shelf. A piece of onionskin fell from between the pages to the floor. It was a letter, typewritten on what appeared to be a manual Olivetti or Brother, from the author of the collection. The letter was addressed to Strauss, thanking him for contributing to the book, and informing him that his section began on page 238.

Chapter Seven

Solid

E., a 34-year-old executive, grew up in Brooklyn. His father,
a native of Ferrara, spent six months in Treblinka.

My earliest memory—or one of my most complete memories—has to
do with my dad and the war. The memory also is linked to the birth of my
sister.

We lived in Astoria then, in a walk-up owned by an old Italian couple
who lived on the ground floor. They kept their distance but treated us decently enough. The apartment was pretty run-down, but they repaired the
leaky faucets and the broken heater and the shaky top step the day we
reported the damage. My mother said they probably were afraid of us. But I
noticed how kind they were to my father—smiling and greeting him in Italian if we passed on the stoop—and they didn't play their radio on Friday
nights, until I think my father told them their silence wasn't necessary,
because we weren't religious. At least not very. After that they gave us cookies on Christmas, and once the landlady, after asking my father in Italian if
it was all right, even gave me a chocolate rabbit on Easter. My mother
frowned when I bit into the ear, but my father remarked with approval—we
weren't very well off then, and it didn't take much to impress him—"Ah,
solid."

Out in the tiny backyard the landlords had a fig tree, which they had
planted to celebrate the birth of their first son. (I may have this wrong, but I
think it's a tradition to wrap the discarded umbilical cord of the boy around
the seed of the tree before it's planted. I'm not sure if this is done to protect
the parents' fertility or to guarantee the son long life.) In any case, the
landlords' son was grown—he was almost as old as my own father, who was
in his forties then—so the tree was tall, and the trunk was treated with tar in
the summer to keep the insects from damaging the fruit.

One hot summer day—this was before air-conditioning—our landlords
went to the shore, and my mother suggested we have dinner outside in the
shade of the fig tree. She brought out food that didn't need to be cooked—
egg salad and challah, a bowl of sliced peaches, and a tub of peanuts, which
my father, who never helped with food preparation except to make coffee—

he was very particular about his coffee—actually volunteered to shell. He sat in a webbed lawn chair, the tub in his lap, and he offered us peanuts, two at a time—first to my mother, who smiled as she accepted them—then to me. Only after he fed us first did he pop a peanut into his own mouth. I was only four, but already I had noticed my father had the habit of making sure there was something on my plate before he picked up his fork.

He was tapping one of those stubborn single peanuts against the metal of the lawn chair when I noticed it. I'd seen it before, I guess, but never before had it seemed so blue against his pale skin.

"Somebody wrote on your arm," I told my father.

The minute the comment came out of my mouth, I knew it was the wrong thing to say. A squirrel scrambled up the fig tree, its claws scratching the tar. The backyard became so quiet you could hear the grass rustling.

"That's my number," my father said.

"Where'd you get it?" I asked.

My mother made a noise, as if she were about to say something, but my father cut her off. "In the war."

"Neat!" I was about to say, but something stopped me. "What's it for?"

"It's like a name," my father said.

"Where's yours?" I asked my mother, and she looked down at the peaches she was slicing, as if she was ashamed.

"I don't have one," she said.

To make her feel better I stuck out my arm. "I don't have one either. See?"

My father pushed his glasses up and pretended to inspect me. "Good," he said. "Have a peanut."

But I refused the peanut and turned back to my mother. All of a sudden she looked different—fuller, softer, distracted.

"Are you going to have a baby?" I asked her.

Her face turned red. "Enough questions," she said.

For five years I was the only child. I stayed home with my mother, just the two of us—my father always worked late—and I should have gotten closer to her, but the minute my father came through the door and hugged me—he always kissed and hugged me first—I knew I was first and foremost my father's child. My mother was the odd one out. Things changed when my sister was born. My mother fussed over her all day long, obviously preferring my sister to me, just as my father—although he loved them, please don't get me wrong—seemed to prefer me to my mother and my sister. So the alliances in our family were clear: On one side were the men, and on the other, the women.

The first year after my sister was born I got lonely. She was colicky and peevish and my mother seemed to spend all day—and sometimes half the night—trying to keep her from crying. One night—it must have been one of those nights when my sister kept wailing—I kept falling asleep and waking back up, and I had a weird dream. There was a little boy—all white and waxy, a ghost boy—standing in a tall doorway. Behind him was a stairway, and beyond that, even though I couldn't see it, I knew there were dozens and dozens of rooms, all empty, all waiting. At first I thought he was my shadow, or another version of me. Because he looked like me. But then I also saw myself standing at the bottom of the stairs, and I knew the boy was a separate person.

I might have forgotten that dream, but my sister began crying, and I woke up with the feeling that the dream-boy stood in the same room with me—for just a moment—before he disappeared again. The next day, when my mother was feeding my sister, I remembered the boy and I decided to play with him. I had some metal cars and a little wooden train, and I took them out, and from then on I wasn't lonely, because I had an imaginary playmate. I called him by my full name, my real name. No one ever called me by my proper first name; my parents had given me a nickname when I was small, and it has stuck ever since.

On weekends my mother would try to catch up on all the sleep she lost during the week, and my father spent time with me. One day my mother and the baby were napping. I was playing on the front-room rug—it was Oriental and had an elaborate pattern I would use as a racetrack for my cars—and my father came and stood over me. He seemed so tall when I looked up. For a second I was scared of him. I remembered the time we went to the Catskills for the weekend to visit my mother's sister and her husband, who had a cabin on the lake. Outside of the cabin was a burrow hole, and every morning when we sat on the deck to eat our breakfast we saw a chipmunk stick out his head, then scurry over to eat the Cheerios and Wheaties that had fallen through the slats of the picnic table. One morning before breakfast—I don't know why—I went outside, and before I knew it I had stuffed the hole with enough dirt to smother the chipmunk inside. Then I looked up and saw my father standing over me on the deck.

"What are you doing?" he asked.

Instead of saying, *I don't know*—because really, I had no idea what possessed me—I lied and said, "I was trying to make the hole look nice."

The look in his eyes made me realize I had done something wrong. "Think," my father said. "*Think* before you do things. Now uncover it."

I undug the sand and grass until my nails were black with dirt and my fingers rubbed raw and red. My mother grew angry because she just had given me a bath. For weeks afterward I felt as though my father was watching me and censoring my every word and movement. Then that feeling went away.

But for some reason the feeling returned when he stood over me on the carpet that one afternoon. I found myself hating him for knowing I wasn't perfect and for finding me guilty of doing something destructive. So I ignored him, until he made it clear he hadn't come to yell at me or scold me, but to take me out for ice cream.

"Can E. come too?" I asked.

Then there was that silence, just like the time in the backyard, only this time instead of the squirrels and the grass, I could hear the footsteps of the tenant on the third floor and the clock ticking on top of the mantel.

"Who's that?" my father asked.

"My friend."

"Where does he live?"

"Here."

"A friend who is pretend, then," my father said.

"Is he pretend or real if he comes in a dream?"

"He comes in a dream?" my father asked. "Does he ever say anything? In the dream?"

I shrugged. "I don't remember." Then, because my father looked down at the pattern on the chair and seemed so disappointed, I lied and said, "Oh, yeah, I forgot. He said to tell you hi, Daddy."

My father got up and opened the door to my parents' bedroom, which was right off the front room. I saw my mother's stockinged feet on the bed. They looked strange, like they belonged to a corpse or to a pair of legs disconnected from a body. My father sat down by her feet. He put his head in his hands. And out of him came horrible sounds—like an animal. The whole house seemed to be shaking. Everything in our house—the furniture and the carpet and even the few books on the shelves—was so heavy and ornate, as if my parents were afraid that a strong wind might come and blow everything in the house away. Yet even the couch and the hutch in the dining room where my mother kept all her special plates seemed to tremble.

My mother's feet stirred. She bolted up. She started to rush into my sister's bedroom, then stopped when she saw it was my father crying, not the baby.

She glared out the door at me. "What did you do to him?" she demanded.

"I didn't do anything," I said.

"You made him upset. Can't you see how upset you made him?" and my father kept crying, and then, from the other side of the house, my sister started screaming. My mother ran to get her, and the configuration seemed to represent something—my mother and sister in one room, my father and I sitting separate from them and also from each other. Then my mother came back in with the howling baby, tears on her face from the stress and lack of sleep, and wanted to know what was happening. *"What's happening?"* she kept asking. *"Oh God, what's happening?"*

What happened next? My father blew his nose, went into the bath-room, and threw water on his face.

"Ice-cream time," he told me. "Leave your friend here." And we left the house.

In retrospect it seems romantic, even contrived—a story some boy might make up to win himself the sympathy of a girlfriend. Yet it was true. I don't know how I intuited my father had another son, with another woman—before the war—who had the same name as me. It must have been something I overheard—late one night when my parents thought I was asleep—or maybe something referred to in passing by my mother's parents (who always seemed suspicious of my father, until he started making money hand over fist, and then he could do no wrong). Maybe even as a child I could see my parents were a little mismatched—at least in terms of age (he's fifteen years older than she is; they met when my mother went to Europe with the Red Cross after the war; people sometimes would take my father for my grandfather, which embarrassed me). Maybe something that passed be-tween my father and our landlords—although it was spoken in Italian, which I could only understand in bits and pieces—gave it away. Maybe it was the way my father sat in his chair, sometimes, and looked so sad, as if he were looking down a long dark well at some treasure that had fallen and couldn't be recovered. Or maybe—and here, I suppose, might be the beginning or end of any faith I have—that vision of the waxy-skinned boy really was a visit from beyond the grave.

But in any case—you know how the origin of knowledge sometimes is a haze?—I think I knew of the other son even though no one directly spoke of him until my mother sat me down when I was eight or nine and told me that during the war my father had *lost his family*—that's the expression she used, *lost his family*—and she said, *"Another boy just like you, do you under-stand?"* I remember nodding. I remember nodding again when she told me never to talk to my father about it unless he started talking about it first. *"Do you promise?"* she asked, and I said yes. I always said yes.

The older I grew the more I could see that I was meant to take the place of the other boy, and therefore I had to be doubly smart—doubly good—doubly polite and doubly wonderful—if I didn't want to let anybody down. And I was good, so good that even my mother—who I knew on some subconscious level was bothered by my father's past because it made her the second wife, and therefore only second-best—probably felt indebted to that first boy. It made her job with me that much easier.

Until I was a teenager I thought only about the boy, as if he had come into the world by osmosis. And then—with the onslaught of adolescent hor-mones—it suddenly dawned on me that my father had been married before, to a woman who was not my mother. The idea intrigued me. I used to lie in bed and try to imagine her. She always surfaced as the opposite of my mother—hot and dark and throaty-voiced, her blouse opened at her throat. She played a big role in my teenage sexual fantasies.

I don't know why I'm telling you this. You asked me at the beginning of this session if I ever was ashamed of being my father's son, and this probably answers it—yes, certainly I was ashamed that I could cook up this wild fantasy about the equivalent of my own stepmother, conveniently forgetting she had been destroyed. Of course, I didn't know that then. I knew she was dead, but I didn't want to think about how or why, and neither of my parents told me anything that would keep my thoughts in check. I doubt I would have harbored those fantasies had my father done any justice to her memory—or even just acknowledged her. Why did he hide her, as if she were something shameful that ought to be hung in the closet sheathed in a bag full of mothballs and cedar chips? But people do what they have to do—I don't want you to think that I'm being critical of my parents. I mean, this was my father's experience and he had his own way of dealing with it, which was to keep totally quiet about it—and I knew it was wrong to judge.

Still, I judged. When I was sixteen I started going out with girls, and the fantasy fell away, and in its place came this nagging feeling of responsibility toward women, as if they needed to be protected against all men, including me—because men were the ones who had the destructive impulse, or at least, the power to do the most harm. I was always very careful, always very respectful of girls—too respectful, I think. In any case, I had trouble being forward. I didn't like playing the aggressor.

At the crudest level you could say I went in search of information about my father's wife and son, because they stood in the way of my getting on with girls.

By this time we lived in Park Slope, and only one other kid in my high-school class—a boy—had parents who were survivors. Or at least he was the only one who admitted to it. His mother and father had been in Birkenau and got married after the liberation. We compared notes. He had it much worse than me. When I complained—*"You know, they never talk about it, but yet you can't do anything, can't play with an imaginary friend, push a toy train around the carpet, write a girl's phone number with pen on your arm, without it all reverberating back to that"*—he told me how good I had it. His parents were nuts about it, he said—talked about it nonstop, utterly obsessive, and he grew up wishing they would just shut up about it and get on with their lives.

He told me I could find out what had happened to my relatives by calling the New York Public Library and asking one of the archivists to help find the records. It took over a month for the librarian to call me back, but one Saturday—under the pretext of going into the city to consult college catalogs—I took the train and got off at Forty-second Street. I held my breath when I walked up the long stretch of stairs to the front entrance between the stone lions—what are they called? Patience and Fortitude? I came back down a different person.

All the archivist showed me was a photocopy of a transport list. But it really was a shock—like a sock in the gut, maybe the way people feel when they see their parent's name inscribed for the first time on a headstone—to spot my father's name typed halfway down on the page. What was even weirder was to see my own name two lines below.

My brother's—I mean, my stepbrother's—name was in the Italian version. He was five. My mother—I mean, his mother—was twenty-seven. Her first name was G——. Her maiden name was L——. Sometimes names can be deceptive (you know what I mean, don't you, how you meet a Hoffman or a Klein or a Kraus and you think you're dealing with—well, you know, one of your own?), but I didn't think L—— was throwing off false signals. She must have been Italian—you know, true Italian, not like my father, who when he dared to say anything at all about his past talked about how his parents came down from Graz to open a branch of the family textile factory and sometimes shared the story about how isolated he felt being the only child at his *scuola* who did not eagerly await, each year, the arrival of Babbo Natale.

She must have been Catholic. This would have been even more romantic (you know how it is when you're a teenager—the very idea of being destroyed for love is intensely appealing) if it hadn't been so brutally true—that the only reason she was put on the train was because she married him.

When I told my sister she looked disgusted. She told me the whole thing was creepy—why did I have to go digging it up?—and none of my business, and that I had better not say anything to my mother about nosing around in my father's past, because it would hurt her feelings. My sister didn't care what I told my father; she never was close to him anyway, and there always was a lot of friction between them, especially after she turned thirteen, and my father, who seemed to equate teenage boys with the very forces of evil, began restricting where she could go and who she could see—and the antipathy between them flared up again after she went away to college, where she developed an eating disorder and had to be hospitalized.

I was close to my father—I still am—but I've had my own share of trouble talking to him. Besides, I had promised my mother I would keep quiet. I never could bring myself to ask why, at the start of June, he always looked so sad, as if this was his time to remember—her birthday maybe, or the boy's, or was it their wedding anniversary, or could this have been the last time he saw her, and not even knowing what day she died, he had to remember a long stretch of days, instead of just one, as her *jahrzeit?* I wanted to ask if he loved her more than my own mother and why he gave me the same name as the boy. (It had been his own father's name, so I guess he wanted to keep it alive.) But I said nothing. Maybe it suited me more to cook up fantasies.

I imagined the boy as an earlier version of myself. I saw his sturdy little calves and sensible socks, the leather shoes that connected with the black-and-white ball that he must have kicked around the town square. I imagined him eating biscotti dunked in cocoa, maybe even dropping rocks into a deep stone well and listening to the water plop as the stone hit the surface. His mother, I thought, should have been my mother. After the sexual fantasy faded, she became a dream—the woman in the white dress who waited by the lace-curtained windows for her son to come home, while soup simmered on the stove and pigeons cooed on the red-tiled roof. And my father—my link to all this—strangely never came into the picture, except years later, when I fantasized he would take me on a trip back to Italy, where he would show me the textile warehouse his father had set up, and maybe a monastery or a crawl space where he hid with his wife and child when a roundup began, and the home of the man he believed snitched on them for the measly bounty of a few thousand lire a head.

But my father never said anything and so neither did I. None of it came up until my early thirties, when I got involved with a woman. Her name was Jeanne. We had been classmates at Cornell, both premed, both of us seeing someone else. Years afterward I was working for a drug company in N—— that was coming under fire for manufacturing an anti-depressant that had bad side effects. We were trying to gather some support for the drug from the medical community, and I met Jeanne again at a conference. She had become a shrink. Excuse me, a psychiatrist. And yes, she had done a lot of research on posttraumatic psychosis and even had a healthy share of Holocaust survivors and incest victims and Vietnam veterans among her clients.

I have to admit her profession made me nervous. But I liked and respected her. We got to be good friends, and then we became something more than that. In many ways I was more compatible with her than I suspect I'll ever be with anyone else—we both liked the same kinds of food and music and books, and we both had a sober, clinical sort of temperament. So we started talking marriage. She took me home to Short Hills to meet her parents. I took her back to Brooklyn to meet mine.

The parents did us in. Her parents were intensely religious; she had rejected it all, but then she brought home the son of a survivor like a prize. I can't tell you how they fawned over me. It still makes me ill to think of it. And my parents—well, they still were disappointed I hadn't gone through medical school; here was the doctor they didn't get when I ditched premed to study religion (*"Of all things!"* my mother said, and my father shook his head), then finally "saw the light" and went for my MBA. They loved Jeanne. They were crazy about Jeanne. She could do no wrong.

From our parents' perspective, it was just too good to be true. But something, at least from my point of view, was missing. It just didn't seem right. Jeanne seemed like the sister my real sister had never been for me. This can't be the real thing, I thought. Because when I thought of Jeanne my heart stopped, not from love, but from fear: of what more-daring side of myself I might lose or never discover if I married her. I thought we were drawn together more out of some weird kind of guilt and the desire to let Mom and Dad pull our strings. I don't deny it: More than once in my life my parents have called the shots, and I've let them do it.

We parted on bad terms. I had let it go too far; by then we were engaged.

The worst part of the end of that relationship was telling my parents. I drove back into Brooklyn; it was a gloomy evening and the next day was my parents' wedding anniversary, which only rubbed salt into the wound. I knew in the long run it was the right move—I wasn't crazy enough about her, there wasn't that gut feeling—yet breaking it off left me feeling more depressed than I ever had been in my life. I had just turned thirty-one. I felt tired.

I went to my father's office first. He works in the carpet business. It was late. He had sent the secretary home, but he still had a few phone calls to make. I sat out in the lobby. I dreaded telling him—knew how disappointed he would be—and that made me angry. I thought: *Why is this any of his business? It's my life. I'm the one who has to live it.*

He got off the phone and waved me in. "What's the matter?" he asked the minute he saw me.

"Dad," I said. "About Jeanne."

"She's sick?" he asked, and I said, "No."

"Then what?" he asked.

"No go," I said. "It's off."

He had a pencil in his hand, and he put it down on the desk. "Well. Did she put an end to it or did you?"

"She did," I said, which wasn't exactly true, although I let her have the final word, as if that were any satisfaction. "But I wanted her to."

"But why did you want her to?" he asked.

"I don't know. I can't explain."

My father shrugged. "So. What do you want me to say?"

I shrugged back. "I don't know," I said. I looked around the office (the battered shades and the old steel desk, all testimony to the sacrifices he had made to be the good provider), and I remembered the way he never came home until late at night and always worked—in a Jewish neighborhood, no less—every Saturday. Around his neck hung a yellow measuring tape, and I remembered how ashamed I always had felt of that tape, that badge of the working class, which he would not give up wearing, even after he stopped crawling around on his hands and knees across the floor because he had ten salesmen underneath him to do the dirty business.

I never back-talked my father in my entire life, but all of a sudden I was the smart-ass teenager I never felt I had the right to be. "Why should I say anything to you?" I asked. "You never talk to me."

"What do you want me to say?"

"Why don't you ever talk to me about anything important?" I asked.

"What's important?" he said.

"Dad," I said. "Come on." It seemed so much easier to impute all my questions to Jeanne. I said, "Even Jeanne said it was sick—unhealthy—the way you don't talk about what happened to you."

"What do you want me to do?" he asked. "Go nuts with grief in front of you?"

I told him I just wanted to feel sorry for him, and he said *save your pity.* "Just save your pity," he said.

"But how can you get up in the morning?" I asked him. (This was becoming a big problem for me, because I couldn't sleep well at night.)

"What's the alternative?" he asked.

I knew the alternative was suicide. Truth to tell, I often wondered why he hadn't committed it—and what I would have done in his place. *Just tell me how to live,* I felt like begging him. Instead, I asked him the real question I had been wanting to ask for years: How could he have gotten through all that?

I thought he would tell me he believed in some kind of God, terrible as He might be, or that he hung on by imagining another life for himself.

Instead, my father told me he was given a screwdriver. He broke open jaws and dug gold out of teeth.

Plenty did worse, I know it. Still, it made me so scared my hands tingled. And when I asked him how he did it, he answered, "It was easier than you think."

And now here I sit. In many respects I feel just like any other person. I get up every morning and report to work. On Saturdays I clean my car. I run errands. Twice a month I visit my parents. The visits are sometimes dull. Other times they're aggravating. Most of the time they're pleasant enough.

On the sheet of questions you sent, you asked if I ever fantasized about having a so-called "normal" family. The answer, I guess, is that I never wanted to be anyone else's son. Well, maybe most of the time I felt that way. Because when I was a boy and my father reached out his hand to ruffle my hair, there seemed to be electricity between us—a current that coursed deeper than the average one between a parent and a child. When he passed me food at the dinner table, when he hugged me when I got into Cornell, when he shook my hand that first vacation I came home, it was with an intensity that I never saw or felt when I looked at my friends and their fathers. Everything meant more between us. I wouldn't have given that up for anything. Yet I felt guilty about that privilege, because I knew the source of the strong emotion between us came from something evil.

After I broke with Jeanne, a month later there was a fallout in the company I worked for—about another product that was doing more harm than good and also because of business practices I considered unethical— my father stuck by me. He was the one who told me to do the right thing, even if it cost me the job, which it did. He helped me out financially. He asked me one more time if I wanted to come into the business with him, even though I knew it cost him his pride to ask me again after I already had told him I wasn't interested.

I love my father. And yet the fierceness between us seems to have gotten in the way of my forming other relationships. I felt I might have had a chance at it with Jeanne if only he wasn't who he was, or rather, if what happened to him hadn't happened. But then I think Jeanne probably wouldn't have been interested in me at all if I weren't my father's son. I know because she took an inordinate amount of interest in my dad, and she always wanted me to tell her my dreams in the morning. I don't like to admit this, but I often have nightmares and insomnia so persistent it sometimes makes me feel crazy.

I have trouble getting close to anyone. I would like to meet someone who would value the real me—not some romantic victim of evil (which, if you think about it, lurks everywhere and isn't that hard to find in everyday life). I have a little pact with myself—if I ever get serious with someone again, I won't tell the woman about my father until I'm sure I love her. Because I don't want my father getting in the way. After Jeanne, I realized there were plenty of people for whom the grand scale of such suffering has endless fascination. People want to be attached to it, without taking any of the consequences. Maybe in that sense I'm as guilty as all the rest. After all, it's my father's experience. It's not mine. I keep telling myself it's not mine. Yet it's me. It still seems like some part of me went through something too— but I'm not sure what that something is.

I don't want you to think this issue dominates my life. Days, weeks go by—I fly to Columbus or Saint Louis for a conference—and I don't think about it. But then it comes back, in a flash, always at some inappropriate moment—at a company reception, or in the middle of a meeting, I look across the table and know I'm the only person in the room who has to deal with this. And then comes another flash, which helps me get through it—the realization that they all have their own burdens to live with too. That's when I appreciate the obligation of being my father's son, because I feel that without this trigger of sympathy inside me, I couldn't relate to the rest of the world.

Yet I'm ashamed that it's only inherited pain. I've grown up believing that something awful should happen to me, that it's only a matter of time before God puts me to the test. I keep waiting and wondering why my father can sleep at night and why I get the nightmares, the bad dreams that should have belonged to him. I dream I'm standing at the edge of a cliff—no, a ravine—and I keep standing and waiting for the bullet to come, or the hand that will push me over.

Chapter Eight

Lower and Lower

I replaced the onionskin letter, then slipped the book back on the shelf. The shower squeaked off. I thought about the "shower rooms" in the crematoria. My face flushed and my ankles felt numb. I had the urge to storm the bathroom—to run in and embrace Strauss.

Instead, I went downstairs to make him coffee.

As I slowly lowered my feet upon each step, I thought it was little wonder I felt like I knew Strauss well right from the first. His was the last section I read. But I only had gotten halfway through, putting down my blue pencil when I got to the girlfriend named Jeanne. My relief to pass the project on to someone else had been immense. With the exception of Strauss's section—which had an even, level tone that contrasted with the voice of all the rest of the sons and daughters interviewed—the whole manuscript hummed with anxiety. Some of those interviewed had joined kibbutzes; others had joined ashrams. One was a concert pianist who specialized in playing music written by people destroyed in the camps. Another had gone off the deep end and had multiple suicide attempts. All of them loved and hated their parents with a fury that would have shocked me if I hadn't felt the same intensity toward my own.

The drip coffee maker—Swedish—sat beside the Jenn-Air range. Strauss hadn't washed it. I dumped the grounds, which were tinged with white mold, then grabbed a sponge. Housework always helped clear my head. I scrubbed the basket and the glass pot. If I could have done so without causing commentary, I might have run eight ounces of vinegar through the machine. Something told me Strauss was not the type to regularly clean out the filter system.

In the refrigerator I found a six-pack of Czech beer down to its last two bottles, a half dozen eggs far beyond their expiration date (I took matters into my own hands and chucked them into the wastebasket), two cans of picante V-8, more root beer (Dr. Brown's), and some tiny containers of Chinese takeout that probably dated back from last week. I tossed those too. The coffee beans, dark and rough, sat in a Rubbermaid container on the freezer door. I peered into the cold compartment long enough to find out Strauss liked pierogies and took pity on the Girl Scouts, buying enough thin mints to necessitate stowing some in the freezer.

But why was I thinking of Girl Scout cookies at such a dire time? Because I was afraid to let myself think about what I'd read, and because my self-centeredness and ignorance embarrassed me. Since my own father had emigrated as a teenager, I simply had assumed Strauss's father had done the same. Yet once they "became American," Daddy and all of my uncles had served in World War II. Where had I imagined Strauss's own dad had been—Fort Dix or Valley Forge? Playing bocce beneath the vineyard cypress trees? Wearing a black shirt and saluting Il Duce? Why hadn't it even occurred to me that his father could have gotten left behind? In the one college course I took in modern European history, we had learned that the destruction of Jews in Italy was not as thorough as it had been in other countries—but we also had read an account of the cleansing of the Venetian ghetto and the moving story of a physician who committed suicide rather than surrender the names of hundreds of other Jews left in that storybook city. I knew that the husband of one of my favorite authors, Natalia Ginzburg, had been arrested and died in prison, leaving her to care for three children. Countless times I had read and reread Giorgio Bassani's beautiful novella, *The Gold-Rimmed Spectacles*, in which the hounding of the homosexual doctor became a metaphor for the eventual persecution of the Jews by Fascist forces.

While Strauss was shaving—I was pretty sure that was what men did after they showered—I ground the beans, filled the pot with water, and then dripped the coffee, hoping that when he came downstairs he would be so pleased and distracted by the rich smell of java roasting that he wouldn't notice I was looking at him in a different way. If there was one thing I felt moral about, it was the right to privacy. But I had just violated Strauss's, and now I would have to pay. I wouldn't be able to joke about Scrooge McDuck or laugh when Strauss told his own occasional mild Jewish joke (the rabbi always one-upping the minister and the priest), which he insisted (and I agreed) was a harmless practice. Worse, I would have to wonder—on a daily basis—if the very fear he had expressed in the interview (reading it *had* made him seem more interesting; how could it not?) affected my feelings for him. Even worse, I would have to wonder—or cease to wonder—what strange pushes and pulls from his past affected his feelings for me.

The immediate dilemma—of having to hide the knowledge I wasn't supposed to have—was a big one. *Save your pity,* his father had said. So mine would have to go into the bank, until Strauss asked me to withdraw it. From that moment on, I knew I would be waiting for him to tell me the story, plagued with a tremendous amount of guilt for using his father's bad fortune as a thermometer of his romantic interest in me.

Everyone had a right to secrets. But when you grew close to someone, I thought, wasn't the list supposed to grow shorter, not longer? In addition to the Rodgers and Hammerstein tapes, there were plenty of things I'd kept hidden from Strauss already. Under my bed I had stowed my chapters of *Stop It Some More.* I hadn't told Strauss that in my mother's house there was a toilet (always referred to, in reverent tones, as *the Commode*—as if it were some technological wonder) that flushed only when you pulled on a shot-bead chain suspended from the ceiling. I stopped wearing my miraculous medal the moment I began seeing him. I said nothing about my abortion. I didn't disclose how close I was to Dodie. I put a thick blanket over my bad feelings toward my mother and father.

Nor did I tell him I had made my own little contribution to the annals of anti-Semitism.

On that hot July Saturday in 1976 (the year the whole world seemed wrapped in bicentennial red, white, and blue), my father was working overtime and Carol, my mother, and I were sweating in the kitchen, stuffing ricotta into manicotti shells. My mother, who claimed she could smell trouble a mile off, heard a car door out front. She wiped her hands on her apron, went into the front room, and returned to the kitchen, whispering, *"Polizia.* What'd you do now?"

"Don't look at me," Carol said—an unnecessary command, since my mother was staring straight at me.

"I didn't do nothing—" I said, before I blurted out, "They're at the wrong house."

"You know something," my mother said. "What were you up to last night?"

Rather than admit I was flat on my back next to Runway Number Two at Tweed New Haven Airport with Tony Adano on top of me, I told her what happened afterward. Tony drove me home by the back alley of Schlottmann's Dry Goods, where I had the bad fortune of witnessing my cousin Jocko shaking a can of black spray paint. The car passed too quickly for me to figure out what Jocko actually did. But Schlottmann just had fired Jocko's girlfriend for skimming a few bucks every day from the cash register, and what use Jocko had for spray paint I could well guess.

I hinted as much to my mother. Mama yanked Carol up. "Go tell Auntie Beppina," she said. Like me, Carol had grown up on a steady diet of *Hawaii Five-O, The Mod Squad,* and other cop shows, so she rose to the melodrama of the occasion and bolted out the back door as if the success of this hour-long plot depended on it. Mama turned back to me. "And you—you. You don't know nothing. You don't say nothing—"

"But, Ma—"

"Family first. Keep your mouth shut. Let Uncle Gianni fix Jocko's cart."

A loud knock thudded on the front door. My mother turned off the stove burners and went to the front. From the kitchen I saw her crack the door. I cringed when I saw the cop was black.

The officer started to say something, but Mama interrupted. "Let me see your badge," she said, as if the only way a black guy could become an officer of the law was by renting a police costume from the Halloween store on Temple Street.

The cop produced his badge. Mama leaned over and read the officer's name the way she read the church bulletin and her holy cards—silently moving her lips.

The cop finally snapped his badge away. "You Mrs. Diodetto?"

"That's my name."

"Like to talk to your son."

"He's not home," Mama said, not bothering to add that her son—whoever he was—had yet to be born.

"Where's he at?" the cop asked. "A friend's? Down the corner?" The cop looked over Mama's shoulder and pointed at me. "She the sister? You girl, you know where your brother at right now? Or where he at last night?"

My mouth started to open, then closed when Mama turned and gave me a murderous look.

"Which son of mine you looking for anyway?" she asked the cop.

"Name's Gia-*como.*"

"*Gia*-como," Mama corrected him. "My nephew. Two doors down."

Satisfied she had stalled the cop long enough for Jocko to hide, Mama shut the door and came back in, wiping the sweat off her brow with the back of her arm.

"Ma," I said.

"What?"

"Jocko sprayed a Nazi sign. On Schlottmann's."

Mama's forehead wrinkled. "You sure? You saw?"

"Not positive. But I think so."

"What'd he do that for?"

"You know his girlfriend, Paola—the one they call P.T.?"

"In the fishnet stockings? Don't ever let me catch you in those fishnets. *Madonna,* that girl means trouble."

"Schlottmann fired her," I said. "For stealing."

"So Jocko sprays a Nazi sign? He could have sent her a valentine, it would have been safer and cheaper. *Santa Maria,* what a stupid kid! And that Schlottmann—"

"What about him?"

Mama thought about it. "I guess he's seen that sign before."

Schlottmann had an accent. Some people said he even wore the numbers. I knew I was supposed to feel sorry for him. But the truth was I disliked him, even hated him—because all those years my mother had paraded me in and out of his shop to buy my back-to-school wardrobe: a pair of black patent-leather Mary Janes, red rubber boots, a wool plaid kilt fastened with a gold safety pin, and a white cotton blouse with a Peter Pan collar. Schlottmann looked scornfully at my mother when she complained loudly in Italian about the prices, as if he could not understand from her intonation the gist of her dissatisfaction.

I hated Schlottmann because once Mama sent me down to his store and I couldn't find what I was looking for. When he came up behind me— certain, I'm sure, that I was wandering up and down the aisles with the intention to shoplift—and asked me what I was looking for, I was so scared of him I couldn't remember the word for lightbulb in English. I felt like such a tongue-tied idiot—so stupid, so unworthy of ever moving beyond my mother—and I blamed him for making me feel ashamed.

I hated Schlottmann because my mother brought me to his store to buy my first bra, and she insisted on coming into the one dressing room, where the curtain didn't even close all the way, and after I finally got the stupid thing on, she said loudly—in English, this time: "That doesn't fit—I *told* you to try on the smaller one first."

Schlottmann heard her, and I couldn't stand him for that. But the spray paint changed everything. Schlottmann suddenly became someone else for me—not the man I hated, but the man I was supposed to side with. It was a miraculous metamorphosis. But I had seen it happen countless times before—the way an obnoxious great-aunt who contracted cancer or an utterly loathsome kid at school who got creamed in a car accident suddenly became a saint.

"Stupid kid," my mother repeated. For even Mama, who had little tolerance for Schlottmann—who always said he should have moved out of the neighborhood while the going was good—realized the gravity of that swastika on the back-alley door. *Not for nothing* had Uncle Gianni spent four years as a sous-chef on a submarine in the Pacific. *Not for nothing* had my own father sweated to death on radio duty at Fort Bragg, playing poker to combat only boredom, not enemy soldiers, as he waited, along with the rest of the world, for the war to end.

That was the line that Uncle Gianni took when he came home and found out Jocko had just missed getting sent to juvenile detention because *there weren't any witnesses.* All the way up and down the street you could hear Uncle Gianni yelling, his voice rising to a higher pitch with each exclamation:

You stupid fucking kid!
We fought a war over that!
I shit in a pot for four years!
Your uncle got the skin cancer!
My best friend lost his leg!
Your girlfriend's a fucking slut!
You're heading straight for jail!

Then arriving back where he had started, Gianni yelled the whole argument out, point by point, all over again.

You stupid fucking kid!

Etc.

The hollering went on for fifteen minutes or so—long enough, at least, for my father to use *the Commode* after dinner, which usually was a quarter of an hour operation, and probably long enough to make Jocko wish he had been sent to J.D. rather than subjected to the wrath of his own dad. Then the voices faded and my own parents started snapping at one another and I went outside and sat on the stoop to watch the fireflies hang and blink, hang and blink. The whiz and pop of Roman candles—set off illegally by my schoolmates over the airport marshes—was punctuated by the thud of M-80s in the distance.

On the front porch of Gianni and Beppina's house sat Dodie, a yellow number-two pencil tucked behind his ear as he studied his homework in the half-dark. He was one of two students at our high school chosen to take accelerated math in a special summer program held at Southern Connecticut State College. Auntie Beppina and Zio Gianni let him go only after determining *it wouldn't cost them nothing.*

I went over. Dodie and I were friendly to each other at home, but we kept our distance from one another in high school—he was top-job dork material, while I was still making up my mind if I was a pothead or an egghead or just another slut from the shore. But between us—especially at family gatherings—there was still an understanding that we were the only sane ones on the street and that we would have to stick together.

"Hey," I said. "Whatcha doing?"

"Calculus."

Although math was Dodie's forte, it was my downfall. Along with PE, at which I was hopeless, algebra was the biggest barrier to my getting a college scholarship—unless you counted the way I dressed and talked. My speech—and even Dodie's, until he went off to Duke—was laced with obscenities and fraught with double and sometimes even triple negatives.

I cocked my head toward the back porch to get Dodie's read on the Jocko situation. He shrugged.

"You knew he did it," Dodie said. "But you didn't say nothing?"

"A cop came over. A black cop—"

"I know. I've heard about nothing but all day—"

"And my mother, she told me to *stai zitta*."

Dodie shrugged again.

"Don't look at me that way, Dodie. She's my mother."

"Yeah," Dodie said. "*She's* your mother. And if you keep on doing what she tells you, you'll never get out of your father's house."

The force of Dodie's disapproval was so strong, I almost turned and walked away. But I stood my ground and told him, "I didn't do nothing wrong. It wasn't me who used the spray paint. And I'm stuck living where I'm living, so how the fuck am I supposed to live like I'm somewhere else?"

Then Dodie put down his calculus book and we got into an argument—our first exposure to philosophy, other than the brief foray into Saint Thomas Aquinas's teleological proof presented to us in CYO by a visiting Jesuit from Yale Divinity School, who blinked when he walked into the church basement and saw us slouched on the green folding chairs, the girls dressed in halter tops and miniskirts and the boys in their muscle T-shirts and holey dungarees. Although we didn't know it at the time, that night Dodie and I fought about our responsibility to family versus our responsibility to ourselves and society. Then we sat silent on the front porch until long after sunset, watching the moon hang like a big white china plate in the sky. That was the last time I ever talked about that incident with anyone. But I thought about it from time to time, especially when I got stuck with those Holocaust manuscripts at work—almost as if God had handed them to me as a penance. I even looked for a testimony from Schlottmann inside the manuscripts. But I found nothing.

Schlottmann kept silent. He washed off the black paint from his back door and continued as before. Business as usual. Some people said he should have taken the hint and gotten out of the neighborhood. He should have taken it years ago. "This isn't Westville," my mother said, as if it needed to be pointed out that our neighborhood was Sicilian to the core, its main drag lined with Catholic churches and *panetterie* and *tabaccherie,* instead of delicatessens and the Hadassah thrift shop, the Mishkan Israel cemetery, and a low brick building—unmarked—where people who seemed foreign, almost alien, gathered to worship on what we thought was the wrong day of the week.

When Strauss came downstairs and leaned in the doorway of the kitchen, I greeted him with a steaming blue-stoneware mug. As he accepted it, I realized this was another first in my life. The previous night for the first time I had made a bed with a man. And this morning Elisabetta Diodetto—who had vowed never to serve food to a man after years of waiting on her father at the table—served a guy coffee.

And got thanked for it too.

Strauss leaned against the counter and sipped his coffee. I leaned against the opposite counter and drank a few sips from my own cup. We smiled, shyly, at each other. Finally, because it seemed important to admit to something, I said, "I've discovered your deepest, darkest secret."

"And what might that be?"

"You own a Petula Clark album."

"That's right."

"And Herb Alpert's *A Taste of Honey*—"

"I won't deny it."

"You play baseball."

"I've already admitted to that."

"And patronize the Girl Scouts who set up card tables in front of the grocery store. You also have three illegitimate children."

"You've covered a lot of ground this morning."

"That was a long shower you took."

"Fucking on the floor—as you called it—gave me kinks in my back." He smiled. "Lisar, you were spying on me."

"Guilty."

"And now you'll have to pay."

"How?"

He came over to me and put down his coffee. He took mine from me and pushed it back on the counter. "By telling me yours."

"Never."

He stood in front of me, close, so I felt the drawer handle on the small of my back. He put his arm around me and his fingers pressed against the top of my neck, brushing against my still-wet hair. "I'll have to guess, then." He paused. "I'm hoping—almost to the point of praying—you like older men."

"Certain customers," I said, "have been known to please me."

"And you like to wear men's clothing."

"From time to time."

"You have a pierced navel. What? You don't? I thought I felt something hard down here last night." His hand was inside my shirt, his own denim shirt, caressing my tummy. "Was it here?"

"No."

"Here?"

"No." I knew this sort of coy innuendo was silly. But I liked it. It reminded me of the old TV commercials for deodorant soap that showed handsome, healthy, muscled men taking a shower. Parked in front of the boob tube, Carol and I used to gawk and hoot at those hunks—and provided Mama was out of earshot, we dared the cameramen to go *lower, lower, lower.*

I wanted Strauss to go lower and lower. I wanted everything I had learned about him to dissolve in the act. Making love makes people stupid, and I wouldn't have minded going dumb for the next half hour. But then I remembered—again—the birth-control issue, and I regretfully moved his hand away. "I got you coffee," I said. "Now give me something to eat. Unless you have a pack of condoms upstairs—"

"I've never used one in my life. But now you'll really think I'm hopeless for making the woman always take responsibility."

"Just as long as you don't tell the waiter, 'She'll have the fish,' we'll get along all right."

"She'll have the granola, then," Strauss said, and pulled down a box. In the cabinet I saw three more boxes of the same brand.

"Don't tell me," I said. "You have the same thing for breakfast every day."

He confessed he did. To further incriminate himself, he told me that on weekends he put coconut on top. On holidays—M&Ms.

"Plain or nut?"

"Both."

"That's sad, you know."

"A guy's got to take his pleasure where he can find it."

"So what do we get today?"

"Coconut *and* M&Ms, of course."

"Hedonist."

We took fresh coffee and our cereal bowls out to the dining area and sat at the glass table in front of the gargoyle print. Then, for some reason, I felt awkward, embarrassed about my body, as if eating candy-laden granola with a man was a more intimate act than taking off my clothes for him. It certainly had the potential to be more fattening. Strauss really had loaded on those M&Ms.

"So what's with all the Confucius and Boethius on your bookcase?" I asked.

"I switched to religion after pulling out of premed."

"What did your parents make of that?"

"It was the sixties," Strauss said. "The late sixties—"

"I repeat: What did your parents make of that?"

"Well—if you must know. Not much. But they kept it to themselves. I guess they hoped it was a phase."

"I guess it was."

"I'm not so sure."

"You can't tell me you use Augustine to do a better job at Boorman."

Strauss admitted that the author of *The City of God* didn't figure much into corporate politics. "You, however, do," he said.

I balanced a green M&M on the end of my spoon. "I guess this is the start of our little talk."

"Would you rather wait?"

"Let's get it over with," I said.

Strauss really had been going to too many meetings. In any case, he asked if he could *hold the floor first*. He said he had given it a lot of thought and what he thought was that there wasn't anything wrong with our *enjoying each other's company*. Others, of course, might misinterpret the situation as *an abuse of power*. There was a common perception that most people couldn't *maintain their professionalism under these circumstances*.

Everything he said from that point onward was prefaced with qualifiers: *I hope I don't need to tell you . . . it would be best if we both agreed . . . you know and I know . . . it goes without saying. . . .*

But it didn't go without saying. For a full five minutes he went on and on, trying to impress upon me the need for caution and telling me that no matter how much we both abhorred the dishonesty involved in such a situation, it was unavoidable, because we both would suffer if this should get out.

"For now, at least, this can't get out," he said. "Now. Your turn to speak."

I looked down at my almost-empty cereal bowl. I couldn't believe I had eaten all those M&Ms. I picked up a lone piece of oat and examined it under the dining-room light. I knew that what he was saying was right. But I didn't necessarily like the way he was telling me. It seemed impossible to link his lecturing style back to the much more vulnerable voice I'd read just half an hour before.

"I don't have anything to add to the discussion," I said.

"I can't believe that. Of you."

"You think I have a big mouth, don't you?"

"I think you have strong opinions."

"And you don't like that."

"Not at all. I just invited you to voice those opinions."

"All right," I said. "My opinion is that it's nobody's business but ours what we do off-hours."

"A year ago, maybe, the company would have frowned but looked the other way. But once the new policy is put into place—"

"The policy makes a clear distinction between unwanted advances and consensual relationships."

"It says *no supervisor shall insinuate, either explicitly or implicitly, that an employee's submission to—*"

"Please stop," I told Strauss, finishing the phrase in my head: *or rejection of sexual advances will in any way influence any personnel decision regarding that individual's employment.* "It's obvious we've both taken the policy home and practically memorized it. And if you're worried about Peggy—"

"Of course I'm concerned. She's not without compassion, but this sort of thing wouldn't sit well with her at all. I wouldn't want this getting back—in the wrong way—to Peg. I owe a lot to her—"

"You also owe something to yourself. You have a right to be happy."

"I don't think you understand. I lost my position before under very uncomfortable circumstances. And it's not what you're thinking—"

"*What* am I thinking? You always seem to know what I'm thinking."

"That I made a move on someone. It had to do with something much more unethical. Not that making a move on someone—without caring for them—*isn't* unethical."

"What happened?"

"I can't talk about it. There was a legal settlement—"

"Hush money?"

"Do I act like someone who would take hush money?"

"Then were you let go because you *wouldn't* hush up?"

"Forget that. For now. For now we're at Boorman, and in due course, I can speak to Peg—"

"Are you nuts?" I asked, and when he looked offended I said,

"Strauss, you're not the only one who wants to keep his—I mean her—job."

"But Lisar. Maybe I've misunderstood you, but I had the feeling you weren't totally wedded to your position at Boorman."

"Last night you implied as much about yourself."

His face flushed. "I regret if I gave you that mistaken impression."

I put down my spoon with a clang. "This isn't a power breakfast. Could you please stop talking to me like we're negotiating some kind of inner-office political coup?"

"It's habit."

"Break it. The bottom line is, we both need to eat and support ourselves. Which means we just keep quiet about it. And no one will guess. Really. Believe me. Unless you take me to the office Christmas party and smooch me in front of the CEO and all his minions."

Strauss told me I obviously had yet to attend the end-of-the-year Boorman gala—but once I'd gone, I'd immediately see it was hardly the sort of thing any caring man would inflict upon a date. He also said that by the end of the year we would *have a better read* on how we felt about this whole situation and by then we both might feel differently about *bringing it out into fresh air.*

I didn't want to tell Strauss our secret was guarded by the fact that I was an excellent actress when I needed to be and that the general office consensus was that he and Peggy were birds of a feather: She was interested in women, while he was not. Rumors sometimes were useful. Had I dared to be so bold—to throw any busybodies off the track—I might have dropped a few hints to that effect myself. But I held my tongue and let others wag away. And the next time I stayed overnight with Strauss, I noted with dismay he had taken a cautionary measure against my own curiosity by removing *The Cursed Generation* from his shelf.

I went on the pill. Strauss went on the road. When he returned, he picked me up at my apartment and brought me back to his place, where he uncorked another bottle of California wine and announced he had brought me back a present. The gift came wrapped in a pale pink silk pouch—an equally pale pink and silky chemise with spaghetti straps. I did the modest-girl routine and retired to the bathroom to try it on. It fit perfectly.

No man had ever given me such a gift. But I knew the protocol: I was expected to model it. Through the cracked bathroom door I announced, "I'm coming out."

"I'm ready."

"Are you sure?"

"I think I can handle it."

I tiptoed around the corner and peeked my head into the bedroom, where I found him lying on his bed with his hands propped beneath his head. He had taken off his coat and loosened his tie. I caught a glance of myself in the mirror—the creamy pink chemise was the exact opposite of what I imagined was the color of lust—and tried not to laugh.

"Do you like it?" he asked.

"Beats an apron."

He threw a pillow at me.

"If there's more where this came from—"

"There may be if you behave—or misbehave—"

"—I feel obliged to warn you—record it in the minutes—I don't do wires. Or leopard skin. A modest cheetah print might be acceptable on the top, but not on the bottom."

"I can't quite picture you as a large jungle cat, Lisar."

"And I don't dance to *Bolero*. Although I *did* dress up as the Cowardly Lion once for Halloween. My cousin kept stepping on my tail. . . . But you—you actually went into a store and picked this out?"

"Why not?"

"Weren't you embarrassed?" I asked, thinking about how mortified I always was just to try on a bra in a department store and how I always cringed when the salesladies with their half-glasses on chains around their necks hovered outside the dressing-room door and said, "Are you finding the right fit, honey?" I smoothed down the chemise. "Weren't you afraid they might think you're a cross-dresser?"

"It's not my size."

"How did you know which size to get?"

"Checked your bra when you were in the shower. I hope you don't mind?"

I didn't mind. I had a respectable number—neither too large nor too small. When Strauss gave me more gifts and said, "Wear this? For me?" I obliged him. Then I found I was starting to do more than just play along. I liked going into the bathroom and then making my grand entrance into the bedroom; I liked straddling him on the bed and slowly taking off his loosened tie, and unbuttoning his shirt, and undressing him while still wearing what he had dressed me up in. I liked the way he fucked me with the outfit torn aside—never totally taken off—the straps in disarray, the pants pulled down only halfway. It was his game. His fantasy. But after a while it became mine too, and we got into a groove that felt too good to break, full of rhythmic breathing and muffled bed thumps and intense cries that practically made the skylight shake until he put his hand over my mouth and whispered, "Shh, I have neighbors."

Afterward I always fell asleep, a habit noted by Strauss, who was that rarity among men that most women, at least in magazine advice columns, seemed to long for—the kind of guy who liked to talk and cuddle.

These sessions thrilled and bothered me. I went home and read Betty Friedan. I checked if Gloria Steinem had anything to say about sleeping with the boss. I thought Simone de Beauvoir did it with Sartre, and he was hardly a big proponent of women's rights. I remembered Hannah Arendt made it with Heidegger, and he was a Nazi. Then I thought: Fuck it, Strauss is a nice guy, he's my friend, this feels good, and why shouldn't I enjoy my body? It's just as much a part of me as my mind. And why shouldn't I enjoy making Strauss feel good? It was the first time in my life I had ever even cared if it felt right for the other person. Why did I have to think about the oppression of women while his tongue was in my mouth and his hands were running through my hair? We already had agreed to bar the lawyers from our bedroom. But if that old theory was correct that there were six people present at every act of love—the lovers and both sets of their parents—then the bedroom was crowded enough without me bringing in some social scientist to sit on my shoulder and evaluate my feminist or antifeminist behavior.

Wear this? For me?

Well, maybe. But more and more I found I was wearing it for myself. The chemise was followed by a pale-green camisole and tap-pant set, a black full slip, and lace bras. I took the hint. I retired my saggy old Bestform bras to the back of my drawer, tossed out my Jockeys, and underneath my professional Monday–Friday garb, I wore what Strauss gave me to work. Late one afternoon I was deep into a grant proposal—trying to clean up some clotted, circular prose—when I was distracted by the feel of silk under my blouse. I remembered how one night I came over to his place—after working out at the gym so late the security guards came around to lock up and I couldn't get into the shower. I showed up at his door a sweaty, disheveled mess. "Don't touch me," I said. "Don't even kiss me." Without a word, he pulled me inside by the hand and led me upstairs, where he ran a bath. "Take off your clothes," he said, as he went into the hall and fetched a couple of fluffy white towels and a washcloth from the linen closet. I stripped off my leotard and bike shorts, got into the tub, and turned off the water. I was surprised when Strauss came back in and knelt by the tub.

"Humor me," he said, then rolled up his sleeves—he still had on his pressed shirt from work, Egyptian cotton with a windowpane pattern—and he dunked the washcloth into the water. I leaned back and let him dribble warm water over my body. After a while he admitted that before we went to bed together this was his fantasy: to give me a bath, to soap my back and squeeze warm water off a washcloth over my breasts.

"I wanted you to screw me on your desk," I said—which really wasn't true, but I thought it would make interesting research for the latest chapter of my novel. My Don Juan character now sat in the waiting room of his chiropractor, having discovered it was murder on his spine to have sex on hard surfaces.

"There are too many important papers on my desk," Strauss said. "Such as your biannual employee evaluation."

"But I haven't been at Boorman for six months."

"Doesn't matter. Everyone gets evaluated at the same time."

"Did I pass?" I asked.

"On a flying carpet. All eights and nines except for collegiality—"

"What'd you rate me on that, zilch?"

"Six."

"Six! Change it."

"I won't. You're argumentative."

"With who?"

He smiled. "Your immediate superior."

I splashed him with water. "I am *not*—"

"See? Not that I don't enjoy it. But I do think you should eat your lunch—I've noticed you get a little cranky with me in the afternoon; maybe it's a blood-sugar problem. As for getting along with your *inferiors,* it's been reported you have yet to attend a single Tupperware party—"

"I beg your pardon. I have a lot of allies in Editorial. I clean out Mr. Coffee and the refrigerator *and* the microwave, so I feel like I deserve at least a seven—"

"An evaluation is like a letter of recommendation, Lisar. It has to have one slightly less positive thing so the rest of the superlatives sound believable."

"What are the superlatives?"

"Works overtime—and more. Gives her all to the task at hand. Pays close attention to detail."

I slipped down farther in the bathtub—he'd made the water awfully hot, which made me feel lazy and desirous—and opened my legs. "Shut up," I murmured. "I hate the office. Soap me here. There. Oh God. Right there."

"Shameless," Strauss said. "That's your middle name."

Sitting at my desk at Boorman, the memory of the warm water and the washcloth was so strong and real, and I was so distracted from the manuscript, I was afraid I'd have to run into the bathroom and do something wild that would cost me my job if I got caught. I closed my office door. I knew Strauss would be at his desk that morning, and in spite of our agreement that we would not engage in unprofessional behavior while on the job, I logged on to All-in-1 and shot through the following message.

Are you there?

After a ten-minute delay, Strauss gave me a cautious answer. *Yes.*

Alone?

Yes.

Thinking about me?

Another five-minute delay. *I am now.*

Tell me what you're thinking.

The answer shot back fast. *Follow me home. 12:30.*

What if I don't?

Expect another kind of pink slip.

I prefer the kind I already have.

I might have worn that pink chemise that afternoon—had he not met me in his driveway and bent down through my opened car window, his voice anything but authoritative as he said, "I'm embarrassed. I forgot. It's Wednesday. The cleaning woman is here. She's got soap all over the kitchen floor."

"I guess it's a no-go then. Let's take a walk along the creek."

"You'll get mud all over your shoes."

"They'll come clean."

He held my hand as we went around the back into the shade of the trees. After a few moments of walking in silence, he told me, "I shouldn't have sent you that message."

"I deleted it," I said. But if the truth be told, I had hesitated more than a few seconds before I pointed my cursor to kill off that missive from *Strauss, E.* I told myself I would have been a complete fool if I hadn't at least *contemplated* hanging on to it. You never knew when you might need some powerful ammunition. But I hated the Fourth of July, and firecrackers—even the mild sparklers and the shower-of-spark explosives named Jade Flower or Lotus Blossom that Jocko called "girly crackers"—always made me nervous. Guns terrified me. I couldn't even imagine holding one in my hand, much less pulling the trigger.

"I deleted everything," I said. "I'm not interested in—you know, what we've talked about before. Using sex as a weapon."

"I'm not either."

"So why do we have to talk like this?"

"Because, Lisar, we talked like *that*—"

"But we're friends. And I want to trust you."

"I want to trust you too."

"So let's forget about it," I said.

"Could I say one more word on the topic?"

Knowing Strauss's definition of one more word probably could run the entire length of *Webster's Unabridged,* I firmly told him, "No, you may not."

The walk we took that afternoon was peaceful and pleasant. But afterward I forgot to scrape the mud off my heels with a Kleenex, and when I got back to the office the secretary said, "Lisa, what happened to your shoes?"

I looked down. "Oh," I said blithely, "didn't you know the CEO's got a whiskey still in the woods? I spent the lunch hour with him, swilling moonshine."

That story made the complete rounds of Editorial within half an hour, with everyone snickering at what an unlikely couple the notoriously hard-drinking CEO and Lisa "Cheap Date" Diodetto would make. Back at my desk, I congratulated myself on thinking fast—but I also swore I'd never let myself get into a situation like that again. What if next time I couldn't come up with a smart-alecky answer? What if Strauss was tracking mud—right at that very moment—up and down Boorman's heavy-duty industrial carpet?

The amber glow of my computer gave me a headache that afternoon. I couldn't concentrate on my work. Maybe I did have a blood-sugar problem, I thought. Maybe I shouldn't have skipped lunch. Maybe I needed more caffeine.

By quitting time, I faced facts: I was in love with Eben Strauss, and it was making me nauseous.

By the end of August I knew Strauss kept his dish towels in the bottom cabinet by the sink, his aspirin was in the nightstand, his shot glass sat in the basket on top of the refrigerator, and the oolong tea that I liked—and that Strauss bought at Macy's just for me—was in the white canister with the rubber seal next to the coffee maker. I knew which drawer held his socks and which drawer held his underwear. I knew he put his pants on right leg first and knotted his tie without looking in the mirror, then did a quick check. I knew he loved to be teased, that he liked a hand on his waist and a finger looped under his belt and my other hand on the back of his neck when we kissed.

Strauss's cleaning woman came once a week. But when I visited, I found gray buildup behind the faucet, three-month-old issues of *The Economist* on the coffee table, and coffee grounds scattered beneath the dusty, empty fruit bowl on the counter, and I found myself taking over the role Dodie always played when he visited me: fixing and tidying when Strauss was on the phone or in the bathroom, and happy when he came back and told me, "Looks good in here. Nice. Did you change something?" Why did I find this so gratifying? Why did I want to turn to him and say *I am carrying your child?* Why didn't I put down my sponge and give him a swift kick in the shin instead of a French kiss?

For years I watched my mother, under the despotic reign of my father, press her lips together until they became thin as well-worn credit cards, and I swore I'd never hold my tongue for a man. I told myself—and plenty of others—that I would never get trapped in a relationship where the man controlled what did or didn't get said, usually by means of wielding his wallet. I told myself I'd never be like Carol, who sneaked home the back way from the Boston Post Road shoe stores and buried the new pumps she bought at the back of the closet because Al Dante would hit the roof if he found out she had spent some of his bowling money on new heels—or any heels, for that matter—to wear to the next wedding. I swore I'd never get like my mother, who stashed away the last ten from her weekly grocery allowance in an old Kotex box, where she rightly figured my father would never look. I swore I'd never hide anything from a man. He could like me—and everything that went along with me—or lump me. That was his choice.

Yet if ever I felt subtly under a man's thumb, it was with Strauss. I didn't like that. But I loved that when I saw him in the hall at Boorman, my stomach dropped. I loved the way his name felt fresh on my tongue, odd and tangy as an Altoid's. In all fairness, we both were aware of the discrepancy in this—a moment after making love, I called him by his last name, as if he were a drill sergeant barking out orders at boot camp. He said maybe I should call him something else—but he never went by Eben, and it had been years since anyone other than his parents and sister called him Ibby.

"How about your other girlfriends?" I asked. "What did they call you?"

"Before or after they broke up with me?"

"Did they always break up with you?"

"Maybe."

"Why? Because you weren't a good cook?"

"No, no."

"You drove too fast."

"Never an issue."

"What then?"

"Actually, I've been accused of being domineering."

"You?" I said, in mock disbelief. "Domineering?"

"And I was trying so hard to conceal it." He paused. "Another time I was told I was *too much there*. Whatever that means." He took my hand in his and traced the lines inside my palm. "And you?" he asked. "I can't imagine why they'd break it off with you. Unless they got sick of your backtalk."

"Oh, they never stick around," I said. "Besides, I've never been sorry to get rid of them."

Strauss was quiet for a moment. "You've never felt serious about someone before?"

I shook my head.

He hesitated. "Maybe you will, someday."

"Maybe."

"Can I take you into New York next weekend?"

I assumed he meant to meet his parents. But I wasn't disappointed when I answered yes and he told me good, because he already had booked a room at the Pierre and gotten tickets to Lincoln Center for a visiting production of *Rigoletto*.

"For your twenty-fifth and third-month birthday," he said.

"How did you know it was coming up?"

"You forgot. I have access to your personnel file."

I blushed. For now he knew my middle name was Assunta.

Chapter Nine

A Thunderously Dumb Guy

My phone rang just as Strauss picked up my suitcase to carry it down to his car.

"Skip it," I said.

"But it might be something important. It might be your mother—"

I put up my hands to push Strauss out the door. But then the answering machine clicked on and Al announced, "Yo! Lise! Had the baby!"

"Have a seat," I told Strauss, dropping my keys and purse. I ran to pick up the phone. "Congratulations, Al."

"He came early," Al said.

"So it was the famed boy, after all?"

"We're looking at a sizable wiener here—"

In the background Carol said, "Al! Al! Cut it out!"

"So who does he look like?" I asked Al. "You?"

"Poor kid, huh? Hold on for Carol. I can't even remember what color eyes he's got. God, it was something, Lise. You shoulda been here."

"Al started crying," Carol told me when she got on the phone.

"Bullshit!" Al called out.

"It was *so* moving," Carol said.

"Didn't move fast enough!" Al added.

Carol gave me a long account of her sixteen-hour labor, and an even longer report on the last gruesome five minutes—the way Al had to push her legs up past her head, and the grunting and the groaning and the crowning of the baby's head and how the nurses cheered her on and the way the doctor did nothing more than catch the kid and cut the cord, and for that he charged close to fifteen hundred dollars. Then she finally got around to describing Al Dante Junior—how sweet and warm and red he was. "Come and see him."

"I can't," I said. "Until next week. I'm going to New York. I was just leaving when Al called."

"Visiting Dodie?"

I hesitated. "Yup."

"Change your plans."

"Why don't I come see you when you're out of the hospital? I could help you out around the house for a couple of days."

"That would be great. Although you'll probably get grief from Mama about waiting until Monday."

"Is she there?" I asked, wanting to get Mama's tirade over with.

"Are you kidding? Would Al say *wiener* in front of her? She went to church to light a candle to Saint Anne—"

"Why am I not surprised?" I asked. "Tell her I'll call over the week-end."

I got off the phone after Carol made me promise—again, as if I would renege on my vow—to be the godmother. I went into the living room, where Strauss rose hastily from the couch.

"My sister had a baby boy."

"So I gathered."

"My brother-in-law's name is Al."

"I also gathered that."

"His middle name is Dante. They called the baby Al Dante Junior."

"You're making that up. It's a wicked gift you have, Lisar, this penchant for exaggeration."

His eyes fixed on the coffee table. To my horror, I saw I had left out the first chapter of *Stop It Some More,* which I had been editing in red pen right before he came to pick me up.

"You didn't tell me you had literary ambitions," Strauss said.

"How far did you read?"

"Far enough."

"So what'd you think of it?" I asked. "Not much, I guess."

"On the contrary. I thought it was clever. And stylish. But a little too artificially witty. There also are a couple of credibility issues you might want to address."

"You don't think office romance is believable?"

"I don't think this art-shop director—Donna, as you call her—would be quite so flirtatious on her first meeting with the chief financial officer. A grown man of forty probably wouldn't go by Tommy. And I'm not certain Donna needs to wear green glasses to prove she's the artistic type."

I stared at him. "Maybe we can hire you in Editorial."

He raised his eyebrow. "Maybe we can say *doesn't respond well to constructive criticism* on your next employee evaluation."

"You're pissing me off."

"You're overreacting."

"It's just a first draft," I said.

"When can I read more?"

"The story heats up in Chapter Two," I said, heartily glad I hadn't left that Don Juan subplot out on the table.

"I'm sure. Well, it's funny, Lisar. And on the mark. How long have you been working on it?"

"Since I got hired."

He hesitated. "Do you write it on company time?"

"Of course not," I said, although I took company time almost daily to write short passages that appeared brilliant in the midst of inspiration—and complete dogshit one day later.

"That's the same typeface as your printer at work," Strauss said.

"What do you think I'm doing those Saturday afternoons when we're both at Boorman?" I asked, for Strauss and I were known to drag ourselves in on the weekend—always arriving and leaving at separate times—to what I imagined was the silent amusement of the night and weekend watchman, Gussie. "I don't have a computer here. I need to type it and print it."

"I thought you were hard at work on projects for me and Peg."

"Think again," I said.

"Once or twice—before we went out together—I seem to remember you leaping up from your desk to block my view of your printer."

"I was trying to show you my gorgeous body."

"And your stockinged feet? Why don't you buy more comfortable shoes that you don't need to kick off beneath your desk?"

"Why don't you mind your own business?"

He smiled. "I like making you my business." He looked down at my manuscript. "Is writing something you've been burning to do with your life?"

"I don't like to admit to it. Everybody wants to write a novel. And very few people do it right. I want to do it right."

"This is a good start."

"It feels kind of false."

"You said it was a first draft."

"I lied. It's really my third."

"Think of how good it'll be on your fifth."

"Actually, I can only think of how pissed my mother will be when she reads the seventh."

"Why would she be angry? She isn't the one being parodied."

I shrugged. Then something in his tone of voice—too neutral—put me on the alert. "You think I'm parodying you."

"Not at all." But I was sure he saw himself in Thomas "Tommy" Akins, because he immediately switched the subject. "Aren't you glad you picked up the phone? But I guess we need to change our plans."

"I don't want to change. I want to be with you. I'll take Monday and Tuesday off. With your permission, of course."

I reached—again—for my purse and keys. Strauss reached down for my bag, then stopped himself. "Why didn't you tell your sister why you were going to New York?"

My anger—at myself—for leaving that manuscript on the table came blurting out all at once. "I'm going to tell my sister I'm boinking my boss in a hotel room?"

"You might find a more elegant way to put it."

I looked down at the carpet. I clutched my keys. "I'm sorry. I'm confused. I wish I hadn't picked up that phone—"

"I understand. If it makes you feel any better, I felt a little thrown for a loop after my sister had her first baby. There was something . . . disconcerting about it." He paused. "You've complained, but you seem to get along all right with *your* sister and brother-in-law."

"Strauss," I said, "be honest. I have a feeling you don't really like this sister of yours."

"It's her husband I don't like. The guy's a full-time professional Jew . . . Lisar, are you crying?"

"Of course not," I said, digging through my purse for a Kleenex. "I have something in my eye. I need to dust my apartment. Let's take off, okay?"

Except to comment on how every classical deejay in the world felt Saturday morning was just the right time to play chestnuts such as *The Four Seasons* and *Rhapsody in Blue,* both Strauss and I were quiet on the drive into the city. I tried to forget how close I would have been to delivering a child by now, one that neither I nor its father even wanted. I told myself I had done the right thing. The right thing was to be by Strauss's side. He was the only guy who ever had treated me decently, and I didn't think God would object to that.

The entry of the Pierre was long and narrow, carpeted with a light blue and gold runner and lined with cloyingly rococo murals that pictured lush-lipped goddesses in pastoral settings. Beyond the heavy gilt mirrors and the clink of the silverware against bone-china cups in the Café Pierre, and beyond the hushed hallway of the twelfth floor—I was still me and Strauss was still Strauss. He made sure to tell me he found the Café Pierre a bit pretentious, but that certainly put him in another category than me, who never had set foot in the luxurious lobby and whose only knowledge of the hotel came from those discreet black-and-white ads in *The New Yorker*.

The whole thing smacked of a way of life neither one of us had been brought up to live. Yet because Strauss was older than I was—and traveled in different circles—he had grown accustomed to it. I looked away when he tipped the bellhop, just as I suddenly had found myself absorbed in inspecting the huge vase full of daylilies on the counter when Strauss gave his credit card to the clerk upon check-in. I also had every intention of looking away when he cleared the bill upon checkout, although I knew I would be consumed with curiosity to know the price he had paid to put his head next to mine on a Pierre pillow for just one night. The Pierre was not the kind of hotel where they listed the rates on the back of the room door, along with warnings not to smoke in bed and maps that showed where the ice machines and the video arcades and the indoor pool were located.

Our room—which was lightly scented by the fresh flowers on the mantel—overlooked the park and was dominated by a huge gilt mirror opposite the queen-size bed. I moved over to the writing table, where a black lacquer tray held a small stack of heavy cards printed with all the hotel information. I turned the top card over and found the menu of the Café Pierre. I noticed that a single grapefruit cost six dollars. In my head I heard my mother say, *Where's it imported from—the moon?* And then I heard Strauss describing the café as *pretentious,* and I remembered his ex-fiancée—that nebulous piece of competition, the psychiatrist from Short Hills who I imagined always wore crisp white blouses under wool blazers.

My eyes went up to the mirror and connected with his. "You've been here before, haven't you?"

He blinked. "I wish you wouldn't ask me that."

"Okay," I said, for that was close enough to a *yes.* "Scratch that. I didn't ask it."

"I really just came here for lunch one time."

"With another woman."

"Of course with another woman. It wasn't you, was it?"

"You could lie."

"I don't want to lie to you."

"You could say you were here on business."

"Would you believe that?"

"Was I born yesterday?"

"No. That's why we're here, isn't it?"

"I don't know," I said. For all of a sudden I had no idea why I was there. Something felt unnatural and off. The previous evening I had gotten a haircut, and as I parked my hopeless head of curls beneath the beauty-salon dryer, I had picked up the latest issue of *Glamour,* where the lead article cautioned women that taking a vacation with a man often spelled instant death for the relationship. I had read the article word for word, then dismissed it as so much fluff. The author clearly had some ax to grind against a former boyfriend. Yet there I stood in the Pierre, wondering how many rooms the hotel had, all full of couples weighted down with their own fears and grievances, sighing as they undressed to go to bed at night.

"If you came here with someone else," I said, "then why did you bring me here?"

"It's a beautiful hotel. I thought you'd like it. It seemed like the kind of place that would please a woman, any woman. Should I say anything more?"

I had to laugh. "Put down your shovel. You've dug yourself a grave deep enough."

"I think you're being overly sensitive. But I'm sure from reading that story of yours, you think I'm being—what did you call Tommy?—a *thunderously dumb guy*?"

"That was the expression."

Strauss kissed me on the back of my head. "Somebody older is bound to have more experience—"

"How are we defining experience?"

"You know. Serious, or quasi-serious, relationships."

"Like living with other people?"

"I've never done that. Unless you count six weeks of screwing like crazy in a college dorm room—"

"Let's not count that," I said.

"If you have to know—"

"Oh, I don't have to know anything—"

"No, let me say this. I've wanted to tell you this for a while. I was engaged once."

I bit my lip, ashamed of myself. Of course he thought this information was new to me and that it needed to be presented quite carefully, so as not to further hurt my feelings. I tried to joke it off. "So why don't you have a mortage on a split level now and two-point-five kids?"

"It didn't work out, that's all. Some of it had to do with religion—"

"Why? If you were both Jewish?"

"I didn't say she was."

I thought quickly. "You told me once you'd never slept with anyone eligible to attend a DAR meeting, so I just assumed—"

"Well. You assumed right. And there were these parent problems."

"Hers or yours?"

"Both. It was awkward. Hers were—how should I say it? Vastly more upscale?"

"How about stinkingly rich?" I said.

"I knew you'd find the right phrase. And there were other issues."

"Such as?"

"We didn't get along in bed."

"Oh."

"Not the way I get along with you."

"Oh."

"I mean, I know there's more to life than bed."

"Of course."

"It just seemed a good indication of some deeper problem."

I waited for him to expand on the subject, but no elaboration was forthcoming. I moved over to the window and looked down at the flattened yellow tops of taxicabs, the seemingly miniature tourists strolling down the park, and the bright blue Strand Bookseller's stall parked right across the street, which I hoped to check out later. He came up behind me. "It's a beautiful view," I said. I was wearing two-and-a-half-inch heels, and I didn't even have to reach up to give him what I hoped he took for a grateful kiss. I could never stay in the Pierre on my own. But the faster my debts toward Strauss piled up, the more I wanted to know what he wanted back from me, and the more I kept thinking things like, *God, I should make him a nice dinner.*

But I *had* made him a nice dinner. Once. Or at least I tried to. But without my mother—or Dodie—by my side, I wasn't half as good a cook. The veal was tough, the asparagus stringy, I was all apologies, Strauss was all thanks, and after that he never told me his mother spent a lot of time in the kitchen again.

The Met on a Saturday was so packed it felt like Macy's day-after-Thanksgiving sale. After a quick perusal of the map, we hit the Dutch exhibit and then moved over to the impressionist rooms. We both admired the hushed, muted canvases by Degas. Strauss liked the racehorses the best.

"Which is your favorite?" he asked.

I pointed to a blurred pastel of a woman bent over an ironing board. Her hair swung down, hiding her face, and her upper arms seemed tired from the labor. For me, that was art: the ability to make beauty out of sadness.

"But why do you like that one? Do you identify with the woman in the picture?"

The question annoyed me. "Do you identify with the horse?"

"Of course not," Strauss said. The closest he'd ever gotten to a horse in his life was rooming with a polo player at Cornell. He was from a fine Louisville family and sported a Roman numeral after his name.

"Sounds like a jerk," I said.

"I see we have strong opinions."

"What's wrong with that?" I asked. "And why do you think I'd identify with a laundry lady, even if I did tell you my mother actually owns a washboard?"

"Lisar, please. You're so defensive. I—" Strauss stopped. He told me the question was a compliment, of sorts. For he had noticed—and Peg had too—that in spite of my jaded attitude about Boorman and corporate life in general, I had an extremely strong work ethic: When the heat was on, I kept my head down and concentrated on the task.

"Sometimes that's out of competition," I said, "not the work ethic. Sometimes it just feels good to beat out other women."

My use of the word *women* was interesting, Strauss said.

"I work in an all-female department," I reminded him.

"So you do."

"And Karen's job is open."

"She's on leave, Lisar."

"So what? She may never come back."

He frowned. "How do you know?"

I kept my eyes on the washerwoman. "I just don't think she's coming back."

"This is the first I've heard of it."

"If you're inclined to repeat the rumor, just remember you didn't hear it from my big mouth."

"Did she tell you in confidence? If she told you in confidence, then you shouldn't have told me."

We kept on walking through the gallery. Pisarro's admittedly dull takes on the French countryside didn't seem to interest Strauss half as much as what I knew about Karen. He kept his eyes more on the polished floor than on the artwork. "Don't your feet hurt in those heels?" he finally asked me.

"Not at all."

"Let's sit down here for a moment, so you can rest."

"I don't need to rest."

"I need to clean my glasses."

We sat down in the center of the gallery on a foolish tufted pouf that squeaked and groaned under our weight. Sunlight flooded the bleached floor and glinted off the black hair of a group of Asian tourists. A team of Swedes—big and blond as plowhorses—forged after the Asians. A woman walking backward—carrying a miniature French flag to keep her group together—paused in front of a fat Renoir portrait. It was like watching the opening-day parade at the Olympics.

Strauss, of course, was oblivious to all this, for he had reached into his pocket for his handkerchief and taken off his glasses. "Now that you've started, maybe you'd like to finish your story."

I shrugged. The harm already had been done. I didn't see any reason not to tell him why Karen was considering not coming back. "She said her husband might have a chance to join another firm. In White Plains. He'd make a lot more there. Then she could stay home with the baby and still make her mortgage payment."

"That doesn't sound like anything definite to me," Strauss said. "Besides, if she left, she'd owe Boorman a big chunk of back pay."

"Maybe she thinks it's worth it," I said. The methodical way he cleaned his glasses irritated me. "You've already cleaned that lens."

"So I have."

"Maybe you should get contacts."

"I can't. I have astigmatism." He put his glasses back on. "I shouldn't ask you this. But did Karen really seem inclined to leave if she had the chance?"

"I didn't discourage her," I said.

"What are you driving at?"

"I mean—*in case it hasn't crossed your mind*—I wouldn't mind moving into her office."

"I am not dense. It's done more than cross my mind." He pushed up his glasses. "It would be a good promotion for you."

"Yes."

"But you can't go for it, of course."

I shifted my position and the pouf let out an angry groan. "What do you mean? Of course I'll go for it."

"You haven't been on board long enough. There are plenty of women in your department who have been there much longer than you—"

"They don't have the drive. Or the initiative. Besides, I'm the logical replacement. I'm assistant manager. And even you said Peg thought I was a workhorse. And liked me." I pinched him on his sleeve. "Maybe *you* don't like me enough."

"But Lisar—that's the problem—I do—" He lowered his voice, although no one could possibly overhear us in the echoing din of that crowded gallery. "Don't you see how complicated that would be? What an awkward position you'd place me in?"

"Nobody knows."

"But if it should come out. If people thought you moved up due to unfair means, it would be very unpleasant for you."

"You mean, it would be unpleasant for *you.*"

"For both of us. Besides, the search will have to be advertised, at least locally, because of affirmative action. And please let's not get into that issue again—"

The one and only time we had ventured onto that topic, it had quickly degenerated into a heated discussion about why Jews weren't considered minorities. I said they should be and he said they should not.

Jews are hardly the minority in New York, Lisar.

Boorman isn't New York. Boorman closes on Good Friday.

Yes, so all the executives can go golfing, provided the course still isn't under snow and ice.

Do they ask you along?

Of course not. Everyone knows how hopeless my golf game is.

Do they ask once-upon-a-pro Peg?

No. But I can't blame them. I hope you don't think I'm a chauvinist, but there's something humiliating about being walloped on the green by a fifty-five-year-old woman. I work on Good Friday morning and so does Peg. Then she takes me out to lunch and goes off to do her eighteen holes with— with someone else.

Because he seemed irritated, I hadn't dared pursue the subject. But now I said to him, "You know, Strauss, you never told me if Peg orders fish sticks or steak at those Good Friday lunches."

"Oh, for God's sake, Lisar. Peg's as Protestant as they come. Besides, you yourself ate the meatballs—two weeks ago—when we went out to Friday dinner."

Ever since that first date—when I had foolishly announced I kept meatless Fridays—I had taken great care not to slip up and prove myself a liar. I must have had too much wine before I ordered. "Why didn't you stop me?"

"I remembered after the fact."

"Thank you for pointing my sins out."

"I forgive you."

"You're not God," I said.

"I never claimed to be—"

"And I don't want to argue about meatballs in the middle of the Metropolitan Museum—"

"Neither do I." He rose from the pouf and held out his hand to me, which I grudgingly accepted.

But I could tell he was brooding about my gossip as we walked down a long corridor lined with pastels. We finished up the impressionist rooms in silence, and by the time we got to the bolder colors that signaled the approach of the Fauves, Strauss said, "I'm just surprised, that's all. You just told me you'd give anything to write your book—"

"How do you propose I'd pay off my student loans doing that?"

"—and you've never seemed totally attached to your job at Boorman."

"But, Strauss," I said. "You seem frustrated with it too."

"I am not frustrated. I don't know why you think I'm frustrated. I've never spoken against the company once to you."

"Just a feeling," I said.

"And what gives you that feeling?"

"For starters, you're hanging out with me, and you know I don't totally buy into the Boorman party line."

"No one totally buys into the party line. You play along with it to get ahead."

"You just criticized me for wanting to get ahead."

He sidestepped that one. "You know I can't very well complain about work—" he said, stopping just short of saying *to you*. But we both knew what he meant: Management should not bitch about the corporation to underlings. Management should show company loyalty at all times. Management should not look at the devil in a Gauguin painting and say—as I did—"Ha, doesn't that look just like the CEO?" Management should not lead the flocks down to the display of arms and armor and remark—as I did again—that a sword of tempered steel and a flintlock musket would come in handy at one of Boorman's contentious staff meetings.

Strauss actually laughed. So I dared to tease him. "You'd look mighty fine in one of those Joan of Arc helmets," I told him.

"You might be better suited to that outfit, since you're feeling so feisty all of a sudden. Besides, isn't that a typical Catholic schoolgirl fantasy, to play Joan of Arc?"

I told him no: it was to be the ultimate in the madonna/whore dichotomy, Maria in *The Sound of Music*, because she got to be a nun, but fuck the handsome captain too. It went without mentioning—although I was dumb enough to actually say it—that in the magical world of Rodgers and Hammerstein, as in the dream world of *Jane Eyre,* no one blew the whistle when the master of the house made a move on the governess. "Nobody called *that* sexual harassment," I said.

It was hard to tell which man most strongly—and silently—disapproved of my behavior: Strauss, who gave me one of his impassive stares, or the security guard positioned like a statue in the far doorway, who glared at me as I stepped back and bumped into a sign that described the roped-off exhibit: some contraption that was forerunner of the cannon.

"Look out," Strauss said. "You might set that thing off."

I turned to steady the sign. "I think I've already caused enough trouble for one afternoon."

"I couldn't agree with you more." He pushed back his cuff and looked at his watch. "Shall we go?"

"Wait a second. There must be a muzzle in here somewhere—"

"You have my permission to steal it—and wear it—"

"How do you know I don't want to put it on you?"

"—on the way out." He pointed toward the door.

As we exited the room under the close scrutiny of the guard, we passed beneath a large red and black standard that reminded me of the flag hanging from the front of the Von Trapp family mansion when Maria and the Captain came back flushed and glowing from their honeymoon. Only then did I remember that the backdrop of *The Sound of Music* was the German occupation of Austria, to which Rodgers and Hammerstein also gave a ludicrous fairy-tale ending. Strauss probably was appalled by such a naive portrayal of the Nazi era. I couldn't blame him. Anyone whose father—or mother—had suffered in the war could hardly be expected to sit back with a bucket of popcorn in the movie theater and enjoy watching the dashing Christopher Plummer come out from behind the gravestones (in his jaunty Austrian felt hat) to wrestle the gun away from the Nazi youth telegram boy. Lacking such emotional baggage, Carol and I had loved the movie simply for its improbable outcome, which promised that a poor girl with a flat chest could beat out a rich baroness with cleavage.

We left the museum, stepping around the tourists sitting on the long stone steps and the bold pigeons that stalked up and down the sidewalk, their eyes on the lookout for bits of hot-dog buns and cast-off soft pretzels.

As the M3 bus roared off the curb, I offered Strauss my hand. "Let's walk back."

"You don't exactly have hiking boots on," he said.

"You don't like these shoes, do you?"

"Heels are not safe. If someone ran after you, you'd never be able to escape."

"You're here to protect me. And scold me."

"The scolding is for your own good."

"How do you know my good?" I asked. "I don't pretend to know yours."

"I don't think you do. Otherwise you would listen to what I have to say. Lisar, I want you to listen to what I have to say, put aside these jokes for half a second about wanting to be Julie Andrews—"

"I don't want to be Julie Andrews," I said. "She has a flat chest and a butch haircut!" I walked quickly by the museum fountain, as if to prove to Strauss I really could do the twelve-minute mile with a man hot on my too-high heels.

"Listen to me, Lisar—"

"I'm listening," I said, and kept on marching.

"Slow down, please. You're going to twist your ankle—"

"These are only two-and-a-half-inch heels!" I said, and purposefully stopped to look him dead-level in the eye.

He frowned at me. "You know this is precisely what I've been trying to tell you all along. We don't live in the world of American musical theater, or in the pages of some eighteenth-century novel—"

"*Jane Eyre* is nineteenth-century."

From the annoyed way he pushed up his glasses, I could tell he hadn't read it. "Whatever. This is the twentieth century and the fact is, some people wouldn't look very kindly on what's happening between you and me. At some point it will have to change."

"So how are you proposing a change?"

"I'm not proposing a change—just yet. I'm concerned now that someone else will put it to a stop. And I hope I don't need to name names."

"You needn't name names," I said.

"Although you're certainly throwing names around left and right today."

"What do you mean by that?"

Strauss took my elbow and put his head down close to mine, as if the very pigeons scattering in front of us could be offended. "Did you or did you not practically yell the word *butch* back there on the sidewalk?"

"This is New York, people know who they are, and since when are you such an advocate of gay rights anyway?"

"I'm not advocating anything. I'm just pointing out a truth."

"And what is that truth, pray tell?"

"That people don't like to be called names."

"But, Strauss, gays call themselves all sorts of names. You just don't know because nobody in your family swings that way."

"I work for Peg." It was the first time he'd ever acknowledged Peg was a lesbian, and his face flushed as if he had just given some big secret away. He was so uptight about the whole thing, I felt like laughing.

"What does she have to say on the subject?" I asked.

"I'm not at liberty to discuss it—"

"Strauss, my cousin calls himself, point-blank, a *faggot*," I said, careful this time to lower my voice when I got to the questionable word, although the roar of yet another bus pulling off from the curb and the clack of my heels on the sidewalk did more than enough to cover me.

"Why do you suppose he does that?"

"That's a rhetorical question, I hope?"

"Lisar. Slow down here. I don't mean to play Mr. Rogers—"

"I hope not. You'd look like shit in one of those cardigan sweaters—"

"Or the thought police. I'm not above laughing at a good Jewish joke—"

"But only if you tell it, right? If a goy told it, you'd get all bent out of shape—"

"—if a goy told it, the punchline would be something ugly, like, *because the air is free!*"

I grabbed his arm—tightly—and said, "Now, you hold it. What are we really discussing here?"

"Why you made me the chief financial officer in your novel!"

"But, Strauss! Don't be so paranoid! It's fiction!"

"I have a Thomas Eakins print on my wall!"

"But you're not Tommy Akins, you're the root-beer-swilling Casanova in the second chapter, and if you don't believe me, you can read it yourself—"

"I can hardly wait to get my hands on it."

"And speaking of name-calling," I said, eager to change the subject, "you needn't be so self-righteous, considering what you called your own brother-in-law just a few hours ago."

"What did I call him but what he is?" Strauss asked. Then he stopped. "All right. Maybe. Maybe you have a point."

I shrugged. It was hot on the sidewalk and I wanted to do anything else but fight. To make peace, I told him maybe I was out of line to say *butch* too loudly in public. "I would never call my cousin the names he calls himself. I call him *gay*. But we both say *straight*."

After a moment Strauss—probably to smooth over some of the tension bristling between us—admitted that he said *straight* too, even though he knew it was probably not the most felicitous term to use, because it implied that everything else was crooked.

"Do you think it's crooked?" I asked.

"No. I mean, I know it's not the norm—I mean, I know *I'm* not the norm either, at least at Boorman—"

"That's quite all right," I said. "I'll still talk to you, even if you don't do eighteen holes on Good Friday."

"That's tolerant of you."

"I might even make you some Mrs. Paul's fish sticks when I get back from Confession."

"You don't go to Confession."

"I've gone once in the past seven years. But remind me to stop in Saint Patrick's if and when we pass. I have to go again."

"What grievous sins have you committed?" he asked. "Besides mouthing off left and right to me?"

"I agreed to be godmother to my sister's baby. I have to make confession before the baptism."

"What will you confess to then?"

"It's private. Between me and God. Like prayer."

We walked along quietly for a while. Then Strauss said, "It must feel good. Prayer, I mean."

"I wouldn't know."

He stopped on the sidewalk. "But you do it. At night. I thought I saw you—in bed—once or twice—" Strauss shrugged, then started to show me a sign of the cross. If I hadn't been so dismayed to have my secret discovered—and if we just hadn't had such an uncomfortable argument—I would have howled with laughter when he touched his right shoulder before he went for his left.

"Your bedroom is dark," I said. "How can you see anything?"

"You forget the skylight."

"All right. So the skylight."

"It doesn't bother me, you know."

"Gee. Good thing. Otherwise this relationship would be up shit creek on a small canoe, wouldn't it?"

"You've probably never been in a canoe in your life, except in your naughty imagination, with this Thomas Akins character. By the way, those boats are called *sculls*."

"Thank you, Harvard. I'm aware of the terminology."

We walked along in silence. Then Strauss said, "Actually, I'm a little envious."

"What of—Thomas Akins's superb sculling abilities?"

"Stop. The prayer thing. You don't have to turn away. In bed. Why do you turn away?"

"Because—because I can't talk to you and God at the same time. Now forget it. You don't get it."

"But I do get it. Give me some credit here. I get it better than you think."

I took his hand. He squeezed my palm and I squeezed his back. This seemed a much better way of ending our first fight (which I was ashamed to say I actually found rather invigorating) than smoothing it over with a banal corporate phrase, such as *let us agree to disagree*. But I gathered there was trouble ahead: We were both stubborn, neither one of us liked to apologize, and any subsequent truces we had were bound to be uneasy.

Back at the Pierre we sipped on room-service-delivered white wine, and I slid into the long black dress with the chiffon sleeves and the zipper that traveled up the back like an insidious snake, which Strauss agreed to have the pleasure of zipping me into if he could have the pleasure of unzipping me out of it later. We went to an Italian restaurant for dinner—where I tussled with Strauss over how much food I should eat (*You sound like my mother—the minute I come in the door she says "Too fat!" or "Too skinny!"*)—and to Lincoln Center for a *Rigoletto* that I enjoyed more than anything because it was the first time in my life I didn't have to sit through three acts in a seat so high—the fifth or sixth balcony—it induced nose-bleeds.

The moment the overture began, I settled back into my seat and wondered why, since moving to Ossining, I hadn't returned to New York to enjoy some of the culture that used to form the basis of my weekend diet (probably because the price of the tickets precluded buying groceries). As a student in Bronxville I had learned all the tricks—showing up an hour before the performance at Weill to nab five-dollar seats, and waiting beneath the overhang at Lincoln Center for the ticket scalpers. I went to Shakespeare in the Park and visited museums on the one weekday that offered free admission. I hit the public library every Saturday morning and cleaned out the office once a month for unmailed reviewers' copies. I used to go to plays and concerts more often than I cooked myself a decent dinner. In many ways it had been a squalid life—but the art (perhaps because it took me out of my rodent-and-roach-infested apartment) made me feel it was worth trying to stick it out in the city.

The moment I moved to Ossining that all changed. It seemed a drag to take the train into Manhattan on Friday nights; the couple of times I went in on Saturdays I spent hours at Macy's and Bloomingdale's and the sample sales to find the right outfits for work. When I thought of how often I used to brave my fear of heights to teeter on the top tier of Carnegie Hall, I marveled at more than the thought of the famed acoustics.

My life had changed, and I wasn't sure it was for the better. Monday through Friday would be dull no matter where I worked. But my weekends weren't charged with music and drama and dance and literature anymore. I had an apartment nice enough to keep neat. I had to drop my suits and silk blouses at the dry cleaner's. I had to replace the panty hose that had ruptured runs. I had to work out every night to convince myself I still looked decent enough for any man to look at me, and when a man— Strauss—finally looked, I ended up with lingerie so delicate I had to hand-wash it every night.

I hadn't turned on my stereo, it seemed, in weeks. But at least I had made some headway into my novel—and I vowed that when I got home I would change that facile plot once and for all. The opera, which raked up all the passion that had come to an absolutely stultifying rest in the sub-urbs, made me vow to go deeper. Why did I always have to go for the yucks? Why shouldn't I write something as profoundly tragic as *Rigoletto*? The story of a hunchback man whose quest for revenge resulted in the loss of his beloved daughter moved me beyond belief. The tears I had held back that morning returned to clutch at my eyes when Gilda sang *Il mio nome,* and I had to borrow Strauss's handkerchief at the end. I wept through the prolonged applause and the numerous bows. We were sitting so close to the stage that the long-stemmed roses flung at the soprano almost pelted me on the head.

"That was wonderful," I told Strauss, and in a response infinitely more sober than mine, he said the plot was less than credible, as it always was in opera—but he was moved by the music and especially the horrible moment when Rigoletto discovered his daughter's body in a sack.

"But you didn't cry," I said.

"You've done enough of that for both of us," he said, holding his wet handkerchief by the corners, as if he were a prisoner coming forth from his hiding place, giving the signal to surrender.

"Do you ever?" I asked. "Cry? Why don't men cry?"

"Because you learn at an early age to put a lid on it."

"I could never put a lid on it."

"Duly noted," he said, and carefully folded his soggy handkerchief before he bunched it up into his pocket.

Outside on the street, Strauss wanted to catch a cab, but I wanted to walk back, and we bickered—gently this time—about just how safe it was to walk along the park at night. "Give in to me," I said, and he did, but he put his arm around me, as if this would ward off all potential muggers and rapists and homeless people shaking tin cans. I wanted to drink it all in— the curved purple neon lights of the coffee bars opposite Lincoln Center, the dark steps of the brownstones on Sixty-fourth, the black boots and leather jackets of the students hanging out at the Columbus Circle subway stop, and even the smell of dung that pervaded the lower end of the park where the horse-drawn carriages were parked—an odor that prompted Strauss to lead me across the street so we could walk by the Saint Moritz and the back end of the Plaza rather than listen to the horse cabbies in their top hats and roses hawk us for a midnight trot around the park.

Strauss squeezed my shoulder. "What are you thinking of, birthday girl?"

I held him tight. "That you would look like an ass in a leather jacket," I said, and gave him a big kiss.

"I look even more ridiculous in a yarmulke."

I put my hand on his shirt. "But you look like a million bucks in a tie. I like this tie."

A slight smile spread across his face. "You wouldn't happen to have seen another tie of mine lately?"

"I see you wear a new tie every day."

"This one is black with red diamonds?"

"Sounds ugly," I said. "Maybe you should be glad you lost it—"

"Ah, I didn't say I lost it."

And I didn't say I stole it. Instead, I thanked him for such a wonderful belated birthday celebration. I offered him a long account of my real birthday at home with Carol and my mother and told him all about Security Man, except for the part about how Dodie and I flung him into the ditch. When we hit the stoplight at Fifth, I even told him about my father's birthday whacks.

"I'm surprised you mentioned that," Strauss said. "You hardly ever talk about your father."

"What's to say? He drove a Ford and aspired to a Buick. And now he's dead. And when he was alive, he was never home. He was always working."

"My father wasn't home much either."

The taxis lurched to a stop and we crossed Fifth. On the other side, Strauss said he could tell I didn't get along with my mother—

"That's the understatement of the year," I said.

"Did you get along any better with your father?"

"No. Neither did my mother."

"Surely something was there between them."

"It's called Catholicism. Which says, *Thou shalt not divorce.*"

"You never saw any—" and I hooted after Strauss said *displays of affection?*

"Sure," I said. "You could tell when they had their annual sex. Because in the morning my mother would strip the sheets and storm the house with a sponge and a can of Jubilee. By noon she would have mopped the floor, scraped the streaks off the window with ammonia and a razor blade, and vacuumed all the floors and ceilings—"

"Oh, Lise. You really know how to exaggerate."

"This is not a story," I said, glad I hadn't gone so far as to tell him about the evil rubber hose snaking down from my mother's douche bag, which always hung from the shower head the morning after my father forced her—for she did not seem to welcome his advances in any way, shape, or fashion—to discharge her conjugal duties. The whole house smelled—for the rest of the morning—of white vinegar.

"Why do you think I only have one sister?" I asked Strauss—not mentioning my mother's miscarriages—for he already knew about my fifty-five first cousins and the fact that some of my aunts and uncles had nine or ten children each.

"I only have one sister too," Strauss reminded me. "Of course, that's due to birth control."

"Are you sure of that?"

"Positive. My father told me when he taught me about sex."

"Your *father* taught you about sex?"

"Of course. Who taught you?"

"Boys," I said.

"Couldn't you ask your sister?"

"She was fat. She didn't get asked out much."

"Have you always been so thin?" Strauss asked.

"It's a recent phenomenon."

"You don't take diet pills, do you?"

"Why are you so focused on my weight? Just because your sister had an eating disorder—"

"I never told you my sister had an eating disorder."

I thought hard and fast. "Yes, you did. That first time we went out. You said she obsessed about food."

"I meant her marriage—the whole kosher thing—gives her a socially acceptable method of watching her food intake. But you're not far off-track. She did have a problem once. A big problem. While she was at Brandeis."

"She would have had good company at Sarah Lawrence," I said. "Although along with the anorexics, there also was a big contingent of girls who decided fat was a feminist issue after they put on the freshman fifteen."

I failed to tell Strauss that as a transfer student, I was guilty of putting on the junior year twelve-and-one-half. Thank God that after college I suffered from abject poverty, or I probably would have gained even more. In Brooklyn I had shed that extra dozen pounds by walking everywhere to save the subway fare and from eating in ways that were practically an advertisement for how to suffer from malnutrition.

"Is your sister okay now?" I asked.

"What's okay? She's married to Zalman—that's his name, the man I called the professional Jew, and don't give me any more lip about that, Lisar. He keeps a close eye on her."

"He sounds pretty horrible. But he can't be all that bad if she's still with him, right?"

"She could never get by on her own. She'd fall apart."

"You once said the same about your parents. If one of them died."

"That's different. My parents have something different with each other."

"You mean love."

"Well, yes. They don't say it, but you can feel it."

"How?"

"They still sleep together. I mean, more than sleep—"

"Go on!" I said. "How old is your dad again?"

"Seventy-nine next week—"

"Strauss, that's impossible."

"It is not impossible."

"How do you know? Point-blank, do you ask? Or do you just imagine?"

Strauss said he was just as squeamish as the next person when it came to imagining his parents. He knew only because a couple of years ago his father had gone in for what he thought was a routine hernia repair done on an outpatient basis. But something undisclosed had gone wrong, and when Strauss ended up visiting his dad in the hospital two days later, he had sneaked a look at the chart and saw, to his amazement, that his father had undergone surgery for a penile implant.

"Can I laugh now?" I asked.

"Sure. Go ahead." Strauss actually smiled too, but sadly, as if he was afraid of getting old—well, who wasn't afraid?—and of having basic human desires that the body no longer could respond to on its own.

The lobby of the Pierre seemed even more imposing in the dark, like one of the French provincial period rooms at the Met. As we rode the elevator in silence, I wanted to know why Strauss had come for lunch here with his fiancée—had her vastly upscale parents hosted a party to celebrate their engagement? Somehow it gave me pleasure to imagine Strauss squirming as somebody else picked up the tab, which undoubtedly was enormous. But it did not give me any pleasure at all—even if he *were* telling the truth and hadn't found much joy in the process—to imagine Strauss and his fiancée in bed.

The room felt stuffy when we entered. But the air-conditioning, forced out of vents along the ceiling, felt cold on my back. While Strauss was in the bathroom, I sat at the writing table and gazed out the sheer curtains. The park was now nothing but a big stretch of blackness ending in tiny squares of light from apartment houses on the west side. The distance was too great to make out any human figures.

Strauss came out and leaned in the bathroom doorway. "It's nice to see you sitting there."

"Did you think I'd run away?"

"I hope you won't. Before you have a chance to open a present."

"Another present?"

"You said you didn't like growing older. Maybe this will take away some of the sting."

"You shouldn't have," I said, and he laughed and told me that just for that false and feeble remark, I could root through his suitcase and find it myself.

"I really don't want to root through your clothes, Strauss."

"Don't you, Lise? I thought you liked that."

"A suitcase is different than a closet—"

"Aha. Now I've caught you."

"You haven't caught me at anything." I got up and hesitated in front of his bag. It was unzipped. I opened the top and slowly put my hands in. Then I pulled them out.

"I'm not going to do that," I said. "If it's a gift, then give it to me, goddammit."

"Emily Post would be appalled by your language."

"I'll send you a handwritten thank-you afterward."

"How will you sign it?"

"*Yours.*"

"We have a deal." He came over and reached into the suitcase. I could tell he was embarrassed—because he didn't look at me—as he handed me a velvet jewelry box.

I also was embarrassed. Because it was the wrong size, the box. Too big to hold what I suddenly knew I wanted from him and just as suddenly feared he would never give me. And I didn't want him to see that on my face. How could I keep a feeling as strong as that off my face?

As I pried open the emerald-green box, I caught a glimpse of a gold chain, so fine and delicate it looked like the slightest touch could make it break. Then the lid snapped shut on my finger like a dog's bite.

"Ouch," I said.

"Careful."

"Shit," I said, tears in my eyes. "It's lovely. Thank you."

"Are you all right?"

"Here. You open it. I'm frightened to do it again."

The bite of the box lid had been a distraction, and a good excuse for my tears. Strauss kissed my finger before he reopened the box. I stood in front of the mirror as he put the chain on me. But his big klutzy fingers fumbled so long with the clasp I was afraid he would notice—for the first time—the unavoidable rough stubble left behind on the back of my neck. It seemed shameful to be a woman whose hairdresser always grimly got out the electric razor after putting down the scissors.

The chain looked chaste and delicate against my black dress. Strauss apologized for not giving it to me earlier, because then I could have worn it to *Rigoletto*.

"And then some thug from Hoboken could have yanked it off my neck on that perilous walk home," I said.

"It really would have been more prudent to take a cab," Strauss said, and he went on and on about the craftiness of the criminal mind, how it only took one second with your guard down and they had you, theft and violence lurked everywhere looking for a victim, and much as he did not like to even say the word, the word was worth saying and reminding myself of from time to time: A woman on her own needed to protect herself from rape.

I sat down during his lecture because my feet really hurt. Then I asked, "Have you ever considered a career as an officer of the law?"

"No."

"Chief of police, then?"

He frowned. "Jews don't become cops any more than they become professional football players."

"You're perpetuating stereotypes."

"I'm telling you God's honest truth."

"Too bad," I said, as I took off my shoes and stretched my aching toes. "You know I have a secret thing for cops."

"Is that why you flirt with the night guard at Boorman?"

"I was trying to throw Gussie offtrack."

"I think Gus was on the right track before even you and I were."

Strauss smiled. "I could have killed him that night he called me your shadow—"

"He's definitely on to us. He's winked at me a couple of times when I went in on Saturday. Does he wink at you, Strauss?"

"I doubt he finds me worth winking at." Strauss loosened his tie and slowly unknotted it. He draped it over the chair, took off his jacket, hung it over the wooden valet, and unbuttoned his cuffs.

"Has a man ever come on to you?" I asked.

"Why do you ask such questions?"

"Just curious. If you don't want to answer, then don't."

"I'll answer. I don't have a problem with answering." But he obviously did, because he said, "Once, maybe."

"What's maybe? Coming on is either a definite yes or a no."

"Not if you're eighteen and you don't have a clue what's happening."

"Was it a professor?"

"How did you guess?"

"Were you interested?"

"I was appalled."

"I thought you were Mr. Tolerant."

"It was an abuse of power, that's why it bothered me." In the mirror, I could see his face flushing. "The other thing bothered me less. I mean, it made me uncomfortable. I didn't even know what two men did together."

Strauss slipped off his loafers and put them in the closet. Then he did something endearing: He picked up my shoes and placed them next to his in the closet, taking care to line them up in a neat row.

"How about you?" he asked. "Is it true that all women have a so-called *lesbian episode*?"

"Where did you learn that?"

"*The Diary of Anne Frank.* The scene, do you remember, where she suggests to the other girl that they feel each other's breasts?"

"I remember. I've never done that, though. My, you look relieved. What would you have done if I said I'd made it with another woman?"

"You haven't. You just said you hadn't, so it's a moot point. Unless you're still curious."

"Everybody's at least a little curious."

"Of course, but that doesn't mean everyone acts upon it. It's just a line I wouldn't cross."

The air-conditioner clicked off. "I slept with a teacher once," I blurted out.

When Strauss pressed me, I told him about my creative-writing teacher at Sarah Lawrence, who had leaned forward in his desk chair as he criticized the characters and the conflict in my short story as farfetched and facile. " 'If you want to be a good writer,' he told me, 'you need to get your heart broken.' "

"And don't tell me," Strauss said. "He wanted to be the one who broke it. Did he?"

I hesitated. Something strange had occurred that afternoon—besides the professor's impotence. Only in retrospect did this episode seem even remotely comic even to me, who liked more than anything a good laugh: the motel room in Rye, the squeak of the battered box springs, how his breathing became so belabored he actually started to snort, and the way he had kept coming at me, over and over, not accepting the failure of his own body, until I finally said, "Look, I think this is a futile attempt we have here."

"Don't worry," he said. "You'll still ace the class—provided you don't put this in your next story." Up until then I hadn't been that concerned about my grade, but all of a sudden I thought, *Oh . . . is this what he thinks this whole thing's been about?*

"I don't want to ace your class," I lied. And then I told the truth: "You're a lousy teacher."

"And you're a lousy writer," he said, "and an even lousier lay. Get dressed and I'll take you home."

My feet had felt ice-cold on the tile in the bathroom. When I looked in the mirror, my eyes seemed off-focus, as if to prove I was nothing but confused about why I had done what I just had done and why he had tried to do what he had just tried to do. What could I possibly have been looking for with this man so old his very pubic hair was going gray? What emptiness in his life had led him out of his marriage bed? What was his wife like? Who called him Dad? I would have felt sorry for the kids who called him Dad if I had not felt so in despair about myself.

"He didn't break my heart," I told Strauss. "He did something worse. He broke my spirit. For a while, at least. He couldn't do it, and afterward he told me I would never write anything worth reading."

"That's a cruel thing to do. To a young girl."

"The toilet paper was blue . . . in the bathroom . . . afterward . . . and the dye stung my eyes. I couldn't stop crying. Really, it was worse than tonight at *Rigoletto*—"

"That's hard to believe."

"I definitely have a lot of sobbing inside me," I said. Then I laughed. "But not enough to get me onto the best-seller list."

"Well. Who said the pen is mightier than the sword? Now you can have your revenge. Make him a character in your book."

"I don't think writing should be revenge. Or therapy."

"What should it be, then?"

"I don't know. Sometimes I think it's mental illness. A weird noise in your head. Like voices that come from a god . . . Oy, stop looking at me like I'm some berserk Joan of Arc—"

"If the helmet fits." Strauss smiled. Then the next moment he frowned. "About your book. You haven't portrayed yourself in a very flattering light."

"You really don't like those green glasses, do you?"

"Forget the glasses."

"When you remember they're *characters*, not people in real life."

"What I mean to say is, this Donna should be a little less critical of the corporation. You might want to tone down your descriptions of the caricatures she draws during staff meetings—"

"But she wants to be a cartoonist."

"But she has to acknowledge that people are going to grow and change—"

"But you just read the first chapter. Besides, in really great stories—like, like, *Peter Rabbit*!—the characters don't change, they just keep making the same stupid mistakes, and if you want stories about spiritual growth, go read Dostoyevsky—you notice *he's* not banging off the bestseller list. And name me one great novel that has a co-author!"

"I wouldn't presume to co-author. But I might suggest you get rid of this root-beer detail you spoke of that's supposedly in the second chapter."

"Maybe I'll just burn the whole manuscript."

"Don't do anything hasty," he said—but I noticed he didn't offer to come in with a fire hose and put out the flames should I be so inclined to play the arsonist. His disapproval—or maybe his fear of the way I might have portrayed him in the book—was palpable. I felt guilty. But I told myself my decision to ditch the juicy subplot had nothing whatsoever to do with his approval or censure. The Casanova stuff was too *facile and far-fetched*—and more important, heartless—to hold much interest even to me, who enjoyed subverting the reality of Boorman while leaving in enough key details so I undoubtedly would be physically escorted off the grounds of the corporate headquarters if the manuscript ever saw the light of day. If Strauss's death wish at Boorman was sleeping with yours truly, *Stop It Some More* clearly represented mine.

As promised, Strauss helped me with the zipper of my dress, but he patted me on the shoulder after he pulled it down, and all the little signals we gave off to one another made it clear that for the first time since we started staying with one another, we weren't going to make love when we went to bed. He moved away to take off his shirt, and after struggling with the clasp on the chain, I undressed without looking at him and did not don any of the lingerie he had given me. He also undressed without looking at me. We both got into bed, and Strauss let me have the side closest to the bathroom even though he was the one who always seemed to prowl around during the night, not me. Then he did something that irritated me—he got up to check the locks on the door to make sure we were bolted in tight. He took so long to check, I suspected—then became certain—he was squinting at the discreet card the Pierre posted on the back of the door to mark the emergency fire exits. He couldn't see very well with his glasses off, and only the dimmest of light came into the room through the still-open shades.

"Strauss," I said. "I know what you're doing, and I don't like it."

"You'll thank me if the hotel goes up in flames. Just remember to crouch down and take a right to get to the nearest stairs. I'll take the room key in case we have to crawl back."

"Are you done doing your fireman imitation?"

"Yes. But I warn you, it's supposed to rain tomorrow. Already I'm dreaming of saving you from drowning in a puddle."

I laughed. So did he. But neither of us turned to one another once we were under the covers, and finally he just took my hand.

"Tired?" he asked.

"Yes."

"Will you be hurt if I don't touch you?"

"No, no, not at all," I said, and the honesty of this hurt me more than if he had grabbed me tight enough to bruise me.

I gave him a kiss on the cheek. He put his arm around me. Within minutes his breathing became steady. Locked under his arm, I envied his fall into the dream world. I couldn't go to sleep. I lay there thinking: *I don't want to make love with him. I want to marry him.* That those two feelings seemed so linked together confirmed my worst fears about permanent relationships. Although I suddenly found myself longing for it, I was afraid that marriage to Strauss would be like wonderfully warm, soapy bathwater that bit by bit turned colder and colder, each bank of white foamy bubbles shriveling up and wearing away. If I married him I would have to quit my job. I'd have to find another—or stay at home like Carol and my mother and Strauss's sister and his mother. Maybe that wouldn't be so bad. But I knew if I stayed home I would only pretend to be keeping house. The minute he left in the morning, I'd dash upstairs and get cracking on my novel. I'd sit in front of a notebook and a cup of cold coffee all day, and it would be only a matter of weeks before I began living in a very strange place inside my head, talking to myself like some antisocial entity who never had a lunch date, weeping at the beauty and majesty of my own melodramatic words, or worse—shooting off one-liners like a comedienne given her first break on national TV and fighting for her life to win the audience. Meanwhile, the carpets and kitchen floor would collect dust; green slime would creep forward, like a growing worm, on the tracks of the shower door. Four o'clock would roll around and I'd have to rush down to the kitchen and preheat the oven, because somebody in the family had to make dinner. My neck would be more knotted—with tension—than my apron strings. I'd get out a bottle of fine wine and think, *I really need to let this chardonnay breathe*—but because I was afraid Strauss would comment on how much I had slugged, I'd end up drinking jug wine to relax, pouring more down my throat than into whatever sauce I was fixing. Dinner would simmer as close to perfection as a chef like me would ever get it—and then it would burn. Strauss would come home late, and the minute he opened the front door I'd realize just how tightly I'd been cooped up all day, and I would want to run out of it.

Any progress today? he'd ask, and because any progress made—on any piece of writing—might collapse like a cobweb hit by a broom the very next morning, I'd have to be honest and tell him, *I don't know.*

He would say: *You just have to keep on trying.*

He would say: *Maybe you ought to take a course at the local community college on how to write a book and really finish it.*

He would say: *The floor is filthy and the laundry isn't done. I don't ask for much, Lisar, but can't you find a better balance between this dream you have and the more pressing concerns that keep life running smoothly in this house from day to day?*

Then I'd doubt myself. I'd start mopping the floor to avoid writing, and then how soon would it be before I did nothing all day but dust and sweep and deliver his dry cleaning? How soon would it be—in fact, he already seemed to have started—before Strauss, who paid all the bills, would begin telling me to stop doing this or that or the other? How soon would it be before he started nagging me to go off the pill and get pregnant? How soon before I began making excuses not to visit his parents on Saturdays, before he began welcoming those trips out of town as a relief from having to work all day and then come home to a crying child and an embittered wife? How soon before the whole house smelled of diapers and disappointment, and lovemaking came about only to satisfy the urge, not prompted at all by the desire to please the other person?

Why in the world would I want that with any man? But Strauss wasn't just any man, and I wasn't just any woman. That wouldn't be us, I thought. We would go to Italy . . . and make love under an arbor, while the moonlight shone through the trellis and the night sparkled with Tuscan stars! We would stroll through Sleepy Hollow and walk along the Palisades—while Strauss praised my latest writing endeavors as utterly brilliant, beyond compare, and while I smiled demurely and refrained from saying inappropriate words like *butch* and *faggot*! We would have a baby— and she would wear a sailor dress and chase sea gulls on the beach. How neat and clean our house would be! How sweet the summer cottage on the lake with the wide white porch and rockers! How easy every night—because nothing in the world was wrong—to thank God in our prayers. . . .

If it was just as easy for me to imagine happiness as sadness, then why did sadness seem more real? Because it was 1:00 A.M. and I wanted to be dreaming, but couldn't? Or because the darkness only spoke a scary truth, that so many things happened in spite of my imagination or will, and that there really was something to be said for the way fate was already spelled out in the stars? I lay there listening to the traffic rushing by on Fifth Avenue, and the sound seemed more muted—but just as senseless— as the noise in my heart. I felt like a city that could not sleep. Yet I must have drifted off, because during the night I stretched out my leg and realized Strauss wasn't beside me. When I opened my eyes, the dark was turning to dawn, and he was sitting across the room in the chair, watching over me the way angels were said to guard a person who lay gravely ill in a hospital bed. I would have spoken—I would have told him I loved him— had it not felt so profane to disturb the silence.

Chapter Ten

The Woman in the Ingres,
The Woman in the Whistler

In the morning we made love the way I imagined newlyweds came together on their wedding night—more from obligation than desire. Then we had breakfast—coffee and rolls—lounging in bed. Strauss had arranged for a late checkout of four o'clock. "What should we do for the rest of the morning?" he asked. "The Frick doesn't open until one."

I nudged him in the ribs. "Why don't you introduce me to your parents?"

"They're in Jersey, at my sister's. But didn't you promise to call your mother?"

"I'll call her. When you're in the shower. Take a long shower."

"Do you want to give your cousin a call?"

A call to Dodie was long overdue. The thought made me feel ashamed—as if I hadn't been a good friend—until I realized that Dodie hadn't called me either. He must have gotten totally swept up by his partner too.

For a moment I tried to picture Strauss and Dodie together, and it was like trying to force a puzzle piece into the wrong place. But why? Strauss and Dodie had more in common with one another—the world of business—than I had with either one of them. They both knew what T-bills and municipal bonds were. They could crunch numbers until the little fuckers practically screamed. They both liked baseball, for Christ's sake. Yet the idea of them in the same room—sitting over espresso in some downtown bar, or eating stuffed croissants in a charming Greenwich Village bakery—distressed me. Dodie and I had our own language, our own way of being, that the mere presence of Strauss would alter and strain. Dodie would feel compelled to straighten up, wash out his mouth with soap, and put on the persona he assumed to go to work—there would be no *"Bella Ciao,"* no talk of butt-fucking Prince Charles—and I would have to put a lid on my exuberance too. The more I thought about it, the more I could not imagine a more awkward morning.

"You might not like him," I told Strauss.

"Why not?"

"He just brings out the naughty in me."

"I thought that was my job."

"We're really not that close anymore," I said.

"But you were close once, weren't you? You told me you were."

"Now he's got his own life."

"Does he live with someone?"

"I think he'd maybe like to."

"It would be a smart move on his part."

"Why?"

"Because of AIDS," Strauss said.

"That's hardly a reason to move in with someone."

"It's certainly a reason to change your behavior."

He doesn't have *behavior,* I felt like telling Strauss. But when I tried to find a synonym for the offending word, the only thing I could come up with was *conduct,* which sounded even more censorious, and I decided I couldn't blame Strauss for the failures of the English language, other than to remind him that Dodie simply had relationships with other people. "Just like you and me. In fact, right now he's seriously seeing someone. So I'd rather not call him. I wouldn't want to get in his way."

Strauss paused. "Could I ask you something personal?"

"I should hope so. Since we're lying naked in bed."

Naked in bed was a vulnerable position, to be sure. Strauss had moved the breakfast tray onto the floor. So there was nothing between us—no wall, no sheet, no coffee cups, no place to hide—when Strauss turned over my arm and looked down at the whitish pin pricks in the crook of my elbow that hadn't healed since Sarah Lawrence.

"I just noticed this—a few moments ago, and I don't know why I didn't see it before—on your arm. What is this from?"

I bit my lip. "Why are you asking me that?"

"For my own peace of mind. You told me you did drugs with him. He's gay. There's a link now."

"You don't have to remind me. We really just smoked pot together."

"But what are these marks from? Were you sick at some point in your life that you needed an IV?"

I told him a truth that evaded the real question. "I donated blood plasma so I could buy books for my college courses. The marks from the needle never went away."

I got up from the bed and went over to my suitcase, where I pulled on a silky robe that I regretted having brought—because Strauss, of course, was the one who gave it to me. In the mirror above the chest of drawers I saw Strauss watching me, and I felt like he saw through the Lisa he knew all the way down to the girl who had pressed her lips around countless joints and pipes and bong hoses, who stuck straws up her nose and one intravenous needle in her arm, which came courtesy of the very cousin he suggested we meet.

Strauss cleared his throat and the sound annoyed me, because it signaled the prelude of yet another lecture. And it ran like this: Strauss was sorry that sometimes things seemed a little touchy—a little off-kilter—between us. But it was only natural considering we had grown up in radically different ways—in different decades and even different faiths—and from what Strauss could make out, there was a rather significant economic gap between us—

When he said *economic gap,* I breathed a sigh of relief. For then I knew he had seen in me not the drug-sucking slut, but just a snotty kid who grew up wearing hand-me-downs from third cousins and jeans purchased from a bin at Railroad Salvage, who once confided, at college, to the only black friend she ever had, "Whenever I go into Macy's I have the insane urge to steal everything" and who cringed like the fool that she was when her friend stepped back and asked, "Why do you automatically assume that I would feel that way too?"

"But, Strauss," I said. "We don't have an economic gap. You grew up just as bad off as I did."

"For a while."

"You said you felt uncomfortable around your fiancée's parents because they were wealthy."

"There are different ways of being wealthy, Lisar—or at least of spending money or holding on to it."

"You said your mother mopped the floor on her hands and knees."

"*Waxes* it. She does own a mop."

"And you said you were embarrassed by the measuring tape your father wore around his neck—"

"I never told you that. How did you know that?"

I didn't answer. It had slid out of my mouth before I could catch it, like a snake slithered out of a hole in the ground.

"I've never told you that, I'm positive. And last night you said my sister was anorexic. I've never told you Rache was anorexic. Or that Jeanne was Jewish—"

"Can I tell you something now?"

"I think you'd better."

"But I couldn't tell you before. I just couldn't, believe me. When I worked in publishing—oh God, I was the proofreader on that book. With that interview. About your father."

The look in his eyes was too awful to bear. I switched my eyes to the mirror, and not even able to stand that, I looked out onto the park, at the tops of trees and the wide expanse of lawn that led to the carousel and zoo.

"I forgot you worked in publishing," he said.

"Well. I did. That was the house."

"Small world," Strauss finally said. Then he added, "You should have told me, Lisar."

"I don't know why I didn't. I mean, I can't tell you why I didn't. Please don't make me say why."

From the hallway came the voices of people passing by—a man and a woman, engaged in some dispute about the room key. Strauss looked to the door and then looked back at me. With a calmness that dismayed me, he told me that I could take a shower first.

"You're angry," I said.

"Go ahead, Lise. Please. If you have any feeling at all for me—"

"What do you mean? Of course I have feelings for you—"

"You'll just give me a few minutes to myself."

I didn't hesitate a second before I was in the shower, the bathroom door shut tight and the water on blasting to cover up the sound of my own weeping. Now I was sure it was love, because he had the power to reduce me in a second to such ragged tears. *Lisa,* I thought, *now you've done it. You've blown it. The man is pissed.* It was too much to handle to look around the bathroom after getting out of the steamy shower and to see what a concerted effort Strauss had made not to be a bathroom slob—just for me—and to realize, after opening my cosmetics case, that I forgot to take my birth-control pill yesterday morning. I sucked in my breath and took two pills at once, chewing them to bits, as if this would make them twice as effective.

Then I wondered what it would be like to have a child with Strauss. It was easy, really, to imagine him wearily rolling out of bed in the middle of the night—for unlike Al Dante, he would be the kind of father who took turns with the feedings—and bumping into the bassinet before he bent down and scooped the wet, bawling infant from its blankets. I could hear the tape on both sides of the diaper rip open, and his soft voice trying to soothe the baby, and actually trying to reason with the irrational little creature, asking him or her to please be patient, for the agenda called for a diaper change first, and a bottle second. I saw him down on his hands and knees, patiently building a tower out of alphabet blocks that the toddler would keep pushing over. "The point is to build," he would say. "Not break." I pictured him rushing over to an electrical outlet (covered and taped) and firmly taking a little hand away, saying, "No, no, you know that's wrong, so why are you doing it?" as if a child were born with moral sense—or as if a father really could instill it.

When I came out of the bathroom—dreading meeting him, and almost hoping he had gone to get some ice or fetch a newspaper—Strauss looked anything but fatherly. He was sitting on the end of the bed wearing his shirt from the day before and his undershorts, which made him look about as vulnerable as a patient on a doctor's examination table. His glasses were off, and I wondered if while I was in the shower he had felt so depressed he needed to lie back on the bed and close his eyes.

"Let's not fight, Lise," he said. "I'd like to get along with you."

My voice felt stiff as day-old frosting as I said, "I also want to get along with you."

"I know it's not easy sometimes. For either of us. But it's worth trying."

"I am trying. I'm just fucking up, that's all."

"Come here. Sit down." I sat down next to him on the mattress and tried to rearrange the towel around me in a more modest way.

"About the book. About that whole part of my life—I'm ashamed of not talking about it with you. But I don't think it was right of you to hide that you knew of it from me."

"But it was your business. We're all entitled to privacy, that's why I never brought it up. In the beginning I didn't even link you back to it, and when I did, it was too late. Besides, *you* talked, Strauss. If you didn't want anyone to know, why did you consent to the interview?"

Strauss shrugged. "I don't know. No, I do know. My father always got letters in the mail from shrinks or writers—you might not like that he called them nosy writers, Lise—asking for interviews. It was the first time anyone ever had written to me, acknowledged it had some kind of effect on me. I was tired of being quiet. Now I see why my dad never said anything."

"Does he know you talked?"

"God, no. He never reads anything but the newspaper. He won't find out."

"What if someone shows it to him? Or worse, your mother?"

"It's just not likely."

"What if your sister found it?" I asked, thinking of how pleased my own sister would be to betray some indiscretion of mine to our mother.

"She knows about it. She was angry at first, mostly because I told the whole world—that's what she said to me, '*Why did you tell the whole world?*'—that she had an eating disorder, but then she promised not to say anything to my parents if I never told Zalman—as if I would ever tell Zalman—she once OD'd on diet pills."

"Doesn't he know?"

"That she had a problem with food, yes. Of course. *That* he loves. It's something to hold over her. He thinks he's her savior. But he doesn't know about the pills. That she had to be hospitalized. He wouldn't go for that."

"He sounds like a complete control freak, if he thinks he can change her past."

"I told you he was extreme. But let's not talk about it anymore. I mean, if that's all right with you. I need to shower. And you need to call your mother."

"She's probably at church," I said.

Only after I heard the water going—and after I tried my mother's house twice without any answer—did I remember, too late, the following point: Strauss also had snooped on me. He had gone into my personnel files for less-than-professional reasons. He had picked up my manuscript from the coffee table and read it while I was on the phone with Al Dante. Of course, there was a big difference between *The Cursed Generation* and *Stop It Some More.* That more than anything seemed to throw into relief the whole foolishness of what I was writing. Who cared about a too-cute office flirtation when wars raged on the planet? Why couldn't I write about something more earth-shattering, like ghosts beyond the grave, blue numbers, seeing your own name on a transport list?

Because it hadn't happened to me.

I could steal it though, I thought. Or borrow it. Really it would just be *appropriating* it for a higher cause. And although the theft might come from the devil, wouldn't the crime be redeemed by dedicating the whole thing to God?

Interesting rationalization, Lisar.

Most Machiavellian! I heard Dodie say.

The rest of the day was about as civilized as an ice-cream headache. Strauss helped me fasten on the necklace. He was such a klutz he couldn't get the clasp and so patient he kept trying over and over again, until I chided him for being clumsy and he chided me for being so antsy I couldn't sit still for two seconds. As we walked to the Barnes & Noble on Forty-eighth Street, a throng of parishioners and tourists came down the stone steps of Saint Patrick's. "Here's your chance for Confession," Strauss reminded me.

"Confession isn't heard on Sundays," I said, suddenly longing for what I couldn't have: a quick consultation with the priest who absolved me of my sins last time I went down on my knees to God.

At the bookstore I told Strauss, "Now it's my turn to give you a gift."

I picked out his reading material for the next few weeks, over his strong avowal that the only thing he really wanted and needed to read was the second chapter of Lisa Diodetto's lusty opus. "I told you, I'm torching it," I said as I bent down on my hands and knees to find something to keep him really busy—a black Penguin edition of *Anna Karenina* that showed, on the cover, a troika gliding through a blizzard.

He looked dismayed. "That's a lot of words," he said. "Besides, isn't that the one where she throws herself under the train?"

"You'll love it. You remind me of the character Levin," I told him (not mentioning, of course, that I skipped over the long, dull sections—and there were many—where Levin pondered agricultural economy. Nor did I tell him that the scene where Levin's wife, Kitty, painfully delivers their first baby was so convincingly written it made me swear I'd never have children).

We rounded the corner and I saw Strauss's eye fix upon the very book we'd been arguing about yesterday—*Jane Eyre.* "Forget that," I said. "You wouldn't approve of that. There's a scene where the hero cross-dresses as a Gypsy. Give me that book. I'm paying for *Anna.* She's a gift."

After another round of coffee—and rye sandwiches laden with roast beef and pastrami—we visited the Frick. The coolness of the lobby, after the heat of the street, seemed to soothe both of us. Strauss pressed the admission sticker directly above my left breast, plastering the gold chain to my blouse.

We walked through the museum in silence. Here it was possible to believe that on this late-summer weekend all of New York had escaped for one last time to the Hamptons or the Adirondacks. Only a few others were moving through the Boucher Room, which was paneled with scenes of fluffy Cupid-looking children so pretty they made me want to get sick all over Henry Clay Frick's beautiful Oriental carpets. We were the only English-speaking tourists in the Fragonard Room, full of canvases that Strauss, who had purchased one of the fifty-cent museum guides, clearly seemed embarrassed to inform me were collectively titled "The Progress of Love." Out in the vestibule, we were the only ones to linger in front of the luminous Vermeers by the stairs—"Officer and Laughing Girl" and "Girl Interrupted at Her Music"—and to examine, for more than five minutes, the enchanting woman in blue by Ingres, whose finger coyly posed on the underside of her chin seemed to invite us to admire her and indicated she had a secret she wanted to share—which would never get said.

In the enamel room, the blue and yellow tiles reminded me of my mother's fruit bowl—perpetually full of wax bananas and dusty fake Concord grapes. But these plates documented the birth and death of Christ— scenes lovingly crafted by guild artisans known as the *Workshop of the Master of Large Foreheads* and the *Workshop of the Master of the Passion.* I felt Catholicism emanating from every pore in my body. I wondered how Strauss reacted to these repeated images of the Annunciation, the Adoration of the Magi, the Madonna and Child, the Crucifixion, the Deposition. What was it like not to believe in Christ in a world full of crosses? I thought about all the gold and silver crucifixes I had, lying dormant in my jewelry box (gifts from Auntie Beppina on my name day and Holy Communion and Confirmation), and the miraculous medal I wore after I had the abortion and was making a concerted effort to change my ways.

I turned away from the enamels. Of all the sufferings of Christ (which we catechism kids had to repeat in chronological order as we made the Stations of the Cross), the one that most plagued my childhood imagination was the crowning of the thorns. The enamels were so bright and vivid that the thorns seemed to pierce my own skull. Either that or the double dose of hormones I took that morning was getting to me.

"What's the matter?" Strauss asked.

"I have a headache."

"You can't be getting your—"

"No. I forgot to take my pill yesterday and I had to take two this morning. Please stop frowning at me. I'm only human and I make mistakes."

"I wish you'd be more careful. You have been careful up to now, haven't you? Lisar, you really look ill. Do you want to sit down?"

"Not in here. This Christian stuff is creeping me out. Doesn't it bother you?"

"I prefer it to the mall at Christmas," he said, putting his arm around me and ushering me into the next room.

After we sat down in the huge hall dominated by some Turner harbor scenes, we continued our tour and ended up in the East Gallery all by ourselves. Strauss admired a long portrait of a woman in black by Whistler. "Very elegant," he said.

"She looks constrained to me." The woman was painted in profile and proudly lifted her chin to show her independent nature. Nevertheless, her bosom thrust forward and her belly seemed unnaturally pulled in. "She probably had on a whalebone corset and fainted every five minutes."

Strauss gestured at the accompanying portrait on the other side of the door—a tall, thin man in white gloves and cravat who held a cane. "He doesn't look too happy either."

"Maybe they're married," I said.

Strauss frowned. "Maybe they're not."

He consulted his guidebook. He told me the man—Robert, Comte de Montesquiou-Fezensac—served as the model for Proust's Baron de Charlus.

I was tempted to snort and tell Strauss—who had never read Proust—that Charlus seduced boys. When Strauss read in the brochure that the other portrait was of a mistress of Whistler's agent named Rosa de Cambrier, I also was tempted to tell him Rosa looked more like a man to me than a woman.

"Which woman do you think is more attractive?" I asked Strauss. "The woman in the Ingres or the woman in the Whistler?"

"Is that a trick question?"

"Are you evading it?"

"Which one do *you* think is more attractive?"

"This one," I lied, pointing to the Whistler, perhaps because the woman's black dress reflected my somber mood at the moment.

"You look like the girl in the other portrait."

"You think?"

"I know."

"But she's so chubby."

"How can you say that? This woman here looks emaciated to me."

When we exited the gallery, we passed by the Ingres again, and I slipped into a habit I had—one I desperately wanted to break—of comparing myself to other women, even if they were two-dimensional portraits hanging on the wall posing no threat whatsoever to me. Strauss was right—the woman in the Ingres had my intensely pale skin and brown hair; she had my round face and the big eyes that looked like any moment they would begin to weep. But she was plumper—and much prettier—than I was, and her shiny, luxurious blue dress and jeweled bracelet bespoke an elegance I'd never attain. Her lips were permanently pressed together. She'd never stick her foot in *her* mouth.

Back at the Pierre, Strauss got me two aspirin and stood over me while I downed them with water. We packed our bags and were silent during the long wait for the elevator. In the lobby, we had the bad fortune of bumping into a wedding party. Who got married on a Sunday? I thought, until I realized either the bride or the groom—or both parties involved—probably were Jewish. But the bride, the kind of woman who didn't realize how carefully you had to dress after you turned thirty, had the appearance of an Irish maid gussied up in some hideous concoction of cut-through lace and seed pearls and hooped tulle that made her look like Zsa Zsa Gabor on top and Scarlett O'Hara on the bottom. Just like both of those commanding ladies, the bride had her hands on her hips and was bossing the groom—an ugly duck in a yellow cummerbund—to check on the flower arrangements before they entered the Café. "I *told* them I didn't want the centerpieces in the *center* of the table," she kept repeating.

I averted my eyes. Strauss also looked away. He at least could concentrate on clearing the bill. At that moment I wouldn't have dreamed of looking over his shoulder at the room charge. I needed no further proof at this point that it had been a high-stakes kind of weekend.

After asking for the car to be brought around, Strauss ran back inside. He said he forgot to *leave something* for the maids. He left me standing next to the bellhop, my ears ringing from the sound of cars honking in stalled traffic.

I stood there awkwardly for a few minutes, feeling decidedly shabby in comparison to the well-dressed people who were entering the hotel, probably to attend that fatal wedding reception. I thought, *if I married Strauss* . . . well, we'd have to elope. No one in my family would behave themselves at our wedding; Strauss's parents probably would not approve of me, his brother-in-law would go ballistic, and we would hardly have the blessing of the folks at Boorman. So who would stand up with us, besides the rabbi or the priest or the third guy in the joke? Yes, it would have to be the third guy, a minister—some Unitarian in sandals—because neither one of us would give in and convert.

It was easier to be Strauss's lover. Or so I thought until (in one of those coincidences I could blame only on the stars) a cab pulled up to the curb, and who stepped out but the new fool in charge of Boorman's advertising team—Ed "Hook" Roberts—who clearly did not recognize me even though I recognized him. He looked like the kind of macho man who went to sports bars after hours to belt back a few brewskies. His fullback shoulders and beefy neck gave him the appearance of a state trooper. All he needed was a pair of mirrored shades, a Smoky Mountain hat with a black plastic chin strap, and a radar gun, and he'd be all set to pull you over and request to *see your license, ma'am—clocked you at eighty.*

Hook paid the driver and reached his hand into the backseat to help his wife (I spotted a wedding band and an engagement ring with a diamond big as a hoppy-toad on her carefully manicured hand). He began to brush past me and the bellboy, who stood beneath the shade of the canopy. Yet who should come through the revolving door right at that moment but my partner in crime.

"Yo, Strauss," Hook Roberts boomed, and actually echoed Strauss's words from this morning. "Small world."

"Isn't it," Strauss said, and his hand seemed unnaturally pale when he reached out to accept Hook's handshake. He then greeted Hook's wife. Her name was Lorraine.

"We're here for a wedding," Hook said, leaving plenty of room for Strauss to explain what had brought him into the city. Then came the moment when Strauss looked beyond them and sized up the situation— the moment when he had to decide whether to acknowledge me or ignore me. "No," I silently mouthed, and shook my head, trying to let him know I hadn't been spotted. But he already had decided to do the right thing, of course.

"Do you know Lisar Diodetto?" Strauss said, carefully using my whole name and also carefully admitting—up front—that I was in the Editorial department.

"What was your name again? Oh Lee-*sa!* No, I haven't had that pleasure," Hook said, although he had met me just the week before on his introductory whirlwind tour through Boorman. He turned to check me out. He saw the suitcases at my feet and the bellhop next to me, from which he clearly could tell we hadn't been there just to dine at the Café Pierre, where a cup of coffee cost more than a paperback book, and an appetizer more than a hardcover.

"It's a pleasure," Hook repeated as he shook my hand, then introduced me to his *cara sposa,* who looked like she had just risen from a Wolff tanning bed to don her Talbot's special-occasion beaded dress. Lorraine took my hand with just the slightest touch of her pale French-manicured fingertips and waited for Hook to release us. But Hook clearly was having a merry time watching our discomfort. After finding out that we went to Lincoln Center last night (*No kidding, you guys really like opera? Or is it just him, Lisa, and you're along for the ride?*), he pointed to my left breast, where I had stupidly left on my Frick admission sticker, and said, "You left your handle off the name tag; you traveling incognito?" Lorraine stood there, looking bored, undoubtedly inured to his buffoonery, while he smiled and laughed like a great-uncle razzing the groom at a wedding and did everything short of winking at Strauss and clapping him on the back. That was how I knew for sure that Strauss—the sole bachelor of the upper echelon at Boorman—was probably the butt of many a single-man joke and the object of ugly speculation when the bigwigs got together, rumors that already had reached Hook, who'd *been on board* less than one week.

Strauss handled the whole thing well, but I could tell he was relieved when the valet pulled the Audi up to the curb. More handshakes were exchanged all around, and then Strauss ushered me into the front seat. Strauss was so distracted he practically pulled away from the hotel without tipping the poor schmuck who had to bring the car around.

He sighed as he edged—and then lurched—the car out onto Fifth Avenue.

"I'm sorry that happened."

"Bad timing," I said. "You couldn't control it."

"I got rattled."

"I did too," I said. "I mean, I hated the way he looked at me—"

"You see what I mean now," Strauss said.

I stared out the window, and what I envisioned gave plenty of competition to the stark mannequins posed in grotesque postures in the Henri Bendel storefront. Within twenty-four hours Strauss and I would be crushed—mortar-and-pestle style—in Boorman's rumor mill. Strauss would be criticized by some—but admired by others—for screwing one of the *gals* in Editorial. I would be marked as the office hussy. Bets would be taken on how soon I would be promoted and how soon I would become the proverbial day-old doughnut that not even the cleaning woman would deign to eat when she found it stale and dusty by the coffee machine in the early morning. Both of us could plan on getting drubbed down—either publicly or privately—by Peggy.

"Yes, I see," I was about to say, when Strauss said, "Of all the people to spot us, it would have to be that sonofabitch."

Except for that crack at his brother-in-law, this was the harshest thing I'd ever heard Strauss say. His hostility toward Hook seemed to surface out of a sense of chivalry (which was about as hip as the handkerchief in his pants pocket, but I couldn't help what I liked, so why fight it?). His hatred also seemed to stem from a feeling of inadequacy. Strauss probably didn't like those linebacker types any more than I liked the Betty Crockers who surrounded me in Editorial—because they made us question just how manly-man or girly-girl we were. A man like Strauss, who always returned his library materials on time, naturally would loathe a no-necker like Hook, who surely would take the prize for doing the most push-ups at the next company retreat.

"So I guess you didn't head the search committee who hired Hook," I said.

"If you only knew. How strongly Peg went to bat to keep them from hiring him—"

"Did you join in?"

"What do you think?"

I bit my lip. "Why did you introduce me?"

Strauss had that pained look in his eyes that came from trying to concentrate on driving and conduct a serious conversation at the same time. "Because when you try to hide something, it looks like you're doing wrong even when you're not."

"But I shook my head at you," I said. "I don't think he saw me. And if he did, I don't think he knew who I was. He didn't remember me."

"He was pretending not to remember you, so he could lean over and inspect what he called your name tag—which was an excuse to stare at your breasts."

"So that wasn't my imagination; I thought he was checking out my boobs too—oh, Strauss, watch out for that cab!"

Strauss hit the brakes and my hand flew up to the dashboard to brace myself. A cacophony of car horns began and ended.

"Are you okay?" Strauss asked.

I nodded, although I was feeling green from the sudden lurch of the car. "Just drive," I said. "Just drive carefully." Because I wanted to get home in one piece, although I was certain now that Boorman would be more than willing to pay for my funeral.

"There's a very simple solution to all this," Strauss said.

"What?"

"Let me handle it."

"I don't want you to handle it. How are you going to handle it?"

"I'll talk to Peg."

"Are you nuts? I don't want you to talk about me to Peg."

"Peg is a human being. I have a good relationship with her. But she has certain *idears*—that I don't always agree with—about the way people should interact—"

"Tell me the truth. Does she disapprove of me?"

"But what are you talking about, she's practically adopted you, look at how close you've gotten to her in just the short amount of time you've been on board—"

"You're the one who reminds her to take her Dramamine."

"She's obviously taken some sort of shine to you, with this dear-sir-and-madam stuff, and I'm warning you, she's going to ask you to go golfing—"

"Tell her I don't play—"

"I don't tell her anything, and when you do come into the conversation, I wait it out because I don't dare change the subject. But now this has got to stop once and for all. Now that it isn't necessary to hide it, it's best to explain the situation. Put it above board."

"I'm not comfortable with that," I said.

"I am."

"I'm not."

"I thought we agreed to get along with one another, Lisar."

"That doesn't mean we have to go along with what *you* say."

"It's a long ride home," Strauss said. "Think about it. And if you can't see it from my point of view, then be prepared to present an alternative battle plan."

Although I'd always been pretty good at games of strategy—so good that by age nine only Dodie could sustain a game of checkers with me that lasted more than a quarter of an hour—I could not see more than one uncertain move ahead in this tournament. The only thing I knew for certain was that Strauss was getting bossy—in a way I didn't like—which meant all of a sudden Strauss (not Hook) seemed like the opponent who had backed me into the corner and made me sweat my next turn.

I tried to concentrate on Hook. What were the odds he would leak something at the office? Very strong. He was new; he probably was aware that Strauss and Peggy had opposed hiring him; he would have nothing at all to lose by contributing an interesting factoid to the humdrum lore at Boorman, unless he wanted to hang on to the information for blackmail. There seemed no reasonable way—beyond putting cement shoes on Hook and sinking him to the bottom of the Hudson River—to silence him.

At my place Strauss pulled into a shady spot in the parking lot and killed the engine. Neither one of us moved.

"Well?" Strauss said.

"I need more time."

"I guess you'll have it, whether I like it or not."

"What do you mean?" I asked.

"Don't you remember you're going home tomorrow? And I'm in Atlanta for the rest of the week? I'd rather not talk about something sensitive like this on the phone with Peg."

I nodded. With relief. But then I realized that come Wednesday I would be at Boorman without Strauss around to protect me if Peggy should blow a cork. Who would she go after more vigorously—him or me?

"I wish you weren't going away for so long," I said.

"And next weekend. It's my father's birthday. I have to take him to a doubleheader at Yankee Stadium."

"Well. Bring back a Cracker Jack surprise for me."

He hesitated. "This is awful timing. I wanted to take you home—"

"Don't feel obliged."

"I mean, I would like you to come home and meet my parents. Do you want to?"

"Of course. Yes."

"But this coming weekend is out. My sister and her family will be at my parents' too. It would be too much—"

"You mean your brother-in-law would object to my presence."

"Don't be ridiculous. I don't give a goddamn what he thinks. Nor would my parents. It just doesn't seem like the right time, the proper forum—" He stopped. "Trust me. It's got nothing to do with what happened in New York."

"What did happen?" I asked. "In New York?"

"I don't know. I just felt like we had turned some kind of corner. And now it's got to change; please let me hold the floor just one more minute without interrupting—"

"I'm not interrupting!"

Strauss looked down at the steering wheel and he shamed me by telling me that although he had doubted it—and maybe even fought against it almost every step of the way—he now knew he *cared for me, very deeply,* and corrected himself by hurriedly saying, "I mean, all weekend I've been trying to tell you I love you." Before I could open my mouth to answer, he held up his hand and announced, "You don't have to say anything back. Yet. Don't say anything."

I sat there, amazed that he would try to shut me up at such a moment. With a flush I remembered how he said, *"Let me handle it."* Was that selflessness—wanting to save us both from harm—or just another power trip for him? He always picked up the check. He drove. We slept in his bed. Even though he whispered it with what I thought was love in his voice, he had ordered me to lie still in bed that morning and had insisted on working me over like there was no tomorrow. He had given me a pink slip, and I wore it.

I wore it.

"I need to get out of this car," I said, and reached for the lever. But I couldn't open the door.

"Are you all right?" he asked.

"Flip the locks."

"But you don't look well."

"Please let me go, Strauss."

He popped the locks and his voice was officious when he said, "I'll bring your bag upstairs."

"I can carry it myself," I said.

I heard the locks pop back down again. I gasped. "Open the door, and I'm not saying please this time!"

"Goddammit, Lisar, you're not going anywhere until you tell me why you're being so stubborn."

"Because you always want to do everything for me!"

"Maybe it's because I care for you. I just told you I love you!"

"What kind of way was that?—telling me you doubted it and fought it—and admitting it like it was some kind of sin! Or a crime, because you can't control it or walk it upstairs like my suitcase! Why did you say *don't say anything* just now? What if I wanted to say I loved you back?"

"Then you would have said it, wouldn't you? You're not exactly one to hold your tongue."

"I have been holding my tongue for weeks."

"How? By describing this weekend—right to my face—as *boinking your boss*? And writing—behind my back—a novel that pokes fun at our relationship?"

"You haven't read my novel! How do you know you're even a character in it?"

"Because you told me I was, remember?"

"How do you know my novel isn't about love—"

"Because you gave it a pornographic title!"

"So what? Fucking and love can go together—sometimes at least!"

"That's nice to know, Lisar. Save that line, why don't you, for that thunderously dumb guy in your book who has such trouble expressing his feelings!"

I looked out the window and thought this was a strange kind of love that kept us sitting in a parked car hurling insults at each other like a couple of bored kids lighting cherry bombs on Independence Day. Strauss popped the locks, reached under the dash, and pulled the lever that opened the trunk. I got out of the car and tried not to slam the door. My suitcase was incredibly heavy, which I felt compelled to blame on him. I told myself I wouldn't have needed half my makeup—and the shoes and the clothes—if he didn't make me feel so concerned about the way I looked. But was he that concerned? Or had I just projected all my own concerns onto him?

It was too complicated to think of. "Fuck it!" I muttered, and tried not to slap down the trunk, but it didn't close and I had to push on it with two hands. The Audi shook from the resulting slam.

I dragged the suitcase around to the driver's side and tapped on the window. He reached for the button and opened it halfway—not enough for me to lean in and kiss him, had I been so inclined, which needless to say, I wasn't.

"Will you be in at all tomorrow?" I asked.

He shook his head.

"But you'll call me?" I asked.

"Of course. I always call you. But maybe you think that's controlling too."

"I don't."

"I believe you do."

"Please," I said. "Stop this. You're misconstruing everything I say. It's all Hook's fault. You're upset and I'm upset, about Hook seeing us—"

"That was inevitable. We can't keep it a secret forever."

"Let me think about what you said. About talking to Peg. I want to do the right thing."

"So do I," Strauss said. "Just remember it's better to take hold of the situation before it takes hold of you."

"Maybe he won't say anything."

"Don't count on it."

I put my hand through the window, knowing Strauss would have to take it. "Thank you. For the weekend—"

He shook his head to cut me off. Our hands clasped for a moment, then broke apart. He pressed the button to roll up the window, then changed his mind and rolled the window back down.

"I know you have that tie of mine," he said quietly.

I smiled. "So what if I do?"

"Keep it. For now."

"Can I wear it?"

"It wouldn't become you."

His voice sounded so sad I immediately put my hand to the gold chain around my neck. "This does. Thank you. I won't take it off."

Finally, he smiled. He nodded. "Now get out of here before I run you over with the car."

"But I haven't told you I loved you yet," I started to say. But he already had closed the window and was revving up the engine. I didn't look back when I hauled my suitcase and dress bag up the stairwell, but I knew he was waiting there—like he always did—the proverbial good boy your mother always wanted you to date, who waited to make sure *you got in all right* before he drove off.

Fortunately I made it upstairs without blubbering like a baby. Once I got past my dead-bolt locks I knew I wouldn't even stop to do the usual routine after being away for the weekend—pee and read the mail after checking my apartment to see if a serial murderer was lying in wait in the closet. I planned to collapse on the couch and cry my eyes out for a reason I couldn't determine.

But right after I came in the door, I saw the red light on my answering machine flashing twice, and out of curiosity I picked it up. The first message was from the public library; one of the novels I had checked out had been recalled. The second message was from Dodie. "Hey, Lise. Just checking in. Give me a call whenever."

Whenever, I decided, would be right now. But it had been so long since I'd phoned Dodie that I couldn't remember if his number ended with two-five or five-two. I actually had to look it up in my address book.

Dodie's voice was high and rushed when he answered, and I was relieved I hadn't arranged a meeting between him and Strauss. He sounded coked up.

"I'm interrupting something," I said.

"Not at all."

"You have company."

"I do. I do."

"I'll get off. Call me back when you have time."

"You okay?"

"Sure," I said. "I just need some cheering up, that's all."

"Come see me—see us—next weekend."

"Who's us?"

"He's sitting right here. And he's a sight to behold."

"I'll pass."

"No, come. And bring your beau too."

"I think I'd better come solo."

"Uh-oh," Dodie said. "I was afraid of that. Did you get into a fight?"

"He just threatened to run me over with his car."

"So when are you getting married?"

"I'll bring a bottle of Mumm's if he proposes between now and then."

Dodie's friend had a house just beyond Bay Shore. The friend also had a boat, and I was invited to sleep on board.

"Don't tell me," I said. "It's a rowboat."

"No, no, no."

"A canoe."

"Nope."

"An air mattress."

Dodie laughed slyly. "It's a yacht. The size of a ranch house in Rye."

"You slut," I said. "I'll be there."

Chapter Eleven

Then the Girls Could Rule the Sea

My brief visit home to meet the latest Al Dante began with a fight with my mother, who rightly claimed I shouldn't just show up on her doorstep without warning (to which I replied, *So get an answering machine. I will* buy *you an answering machine!*), and ended with Mama making me a ginger-ale ice-cream float—as if I were a teenager stuck in bed with bad menstrual cramps on the night of the prom. Mama's generosity was inspired by the inexplicable tears I shed after I handed Junior back to Carol.

"You don't have to feel sorry for me," I told Mama as she pulled out the store-brand ice cream and the generic ginger ale.

"Who feels for you?" Mama said. "I want one of these sodas myself. *Madonna,* I meant to take some straws from the Wawa market last time I walked past—go call Auntie Beppina and ask to borrow a couple. Tell her I'll bring 'em back after church—"

"Mama, straws are like Kleenex—you don't borrow them, you use them and chuck 'em in the trash."

"Like Carol—with those disposed diapers! In my day, hot water and a washboard. Never would you even dream of throwing nothing out."

Walking through the back door of Boorman on Wednesday, I felt off-kilter. But my lack of balance had nothing to do with my heel height. I felt like I was in junior high school again and one of my worst enemies had ratted to the teacher that I had let a boy paw me in the janitor's closet. Any minute I expected the intercom to crackle and the office secretary to announce to the delight of the entire algebra class: *Elisabetta Diodetto: Report at once to the principal's office!*

Nothing happened, of course. I rearranged my paper clips, reloaded my stapler, and business proceeded as usual. But the thought that something evil was beginning to brew left me feeling so weak in the knees I actually welcomed, at the end of the day, the smarmy voice of Hook Roberts calling out to me in the parking lot.

"Hello, Miss D.!"

I turned. His car—a royal blue Camaro—was parked one row back from mine.

"Hi there," I said, and started raking through my purse to find my car keys.

He came over to my Toyota. "We seem to be bumping into each other a lot."

"Oh," I said. "I wouldn't say *a lot*."

He gave a quick glance over his shoulder. "Enjoy New York?"

"Was I in New York?"

"Funny, I was sure that was you I saw. With a traveling companion."

"What traveling companion?"

Hook smiled. "Am I reading this right? I didn't see you guys over the weekend, even though you saw me?"

I hesitated and looked over in the executive lot, where I pictured Strauss's Audi—subtle and silver and dependable—sitting there as a warning, which of course I did not heed.

"I think you might be reading that right," I told Hook.

"Mum's the word then, Lisa."

"I certainly hope so," I said, racking my brains for a way to win him over. He seemed fool enough to fall for a little flirtation, so I stepped in closer, gave him my best Miss America smile, and asked how he had enjoyed his wedding.

"It was the usual folderol."

"Why did your friends get married on a Sunday?"

"Not friends. A cousin. On my wife's side. And that's exactly what I said to Lorraine when the invitation came. I said, who's this girl marrying, a Hindu? What's on the menu at the reception, chicken vindaloo?"

Here was a thunderously dumb guy if ever one was invented, I thought.

He kept on going. "But these kids were Catholic all the way. Just had trouble booking on the right day of the week." He winked. "Shotgun wedding."

"So that explained her hoop dress—"

"Ha! Did you get a load of that dress in the lobby? I said to Lorraine, you can hide a lot of belly under a hoopskirt like that. I said to her, just think of what a huge market that must be, wedding gowns for girls who say their vows for two—but you've probably never seen an ad for that in *Modern Bride* magazine."

"I don't subscribe to that particular publication."

"You could stay up all night just thinking of the challenges involved in that ad campaign."

"I'll leave that to you," I said. "Since I like to get a good night's sleep."

He grinned. "I'm sure you do."

I held his smile—for a moment—with my own clenched smile. Then I turned my key in the car lock. I pulled on the lever, but the door didn't open.

"You just shut yourself out," Hook said.

"Funny," I said. "I must have forgotten to lock it this morning."

"Make sure you look in the backseat."

"Excuse me?"

"The backseat. That's where men up to no good are supposed to be hiding."

I opened the door without looking in.

"Before you go," Hook said, "I have some new projects coming up. Might need some help on your end."

"Sounds good," I said. "Clear it with Peggy. I mean, Dr. Schoenbarger."

"Not someone else? Who shall remain nameless?"

"Dr. Schoenbarger," I repeated.

"Oh, excuse me. Being new and all, it may take a while to figure out the chain of command."

"I'm sure you'll master it," I said, and got into my car. It was all I could do to keep myself from backing out right into him and breaking his sturdy state-trooperlike legs.

Strauss called later that evening. After some stilted conversation about holdups at the Atlanta airport, he asked me to report *my take on the situation* at work.

"No one seems to know."

"Did you see Hook today?"

"He stopped me in the parking lot."

"Christ."

"He said he wouldn't say anything. About seeing us."

"How did he say it?"

I gave Strauss a sanitized account of my exchange with Hook.

"The man's a snake in the grass, Lisar. I'm talking to Peg when I come back."

"I don't like the idea of you talking about me with her," I said.

"We could make it a three-way conversation."

"What a nightmare!"

"I could do most of the talking."

I knew too well he could. "I'd rather speak for myself."

"Together or separately?"

"Wait. I didn't tell you yes to either. You said I had until Monday."

"Monday, then. No later." I bristled until he added, a half second later, a polite *please*. "Did you speak to Karen today?" he asked.

"She hasn't had her baby."

"I'm more interested in her husband."

"He has very white teeth."

There was a silence.

"Strauss," I finally said, "you're the only person I know who can brood—audibly—over the telephone. Lighten up."

"All right. How was your visit home?"

"The usual. Except for the baby. I love the baby."

"Of course." He cleared his throat. "When you went home—were you able to talk to anyone? About anything important?"

"How could I talk? What could I say? Everybody was busy fussing over Junior. I didn't want to steal my sister's thunder."

"How is it stealing your sister's thunder to simply say you've met someone?"

Because I'd have to say your name and explain who you are, I felt like telling him, *and best be sure your P.J. brother-in-law isn't the only one who'd raise a few fireworks over that.*

"My mother made me an ice-cream float," I said. "Like I was a kid sick in bed."

"What you're trying to say, maybe, is that your family wouldn't be well-disposed to our relationship?"

"Don't be ridiculous," I blurted out. "My mother's so desperate for me to get married, anything in pants will do."

Was the silence that followed that remark censorious or amused? "I'm getting off the phone now," I said, and did.

He called me back ten seconds later. "That's useful information," he said, and returned the favor of hanging up in my face.

The next weekend on the hot drive down to Long Island, I didn't know which I missed most: air-conditioning or a tape deck or just a rubber band to pull back my tangled hair. With all the windows down, my humidified curls whipped around my head. My shorts and shirt were drenched with sweat, and my ears hurt from the roar of passing eighteen-wheelers. My boom box, which I strapped into the passenger seat with the safety belt, could hardly project over the constant sound of the traffic. The speakers warbled in and out and the highest notes vibrated.

I had every intention of giving, for the first time, an intellectual ear to Benjamin Britten's take on *The Turn of the Screw*, which I had purchased half price at Tower. But after ten minutes I was bored and irritated by the wild swings of the overture, the incoherence of each aria, the too-trained voices that seemed to mock the listener, who had no idea where the next phrase would go. That the opera was sung in English, not Italian, also got on my nerves. I thought of *Rigoletto*. Verdi's glorious version of the travails of a bitter hunchback was proof that no good ever came from secrets. *The Turn of the Screw*, maybe, was a cautionary tale that a woman should never get too hot and bothered over a guy, especially when he was a dead man. With my eyes still on the road, I reached over to my boom box, popped out the Benjamin Britten, and put in some Beatles. Songs like "Love Me Do" and "Paperback Writer" seemed to take me even faster to the beach.

The community where Dodie's friend lived was called Shore Line. Two lefts after the entrance, Dodie had said, then take a right toward the water and continue down the road for a mile until you reach a sign that says North Lagoon. But the roads were circular and forked off one another. I got lost in a tangle of pine trees and houses with slanted roofs whose interiors probably looked like something out of *Architectural Digest*. In the winding driveways sat Jags and BMWs and some Italian-looking sports cars I couldn't even begin to identify. I couldn't help it: Suddenly I heard Strauss's voice—quiet and wry, describing his former classmates at Harvard as obscenely wealthy—and I came to the conclusion that Dodie had been bought. Then I tried to erase this impression.

No can do, Lisa.

Well? I thought to myself. So what if Dodie was going out with someone who was rolling in it—no, *wallowing* in it? Didn't Strauss have a lot of money, even if he didn't flash it? And didn't Dodie work for nothing but obscenely wealthy people, every day? If anything, I should have been surprised he hadn't gotten caught up with one of them before this.

All week long—when I wasn't stewing about my problems with Strauss and Boorman, and waiting for Karen to give me more news—I'd been thinking about Dodie's latest. At times Dodie and I had discussed, probably too frankly, our relationships with others. We knew their names and professions and salaries, their tastes in music and literature, their faults and bad habits, and their relative worth in bed. Just as I knew that Dodie had never dated anyone taller than him—which, because he was all of five foot eight, severely limited the field—I also knew that his friends were always younger than him. The one I got to know best, of course, was George, who had a slight build, a soft voice, and an insider's knowledge of where to buy saffron for a great price. I had met maybe half a dozen other friends—who seemed puzzled, but tolerant, of my presence in Dodie's life—but I always had kept the image of George in my mind when I wanted to picture Dodie's lovers, probably because it was an image I felt comfortable with.

The clean white sign for North Lagoon, with its silver script, inspired another picture. This time I imagined that Dodie's friend was older, maybe even silver-haired. After I had gone a block along the beach road, I shook my head, as if to rattle the sign for North Lagoon out of my head and bring into focus the real inspiration for this image: Strauss. As I peered at the numbers on the mailboxes, I formed one last string of pictures of Dodie's friend, and they all were of a gay version of Strauss—Strauss with a better haircut, Strauss in chinos, Strauss in contact lenses, Strauss with a shiny clean faucet, Strauss in Docksiders with no socks underneath.

Then I thought, *Lisa, you are fucking absurd. Stop it right now. Just stop it.*

A low-slung blue sports car—a convertible—was parked in the driveway. The house was an A-frame, painted antique blue. The windows were floor-to-ceiling and covered with white sheers that I expected any minute would pull back when the people inside realized I needed to be welcomed. But no one came out of the house, even after I hoisted my duffel bag and boom box (a safety precaution I automatically performed after living so long in New York) out of the car and knocked on the front door twice, then three times.

I took up my gear and went around the back. The house was set high above the water. A flight of rough-hewn log stairs led down to a private dock, where the yacht Dodie had promised—a big white gleaming thing called *The Young Girl*—was anchored. The boat came as no surprise. Its owner did. He and Dodie were sitting on matching chaise longues on the boat's deck, and when the man saw me he nudged Dodie, and they both stood and waved. The man had six inches—although probably not more than an extra year—on Dodie. Even at that distance, I could tell Dodie's new friend was the kind of material who could take any girl's—or guy's— breath away.

"Come on down!" Dodie called.

I hauled my duffel bag and boom box down the precarious flight of stairs to the dock, and then scrambled up the plank leading to the boat, sweaty and out of breath. Dodie gave me my usual hug, but no kiss.

"This is 800," he said.

What could I say? I said nothing. 800 was a knockout. He was dressed in chino shorts and a maroon polo that seemed tailor-made to fit his lean, tight body. But the dark five o'clock shadow on his beautiful chiseled face betrayed the fact that his hair—a gleaming blond—had been bleached. No matter. It was still sexy. Almost too sexy. Dodie had hit the jackpot, and his playful eyes, as they looked at me, seemed to jing and whiz like the slot machines at Atlantic City.

"Lisa, right?" 800 asked.

"Right," I said, and shook his hand. In an instant, looking into 800's mirrored sunglasses, I knew I should not question his odd name. I also came to the instant conclusion that I didn't like him.

The feeling—of dislike, at least—didn't seem to be mutual. 800 obviously was so used to being a popular guy, he didn't pick up on the bad vibes I probably was emanating. After I shook his hand—too quickly, trying to avoid my own distorted reflection in his sunglasses, which made me look fat—I became ridiculously conscious of my breasts. Maybe it was because my T-shirt was soaked with sweat and plastered against every curve of my body, but I hadn't been so aware of being a girl since the time I went to a pool party in sixth grade and some boys lapped their tongues and said "Ooh la la" when I took off my shirt. I was only 32A back then, but I wished at that moment that I could cut off my breasts and never have to deal with all the rest of the stuff that inevitably would happen once they got bigger—which (fortunately) they did.

Dodie got me a director's chair, which forced me to sit up straight. I felt hot from the drive and peeved that Dodie did not come around to the front of the house to meet me.

"A drink?" 800 asked.

"Whatever you're having."

It was Long Island Iced Tea. Knowing how susceptible I was to alcohol, Dodie called out, "Not so strong," to 800, who disappeared below deck with the comment, "I make no promises."

I sat there with Dodie, the sun beating down on my knees, and looked out over the water, which shimmered in the light. A gleam of silver shone on the roof of the house on the next lot—which was at least one acre over, partially hidden behind a windbreak of cypresses. Dodie stretched out his legs—like 800, he was wearing loafers without socks, which made me feel like an ass for wearing white tubes underneath my Reeboks.

"So what do you think, Lise?"

"Handsome," I admitted.

"You can do better than that."

"All right. So he's Adonis. But why's he called 800?"

"It's short for Hot Fuck."

"Huh?" I asked.

"1–800–Hot–Fukk. Fuck with two *K's* instead of a *C.*"

"Doesn't he know how to spell?"

"He went to Yale."

"Big deal. My beau went to Harvard."

"Competitive, aren't we? But more on your Cambridge man later. 800 has to spell it wrong so he gets away with it with the FCC. It's a phone-order business. For sex toys."

"He takes orders for dildos for a living?"

Dodie gave me a long, alcohol-induced laugh. "He owns the company. He's never answered one of the phones in his life."

"Oh," I said. "Now I can rest easy."

Below deck, 800—or Hot Fuck—was breaking up tray after tray of ice cubes. I heard the cubes tinkle into each glass.

"What's his real name?" I asked.

"Homer Francis."

"I'll stick to 800."

Dodie always had insisted on the importance of not mixing the personal with the professional, of accepting only certain kinds of favors from clients, such as extra tickets and use of country-club facilities, but not becoming too close to anyone, especially not becoming what he called a *capon* for the old ladies who wanted a sexless escort service when their husbands left town. Although I certainly wasn't in a position to criticize anyone for blurring the distinction between work and social life, I asked, "Your client?"

"Yup."

I shrugged. "Beats the bar scene."

"We've sworn off that."

We so soon? I wanted to ask. But I didn't. I felt an unfounded, unsettling envy rising up inside me, that Dodie could sit there and say *we* while I sat miles apart from Strauss.

800 may have owned a million-dollar company—which explained how he owned that cute car and the gorgeous house and this ostentatious boat—but that did nothing to explain how he came to own Dodie. Although he had decent enough manners, he also showed he knew too well the privileges accorded to the wealthy and the beautiful. He called me *Cuz*

and called Dodie *Bugle Boy* and *Duck Head,* which I suspected had less to
do with Dodie's choice of clothes than the activities he engaged in with
800 once his clothes had been shed. Dodie, in turn, called him *H.F.* or
Homer or *Eight-Oh-Oh* with a touch of undue respect. When I stopped to
think about it, I realized that Dodie always had worn the pants in our
relationship. He had talked more, chosen the restaurants, dispensed the
drugs, bought the drinks. I had never seen Dodie play the boy before. It
bothered me.

Then I wondered what Dodie would make of me and Strauss. *Not
much,* I thought. *But what's it any of his goddamn business? Who on the
outside knows what's going on in any relationship? For that matter, who on
the inside knows a blessed thing either?*

I slurped to the bottom of my Long Island Iced Tea in five minutes
flat.

"Long time since you've had a drink, Lise?" Dodie asked.

"Get your cuz another," 800 told him.

With that comment, I felt intense relief not to be sitting in Park
Slope with my knees pressed too firmly together, having to monitor everything I did and said to win over Strauss's mother and father. I didn't give a
damn what 800 thought of me. I drank—and drank—until it was no longer
a conscious decision to tie a good one on. To the delight of 800 and
Dodie—who also seemed eager to drown whatever sorrows they had—I got
wasted.

800 started to grow on me, probably because he seemed the perfect
antidote to the conservative duds who worked at Boorman. He had a huge
repertoire of rude regional jokes (*Why's it called a toothbrush instead of a
teethbrush? It was invented in West Virginia!*) and pulled out puns like a
magician drew scarves from his pockets. But he preempted my usual role.
The kind of repartee that Dodie and I usually engaged in wouldn't fly here.
All the push and pull was between 800 and Dodie, and a lot of their joking
seemed to revolve around references back to New Haven. Only instead of
comparing versions of the city, as Dodie and I did, 800 and Dodie contrasted them. What irritated me about the whole thing was the obvious
delight Dodie took in landing a Yale boy, who clearly had not been a
scholarship student.

"I'll bet you never once crossed the Q the whole time you went to
school there," I told 800.

"What's the Q?" 800 asked.

I shrugged and let Dodie explain. The Q Bridge was the long elevated
stretch of highway that separated the marshes and the gated liquor stores
and the shoemaker shops of our old neighborhood from what Dodie and I

used to envision as the wealthy, ivy-walled paradise of downtown New
Haven. When we were small, our parents hated to drive the Q, for it had
no shoulder to pull over on in case the car broke down (and ours broke
down plenty), and because the Q took us over New Haven Harbor, which
always gave off a foul smell no matter how low or high the tide. The Q
intrigued me. I got ushered into downtown New Haven only two or three
times a year by my father: to attend the Columbus Day parade and La
Festa di Santa Maria Maddalena on Wooster Square, and to see the
Christmas window decorations at Macy's. Once, on the Q, we rode in a
hushed limousine with the lights on low following the hearse that contained my grandfather's body. Our family, for some unknown reason, always was buried in Saint Lawrence Cemetery, those green-gated acres that
stretched beyond the Yale Bowl.

The Q's very name always seemed mysterious to me, perhaps because
my mother could not pronounce the ancient Indian word *Quinnipiac*—
and so she shortened it, like many other Italians, to simply *the Q*. But she
couldn't even say that single letter right. She said *Cu—Cu Bridge*—pro-
nouncing the Q the same way vo-tech boys used to taunt kids in the high-
school marching band by stretching the damning word *queer* into two
syllables: *cu-weer*.

The Q, perhaps, was most memorable to us under another name:
Suicide Bridge. Yalies who couldn't make the grade were said to jump from
Harkness Tower. But townies—the depressed teens and desperate lovers
who could not face leaping off East Rock to impale themselves on the
jagged stones below—sometimes chose to throw themselves off Q Bridge
into the dull, murky green depths of New Haven Harbor.

As a teenager, I vowed I would kill myself if I never made it out of
New Haven. My worst fear since moving out had been of coming down
with a terminal illness and being forced to go home and die in my father's
house under my mother's care. I had nightmares of getting into a car
accident and ending up a quadriplegic. I envisioned Mama parking me in a
wheelchair, feeding me *acini de pepe,* and wiping my hairy chin half-raw
with a rough paper napkin as *Truth or Consequences* and *Wheel of Fortune*
flickered on her black-and-white TV.

If I ever got deathly ill, I thought, *Strauss would take care of me.* But
then I remembered the snap of the Audi's power locks and I felt confused
and carsick, the way I felt whenever I went home and drove over the Q
Bridge, frightened I would run into a traffic jam when I reached the top.
Heights terrified me. Below me lay the water, beyond that the pink and
green oil tanks on the shore, and far beyond that the rust-brown facade of
the Coliseum and the glare of the Knights of Columbus tower. I thought

about how easy it would be—and yet how hard—to turn the wheel and jump the rail. Which would it take—weakness or strength—to do it?

Darkness engulfed the boat. Then the full moon rose above the trees, pale and silver, and 800 flicked on a switch so the lights strung around the deck—fanciful strings of chili peppers and cacti that gleamed red and green like Christmas-tree bulbs—glowed and winked at us. The mosquitoes came out in droves, and 800 took his lighter to the citronella candles on the table. Neither Dodie nor 800 nor I were inclined to pry ourselves off the deck chairs, except to go below for more drinks and to replenish the wicker plate that held water crackers and brie, which seemed all there was to nibble on. By nine o'clock I was so blitzed I didn't even blink when 800 got up and lowered his fly to pee over the side of the deck into the lagoon.

"Ignore him," Dodie said, his laugh sputtering out like an engine gearing up to go nowhere.

"I'm trying my best," I said. My head spun. "Why do you call this boat"—and to the snorting delight of Dodie, I held back a hiccup, or was it a burp?—"*The Young Girl?*" Then, as if 800 were retarded, I repeated the question.

800's voice sounded disembodied to me. "Gary Puckett."

Puckett. No, fuck it. The metal legs of Dodie's and 800's chairs vibrated on the deck as they shook with laughter and explained—in halting, alternating voices—that at one time 800 had a business partner—or was that a sexual partner?—who had been involved with producing—or was that seducing?—an album made by that group from the sixties called Gary Puckett and the Union Gap.

The story was jumbled, and close to incoherent, and punctuated by snorts of laughter, resulting in Dodie spilling ice down the front of his shirt and 800 disappearing below deck to bring up a cassette tape, which he inserted in my boom box after tossing aside the Beatles cassette too close to the citronella candle—where I would find it melted into a blob of black in the morning. 800 turned off the string of chili-pepper lights, pushed down the PLAY button, and held out his hand to invite Dodie to join him on the dance floor in the pale yellow glow of the candles. The song "This Girl Is a Woman Now" took me back to junior high school and those long, hot afternoons I spent longing for love on the beach, coming home with nothing but a burn that puckered the skin on my shoulders and back.

For more than five years I had lived in or around New York City.

With—and without—Dodie, I had been to gay bars, transvestite hangouts, a Forty-second Street peep show as research for my human-sexuality class, and Saint Mark's to catch the black-leather-and-whips scene—but I had never seen two men slow-dance together before. 800 was the lead. Dodie was in his arms, his head on 800's shoulder, his feet side by side with 800's Docksiders, his legs pressed against 800's thighs. I could not take my eyes off them, and as the song continued, I had the feeling this moment would be locked in my memory forever.

But why? Because the light was yellow. Because the mosquitoes were biting so hard I slapped away blood. Because I remembered a trip Dodie and I made a few years back to the Murray Hill Playhouse where we saw *Cabaret*. I heard Joel Grey's strange hiss, like ice cubes expanding in a glass, in the language that movies and documentaries had taught us to associate only with Hitler (and that Dodie and I both speculated was best suited for weird sex): *Wilkommen*. I remembered the dance with two ladies. And the strange scene in which Sally Bowles and Maximilian and Christopher all danced together, and then they all started to kiss, and the men seemed to become women and the woman became a man. I remembered how much Dodie and I had laughed when the master of ceremonies first introduced the Jewish gorilla as his girlfriend *(I ask you: Eez it a crime to love?)* and how bummed out we felt at the end when the drums rolled and the camera moved slowly across the frosted glass, finally freezing on the armband of a Nazi soldier, the swastika distorted in the image.

It had been a midnight show. Afterward Dodie and I had walked back to his apartment, in what our parents used to disparagingly call *"the wee hours of the morning"* (as if no good could ever come of anything done at 2:00 A.M.). We had been scared walking the deserted streets but tried not to show it. Like Scouts at camp who have to make a midnight trip to the latrine, we walked with our arms around each other and sang to keep up our courage:

Reuben, Reuben, I been thinking
What a great world this would be!
If all the boys would move to China
Then the girls could rule the sea!

How unaccountably happy I had felt on that long walk! How fun it was to drink too much wine when we got back and to step into the cramped bathroom and dress myself in a pair of Dodie's blue-and-white chambray pajamas—described as his *no-sex tonight outfit*. But as I climbed into the bottom, I noticed the pants had a drawstring waist. I was drunk. I remembered thinking, idly, *If Dodie weren't gay and he wasn't my cousin, I would marry him in a heartbeat.*

When I came out, Dodie was drying the wineglasses with a linen towel. "You don't look half-bad in those PJs, Lise."

"You're just saying that because they make me look like a man." I gave him a dizzy smile. "What if I were a man?"

He held up one of the goblets to make sure he had rubbed off the spots with the towel. "*Such* a boner would I have for you, babe," he said, and then we both burst out laughing in a way I knew Eben Strauss would deem "unhealthy."

What would Mr. Eben Strauss make of this? I thought, as the music played and Dodie—perhaps remembering *Cabaret* too—held out his hand toward me and invited me to join him and 800 on the dance floor. I shook my head. Suddenly I pictured Strauss—sitting in right field, drinking a ballpark rip-off-priced beer with his seventy-nine-year-old father, and maybe even eating some Cracker Jacks, a treat my father always bought me at Yankee Stadium. Then I was back on the boat, wondering who was more real—the woman who told Strauss "Bring back a Cracker Jack surprise for me," or the girl who had eyes only for Dodie's erection, visibly pushing against Homer Francis's chinos?

I got up at the end of the song and told them good night. Apparently I was sleeping on the boat. 800 told me to take the room at the bottom of the stairs. Nobody helped me schlepp my duffel bag downstairs to the cabin below, which was paneled in pine, with varnish so thick it shone in the moonlight that came in through the tiny window. The boards were speckled with large dark knots that looked like evil eyes. I used the lavatory, which was outfitted with an aqua toilet and sink and a shower stall with a frosted-glass door that seemed to beg me to open it, as if I could find the answer to all my questions about life waiting inside. But all I found behind the shower-stall door was a bar of white-and-green-striped deodorant soap drying out on the plastic holder.

I left on my T-shirt in case I had to get up and pee during the night, but then the cabin was so stuffy and hot I took it off, knowing nobody was going to get a thrill looking at my body anyway. That body—my body—felt like someone else's body, swaying queasily back and forth on the bunk. I knew the boat was firmly anchored and the water was still as a mirror, yet the cabin seemed to be rocking. The combination of alcohol and hunger dug a deeper hole in my stomach, and to level myself, I thought again of Strauss—the way he put his arm around me from behind and pulled me against his body.

Why wouldn't I want him forever? Because there was a certain bland-
ness about being with a man who covered you with a blanket before he
went off to the kitchen or the bathroom, as if naturally assuming that all
women were modest (or maybe, slightly ashamed of their figures) and
would not want to be viewed too closely on the trip back.

"Why do you always cover me up?" I once asked him.

"I don't know," he said. "It's a reflex. I suppose—well, my mother and
my sister always seem to be cold."

"Maybe they have iron-poor blood."

I tried to picture Strauss's mother, bundled in a cherry-red terry
bathrobe over a modest Miss Elaine nightgown, fixing his father dark coffee and a pile of rye toast coated—on one side only—with margarine. I
tried to imagine Strauss's sister—sitting on her Broyhill sofa in her four-
bedroom split-level in Bergen County—reading *The Little Engine that
Could* to her children beneath a multicolored afghan she purchased at the
last Sisterhood fund-raiser for the temple. These were the women I was
likened to, compared to, whose lives and goals seemed so radically different from my own.

"I'm not like your mother," I told Strauss, sure of this even though I
had absolutely no proof of it. "I'm probably not even like your sister."

"No. You're not. I wouldn't want you to be."

But who did Strauss want me to be? More important, who did I want
to become? Certainly not this—a girl who spent the night shit-faced on a
yacht belonging to a man named Hot Fuck, who had to masturbate herself
to sleep with the tail end of her T-shirt while fantasizing about doing it
with a couple of nameless twins, who felt so lonely after this momentarily
satisfying yet meaningless act she even considered going back up on deck
to talk with the guys and was stopped only by the fear that the guys were
doing it doggy-style on the deck, and whose final thought before she sunk
into a sleep from which she would awake with her head full of pins and
needles and her mouth full of cotton was of a tale called *The Secret
Stranger.*

In Conrad's story, the boat was called *The Sephora,* and the captain
strolled the deck smoking a cigar, then stopped when he discovered what
he thought was a headless corpse floating in those strange, Asiatic waters.
Once "the corpse" slithered up the ladder onto deck, he revealed himself
to be a criminal guilty of mutiny and murder. The captain hid him in a
cabin, risking the safety of his men and himself to save the stranger because he identified with this dark shadow of himself.

I dreamed of *The Sephora,* the moonlit sea, the wet criminal shivering in the corner of the cabin in borrowed pajamas, and a captain who

looked like a sterner, burlier, bearded version of Strauss. In the middle of the night I awoke to a sound that at first I feared was the sound of a violent coitus coming to conclusion, before I realized it was something even more terrible: the ragged edges of weeping. It came from above, a horrible *oh God, oh God* that seemed scraped from someone's most inner space.

Every human being was capable of tears, yet I could not imagine them coming from 800's blue eyes. The weeping belonged to Dodie—his gift freely given to the dark night. I listened. Then it stopped, the boat went quiet, the moonlight streamed in through the porthole, and I fell into a restless sleep that was anything but oblivion.

Chapter Twelve

It's Your Funeral

I was the first to wake the next morning—or rather, the first to make an appearance on deck. Before I went upstairs I slipped on a tank top and shorts and peed a foul-smelling urine into the aqua toilet. Then I splashed a blast of cold water on my drawn skin and cracked lips. The first sip of water I took from the cup of my hands left me queasy, and I resigned myself to a morning—if not an afternoon and an evening—of dry mouth. My hunger was completely gone, but my forehead felt heavy and I craved caffeine.

It was 10:15. I sat on the deck, the floorboards already warm beneath my bare feet. Desiccated lemon slices floated on top of the pale brown liquid left in the glasses. One of the strings of chili pepper and cactus lights had fallen from the guardrail, and on the table next to me was an ashtray soiled with cigarette butts. Once I looked closer, I saw they were a couple of roaches. Dodie and 800 had been smoking dope last night without me.

After a while the sheer curtains on the top floor of the A-frame moved slightly. Dodie's head peeked out. He made a *shh* gesture by raising his finger to his lips, and just before he dropped the curtain I saw a bare leg on a bed behind him.

Dressed in the same clothes he wore the night before, Dodie walked too slowly down the log staircase. He, too, looked like a wreck. He obviously hadn't showered or shaved, and I had the urge to lick the palm of my hand and run it through his rumpled hair, smoothing it back down on his skull.

"Man, I'm hurting," he said. "You got your car keys?"

I patted my shorts pocket and heard the familiar jingle of my Saint Christopher key chain.

"Let's go get some joe," Dodie said.

I cocked my head toward the house.

"Homer doesn't drink coffee," Dodie said. "He's macrobiotic."

My parched mouth opened in disbelief. I extended my first finger, like a gun, toward the ashtray full of roaches.

Dodie shrugged. "He's full of contradictions. Come on," he added, with such impatience that I knew escape from Homer Francis was the name of the game, which I was more than willing to play.

The nearest coffee joint was a Dunkin' Donuts on the main drag. Dodie refused to drink his joe at the counter next to a pair of cops and a retiree who actually wore a baseball cap that said GONE FISHIN'. We ordered four cups, which Dodie held in a cardboard container on his lap as we headed along the main street that ran parallel to the beach.

"No sudden stops," he said, "or I'll never have children."

"You want kids?" I asked.

"Doiyyyy," Dodie said, making the ugly sound we used to let off as teenagers when we wanted to indicate the person we were speaking to—usually one of our parents—was acting completely retarded.

"You'd actually be a good father," I said. "Better than either of ours."

"That wouldn't take much effort, would it?" Dodie asked. He cracked the safety lid on one of the cups and carefully raised it to his lips. After his first sip of coffee he asked, "Do you want to hear my deepest, darkest fantasy?"

"Spare me."

"It's nonsexual in nature."

"Oh," I said. "Then really spare me."

"Eccola, Lisa. Here it is: I go home and tell my father I've gotten a girl into trouble—"

"Don't make me laugh—"

"—and my father claps me on the back. Takes me out for a beer. Or three or four. Or eight. And my mother, she gets down on her knees in front of that white plastic Madonna she's got on top of the Magnavox—"

"They have a Quasar now," I said.

"Oh. How long have they had that?"

"A couple of years, maybe."

Dodie fell silent. I, too, was quiet, as if it were my fault I knew more about his own parents' house than he himself did.

The road beyond Shore Line was two lanes only and shaded on both sides by pine trees. Dodie told me we had a good thirty miles to go before we hit the place he wanted to show me—a wild and beautiful spot that 800 took him to last weekend. For a few minutes we did nothing but drive—quietly, slowly—on this road that bore almost no traffic on a Sunday morning. Then Dodie asked me, "How about you, Lise?"

"What about me?"

"Think you'll ever have kids?"

I swallowed. Dodie looked out the window to hide his embarrassment.

"Carol had her baby," I said. "Last weekend."

"You should have told me."

"It was a boy. I went home. And listened to her sing the praises of motherhood."

"Did your mother join in?" Dodie laughed when I didn't answer. "Were you inspired to follow suit?"

I shrugged, remembering the irrational sob I let loose when I gave Al Dante Junior back to Carol. "I don't know. I mean, I want to someday."

There were breaks in the evergreens along the road. We kept passing in and out of the sunlight, which aggravated my headache.

"What about this guy you're going with now?" Dodie asked.

"What about him?"

Dodie looked at me out of the corner of his eye. "You look like shit, Lise. You must be in love."

I glanced at him out of the side of my sunglasses. "What's your excuse?"

Dodie gave me an odd laugh, thick and sputtery like a blender clogged with sticky stuff the blades wouldn't whirl. "No excuse," he said. "So to return to Mr. Right . . . I really think it's time you 'fessed up about him."

"There's nothing to 'fess."

"But you're so secretive. I'm beginning to think he's what your mother calls a *Negro*—"

"He's not a *Negro*. What a stupid word."

"So why are you hiding him? Where is he this weekend?"

"He went to a doubleheader at Yankee Stadium."

"Sounds like he has potential," Dodie said. "Why don't you marry him?"

"Because—because sometimes he bores me," I blurted out.

"Oh. Then you really ought to marry him, because you know exactly what you're getting into."

I tried to laugh, but my mouth and throat felt too tight. "Why would I want to get married, anyway?" I asked.

"Because you're getting too old for this shit—"

"*Et tu,* Peter Pan?"

"—and because you like a man telling you what to do—"

I started to squawk but swallowed it when Dodie said, "—if only because you like to buck against it."

"Bingo," I said.

Dodie fell quiet for a moment. Then he told me he would love to see me happy—although why he thought marriage was the ticket to la-la land was beyond me—and that he thought I needed to start thinking about playing it safe, viewing the long run, working toward being more secure. "Besides," he added, "I'd like to see what you'd do to a man, Lise."

I kept quiet. For the first time in my life I was frightened of what a man could do to *me*—or what I would *let* him do to me.

"So what else does this guy do, besides bore you?" Dodie asked.

"*Bore* isn't the right word," I said, even though Strauss did have all the hallmarks of the kind of man I often saw standing in the lobby of a concert hall, patiently waiting for his wife to come out of the ladies' room. "He's just so decent—"

"And you want a bad boy—"

"And gentle—"

"What do you want him to do—break your hips?"

"And polite! How can I marry someone polite, who doesn't even say *shit* when he drops something on the floor, and then the next minute—he's so friggin' bossy!—he turns around and tells me to fetch it for him, please! How am I going to have a really good fight with him—and win it?"

"Find the right button," Dodie said, "and push it." He flipped down the visor. "I take it this isn't a nice Italian boy we have here?"

"Nice *Jewish* boy," I said.

"Oh," Dodie said. "Can I watch when you break the news to your mother?"

"No, you may not."

"*Are* you going to break it to her?"

"Why would I?"

"Because that's what you do," Dodie said. "If you're straight. And you're serious. You take the other person home."

Suddenly I realized the gravity of the situation: The moment I accepted Strauss's invitation to meet his parents, I would have to reciprocate. "God," I blurted out, "I guess I'll have to—"

Dodie smiled. "I knew it. I just knew it, there are diamonds on the horizon—"

"Look out, Dodici," I said, "or I'll name my firstborn after you."

For half a second this appalling thought shut Dodie up. He looked out the window at the pines, which were beginning to thin, so we could see through the trees to the white dunes along the beach. Then he reminded me, "Jews don't do that—name after someone living."

"He's named after his dead brother."

"What did his brother die of?"

"It's too complicated to go into. I just know the brother was named after his grandfather—"

"Lisa, please. *What* is this man's name?"

"He goes by his last name—"

"And what do you call him?"

"His last name—"

"Oh, man! Lise! Isn't that just like you, to sit on a guy's face and then call him *sir*—"

"I don't call him *sir!* I call him Strauss."

"Strauss, huh?" Dodie said. "What's his grandfather's name—Johann?" Dodie hummed a Viennese waltz. "Richard? Levi? Nathan? Wow, Nathan Straus, the guy behind Macy's—"

"Don't start getting wild, Dodie. His father has a family business. He sells carpet in Brooklyn."

"Home or industrial?"

"I don't know. And what do I care?"

Dodie knocked his hand against his forehead. "Because—you *ignoranus*—there's a big difference between his father managing big-time jobs like hospitals and airports and him offering penny-pinching housewives like your sister three rooms for the price of two and the hallway runners for free."

Because my own father had put down cement, it had suited my imagination just fine to picture Strauss's dad on his hands and knees driving in carpet tacks. Now I wasn't so sure that was the case. "His parents live in Park Slope," I told Dodie. "I guess he must be some kind of contractor."

"And this man of yours, he's in the rug business too?"

"Not exactly."

"So how does he earn his living?"

I hesitated. "By going to a lot of meetings."

"Sounds like he has a healthy salary."

I squinted, flipped down the visor, and admitted I knew this much about Strauss's financial state: "He has to do his taxes on a quarterly basis."

"Now we're talking," Dodie said.

"But that's not why I'm going out with him," I added.

"I didn't say it was."

"I wish he made less money."

"Are you out to lunch?"

"But, Dodie. It's a power thing. It makes me nervous. He always picks up the check."

"Christ," Dodie said. "Can't you find something better to complain about?"

"But then he's in control."

"Lise, somebody's *always* in control, whether it's obvious or not—"

"But it's supposed to be fifty-fifty, or at least sixty-forty, or at least more balanced—"

"You want balance, take t'ai chi." Dodie sipped more coffee and replaced the lid. "So where'd you meet him, the gym?"

"Nope."

"A bar? A personal ad?" Dodie paused. When I didn't answer he said, "Don't tell me what I think you're about to tell me."

"All right, so he works with me."

"In another division," Dodie prompted me.

"Sort of."

"You told me everyone in the Editorial division kept tampons in the bottom desk drawer." Dodie took a quick look at my face. He drew in his breath. "Lisa, you're sleeping with your boss—"

"So what if I am! He's not married!"

"That's never stopped you before—"

"And he's under forty—"

Dodie let out a long, low whistle. "It's your funeral."

"Stop overreacting. It's not like we're fucking on the boardroom table."

"But, Lisa, people aren't blind. They notice this shit. They pick up on the vibes."

"Half the time he's on the road," I told Dodie.

"And the other half he's not. So who knows? Or is this public knowledge and everybody just turns their head?"

"No. I mean yes. I mean, it probably wouldn't be kindly received. We kept it secret up until last weekend. Then somebody spotted us."

"Doing lunch?"

"No."

"In neutral territory?"

"On the sidewalk."

"On the sidewalk in front of *where*?"

"The Pierre."

"The Pierre Hotel? *Madonna mi*, your goose is cooked." Then Dodie laughed. "I've never been in that hotel. What's it like?"

"Oh, Dodie! Tell me what to do. I don't know what to do—"

"You're going to quit your job, is what you're going to do—"

"Are you crazy? Why doesn't he quit?"

"Because he's on top of you, is why. What's his title?"

"VP—"

"VP!"

"There are six VPs at Boorman, and three senior VPs and even an executive VP, and the whole corporation has more layers than my mother's lasagne—"

"But, Lise, a conservative corporation like that—and didn't you tell me there was a frosty dyke somewhere?"

I nodded. "She's right on top of him—"

"And didn't you tell me you were working on some kind of sexual-harassment code?"

"I just edited some of the language, the policy isn't put into place—"

"Oy, how the plot thickens! Lisa, I think you *do* have a bad boy on your hands."

"Really?"

"I mean, this guy's either stupid or a reckless sonofabitch."

"He's anything but," I said.

"A guy in his position? Screwing around with someone in your position? He's risking something. He's risking a lot. But maybe he gets off on the risk. Or maybe you're the one getting off on it. Or maybe you both have a death wish."

"Maybe you should stop playing analyst."

"Well, let me ask you this: Would you still go with him if you didn't have to hide it?"

"It would change things."

"For better or worse?"

"I couldn't say."

"Tell me something else then."

"Like what?"

Dodie asked me the question that Strauss insisted I not answer, at least for the moment. "Tell me you love him."

I hesitated. "I love his elbows," I said. "Do you know what I mean?"

"Can't say that I relate—"

"I mean, I want to stroke them all the time. When I see him in the hallway at Boorman, I want to grab his collar. I want to reach out and touch the cuffs of his shirt—"

"Where does he buy these shirts?" Before I could admit it was Brooks Brothers, Dodie said, "Cut the shit, Lise. Do you or don't you love him?"

"I'm crazy about him, but I don't know why—"

"Does he love you?"

"Yes. He told me. But he said he fought against it."

"That's even better," Dodie said. His eyes lit up. "That's like *Pride and Prejudice!*" Dodie, too, had the hots for Mr. Darcy, and he even had memorized that great passage where Darcy burst in upon the high-spirited Elizabeth and let down his ultradignified guard to passionately confess his feelings. He now quoted it: " 'In vain have I struggled! It will not do! You must allow me to tell you how ardently I admire and love you!' "

"Cut it out."

"Christ! Why can't someone say that to *me*?" Dodie sighed. "Congratulations, Lise."

"Thank you."

Dodie looked out at the scrubby pines along the side of the road. He added, almost under his breath, "Don't undervalue it."

Yes, Mom, I wanted to reply. But something inside me, my throat or my heart, felt so choked up, I was afraid I would begin to cry if I spoke. Finally I eked out an innocuous question—how much longer did I have to keep driving?—and Dodie said we had a while to go yet.

Dodie adjusted the cardboard container of coffee between his legs. His voice sounded pensive as he asked, "How do men—straight men—tell women they're in love with them? I don't ask to be facetious. I truly want to know."

I gave him a facetious answer. "They give you lingerie. That comes on padded hangers. That isn't red. That has a cotton crotch."

"Sounds like somebody has a sister—"

"And they say, *Wear this? For me?*"

"You've got to get him to change the intonation. Get rid of those question marks. You want a man who commands you: *Wear this. For me.*"

"How do you know what I want?"

"You said you wanted rough and rude, not gentle and polite."

"I'm not into being degraded."

"People are degraded every day," Dodie says. "For starters, we get up and go to work. And we say to our boss, 'Good morning, how was your weekend?' when what we really want to say is, 'Last night I dreamed you were lying at the bottom of an elevator shaft, and boy, did you look good there.' Although I guess you don't say that to *your* boss."

"I've told you, he's not really my boss—"

"Can he fire you?"

As I released some of the pressure on the gas pedal, the car slowed down. "Well. Yeah, sure, I guess he could—"

"He's your boss then, baby. And if you're not going to quit your job, you shouldn't forget it."

My stomach felt sick as I thought of how Strauss and I argued the weekend before, the rather uneasy peace we had made by phone while he was in Atlanta, his promise to bring me back the Cracker Jack surprise from Yankee Stadium, the permission I as good as promised to give him to talk to Peggy on Monday. My hand went up to my throat and landed, unconsciously, on the thin gold chain Strauss gave me, which still hung around my neck. Dodie, of course, noticed the gesture.

"Nice necklace. Another present?"

"Could be."

Dodie's eyes went lower. "But I see you left off his lingerie this morning."

I snorted. "You once swore to me you never looked at tits."

"How can I help it? You're letting them all hang out."

"Yeah, after watching you—and Hot Fuck—let it all hang out last night."

"You don't like 800, do you?"

"What do you see in him?" I asked. "Besides his beautiful bod and face?"

"Love is blind."

"And stupid," I added. "I mean, this guy went to Yale, but he can't even spell *fuck* right?"

"I wouldn't knock 800's business if I were you," Dodie said. "You now own significant stock in it, and it's making you money hand over fist." When I clucked my tongue, Dodie said, "Relax. It's a good bet. Especially strong in new-product development."

"Like what—French ticklers that taste like Left Bank croissants?"

"Actually, their latest is a talking dildo."

I paused. "What does it say?"

I was sorry I asked, because Dodie—obviously feeling too mirthful from just a few sips of coffee—got right down to business. He said he was urging 800 to do dildos with accents. He said the Brooklyn version could call out, *Hoddah, hoddah.* He said the Southern version could hillbilly-holler, *Y'all come!* He said the Fourteenth-Street-and-below version could lisp, *I've seen bigger assholes at the last staff meeting.*

"Frankly," I said, "I prefer my dildo to be the strong, silent type."

"For you, then, we offer the ten-inch marital aid known as Big Swede—dumb and hard as a post—possessing the immigrant work ethic—gets the job done right for half the cost—"

"You are *so* full of shit."

"Aren't I, though? And don't you love it. Stop the car. Pull over. Right now. On this stretch."

To the right lay a short, sandy pull-off that at first I thought was a driveway. But it didn't lead anywhere. There was nowhere to park but on the gravel that backed up against a thicket of pine trees and then a stretch of dunes on a lot that was clearly marked with so many for-sale signs it only served to indicate that the going price, even for the Hamptons, was astronomically absurd. The land also was marked as private property, but Dodie told me he spent the afternoon here just last week with 800, and not a soul appeared on the horizon to bother them.

"What about cops?"

"It's Sunday morning. They're in church or Dunkin' Donuts, where they belong. Besides, Homer knows the owner if anyone kicks up a fuss. Let's get on the beach."

Dodie rested the coffee—which was probably cold—on top of the car. I put up the autoshade, because the sun already was rising above the trees. Hot sand sifted between our flip-flops and our feet as we climbed the dunes and walked down the wide expanse of land to the shore, where we sat close to the water like a couple of kids about to build mud castles.

After I finished my first tepid coffee, I used the empty cup to idly dig up big clumps of sand. I tipped the cup and watched the particles run back onto the beach. Then I looked up at Dodie. In the bright sunlight the lines that ran from his nose to his mouth seemed deeper, and his hair, which I thought was cut too short, seemed thinner than the time I saw him last. He was right. We *were* getting old, too old to live like this. I was glad I couldn't see myself.

"What happened last night?" I finally asked, in a roundabout way of telling Dodie: *I heard you weeping.*

Dodie shrugged. "Lovers' quarrel."

"You can't tell me you love a man named Hot Fuck—"

"I told you his real name is Homer Francis. And really, I'm starting to wonder at the nature of your objections."

"But you don't have anything in common with him."

"How do you know?"

"He's not your type," I said, violating the lesson I should have learned way back in eighth grade—never to criticize a friend's romantic interest. "There's something about him that spells trouble," I said. "Don't get into trouble, Dodie—"

"Too late."

Dodie reached over, pulled the empty coffee cup from my hand, and flung it out toward the water, where it lay on the wet sand for a moment before a wave surged up, crumpled it, and took it back to sea. And then my cousin—with whom I had shared my secrets, my toothbrush and razor and bed, and his no-sex-tonight pajamas—told me his latest lover might have looked like King Midas, but what Dodie had given him in return was anything but gold.

My bout with mono in high school was my first taste of mortality, an illness that mocked the slow decline of the body just before death: the breathlessness that came just from sitting up in bed, the disinterest in food, the inertia of my imagination, the lack of awareness of time, the heightened power of memory, the need to sleep and sleep and sleep and the blessed moments before I fell into unconsciousness, in which I seemed to feel the parts of my body shutting down, one by one—the lungs, the mind, the heart.

When Dodie told me he had tested positive, I imagined that same slow decline overcoming his body, and then I felt my own body all too well—the way it began to rock, the way men pray at the Wailing Wall, the way mourners keen. Dodie's hand on my hand seemed the only thing tethering me to the earth.

Then I broke away and put my head in my hands, for my fear of touching Dodie suddenly was strong and even more overwhelming than the sobs that came out of my parched throat—so loud and ragged I wished I still had that empty coffee cup washed out to sea, so I could have scooped up a pile of sand and stuffed it into my mouth, silencing my voice forever.

"Please stop crying," Dodie finally said.

"But I can't. I can't believe it, I don't want to believe it, I'm crying for you—"

"Then put a lid on it. *For me.* Please."

I wiped my nose on my arm. Then—because there was no other option—I blew my nose into the tail of my T-shirt. Dodie looked away. After I finally stopped sniffling, he said, "I knew I shouldn't have told you. At least not without a jumbo box of Kleenex nearby."

He gave me a sad smile. But I didn't dare do anything more than nod, until I finally got a grip and asked, "How long have you known?"

"For sure? A couple of weeks. But since the beginning of summer I had a feeling. I didn't put it together. I didn't want to put it together. That weekend I came up to see you. Remember, I had the runs?"

"You said you'd eaten Mexican—but why didn't you say anything?"

"I didn't know then. Right after I came back I started to think—"

"But you should have said . . . all summer long . . . to carry that around without saying anything—"

"What was there to say? Beyond what I've just told you?"

"I could have helped you. I could have said I was sorry, oh, Dodie, I'm so sorry—"

"What good is sorry going to do me now? Oh. My God. That crying again . . . Lise, stop it. Enough. Really."

"Maybe the test was wrong."

"It wasn't wrong. I have it. And so does Homer."

"He gave it to you," I said.

"George gave it to me."

"Are you sure?"

"How can I be sure—"

"*Ask* him."

"I can't. He's dead."

I put my head back in my arms. "Oh God, oh God—"

"Please stop saying *oh God*—"

"But when did that happen? How did it happen?"

"Pneumonia. His mother called me. Fourth of July. She accused me of giving it to him. That was some great conversation I had with her, trying to tell her it was *her* son who messed around behind *my* back, after we both agreed—oh, Lise, we both agreed we were going to be careful—why didn't he just take a gun and put it to my head? He did me in, I'm sure it was him, but there isn't any way of tracking it, and even the doctor said it could have been sitting around inside me for years. I mean, this stuff about it being in the blood supply is pretty scary."

My stomach dropped. I looked out on the water, and the waves almost seemed to stop coursing in for a moment before the last whitecap crested and broke on the shore. "Dodie," I said, trying to keep my voice level, all the while listening to it get higher and higher. "We shared your razor, remember, when I stayed at your place? I put a Band-Aid on your hand, remember, that time you came down too hard on the Spanish onion? Your nose was bleeding one time when we did some coke—"

"That was a long time ago."

"—and we shot up together, remember, way back at Sarah Lawrence—"

"That was *light-years* ago."

"You said *years*. Sits around inside you for *years*."

"You get it from fucking, Lise, and we've never fucked, so what are you getting all bent out of shape about?"

"But, Dodie." My voice jangled. "That coke. And the poppers. And the needle—and you and me and George, we all smoked off the same bong. . . . Oh God. How am I going to tell Strauss—"

"You aren't. *Don't.* You don't have it."

"But, Dodie. That's wrong. That's worse than George. I could be a loaded gun."

Dodie bit his lip. We looked at one another, then looked away.

"Get the test," Dodie said. "If you're really worried, just get the test and find out for certain. Now calm down. You don't have diarrhea, do you?"

I shook my head.

"Night sweats?"

"I always kick the sheets and blankets off, Strauss says I kick 'em—"

"Nothing swollen along your neck?"

"Is that how you found out?"

"The sweats came first. Then like—lumps, right here—like mono. When I got more runs, I was pretty sure that was it. Still, I kept hoping. God, I kept hoping."

I looked into Dodie's black eyes until I saw, in the wet reflection of his pupils, my own eyes beginning to well up with tears again. I reached out and clasped his hand. We sat there in the hot sun until we couldn't stand the silence any longer. Then Dodie told me he had a weird memory the moment he found out his test results. It was a picture of Zio Gianni standing with his gut hanging out by the chain-link fence at the neighborhood YMCA, hollering at us kids above the rumble of the summer thunder, "Everybody out of the pool! Party's over!"

Just the mere thought of Uncle Gianni—his threatening stomach, his Pacific theater tattoos, the way he squished his beer can in the palm of his hand—scared me. I shuddered. "How are you going to tell your mother?"

"I'm not," Dodie said. "And you aren't either."

"But how will I hide it? When I see her?"

"You're a good actress. Find a way."

The lull of the tide coming in should have soothed me, but every sea gull swoop and caw made my nerves jump. "I'd give anything for a Valium," I told Dodie. "Or a lude—"

"It just so happens I have the next best thing." Dodie looked up and down the deserted beach. Out of his shirt pocket he pulled a plastic Baggie tied with a red-and-white twist—two fingers' worth of pot, which Dodie informed me was the very finest of Hawaiian sinsemilla, borrowed from 800 just that morning. "Now *regardez: Ceci n'est pas une pipe?*" Dodie pulled a very tiny pipe out of his shorts pocket, but I didn't laugh. I kept staring at the mouthpiece until he looked at me and in a split second he read my mind—that I was frightened to share it with him.

"I don't blame you," he said.

He went down to the ocean and dredged the pipe in the salt water,

then wiped the outside of the pipe on his T-shirt. He waited awhile for it to
dry inside, then packed the pipe and handed it to me. I put it in my mouth
and turned my head away from the water and the wind, and he tilted a
silver lighter—also probably swiped from 800—down toward the bowl and
lit up the pot. I took a megasuck of breath. It was the smoothest dope I
had ever smoked. It hardly burned my throat, and it left me feeling like I
was levitating toward the sky, like the slumber parties at which girls
chanted incantations and then lifted one girl's body up, on two fingers
alone, toward the ceiling. I passed the pipe to Dodie. The waves lapped the
sand, the grass rustled on the dunes, and Dodie's body seemed close and
far away from mine at the same time. We sat there for what seemed like
forever.

"I've got to get out of this sun," I finally said.

Dodie gave me a hand up. He offered to drive—slowly—back to the
boat. But even though he clearly was in better shape, I hung on to my
keys. I wanted to drive. Dodie had already taken me, on that morning,
plenty of places I did not want to go.

The beach was wide, and it took awhile to climb back up to the
dunes. Our feet sank so deep it seemed as if our flip-flops would leave a
permanent impression on the sand. As Dodie and I rounded over the last
dune, the sea oats cutting and chafing at our calves, I looked over at my
Toyota, unable to believe my eyes. In my eagerness to get out on the beach
and drink my coffee, I had turned the autoshade the wrong way. In large
red capital letters it read: NEED HELP. PLEASE CALL POLICE.

"Smart move, Lise," Dodie said, as we climbed into the car. "Good
thing no coppers drove by."

I started the engine.

"You might want to take down that autoshade before you start to
drive," Dodie suggested, "unless you really want to get arrested."

The mere thought of being dragged into the station—booked for tres-
passing and possession and perhaps losing my job if Boorman ever ordered
an updated background check—made my stomach turn. I thrust my hands
against the handle, jacked the car door open, and left a stupendous puddle
of yellow and green vomit on the gravel.

Riding side by side in the hot Toyota—my mouth still coated with
vomit, and our bodies coated with nervous sweat—I noticed what had
been disguised in the fresh salt air on the beach: My cousin and I smelled
like low tide beneath the Q Bridge. As we drove through a tiny town
outside Shore Line, church bells were pealing. It was Sunday morning,
and even in the Hamptons, some people on earth still went to church.
Back home our mothers already had been to mass and knelt side by side at

the altar, their mouths open to receive the host. They were probably sitting down to Sunday dinner while we were on the beach blowing weed, my autoshade an open invitation to the law to come mug us and fingerprint us and park us in front of a black phone on an otherwise bare table so we could make our one phone call to someone in the law-abiding world. Dodie wouldn't have hesitated a moment before he dialed 800's number. But who would I have called had I gotten arrested?

The church bells continued to ring as inside myself I repeated like a mantra the name of the man I suddenly knew I was about to lose: *Eben, Eben, Eben.*

Chapter Thirteen

That's Your Real Name

Back at home—where I was surprised to find no messages on my answering machine—I finally faced the enormous question: how to deal with Strauss? To buy time I unplugged the phone on Sunday evening. After a sweaty, restless night of half-sleep, I called in sick to work on Monday morning, then made an appointment at a public health clinic in Tarrytown for that afternoon—the earliest they could get me in, the receptionist claimed, even though I told her it was an emergency, *a real emergency*.

When the long, throaty chirp of the phone pierced the silence of my apartment at 10:00 A.M., I dropped my rosary beads. I'd been doing rounds of Hail Marys, just to calm myself down. I had promised God I would read the Bible from cover to cover, from *In the beginning* or *Let there be light* or whatever that first chapter said, all the way up to the headless horsemen and all that wild Jungian stuff in Revelation—if only He would save Dodie and me, and if only there was a way to hide my exposure to that disease from Strauss.

My voice cracked like an adolescent boy's when I picked up the receiver and said hello.

"Where have you been?" Strauss asked—quietly, to protect against secretaries with big ears. "I called you—several times—last night."

"I unplugged the phone. I went to bed early. I'm not feeling well."

"I figured as much this morning, when I saw you hadn't logged in."

"I see you have your ways of checking up on me."

"I was worried," he said, in a tone that suggested he had spent the weekend stewing about our relationship, while I had been boozing and masturbating and smoking dope and discovering I might have a fatal disease associated with boy hookers and heroin addicts. "I almost came over last night, but I didn't want to risk your wrath."

Because my voice broke again when I told him I felt under the weather, Strauss asked me if I had a cold. This was as good an excuse as any. To add further validity to my sickbed claims, I recklessly added, "I have cramps too." The moment I said it I hoped he didn't remember I just had my period two weeks before.

But he did. "I thought you—"

"It's irregular," I told him.

"You should see a doctor about that."

"I'm going this afternoon."

I heard the creak of his desk chair. "I've told Peg I need to talk to her this afternoon."

"Strauss, don't. Please. I thought we were going to do it together."

"Oh. Is that what you decided?"

"Yes," I said quickly, and he seemed relieved, almost cheerful after that.

"Can I see you tonight?" he asked.

"Actually, I was thinking about retreating into a hut—"

"Just to talk," Strauss said. When his voice lowered and he said, "I give good back rubs," I heard Dodie warning, *Don't undervalue it,* and I began to realize the worth of everything I was on the verge of losing.

"How was your weekend?" I asked, to change the subject.

Strauss said it was fine. He said birthdays always were emotional for his father. He said his nephew walloped him at Uncle Wiggly (sending him several times back to the Cluck-Cluck Chicken House), the twins got carsick and threw up twice—that was two times each, four times all together—his sister was a nervous wreck, his brother-in-law was his usual pompous self, his mother made too much food, the front room smelled of lemon floor wax, the Yankees won one, lost one, and he sneaked into my office very early, before anyone arrived, and left a little something on my desk.

"Lisar."

"What."

"I've missed you."

"I missed you too."

"My parents are eager to meet you."

"You told them?"

"I took the liberty."

I just knew it, there are diamonds on the horizon—

"Congratulations," he added. "You didn't even have to be there to win them over. Within half an hour of my getting home, you were already lovingly referred to as—I hope you don't blister at the epithet—*Ibby's girl.*"

When I got off the phone—promising to call him back later that night—I fingered the blue glass beads of my rosary (a gift from Auntie Beppina on my Confirmation) one last time before I put them away in their plastic pouch. Then I stashed the rosary in my top drawer, under-neath the tie I swiped from Strauss and right beside the brown vial of tiny white sleeping pills I knew I was going to get addicted to in the upcoming weeks. I slathered cold cream on my face, which looked crisped in the mirror. The tight sunburn on my cheeks and shoulders—a dead giveaway that I had spent time on the beach—now could be added to all the other things I'd never be able to hide from Strauss.

I had to come up with something good. A really credible story. Know-ing I didn't have the guts to level with him, I tried to think of ways I could avoid sleeping with Strauss until my test came back clean. I figured a good case of imaginary flu—on top of the period and the cramps—ought to keep him at bay for four or five days at most, long enough to get the results back from the lab. After all those years of trying to weasel my way out of the humiliation of high-school gym, I had become skilled at feigning illness. By affecting some scratchiness in the throat and not washing my face and hair, I knew I could look and sound like the worst of patients.

But what if he showed up at my apartment feeling amorous? Not that he would ever force me. A man like him would never force me. But what if he just wanted to make me feel good? What if he knew—as he probably did, since he trained as premed—that a really sharp orgasm could send even the worst of cramps on their merry way? What if he said, *Just relax and let me take care of you. You know I like to take care of you. . . .*

I told myself: If I already had it, then Strauss probably already had it. If I didn't have it, then Strauss couldn't get it, unless he was screwing someone else behind my back, which he would never do—any more than I would do to him. It hit me, like a dodgeball thrown right into my tummy during recess, that therein was proof I loved him. I wanted to be faithful to him. I wanted him to be faithful to me. And if we were faithful to each other, we could just go on sleeping with each other without anything changing for better or worse, so why should I risk telling him?

As an old proverb put it: *The fish that keeps its mouth shut can't get caught.* I told myself I'd get the test and then clam up.

At the clinic, the patient-registration sheet asked me to identify my-self. On the first dotted line I wrote the same altered name I had the presence of mind to give the receptionist on the phone: *Elisa Dodici.*

Why are you here? the patient-information chart asked.

Confidential, I wrote.

Only in the examination room, sitting on the crinkling wax-paper liner that covered the table, did I tell the nurse—a woman with too-white hair and pink lips—that I needed a test for AIDS. She pursed her lips and said she would get the equipment. When she returned, she did not speak to me while she scrubbed and then suited up in her rubber gloves. I didn't look at her when she hiked the cuff of my white shirt higher, swabbed my inner arm with a yellow sterilization compound, and stabbed the needle into my vein. I made the mistake of looking at the vial of blackish-red blood after she capped it and placed it in the holder by the sink, and my head went lighter than air. The small package from which she took the vial was marked ELISA.

"I think I'm going to faint," I told the nurse, who was scrubbing her hands again. She turned toward me and commanded, "Lie back. Lie back right now on the table."

I obeyed. She exited the room, closing the door behind her. I stared at the stippled tiles on the ceiling—thinking, How could this be happening to me? Me, to whom the dentist always said, "Looking good—not a single cavity" and to whom the gynecologist always chirped, "Your cervix is pink and healthy"? Then there came a frightening knock on the door—strictly *pro forma,* because it was not followed by the polite question, "May I come in?" The doctor charged in, holding my chart. He had on the ominous white coat that had scared me ever since I was five and had to get my shots to enter elementary school. I was relieved to see that he was close to Strauss's age—not old and bald like the doctors who had brusquely examined me as a child. But any hopes I harbored that he would be more understanding were shot to hell when he addressed me as *young lady.*

"Hello, young lady." He closed the door, drew up a stool, and scooted over to me, all the while looking at my chart. "Elisa," he said. "That's your real name?"

I nodded and knew he didn't believe me.

"I'm Dr. O'Brien. How long have you had these fainting spells?"

"I don't have fainting spells."

"The nurse said you almost passed out."

"I haven't fainted in years. I saw the blood. I got scared."

Admitting to fear seemed like the most intimate thing I could confess—that is, until Dr. O'Brien started his questions. He had a whole list of them on his clipboard, and at first he ran through the same ones Dodie asked, about the diarrhea and the night sweats and the lumps.

"I don't have any symptoms," I said.

Dr. O'Brien cleared his throat. He wanted to know why I was getting the test. "Have you had sexual contact with someone who has the disease?"

I shook my head, making the wax-paper liner on the table crinkle.

"Intercourse with a known homosexual?"

I shook my head. More crinkling.

"Known bisexual?"

"Maybe in college. I'm not certain."

"Strictly vaginal sex?"

"Say what?"

"Was there anal penetration?"

"Ouch," I said.

"Just answer the question."

"I've never done that," I said. "That scares me—"

"Sex with a known drug user?"

"Listen," I said. I tried to explain. I told him I had a friend—a male friend—who had the virus. With him I'd shared a razor and silverware and a toothbrush. Once I'd bandaged his finger after he got cut slicing a Spanish onion—

At that point the doctor interrupted. "Unless you had an open sore when you changed his bandage, what you're describing doesn't sound life-threatening to me. There are only two ways this friend could have transmitted it to you: sexual contact or intravenous drug use."

"All right. We shared a needle."

"How many times?"

"Just once."

"Did anyone else share it?"

"Just us," I said.

"When was this?"

"I don't know. Nineteen-eighty. Eighty-one? It might have been in eighty-two."

"Are you sexually active now?"

Why did I feel like a slut when I said yes?

"Multiple partners?"

"Not at the moment."

"But at other times, yes? And is there a partner now?"

To hear Strauss described as a *partner* made me bristle, and I suddenly saw why Dodie always had despised the term, because it reduced the other person to merely his sexual function. *Boyfriend* also was stupid and adolescent and demeaning. There just were no acceptable names for lovers outside of the marriage bond.

"There's somebody," I said. "But I don't want to tell him any of this."

The wheels on his stool creaked as Dr. O'Brien moved back slightly from the table. "That's your decision."

"I mean, if I test positive, of course I'll have to tell him. How long do I have to wait for the results?"

"You're not off the hook with this test. It isn't foolproof. There are false negatives and even some positives. If this one is negative, you'll have to have another in six months."

"Six months!" I thought, *I can't pretend to have my period for six months. I can't even have the flu for that long, and Strauss knows I've already had mono, so now I'm up the creek.* I started to sit up, felt light-headed, and lay back down again. "You don't get it; this is a serious relationship. I can't tell him. I mean, I love him. Can't you tell me what the chances are that I have it?"

He looked annoyed. "If it was just that one needle—and a Band-Aid—the chances are slim you have it. Your other behavior, it seems to me, has put you at greater risk."

"What other behavior?"

"You've talked of multiple partners. Some of whose sexual activity you don't seem entirely sure of. And they in turn have been with others whose activity you have no way of monitoring."

I turned my head and watched as he scribbled something on the clipboard. Just as I suspected, he wore a wedding band on his left hand.

"How many sexual partners—total—have you had?" he asked.

"I don't know. I don't keep track. I mean, after five it seemed like there wasn't any reason to count, and after ten there didn't seem any reason to stop, because I'd never get myself back again, and God, what's with this interrogation? You're not my conscience. I have my own conscience."

"For your own good and the good of others, then, I hope you'll listen to it." He stood up. "The current Board of Health recommendation is that you notify everyone you've been with for the past five years—"

"Five years!" I said, thinking of Davey and Brian and the impotent professor and all the others on my dance card, a long list that seemed to go on and on, like *le donne di Don Giovanni,* and made me realize that when it came to promiscuity, I could give Dodie a real run for the money. "But that's only if I test positive, right?"

"That's up to you." His voice was irritated. "If you can't or won't call them, you can write down their names, and someone from the Board will notify them to have a test. It's done confidentially. No one can trace it back to you."

He went into the drawer beside the sink and took out a card, preprinted with the Board of Health number, which I was supposed to call in seventy-two hours for my results and with any other information I might want to share with the counselor who was on the other end of the line. He held the card over me like a threat. "Sit up now, please. But keep your head down."

He gave me a spiel about condoms. About monogamous relationships. About the percentage of false negatives and positives. The nurse
brought some juice. I paid by cash at the desk and slunk out the front
door. On the way home I stopped at a 7-Eleven and bought a pack of
Trojans and a Little Debbie crumb cake. To this I added a last-minute
impulse purchase—a Big Joe to Go cup of hazelnut coffee. I sat out in the
parking lot trying to nurse my cares away with this comfort food. By the
time I got back it was five-thirty, and the way the light waned in my living-
room window reminded me that fall and winter were coming. I thought of
pumpkins and turkeys and tinsel, and how the great chain of sexual connections suddenly seemed like a string of Christmas lights—one dysfunc-
tional bulb could cause the entire series to go dark within an instant.

I stored the Trojans beneath my bed.

Just like my mother, I always kept a coffee cup full of dull yellow
pencils and a light-green steno pad by the phone, although I rarely had to
write down any messages. I took up the steno pad and a pencil and sat
down on my couch to record the names of my sexual partners. Then I
tossed the steno pad aside, got out a college-ruled legal pad, and started to
cover the page with names. I also listed the few addresses I had or remembered, most of which amounted to nothing more specific than the bor-
oughs of New York. I saw I had done more men from Brooklyn than from
Manhattan, and more men from Manhattan than the Bronx. I saw I had
never had anything more than oral sex with anyone from Staten Island. I
saw I had never slept with a doctor, or a lawyer, or a priest, or an Asian,
or—post–high school, at least—any man with less than a high-school di-
ploma. I saw I had a bad pattern of getting involved with ugly Eastern
European men, who drank too much and growled *Leee-za, Leee-za* as they
pumped away at me, and who always looked clinically depressed when
they were finished, as if the physical exertion of fucking me had brought
them to the point where they needed to jump over a cliff. I saw I had tried
on men the way some women tried on clothes in a department store—
carelessly leaving them draped on hooks or rumpled on the dressing-room
floor until the saleswoman could rescue them and put them back onto the
hanger.

Right before the end of the list—which I hoped was comprehensive,
because the thought of even one more name was utterly staggering—I
thought how strange it would be to send this sheet of paper to my mother,
unsigned, so she would open it and say, "*Madonna*, the weird things you
get in the mail these days—do you suppose this is part of one of those
wacky chain letters?"

I chewed on the end of the pencil. There was one more line left. I pressed my finger hard on the pencil and added the name of the man, with the exact address and the phone number I had memorized within a week after I began dating him: *Eben Strauss.*

Then I drew in my breath, full of hope, and thought: Why not? Why not have the Board of Health call Strauss and tell him that an anonymous former partner had submitted his name for testing, so that Strauss would be forced to come to me, as he no doubt would, and say, "Lisar. I have something awful to tell you. Please keep an open mind. Please listen."

This plan momentarily struck me as the ideal solution. But as I stared at the last line on the legal pad, I realized I had no idea how many women Strauss had taken into bed before me. I knew there was a steady girl in college—described rather ruefully as *Well, you only fall in love like that once in your life, thank God*—and in his twenties, someone he said he hadn't cared for, and in his early thirties, the psychiatrist to whom he had been briefly engaged until he decided it wasn't right. But since then? Since the fiancée? Strauss was thirty-six, the age at which his parents more than expected him to be married, the age at which the number of adventures usually began declining as opposed to escalating. He had already *sown his oats.* But where? With who? How many?

There hasn't been anyone else. In quite some time.

I bit the end of the pencil so hard the eraser came off in my mouth. I spit it out. It was no use. Strauss and I obviously had not shared the same circulation rate. One call from the Board of Health and he would either intuit the identity of the *anonymous party,* or else he would show up at my apartment, take one look at my ashen, penitent face, and find out.

I picked up the phone and called Strauss. He arrived at my apartment an hour and a half later. And then he showed me just how rough and rude he could play. In fifteen swift minutes our relationship was over.

Chapter Fourteen

Hurts Is a Verb, Not a Possessive

In the long dim months to come, I would play and replay that conversation, like a foreign-language cassette that spoke a dialogue I needed to repeat but couldn't master. I remembered every last hateful, hurtful, blown-out-of-proportion line we uttered, beginning with the undignified *ouch!* that escaped my lips when he first embraced me and the palm of his hand—like the press of an iron—came down against my sunburned back.

"Did I hurt you?" he asked, pulling away and holding me at arm's length, his head bent so he could see me better in the dark of the hallway. "You look awful, Lisar. I mean, not yourself."

"I went to the doctor."

"What did he—" Strauss stopped. "Excuse me. I've been hanging around Peg all day. What did he *or she* say?"

"It was a he," I said. "And he told me bad news."

Strauss blinked. "About your period?"

"I don't have my period."

He pushed up his glasses. "But I'm confused. On the phone. You said you did." He hesitated. "Is it late? Are you trying to tell me it's late?"

For a second I paused. I hadn't even thought of that one—the oldest ruse in the book, performed by countless wily heroines in nineteenth-century novels: snaring a man into marriage by faking pregnancy. The setup was perfect: In the Frick I'd told Strauss I'd forgotten to take my pill. That such fraud was beneath me, but not my depraved imagination, sent me even further into despair about myself. I swallowed hard and told him, "It isn't late."

"Oh," he said. He gave me a sad smile. "Help me out here, Lisar, with my dumb-guy etiquette. I guess I'm supposed to say I'm relieved."

I bit my lip. "I wouldn't know. What a man was supposed to say—"

"Of course not."

I took a step backward. "I need to tell you something."

He looked at me expectantly.

My voice faltered. "I'm trying to do the right thing."

"Of course."

"Why 'of course'?"

"Because that's the kind of person you are."

I shook my head. He stared at me for a moment, then looked back at the door, almost as if he wished he had never come into my apartment in the first place. "What do you want to tell me?"

"Anything but what I have to tell you."

His hand went up to his jacket. I had seen him do that at Boorman: touch his lapel, and then his tie—as if it were a talisman—before he went into an important meeting. "Sit down, please," he said.

I took the couch. He took the chair. I started to speak, then put my knuckles up to my mouth. Strauss held out the Kleenex I had parked on the coffee table—I'd already gone through half a box that morning. I took the box, grabbed a tissue, and blew my nose.

He winced. "Something happened at work while I was gone, didn't it?"

"It doesn't have to do with work," I said.

"What does it have to do with, then?"

"This weekend—"

"Where were you this weekend, anyway?"

I dropped the Kleenex to my lap. "I was at the beach. I went with my cousin to the beach."

Strauss gave me a hard look. Then he reached over and turned on the floor lamp. "I thought that was a sunburn on your face," he said, in the same disapproving tone my father had used when Carol and I came home—*red as a couple of Maine lobsters!*—after baking ourselves on the scorched, gravelly sand at Lighthouse Beach. "Why didn't your cousin give you some sunscreen?"

"Stop blaming him."

Strauss looked annoyed. "Who's blaming him? I don't even *know* him—"

"It's my fault, it's all my fault—"

"*What* is your fault, Lisar?"

I told him. And after I told him, the refrigerator in the kitchen let off a sudden hum—like a low, far-off droning of a bomber plane—and then the sound spiraled down to silence, which was followed by Strauss's thin-wire whip of question after question I didn't want to answer: *Why did you lie? Even if you did shoot up only once, once is enough, isn't it? But if it was only once, the chances are slim, unless you've done other things to put yourself at risk? What else have you done? What else haven't you told me?*

"I slept with a lot of guys," I said.

He started to say something, then stopped. "How many?" he finally asked. "Be honest, that's all I'm asking from you now."

"Enough to fill up a sheet of paper," I said.

He put his forehead against his hand. "You're joking, I hope."

"Why would I joke about something like that?"

"A better question is why would you *do* something like that?"

"You wouldn't ask me why if I were a guy—"

"Don't change the subject. This has nothing to do with being male or female."

"It has to do with a double standard."

"It has to do with—I don't know what to call it but self-respect—"

"You said yourself you'd once been with someone you hadn't cared for—"

"—and sheer numbers. *The numbers.*"

I clutched the box of Kleenex on my lap. "What about your numbers? How many women have you been with?"

"I don't owe you that information."

"But I owe it to you?"

"You do, and you know it, or else you wouldn't have initiated this conversation—but what is eight to your what? Two dozen?"

"One-third."

He glared at me. "I can do my math, Lisar."

I pressed my foot hard against the leg of the coffee table. "All right. So I made some mistakes—"

"But in this day and age, to make mistakes of that magnitude—haven't you been reading the newspaper? And the dishonesty of not telling me, that's what I can't stand. The lying. And beyond that . . . to be so reckless with yourself—"

I shoved the box of Kleenex onto the couch cushion. "You didn't mind my recklessness when you pushed me onto your carpet."

"Wait a second," he said. "I didn't push . . . I didn't set out to hurt you. I never set out to hurt you, and now I see there's this hurtful hidden side of you—no, don't interrupt me—that shows a real want of judgment, a lack of moral sense, and what in God's name are you praying for at night, Lisar—"

"For forgiveness! Because I had an abortion!"

My face felt on fire from my sunburn. I had a good long time to savor the sensation, because Strauss sat there, for several moments, in silence.

Finally he looked down at the back of his hand and asked, "Was it mine?"

"*Ours.*"

"How could you have—"

"But it wasn't yours—I mean ours—whatever name you want to call it—"

"Whose, then?" Strauss said. "Or shouldn't I ask?"

"It was right before I met you. Remember you asked me if I'd been involved with someone else in New York—"

"He forced you to have it?"

"I never told him. The man was married, and don't give me that look, Strauss! You thought I was married when you first met me, and that never stopped you from coming down to my office—"

"I came down to your office in a professional capacity—"

"Did you?" I asked, surprised at the threatening tone that came out of my mouth.

"—and I never would have . . . initiated a relationship with you . . . if I had thought you were married—"

"What do you know about marriage?"

"I can use my imagination!" Strauss said. "I have used my imagination on that point, Lisar, more than once. Use your imagination now: Can't you see how wrong that was of you, to come between two people?"

"Use yours: What if the two people are grossly unhappy? What if you had married this other woman, this fiancée of yours, and were utterly miserable and then you met me—"

"And got just as miserable with you?" His face flushed. "Stop putting me into these hypothetical situations to deflect attention from your own mistakes—"

I leaned forward on the couch. "Who are you to judge? You have no idea what it's like to go into a clinic and make that kind of choice—do you think I felt good about it, do you think it was any kind of choice at all? What was I supposed to do, go home and have the baby in front of my sister, who couldn't even get pregnant, and live with my mother for the rest of my life? Oh, what do you know about *anything*, sitting there in your coat and tie? You're a man—"

"Why do you say *you're a man* as if it's a fault? What kind of man do you expect would understand even half of what you've told me? And don't tell me your cousin—"

"I will tell you my cousin!" I said. "He's a better man than you are. He at least has compassion; he at least understands that people make mistakes! He at least stood by me. How could I ever have thought you would stand by me?"

"How could I ever have thought . . ." Strauss's voice trailed off. "All right. Let's put a stop to this right now. We've both said enough."

"More than enough."

We hesitated, as if we were listening to the echo of our own words against the walls. Then we both stood. Because I was in my stockinged feet—without the benefit of higher heels—I had to lift my chin to look him dead-level in the face.

Strauss held out his hand—not for my hand, but for the phone number of the Board of Health. Or the clinic. Where, he said, he hoped a man could be tested confidentially.

"They give you a number," I said. "Or you can use a false name."

"Like a criminal."

"Exactly," I said. "You take this test, and then you have to take another in six months."

I handed him the card. I already had the number memorized. He tucked it into the inside pocket of his coat.

"About work," he said, in a voice that sounded too purposefully cool, the way my own voice had frosted over not to show my fear when I once had to tell a guy on the subway platform, *Here's the money in my wallet, I'm giving you all the money in my wallet, now please step away.*

"What about work?" I asked, trying to control the shakiness in my own throat.

He spoke carefully, as if he suspected I would memorize his words to use against him at some later date. "I blame myself for a lot of this," he said. "For most of this. It's obvious that this has been a mistake from the word go, that I—that *we*—both used poor judgment. I want you to know I won't use this against you at work. But I think you should promise me the same."

"You have my word."

"If nothing else, we owe that much to each other."

"I just gave you my word," I said. "For all you think my word is worth."

He hesitated. "I want to trust you on this."

"You're just saying that because you're afraid I'm going to do you in."

"You have . . . you may have some ammunition, but—"

"But what? You have the corner office. And you could drive me right out of mine—"

"That would be indecent," he said. "You don't know me very well if you think I'm capable of that."

"Anyone is capable of anything."

"But to live like you are—to *live* like you're capable—is wrong. I need to go to bed at night and not be sorry for what I've done that day."

"You can't sleep at night anyway," I said. Then—because there didn't seem any point in trying to hold it back any longer—I started crying again. "I hope you lose even more sleep over this one."

"But I never wanted to hurt you," he repeated. "Look at me. Look at what you've done here, Lisar." But I couldn't—I had to look away—because suddenly there seemed no more wrenching sight in the world than a man on the edge of tears.

Gray fog rolled into Westchester every morning; thick rain fell all that September. As autumn came, I tore off the pages on my desk calendar and remembered the depression that always came with winter, the despair I used to feel as I shoveled my parents' long, wide driveway after the fifth or sixth bad snowstorm of the season. When I propped the wet metal shovel against the wall of the garage, I used to look longingly at our red-and-white-striped beach umbrella—covered with cobwebs—that lay folded on our old redwood picnic table, and my feet never felt so soggy nor my hands so numb with cold than when I thought of all the months left of winter before I could nestle my body in the sand and gaze up into the star-shape spokes of that beach umbrella.

That was the way I felt after Strauss walked out of my apartment: like I'd never be warm again.

In the dark hours of the morning, when the alarm carved its insistent monotone into my dreams, I hit the button and rolled over, so groggy from the sleeping pill I took the night before that I often fell back into a deep slumber. I forced myself to roll out and stumble into the kitchen to plug in the percolator, which I had set up with coffee and water the night before. While the coffee maker did its happy little song-and-dance routine, I blasted myself awake with a shower so hot the mirror stayed steamed for close to half an hour. I ate a granola bar and drank two cups of coffee while slumped on the couch in my bathrobe. I spent fifteen minutes getting dressed and made up (on the off chance I bumped into exactly who I was trying to avoid at work). After pulling on my gloves and coat, I raced downstairs and started the car. Even on the grayest, cloudiest of days, I wore sunglasses, because I routinely wept on the way to work.

At Boorman—much as I tried—I couldn't avoid Strauss. I looked into the rearview mirror and saw his Audi trailing mine, three cars back, on the long driveway that led to the parking lot. I came careening out of the ladies' room and practically knocked him down along with a squadron of statisticians, a bowling ball to their ten pins. To brace myself for those unexpected meetings, I always looked for his car when I swung by the VIP lot. When the Audi was gone for days at a time, I thanked God for inventing places like Springfield and Saint Louis and Kansas City, because Strauss was there and that meant I could roam around the halls of Boorman without bumping into him as I delivered a report to another office or headed to the cafeteria. But I also was depressed because I knew that was one more day I wouldn't see him, one less chance that he would stop me— call me—and say, *This is ridiculous, I've been a fool (and you've been an even bigger one!), but what are you doing tonight, what are you doing for the rest of your life, do you want to get back together again?*

He proved stubborn, and so did I. I, too, did not pick up the phone or log on to my computer to send him a message. Instead, when I opened my desk drawer at work, I stared at the Cracker Jack surprise he left on my desk early in the morning on that day we broke up. The surprise came wrapped in a thin paper packet printed with repeated images of the Cracker Jack sailor boy, and the bulbous shape within turned out to be a miniature blue whistle imprinted on the side with the word POLICE. Sometimes I imagined that if I raised the whistle to my lips and blew, he would hear the lame, sputtery sound that crescendoed into a high trill, and like a dog responding to his owner, he would run to me.

So why didn't I whistle for him, especially after my initial test came back clean? Why didn't I try to talk to him instead of waiting for him to talk to me?

"Lisa," Dodie told me on the phone. "Forget whose fault it is. You're negative, which means he's probably negative, so call him and declare a truce."

"I can't. I won't. I'm not going to yodel up to him on his moral high ground. I don't even know why I want to be with him anymore." Just to test how credible it sounded—as well as to gauge its dramatic qualities—I quoted one of Donna Dilano's lines from *Stop It Some More,* which I was considering retitling *If I'm Hearing You Correctly, You're Saying It's Over.* "I already had a father," I told Dodie, "and I don't need another man around to make me feel like shit!"

"Christ, I hope you didn't say *that* soap-opera line to him."

"I didn't!" I said, not bothering to report that Strauss and I had exchanged more than a few other choice phrases that could have been straight off a *General Hospital* episode.

"If you *did* say that," Dodie assured me, "you can as good as count it over."

"It is over. But if it's over, why does he keep watching me? I'm sure, at work, he's watching me."

"Of course he's watching you. He's probably scared shitless you're going to blow him out of the water."

"But I promised not to."

"Maybe he's looking for a chance to give you the boot."

"He promised he wouldn't."

"You must still be crazy in love with each other if you're holding to those kinds of promises."

Maybe we were. But love lived next door to hate. There was nothing to keep either one of us from holding a gun to the other's head and firing. The whole thing seemed as simple (and as complex) as Dr. Seuss's anti-Iron Curtain manifesto, *The Butter Battle Book*—in which the respective enemies climbed up on the wall, each holding their Big-Boy Boomeroos, and threatened to blow each other into pork and wee beans. Which side would drop it?

"Every day when I go into work," I told Dodie, "I'm terrified I'm going to get the can."

"He's more likely to get it than you are. Although you never know." Dodie cleared his throat. He had a lot of phlegm in his throat lately. "What news from the feminist contingent, such as it may be at Boorman?"

"Doctor Peg's been out a lot. I think she's at Hilton Head, trying to squeeze in every last moment of golf season."

"You're lucky she didn't boink you over your bimbo head with her five-iron."

"To think that we came within twenty-four hours of telling her. . . . well, either she's blessedly oblivious, or she's just acting that way."

Dr. Peggy Schoenbarger had more than just a physical resemblance to Beatrix Potter. The more I watched her, the more I thought she was acting like the omniscient author, manipulating me and Strauss like a couple of fierce bad rabbits—determined to push us into a hole until we gave up and confessed. At the end of September she started toying with me. She called me to her office one day and I noticed, with a start, that my quarterly employee evaluation—the one Strauss had prepared—was on her desk.

"I've heard a rumor, Ms. Diodetto," she said.

My knees weakened. I sat down and pressed my thighs together so hard that later I would find a small bruise along the inside of my kneecap. "You don't strike me as the type of person who listens to rumors, Dr. Schoenbarger."

"I don't usually. Nor do I repeat them. But this one interested me. And I think I will listen to this one and repeat it back to you, just to get your reaction." She gave me a prescient pause. "It concerns Mr. Strauss."

"Oh."

"Mr. Strauss seems to think Karen might not be coming back."

"Oh."

"In which case her position would be vacant. In which case, you'd be the logical replacement." She watched me carefully. "Mr. Strauss seemed to be of the mind that you'd be interested."

"He did?"

"Aren't you? It's been noted you're here almost every weekend."

I was there all right—and so was my fictional alter ego. *Donna Dilano was having the time of her life. If she couldn't be a professional cartoonist, at least the savage caricatures she drew of Thomas Akins (who had most cruelly jilted her) functioned both as therapy and revenge!*

"And you've shown a lot of dedication," Peggy said. "On your last performance evaluation Mr. Strauss praised your doggedness—"

That hardly sounded like a compliment.

"—and your hard work. I forgot how he put it. The phrasing seemed a little poetic coming from Eben."

Peg thought it was poetic; I knew it was pure plagiarism, because Strauss, as a little inside joke between the two of us, had gone back and rewritten the evaluation to quote the first chapter of *Stop It Some More* almost verbatim—changing only the tense and the name:

Donna Dilano proved herself to be the kind of employee who never took the last cup of coffee and left the glass pot on the burner.

Lisa Diodetto has proven herself to be the kind of employee who never takes the last cup of coffee and leaves the pot on the burner.

"Here it is," she said, flipping through the evaluation. "Something about coffee. So you like your coffee. Eben also is partial to it. Caffeine is bad for your health. It puts a tremendous strain on your heart. But let me get to the point—"

"Please do," I said. "I mean, I'm eager to hear what you have to say."

She raised an eyebrow. "There are some concerns about your—how shall I say this?—*attitude.*"

"I don't have an attitude," I said. "I have . . . strong opinions."

"Which get voiced, loud and clear? Especially after lunch?"

"Lunch?"

"Mr. Strauss seems to think you don't eat enough—"

"What?"

"—and that in the afternoon your blood sugar drops and you encounter some problems with authority."

"That's ridiculous."

"That's what I told him. Although I do think you can stand to eat more. Quite a bit more." Peg quickly turned the page on my evaluation, as if embarrassed to have caught herself breaking one of the cardinal rules of feminism, which stated that a woman should never comment on another woman's weight. "Now, let's look at this category of collegiality. Mr. Strauss wrote: *In due time, Ms. Diodetto will better understand the dynamics of corporate life.* What does this mean?"

"I have no idea. Maybe Mr. Strauss wrote that after *he* skipped his graham crackers and milk."

She gave me a level gaze.

"I've noticed he has a problem with clarity in his prose," I added.

"He can be a bit windy in his memos. But this is a low score here. A six."

"Mr. Strauss is a hard judge."

"But a fair one, don't you think?"

"Not all of the time."

"You didn't agree with the score? You signed it."

"I didn't want to argue. I don't like arguing with him."

"That's not his side of the story. He said he wrote that of you because you *were* argumentative. So are you or aren't you?"

"What?"

"Argumentative with him?"

Sometimes I could surprise even myself with my own chutzpah. "I hope you don't mind me making sexist generalizations, Dr. Schoenbarger."

"Proceed."

"But when a man says a woman is argumentative, it's usually because she doesn't agree one hundred and one percent with something he has to say."

She cracked a grim smile. I wondered how many stubborn run-ins she herself had with Strauss in the back of those stretch limousines.

"We'll have to get you out on the green sometime, Ms. Diodetto. Mr. Strauss has an awful slice. How are you with a driver?"

"Merciless," I assured her, and with that remark, I was as good as promoted. I also was as good as fucked.

"Eighteen holes," she said, "come spring."

I gulped. The only time I'd ever been on a golf course—other than the Putt-Putt variety—was to illegally bellywhop on my sled down the

steep slopes of the municipal golf course. Not a single item in my wardrobe was kelly green. I was sure I'd look as foolish as Benjamin Bunny in a
tam-o'-shanter. But there was no backing out now. Peg's eyes seemed to
gleam at the very thought of my beating the pants off Strauss.

          October was another rainy mess, and most of the leaves were
down by the time the secretaries threw a loathsome baby shower for
Karen (*Now, each one of you women—even the ones who don't have children—write down a few words of advice and encouragement for Karen on a
three-by-five card, and we'll put all these cards into a little book that she can
enjoy reading during her two A.M. feedings!*). After Karen gave birth to a
boy—and I got used to the idea that she'd be returning at the end of her
six-week maternity leave—I got called down to Human Resources by the
chief honcho, a man with the country-western handle of Wayne Lamarr.
As I walked into his office, my heart thumped to see the inscrutable Dr.
Margaret Schoenbarger also sitting there. *This is it,* I thought, *I am out
the door.*
     "Greetings, Ms. Diodetto," she said.
     I tried to say *hi,* but the odd syllable that came out of my mouth
sounded more like *hoy!* I nodded at Wayne Lamarr, and to distract myself I
wondered if he was from Tennessee or Kentucky.
     Mr. Lamarr greeted me cordially in a New Jersey accent and asked
me to sit down. I lowered myself into the visitor's throne opposite his desk
as if it were an electric chair.
     "We're waiting on Mr. Strauss," Mr. Lamarr told me, and I immedi-
ately looked around for the wastebasket, terrified I would throw up. After
two quivery minutes—during which time Mr. Lamarr and Dr. Peg vigorously debated the real reason behind the rising green fees at the local
country club—Strauss strode in. I bolted up from my chair as if the priest
had entered the room during catechism assembly and the nuns had commanded, "Stand for Father!"
     Strauss saved me by shaking my hand and telling me in a deliberately
calm voice, "Please sit down. This is very nice news we have for you here."
     He let Mr. Wayne Lamarr deliver it. Karen had decided that mother-
hood took precedence over her career (here Peggy frowned) and given her
notice. After consultation with all parties concerned, Human Resources
was pleased to offer me Karen's former position.
     I didn't dare look at anyone but Mr. Lamarr. "I thought it had to be
advertised," I said. "Because of affirmative action."
     The way Mr. Lamarr focused on his pencil holder made it clear that

the trio of executives assembled here *had some concerns* about this very issue. "We're getting around that by—"

"We're not getting around anything," Peg interrupted. "We're treating this as an internal promotion. Besides, she's a woman—"

I saw Strauss's loafer shift forward on the carpet.

"—and no one can—or *should*—object to having more women in management positions at Boorman," Peggy finished.

A hostile testosterone-laden silence followed. "I accept," I blurted out—two words that probably cost me a thousand dollars each in terms of salary negotiation. "I mean, I'm interested," I said. "Could you outline the responsibilities and the compensation, please?"

During the conversation that ensued, I tried to determine how vigorously—and using what means besides the affirmative-action argument—Strauss had tried to block my promotion. I finally concluded he had done just the opposite, probably to avoid creating suspicion about his own bad behavior. He played it cool throughout the whole meeting. When it was his turn to speak, he only said, "You should know by now what I expect of you, Lisar."

At this mention of my mispronounced name, Dr. Schoenbarger looked at me closely, as if she had just been informed she had been calling me by the wrong handle since my first day at Boorman. I recrossed my legs and felt sweat collecting in my panty-hose crotch.

Formal notification of my promotion came in a letter—typed on twenty-pound cream letterhead—signed *Eben Strauss* and *Dr. Margaret Schoenbarger*. Formal acceptance consisted of my typed letter back to Peggy and Strauss thanking them for their confidence in my work and promising to live up to their highest expectations. I did not mention the glaring typo I found in their letter just above the salutation (*Dear Ms. Diodetto*), which said *Research and Developement*. I proofread my letter twenty times before I asked the secretary—in a tone of voice that I hoped conveyed my new authority—to deliver it.

Being a boss, I found, was not easy. First of all, I couldn't be late to work. *Greetings* got dropped from my vocabulary; I ceased referring to the CEO as *Booze-Hound Dick*. I had to hang around at the office later than everyone else (which I always did anyway), and nobody in my own department suggested doughnut runs or chats about weekend activities over the Mr. Coffee machine. My coworkers—now my subordinates—were sometimes truculent and other times so eager to kiss my ass I knew they were about to ask for next Friday and the following Monday off, if that was okay by me? Only half of them congratulated me with any sincerity after my promotion was announced in a staff meeting.

I tried to convince myself that nobody at Boorman—except Hook and probably Gussie and now maybe even Peggy—knew about me and Strauss. That wishful thinking got squashed on the sunny November day that Karen came back to show off her new baby. When she brought the plastic carrier filled with her sleeping, swaddled infant into the office she once used to occupy, I felt awkward. The moment I moved into her old space, I had the housekeeping staff replace the blinds, strip the prints off the walls, and move all the furniture around—the way divorced people were reported to redecorate the moment the spouse moved out of the picture. I thought this would bother Karen. But she merely put the baby in its carrier down by my desk and told me it was great to see me.

"Do you mind if I shut this door?" she asked.

"Not at all."

"One of the reasons I came today was because I thought we should have a little chat."

Little chat certainly sounded threatening. As she shut the door, I reminded myself that I was in the power seat now—the office chair—while she was relegated to the straight-back chair that was clearly the visitor's spot. I asked her how she was feeling, admired her baby (a sweet, chubby-cheeked muffin with fingers so precious I couldn't resist leaning over to stroke them), and thanked her for recommending me for her old position.

Karen told me she had every confidence that I could *steer through a storm.* Continuing the nautical theme—but mixing metaphors to the point where I had to wonder how much sleep she really was getting at night—she told me, "We have a first-rate crew here, and even though we may have a few unhappy campers in our division, we have lots of support from the commanders up top." She paused. "Things change, of course, when you're the one who has to give the orders."

I nodded.

"You really have to watch what you say and do."

"That's right."

"I hope you don't mind a little advice."

"Not at all."

"I mean it in a friendly way."

"Of course."

"I don't work here anymore, so I don't have an ulterior motive—"

I acknowledged the truth of that statement. The baby gurgled and sighed. After a quick look downward to check on her new job and life, Karen told me hurriedly that she thought I should know that some of the girls in the office were bound to be difficult because they felt I did not deserve this promotion.

My face grew hot. "I don't see why. I work just as hard, if not harder, than everyone else. After all, I'm in here every weekend—"

"Lisa, please. I recommended you for this job, I want you to succeed, I'm trying to help. I just think you need to be careful. There's this gossip—"

"Gossip about what?"

"Totally unwarranted, I'm sure. That you're involved with someone on top."

"That isn't true," I told Karen, thankful for once I wasn't lying, but scared that the oil slick of gossip had spread so far that even someone who no longer worked on the premises was privy to the information. Because I knew that after she left my office she would make the rounds of the entire company to show off her baby (sharing her news and perhaps disseminating some of mine with the lead-in phrase, *I don't want to spread rumors, but . . .*), I told her, "In fact, I'm dating someone in the city. He's my financial adviser. We're pretty serious about each other."

"Oh, how wonderful," she said. "I'm glad to hear that."

"We're talking marriage—"

"How wonderful!" she repeated. "Lisa, I'm so pleased for you. You really deserve to be happy."

I gave her a tight smile. "I wouldn't mind knowing where you heard that other story."

Karen shook her head and said she was sorry she ever brought this up in the first place. "I never believed that story about you anyway," she said, leaning down to stroke her baby's foot. "Just for a laugh, they said it was Mr. Strauss—"

I tried to eke out a chuckle, but only a pig-snort surfaced from my nose and mouth.

"I know how he bores you, Lisa. And who would do such a stupid thing with Dr. Schoenbarger standing right there as—what did you call her that time?—*chieftess of the feminist police*? Besides—not that it matters— everyone knows Mr. Strauss is probably gay—"

"What makes you think that?" I asked.

Fortunately Karen was too engrossed in her own baby to pick up on the sharpness in my voice. "In all the years I've worked here, he's never once been seen with a woman. He's never brought a date to the Christmas party—"

"Maybe he just dates Jews."

"Oh. That would make sense."

"Why would that make sense?"

Karen looked embarrassed. "I just meant I never thought of that issue."

"Oh," I said. "I thought maybe you were expressing disapproval of interfaith relationships."

"Why would I be opposed to interfaith relationships? You know my husband is Methodist and I grew up in the Congregational church."

"*That* must present some real problems."

"They're not insurmountable. What I meant to say was that I forgot Mr. Strauss was Jewish."

"But you remembered that he was a probable homosexual."

She looked at me closely. "Did I say something to offend you? Lisa, now I'm quite sure I've said something offensive to you—"

"Not at all," I said, quickly trying to cover my tracks. "You know, I have a cousin who's gay—"

"I'm so sorry."

"—and my boyfriend—well, really, just between you and me, my *fiancé*—he's Jewish, that's all, and ever since I've been dating him I've gotten kind of sensitive to . . . um . . . religious issues. . . ."

Karen looked worried. "I hope you know what you're getting into, Lisa. I mean, I wish you the best of luck."

I gave Karen another smile that made my lips hurt and turned the conversation back toward her baby. Karen sat there singing the praises of breast-feeding so long I was sure her boobs would start leaking milk all over her monogrammed sweater. She finally wound up her La Leche League lecture by saying, "Where has the time gone? I promised to stop in and say hello to everyone. I suppose I'll start with Mr. Strauss."

Although I knew it might get me into deep doo-doo, I just couldn't resist. "You really think Mr. Strauss is gay?" I asked.

"Don't you?"

"I'm usually pretty dense about that kind of stuff," I told her. "But I'm curious. How you get that impression. Of a guy's gayness. Or gaiety. Or whatever you want to call it."

"Well. Little things. For starters, he's a good dresser—"

"Oh, I don't know about that. He's got some ugly ties."

"And he sent me flowers when I was told to stay in bed. And flowers again when the baby was born. I mean, he's just too nice to be straight—"

"Now, now," I said. "What does that say about your attitude toward men?"

"Well, Lisa," she said, "*your* attitude toward men is very clear."

"What is my attitude?" I asked. "Tell me."

It was my good fortune that the baby chose this moment first to gurgle, then to open its mouth and throw up—a big yellow cheesy gob that looked and smelled revolting.

"Oh God," Karen said. "How awful. I'm so sorry—"

"Quite all right," I said, thrilled she would have to clean the vomit up.

The baby started to cry.

"We'll be leaving now," Karen said.

"Of course." I smiled, wished Karen well, and told her good luck with her baby—but I did not chuck his cheery little upchucked chin before I sent them on their way. As my final send-off, I pleasantly threatened her, "I'll be sure to invite you to my bridal shower."

After she departed, leaving the sour smell of her baby behind, I clutched one of my blue pencils so hard it snapped between my fingers. Then I logged on to my word-processing program and began updating my résumé. Two hours later I was in the ladies' room, and a designer from the art shop stopped me. She ducked her head to check if there were any feet beneath the stall doors before she whispered, "I know it's supposed to be a secret—but congratulations, I heard you're tying the knot!"

Strauss and I got our comeuppance at the next divisional meeting, held in the small auditorium, where Human Resources was due to present the new sexual-harassment code. Attendance was de rigueur. For legal reasons—*Boorman Pharmaceuticals is required by law to fully educate each of its employees about the policies and procedures of said sexual-harassment code*—roll was taken; we each were required to sign our names on a numbered legal sheet before we sat down. I deliberately straggled behind. Strauss's overly bold signature was on line 23. I was number 27—and also number 28, because as I signed my name I took wild glances up and down the auditorium to find out where he was sitting so I could snag a seat on the other side of the room. My signature ended up spilling onto two lines and looked like it came from the pen of a split personality.

My efforts went for naught; Mr. Wayne Lamarr waved me down to the front. Just in case there were any questions on the wording, he asked me (as the editor who put the seal on the final draft) to sit in the front row—along with the social worker who was going to give us a canned presentation, a company lawyer, and our leaders, Dr. Peggy Schoenbarger and Eben Strauss.

That morning—knowing I would see Strauss in this most absurd of settings—I had deliberately donned a mixture of the provocative and the respectable. Over the Natori bra and underwear Strauss had given me, I put on a semitransparent silk blouse and a black skirt, making the whole thing look chaste by covering it up with a long wool jacket in pristine pastel blue.

Although my skirt was above the knee, it was not high enough to warrant the sober, level stare I got from Dr. Schoenbarger as I passed by. At that moment I was sure she knew something more than she had last week. My face flushed as I headed for the last seat in the row, which would, of course, happen to be right next to Strauss.

"Good morning," Strauss said, in a tone at least thirty-five degrees chillier than the tone he used to greet me that first dawn I woke up in his bed.

"Good morning," I repeated.

He looked away when I sat down, taking his elbow off the armrest to make sure it didn't brush against me. I looked at his legs—I, at least, bore no ill will toward *his* knees—and tried hard not to look at his hands. I wanted to touch his hand. Maybe he wanted the same, because he looked down at my fingers, gripped all too tightly around my pen and legal pad.

I dropped my pen to the pad, as if to say, *Not to fear—I don't plan on taking notes.*

"How are you?" he asked.

"Fine. You?"

"The same." He paused. "Everything going smoothly in your office?"

"Of course."

That is, when my blood sugar isn't dropping. After I skip lunch.

He adjusted the cuff on his shirt. I noticed it was a little dingy. "You know to speak to Peg if there are problems."

"I don't need to speak to Peg," I said. "Unless Peg has said something critical to you . . ."

"Nothing critical has been said of you," he told me in a mild voice. "You have nothing to worry about on that count." Then he turned to the person next to him—one of the corporation lawyers—to give him equal time.

I bit my lip and wished I could ask him: What does Peg know? And who—if anyone—is going to pay for it? My stomach curled into a tight ball. I wished I had called in sick to work, so I could have attended the session the following day for the Finance division. How could I ever have believed that Research and Development—the brains as opposed to the brawn—was the most exciting division at Boorman? I turned around and quickly inspected the auditorium. Among the dull sea of faces in R&D, a definite pattern emerged: Women without any power—i.e., the secretaries and everyone in Editorial—sat stage left. In the middle bank of chairs sat women with slightly higher responsibilities—some of the lab technicians and the director of the art shop (who, I felt like pointing out to Strauss, wore hot-pink glasses, not green)—and the bespectacled scientists. Stage right sat whatever good old boys could be found in our division—some of the guys who worked below Strauss on positioning the latest drugs on the market. I couldn't even figure out what those guys did all day, besides hustling paperwork around the headquarters of the FDA and being wined and dined by university deans eager to get corporate sponsorship for the labs at their own major research institutions.

My mood felt vinegary as the cafeteria's cole slaw and turned even more sour after the meeting was called to order by Dr. Peggy Schoenbarger.

The presentation consisted of a windy introduction by Wayne Lamarr and a clipped message from Peggy about how sexual harassment was against the law and would not be tolerated. The social worker trotted out a few innocuous platitudes, and then we were shown a film. Strauss and I never even went to the movies together, I thought as the lights went down and the video machine began to flicker.

I knew this film would be about fifteen minutes long, just like the "shorts" they used to show before the feature presentation at the Roger Sherman Cinema to convince the audience they'd gotten their money's worth—the documentaries with educational overtones, which seemed purposefully made to encourage the unruly kids in the front rows to throw popcorn at the screen and inspire horny teenagers, slunk down in the backseats beneath the balcony, to get grabby. The officious tones of the conarrators (a plain brunette in a red jacket and a man in a blue blazer, who on closer inspection looked remarkably like the Tidy Bowl Man) brought to mind the movies shown to us in junior-high-school health class over the strenuous objections of our local priests, the Archbishop of Hartford, and even some of our mothers whose English was good enough to raise a protest. These movies warned about the dangers of drug and alcohol abuse. They defined the terms *syphilis* and *gonorrhea*. They explained how babies were made and even showed us a scene that made my ears ring and the blood flow to my feet: the last three minutes of a natural childbirth. Although I had tried to laugh along with the rest of the kids, the labor seemed all too real. My heart had pounded with fear and I had bit my lip to keep from crying out when the bloody infant, still attached to a pulsing purple umbilical cord, was triumphantly lifted by the father and placed on the belly of the mother.

Boorman's featured presentation failed to move me. It was a low-budget affair that showed various scenes of inappropriate verbal and physical behavior, such as men calling women *sweetheart, honey,* and *sugar pie,* men standing too close to women at the Xerox machine, and men winking at women across the conference table. After each scene a question was flashed on the screen—IS THIS HARASSMENT?—always followed by another screen that firmly told us YES. Although the conarrators spoke of *subtle coercion,* the advances shown were obvious enough to fly at any cocktail bar's happy hour. The plot was predictable and the characters no more complex than horny white heterosexual Midwestern males in Arrow shirts and Van Heusen slacks and their modest female coparts in polyester dresses. One guy looked vaguely like Hook Roberts, but this was about as close to realism as this movie was going to get.

I wasn't so naive that I thought such power plays between men and women never happened. But it galled me to think that someone would try to reduce my relationship with Strauss down to this. By law the film should have had everything to do with me—but in reality, it had nothing. Nothing. Where was the clatter of a root-beer can falling to the bottom of a vending machine? Where was the aria from *Gianni Schicchi?* Where was the man whose half-brother came to him in the middle of the night? Where was the girl whose mother told her, *Thank God for your health and don't expect nothing more* and whose father would rather have had his balls cut off with a pinking shears than ever once tell his daughter he loved her? Where was the boredom that came from sitting in front of a computer terminal for hours? The claustrophobia of entering the workplace before the sun even rose above the trees and leaving only after the day had long gone dark, and the sad moment when you realized the headlights of the car promised only to take you back to a cold apartment? Where was the guilt and the loneliness and the desire every human being on earth had to be held in someone else's arms, to hear a lover call your name and whisper, *Listen to the rain?*

We were sitting in the dark. I sensed Strauss's arm next to mine. He had on one of those wool jackets I loved to stroke. The moment the lights went back on, I saw a long strand of brown hair on his left sleeve. I blinked, and stopped myself just in time from reaching out to pluck it.

It was my hair. Mine. And I couldn't be certain, but I thought that was the jacket he wore the afternoon he came back from Omaha, the one I stripped him of when we fell to the floor of his apartment, and he shoved the pillow under me, and said, *Oh God Jesus, you feel so good,* while I said, *Oh God, yes God, give it to me give it to me, this is what I need . . .*

You'd think, by now, that Strauss would have taken that jacket to the dry cleaner's. You'd also think, in the heat of the moment, we would have come up with something more original to say. In bed, maybe, everyone became a stock character. But the reasons people went between the sheets—now, there was a story worth telling. And not surprisingly, this was exactly what the movie didn't illustrate.

After the movie the social worker took the podium and told us what we had just learned: that unwanted attention and unwelcome advances made for a hostile work environment, and a hostile work environment would not be tolerated by the top management of Boorman. She talked about the need to create a productive working atmosphere and to form healthy relationships with those outside the office. Nobody asked her for a definition of the term *healthy relationship.*

The actual sexual-harassment document—twenty-six pages long, and printed in enough copies to kill an acre of redwoods—was passed around for inspection. Key points were read aloud by Mr. Wayne Lamarr and the corporate lawyer. We were all urged to *study* the document and refer any questions—or grievances—to Mr. Lamarr, who would field our inquiries in strict confidence. Any questions?

Stage left remained silent. The folks in the middle bank of seats decided to maintain professional decorum, but stage-right male hands shot up all over the place. It was obvious the guys had trouble with the whole code, which they expressed by stabbing their forefingers at the document and questioning the wording, posing hypothetical situations (*Now say I call my secretary* honey—*is that harassment? I call my wife* honey. *I call my mother* honey, *for Christ's sake!*).

In his responses, Mr. Lamarr sang the company line. Dr. Peggy Schoenbarger provided backup in her forbidding alto. The social worker kept referring back to scenes in the movie, Strauss remained silent, and when I was asked to offer a comment on the phrasing of section sixteen, I graciously deferred to the lawyer, who, after giving us a tedious explanation of *quid pro quo,* then pontificated for fifteen minutes on everything from equal opportunity to single-sex harassment to whether gay men should be allowed to be Boy Scout leaders, until Mr. Wayne Lamarr cut him off.

"Any closing remarks?" he asked.

Just to prove she was the head honcho, Peggy stood and repeated, "Any more questions?" with a finality that made it clear that whoever prolonged this meeting another second risked being drawn and quartered. Peggy nodded and pronounced the meeting adjourned—a command that had the same effect as a priest saying, "Mass has ended. Go in peace." The cushioned seats snapped back, people laughed and grumbled and called across the room to one another, and Strauss surprised me by saying, "That should give you plenty of material for your novel, Lisar," before he stood up and walked away. I bolted for the bathroom, having drunk far too much coffee again.

On the way out of the ladies', I had the misfortune to pass Strauss and Peggy—both giving off extremely bad body language—as they walked back to their executive suite. At first it seemed to me that Peggy was a teacher marching an unruly student down the hall. Then she metamorphosed into a bodyguard in a bulletproof vest, protecting some celebrity from the prying eyes of the paparazzi. *She's pissed, I thought. But she's going to save him. She wants to whomp his ass on the golf course. She needs somebody to remind her to take her Dramamine.*

I felt sick—and vulnerable to her wrath and scorn—until I realized that in order to save Strauss, she had to save me, whether it agreed with her principles or not. For the moment, I was safe.

I felt better after I ate lunch. Maybe there was something to be said for Strauss's blood-sugar theory. In the afternoon I wouldn't have gotten so annoyed that the women in Editorial were wasting company time doing a trash-town number on the new sexual-harassment policy if they hadn't so inconveniently interrupted my own hard work. Inspired by Strauss's comment about my novel, I had clicked back into my personal files and was deep into a really hot reconciliation scene between Thomas Akins and Donna Dilano:

"Take off those goddamn glasses," Thomas growled, before he threw the power locks of his Saab, flicked Donna's leather seat into the recline position, and fucked Donna until she saw more stars than . . . than . . . who?—the learned astronomer in Whitman's poem?—Galileo?—an Iowa farm boy lying in a dark cornfield?—a group of grammar-school children on a field trip to the Hartford observatory?

The piercing laughter of my coworkers zapped my concentration and made me unable to decide on any of those poor choices. My office door was cracked just an inch open, but even over the *whoomp-ah-whoomp-ah* of the Xerox machine, I could hear a trio of them reenacting some of the absurd scenarios played out in the orange-colored film.

Look out, I'm about to call you honey!
Can I pat you on the shoulder, dollcakes?
Depends on if your name is Steve . . . ?
You know you'd be flat on top of the boardroom table in no time if he wanted it—

How about that new guy in advertising, the one in the Camaro—
I'd pay him to harass me.

The hair bristled on the back of my neck. Was it possible that some women found Hook Roberts attractive? That more than anything almost sent me out there, à la Schoenbarger, to put a stop to their nonsense, but then I realized that if I weren't the boss—and Strauss's ex-lunch-hour-quickie—I, too, would be out there, joining in the conversation, if not leading the way with my comments: *I bet the CEO flies his whores in from France on the Concorde! Hook Roberts can whack off in my pencil cup for all I care! Lunch-hour sex at Boorman?—just working here already gives me enough problems with my digestive processes!*

I ground my heels into the carpet and kept my butt parked on my ergonomically correct office chair. I kept my ears peeled, waiting to hear my name mentioned—or Strauss's—but the trio of giggling women remained prudent enough not to refer to either one of us. Everybody wanted to keep their jobs, I thought—including me. Christmas was coming, after all, and they had to buy presents. Lately that was all they talked about, these women—the married ones may have complained about their husbands, the sole divorcée did a routine number on her ex, and the single ones bemoaned the lack of good dates, but they all agreed on one thing: Food and holidays took top priority. I sat there listening, both wanting to scorn them and join them, before I gritted my teeth and returned to the computer, scrolling up to just before Thomas Akins screwed Donna Dilano right out of the solar system and straight up the Milky Way. I wrote:

Donna Dilano felt anything but love as she stared into Thomas Akins's eyes, which were grayer than the pots her mother used to boil spaghetti in (change later, don't end in preposition). "Let me out of this car, you self-righteous, moralizing prick!" she growled.

"Take off those goddamn glasses!" Thomas growled—

But *Donna* just growled. So Thomas couldn't growl, could he? unless I wrote:

"Take off those goddamn glasses!" Thomas growled back.

In any case, there was a whole lot of growling going on.

I stared at the screen in amazement. Was it possible that I had just written something even more preposterous and simplistic than the sexual-harassment movie?

Yup.

Was it true that it was easier to be an editor than a writer?

Maybe.

What was my sage editorial opinion on what I had just written?

This scene sucks the big one, I thought. But unless I wanted to abandon my dream altogether of writing something worth reading, there was no other option but to delete and proceed, delete and proceed. I kept on going.

That week it was double the fun and double the agony at Boorman, at least when it came to meetings with Strauss. On Thursday Strauss—as VP for new product development—was going to preside over a conference with the Marketing division, where Hook Roberts would unveil the preliminary boards for a new ad campaign. Boorman was launching a *new and improved* version of their standard over-the-counter pain reliever. An unusual hushy-hushness had surrounded the marketing of this pain-killer—for instance, I routinely saw the ad boards before they went into production at the art shop, but this time I hadn't been allowed a glimpse. This was Hook Roberts's first big chance to woo and win over the upper levels of Boorman with his *vision*. I hated that word, which implied that creating a nine-by-eleven ad for a glossy magazine was equal to Saint Teresa swooning in ecstasy.

To avoid bumping into Strauss in the hall, I waited until one minute before the meeting was due to start before I gathered my mechanical pencil and leather binder and marched down the hall. Just my luck his strategy was identical to mine. We rounded the corner at opposite ends of the hall at the exact same moment, and so we had the long length of carpet to traverse and pretend we had not noticed one another, until the moment when we both reached the glass door that led to the meeting room.

"Good afternoon," he said, then lunged to open the door. I was careful not to brush against him as I passed.

I hoped I was imagining it, but everyone in the meeting room seemed to fall silent as we came through the door. I took a chair far down on the right-hand side of the table. Strauss frowned at the folks still messing around at the coffee maker. He had a three o'clock train to catch, so he asked those who were presenting to be brief. As if to mock him, the coffee maker let loose a wild rip of burps and gurgles. Everyone laughed. Even I had to look down at the table and smile when Strauss said, "Anyone mind if I unplug this goddamn thing?"

It seemed to me that Strauss had been doing a fair amount of swearing lately. In any case, he muttered a barely audible *shit* as he rocked the reluctant plug of Mr. Coffee out of the stubborn socket. He took his seat at the head of the table. I wondered where he was off to that night. Probably taking the Metroliner down to D.C. Good thing I wasn't going along—he obviously was in a foul mood and we'd probably only get into another fight about Maria Von Trapp in the National Portrait Gallery.

"Floor's all yours, Hook," Strauss said.

"Thank you, sir," Hook said, and rose from his chair. I half-expected him to adjust himself before he went over to the easel covered in black cloth. Contrary to Strauss's explicit instructions, he gave a very unbrief speech about the need to infiltrate the market and saturate the public with information about this new and improved product. He said it was time for Boorman to stop pussyfooting around and to take an aggressive stance with consumers who were too stupid to figure out why they bought what they bought anyway. It was Boorman's job to appeal to their gut instincts, make 'em sit up and pay attention, go for the gusto, grab life by the beans, etc., etc.

From where I was sitting, I couldn't see Strauss, but I knew he was lifting his cuff and looking impatiently at his watch, because Hook finally put a lid on his bullshit, stood in front of the easel, and yanked down the black cloth that covered the art boards as if he were ripping an evening gown off a starlet he was about to mount and penetrate. Underneath the cloth was a photograph of the very kind of starlet I imagined would drive Hook wild: a blond, white-shouldered, heaving-bosomed woman wrapped in a black velvet cloth, whose puckered lips seemed to invite her audience to respond to the ungrammatical message written right above her:

JUST TELL ME WHERE IT HURT'S

Silence reigned after the unveiling. We all scrutinized the photo, and a few audible sighs from around the room made it clear that this bombshell had captured the imagination of most of the men. A few of them actually pulled their chairs closer in to the table.

"Any comments?" Strauss asked, in a voice so neutral I knew he was appalled.

There was a long pause. Then I opened my big mouth and said, "*Hurts* is a verb, not a possessive."

Hook waved his hand as if I had just made some irrelevant point. "In other words, switch the apostrophe?"

I wondered where he went to college. "No apostrophe is necessary at all," I said.

"Thank you, Editorial," Hook said.

"You're most welcome," I said.

Strauss frowned. "Any comments on the content?"

Everyone hesitated. Then Strauss's question was taken as an open invitation for mirth. There was laughter and ribald comments. After all, we worked for a corporation that had made its biggest buck off a lubricant to relieve vaginal dryness. Since I'd been with Boorman, we had launched or modified ad campaigns for all sorts of weird, embarrassing products that probably made the majority of consumers mumble and flush as they placed their order with their local druggist—antibiotics targeted for bladder infections, a solution to dissolve excessive earwax, hemorrhoid pads, and a medicated douche to ease the itching due to herpes and genital warts. But we never had marketed any of those products in quite this way before. The big-boobed starlet in velvet definitely was something new, and every man at the meeting was eager to voice an opinion on her, their comments only slightly tempered by the fact that three—counting me—women who didn't have half as big breasts were sitting at the table.

Finally I couldn't stand it anymore. I pointed out that half the world was female and that the ad targeted the male consumer only.

Hook gave me a snarky smile. "Good point, Editorial," he said. He took down the board of boobs. Underneath, there was another photo—all muscle and bulging crotch. It showed a sweaty Joe in boxer shorts rubbing his aching bicep. Underneath was written the same message that had crowned the starlet:

JUST TELL ME WHERE IT HURT'S

"You like this one better, Lisa?" Hook said.

"Not half-bad," I said, and took up my pencil. "Got his phone number?"

Strauss let me enjoy my triumph as class clown until the laughter died down. Then he asked Hook, "What are we selling here, sex or drugs?"

"It ain't rock 'n' roll," Hook said.

"You know Peggy will never go for this."

"What's Peggy got to do with it?" Hook asked sharply. Then he must have remembered how complicated the chain of command was at Boorman: what displeased Peggy might also displease the CEO, etc. "No offense, Strauss," he said, "but Peg's idea of a zippy ad probably is a full-page diagram of the molecular structure—or whatever you call it—of a drug."

Strauss was not amused. He reminded Hook that Boorman always had presented itself as a prudent, conservative corporation concerned with the health and welfare of the American family, and ads such as these did nothing to support that reputation.

"Maybe it's time to change tactics," said Hook. "Swing with the times. Sex sells movies and books—"

"So do swastikas," Strauss said, "but does that mean you would use them as an advertising tactic?"

"Hey, I never suggested that," Hook said.

Everybody went quiet. I looked down at the table, suddenly fascinated by the whirls and swirls in the wood grain. I actually would have felt
bad for Hook if I hadn't felt so sorry for Strauss. I knew more than anything he hated to lose his cool, and there he sat, right in front of me,
displaying exactly the kind of behavior he had roundly criticized in his own
brother-in-law. Yet the remark had been made. He could not take it back.

Men (I had noticed over the years) had a real knack for dodging
apologies. I was surprised when Strauss said in a tired voice, "I spoke out
of turn. I mean, out of line."

"No big deal," Hook said.

After a moment Strauss looked at his watch and said, "I've really got
to get that train. We'll have to discuss this when I get back, Hook. Meeting
adjourned, unless you guys want to stick around and talk."

I kept my eyes on the table as he left the room. It just so happened
that the guys *did* want to stick around and talk—more about the breasty
starlet than about the viability of the ad campaign itself. I waited until I
was sure Strauss was halfway back to his office before I got up from the
table and made for the ladies' room, where I got out my comb and tried to
do something with my hopeless hair. I was joined at the sink by one of the
new ad reps, a recent college grad who had sat silently across the table
from me at the meeting. She obviously wasn't *au courant* about office
gossip, because as she washed her hands she asked, "What's the matter
with Strauss?"

I shrugged. "Maybe he's doing drugs."

She laughed. "Why did he say that about the swastikas?"

"He's Jewish."

"Well I *know* that," she said. "I have two eyes in my head. I mean,
why does he have to be so sensitive about it?"

As she scrubbed her hands with overly fragranced soap, I caught her
eye in the mirror. "What'd you think of those ads?" I asked her.

"I thought that first one was disgusting—"

"So why didn't you say so?"

"I just got here. It took me four months to find a job after I graduated—"

"What'd you think of the second ad?" I asked.

She smiled. "Total one-eighty. I mean, once Hook unveiled that guy,
I thought, okay, I'm human too, and I don't mind looking at this muscled
hunk at all. Did you?"

"Did I what?"

"Mind looking at him."

"I don't like looking at things I can't have," I said. But when I held my comb slack for a moment, I saw in the mirror a woman who wanted just that: who would give anything to go catch that train with Strauss.

"Doing anything on Friday night?" I asked the ad rep.

She looked apologetic. "Standing date. With my long-standing boyfriend."

"Too bad," I said. "I was hoping you might want to go pick up a couple of good ones in a bar."

She laughed. "If this beau doesn't propose soon," she said, "I might take you up on that offer. But didn't I hear *you* were getting married? I swear someone told me the other day you're getting married. To a stockbroker in New York."

"That's supposed to be a secret," I said.

"I won't tell anyone," she said. "If you want, I could spread a rumor that it's just a rumor—"

"You don't have to do that," I said. "It's just—I'm not so sure this relationship is going to pan out, and I don't want to close off all my other options."

"Namely—Hook Roberts?"

"Hook!" I said. "Gag me with a comb, girl." I mimed sticking my Goody unbreakable into my mouth.

She looked at me in wonder. "Sleeping with him wouldn't gag some women."

"Hopefully his wife is among them."

"He's married? God, he sure doesn't act like it. At that meeting he really was honing in on you."

"Go on."

"No, straight stuff. Weren't you flirting back?"

"God, no—was I?"

"Come to think of it," she said, "that's probably why Strauss got pissed."

My heart seemed to stop for a second. "Why should that piss him?"

"He seems kind of uptight."

I nodded. "He's definitely someone who doesn't believe in sex outside of the marriage bond."

"But I heard he was involved with someone in your department."

"*Right,*" I said. "But she went on maternity leave after he knocked her up—"

"Are you serious? Come on, you're shittin' me now."

I nodded again, and we both burst into laughter. Then she pointed to the sink. "Oh, my God. Look at that."

I gazed down. Strand upon strand of my thick, uncontrollable hair crisscrossed the sink. As I hurried to clean up the hair with some paper towels, I told her, "Hormone drop-off. I just went off the pill."

"That's supposed to happen after you have a baby too," she said. "Between that and the fat, it's enough to make you want to get sterilized."

"Or go lesbian."

"I wouldn't go *that* far."

"Me neither," I said. "Although it sure would make my life a lot easier."

She watched me sorrowfully as I stuffed the paper towels into the wastebasket. "Maybe we could do a bar on some *Saturday* night," she said.

I shrugged. All of a sudden I no longer wanted *a couple of good ones.* I only wanted one. But I couldn't have him and he couldn't have me, and my only consolation out of the whole business was that neither one of us could have anyone else until our second tests came back clean. For six months, at least, I was spared the gnawing pains of jealousy. But I developed my own substitute form of it: hunger.

Chapter Fifteen

I Pray

Maybe it started right there in the ladies' room, when I felt my comb was already down my throat, rendering me incapable of suggesting *"Let's do lunch"* to this woman who obviously wanted to be my friend. More than likely it began that night at the gym. As my left foot hit the rubber track of the treadmill, I felt a hard spot—a toughness on my sole— that became a definite ache before I even dented five minutes into my favorite program: the Colorado Rockies Jog. As the machine picked up pace and I began the uphill portion of the routine, the ache turned into a definite pinprick of pain; the faster and harder I ran, the more it felt like a nail was being driven into the bottom of my foot. It hurt so badly I had to get off the treadmill, remount the Exercycle, adjust the pedal so the ball of my foot wouldn't get too much pressure, and clock another half hour mindlessly cycling just to burn the requisite amount of calories.

In the locker room, I sat with my foot in my hand and pressed lightly on a hard ring of skin that dotted the bottom. Even though my first test came back clean, I still couldn't believe that I didn't have AIDS. Every morning I looked inside my mouth for the milky white signs of thrush; every night my fingers traced the lymph nodes along my neck for signs of swelling. The merest hint of diarrhea sent me into a panic. This weird callus on my foot had to be the first sign of terminal illness.

So what did I do? I bit my lip and ignored it. I put my two- and three-inch heels aside and wore my most sensible pumps to work. But still the bottom of my foot burned like crazy. A week later—only because I had to get back on that treadmill to keep myself from blimping out—I found myself in the podiatrist's office. As the doctor directed the beam of his lamp onto the bottom of my foot, I winced when I saw I'd forgotten to shave the hideous black hairs that grew on my big-toe knuckle.

"You've got a plantar wart," the doctor said. "You have two choices: either live with the pain or have it removed—but chances are it'll grow back."

"Sounds like a metaphor for my life," I said.

"Pardon me?"

Already feeling queasy, I told him, "Dig it out. Now."

"Did you drive yourself here?" he asked. "Because you won't be able to put pressure on your foot once I'm done with you."

He looked at me sympathetically. He was kind of cute, for a doctor—thirties-ish, sandy brown hair, gold-rimmed glasses, and, best of all, no wedding ring. What was it like to sleep with a podiatrist? Very few women in the world, after all, had the opportunity to find out. I made a mental note to give myself a pedicure that weekend and made an appointment to return on Monday.

But Monday found me singing an altogether different tune about the foot-doctor profession. I wondered who could ever go to bed with such a sadist, a man who got his rocks off delivering such searing pain. A sharp whimper escaped me as the doctor needled the anesthetic into my sole, and my heart beat wildly as he turned on the whirring drill-like instrument. He left me passed out on the table after displaying to me, in a shiny silver pan, the bloody stump of hardened skin he had extracted.

The nurse held a vial of foul-smelling salts beneath my nose. I came to and took a cab home. After I limped up all twenty-six stairs to my apartment, I wept when I looked in the freezer and discovered I hadn't filled one of the ice-cube trays last time I fixed myself a bourbon and water, which left me with only eight measly cubes from the second tray to pack my aching foot. I sat on the couch with my foot propped, and as I waited for the ice cubes to form in the freezer—two or three hours, I figured, at the very least—my loneliness seemed as acute and stabbing as the anesthetic injection I had just suffered. Who were my real friends? I thought. Where was my family? I didn't even know my neighbors. I could have called Strauss—although I didn't have the least idea what I would say—and hope that he would come sit by my bedside (after all, there was nothing moral attached to a plantar wart, although he probably could find something illicit about it if I gave him half a chance).

I could have called my mother. I could have called her but didn't, which seemed to sum up in a nutshell our relationship.

I could have called Dodie, and while he was sure to sympathize, I knew his mind would be on far worse things—among them, a breakup with Homer—than my trivial foot blister. I was trying (all the while denying why) to train myself not to turn to Dodie with my problems. I had to learn to stand on my own. But when my despair became overwhelming, I finally buzzed Carol.

"Yo, Lise," Al said. "What's shakin'?"

"I'm in massive pain."

"What, your brain finally explode or what?"

"I got a wart removed from my foot and I ran out of ice cubes."

"Pack of peas," Al said.

"What?"

"You got a pack of frozen peas? Carol sat on 'em after her episiotomy. Doctor's screwball idea. He goes to her, 'Forget the ice, a pack of peas fits just right down there.' "

"This is my *foot* we're talking about, Al, not my crotch." I frowned. "Did you eat those peas afterward?"

"Your mother did. They were wrapped in a Ziploc bag; still, I think she went a little too far—"

"Lemme talk to Carol. Now."

"She's at your mother's." Al must have taken the mute off the Zenith, because the roar of Monday Night Football suddenly filled the air. "Mondays she clears out and lets me watch the game."

"Who's playing?"

"Jets and the Cowboys."

"Who you for?"

"You gotta ask?"

"What's the score?"

"Why don't you turn it on and see for yourself? Lotta good butt shots on the guys, Lise."

"Oh, yeah?" I asked. "What's the station?"

I turned on the game and found Al had spoken true: The huddle provided more than enough excitement to keep me watching into overtime. The Jets got clobbered and I was sure Al felt beaten too, because I already knew—straight from the source's mouth—that after being banished from the house on Monday evenings, Carol refused to perform her conjugal duties. "Runs me out of the house," she complained, "totally stinks of Old Milwaukee, and then he expects me to put out? Dream on, big dummy."

Two sick days and a bottle of aspirin later, I returned to work with a bloody gauze bandage on my foot, which shriveled and constricted as the skin on my sole dried and hardened. During the two-week period when I couldn't work out at the gym, I strictly monitored my caloric intake. For breakfast I cut the amount of cereal I poured into the bowl in half. I delayed—or skipped—lunch. I didn't visit the break room because I'd have to pass by the vending machines, where the smashed white sticky buns hung next to the cheerful yellow and orange bags of nacho-cheese chips and the bright blue-and-white Nestlé's Crunch bars seemed to beckon me to drop my quarters into the slot. For dinner I ate a pack of melba toast and two hard-boiled eggs washed down with a one-calorie root beer. I gnawed on more raw vegetables than Peter Rabbit ate on his ill-fated trip to Mr. McGregor's garden. Unlike Peter, I did not lose my new blue jacket in pursuit of cabbages and potatoes—but I did find what I considered a compelling story:

After her painful breakup with Thomas Akins, Donna Dilano went on a diet. She found starvation—even more than exercise—a very effective weight-loss method. At first it was a game she played with herself—how many hours could go by before food passed her lips? Then not eating—denying herself meals—became an overwhelming interest. Just looking at food made her sick. The employee cafeteria—with its smell of bacon bits and fried potatoes and fish sticks—disgusted her to the point where she didn't want to show her face there anymore. At home she sucked on pretzels so slowly she could make a single Rold Gold Thinnee last for over an hour. A celery stick could take her through the afternoon and the entire evening. If she truly got ravenous—began to cry at the thought of food, but not want to consume any—she went into the kitchen and took down the kosher salt. Following the advice of several women's magazines (which she publicly professed to scorn but secretly read religiously), Donna formerly had used kosher salt mixed with olive oil as an economical substitute for expensive beauty-counter ex-foliants. Now she found that just a spoonful of said kosher salt, plunged into her mouth until she gagged and spit it into the sink, was an effective dietary aid. She slept with her forefinger tucked between her lips and woke in the morning with her cuticle torn and red. This was all the nourishment she would allow her sorry self. The fat dripped off her body like wax from a candle. Her Pappagallo pumps became loose at the ankle. She had to use a matte knife to puncture another hole in her leather belt (which already was stamped in gold: EXTRA SMALL). She used a yellow measuring tape to get the numbers on her forearm and her calves and her stomach and her neck. . . .

Donna lost twenty-five pounds. I shed seven. But what a seven! My thighs no longer touched. My kneecaps and elbows hardened. I felt my rib cage as I showered. For the first time in my life I started to see some cheekbones—the kind for which some women paid plastic surgeons thousands—and I was determined not to bury them beneath fat ever again.

At Sarah Lawrence, girls had dieted until they stopped their periods. I wondered how much I'd have to lose to put an end to my curse. That would be a happy day, I thought, and imagined tossing all my tampons and minipads and Midol and that blasted pack of Trojans I'd purchased on the way home from the public health clinic—which of course I hadn't used, but still felt compelled to hang on to in case some fortuitous encounter with a romantic hero transpired. Fat chance. My period came and went, with its usual share of cramps, tears, and bloated bitchiness. I was tired and short-tempered at work.

Dropping seven pounds had its downside. My bras didn't fit me right. My feet and hands felt numb from cold—iron-poor blood had set in again—and I couldn't wear enough layers against the frigid weather. My fingernails looked ridged and yellow, which I disguised with pale pink polish. I found myself rooting through the boxes in my closet to rediscover some of my college outfits, which I never had the heart to throw out.

This was how sick Donna became: Into the trash went all the ice cream and meat-loaf dinners from her freezer, the stale crackers and cans of pâté she did not want to tempt herself to eat, the expired food coupons she clipped from the Sunday paper, the panty hose that no longer hugged her thin thighs, the makeup that no longer matched her wan skin, the antiperspirant that no longer masked her body odor—because suddenly Donna seemed to be giving off a different kind of smell, which she knew resembled mold on sweet potatoes and was not pleasant. Her winter coat, two sizes too big, looked like a maternity garment. She couldn't bring herself to wear gauze; the wind might have blown her away.

"Lisa, you're skinny enough to see through," my secretary told me. "Hardly a heavyweight," the nurse remarked when I stood on the scale at the gynecologist's and barely tipped one hundred and three. "Great muscle definition," one of the trainers at the gym commented, which only made me spend ten more strenuous minutes with the Pacer.

I thought I looked good. I thought of myself as another person. I was Lisa, but I was also Donna—the girl who had whittled away her body and her friends and her lover, who put her sore feet on the treadmill and jogged until she practically heard her bones clack together like a mallet on a xylophone, her stomach shaking like a seed within a dried gourd, her dull, strawlike hair soaked with sweat, and her heart ready to stop.

At the end of November, three months after I learned my first ELISA was negative, I cheated and got another test. When I got the second negative, I decided to go to church. But I didn't even know where the Catholic church was in Ossining, and I was forced to look it up—like it was an appliance store or a Midas Muffler station—in the phone book.

The Church of the Archangel Gabriel was off a secluded road, hidden behind fir trees. Only the white spire and a too tasteful wooden sign with gold lettering gave its presence away, a subtle reminder that I was miles from my childhood parish. My mother's church, situated on a busy street corner, smelled of incense and beeswax and floor polish, and on holidays it reeked of mothballs from the furs the ladies wore and (supposedly to cover up that evil smell) the even more noxious smell of their Jungle Gardenia perfume.

I parked in the small lot—empty on this Wednesday evening except for a beat-up Ford that probably belonged to the rectory housekeeper. The carved wooden doors thudded behind me when I stepped into the hushed vestibule. I dipped my first finger into the glass font and tried to feel the healing power of the holy water come over me as I made the sign of the cross. Only then did I feel fit to enter the church. My feet were shod in low pumps that made a soft padding sound on the red carpet. I sat in one of the back pews. I didn't go so far as to kneel, but I bowed my head, remembering the part of mass when the parishioners say, *Lord, I am not worthy . . . but only say the word and I shall be healed.* Then I lifted my eyes. The altar was dim, lit only by the flicker of votives. Outside, darkness already had fallen; the stained-glass windows were a dull plum and deep green; the tabernacle glowed; the crucifix was illuminated from below.

I wanted to give God thanks, but I no longer knew how. I went down on my knees, clasped my hands against my forehead, and was reduced to a guilty litany. *I pray, I pray,* I whispered inside myself, as if the assertion were equivalent to the act, and as if I knew who or what I could possibly be praying for. My knuckles were white and wet from my weeping when I rose, blew my nose, and walked up the right aisle to the transept. I wanted to light a candle for Dodie. But when I reached into my purse, I realized I hadn't swung by the bank in days. I had a twenty, no change, and I needed gas on the way home. My penitence—my resolution—was short-lived. I hoped God loved a thief. I took a thin stick from the metal box of cinders, held it to a burning candle, and lit all the votives, from the small to the large—fifty, maybe a hundred bucks' worth—for Dodie. Then I slunk from the church like a criminal.

"How very Genet," Dodie said when he came to spend the weekend and to celebrate—in advance—Christmas and New Year's. I picked up Dodie at the Ossining train station not in my Toyota with a lobotomized, inflatable man in the backseat, but in a brand-new set of wheels I had purchased—on a wild impulse—the previous weekend.

That Saturday I had received through the mail my summons to the Boorman holiday party. The wording—*You and your guest are cordially invited*—had made my stomach gnaw with loneliness. But as I went to tack the invitation on my refrigerator door, I spied the Toyota salesman's card still hanging beneath the MONEY STINKS magnet. Well, I thought, why else had I kept it there, if not for what my mother called *the day that rains?* A moment later I was on the phone with the salesman. He was there. On the lot. Until seven-thirty that evening.

I went shopping for a man and ended up buying a Jeep.

I walked into the dealership, strode up to my gentleman of the hour, and held out my hand. His name was Bill—Bill Walker, a handle that sounded so bland I wondered if it was an alias. I reintroduced myself, giving him a smile that led him to say, "Sure, I remember you. What'd you have in mind this afternoon?"

"I just thought it was time for a look around."

"Corolla still treatin' you right?"

"It's done the trick."

"Looking to upgrade now?"

"Maybe," I said, and when he went into his office to get his coat, I spied the back of a picture frame on his desk. When he came out, I tried to spot if he wore a wedding ring, but he pulled on his left glove first.

Bill and I went onto the lot. It was a mild day. Although the trees were lined with white, patches of grass shone through the snow on the ground, and the sun glinted off the smooth, waxy hoods of the new cars. Bill walked me up and down the rows. He talked horsepower and power steering and list price. He gave me the bit about the floor mats and the radio and the various option packages.

"See anything you want to test drive?" he asked, and as I pointed toward a light-blue Celica—clearly way beyond my price range—I saw over his shoulder a row of Jeeps, cute and silly as the amusement cars that Carol and I used to ride at Lighthouse Beach. I was sure their horns made a funny sound: *a-whoogga-a-whoogga.*

When Bill went back into the showroom to get a license plate to fix on the Celica, I hustled over and peered into the bright blue Jeep on the end. It was utterly impractical: seated only two, and the wind probably whistled through the doors, but I imagined a girl could feel like King of the Road sitting up so high. The big wide tires looked like they'd really grip the road, which had been icy of late. From this standpoint, the Jeep suddenly seemed the very thing I needed: It was exceptionally safe.

"I've changed my mind," I said when Bill came out. "I want to take this little thing for a spin."

He looked surprised. But when he saw how dead-set I was on climbing in, he opened the door for me, fixed the license plates on the back and front, and went back into the dealership to fetch the key. He got in beside me, already starting to talk serious—some shit about the engine, which I didn't listen to—as if I gave a damn about the inner workings of this all-terrain vehicle, when I was having so much fun tooling it down the street, pretending I was an archaeologist, a safari hunter, a desert explorer, an anthropologist in the wilds, a regular Margaret Mead or Jane Goodall, who was practically on the verge of singing the theme song from *Born Free.*

When we got back to the lot, I test-drove the Celica and a couple of low-range vehicles just for show, then asked for the literature on the Jeep. Bill wouldn't leave me alone in his office even though I told him I needed fifteen minutes or so to look over the manufacturer's material. As I browsed through the pages, I chatted with him about his job before I started flirting him down on the price—first seven-fifty, then a thousand, and then another five hundred on top of that—and once I got him that low, I knew I couldn't cocktease him any lower without walking off the lot, and I asked what he'd take on a trade. My heart in my mouth, I signed on for yet another round of monthly payments, and as I drove off the lot I thought: Why would a girl need a man named Bill Walker or Ibby Strauss or any other guy for that matter, when she could drive a Jeep?

Then I realized that I hadn't called State Farm. I wondered if I was driving an uninsured vehicle down an icy street. Of more immediate concern: I was cold. Really cold. I fiddled with the buttons on the dashboard and thought: *Lisa, you are so stupid—in the dead of summer you buy a car without air-conditioning, and at the start of winter, a vehicle that has no fucking heat!*

Dodie stopped dead in his tracks when he saw my Jeep sitting in the parking lot of the Ossining train station. "You've got to be kidding," he said, when I slipped the key into the driver's door to prove my ownership. "What is this? You hate Hemingway."

"Yeah, but I always loved watching that safari show, *Daktari.*"

Dodie climbed into the passenger seat. He cupped his hands around his mouth and blared into his mock trumpet the first few bars of the music that opened the *National Geographic* series, ending with a couple of spitty fart sounds blasted against the palm of his hand. "You gotta wonder about people who play brass instruments," he said, and I laughed, remembering how far from lighthearted we both felt the last time we were in my car together. Then I knew why I got rid of my Toyota—it was nothing but a reminder of that morning when everything seemed to change for the worse, and a memory of that drive so long ago with Security Man mocking us in the backseat.

"What possessed you?" Dodie asked, as we started for my place.

"I wanted the car dealer to take me to the office Christmas party."

"Did you get your date?"

"I think he's married now."

"So as a reaction, you went out and bought this butchbuggy?"

I squinted my eyes at him. "What'd you call my Jeep?"

Dodie held his head in his hands. "Lise, Lise, you're so naive! I mean, this is like me driving the Oscar Mayer wienermobile down the street—"

"I don't get what you're saying."

"A Jeep is a statement. That you're on the dyke squad—"

"Bull*shit,* Dodie."

"This is bullshit you'd better believe, sweetie."

"It's not like I'm wearing combat boots," I said. "Or a bunch of keys on my belt loop."

"I don't know," Dodie said, shaking his head in a nifty imitation of my mother. "Your hair, it's kinda short. You got the muscles. And no boyfriend."

I fell quiet.

"Still a sore spot?" Dodie asked.

"Let's not talk about it," I said.

So of course, it was one of the first things to come up while we made dinner—baked eggplant and risotto with basil and tomato chunks—and while we were chilling the champagne that Dodie matter-of-factly announced he brought as a way of celebrating the results of my second test, inconclusive as it still was. Tears came to my eyes when he slipped the champagne bottle in my refrigerator. Dodie also had cheated and taken a second test before his six-month mark. His was positive again.

Dodie sliced the eggplant; I chopped the tomatoes. Out of the corner of his eye, Dodie gave me the once-over.

"You'd better eat most of this," he said.

"No, *you'd* better eat most of it," I said, because Dodie's doctor had ordered him to keep up his weight.

"You've really gotten skinny," Dodie said.

"I only lost seven pounds."

"Looks closer to ten or fifteen to me."

"Great."

"You aren't making yourself throw up or anything, like those Sarah Lawrence princesses?"

"Yeah, last week I got an invitation to my reunion, and I'm such a *dedicated* alum—so loyal to my alma mater—that I've been riding the porcelain bus ever since."

Dodie laughed and opened my cabinet. "What's with this kosher salt?"

"Part of a feminine beauty ritual."

"I thought you might be converting."

"I think it's safe to say I'm not."

I shoved the kosher salt aside and pulled down the Morton's. My mother always had bought store-brand salt, and I had vowed that when I grew up, I would pay the extra five cents just to get the midnight-blue container that offered in delicate cursive script this melancholy reminder: *When it rains, it pours.*

Dodie examined the bob-haired Morton's salt girl sheltered beneath her big umbrella. He fell quiet as he sprinkled salt on the eggplant slices, and I knew I was in for a serious chat. I got out an onion, hacked off the wrong end—the crying end—and dug my nails under the skin, peeling back the brown papery wrapper.

"Listen, Lise," Dodie said. "I've been thinking. I feel bad about what happened between you and this Strauss guy—"

"It's not your fault," I said, as I sawed away at the onion. "You didn't ask to get sick."

"But I should never have told you," Dodie said. "I could have hid it, and then you wouldn't have felt like you were hiding something from him."

"You did the right thing," I said. "You told me. And I did the right thing. I told him. He was the one who couldn't deal."

I put down the knife for a second to wipe my watery eyes with the back of my hand. Dodie got out the eggs and cracked them against the counter, slowly letting the whites slip into the bowl before the yolks plopped to the bottom. This created a sick sucking sound that made me wince, and I was glad when he got out the egg beater, even if he did use it to goose me.

"Stop harassing me," I said.

"*I'm* not the one harassing you, Lise."

"And forget Strauss."

"Can you say that with a little more conviction in your voice?" Dodie asked.

A year—or two years—ago, Dodie and I would have gotten drunk or stoned or danced all night in some sleazy club to purge the old boyfriend from my system. Instead, Dodie beat the eggs and dredged the eggplant while I pressed my palm on the dull side of the blade and furiously diced until the onions ceased to look like solid matter and resembled a pool of liquid.

"Lise?"

I bit my lip. "Don't."

"No, come on, serious now. This is Dodie Daddy talking."

"All right. Speak."

Dodie went into my refrigerator and pulled out a bag of carrots. "My opinion is that if you still love him—and I think you do—you should call him, especially since now you're to the halfway point. I'm sure you're negative. Tell him you've gotten this second negative. Ask to talk."

I let out a bleat. "You gotta be kidding," I said. "I don't grovel."

"Who said *grovel*? The word is *compromise*."

"That's not in my vocabulary. Or his either."

"Sounds like you were made for each other," Dodie said. He began to hum as he took up my rusty peeler. I could tell he was playing a game with himself, trying to get the longest possible peel off each stroke of the carrot.

"Why do I have to make the first move?" I asked.

"You're the woman. You're the woman, aren't you?"

I looked down at myself, as if I'd find confirmation of this sitting on my chest. Then I looked at Dodie and said, "How sexist can you get?"

Dodie gave me his best locker-room *duh* sound. "Gay, but a guy at heart."

"Fuck guys," I said. "Gay and straight. Why can't guys say they're sorry?"

"Because their pricks will fall off if they even *think* of the word. And if they *said* it, they might spontaneously combust."

I laughed hysterically—much louder than necessary, as Dodie pointed out.

"What's it to you whether I hook up with him or not?"

"Life is short."

Ain't that profound, I felt like saying. But I didn't. I listened when Dodie told me, "Lise, I want you to be happy—"

"I am happy," I said. This was no lie—I had always loved being in the kitchen with Dodie, surrounded by a sea of green and orange and yellow vegetables. Moments like this seemed like natural happiness. But such happiness wouldn't last. As I dumped the onions into the oil-coated frying pan, my hands felt heavy on my wrists when I thought of how lonely I would be after Dodie left my apartment, the emptiness deep and low as the sound a bow drew on the strings of a bass. I had told him, *Dodie, I'll take care of you if you get sick, really sick,* and he'd said, *You've got to be kidding, I wouldn't inflict that on my worst enemy, I just pray it's quick when it comes, sometimes I just want it to hit me like lightning, I can't stand this too much longer, it's like waking up on death row every morning, and the more I want to live, the more I wish the guards would come and take me away.*

Dodie's presence in my kitchen reminded me it was possible to miss a man even when he stood right beside you. I could stand alone, I thought—but did I want to? *I didn't want to.* I tried to make my voice sound casual—flippant, almost—when I asked Dodie, "How would you try to get back together with him? If you were me."

Dodie perked up. He liked to map out battle plans. "What would he go for? Some kind of sweet talk or something?"

I shook my head.

"Tears?"

"He's already gotten that." I put the cutting board in the sink. "Would you call him?"

"No way. Don't ever do anything important over the phone. This has to be face to face. Keep it professional, maybe, at first. Sling the lingo. Talk about the recent miscommunication between you two—"

I groaned.

"No, seriously. Give him the line about wanting to be a better team player—"

"When and where am I supposed to do this? He asked me not to call him at home—"

"Ask for an appointment at the office."

"I'd have to go through his secretary."

Dodie put down the carrot peeler. "Didn't you say you had a Christmas party coming up?"

I nodded. I grabbed his forearm. "Be my date."

"No way, girl. You're going solo. And dancing with him. And pray he doesn't bring another woman."

"He never brings another woman," I said. "I know that for certain."

Dodie's eyes sparkled. " 'Tis the season for forgiveness," he said, and grabbed my hand. "Show me what you're going to wear."

We headed for my closet. After fifteen minutes of bickering, we agreed only on one thing: the next day we'd go shopping.

Chapter Sixteen

She's Positive He's Not

       Boorman's holiday party was held on Friday night in the employee cafeteria. It was beginning to snow when I pulled back into the jammed parking lot—more than fashionably late—at 8:00 P.M. Across the rolling lawn burned the yellow lights from the laboratory, ominously sunk into the ground as if it were a nuclear bunker. The guys in R&D were pulling a second shift again. Boorman hadn't concerned itself with developing an AIDS test. But rumor had it that R&D was madly at work on a new AIDS therapy—something called *Compound Q*, which was derived from the Chinese cucumber. A good comedian, I was sure, could find some material in that.

       Looking at the lab, I was reminded of why Dodie had changed the complexion of my entire investment portfolio. Although he had broken up with Homer, he had kept me in sex toys (claiming that fear would make the market for vibrators and other marital aids absolutely soar). But he also had snapped up stock of corporations that manufactured rubber gloves and condoms and the tightly sealed plastic disposable containers I was starting to see in every doctor's office, the ones labeled BIOHAZARD. "If something happens to me," he said, "make sure you stay in this stuff."

       "I don't want to be in that stuff."

       "Use your head. Somebody's going to make a mint off this thing."

       "Why me?"

       "Why not?"

       "It doesn't seem right."

       "So make the money and give it to Mother Teresa. She won't ask you where you got it."

       The party officially had started at seven. Gussie—who'd been extra nice to me ever since late September, when he hesitantly asked, *Lost your shadow?* and I only nodded and blew my nose—guarded the back door. When I signed in, he was sampling a pig-in-a-blanket off a paper plate full of hors d'oeuvres. Beside him sat a plastic cup full of foamy sea-green liquid that looked more like Saint Patrick's Day brew than wassail. Appar-

ently there had been a colossal power struggle on the entertainment committee over how much—if any—alcohol would be served. The squabble
was quickly resolved by the CEO, who put his own drunken foot down and
said, "Whoever wants to drink can drink, and the lily-livers who don't can
swill punch."

"What say, Miss Lisa?" Gussie asked.

"I say: How come you can't come to the party?"

"Somebody's got to guard the gates." He looked over my shoulder
into the parking lot. "You got a designated driver tonight?"

"Nope," I answered, and took off down the hall after promising Gussie I wouldn't have too much to drink.

The back hallways were hushed except for the buzz of the ventilation
fans and the far-off sound of a phone pealing in one of the hotshot's
offices. It was hard to walk in my heels, and it didn't help that my emerald-
green velvet dress hugged my butt tighter than the hands of a lover. The
dress was purchased at Saks with Dodie's approval and my credit card and
with the implicit plan of returning it the day after the party. Inside the
right sleeve was pinned the price tag. Tucked inside the underarms were
pads to absorb sweat. Whatever I did, I couldn't spill on this dress, or else I
would have to shell out four hundred dollars for three hours' worth of
looking like a knockout.

When I took off my coat in the crowded cloakroom, I noted I was a
victim of static cling. I smoothed my skirt down my thighs and took a deep
breath before I made my grand entrance. At the double doors where employees usually lined up to grab their plastic turquoise trays and bent
silverware, a short receiving line had formed. I peered into the cafeteria.
The fluorescent lights, kept off for this event in favor of hurricane candles,
were festooned with holly berries, ivy, and mistletoe. Tinsel icicles glittered down from the bulletin board that usually displayed the thermometer
gauging the company's contributions to United Way, announcements that
Maryann in Marketing was selling Girl Scout cookies for her daughter,
and Bob in sales was looking to sacrifice a complete cherry-wood dining-
room set for only $600. Gone were the proud proclamations that Boorman
was an Equal Opportunity Employer and that sexual harassment was illegal and would be prosecuted to the fullest extent of the law. They had
been replaced by a multicolored glitter banner that sparked *Noel, Noel!*

A huge evergreen, glimmering with rainbow-colored lights, had been
erected on the tile floor where the salad bar usually reigned. The tables
were covered with green paper, the swinging doors were gift-wrapped in
boldly striped foil and brazen red bows, and the only parts of the cafeteria

not transformed into some kind of evocation of the winter-wonderland
theme were the dull tile floor and the stark orange plastic chairs, which
violently clashed with all the red and green decorations.

Although the affair was billed—with characteristic corporate attempts at cultural sensitivity—as a *holiday party,* this doo-rah clearly was
nothing more than a Christmas celebration, which gave the few non-
Christians at Boorman (a handful of Jews, some Muslims and Hindus and
probably even a few Buddhists, all scientists in R&D) a convenient excuse
to boycott this event. As I stood on line to shake the hand of the cheesy
CEO and his wife—who were dressed in Barney's best with his-and-hers
Mr. and Mrs. Santa Claus hats cocked jauntily on their heads—I thanked
God that Strauss, as part of top management, could never weasel his way
out of showing his face at this fiesta.

I wondered how it felt to be Jewish at a Christmas party. I imagined it
was a little like being the only white girl on the basketball court at Roger
Sherman High, knowing no one was going to throw me the ball, but loping
up and down from basket to basket like a useless dope anyway, because if I
got lower than a C in gym I'd lose whatever slim chance I already had of
getting a full college scholarship. Then I imagined it was the way Dodie
felt at Carol's wedding, his eyes stubbornly lowered toward his melting
spumoni, as the deejay goaded all eligible bachelors onto the dance floor.

I felt the price tag on my dress inching forward as I shook the CEO's
hand. I gave him a gracious smile and adjusted my cuff. The moment I was
free of the receiving line I spotted Strauss far across the room. I smiled
again—until I saw on his elbow the hand of an unknown blonde in a blue
mandarin-collar dress, who hovered next to him like a bee honing in on
pollen.

I, too, could be beelike. I buzzed for a table at the opposite corner of
the room, where I joined the Editorial division and the art-shop designers.
I smiled and laughed and met all my coworkers' spouses and significant
others, whose names I forgot the moment they were spoken.

"We're taking bets on how much you're going to eat tonight, Lisa."

"Save it for the bingo hall," I said, because I was determined not to
eat—or drink—anything. I made up my mind I would stick this party out
for an hour—not only to fulfill the minimum face-time requirements, but
also to avoid having to explain my abrupt departure to Gussie. Of course, I
could have steered clear of the security guard altogether by sneaking out
the front doors, which had to be unlocked from the inside because of fire
regulations. But it was a real hike from the front of headquarters to the
parking lot, a walk I wasn't eager to make in the snow considering I had on
three-inch stilettos.

After a few discreet glances across the room I was able to discern 1) Strauss's date had a good ten years on me, 2) that was blond out of the bottle, thank you very much, 3) my butt was in vastly better shape than hers, and 4) her flimsy rayon dress closed up the back with absurd frog buttons that would be more appropriate on a Chinatown quilted jacket. I felt like marching right up to her and pointing out something I was sure she hadn't noticed: Strauss's big hands and thick fingers. *"En garde,"* I'd confide in her. "He went to Harvard, but he can't handle a bra hook. It'll probably take him half an hour to get you out of that outfit."

Then I felt a tightness in my chest—a breathlessness that mimicked a heart attack—as I remembered that pale pink chemise flying through the air like a silken parachute across the bed, and Strauss saying, *Wear this? For me?*

What I *wouldn't* wear—what I *wouldn't* take off—for him. But why was love so demented? I sat there and told myself, *Right, Lise, this is what your life's come down to—trying but not even succeeding at seducing a man whose parents call him Ibby, a man who actually put on a tie to go out to dinner, a man who was old enough to wank himself blind before you even were born, a man who makes you feel ashamed of where you come from and who you are and who holds you responsible for things you did before you knew enough to put that self-destructive shit behind you. And he's your boss. He's still your boss. Are you crazy?*

Waiters circulated with trays. I declined all offers of drink. Not a smidgen of food—the bacon-wrapped scallops, the spanakopita, the honey-mustard chicken on a stick—passed my lips. My butt was glued to my chair. I made distracted conversation with the person on my right, then the person on my left. But all the while my mind was on Strauss's date. I was sure he met her flying first-class to Indianapolis. I was sure she was a stewardess—*oh, pardon me!—flight attendant.* I was sure she smiled a crinkly lipsticked grin as she offered him a blanket and a pillow and paper slippers for his little tootsies. She probably fetched him magazines and drinks and brushed him with her breasts as she leaned over to refill his cup with tepid black coffee. If you pressed her belly button she'd probably open her mouth like a Chatty Cathy doll and repeat the lines I had come to memorize not through my own extensive air-travel experience (I'd only been on a plane once in my life, to visit Key West with Dodie) but by watching too many made-for-TV movies: *All seats and tray tables must be in the forward position. In the unlikely event of a water landing . . .*

With my back carefully turned toward Strauss (who was obliged to work the room and circulate), I smiled and laughed some more and told a few dumb Ronald Reagan jokes to a spouse after carefully determining he didn't vote Republican. When Karen showed up with her family, I called the baby *she* instead of *he*, emitted the requisite oohs and aahs, and then told Karen everything was under control at the office, so she could rest easy. An older woman from Accounts Receivable told me, "Wait 'til you have your own baby, honey—you'll find out you don't get any rest whatsoever!" This remark sent me over to the next table, which should have had a sign over it saying SINGLES ONLY. I hovered in the corner with the rest of *the girls* from the Editorial department, finally giving in to boredom enough to sip some mulled wine, but not enough to actually eat a cheese puff or a blackened shrimp or a dainty cucumber sandwich. Soon, canned music began playing through the audio system. I hoped the cleared-out space in the back of the cafeteria was not reserved for dancing, because never in my life had I felt so utterly depressed about not having a partner.

My misery was heightened by the forced jollity of the talk. I felt like the only person on the planet who did not spend December making gingerbread and fudge, combing the malls for hours in quest of the perfect present for her sister or brother, and relishing the thought of spending the holidays at the warmth of their family hearth. I planned to drive home on Christmas Eve and try not to complain to my mother about the stink of the smelts she always served the night before Christmas. I planned to attend midnight mass and sleep as late as I could until the wailing of Junior—a boy as stocky and belligerent as Al Dante—woke me. Then I planned on going downstairs and eating one very select Whitman chocolate from the box my mother always splurged and purchased every Christmas, and drinking a pot of coffee to get me through the rest of the day, until I went back to Ossining that night, probably after fighting with both my mother and Carol and exchanging a few harsh words with Auntie Beppina, who always had held a grudge against me because Dodie was gay—as if it were my duty to straighten him out.

The sour singing of Mel Torme—and just the thought of all the MSG in the hors d'oeuvres—made my head pound. I'd never seen so many glittering angora sweaters, gold-lamé tops, jingle-bell necklaces, and Jolly Old Saint Nicholas earrings gathered under one roof in my life. But I couldn't cut out too early. Although roll hadn't been taken, every employee's business card had been put into a clear plastic container exactly like the revolving drum used at catechism bingo. An hour after I got there, the CEO stepped up to the microphone to begin a drawing for door prizes. The announced purpose of this: to show Boorman's appreciation of our hard work throughout the year. The real purpose: to humiliate those who had the good sense to stay home. I had to stay. It would not have been good politics to have the by-now bourbon-bombed CEO pull my business card and announce my name over and over again until it was apparent that I had not shown up to claim the cheesecake or the complimentary movie tickets or the vouchers for two dinners at the most exclusive seafood restaurant in town.

After one of the cafeteria lunch ladies gushingly accepted from the CEO the final door prize—two round-trip tickets to anywhere in the continental United States—I joined in the applause and turned away. But my gaze gravitated in exactly the wrong direction. For a horrible moment, as he made pained conversation with Hook Roberts (the blonde still hovering by his side like an about-to-land helicopter), I caught Strauss's eye.

Judy Garland wished us a merry little Christmas. Strauss turned away toward the shellacked-silver wreath that surrounded the Seth Thomas clock above the door, and my eyes turned onto a tray full of pfeffernüsse nobody dared to eat, because the powdered sugar would leave white spots all over their dry-clean-only holiday outfits—but not before locking, again just for a moment, with Hook Roberts's eyes.

Hook disengaged himself from his conversation with Strauss and came over to me. I was standing against a pillar, and Hook positioned himself right in front of me, his champagne glass all but emptied and cocked at a dangerous angle, as if it were about to tip the last bit of bubbly onto his Santa Claus tie.

"Has the party started?" Hook asked me.

"Is this a party?" I asked. "I hadn't noticed."

"Where's your holiday spirit?"

"I left it at the dry cleaner's."

Hook laughed and downed the last drop of champagne. "I sure didn't." He snagged a waitress. "Hey, hon, trade you this one for two." He put his empty glass on the tray and, against my will, armed me with a glass of champagne.

"Here by yourself?" he asked.

"Looks that way."

"Where's your fiancé?" he asked.

"Where'd you hear I had a fiancé?" I blurted out.

"Don't you?"

I didn't answer. Hook stared at me intently. Then he smiled. "Ah, aren't you a smart cookie, Lisa. And wasn't he a convenient rumor—"

"Where's your wife?" I interrupted him.

"Lorraine's home watering the plants."

"You married a gardener?"

"I married a woman who doesn't like office parties."

"Can't say I blame her."

Hook glanced back over his shoulder at Strauss and the stewardess. "They ought to have a rule, employees only. Don't you think there ought to be a rule: Spouses and dates—and *fiancés*—get to stay home and watch *It's a Wonderful Life* for the fifty-millionth time on TV?"

I took a slug of champagne. The bubbles coursed up my nose like I had just plunged into a swimming pool and forgotten to hold my breath.

"Maybe I'll suggest that to Strauss at our next meeting," Hook said. "Then again, maybe not. I might get a bad reaction."

"You might."

Hook leaned in toward me. "Strauss is a pretty touchy character these days, isn't he?" He looked over at the blonde, then raised his eyebrow at me. "Any idea what's eating him?"

I was dangerously close to throwing my champagne in Hook's face. "I haven't the foggiest. I don't have touch to do with him."

Hook's lips parted into a smile. I corrected myself. "I mean *much*. Much to do with him."

"I must have misread the situation."

"You seem to have a habit of doing that," I said. "As well as the bad habit of spreading gossip."

"Don't blame me. I kept my word."

"Right."

"Honest Injun. Even your former traveling companion knows that. You want to know who blew your cover with dear darling Doctor?"

I hesitated.

"Give me the next dance," Hook said, "and I'll tell you all about it."

The floor had cleared, and a few of the more daring couples—from the looks of it, mostly older folks who wanted to show they still knew how to cut the rug—were swaying to Perry Como. I was right when I had Strauss pegged as a nondancer. He wasn't up there. But maybe he'd lead up the blonde in half a second. Although my reason told me I should extricate myself from this encounter with Hook, I suddenly wanted and needed to beat Strauss up to the dance floor. I couldn't think of a bigger slap in his face than taking my first turn around with Hook. I hadn't had a good flirt in a long time, and judging from his glazed eyes, I figured Hook wouldn't remember much of this in the morning. Hook had some useful information. Three minutes in his arms and that information was mine.

"The next one might be fast," I said.

"You like it slow?"

I put down my drink, suddenly light-headed, and thought, *Good God, girl, sober up. Get something to eat. Move away from this man. Just move away.* But how could I move other than in Hook's arms? He had me out on the dance floor before I knew it. I didn't recognize either the singer or the song. I only knew Hook was a smooth dancer and I was a bumbler.

"Relax," he said.

"I am relaxed."

"You keep poking me with those witchy shoes of yours. You're supposed to let the man lead."

"So lead."

"So follow. There you go. That's right. You've got it."

"No, you've got it."

He brought his head down closer to mine. "Got what?"

"What I want to know."

He laughed and took me to the back of the dance floor. "I'm surprised you haven't figured it out."

I racked my brains.

"Use your head," Hook said.

"Karen," I said.

"Who's that? That schoolmarm who had your job before you? Nah."

"Somebody in computer support?"

"Did you and someone else leave a mail trail? Very indiscreet of you, I'd say."

"I give up."

"No, keep guessing."

"Male or female?" I asked. "Animal or vegetable?"

"Pure manly man. Armed and extremely dangerous."

"Who are you talking about?"

"The night and weekend watchman."

"Gussie?"

"None other."

"How do you know any of this?"

"I surmised a lot, and Frau Doctor herself filled in the gaps. In our confidential little meeting. This afternoon."

My heart thumped and Hook stepped on my toe. "Ow!"

"Keep dancing."

"You met with Peggy this afternoon?"

"I say no more."

"Come on," I said. "Finish what you started."

"Dance is over, Lisa."

And it was. But Hook took pity on me—or so he said—and led me back to where we had started—a table suddenly surrounded by empty chairs because everybody wanted to swing to Elvis.

"What did you tell Peggy?" I asked.

"I told her nothing."

"What did Peggy tell you?"

"Corporate reorganization was high on the conversational agenda."

"Cut the shit. Get to Gussie."

"I didn't get this from her mouth. But rumors fly. People see things, such as your lovebird looks in the hall, and a couple of matching muddy shoeprints on the carpet—ha! I'm not even going to ask what you two naughty children were up to *that* day. You should have realized it would go any-which-way back to Peg. Word is she went back and checked the sign-out log over the summer that showed Strauss following you out the door almost every night he was in town—"

"That doesn't prove anything."

"You were in the building with him almost every weekend."

"I was working. So was the treasurer. And the comptroller. So were some of the janitors—"

"Ha! You could have messed with any of those guys—you could have done the goddamn CEO—without a murmur. But you played with the Doctor's pet boy—"

"He's not her pet—"

"What's the matter with you? Didn't you realize she thought he was golden? Mister Do-No-Wrong? Mister Upright? Mister Morality Incarnate? Everybody knows he lost his job once for blowing the whistle at that lab in Princeton—what were they manufacturing? Faulty IUDs? Something that was making women really sick. Shit, I don't remember. The Doctor hired him thinking he was some great defender of the feminist cause, and then she finds out he's been screwing some girl who coincidentally gets promoted? You can imagine how well that sat with her." Hook laughed. "Shut your mouth, girl. You're catching flies. And relax. She's known for weeks. He's all set to take the rap, not you."

"He's fired?"

"Temporarily removed from the premises. Commonly known as being sent to Siberia. Taipei, really. A three-month stint. Boorman's doing a kamikaze on the Oriental market. Sayonara, New York. Hello, sushi."

"Taipei is in Taiwan," I told Hook. "It's Chinese, not Japanese."

"What the fuck's the difference? They all eat raw fish."

"You've obviously never been there."

"But I know the hotels are first-class. And the women are beautiful. And submissive, I've heard."

"If you like that kind of thing."

"Most men like that."

"Most men," I said, "are wienies. And I'm not talking about this anymore with you."

"*Au contraire,* Lisa. You and I are going to have a lot more chances to discuss this. Why do you think Peg called me into her office?"

"To ask what you knew about—"

"Ha. She got that straight from the source, I'm sure. Mr. Morals came clean the moment she confronted him with it. No, my dear, she wanted to know how I felt about having you work under me."

"What?"

"Expect an interoffice memo. On Monday. From Peggy. I'm in charge of Editorial, effective January one."

I tried not to gasp.

"The look on your face is priceless."

"You should have told me—"

"I just did."

"I can't work for you—"

"So go tell Peg you prefer Strauss's hands-on management style to mine and see how much sympathy you get. On second thought, why don't you just try mine for a while?"

He gave me an evil grin. As Sinatra sang "It's the Most Wonderful Time of the Year" loud enough so I couldn't be overheard, I beckoned toward Hook. He leaned in. Slowly, quietly, with my best beauty-queen smile plastered on my face, I informed him, "Let's get this straight right now, buster: I wouldn't sit on your dick if you paid me a million dollars."

He laughed. "No, but you'd probably suck it for twenty."

I also laughed. But inside I was scrambling for the right comeback. "I don't know," I said. "I got a big mouth. It would take a lot to fill it."

"I'm your man."

"Dream on."

Hook reached over to the table and grabbed a pfeffernüss. "Eat this first," he said. "No man is ever going to jump your bones until you get some meat on them."

He held the powdery cookie before me, and when I refused to lean over and bite the pfeffernüss right from his fingers, he thrust it into my hand, then took one for himself.

I suddenly remembered I was at a party. I turned around and called out to my coworkers who had been laying bets on how much I would eat. "Hey, you guys, watch this," I said, and took a bite of the cookie, sending buttery crumbs—and an avalanche of powdered sugar—down the front of my not-paid-for dress. I half-choked on the pfeffernüss. As I swiped a napkin from the table to brush the mess off my dress, I noticed—for the first time that evening—Peggy Schoenbarger standing solo across the room. Her eyes were on me. I could only imagine what she was thinking of me. It couldn't have been much worse than what I thought of myself.

Summoned away by some guys in advertising, Hook left me with an empty glass of champagne. The hors d'oeuvres got eaten, the flower arrangements were auctioned off for charity, the CEO made a fatuous speech about the dedication and commitment of Boorman's employees, and then the music returned. Burl Ives singing and swinging to "Jingle Bell Rock" was the last straw for me. I took my black-velvet clutch purse into the bathroom. As I stared into the mirror, I saw my dress was destined to be delivered not back to Saks, but to the dry cleaner's. I also noted my hair and makeup were beyond repair. Maybe it was just the lights, but my skin seemed greenish-yellow, like curry powder stained on a spatula—and my curls were so frizzed they looked like a bad mall perm. Champagne may sparkle in the glass, but it dulled the eyes. And what my eyes saw, they didn't like.

It was time to call it a night.

The cloakroom was small and cluttered. I kicked off my stiletto heels and almost grew dizzy with relief, the way I used to feel after unlacing my wobbly skates after a half hour at the ice rink. My feet were back on the ground. I felt safe. In the vast crush of jackets and boots—worn in case that light snow turned to a blizzard—I located my coat and was just pulling it off the metal hanger when who should come in behind me but Strauss.

My coat slipped off the hanger and fell to the floor. After I leaned over to retrieve it by the collar, I stood up and looked him straight in the eye for the first time in months. I might have bad morals, I thought, but in comparison to that blowsy blonde, boy, did I look *good.*

Or did I?

"Leaving early?" he asked, and the quietness of his voice disarmed me. The carol playing in the background, "Rudolph the Red-Nosed Reindeer," seemed loud and ridiculous, and I listened to it—and resented the way he made me hear it—through Strauss's ears, as tacky and goyish.

"I don't like these kinds of parties," I reminded him.

"Neither do I," he said, as if he were confessing something new to me—me, who knew he preferred a quiet dinner or an evening at home with Palestrina playing softly on the stereo to parties or dances or pool halls or anything that resembled a Carnival cruise atmosphere. *Once you've done a Boorman holiday party, you'll immediately see it's hardly the sort of thing any caring man would inflict upon a date.*

As Strauss looked over his shoulder, I suspected his date was a decoy for me—just as my fiancé had been a blind for Strauss. But the blonde wasn't fictional. She was a living, breathing specimen of womanhood, who probably was primping in the bathroom before she made her appearance at the cloakroom door. She'd better do something about that hair of hers, I thought, if she wanted to score with Strauss tonight. She'd better have an arsenal of Trojans in her purse just in case he wasn't carrying a safe in his back pocket. Then I wondered how she got into the dress with all the frog-closure buttons up the back. Maybe Strauss was the one who buttoned her into it.

I was determined to be adult about this. As if it were a big vitamin that refused to go all the way down, I swallowed my jealousy partway and asked Strauss if he had a *nice holiday.* Somehow I couldn't eke out the word Hanukkah when there was a goofy Christmas tune playing in the background.

"I did," he said. "Thank you for asking."

"You're welcome."

He pushed up his glasses. He always did that when he got nervous. Finally, after another glance over his shoulder, he said, "Lisar—"

Why did just the mention of my mispronounced name, coming from his mouth, make my heart feel so warm?

"It's none of my business," he continued, "but I can't help noticing—you've gotten awfully thin. You haven't been ill, have you?"

Couldn't be finer, I felt like telling him. Then I remembered how Hook had told me to get some meat on my bones, and I recalled that specter of myself in the bathroom mirror, and I suddenly realized I didn't look good—I looked awful. I also suspected Strauss was asking me a coded question, and my heart went cold with anger. I was tempted to say, *Yes, yes, I have been sick, deathly sick.* Then, instead of going home and taking off the chief stewardess's dress, he'd reach for the phone and schedule his second ELISA.

I told him, "I took a second test and I don't have it, if that's what you're asking."

He blinked. "That wasn't what I was asking. But of course, I'm relieved. For you."

"Thank you," I said.

Was that all it came down to: civility and decency? No, there was something more. There must have been jealousy, still, within him—for why else would his face flush when he added, "Watch out for Hook, Lisar."

"I'm a big girl," I said to Strauss. "I can take care of myself."

"I think it's only fair to warn you. Peg has her eyes on you—"

I took in a sharp breath. "Is that why you're being sent to China?"

"How did you know?"

"Hook just told me."

"He can't keep his mouth shut, can he?"

"You were the one who told!" I said.

"Goddammit. I had to."

"Tell me what you told Peggy."

"The conversation was confidential."

"But, Strauss, you took the rap—"

"It wasn't a rap." He trotted out the company line. "This trip is a good opportunity for both me and Boorman. I want to take it."

"I hope it's productive," I said. "And I certainly appreciate your advice."

For a moment I had the odd feeling that Strauss was about to lean forward to hold my coat so I didn't have to struggle into the sleeves, but he didn't. I left my coat off, as if I had no intention of leaving. Rudolph the Red-Nosed Reindeer went down in history and was promptly followed by some wild meowing. It was a ridiculous version of "Jingle Bells," supposedly sung by a passel of cats, and appropriately, it announced the arrival of Strauss's date directly behind him in the doorway. *First place the mask on yourself, then administer to your child. . . . To adjust the length, pull on the strap . . .*

I looked directly in her face, for I wanted to know exactly what kind of model Strauss had traded me in for. Do my eyes deceive me, I thought, or am I looking at a woman who sings soprano in the Presbyterian church choir? Of course, she might have had a nose job on top of that bad dye job, but I was almost positive she'd never make the mattress shake in an excess of glee, as I did, when Strauss told this dumb joke: *Why did the bee wear a yarmulke? He didn't want to be taken for a WASP!*

She smiled. Strauss didn't look at either one of us. For a moment I feared he was going to introduce me to her. But courtesy failed him.

"Hello," she said, in the kind of soft, feminine voice I'd never have.

"Hi," I said. In the moment of silence that followed, I decided to take matters into my own hands. "My name is Lisa," I said, hoping this might ring more than a few jingle bells with her.

"Where are my manners?" Strauss said.

"Yes," I asked, "where are they?"

He introduced me to Miranda Anderson—the kind of pretty, storybook name I'd always wished I had. Only he said it *Mirandar*, and never did a final *R* so break my heart.

"Your last name sounds familiar," I heard myself say.

She looked at me as if I were retarded. "It's a common last name," she said. "But maybe you know my brother, Paul? He's a statistician at Boorman."

I thought a moment before I finally found the connection between Paul and Strauss. "The catcher on the corporate baseball team?" I asked.

"How did you know?"

"I'm a secret cheerleader," I told her, and as I reached to take her outstretched hand, my cuff pulled back and the price tag of my dress inched forth.

"Oh, my God," I said. "I left on the label." I stuffed it back in.

Miranda smiled—a very pretty smile, if I did say so myself. But Strauss frowned, as if he had caught me shoplifting the dress—which he had, after a fashion. I hastily draped my coat over my arm. I picked up my shoes, and for some reason I put them on my hands instead of my feet, the stiletto heels forming a couple of gargoylelike claws. Strauss once criticized me for wearing these very shoes. *What's the matter,* I had asked, *you don't want me to be taller than you? No,* he'd said. *I want you to be safe. If someone pursued you, you wouldn't be able to get away.*

Not much danger of being pursued tonight. Strauss merely stepped out of my way to let me through, dismissing me with a quiet, "Merry Christmas, Lisar."

"I doubt it," I answered. My only consolation as I walked quickly through the back halls of Boorman was that I noticed Strauss had not taken Miranda's coat off the hanger and helped her into it.

Boorman's industrial carpeting felt rough beneath my stockinged feet. Although I headed in that direction, I had no intention of leaving by the back door. I could not face Gussie with tears streaming down my face. I could not take off solo in a Jeep while Strauss followed me (Miranda riding shotgun) in his Audi. I didn't dare drive. I felt drop-dead drunk—or at least I hoped I was drunk, because if I didn't have alcohol to blame for my emotions, I really was in deep psychological shit.

At the back of the building I took a detour into my office. Strauss's office looked out onto the fountain and the rolling lawns. Mine had that excellent view of the parking lot. I tossed my heels beneath my desk, sat down on my chair, blew my nose, and looked out. The cars were dusted with a fine coat of snow. After a few minutes I heard Strauss and Miranda pass by my office, and then I saw them cross the asphalt—but not too far, for Strauss had a reserved spot in the VIP lot. His Audi was parked right beneath the streetlight.

You park beneath a light, don't you, when you go out at night? I wish you'd do that. It's safer.

Strauss unlocked the passenger side first. I remembered how he always used to put his hand on my back, as if he were afraid I would bolt away from him in the split second it took him to open the car door. I watched him. He held the door open. But he did not touch her.

Then—inexplicably—he dashed back out of my sight toward Boorman's back door. After a few moments he came back out again. I watched him brush the snow off his windshield and get in. The Audi started, warmed up, and then took off.

After they left, I sat and looked out onto the night. How wonderful to believe, I thought—in a star that shone so bright it led three kings to a manger, in a cruse of oil that lasted eight days and nights instead of one. But there were only the cold lights of the lab burning below the hill. Then they, too, began to go out, one by one, and the snow began to fall again, and I sat there, all by myself, in the dark. I listened to the hum of my humidifier and the buzz of the fluorescent lights in the hall and my own breathing.

But it wasn't all my breathing. My breath had been joined by someone else's.

I turned. In the doorway stood Hook, and in his hands were two more glasses of champagne.

"Thought I might find you here, Lisa," he said.

I sucked in my breath.

That was the moment when I realized the truth of what Dodie and the feminists had been telling me all along: There were other ways to play with the boys than by taking off your clothes and dancing naked for them. And that was the moment when I proved the falsehood of Strauss's high-heel theory. There were times in a girl's life when a three-inch stiletto could come in mighty handy.

As Hook moved forward, I reached down below my desk.

Chapter Seventeen

Home for Christmas

To get myself in the holiday mood, I listened to WAVZ while driving on the Merritt Parkway to my mother's house. It was the day before Christmas, and the annoying jazzed-up versions of traditional carols were punctuated by even more-obnoxious commercials from Crazy Eddie, Bradlees, and Caldor, furniture stores up and down the Boston Post Road, and every Ford and Chevy dealership between here and kingdom come. Good thing I'm not still going with Strauss, I thought. Good thing I haven't married him, or any other man for that matter. I couldn't imagine spending every December for the rest of my life walking the men's department, trying to pick out the perfect tie. I couldn't picture myself trying to look happy when my husband got me a sweater in exactly the wrong cut and color.

Only when I reached the Milford town line—less than a half hour from my mother's house—did I admit that this was exactly my problem. I *could* imagine it. And I wanted it—not the drudge of Christmas shopping for a man, or throwing his undies into the wash along with mine, or even the dubious pleasure of cooking him (or rather, *us*—since both people in a couple had to eat) a well-balanced dinner complete with green vegetables every night. I wanted the man himself—not just as a lover, but as a friend. Failing that, I was thinking—seriously—about buying a vibrator. But I knew the moment I threw the switch, I'd be incapable of anything beyond giggling, and I'd have to stow the damn thing beneath my bed, next to the Trojans and the ninth draft of *Stop It Some More*.

As I pulled up in my mother's driveway, some velvety-voiced asshole started crooning about the joys of coming home for Christmas. I snapped off the radio. Well, there I was. Home. But where was my mother? The back door was locked, the lights were off, and the curtains were drawn. Wasn't that just like Mama? I told her I was going to pull in around three, and she chose that time to make her one trip of the day to Stop & Shop. She probably was still smarting from the joyous smile I had given her five years ago in the Sarah Lawrence dorm room, when I gleefully surrendered my house key.

My hands felt cold and frozen as I knocked, one last time, on the back door. I felt like climbing back into my Jeep and gunning it back to New York, but I settled for a more sane solution: walking two blocks down to Carol's house. I deliberately took the back way so I didn't have to pass by the house where Dodie grew up. I didn't want to bump into Auntie Beppina or Uncle Gianni.

I'd almost forgotten how vulgar the Christmas decorations in my old neighborhood could be. In yards already cluttered with statues of Saint Francis of Assisi and Mary on a half shell, our neighbors planted reindeer—all eight of them, and some even had the odd Rudolph in the lead—pulling sleighs full of jolly Saint Nick and his sack of toys. Plastic Dickensian lamplighters and caroling Brits sang with pursed lips the songs of the season. My favorite were the displays that mixed the religious and the secular themes—Frosty the Snowman rather than the ox or the ass admiring the Christ child in the manger. Also high on my list were the crèches with only two kings instead of three (because the third wise man was black, and they didn't belong in this neighborhood). All of this was brilliantly lit at night, so our street looked like Luna Park in Coney Island's heyday, and pilots probably used it as a marker when touching down at Tweed New Haven Airport. It was a wonder we didn't have a Cessna or a Piper occasionally mistake our street for an actual runway.

Christmas was the only time of the year I gave thanks that my parents were cheap. Through all of this, our house stayed dark. In fact, darker. My parents always scrimped on electricity—refusing to own a dishwasher or a coffee maker or a blender—and Mama used the holiday season as an excuse to eat by candlelight. She bought votives for three cents apiece at the Christmas bazaar—which went down to five for a dime, if any were left on the table during the last hour.

My sister, Carol, also was too thrifty to pay a huge electric bill. But she made up for it in other ways. Cutout silver snowflakes sparkled on her front window. A pasteboard Santa, winking merrily as he shouldered his heavy sack, hung on her front door. I knocked firmly on his fat belly—loud enough to be heard, but not loud enough to wake the baby if he was sleeping. But why was I concerned about the baby? The TV was on loud enough to filter through the front door. It was soap-opera time.

Ever the stickler for security—Al had her well-trained on this count—Carol peeked through the lace curtains. Carol owned nothing worth stealing. But after an episode on a crowded public bus when a guy pushed himself too hard against her, Carol had become deathly afraid of being raped. In spite of my lifelong flirtation with danger—and my modified gang-bang fantasies with the twins—so was I. That episode with Hook—thankfully aborted when he saw the murder weapon I brought up from below my desk—proved just how frightening men could be. Hook had laughed and said, "Take it easy! Just wanted to see if you wanted another drink!" but I noticed he shielded his family jewels with a glass of champagne just in case I decided to get serious. That night he had forced me to leave by the back door whether I wanted to or not. Never was I so thankful that Gussie's eyes—and gun—were watching over me—until I had to sign my name below Strauss's and Miranda's on the log.

Gussie kept his eye on the pen as I signed, and afterward, he examined the signature. "Funny, Miss Lisa," he said. "Doesn't look like you had too much to drink."

"Who said I did?"

"Mr. Strauss."

"What?"

"Not in so many words. But he did ask me to make sure you got home all right. First he checked the sign-out log—everybody seems interested in that sign-out log all of a sudden—and outside I saw him looking in the snow for footprints. Then he came back in here—why do you think he came back here, trying to figure out whether you left?"

"Maybe he wants to steal my Jeep."

"Oh, no. He definitely doesn't like that Jeep of yours. At least not half as much as Dr. Schoenbarger. Twice I've seen her out there, giving it the once-over."

"Did she kick all four of my tires?"

"No, but once I came back from the men's room and I saw Mr. Strauss reach in—it was a foggy Saturday morning—and turn off your lights. 'Good thing Miss Lisa left that door unlocked,' I told him when he came in, and he said he was surprised a car like that even had locks, never mind a safety belt—"

"Next time tell him I have a DieHard battery."

Gussie held up his hands. "I mind my own business."

I peered down the hall to make sure no one was coming. "Mind mine a little bit more."

He smiled. "When are you getting married?"

"Who is spreading these vicious rumors?" I asked.

"I got it—indirectly—from Mr. Strauss. At first I thought he got it from Dr. Schoenbarger—"

"I'm sure he did."

"But now I'm starting to think he got it from Mr. Anderson."

"Such gossip is bad for morale," I said, and gave Gussie my arm. "Walk me out to the lot, will you? And shoot Mr. Roberts—right in the breadbasket, you got me?—if you see him leap out from behind a car."

"It would be a pleasure," Gussie said.

　　　　　Carol unlocked the dead bolt and chain and cracked the door. "Shh. The baby's finally down."

I did a dramatic tiptoe inside. Once in the living room, I slipped off my coat, smiling.

"Ewww," Carol said. "What happened to you?"

My smile instantly disappeared. "What do you mean?"

"You're so skinny—"

"I am not!"

"You are too. You look sick—"

"I'm not sick—"

"—like you crawled out of a concentration camp."

Now it was my turn to draw in my breath, to feel the sharp pull of my bones against my lungs. Maybe Carol had more smarts than I gave her credit for. Or some kind of sisterly ESP. As if to confirm that my thinness was in response to Strauss's rejection, a husky-throated woman in too much mascara and a choker fashioned from oversize pink pearls appeared on Carol's Zenith console and bemoaned, "I should have known he never loved me."

After the bitter cold outside, Carol's living room felt overheated. I was afraid I was going to faint. I wanted to go over the edge, but I was damned if I would do it while *The Guiding Light* was playing.

"Lisa, sit down," Carol said, snapping off the TV. The soap opera faded, then disappeared altogether. Now I had no excuse. I sat down on the couch, landing on a squeaky toy—a cheerful pink pig with a purple bow around his neck. The pig squealed, but I didn't laugh and neither did Carol. Carol sat next to me. She hesitated before she put her hand on my hand, and then she put her arm around me. Nobody had touched me in such a gentle way in months. Carol and I hadn't touched each other in years. But I put my head on her shoulder (where else was I going to put it? it felt so heavy it just needed to go down somewhere) and I started to cry.

Between sobs I said, "Oh, God, I'm in trouble—"

"Lisa! You're pregnant!"

"No, I feel sick, I just feel so sick—"

"Say what's wrong. Tell me what's wrong. Do you have cancer or something?"

After Carol got me some Kleenex, I told her *sick in the head.*

"Oh," Carol said. *"That."* She seemed relieved. "You could go to a doctor. There are doctors for that."

"I know."

"Why don't you go then?" she asked. She paused. "I went to one."

"You! You went! Why?"

For a moment, while Carol hesitated, I thought she was about to confess something was wrong with her marriage. Just as those with an illness sometimes unconsciously wished it on others, I wanted my sister to blurt out, *Al's been screwing another woman and he's going to leave me!*

Instead, Carol confessed she went to a shrink after she gave birth to Al Dante Junior and postpartum blues flattened her like a tractor. "I couldn't help it, I just felt all weird and crazy, like I was going to kill somebody, and then I would cry and cry and cry, and I felt like I couldn't get up from the bed."

"So what happened when you went to the shrink?"

"He gave me drugs."

"Oh, they always give women drugs—"

"Fuck it, I wanted them. I would have swallowed the whole bottle and then some just to feel like myself again—"

"They worked?"

"Man, they're great," Carol said.

"What's the brand name?"

Carol held up her finger and tiptoed into the bathroom off the kitchen, where she tried—unsuccessfully—to quietly open her squeaky medicine cabinet. She came back holding a brown vial.

"I don't know how to pronounce it," she said.

"You said they work?"

"Like a charm."

"Any side effects?"

Carol hesitated. "They lessen your sex drive."

"I'll take two," I said. "You got anything to eat?"

Carol gave me half—half only, because I was so skinny more might knock me out—then popped her third one of the day. We went into the kitchen and downed the pills with water. She got out a jar of Skippy peanut butter and a Hershey bar she admitted she was saving for Al's bowling night, as a reward for dealing all morning, afternoon, and then into the evening with a fussy, demanding Al Junior.

"The baby drives me nuts, Lisa," she said. "And then I feel so guilty because I prayed to have him! And I waited so long for him! And now that he's here all he does is cry and cry! And I can't figure out what he wants from me, and he pisses me off, and I think how could I ever have wanted him in the first place?"

"Sounds more like a husband than a baby," I said.

"At least Junior takes *naps*. Al's always in my face."

"What's he bitchin' about now?"

"He wants to—you know—have sex."

I slapped my face to indicate disbelief.

"Lisa, I'm exhausted from this baby. I have zero interest in anything—you know—below the belt. But if I don't—you know—keep him happy in bed, then he doesn't help out with the housework and I'm even more exhausted."

"So what are you saying? If you give him a blow job once a week, he'll take out the garbage?"

"Lisa!"

"If you swallow, will he wash the dishes?"

"Why do you always have to be so crude and disgusting?"

"Because life is crude and disgusting."

"All I can say is, Al better come through on Christmas, or he's fucked."

"Or not fucked," I said, and Carol and I both screamed with laughter. We split the chocolate into bite-size pieces, which we dipped into the peanut butter and chewed quickly and stickily. In two minutes flat, only slivers were left behind on the foil wrapper. As I picked up the wrapper and licked it, I wondered what Al was like in bed.

In the back room, the baby started to cluck. Carol sighed, went to the refrigerator, and got out a bottle of formula, which she parked in a small saucepan of water on the stove. She turned the burner on low, then went to get the baby. While she was gone, I examined the bottle of pills on the table. So this was why she stopped breastfeeding, I thought. Well, more power to her. A happy mother made for a happier baby.

That half of a pill sure made *me* feel happy. It also made me hungry. I dipped one of my fingers into the jar and licked the peanut butter off my top knuckle and fingernail. Then I stuck two fingers in, and before I knew it, my whole hand was in there, all five fingers, pulling up the peanut butter like I was back in one of the Sarah Lawrence art studios on the first day of sculpture class, drawing out from the corrugated barrel covered in damp plastic a handful of cold, wet clay. The art teacher urged us to use our imaginations. Some girls, obviously lacking in creativity, made Girl Scout–style pinch pots. Some made delicate sleeping kitty cats; others did big bruising dogs along the order of Siberian huskies and Newfoundlands. The majority, most of them city girls whose closest encounter with a horse probably came from walking past the old nags who dragged the carriages around Central Park, made lean and muscular wild stallions. I made a male nude. His penis fell off when we baked it in the kiln. The teacher couldn't find it in the oven. Still, I got an A.

"It's a man, isn't it?" Carol asked, after she came back in and I did my duty of admiring the wiry hair, sturdy legs, and smooth, pink cheeks of Al Dante Junior.

"What do you mean?" I asked.

"I mean, isn't it a guy?" Carol sounded hopeful. "A guy you've gone crazy about?"

"Don't tell Mama."

"Are you nuts? I don't tell her nothing."

Carol sat across the table from me, one arm cradling the baby and the other hand tilting the bottle toward the baby's fast-sucking mouth, and waited for me to tell my story. This she could deal with: a woman going bonkers over a man. What she probably couldn't grapple with were the specifics—that is, of who Strauss was, or how we came together, or how we broke apart—especially all the stuff that had to do with Dodie. I already had vowed, and I would keep my promise, that I would not tell Carol—nor Auntie Beppina, nor my mother—anything about Dodie.

"So," Carol said, "who is he?" To tempt me to talk, she gestured with her chin over at her own famed Christmas Whitman's Sampler, which sat under a stack of mail on the kitchen table. I pulled out the yellow box, took off the top, and folded back the brown tissue paper to reveal a plastic tray—already half picked over—of nuts and creams and turtles. I contemplated long and hard, deliberately avoiding the dreaded cherry bomb—before I made my choice, a dark chocolate mound full of gooey orange cream. Then I watched Carol's eyes light upon a caramel, which I picked out and leaned across the table to slip between her grateful, expectant lips.

"It's my boss," I told Carol.

"Oh my God!" Carol garbled, biting so hard on the caramel it split in two. A gooey-stringed half fell onto Al Dante Junior's diaper. She rescued it before it bounced to the ground. "Is he married?"

I tried to sound indignant. "No."

"How old—"

"Not that old—"

Al had nine years on my sister. "Seven, eight years' age difference I can understand," Carol said. "But don't you think it's weird when women go with guys who could be their fathers?"

I laughed—slowly, lazily, carelessly—because Carol's magic pill really was starting to kick in.

"Yeah," I said. "I do think that's weird."

"I mean, we already had one father," Carol said. "And look at what a disaster he was."

"Daddy wasn't that bad," I was surprised to hear myself saying. "At least he never walked out on us."

"This guy walked out? Screw him."

"That's my problem. I still want to."

"Lisa! You screwed him? I mean, he screwed you?"

"And how—"

"I can't believe it," Carol said.

"What do you think I did with him? Tucked him in for nighty-night with a kiss?"

"You should wait until you're married—or at least engaged."

I shrugged. "You were the one who just asked me if I was pregnant."

"But that was before I knew it was your boss." Carol also shrugged. Maybe her pill was kicking in too. "You sure know how to pick 'em, Lisa."

"Yeah."

"Why do you do this shit to yourself?"

I laughed again. "I honestly don't know."

And Carol, obviously, didn't care. "Damn, this caramel is good," she said. "Find me a turtle."

"There aren't any left."

"Go down to the next level."

This seemed like the height of decadence. Mama never let us go onto the second tray of a Sampler until we had finished every single last piece—including that noxious cherry bomb—on the first.

In between coconuts and creams and nuts, Carol told "Mama stories"—which usually consisted of Carol's complaints and grudges against our mother, but which sometimes also contained choice anecdotes about how Mama had butchered, once again, the English language. We laughed and laughed. Then I held Al Junior while Carol pulled out the stuffed peppers she had prepared for dinner. Junior was a warm and milky bundle. After I patted him for a few seconds on my shoulder, he let out a humongous belch. "Like father, like son," Carol said—for Al was known for how loud he could let it rip. "He does it just to *schif* me out."

As we sat there giggling, I thought of how Strauss probably would disapprove of this low-class humor, and I thought I was much better off without his uptight self sitting there judging Al's killer burps (which, truth to tell, would have been a lot better than his judging Al's equally famous farts). I wondered what Strauss would make of my family. *Not much,* I thought, and then I added, *Oh, fuck him. Just fuck him.* Although of all the men I had ever gone with since leaving home, Strauss *was* the only one who did not require a translation for the word *schif* or the adjective *schifato.* He even knew that you could grammatically glad-hand the verb *schif:* "I *schif* men" or "Men *schif* me" both meant "Guys gross me out." If there was an equivalent Yiddish verb, I would never discover it.

Carol got me a big sweater—one that she wore when she was pregnant—and told me to put it on so Mama couldn't see how skinny I'd gotten. I stayed there past dark, and finally Mama turned up at the back door.

She took off her coat—without Carol's invitation—and glared at me. "I come home and find there's one of those jeeks—"

"Jeeps," I said.

"—sitting in my driveway."

"You bought a Jeep?" Carol asked me.

Mama didn't give me time to answer the question. "Who do I know's got a Jeep, I'm thinking. I look in the backseat. I'm about to call the police—"

"Didn't you see the New York plates?" I asked.

"So I look in the backseat. But you're not in this Jeep."

"Why do you think you'd find me in the backseat of a Jeep?" I asked my mother.

"So I go inside. I wait and wait for you. But you don't come home. And there's this Jeep in the driveway—"

My teeth started to hurt. "Mother, I told you what time I was coming, and then I get here and find the house locked."

"You know where I am, at three o'clock—"

"I'm not going over to the Stop & Shop and look for you in the frozen peas—"

"I gotta do my shopping."

"So I'm supposed to sit in the driveway and freeze to death?"

"Your sister's got a phone. It's too much for you to pick it up and tell me you own the Jeep in the driveway?"

Bentornato! Welcome home. Mama pointed her chin at me. "What do you think of this baby?"

"What's to think?" I said, as I ran my finger over the baby's soft, plump cheek. "He's a-wonderful. He's a-marvelous."

Mama nodded. "That's right," she said. "You got the right attitude." She pushed up her glasses and squinted at me. "You look different."

"I just ate a lot of chocolate," I said. "It makes my eyes look wild."

Mama squinted even more. "Too skinny. Is that supposed to look chick?"

"Sheeeek," I pronounced it for her, and Carol, to save me from yet another argument with Mama, said, "You can never be too rich or too thin."

Then I laughed, and Carol laughed, and with the hand that wasn't cradling the baby, I blew Mama a big kiss.

She glared at me. "You girls. Crazy." She reached across the table and picked up the pill bottle. "Somebody got a bladder infection?"

At the risk of dropping Al Dante Junior, I slid down in my seat and kicked Carol under the table.

"Yeah, I do," I said.

Mama adjusted her bifocals and inspected the label. "What do they give you nowadays for that?"

"An antibiotic," I said, holding out my one free hand.

Mama clutched the bottle closely. "This must be a new kind, I've never heard of this kind before—"

I kept my hand extended. "You know how they're always developing new drugs—"

"Is this made by your drug company—what's the name of that outfit you work for? But why's it got your name on it, Carol?"

I reached across the table—squeezing Junior far too tightly—and snatched the vial from Mama, then put it into my pocket. "Those pharmacists," I said. "More and more, they're like the alcoholic druggist in *It's a Wonderful Life.*"

"I gotta see that movie this year," Mama said. "Last year they played it opposite *Chipmunks' Christmas on Ice*. I had to miss it." She turned to Carol. "So where's your husband?"

Carol was looking edgy—probably as much from this close call with Mama as from her fear that I was going to steal her pills forever. "How should I know where Al is? Working late."

"Maybe he went Christmas shopping for you," I said.

"Yeah, maybe he went to Tahiti too."

Mama shook her head. "This Christmas stuff. All this wild shopping and all the money getting thrown around—"

"There's nothing wrong with a present every now and then," Carol said, pointedly adding, "especially a present bought at full price."

When we were small, Mama used to claim the Easter bunny was still working his way around to our house and wouldn't arrive until the following night. Then she went out to the drugstore on Monday and bought us cellophane-wrapped baskets, full of hollow chocolate rabbits and marshmallow chicks, for half price. Did she think we were too stupid to notice that the bunny had made it to Jocko and Dodie's house, just two doors down? Did she think we wouldn't notice the big red fifty-percent-off sticker that she forgot to detach before leaving the baskets on our bed, where they greeted us, twenty-four hours too late, after we returned from our first dreary Monday back at school?

I lowered Junior to his carryall and offered him his choice of objects to hold. He sat at my feet, his head bent down and all three of his baby-fat chins pudged out as he kept examining—and dropping—a cardboard toilet-paper roll, as if to prove my mother's theory that children didn't need expensive toys. I knew that for Christmas Mama probably had wrapped up for Junior a few more empty toilet-paper rolls, an egg carton minus the dozen eggs, and a couple of carefully washed tins that once held chicken pot pies, on sale four for a dollar.

For Christmas, I had spent fifteen minutes browsing through a catalog titled HOLIDAY FEVER! provided by Boorman's own top Avon Lady. For my mother I purchased a tin of violet talcum powder that she would sniff once (long and hard as an addict sucked up the last long line of coke) before she relegated it to her bottom drawer. For Carol, I bought a silver hairbrush-and-comb set. For Al, a bowling-ball-on-a-rope soap. For Junior, a stuffed polar bear wearing a ski cap and sunglasses. But the bear came with a label warning AGES 3 & UP. Madame Avon showed displeasure when I asked if I could return it. "There are strict return policies on seasonal items," she told me. "I'm afraid the answer is no, but I hope that won't keep you from ordering with me again."

I felt like telling her to take her Skin-So-Soft and her Pretty Feet and her Silicone Glove and shove all three of them—simultaneously—right up her buttinski. Instead, I put the polar bear in the office Christmas grab bag. Imagine my delight when her soft, greedy hands pulled it out.

Carol married Al Dante knowing he was wedded to last-minute shopping, the infamous Christmas Eve blitz through one of the mall's jewelry stores, where he would pick out something very heavy and very gold, probably vastly overpriced. While Mama (with all the insistence of those bold bumper stickers that commanded REMEMBER THE REASON FOR THE SEASON!) went on and on about how people no longer valued the religious significance of the holiday, I looked down at my chapped hands and wondered what Strauss might have gotten me. In the Frick he had told me he hated the mall. But for his wife, I knew he'd walk it.

• • •

Christmas passed in the same old depressing way. Mama didn't want to stay up late for midnight mass, so I went with her in the morning, half an hour early so we could *get a decent seat.* Mama did two rosaries and gave dirty looks to the holiday-only Catholics who flocked to fill up the church. She probably thought there ought to be a lock on the door to keep them out, or maybe even some sort of traffic cop who stood in the vestibule and pointed to the left or the right side of the church to seat the faithful or the unfaithful, just as wedding ushers seated guests according to the categories of *friends of the bride* or *friends of the groom.* Even when I was small, I always thought it was unfair that the groom's family and friends got the privilege of sitting on the right, while the bride's family got relegated to the unlucky left.

Before mass I amused myself by imagining what would have happened if I had brought Strauss home with me. He would have accompanied us to church—after Mama asked him, "*Sei certo?* Are you sure you want to come, you know this is a Catholic event." When the ushers came around before Communion to collect for the parish, Strauss—who did not have a preprinted collection envelope—would have reached into his wallet to make a healthy donation. Mama would have gasped at the size of the bill he dropped down and stopped the usher to make Strauss change from the basket.

"What *does* your family do on Christmas?" I once asked Strauss, and until he gave me a mischievous pinch on the cheek, I believed him when he said, "We go eat kosher Chinese in Crown Heights." The truth was, his family did celebrate it in their own way. He went home to his parents' house, but his sister didn't. Strauss and his dad had a tradition of putting on their boots and hats and going for a long, mostly silent walk in the afternoon, and when they came back his mother—who'd been cooking up a storm all day—served salmon and roasted red potatoes and homemade egg noodles, and his father always praised the food too much, which made everyone sad, although everyone tried not to show it.

The organ hummed and started up. Mass began. I left my hymnal on the rack. I didn't sing—I had a lousy voice—but I recited all the responses and the prayers, which I knew by heart even though I no longer said them on a weekly basis. My mother glared at me when I didn't get up to receive Communion. I shifted my legs to the right to let everyone else pass by, and a little boy accidentally kicked me so hard in the shins I muttered a blasphemous "shit!" At the end of mass, not trusting the choir to do its duty, my mother accompanied them on "Angels We Have Heard on High." But she just couldn't cut those top-of-the-staff *glorias,* and so she delivered them in an alto monotone that annoyed me.

We went home. Carol and Al and the baby came over, the baby clutching a foam bowling ball and a bright red plastic pin—a present from his father, obviously. Carol had on a getup worthy of my former boss Karen—a checked smock complete with rickrack-lined pockets and a Peter Pan collar. Al had on a white dress shirt, brown textured slacks, and no tie. Instead, he wore too much after-shave, in a musky scent probably marketed under the rude name of *Brut* or *Homme.* Wait until he gets hold of my smelly soap-on-a-rope, I thought. Carol might have to fumigate.

"Nice to see you again, Al," I said—for in my heart, I really did like my brother-in-law. Although he was hardly my type, I could see why Carol had married him. Al exuded a certain primitive sensuality that became evident when he leaned over to kiss me on the cheek and his gut grazed my thin hip in an interesting way.

Al sat on the La-Z-Boy that used to belong to my father.

"What's new?" I asked.

"Nothing much," Al said, picking up the newspaper, and in response to my question, Carol took over. Five minutes and two rolls of developed film later ("Here's Junior tasting his first rice cereal." "Here's Al trying to slip him some beer"), Al came up for air from behind the sports page. With a sly look that revealed Carol already had informed him I was screwing my supervisor, Al asked what was new with me.

"I got a promotion," I said, surprising even myself—for I suddenly remembered that although I had hinted I would be moving up, I had never actually told my family I'd been promoted.

"Oh, yeah?" said Al, and Mama said, "Don't let that get to your head," and Carol sniffed the air and said, "Ma, those smelts from last night still stink, and I mean totally!"

And that was it. No one asked me about my new responsibilities. No one asked when I was promoted or—thank God—how I got there.

While my mother trimmed artichokes in the kitchen and Al flipped the TV channels back and forth between the Pope giving mass in Rome and the first dull quarter of a football game, I sat silent on the sofa—all 103 pounds of me wrapped in a pilly sweater my sister wore when her weight almost topped her husband's. I had nothing to say to anyone. The subject of Strauss was off limits. And here in my family home, where the very thought of Dodie always had been a source of contention, I could not venture onto that topic, nor would I even want to, knowing that Dodie hadn't come home for Christmas in years. He was planning to spend the day with some new friends who also had tested positive.

"Is it a support group?" I asked.

"It's a self-pity club. Where you can whine about your diarrhea and take great pleasure in the fact that you have more immune cells than the next person."

"Do you have the runs again?"

"No, but you're gonna, baby, after eating a too big hunk of your mother's lasagne."

"Once she left off the cheese."

Dodie hesitated. "Wasn't that the Good Friday my dad called me a fairy?" Then he laughed. "Happy holidays, Lise. Eat a smelt or two for me."

Before dinner, Auntie Beppina came over. Uncle Gianni stopped visiting us when my father died. I guess he figured he didn't owe anything to my mother and that it fell to the women to keep up the lines of communication between our two families.

Al watched the game, Al Junior slept, and Carol and my mother fought about whether or not the Church of the Holy Family really needed an interior paint job (Carol was pro-Sherwin-Williams, and my mother thought Father ought to put his pennies away *for the day that rains,* because the parish was dwindling, and if it weren't for those Vietnamese boat people who were starting to come in with all their children, he wouldn't have half so many lining up at mass to receive Communion). Auntie Beppina cornered me in the dining room. I was sitting at the table, folding the lace napkins for dinner. She gripped my arm—after all, she was my *comare,* so she felt she had the right—and demanded, "Well? You talk to him lately?"

"Mm-hmm."

"You seen him?"

"Mm-hmm," I repeated.

"Still good-looking?"

"Better than ever," I said. "And making money on a roll."

Auntie Beppina shook her head. Then she smiled, but sadly. This, at least, she could claim: one son who was handsome, who was well-off, who had never been suspended from school or done time in J.D. But she couldn't claim him to the rest of the world, because this son, unlike the others, had never knocked up a girl from East Haven, or West Haven, or

North Haven, or New Haven. He'd never have children. He'd never wear a wedding ring.

"He called me this morning," Auntie Beppina said, sitting down at the table beside me. "He sounded kind of funny on the phone."

"Maybe he wanted to come home for Christmas."

"I asked him. I ask him every year. He says no."

Auntie Beppina took one of the napkins that I'd folded and refolded it. Then she refolded another. They looked a lot better done her way, and that irked me. I narrowed my eyes at her. She narrowed hers back.

"You don't look good," Auntie Beppina said.

"I had the flu," I said. "I lost weight."

"He's been sick lately too. He got the flu last month same as you. You two always seemed to get sick at the same time—"

My hands blanched. I was sure all the blood had drained from my face, because Auntie Beppina asked, "What is it? What's wrong with you?"

"Nothing's wrong with me."

"Your face is white."

"I have anemia, thanks for reminding me, I've got to go take my iron pill—"

When I got up, she put her hand on my forearm. "Ah, Elisabetta, you tell me what you know. You know something, don't you—"

"I don't know nothing," I said, "except that you're practically breaking my arm. Let go of it."

"Ay," Auntie Beppina said, and let me go. I listened to my own breathing and from the china cabinet behind me, the ticking of my mother's porcelain clock. I examined the Santa Claus tablecloth my mother had laid beneath the yellowed vinyl cover. A hole in Santa's forehead made it look as if a bullet had gone right through his brain.

"I worry about him," Auntie Beppina said.

I shrugged, as if I didn't know what she was talking about.

"I read the papers, you know," Auntie Beppina said. "It's supposed to be bad in New York."

I shrugged again.

"I worry about him," she repeated.

I got up and began to place the napkins around the table.

When I got to the head of the table—where Al was slated to sit— Auntie Beppina said, "I saw on TV the other day you can get over it by hypnosis."

"AIDS?"

"The other thing," Auntie Beppina said.

"Oh," I said. "Yeah. *The other thing.*" I opened the silverware chest and took out the forks. "What does the hypnotist do, wave a pocket watch in front of your face and say, 'You are feeling very heterosexual'—"

From the parlor I heard Al laughing, and I suddenly realized that he and my mother and my sister had been listening to every word that Auntie Beppina and I exchanged. But that didn't stop me. In a fake Viennese accent, I said, "Watch this watch. Now, repeat after me: You vant to make love to a woman—"

Auntie Beppina gasped, as if this was the dirtiest thing she'd ever heard in her life. So I kept on going. "You are dreaming of a couple of big fat juicy tits—"

"Watch it!" my mother called out from the kitchen. "Watch your mouth, talking to your *comare* like that—"

Auntie Beppina called back, "This daughter of yours, she's got a problem with herself—"

"Tell me something new," Mama said, which made me drop the forks back into the silverware chest with a clatter.

"You've got the problem," I said. "You all do! Treating me and Dodie like we're a couple of major fuckups—"

"Lisa," Carol said. "For Christ's sake, it's Christmas. Calm down."

"Or go back to New York," Al said, pissed because the Jets were on a losing streak again.

I lowered the lid of the silverware chest with a bang. "Fine. I'm going, right now."

"You need gas in that Jeep!" Al called out—for he had taken my latest purchase for a test-drive that morning.

"I'm leaving," I said, "if I have to run on empty! I don't belong here."

"You belong," my mother called out. "You belong to this family whether you like it or not—"

"Not!" I said, and made for the stairs to get my duffel bag. But Al—who was probably excited by the tied score in the fourth quarter— jumped up from the recliner and tackled me from behind, laughing as he got a good grip around my waist. I stared into the kitchen at my mother and sister, who sat at the table over the open lid of the Whitman's Sampler.

"Look out," I told Al, "or I'll give it to you right where it hurts—"

Carol shrieked—after all, she wanted more kids—and my mother said, "Look at her, she's so skinny! How'd she get to be so skinny?"

"She said she had the flu," Auntie Beppina said, coming to the door.

"Bullshit," Carol said, plucking a milk chocolate from the plastic tray. "She's in love with her boss. At work."

"Carol!" I said, still struggling to get free of Al. "You bitch. You said you wouldn't tell!"

"*Mannaggia!*" my mother said. "A married man?"

"He's not married!"

"What is he then?" my mother demanded.

"A Jew from Brooklyn!" I shouted.

My mother put her hand over her heart. "*Santa Maria,*" she murmured. "What next?" Then she asked, "How much money does he make?"

Al clearly enjoyed this question to the hilt, for he laughed wildly and held me even closer against his showered, after-shaved body.

I knew I was over the deep end when I deliberately pressed my rump back against his pelvis and felt a strange stirring inside of me.

After all, it had been months since any man touched me.

Al must have been pretty hard up too. In any case, he couldn't have been getting much off the tranquilized version of Carol, because before I broke free and headed for the stairs, I earned the dubious satisfaction of giving my own brother-in-law an erection.

Chapter Eighteen

My Father's House Has Mansions

Although the rest of Editorial was thrilled to come out from under the yoke of Eben Strauss—and probably even celebrated his departure with a round of jelly doughnuts ordered behind my back—I grew incensed at Peggy for sending him off on a three-month junket to the Orient while subjecting me to the supervision of Hook. The carpet practically caught fire from static whenever Hook and I were in the same room together. Hook's smarmy face was in my face all day long, suggesting futile, busywork projects that technically were the responsibility of the advertising staff. I didn't dare complain to anyone. I was afraid Hook would accuse *me* of harassing *him*. Eager to vindicate Strauss, Peggy would step forward and say, "Hmm, Ms. Diodetto does seem to have a bad pattern of becoming involved with her superiors." I pictured myself stripped of my computer and private printer, demoted to a cubicle with only a box of blue pencils, the latest edition of the *PDR*, and *The Chicago Manual of Style* to keep me company.

By Valentine's Day—a miserable holiday that I celebrated only by keeping my daily date with the Pacer—my résumé was flying fast and furious through the mail, but apparently no one wanted the exmistress of Boorman's exiled VP, even if she knew where to place her semicolons. Two months in Taipei stretched into three, and there was talk of another shakedown up top. Rumors. I heard them in the cafeteria. Hook started to back off and even dropped a few hints that he was on to bigger and better things. Good. The guy couldn't get out of my face fast enough. But right behind him loomed the unreadable Dr. Peggy Schoenbarger—cool but courteous—who decided she, not Hook, would be the one who executed my next employee evaluation.

Although I had coated my armpits with three layers of an extra-strength antiperspirant touted as *so effective you can even skip a day!* my blouse already felt damp by the time I got to Peggy's office for our meeting. I took it as a bad sign when she stayed behind her massive desk rather than joining me, as she usually did, at her conference table. "Greetings, Ms. Diodetto," she said, looking up from the pile of papers on her desk. "Sit down."

I perched on the penitent's chair opposite her.

"You don't look well," she said.

"I ate lunch in the cafeteria."

She frowned. "I'm not sure the strictest food sanitation is practiced there." She leaned across her desk and handed me the evaluation. "Look it over first and then we'll talk."

I tried not to let my hands shake as I turned the pages, and I tried not to let her see how quickly I scanned the right side of the page to catch the numbers before I read the comments. I had no cause for worry on the first page—she'd given me eights and nines in every category, and under *attention to detail* she'd even given me something that Strauss had never dreamed of doling out: a perfect ten. I had become a minor heroine with Peggy after I scanned a blue line and honed in on an error that four other pairs of eyes had not caught, the lack of a necessary zero in a formula: .025 when it should have read .0025. Although she was hardly effusive in her praise—rewarding me with a cool *I see that's why we pay you to be at Boorman, Ms. Diodetto*—that little compliment had kept me going through weeks of tedium. It bored me to tears sometimes, but at that moment my job seemed to have some meaning. I had saved somebody from getting hurt, and it felt good to remind myself I wasn't just a loose cannon at Boorman, threatening to explode in every hallway I passed through.

My lowest number, predictably, was under the category of collegiality. Peggy had jacked it up only one point to a seven, and as I stared at it, she dryly remarked that although I had shown "some improvement in that area," from all reports I still seemed to be clashing with my immediate supervisor.

"If you remember, this was the weakest point on your last evaluation. On your last evaluation, you scored six."

"Mr. Strauss scored me," I said. "I mean, he filled it out."

There was a long silence. "You signed off on it," Peggy reminded me.

"But—as I told you before—I didn't want to argue with him. I didn't like arguing with him."

"But you like to argue with Mr. Roberts?"

"I can win against him."

"But you didn't think you could win against Mr. Strauss?"

"I'm not sure what you're saying. Asking for. With that question."

"Just an honest answer will do."

From outside her window the spray of the fountain thudded down on the stone base. "No," I finally said. "I didn't think I could win with Mr. Strauss."

"Just as I thought." She shuffled papers on her desk. "Do you enjoy working for Mr. Roberts?"

"He has a dart board in his office."

"Do you object to his playing on company time?"

"No—I mean, I don't think he should do that—I certainly don't join in—"

"Does he ask you to join him?"

"No, Mr. Roberts already knows he'd better duck when I get a sharp object in my hand—but—what I meant to say is that this dart board represents something about his personality that doesn't quite mesh with mine."

"Do you prefer to work for Mr. Strauss?"

"I do like that Thomas Eakins print on his wall."

"I had no idea you were so interested in interior decorating." She leaned back in her chair. "You understand Mr. Strauss is coming back soon."

I nodded, not daring to open my mouth.

"I need to ask you something, Ms. Diodetto."

Shoot, I silently begged her.

"I need to know if you can work under him and maintain a professional relationship."

"Oh, yes," I said. "I can. I will. But I always have—"

"That's not his side of the story."

I looked down at my hands. "Could I ask—what his story—was?"

"Are you interested in telling me your side?"

"No—not at all—but I'm sure he said things about me that—that weren't true—"

"Whatever Eben is, he isn't a liar."

"I'm not saying that. I'm just saying that when you tell a story, you tell it from your own perspective, and sometimes the facts get mixed up with fiction."

She frowned. "Facts are facts, Ms. Diodetto. I had the plain truth. He said he lost his judgment—took advantage of his position—coerced you—"

"Bullshit!" I said.

A lock of her silvery hair—loose in front—froze in midair. I rushed in to set things right. "What I mean to say is, that's the way it happened in his imagination—"

"Why would he imagine such a thing?"

"Because he's on a guilt trip," I said. "And he likes to act as if he's in charge of everything. The guy has a control problem."

"It's true, Eben can be a poor sport on the golf course—but—" She squinted at me. "Did he or didn't he make the first advance?"

But what was the first advance? The moment we stopped in the hall and I admired his shirt and he frowned at my knees? The All-in-1 messages about our names? The way I denied eating lunch so I could corner an invitation to dinner? His *May I?* before he first kissed me? But he was the one who had to lean down for that kiss, because I had kicked off the heels that usually brought our heads even. . . .

Peggy was staring at me the way a judge peered down at the defendant from the bench.

"He did!" I said. "But maybe I shouldn't say anything more, without a lawyer present—"

"I'll thank you to keep lawyers out of my office."

"You don't like them either?"

"My father was an attorney."

"Ha," I said, genuinely amused.

Peggy adjusted her glasses—like my mother, she wore bifocals—to cop a really good look at me. "You are an intensely nervy young woman, Ms. Diodetto."

What could I say but *thank you*?

"Next thing you'll be asking me for a raise."

I folded my hands in my lap. "I think it might be a smarter move on my part to ask for a letter of recommendation."

"And after I praised your work, how would I describe your behavior and your attitude?"

"I could help you find the wording."

"I'm sure you could. In the meantime, here you sit at Boorman. You're a hard worker, and I'd just as soon not lose you. But I can't abide this kind of thing going on in the workplace. It shows a complete lack of respect for yourself, your coworkers, and the entire corporation—"

"I couldn't agree with you more—"

"—never mind me."

I hung my head. "I'm sorry," I mumbled.

The *hmmphf* she emitted hardly inspired me to feel forgiven. "Is this relationship with Mr. Strauss over and done with, as he reports?"

"Yes. I swear it. It has been for months."

"And have you had your fill of Mr. Roberts and his dart board?"

"More than enough."

"Then get ready to work again for Eben." She looked outside at the squalid March weather and sighed. "A good golf game—just the three of us—might help restore some harmony."

"Who gets to drive the cart?" I asked.

"I usually take the wheel. Eben is a careless driver." She handed me a pen and motioned for me to sign off on the evaluation. I bore down so hard with the ballpoint, I practically ripped through the paper.

"I've been admiring your Jeep, Ms. Diodetto. How many miles do you get to the gallon?"

"I have no idea," I said.

She looked gravely disappointed in me as I handed her back the pen.

Dr. Peggy Schoenbarger was bound and determined to make a Lady Golfer—if not a total feminist—out of me. After I slunk back to my office, I called around to get quotes on lessons. I wanted a female golf pro, but the only one I could find was at the most pricey club in Croton. I swallowed hard and committed to six lessons.

The pro—"call me Barb"—was maybe in her mid-forties and presented the kind of image I'd always associated with women golfers. She was dressed in a polo shirt, plaid skort, terry-cloth socks with pert fuzzy balls on the back, and cleated shoes with laces black and thin as licorice whips. Her deep brown complexion obviously came from the great outdoors, not a tanning bed.

Our first lesson took place indoors at the club's banquet facility. "I've got to warn you," I told Barb. "I've never been on a golf course that doesn't have windmills on it. I don't even know what to call half of these clubs."

"We all have to start somewhere," Barb said. She took each club from the bag and rattled off a bunch of names—*putter, wedge, sand wedge, wood, metal wood.*

"Why do these big ones have socks on them?"

Barb pulled out a wood and divested it of its red-and-white pom-pommed sock. I knew we definitely were talking at cross-purposes when she told me, "The greater the loft, the higher and shorter the shot."

Slice, pull, hook, slant. Hazards and bunkers and doglegs and divots. My relief was intense when she got out a metal contraption meant to serve as a real golf hole (was there a term for that?) and told me, "Today we'll concentrate on putting."

"I won't be good at this," I warned her. "I'm really impatient. The last guy I dated kept making a big deal out of how impatient I was—"

"You'll have to curb that fault on the course. Now, this is called the *sweet spot* on your putter blade . . . this is the lifeline grip . . ."

At first I kept forgetting to concentrate before I hit the dimpled ball toward the cup. My aim was all off. But after ten minutes I was starting to be more on target, and after half an hour I found myself discharging the ball with remarkable accuracy toward the hole. After I smacked in my fifth "hole in one"—from all of nine feet back from the cup—Barb told me she was impressed. Her praise immediately went to my head.

I strutted forward on the runner of artificial turf. I liked this Barb. She struck me as amazingly down-to-earth and approachable for a female jock. As I scooped the ball out of the cup, I told her, "I should admit, I didn't even really want to learn this game. I lied to my boss—or rather, my boss got the impression that I was a golfer—and now I'm going to have to follow through and play. God, this is fun. It's actually relaxing. I didn't realize how tense I was. My spine is completely out of whack. My boss really puts a lot of pressure on me—"

"Can't you find your voice and tell him to ease up?"

"My boss is a woman. At first I thought she had all the bad qualities of a man. But now I get along with her. I mean, I actually think she's kind of cool."

"Eye on the ball. Mouth shut."

I knocked in another hole in one. "Wow. God, I can't tell you how good I feel. This boss of mine, she's great except for this golf thing. Jeez, I've done all sorts of dumb things since I started working there, slacking off, working on my own writing—I'm trying to write a novel, now *that* requires patience—and man, I don't know why I ever did this, but I even had an affair with this guy in the office, and she could have creamed me big time on that one, but she let me get away with it. I mean, there's got to be a God if I got away with that."

"Where do you work?"

"Boorman Pharmaceuticals, just outside of Ossining."

"Put down that iron," she told me. "Let's see how good you are with the driver."

I grabbed what I thought was the most powerful club. "That's your trouble wood," Barb said. "You're teeing off, you're not in the sand trap yet. You want the longest shaft . . ."

Maximum carry and roll. Choke up on the grip. Setup. Handicap. Par. "We'll do this without the ball, of course," Barb said, gesturing toward the banquet hall's chandelier. She demonstrated a perfect swing five or six times, showing me how to bring up the club in an arc. "Now you try."

"Aren't you supposed to shout something when you do this, so everyone ducks out of the way?"

"The word is *fore*."

"How loud do you have to holler—like Tarzan, or something?"

She looked at me like I truly was King of the Apes.

"Well," I said, "maybe I won't vocalize this time. It might interfere
with my concentration."

"That might be a wise choice."

I held on to the club for dear life. But when I brought it back,
somehow I loosened my grip. On my first time teeing off, the club went
winging out of my hands, narrowly missing the lowest crystals on the
chandelier and hitting the opposite wall, nicking the plaster something
wicked.

"I've never seen anyone do that before," Barb remarked.

"Oh my God," I said. "I'm so sorry. I'm hopeless. I give up. I'm going
to tell my boss I was a liar—"

"Nonsense. You don't want to compromise the good relationship you
have with her, do you?"

"No. No. I really like her."

"Then give it another whirl. Remember, you want to send the ball
flying, not the club. But just as a safety precaution, move out from under
the chandelier."

At the end of the hour, Barb told me, "This has been a very interesting session." We went back into her tiny office to set up a time for the next
lesson. On her desk was a double photo frame. On the side facing me
there was a picture of a little girl with brownish skin, long braids, and a
solemn face bent down toward a book.

"I see you're admiring my new daughter," Barb said. "She's going to
arrive next week. From Guatemala."

The girl didn't have to be reading *Peter Rabbit*—nor did I have to look
at the photo on the other side of the frame—for me to make the connection.

It was indeed a small world. I gulped. "It'll probably be hard for her to
get adjusted—what with the language barrier and all."

"She'll have two very doting mothers to watch over her."

Instantly my heart went out to the girl. One mother was bad enough
in my book—but everybody could write a different story about that.

I might add, however, that Dr. Margaret Schoenbarger took a very
nice picture.

• • •

While Strauss was gone, Dodie and I hung out together again. As if to establish that our visits would be tranquil, I didn't take the train down to the city—he came up to bland Ossining to be with me. Although Dodie had sworn off all mind-altering substances except a little alcohol every now and then, a large wad of cannabis got smoked when my six-month negative came back. After we blew the weed, we tunneled through an entire bag of Cape Cod potato chips and half a box of Chicken-in-a-Biscuit crackers, then laughed the kind of demented laughs I had heard mourners—me among them, most notably at my own father's graveside—sometimes let loose at inappropriate intervals during funerals.

Dodie's visits always promised cheese-filled Entenmann's and vanilla nut cream coffee. But they also ushered in the Sunday edition of *The New York Times,* in which the obituaries now came fast and thick: actors, dancers, musicians, even a writer whose manuscript I edited. An epidemic of leukemia seemed to sweep New York that year. A veritable plague of brain tumors. Then the truth finally appeared more and more often on the page, and each time he saw the phrase in black and white, Dodie repeated, "His companion reported . . . his companion reported . . ."

Although Dodie did not admit to being lonely, I could tell he was depressed. He had no companion or partner but his own disease, which lay in wait like a detective determined to sit one more hour in a dark car to catch a criminal in the act.

When Dodie lowered the newspaper to read an article at the top of the page, I gave him surreptitious glances, trying to find traces of his partner on his body and face. Like a teenage girl determined to hide her pregnancy from her parents for as long as possible, Dodie was worried about "showing it." There was a case up with the Justice Department to determine whether employers could legally fire carriers of the virus. One morning in March, as we drove back to my place after taking a long soggy walk through the park, Dodie told me he was sure he'd lose his job if the wrong coworker discovered he was sick and ratted on him.

"Who would do such a thing to you?" I asked.

"Somebody always wants somebody else's office. So mum's the word at work. And I cashed in my life insurance—"

"What'd you do that for? Are you afraid you won't pass the physical?"

"It's not term. It's whole life."

"What's the difference?"

"Oh, my God!"

"What's the matter?"

"Don't you even know what kind of insurance Boorman is giving you? Are you even covered?"

"Of course I'm covered. With some kind, I think. But I don't really need to be, do I? Isn't life insurance just for people who have kids?"

"Lisa, who are your beneficiaries?"

"I can't remember. I think I named my mother—do you think I should rename Al Dante Junior?"

"Please do."

"But my mother needs the money more, although she'd probably squat on it like a hen sits on eggs."

My utter stupidity about finances never failed to frustrate Dodie. He threw up his hands, then gave me a good talking-to about getting under the Allstate umbrella and leaning on Prudential's solid rock.

"If you're such a booster for insurance, then why did you cash yours in?" I asked.

"Because the money will make more invested than sitting there waiting for me to turn seventy and one-half. I'm not turning seventy and one-half, Lisa." He squinted at my hair. "You really need a deep conditioner."

"Does it look that bad?"

"And how. When I got off the train, it was all I could do to keep from singing 'Roll Over, Beethoven.'" He put a finger to the front of my scalp. "Don't look now, but there's a white strand right here." He hesitated. "Jeez Louise, here's another. And another."

When we got home, I took my trusty Tweezerman from the medicine cabinet, and, staring in the bathroom mirror, I plucked out my white hairs. Then I shut the bathroom door against Dodie's prying eyes and pulled a chin whisker. As I examined the creases—seemingly deeper every day— that ran from my nose to my mouth, I thought about the horrors of getting old. White hair. Thinning hair. Age spots. Gnarled fingers. A face, like Dorian Gray's portrait, that reflected all the wrongs I had committed and all the hardships—however trivial in comparison to others'—I had suffered. That life could take such a toll on my looks saddened me, and I could understand why Dodie—who had been blessed with a beauty that far surpassed my own—told me he found some small consolation in dying an early death.

While we washed our hands to make dinner, Dodie told me matter-of-factly that he had named me in his will.

"Cut it out," I said. "I don't want anything from you."

"You wouldn't say that if you knew how much it was." Dodie got out a separate towel to wipe his hands, claiming he did not like the stiffness of the dish towel I already had out, which was real Irish linen.

"Stop playing Mr. Moneybags."

"I'm playing Ralph Touchett. Remember, in *The Portrait of a Lady*?"

Dodie lowered his voice into a book-jacket-copy register. "Tragically dying of consumption, Ralph Touchett bequeathed a grand fortune to his cousin Isabel so she wouldn't have to wed an asshole. So what does Isabel do but turn around and marry a repressed pansy who collects antiques?"

"Pansy's the name of the daughter," I said. "And Henry James would be glad to know you got a lot out of his masterpiece."

"Tut-tut. She should have married what's-his-name—the boring Lord Warburton." Dodie shook his head. Then he looked at me mischievously. "I hope you give your novel a better ending, Lise—because the one you got now sucks rotten eggs."

I clenched the dish towel in my fist. Dodie started backing away from the sink, his arms in front of him to ward me off. I was moving in on him. "Now, Lise. Remember, you gave me the A-okay to dust-mop under your bed while you were in the shower—"

"But I didn't give you permission to snoop!"

"You had serious dust bunnies under there—never mind those Trojans. When are you finally going to get around to using those Trojans so you don't have to write pure porn as a substitute for sex?"

"You had no right reading my novel!"

"Hey, I've been reading it for weeks now! You take long showers!"

"My back is killing me from those fucking golf lessons and pure stress!" I unfurled the dish towel and swatted it at Dodie's head. He ducked, and I swung the towel again, giving him a locker-room slap on the ass.

He laughed. "To quote one of your characters: 'Oh, that feels so good, do it again!' "

"Stop it—"

"—some more!"

"Those are sex scenes!" I said, giving Dodie one swipe of the towel for every lame defense of my novel, which I now knew for certain was complete shit. "I'm a realistic writer! It's not my fault people don't utter stunning dialogue in bed! You have no right spying and no right criticizing—"

"Take it easy, that Irish linen is lethal. Oh, Lise, have mercy, I beg of you, it's not bad for a first draft."

It was close to the twelfth revision. "Really?" I asked.

"Put down that dish towel and I'll give you my honest reaction."

I put it down. Dodie ran his fingers through his hair—I had cuffed him a good one right on the side of the head—and warily walked by me. He opened the refrigerator. He crouched in front of my crisper and frowned at the first thing he pulled out: a moldy cucumber, which he threw into the trash. As he lined up an arsenal of stir-fry vegetables on the counter, he told me my book had some good points that he'd discuss later. In the meantime, he strongly suggested I ditch *Stop It Some More's* sex-in-the-Saab scene, wipe out at least seventy-five percent of the references to onanism, and tone down the heroine's latent attraction to her dumb but well-endowed brother-in-law, who always inexplicably greeted her with the gender-inappropriate phrase, *hey, how's it hanging?* "And get rid of Donna's green eyeglasses, or at least stop mentioning them every other paragraph," he said. "I mean, we get the point that she's supposed to be artsy. The bigger question, at least from my point of view, is why did you make my character Jewish?"

"What!"

"In chapter three, an insufferable faggot—who also conveniently happens to be one of the chosen people—floats in from nowhere—"

"That's not you."

"But he has my haircut."

"But he's tall and you aren't."

"He wears black jeans on the weekends—"

"He wears Italian loafers and you wouldn't be caught dead in them."

"But what is this preachy bullshit speech this gee-gee delivers at the office that compares AIDS to a modern-day Holocaust? I mean, *the vaccine as the long-awaited Messiah?*"

"It's just the first draft!" I lied. "Besides, I want to write about something important, something serious—"

"Then you'd better knock that queen off his moral high horse or your readers will be glad there's AIDS to do it for you."

"All right. Maybe that scene bordered—a little—on the didactic."

"Why can't he do something fun, like whip out his *schlong* to gross out the German dyke who looks like Beatrix Potter—ha! a German dyke who looks like Beatrix Potter? I don't think so, Lise. And just because this Donna girl—and by the way, you probably better change her name so it isn't such an obvious reflection of your own—just because Donna D.'s an aspiring cartoonist, does she always have to be drawing such mean caricatures?"

"She wants to be honest and true!"

"She wants a libel suit, if you ask me. But don't worry. I'll let your boyfriend bring it."

"He's not my boyfriend."

"Was he really a rower at Harvard?"

"But Strauss isn't Thomas Akins, and is there anything at all you like in the book?"

"Sure. Plenty. There are lots of funny scenes. Some of the serious ones are starting to work too."

"Which?" I muttered glumly.

"So far my favorite is when Donna remembers how the nuns told her the Holocaust was a sign from God that the Jews needed to convert. That seemed pretty real to me."

"Maybe that's because it actually happened," I said.

"But you didn't get sent to the rectory, Lise, and you weren't spanked with *The Baltimore Catechism*—do you really have a secret desire to get spanked by *The Baltimore Catechism*?"

"It's fiction, you fuckhead!"

"And you didn't yell *'That's a crock of shit'* when Sister Paul said that."

"Neither did you," I said.

"I was seven, and you were seven, and you believed it and so did I." Dodie got out the knife. "Do you believe the stuff we believed? Why did we place faith for a second in such a God?"

"We didn't have evidence that any other kind existed."

Over a pot of rice and vegetables lightly flavored with sesame oil and soy sauce, Dodie and I argued about the Divine. Now that we were adults we didn't have to believe in the kind of God who sent plagues. But we were too smart—or too cynical—to believe in the kind of God who created paradise. So what were we left with?

"Don't you have a decent Brillo pad?" Dodie asked after dinner. "I can't stand to even touch this rusty thing."

"Leave it," I said. "And get back to fat Pierre."

I had challenged Dodie to make it from one end of *War and Peace* to the other without falling asleep. "Physically impossible," he said, "but I'll try it." As I breezed through seventy pages of a novel about anorexia while simultaneously cruising through a bag of macaroons (somehow the irony escaped me), Dodie yawned and slowly turned the pages of Tolstoy's weightiest opus, occasionally commenting, "Bad move, Andrei," "For a Russian novel, they're speaking enough French," "Isn't anyone good-looking in this story?" and "Who's the hero? I need a romantic hero." At ten o'clock he said, "Life is short, and this book is really long." He winged the black Penguin edition across the room and said, "Enough of this intellectual shit. Move over."

He joined me on the couch and we turned on the TV. Dodie wielded the remote. He channel-surfed so fast I felt assaulted by the bright and cheesy commercials for ineffective deodorants and overpriced cars. The Saturday night movie was *Guess Who's Coming to Dinner?* I sighed over Sidney Poitier. Dodie cruised onto PBS, a channel he claimed to loathe because it was overpopulated with thin, handsome gee-gees posturing as straights. But tonight there was no *Mystery*, no *Masterpiece Theatre,* nor yet another dull Edwardian novel turned into a miniseries. Instead, there was an Indian man in a white turban, a professor at Cambridge, lecturing on the mind–body problem.

Dodie put down the remote and I didn't protest. The man's lilting voice was mesmerizing. Dodie's lips rose a little with pleasure when the man said "experience" and "mysterious" in his singsong way. The professor talked about the overlap between science and religion, the use of positive thinking and meditation to overcome pain and hunger and chronic diseases, the brain as the center of memory and the internalization of time, the human imagination as it creates its God. He talked of a doctor who discovered, while performing delicate surgery on a patient under local anesthesia, that if he gently pressed upon the patient's brain, the patient recalled and reexperienced memories from as far back as infancy. The brain was like a sponge: each press seeped forth another drop of time.

After the lecture was over, Dodie turned off the TV. We sat on the couch with our knees hugged up to our chests, our chins resting on top, and wondered aloud at what memories would spring to the surface if a brain surgeon pressed his fingers upon our minds. This was just another way of reminiscing, but it forced us to be selective and pick out the most important details that could be reexperienced. Dodie began.

What about the time we went to Sea Gull Beach after the hurricane and that huge silvery fish was washed up on shore and your dad dragged it out to the water three or four times before it finally made it back out to sea?

How about that wicked thunderstorm in the first grade when we had to run downstairs and take refuge in the boys' bathroom? That was the first time I'd ever seen a urinal. I remember thinking, Why do boys pee into sinks?

Do you remember levitating in the cellar? Séances in the basement under that bare lightbulb with the string dangling? Playing funeral in the Christmas-tree box?

That ghost story Jocko told about the woman who bought the used car and the previous owner's face kept reappearing in the rearview mirror?

Dodie and I were the perfect partners for this game, because we shared not only our childhood, but our response to it. We both were intrigued by *The Lion, the Witch and the Wardrobe*—another book we did not realize was a Christian parable—me for the pictures, Dodie for the mysterious word *wireless* that he did not understand and that he did not want to define, loving the mystery. We both were moved by *The Diary of Anne Frank*—the hiding, the problems with the parents, the scene where Peter spills the beans, the last page where she talks about her divided self, and that crucial moment that always made me weep, turning the page and reading the sparse paragraph about the Gestapo invading the Secret Annexe—the thought that she died just two months before the liberation of Holland. Dodie and I both loved the idea of a large dog playing a nurse—and the picture of Wendy sewing the shadow back onto Peter's feet, Tinker Bell glowing angrily overhead—in the Arthur Rackham edition of *Peter Pan*. We loved how Pinocchio kept on lying, but by the end of the novel earned the right to be a real boy instead of a puppet.

The more Dodie and I talked and laughed, the more inconceivable it seemed to me that either one of us could ever die. What we shared with one another went too deep to be buried in a grave. If there was a paradise, maybe it was nothing more than memory: the chilled smell of our grandfather's fruit cellar. The crack in the blacktop behind the garage in the shape of Florida. The rough bark of the apple tree that functioned, during games of hide-and-seek, as home base. Blood soup made from the berries on the scraggly bushes that grew in our front yard. The long walk down the aisle together, dressed in white, to receive our First Holy Communion and to receive the blessing from the archbishop as we confirmed our desire to be Catholics for the rest of our lives and to take, as part of that pledge, the name of a saint. The names were supposed to be secret—but I knew Dodie's name and he knew mine. He had taken the name of the captain of the heavenly host, the archangel Michael, while I had chosen the name of the woman who wiped Christ's face as he walked toward Calvary—Veronica—because my imagination was captured by the story of how the imprint of Christ's features came away upon her veil.

Veronica's veil was supposed to be preserved in Saint Peter's in Rome. Dodie said he was thinking about making a pilgrimage to Italy over the summer and wanted to know if I'd come along for at least part of the ride. "Let's do it," I said. "We can flirt with the waiters—"

"Didn't I say *pilgrimage*?"

"Didn't I say *flirt*? It's not a sin if I ask some Luigi in a white shirt what he recommends for the entrée."

Dodie looked pensive. "One can only hope God has better things to worry about than that."

I dropped Dodie at the train station just before noon. I felt his fingers splayed on my back when he hugged me. The train pulled in, slow and wheezing. After Dodie got on, he took the first available seat by the window, and I waved to him through the grimy glass, but he didn't see me. Then the train pulled away.

When I returned home, I realized I was exhausted even though I'd already had three cups of coffee. I wondered if I wasn't just having my usual Sunday blues compounded by a psychosomatic reaction to the big news at work: that Strauss was pulling back into town next week. But my throat was sore. In fact, it was killing me. I gargled with salt—Morton's—and water. A half hour later I gargled again, this time more worried about Dodie than myself. Dodie wasn't supposed to be around anyone sick. He wasn't supposed to go into a day-care center or a doctor's waiting room or sit too long in an airport or a train station or anywhere else where his compromised immune system might latch onto something virulent. Now he had spent twenty-four hours in my contagious presence. But if I called him and told him exactly how lousy I felt, I thought I might trigger his hypochondria, and he'd get sick from the stress more than the actual illness.

I sat down on the couch—only to wake up an hour and a half later. My throat was so raw that when I sipped a drink of water, it felt like swallowing sand. It took all the effort I had to go into the kitchen and make some tea. The faucet felt heavy as cast iron. The spigot was hard to twist, like the sealed top of a salad-dressing bottle yet to be opened. The effort was tremendous just to bend down and fetch a tea bag from the bottom drawer. My wrists hurt. The back of my thighs ached. I felt like someone was sitting on my chest.

I slept the night away, hoping I'd wake up fine in the morning, but instead I woke up late enough so it didn't look good when I called in sick to work—like I probably had a hangover. But I didn't even care. Everything about Boorman seemed trivial. I had a fever and I was coughing. Then I had to do it: call Dodie to tell him I really had something and it was probably contagious. I called, but to my relief (because it meant he wasn't sick—he was at work) no one answered. I left more coughs than words on Dodie's machine, but managed to eke out this croaky message: "Dodici Diodetto: You deliberately left *War and Peace* sitting like a dog turd on my carpet—but can't say I blame you. Call me."

I slept through another morning and afternoon of this, hot and sweaty in my PJs. Then I began to fever-dream, first of a hallway long as the Lincoln Tunnel and lined with yellow tiles on the walls and ceiling. I knew the hall was in a hospital because it smelled like cruciferous vegetables and cottage cheese and iodine and Band-Aids, and because I was wearing a paper gown, tied in the back, and I didn't have anything on underneath. With the lack of shame found only in dreams, I didn't even care—in fact, it kind of intrigued me—that my bare butt could be viewed by all the world. I wanted someone to see me.

At the end of the empty hall was a door. When I pushed it open, Dodie lay in a hospital bed, a paper mask stretched over the bottom of his face. In the corner, Auntie Beppina sat by the window, her hands folded in prayer. Then she disappeared.

Where's your father? I said to Dodie.

Where's your father?

My father's dead, I said.

I can't see my father, Dodie said.

Then I noticed Dodie was blind, his eyes a wash of yellow, like thin pudding.

I gotta go, Dodie said.

Go where? Where you going, Dodie?

No, go. You know, go.

But where were the nurses? There weren't any nurses. I walked over to a box of rubber gloves, but the pair I tried on wouldn't fit. *Fuck it,* I said, and reached beneath the nightstand to pull out a red plastic urinal shaped like a dildo. I didn't even blink when the dildo/urinal said, *Call me the gentleman's friend.*

I propped it by Dodie's emaciated leg, then peeled back the sheet and lifted Dodie's hospital robe. His skin was jaundiced and puckered at the top of his legs. In a sad, abandoned nest of hair lay his genitals, pink with a purplish undertone. I took his penis in my hand, and even though the rest of him was so thin and limp, I felt it harden, and I didn't know what to say or do.

Dodie's smile stretched the elastic cords on his hospital mask. *I know you've always wanted to see my tool,* he said. *Voilà. The lethal weapon.*

I laughed. *It's a monstrous jewel. Oh. It's so big it takes my breath away.*

Dodie's stomach started to shake with laughter, and then his pee came pouring out the moment after I tucked him into the gentleman's friend. Dodie laughed so hard he started to choke, and I stepped back just in time to avoid the phlegm—creamy and viscous as semen—that he coughed onto the bed sheet.

The nurse gasped when she came to the door and saw the gentleman's friend in my hand. *Are you crazy?* she asked. *Don't you know what he has? Get in there and dump that urine out, and don't spill it.*

I was in the bathroom. I was crying so hard, it felt like laughing. I was holding the gentleman's friend the way the priest held the golden cup of wine in his hands, and I was thinking of tilting it back and drinking Dodie's piss like poison. I wanted to pour it over my head and drown in its mess. But I tilted it into the toilet, and when the urine came out brown and tinged with blood—why wasn't there more? There was so very little of it!—I realized I must still like my life, because with true survivor's instinct I washed my hands ten times over.

I woke clammy with sweat. I thrashed and turned and dreamed some more. I was driving my Jeep down a hill. On the opposite side of the street was a string of cars with their lights on, and I knew it was a funeral procession although I did not see the hearse, and the steering wheel went loose in my hands and the gas pedal limp beneath my feet, and the brakes, the brakes, where were the brakes? They were at the beach—*Dodie and I* were at the beach, and we were twelve years old again and the sunlight glinted on Dodie's soft brown hair and the jut of his shoulder blades. Then we were six and running down the alley behind the church after watching *Barabbas*, running as if to outstrip leprosy, knowing disease and death were the ways that God sought you out, and He could always find you. *Stop running. Stop running, Lise!* Dodie shouted. Because at the bottom was a chain-link fence crowned with barbed wire and we were going to hit it. . . .

I woke. I felt like a hand was on my shoulder. *Wake up. Wake up, Lise.* The phone was ringing and ringing. I sat up, and when the phone went quiet and the answering machine picked up, my sister's tight voice broadcast Dodie's death. Carol kept repeating until the tape ran out, *"Oh Lise, you were born on the same day, you were born on the same day . . ."*

The official word was pneumonia, but the unspoken one was suicide—a vial of tranquilizers downed in the span of time between the morning clinic visit that confirmed the presence of pneumonia cells and the afternoon visit to Dodie's private physician, who was on the staff of Saint Luke's and was prepared to check Dodie in. Drowsy and disoriented, Dodie had passed out—*like a girl*—at the doctor's office before he even had a chance to give his name to the receptionist. On the ambulance ride to Saint Luke's, Dodie's heart probably had given out in a midtown traffic jam, to the distress and confusion of the paramedics, and to the relief of Dodie, who did not want to waste away in a ward where death was delivered as regularly as bread—or fall into a sleep from which he would never awake, only to have his corpse rot for days before it was discovered.

Auntie Beppina couldn't stop talking about those tranquilizers. Even after she discovered Dodie had pneumonia and Uncle Gianni told her where and how and why you got that kind of pneumonia, she still said, "But the pills. Why would he take the pills? Where do you get such pills?"

and Carol's face went white, knowing how easy it was to get your hands on a vial and write your own ticket to the grave.

In lieu of flowers, the family asked nothing—only that we didn't say that shameful word *suicide,* because then the priest wouldn't give him a decent burial. I kept my mouth closed—when I wasn't coughing, and I was still coughing pretty badly after driving my Jeep back to Connecticut, ten miles under the speed limit, my mouth dry from the antibiotics I was taking and the terror I felt to be behind the wheel. Anything could happen.

The coffin was closed. No wake. Still, I asked Auntie Beppina if I could see Dodie one last time. She shook her head. "They screwed down the lid," she kept saying. "They screwed down the lid."

But they hadn't. I asked the funeral director. He told me he would open it for a moment if I agreed not to touch Dodie. I no longer wanted to touch Dodie. But I had to see him. It didn't seem real until I saw him. Viewing was the only way I could believe my father was really dead. After I saw Daddy's body, I had moved away from the coffin and cried in the black-and-white-tiled bathroom of that very same funeral home, thanking God I'd never have to look at my father again in this life and know that I did not love him nor did he love me.

And so I looked. And so I saw. And so I nodded. And so I remembered you, Dodie: You who were the altar boy who held the cup of ashes on those cold February mornings that marked the beginning of the days of deprivation known as Lent, when the priest took his thumb and ground the ash into my forehead, reminding me that we came from dust and to dust we would return.

The sun shone on the morning of your funeral. The metal rollers on the back of the hearse clattered like the belt in the butcher shop that delivered the sides of beef to the freezer. Your brothers carried you up the aisle. The priest who heard your first confession gave the blessing. Your mother sobbed in the front pew. Your father was so drunk it was a wonder he could stand straight. Weak-kneed, I coughed so much I was like Poison in a croquet game—everyone moved away.

There was a reading from the Gospel according to John. *In my Father's house are many mansions; if it were not so, I would have told you.*

Your brothers carried you back down the aisle. The hearse glittered in the sunshine, and in the back of the hushed limousine where I sat with my sister's hand in mine, I gazed down on the dull brown water beneath the Q Bridge. The green gates of Saint Lawrence welcomed us into the cemetery. The grave was unmarked but open. Once again the rollers squeaked. Your brothers were confused about where to put you—to the right of the open grave or the left—and almost dropped the coffin. Another reading. Said the Bible: *I am the foolish man, which built his house upon the sand. What do I have left to cling to?* I closed my eyes when they lowered your coffin into the ground. Your father used a shovel to throw the first clods on the lid. Then he kept on shoveling, as if this way he could bury you forever, and Jocko had to reach out and say, "Dad. Dad. What are you doing, Dad? Stop it. *Cut it out.*"

At the party afterward (for no Italian funeral was complete without going back to the house and tackling a basket of rolls and cold meats and a platter of roasted vegetables and sloshing back gallons of liquor), your godmother—my mother—said, "I always said those eyelashes were wasted on a boy." Your cousin—my sister—wiped away tears as she said, "Well, Lisa, now you can get on with your life." And Al, the guy we both had laughed at all these years, was the only one who seemed to understand my grief. He asked me if I wanted to hold Junior.

I shook my head. I was afraid I'd drop him.

"Can I get you something, Lise?" Al asked.

I shook my head again.

"Do you want me to leave you alone?" He sat down next to me. "I'll listen if there's something you want to say."

But there was nothing to say. I sat there with Al until Junior rustled, then let out a whimper, and finally broke into a full-blown wail of distress, and I reacted to the baby's cry the same way I responded to a glorious piece of music—as if someone had stuck a fist down my throat and pulled up from the bottom of my soul my very name.

Chapter Nineteen

Somebunny Loves You

On the day we were scheduled to clean out Dodie's apartment, I made excuses to Auntie Beppina about meeting someone in New York for breakfast so I could get there before she did. My first reason was selfish: I wanted to sit there quietly, for a few minutes, in Dodie's space, the way I would sit in a church. My second reason was more altruistic: I knew I had to get rid of Dodie's drugs and erotic photographs and even 800's talking dildo (if it really existed in the first place) before Auntie Beppina pulled it out of some drawer, asked "What's this?" and pushed the button that would give her an indirect answer: *Y'all come!*

Auntie Beppina probably wouldn't even get it. But why test her?

For years Auntie Beppina had gotten on my nerves; she reminded me too much of my own mother. But I knew Dodie had a soft spot for her. Watching her sob in the cemetery, I had gotten a glimpse of how hard her life was. She was surrounded by men who dumped on her, and the only son who really loved her had taken himself far, far away.

The doorman didn't even know Dodie was dead. He lit another Virginia Slim and said, "Cute little man, fourth floor? No way."

I warned him about Auntie Beppina. I said my aunt was coming, she would arrive in a cab, she wouldn't know what to pay the taxi driver, she would probably be all confused, could he help if she needed it? The doorman shrugged. I gave him a five. He said yes. Then I gave him another five and asked him if he'd help us bring a few bags downstairs later.

"How I know you're his cousin?" he asked, angling for another bill.

"You've seen me before."

"No. Never."

"Yes, you have. I've been introduced to you. I know your name. Your name is Luis."

"Your name is what?"

I pulled out my driver's license, which proved I shared Dodie's last name. For this, Luis let me up as far as Dodie's door. I pulled out the keys, which were sent home to Auntie Beppina along with Dodie's bagged body. "Look, here are the keys," I told Luis, and when he started making noises about the super—*"super no like this"*—I described the entire interior of the apartment to Luis before I opened the door and let him peer inside to verify my account of the decor. Then I told him to please leave me alone, I was getting over bronchitis and his Virginia Slims were aggravating my lungs.

He backed away. I shut the door. My description of Dodie's apartment, of course, was accurate to the T. For years I had loved Dodie's place and suffered from rental envy. I wanted the thin, sophisticated blinds—vertical, not horizontal—that hung on the big front window; the bed, covered in white matelassé, pushed against the back wall; the floor-to-ceiling mirror behind it; and the floor-to-ceiling bookcase with the ladder in front. Dodie always had an eye for where to place things: the spare pharmacy lamp on the big blond table, the terra-cotta candlesticks on the fake mantel, and the whimsical basket full of wooden green apples on the glass end table. The chaise longue in the corner came from Roche-Bobois, and the copper pots that hung above the counter where only two people could eat comfortably came from Williams-Sonoma. These last were a gift from George. What gifts George knew how to give to Dodie! But what gift had I offered? I would never know if it had been me who gave Dodie the pneumonia. I didn't even know how you caught pneumonia. I had bronchitis. But forever I would feel guilty, as if I had handed him a grenade and then backed away. And forever I would love him and hate him for leaving me so abruptly, like the ghost-story boy named Reuben who stepped into the closet and disappeared without a trace.

The Berber rug squished beneath my feet as I walked across the floor. I turned on the pharmacy lamp and sat next to its warm haze for a moment, sorry I had come early. I could have gone to church to say my prayers. I moved over to the window to open the blinds. As I reached for the cord, a cheerful voice said:

Somebunny loves you!

I jumped. My hand still on the cord, I practically pulled the whole sheet of vertical blinds down with me.

I looked behind me, then down, sure I had located the infamous dildo. But the voice had come from a small stuffed bunny dressed in pale blue overalls who sat on the windowsill. He looked impishly at me, one ear bent toward his playful whiskers. When I reached for him, he repeated:

Somebunny loves you!

Oh God, I thought. How creepy. Then, in spite of myself, I laughed. I wondered who—besides George—might have given this loving creature to Dodie. Now I'd never know. No one Dodie had worked with—not a single friend—had attended his funeral. A huge bouquet—which my mother declared *must have broke the bank*—had come from his office; the card read only, *Our deepest regrets. Cowards,* I thought. Then I wondered how many of Dodie's friends even knew—after all, Dodie hadn't known about George until George's mother had called.

Dodie's bed was made very neatly, with not a single wrinkle on the bedspread and the pillows all fluffed and arranged just right, as if he had made a conscious decision to tidy up before he took the pills. I wondered if he had washed the glass he had used to take his final drink of water.

Go on, Lise, I heard him say. *Go on over and take a look at how clean I left the sink!*

"No," I said aloud. The word echoed against the ceiling.

Next to the bed a green light was blinking. Dodie had messages on his answering machine. I walked over. I wasn't sure if I should play the tape. I stopped and thought about what he would have wanted me to do. I thought about how this differed from what he would have *expected* me to do. I reached for the switch, pressed REWIND, heard my own coughing on the machine—the hoarse sound of my voice calling Dodie's name—and then stopped the tape.

From the second kitchen drawer I pulled out a garbage bag. Into the bathroom first. My first impulse was to pocket the over-the-counter sleeping pills and the Baggie full of marijuana. Then I changed my mind. (*I'm going to be a better person now,* I kept thinking. *I'm going to be better.*) Down they went into the toilet, and with one push on the handle they were flushed away. Into the garbage bag went the massage oil and the condoms. The experimental medicine Dodie volunteered to take. Those suggestive—but not really lewd—erotic photography folios. I flipped through them—shamelessly inspecting the men—before I remembered where I was and what I was there for. I tossed them.

I washed my hands. I kept on washing my hands. I looked in the mirrors. I kept expecting some vision—a picture of Dodie standing behind me. I kept expecting to turn around and see him lying on the bed. I thought I'd hear the tea kettle whistle from the kitchen, or a tray of ice cubes clattering into a bowl. Then he would say, *Christ, that funeral was a good joke, wasn't it? Like something out of* The Twilight Zone. But there was nothing but the dull thud of the upstairs tenant's feet shaking the ceiling. Nothing but my own congested breathing. And no note. He must not have planned it, I thought. But then I remembered him telling me, *I would throw myself against the fence. I just want it to hit me like lightning.* And he had cashed in his life insurance. He had left it all—all of it, and I was astounded (when his lawyer called the house in Connecticut to tell me) by how much there was of it, the stocks and the mutual funds and the municipal bonds and the treasury notes—half to Auntie Beppina, and half to me.

After an hour I was pretty sure I'd put everything that would offend Auntie Beppina into one bag. I sealed it and propped it by the door.

Auntie Beppina arrived around eleven o'clock, carrying a big black leather trunk that I feared dated back to the first and only big trip she'd ever taken in her life: from Trapani to Ellis Island.

"You should have waited," she said. "We could have come together."

"I told you, I had to meet someone."

"Who is this someone?"

"Just a friend."

After years of listening to falsehoods from her own kids, Auntie Beppina had mellowed out and learned how to let things go. She did not pursue the identity of this *friend*. She put down the trunk and looked around dubiously. "So small," she said. "How could he have lived in this tiny place?"

"He had a doorman," I said. "And no roaches or rats."

Auntie Beppina looked puzzled, and I explained that for a boy who came to Manhattan with a scholarship degree from Duke and six thousand dollars in student loans, this was not bad at all. For someone under thirty—not a Kennedy—this was even more than all right. By New York standards, Dodie had made it.

She looked around the studio again and asked why anyone would want to live like an animal in such a tiny cage. "So many books," she said. "You two, always with your head in books. Why was your head in books all the time?"

"Uncle Gianni couldn't be bothered coming?" I asked.

"He came."

My stomach felt sick. The last person I wanted to see there was Uncle Gianni. But Auntie Beppina told me he rode the train with her into New York, put her in a cab, then took the train back to New Haven. He would return to New York on the six o'clock train and pick her back up.

This behavior was so utterly *guinea* I couldn't stand it. "Why didn't he just stay?" I asked.

"He said, 'What am I going to do in New York? It's not baseball season.'"

"He could have gone to Radio City and gawked at the Rockettes. He could have come to help."

"Cleaning out is woman's work."

"And what is man's work?"

"To pay for the funeral," Auntie Beppina said, as if this was an admirable feat indeed, for a father to *take care of the arrangements.*

Auntie Beppina's face grew sorrowful again when I told her there was no note. "Nothing for me?" she asked.

"No," I said. "Nor me either. I mean neither. He just didn't seem to leave anything."

Auntie Beppina's expression brightened when I asked her if she would clean out the refrigerator. She could handle this. She also could scrub down the bathroom and leave the place nice for the next person.

"Of course, it's so small, it'll be hard to rent," she said. I didn't tell her the doorman probably was downstairs at that very moment, buttonholing any and all folks who passed by to let them know there was an empty studio upstairs with a street view. By the end of the afternoon he probably could have collected thousands of dollars in bribes from prospective renters, some of whom might even consider killing someone (never mind waiting for someone to die) to muscle their way into such digs.

I made some coffee and ran down to the corner grocery to get more plastic garbage bags. I sorted through the books to find the ones I wanted to keep and then decided I would keep all of them, although I had no idea how I'd get them out of Manhattan back to Ossining. I wrapped the dishes and bagged the linens—all these were going to the Salvation Army. The clothes were what killed me. I hid behind the closet door as I lifted one of Dodie's shirts to my face.

Big mistake.

The collar was soft and marked with a single strand of his hair. I used the sleeve to wipe away my tears. I hoped my aunt didn't see. But what if she did? Auntie Beppina was different from my mother. My mother never cried. At my father's funeral she just stood there with a stubborn look on her face.

Auntie Beppina caught me. Maybe I even wanted her to.

"No use," she said. "No use crying now."

I crunched the sleeve of Dodie's shirt against my cheek. "But I loved him."

"No good," she said. "It wasn't right. You should never have been so close to him. He even said so."

"When?"

"On the phone once. He said, *I got in Lisa's way.* Must have been right after Christmas—"

I blanched, remembering that gruesome Christmas scene with my family. In the end, I hadn't left my mother's house. I had run upstairs and packed my bags and then I let Carol talk me into going back downstairs for dinner. At the table everyone acted as if nothing had happened—and no one mentioned my mysterious man again.

"There was somebody, wasn't there?" Auntie Beppina asked. "This man you talked about. This New York man."

"Not anymore," I said.

"What happened?"

"Oh, what does it matter? We got into a fight."

"One fight! You get married, you have plenty of fights."

"I don't want to fight with my husband."

"Then I guess you'd better stay a secretary for the rest of your life."

"I'm not a secretary!" I told her. "I'm an editor! I manage an entire department!"

"Madonna," Auntie Beppina said. "How come your mother never told me that?"

I bit my lip. Just like Mama, Auntie Beppina seemed to think there were only two kinds of women—working girls (prostitutes, teachers, nurses, secretaries, and librarians) and married ladies (enough said). She seemed to think that because I worked, I wasn't interested in getting married. For a while, maybe, that had been true. I had liked being on my own. My initial interest in marriage stemmed only from curiosity: I wanted to find out why people did it. I don't remember when curiosity turned to loneliness and longing and I began entertaining thoughts about how nice it would be to come home and make dinner—together—with someone who would appreciate my smart mouth but also know how to silence it, every now and then, with a kiss.

In college, the message had been clear: Educated women—Sarah Lawrence women—were supposed to find wifedom (or *wife-dumb,* as it was spelled back then) a dismal prospect. Also to be scorned was motherhood—which had brought Carol so low she had to down pills just to roll out of bed in the morning, but which also inspired her to tell me, *After I squeezed that baby out, I felt like I could do anything.* Women with college degrees were supposed to focus on creative expression and job satisfaction. Yet how could I buy into this party line when *Stop It Some More* was going nowhere and the day-to-day workings of Boorman Pharmaceuticals failed to interest or inspire me? I did not see where showing up at eight-thirty every morning in panty hose and pumps and saying *yes, ma'am* or *no, sir* to Peggy Schoenbarger or Hook Roberts or Eben Strauss empowered me. Why was being married to such a rule-ridden company any better than being married to someone as grim and repressive as my father?

For starters, it earned me a paycheck. I liked supporting myself and not having to account for every penny I spent to someone else. But that didn't stop me from fantasizing about bucking against the authority of Boorman. Why did I want like crazy to waltz into Peggy's office and report, *I'm quitting! I'm eloping with Mr. Strauss! I'm writing a novel—about sexual harassment!*

Pro or con, Ms. Diodetto?

You don't get it—it's a story, not a political tract. It's about everything we don't understand in life: love and God and death and war and why people start to cry when they hear music.

Hmm. Any hot fucking?

Of course. I write only from personal experience. But I'm having trouble making the lesbian encounters sound authentic—

Divest yourself of your miniskirt, Ms. Diodetto. Nothing would give me more pleasure than to introduce you to the raptures of Sapphic sex.

Well—why not? Not for nothing was I the author of *Face Crime!* and *Stop It Some More*—I liked living in my head, where anything could happen at any minute. Working for Boorman had taught me I could easily live on a leash if I still had my imagination.

But if I were married, who would be on the other side of the leash? A man named Ibby. A man who visited his parents twice a month and who flipped his lid if I wore high heels into the city. He would nag me about my all-terrain vehicle (*No wife of mine will drive a Jeep!*)—the shaky steering and the lack of heat and the lack of space to put in a car seat—until I agreed to give up my Jeep (although for a long time I had wanted to trash the inconvenient thing, having no idea why I ever bought it in the first place). He would take me to the car lot and haggle with the dealer until he got me a good price on a safe and sturdy car. *Eat my dust,* I'd say as I got behind the wheel and charged off the lot, and he was such a fast driver he would tail me like a cop and pull his Audi into the driveway behind me, blocking me in. Then we would go into the home where once Ibby thought there were too many rooms, and where I now would hurt his feelings by keeping the photo of Dodie and me singing "Bella Ciao" in my top desk drawer, although I would wrap it in purple cloth the way they shrouded the statues in church during Holy Week, because I would be frightened my cousin would step through the glass and show me a version of myself I both feared and longed to recover. . . .

Oh Dodie! I thought. If Strauss asked me into his home, wouldn't I be hiding? If you came back, would you know where to find me? Would you even think to look in that house, where the doors would be left open on Passover for the coming of Elijah? Would it even occur to you to appear in the rearview mirror of a heavy, sturdy car that—when an eighteen-wheeler passed on the highest bridge in the world—didn't even shiver in the wind?

"Do you believe in ghosts?" I asked Auntie Beppina.

"Certo."

On the table at the foot of Dodie's bed, there was a small black vase. I held it in my hand, rubbing the base back and forth in my palm as if it were a magic lantern. "Do you wish Dodie would come back to you?"

"Gia è venuto. He's already come. In my dreams. Dead children visit in dreams."

"Dodie wasn't a child."

"He was mine." Auntie Beppina sighed. "Parents, too, come in dreams. Don't you dream about your father?"

"No," I said, because I couldn't tell her that the few times I had, my father had his arms around me in a way no father should ever touch his daughter, and I woke up with a start, thinking, *Oh God, I'm such a pervert, how can I be such a pervert?* The only thing that made me rest easy was my sneaking suspicion that everyone else on the planet was one too.

Cup of coffee in her hand, Auntie Beppina sat on the chaise longue. "I dream about my mother and my father all the time."

"Is it the same dream?" I asked.

"Most of the time. It isn't a dream like a story. It's a dream—well, like a dream. More about a place than something happening. We're always in the old town. My mother's in the kitchen in her apron. My father comes home and gives me a kiss on the forehead. There's dust on his boots. The skin's split open on his hands. There's the fountain—with the little trickle of water that dribbled over the stone—and the pink wall of the house, and the stone stairs that felt so warm when you sat on them. Sometimes I see the iron railing, the way it twisted—and the sunlight . . ." Her voice trailed off. "Not like here. It's always so dark here."

"Are you sorry your parents brought you over?"

She looked around Dodie's apartment. "None of this would have happened there."

"You don't think so?"

"I know so."

I pointed out what I considered the obvious. "Auntie Beppina, there are gay guys in Italy too."

"Yes, but they get married and have the children. He could have gotten married and had the children. Now this."

For a second I saw it: Dodie in a Panama hat and some natty seer-sucker suit, posing in front of the church with the kids on Easter Sunday. His arm was around a pretty girl in a white straw hat and a blue and yellow cotton dress. Her long hair came down to her swollen belly. There was a garden, full of tomatoes and snap beans and cucumbers heavy on the vine. There was sunlight.

Then I heard an ominous train whistle in the distance, the cold hard click of heels on the marble church floor, the merry but bigoted sounds of the *festa* in the town square, and in the shadow of an alley, Dodie locking eyes with another man, a sliver of light glinting off the gold rims of his sunglasses . . .

"That wouldn't have worked," I told Auntie Beppina.

"Why not? People do it all the time—"

"It's called a double life—"

"He could have lived it." She squinted at me. "Ah, Lisa. You knew he was sick, he had that awful thing. You should have told me. I'm your *comare,* I always treated you like one of my own, I'm practically your mother—"

"What good would it have done?"

"You can say prayers. I could have had the prayers said—"

My voice tightened. "You think that works?" I asked. "What about all the people who died in wars? You think they didn't pray? Who heard them?"

"God heard them."

"And what the fuck did He do about it?"

Auntie Beppina gasped. She told me to *stai zitta,* imagine talking like that, if only my mother could hear me, such a crack across the face she'd give me, so hard I wouldn't talk for weeks. Then I did shut up. Because suddenly the tickle returned to my throat, and my chest started to hurt, and I began coughing again—those rough coughs that came from deep inside my lungs.

Auntie Beppina got me water. She put her hand on my back and held the glass for me. I took some water into my mouth and spit it back into the glass. I tried two more times before I got some down my throat. Then I dumped everything out of my purse and found one of those foul-smelling lozenges the doctor had given me.

Auntie Beppina stared at me. "You have that cough—you—at the funeral—Elisabetta, you have what Dodici had—"

"It's bronchitis. Dodie had pneumonia, Dodie had—"

Auntie Beppina held up her hand. "We could have called it cancer."

"Call it by its name."

Auntie Beppina shook her head. She sat down. "Oh, you two! Why do you have to live in this crazy New York?"

"Where am I supposed to live?" I asked. "I'm supposed to get on a boat and go back to Sicily?" The romanticized view of the old country she had just given me seemed more bogus than ever, especially when I remembered how she and my mother and my uncles would sit around the wooden kitchen table, prying the meat out of walnut shells with toothpicks, bitterly complaining, *Ah, the heat! Ah, the drought! Ah, the hunger! Ah, the earthquakes!*

"You said you were poor there," I told Auntie Beppina. "You said there was nothing to eat. You complained, all the time, about the earthquakes—"

"But there was sun. People grew up the right way—"

"What's the right way?"

"Not like here." Auntie Beppina shook her finger at me. "You should come home. You don't belong here."

"I don't live here," I said. "I live in Ossining."

"And what kind of life do you live? You're twenty-four—"

"Twenty-five, I'm twenty-five, I'm the same age Dodie was—"

"Twenty-five and still not married, still no kids—"

"Why does everything always have to come down to that?"

"That's why we're here—why else are we here?"

She squinted at me. The sun had just broken through the clouds, and the light in the apartment, suddenly, was far too intense. When she got up to close the blinds, she was treated to the same refrain that had welcomed me.

Somebunny loves you!

She jumped. She looked down at her feet, then onto the windowsill. She picked up the bunny. It repeated the refrain, as if to prove that Dodie loved his mother enough to get rid of that talking dildo before he died, even if he did leave behind the condoms and the muscle-men photos and the almond massage oil—now all flung into the trash—and his wonderful wardrobe and the beautiful furniture and the copper pots—all destined for the Salvation Army, because up until then Auntie Beppina's black trunk remained empty. She hadn't claimed a single thing.

"Isn't this clever," Auntie Beppina murmured. She held the bunny to her chest. *"This* I'll take."

Chapter Twenty

Red Rover, Red Rover, Why Don't You Come Over?

I ended up marrying a careful man—accidentally on purpose.

But let me backtrack. I'm getting ahead of the game.

It began with a phone call on the day I returned to Ossining. The leave of absence that I begged from Hook—and when he gave me trouble, finally arranged with Peg—was over. The trees that stretched their dark, wet branches over the Merritt Parkway a week before had blossomed into a bower of green. The air was crisp; the sky bright blue. It was the kind of day that made you want to hang on to your life forever.

As I drove the winding parkway, I thought there were two kinds of people in the world: those who when confronted with the worst of horrors would throw themselves on the fence, and those who would walk on their mother's bones to keep on living. I was afraid—and relieved—to find I fell into the second category. But the minute I came to this conclusion, I was sure my Jeep would wipe out. I kept looking in the rearview to see if another car was bearing down upon me, its accelerator stuck and its steering wobbly as my emotions, but all I could see in the poorly adjusted mirror was a flash of my own eyes. I was so busy looking behind I didn't pay enough attention ahead, and I almost rear-ended a slow-moving Pontiac.

I arrived in Ossining at the hour of day I'd always hated—the blue hour, four o'clock, when the sun began to retreat from the sky and the day started its long, slow slide into night. My duffel bag felt heavy as a dead body as I dragged it upstairs. The apartment smelled stuffy. I cracked a window in the kitchen. I walked into the living room. I wandered in and out of the bathroom, then leaned in the doorway of the bedroom. I remembered how Carol said she had moved from room to room when she brought Al Dante Junior home from the hospital the first time, to introduce him to his new world.

But no one was cradled in my arms. My apartment felt as hollow as my stomach. I realized, finally, that some of the emptiness I felt was pure hunger. I was ready to eat again. Cook again. Try to do something normal again.

I unzipped my duffel bag. As if I could wash death out of my life, I tossed all my clothes from Connecticut into a wicker basket and descended to the basement laundry room, where I stuffed everything in the Maytag. The black rayon dress I wore to Dodie's funeral bore a label that said DRY CLEAN ONLY. I pushed the dress into the incinerator. I never wanted to wear it again. Then I went back upstairs, stripped my bed of the sweaty sheets I had been lying on when I learned Dodie had died, and remade the bed with fresh white linen. I spent fifteen minutes tossing all the rotten stuff—with many satisfying thuds—out of my refrigerator and into the wastebasket. The bulky black trash bag traced an arc through the air when I winged it into the dumpster.

Because I couldn't stand being alone in the apartment, I gathered my keys and took myself to the grocery store, where I walked up and down the aisles pushing an empty cart, thinking of all the possibilities now open to me. Dodie had left me what I considered an enormous sum of money in stocks and bonds. I didn't need any man to support me. I didn't need Boorman, and Boorman obviously no longer wanted me. I could quit my job and write that novel. I could buy a BMW if the whim should strike. But my golf lessons had taught me more than how to chip and pitch—I had finally learned a little patience. I told myself I wouldn't do anything hasty.

I fetched milk and bread and eggs before I returned to the produce section and selected, after much debate, the choicest I could find of each variety, as if I were a chef about to cook her finest meal ever—for a squadron of vegetarians. I picked a crisp head of celery and a dark, glossy cucumber, bulbous white mushrooms big enough for stuffing, a deep green head of broccoli, several yellow and green squashes, red and golden peppers, a one-pound bag of select California carrots, two cheerful navel oranges, a bunch of bananas, deep-red cherry tomatoes, an avocado that felt slightly soft to the touch, a bag of Cajun peanuts, fresh garlic, and a red onion. Then I pushed my laden cart to the front of the store, where the bag boy proceeded to pack the carrots on top of the bananas.

I glared at him. I knew I was going to be all right—make it *out of the bunker* and back *onto the fairway*—when he asked me, "Do you need help carrying this out, *ma'am*?" and I immediately felt like decking him.

"No, thanks," I said, vowing that when I got home I'd pull out of my scalp those other white strands of hair that had grown in over the past week. But would that do the trick? Or had I finally turned a corner—reached the age where I would forever be known as *ma'am* to young boys?

The thought was frightening. But the one alternative to growing old wasn't looking too good either. In the parking lot, I rearranged all the groceries in the bags before I hoisted them into the back of the Jeep. The thud of the hatch closing reminded me of the click of Dodie's coffin. I got into my Jeep and put my head on the steering wheel, just briefly, before I told myself that I was back in Ossining and it was time to leave my grief behind. No tears, no breakdowns, just put the Jeep in gear and drive.

I drove. The groceries slipped in the back as I rounded the driveway into the apartment complex. Two bags up the stairs at a time, three trips up and down from the parking lot. On the last jog up, I pushed open the door to the apartment with my sneaker and heard a voice. Oh, God, I thought, there's a man in my apartment—the dreaded convict, escaped from Sing Sing, that everyone had been warning me about ever since I moved to the suburbs. Then for a moment I had the weird sense it was Dodie speaking to me from beyond the grave, like that *Twilight Zone* episode that had frightened us so much as kids, in which a little boy made contact with his dead grandmother over a toy telephone.

But the amplification came from the answering machine. I switched it off and picked up the phone. The man called my name. "Lise?"

"Dodie?" I whispered.

"It's Strauss."

"Oh." My stomach shrank. Then I remembered how before I left town I dared to leave a letter with Strauss's secretary (marked CONFIDENTIAL and beginning with the salutation *Dear Eben)*, informing him that I was seeking a position elsewhere and that I hoped when he returned he would be so kind as to write me the recommendation he once promised me. I also remembered I'd never told Strauss my cousin's name. Maybe he thought Dodie was my new lover.

"You sound out of breath," he said.

"I just came in the door. I just got back from Connecticut."

"I guess you didn't get my message—messages—then."

For the first time since getting home, I looked down at the counter and noticed the red light of the answering machine was blinking wildly. I didn't want to rewind the tape. Carol's voice was still on there, telling me over and over again that Dodie was dead.

"I just got back a few days ago," Strauss said. As if I didn't know where he'd been all this time, he said, "From Taiwan."

"Did you like it?" I asked, trying to be polite.

"They eat fish with the head still on."

"Sounds like a swell time."

"It wasn't," Strauss said. He cleared his throat. "I got your letter."

I waited for him to continue.

"I don't suppose it's been a picnic working for Hook."

"You guessed it."

"And so you're on the market again."

"The *job* market."

"Where are you looking?" he asked. "Back in New York? Or Connect-icut, you just said you were in Connecticut?"

Before I could answer, *My plans aren't finalized yet,* he said *he'd hate to lose me,* but then he contradicted himself by adding, "Of course, I'll be happy to write a letter for you. If it isn't too late." He cleared his throat again. "When I came back, I tried to get you on your computer. But you weren't logged on. Peg was the one who mentioned you'd asked for a leave of absence—"

"That's right."

"If you don't mind my asking, were you on an interview?"

That was the excuse I gave to Peggy—in confidence—to avoid open-ing myself up to her stern sympathy and my coworkers' overly curious questions, and also to win myself a longer leave than the two days normally allotted for funerals. The last thing I wanted to admit to Strauss was that I told yet another falsehood, when he already suspected I was a pathological liar. But it couldn't be helped.

"I took the leave for my cousin."

"He was sick?"

"No," I said. "He's dead." That was the first time I'd said it out loud, although I had said it over and over to myself, as if to convince myself it was true. *He's dead, he's dead, Dodie is dead.*

Strauss hesitated before he told me he was sorry—very sorry—for me.

"Thank you," I said.

"Was it bad?"

"He looked like a doll. A wax doll. In the coffin."

"Was he sick a long time?"

"No, he killed himself."

More silence. And in that silence, I imagined disapproval. A dislike of anything emotionally excessive. And a complete lack of sympathy, an in-ability to understand despair.

"How are you holding up?" he asked.

I couldn't answer.

"Are you all right?"

"What do you think?" Like a too sharp pencil, my voice snapped off and broke. "God, what do you think?"

"I don't know. I don't know what to think. Although I've given it a lot of hard thought over the past few months . . ." His voice trailed off. I heard his office chair squeak. "Goddammit, Lisar, I can't figure you out: Are you or aren't you quitting your job here? And what is this stuff I hear about you taking golf lessons?"

"What's it to you?"

"Plenty—"

"What's the matter, afraid I'll beat you on the course?"

"That's a given if what I hear is true—that you're studying with Peg's partner. Are you studying with Peg's partner?"

"No, we're having a torrid lesbian love affair!"

"I hope you're joking—"

"Rumors do fly, don't they?"

"You've started a few false ones yourself," he said.

"What, like your tale about coercing me!"

"I was protecting you—"

"If I want a savior, Strauss, I'll buy a Saint Bernard dog—"

"You don't need a dog—you're getting married!"

I waited, a long while, for my throat to unknot. "I'm not getting married," I said.

We both fell silent. The phone against my ear, I turned and looked back at the counter, where I had put down the gray plastic bags full of mushrooms and celery and carrots—way more than one person ever could eat.

Donna Dilano knew if she cooked and ate alone tonight, she probably would cook and eat alone for the rest of her life. That wouldn't be such a bad thing. But neither would the opposite, so she told Thomas Akins . . .

"I do have a lot of broccoli."

"Excuse me?" Strauss asked.

"Come for dinner," I said. "I mean, would you like to come for dinner?"

"Yes," he said. He would like that.

"Do you want directions?"

"No." For the first time in the conversation, his voice sounded relaxed. "I remember the way."

It was Friday night. No baseball for Strauss. And for me, no meat, and not even any fish, and hardly any talking, because once Strauss knocked (quietly, as if to prove he was doing it humbly) and came in, neither one of us could think of a damn thing to say. His arms were empty, and he just stood there as if to apologize for not bringing the wine. The front hall—small and crowded with my backpack full of overdue library books and my ridiculous blue-and-white golf umbrella—seemed to beat like a heart that had stopped for a moment and now began again, but with hesitation and awkwardness.

"You look different," I finally said. He did seem like a different person, and not just because, in his absence, I had fantasized him into a man who was taller and more aggressive and even a better dresser than his present outfit—a pale blue shirt and foulard tie under a too-heavy tweed wool jacket—indicated. He looked older. Tired. Too thin. His skin seemed dehydrated and a glint of silver shone through the front of his hair.

"Jet lag," he said.

I smiled wanly. "Beats funeral lag." From gazing at myself in the bathroom mirror before he came, and not doing anything more to correct my image than combing down my wild hair, I knew I also looked like a wreck. Why else would he keep staring at me? I suspected he was checking out my own few white hairs that I hadn't tweezed, until I realized he was making a concerted effort *not* to look back toward the door, where I had yet to turn the bolt and put on the safety chain.

"Go ahead," I said. "You can lock it."

After he flipped the lock on the knob and slipped in the chain, I had a feeling he was going to reach for me. But he didn't, and I didn't hang there long enough to make him feel like he had to touch me. Why should I have expected him to want to hold me, after all those months apart? But why else had he left two messages on my answering machine, each of them deliberately neutral, in which he identified himself by his first and last name and asked me to please call him at home—not at the office—when I got back into town, because he very much needed to speak to me. The third message puzzled me. It had come from Brooklyn. He left his parents' phone number and told me, "If I've already left for home—my home— make sure you give your name to my mother or father, and they'll let me know you called."

I knew I shouldn't do it—but of course, I did. While Strauss had made the drive to my apartment, I had called that number in Brooklyn, hoping his parents would give me some clue about those messages. I prayed his father would answer; I had a feeling his mother wouldn't like me. But his mother, of course, was the one who said hello, just as my mother always had answered the phone at our house because it was too much to ask my father (who had worked hard all day long! Ten hours and more!) to get up from his La-Z-Boy and utter a civil greeting to the caller.

I swallowed hard. "Is Eben there?"

"He was here over the weekend," she said. "But who's calling?"

Ibby's girl, I almost said before I chickened out and blurted in Brooklynese, "Mirandar!"

"Mirandar?" she asked, as if I had uttered a name from outer space, or at least one that did not require a final *R.*

I hung up the phone, my heart pounding. That's when I knew that if Strauss ever got around to taking me back to Brooklyn, I'd immediately feel at home. Surely we were destined for one another, if already I was starting trouble with his mother.

When Strauss came into my apartment, his skin sallow and his eyes bruised beneath from lack of sleep, he hardly looked like the kind of man who *had a girl,* no matter what her name. I invited him into the kitchen, where I had taken out of the bags the broccoli and carrots and tomatoes and all the rest of the produce. "It'll take awhile to get this stuff together," I said.

"Let me help."

I gave him a dubious look. Then I handed him a colander and told him to wash the mushrooms. "Wash them good," I said. As I got out a cutting board and a serrated knife, I remembered I still was Boorman's chief editor. "I mean *well.*"

I heard him puncture and rip back the plastic wrap stretched tight over the tub of mushrooms. As I wedged the tomatoes, I watched him out of the corner of my eye. He stood at the sink, gazing down at the mushrooms. The task seemed to paralyze him.

"Is there a preferred way to do this?" he asked. "I mean, do I use a brush?"

"No, your hands. Rub the dirt off with your fingers. And do a good job," I repeated. "They're grown in cow shit—"

"I know. I took botany in college." The mushrooms thudded against the metal colander. Strauss looked around—just like a thunderously dumb guy, he'd forgotten where I kept the wastebasket—and when I pointed under the sink, he nodded and disposed of the plastic tub.

He turned on the spigot and tentatively held a mushroom under the faucet. Water splashed in all directions.

"Care for an apron?" I asked.

"Actually, do you mind if I take off my jacket?"

I didn't watch as he pulled off his jacket—the moment called up too many intimate memories. "Thank you," he said, when I took it from him. "You're welcome," I said, with all the disinterest and efficiency of an airline ticket-counter agent divesting him of his luggage. I headed for the hall closet before I changed my mind and went back into my bedroom. There—it must be confessed—I brought the rough wool of his jacket up to my face, then smoothed my cheek against the satin lining. I drew in my breath. He'd been sweating. Strauss hardly ever sweated.

He was nervous.

And his breast pocket crinkled. I peeked in. The paper was pink, but lighter than a while-you-were-out message slip. I hesitated only a moment before I pulled it out. It was a traffic citation. Dated twenty minutes before. Strauss had been pulled over on his way to see me. For speeding. And fined sixty dollars.

I never felt so pleased in my life. If the past few months seemed to prove I needed someone, every now and then, to remind me to look both ways before I crossed a busy street, this pink slip also proved that if I was looking for a bad boy, I'd found my own version of him. For even Ibby drove fast. And sometimes got a ticket.

I slipped the speeding citation back into his pocket. I put the coat on a hanger and placed it next to the infamous, overpriced Christmas dress I had not dared to return after the dry cleaners shrunk it. When I returned, I found Strauss in rolled-up sleeves, slopping water onto the drainboard and floor. I liked this—not the fact that I probably would have to mop after he got done, but the shirtsleeves. Something about a guy with his cuffs folded back always got to me. I always had liked Strauss's forearms. And his hands—beaded with water when he delivered me a colander full of mushrooms so scrubbed they looked like they had been doused with Mr. Clean and rinsed in ammonia—also pleased me.

"Good enough?" he asked.

"That'll do," I said. "Can you handle the celery now?"

He nodded. But again, he had trouble with the method. At the sink he put the entire head of celery under the faucet and began to rub, with his hands, on the outside.

"Stalk by stalk," I recommended, and provided him with a brush. He did such a wicked scrub number on the celery that strings of green fell off into the sink.

We washed and chopped the vegetables. I put a tablespoon of olive oil in a frying pan.

"What are we making?" Strauss finally asked.

"I don't know," I admitted. "You're probably sick to death of stir-fry."

"I've learned to like my vegetables."

"Is it true they eat rats and dogs in China?"

"Not in first-class hotels."

"Did you stay in a four-star?"

"It was a residence inn. For bewildered foreign businessmen." Strauss said the thing he liked best about the inn—and one of the few things he liked in all of Taiwan—were the sunsets from his balcony. "Other than that, I was miserable."

"I find that hard to believe."

"But I felt so alone. It was like the first week of college—I wrote a lot of letters to my parents—only it went on for months, with no one to talk to. I even thought about keeping some kind of diary—or journal—whatever you call it, just to talk to the page—"

"Did you?" I asked, knowing I wouldn't be able to resist snooping through *that* choice document.

"No."

As I tilted the pan to let the oil cover the bottom, I asked, "Afraid of your feelings?"

"Maybe." He cleared his throat. "It's awful to be tongue-tied."

"I've never had that problem," I said.

No argument on his end with that. "What I meant was, it's distressing not to be able to ask for the simplest of things."

"Didn't you learn any Chinese at all?" I asked, sure I myself never would get beyond *tank you velly much.*

"Hello," Strauss said. "Good-bye. Take me to the Regent. Crazy Western man. Crazy Western girl." He smiled. "I really was miserable, believe me."

"I bet the women were pretty," I said.

"Too pretty."

I dropped the onions into the bottom of the pan, where they spurted and sizzled, practically drowning out Strauss when he said, "But too thin. And altogether too quiet."

I took a spatula and pushed the hissing onions around in the pan. "Mind if I do these vegetables Italian-style?"

"You're the chef."

I pointed toward the spice cabinet. "Get me the basil."

He opened the cabinet. I saw him blink at the kosher salt, then move it aside without comment. He jumbled through the jars. The bottles clacked against the side of the cabinet and against one another.

Finally I said, "I'll give you a hint, Harvard. It's green."

"I'm aware of its color."

"Then what's the holdup?"

"There's a lot of green stuff in here," Strauss said, as he finally located the basil. When he handed it to me, our fingers grazed for a moment.

If this had been a Hollywood picture—or the thirteenth draft of *Stop It Some More*—the romantic hero would have repeated in a manly, but broken voice, *There's a lot of green stuff in here* . . . Then, taking matters into his also-manly hands, he would reach over and shut off the burner, divest the heroine of her apron, grab her by the forearm, kiss her until her lips were bruised, and make wild love to her against the refrigerator until the automatic icer spilled out bucket after bucket of cubes onto the floor.

Strauss and I looked away and kept on cooking. Then we sat down and ate dinner, in strained silence, like some old married couple too exhausted to sustain an extended conversation after a hard day at the office and too badly in need of adding extra fiber to their diet. I left my apron on and forgot to put my napkin in my lap. He apologized when he scraped his knife against the plate. The ice cubes in my water clinked as I tilted back my glass. He asked about a humming noise, and I said it was my heater, which twice that winter had been on the fritz.

Finally, because I saw he was having trouble getting to the point, I said, "I noticed you called me once from your parents' house."

"That's right. I went there. When I got back. Last weekend."

"I'll bet they were glad to see you."

"That got repeated a few times. Yes."

I smiled.

He didn't. "My father—my father has a brain tumor."

"I'm sorry," I said. "Can they operate?"

He shook his head.

"Did you find out when you were in Taiwan?"

"No. He told me when I came back." Strauss pushed a strip of red pepper across his plate with his fork. "By then he already had known a whole month."

"Why didn't he tell you?"

"He has a habit of withholding things." Strauss shrugged. "It's strange. The minute I saw him I just had a feeling; do you know how you sometimes know something without it being spoken?"

"Yes. I know that."

"And then—you know—it gets said and too much comes out."

"What do you mean?"

"Everything came out. While I was gone . . . someone showed him that book—"

"It wasn't me—"

Strauss blinked. "Of course it wasn't you."

"Your sister?"

"No. It was my brother-in-law."

"Ah, the infamous, dislikable brother-in-law. What were his motives?"

"Not pure, I'm sure."

"Care to elaborate?"

"Something to do with my father's will."

"Oh. That's ugly stuff. Did your father get angry? At you, I mean. For talking."

"No. I was surprised. He almost seemed to relish having my side of the story. Although he took issue with more than a few details."

"Such as?"

Strauss hesitated. "He said we were shelling walnuts that afternoon, not peanuts. He said, 'We never had an Oriental carpet in our dining room, the landlords gave you a chocolate Easter egg and not a rabbit, you were not so well-behaved as a child as you would like to think—twice we had to leave restaurants because of your misbehavior, and there was plenty of backtalk when you turned thirteen. From the way you remember, people would think it was you and not me who had the brain tumor, Ib.'"

I smiled. "Is that all?"

"Isn't that enough?"

"I'm sure there's more. You have a look on your face like there's more."

"Well. All right. Since you insist. He said—excuse me for just a moment, Lisar—'You were fooled by that last name, she was Jewish, you were the romantic one who made her Catholic, why would I marry a Catholic? I had enough problems in my life at the time.' And he didn't like what I said about my mother."

"Did she see it?"

"I apologized. More than a few times."

"That must have been an icky scene."

"Not as icky as the one with my father after that."

"So he *was* angry."

"Like I said, too much came out."

"I thought you said he didn't like to talk about himself."

"He didn't. He talked about me. He lectured me about me."

"And how did it feel to be lectured?"

"I got a taste of my own medicine."

"Galling, I'm sure."

"You might have enjoyed seeing me get put in my place." Strauss gave me a sad smile. "Should you still be working on that novel of yours—"

"Of course I'm still working on it," I said, although I had decided for the last time in the grocery store—or maybe even standing over Dodie's open grave—that I was going to make good on my threats once and for all. I would trash the whole thing, start again, and prove that if I wanted to tell a true story, I really *did* have to get my heart broken—if not once, then many times over, and write about that. I would write about that.

Strauss shifted in his chair. I could tell he was still uncomfortable with the prospect of *Stop It Some More* seeing the light of day. "Can I give you some advice about your novel?"

"Maybe."

He hesitated, but only for a moment. "Based on what I learned this weekend, my advice is to use a pseudonym."

"I was contemplating that."

"And think—strongly—about being a little more subtle when you choose names for your characters."

I took up my knife and fork like they were weapons and lit into an onion. He kept on going. "Although you'd have plenty of material if you portrayed everyone the hopeless way they really are."

"Yes. I would. Wouldn't I."

"But I forgot," he said. "You don't need a co-author."

"It's good of you to remember," I said, and popped the onion into my mouth.

He looked like he was going to say something else. But he didn't. We both looked away. This probably was the closest to *pardon my stupidity, stubbornness, lies, hotheadedness, high-mindedness, self-righteousness, and promiscuity* that either one of us ever would get. Unless we said it later.

But what was going to happen later? I couldn't even begin to think of it. For the past week I had been living backward. Just like a woman checking her calendar, again and again, to count back toward her last period, I had been counting backward to the day of Dodie's death and thinking, *Dodie's been dead* X *number of days now.* I knew I would be living in reverse for a while, whispering to myself, *Dodie has been dead two weeks, three weeks, one month,* and that was how it would keep on going, the time growing longer and longer, and the pain becoming more and more like a stone in your shoe that you got used to, because you were in public and had to keep up your demeanor and it would be impolite to bend down, take off your stinky loafer, and pull the stone out. So you suffered in silence.

As I ate my vegetables and rice, I wished Strauss would lean over and take my hand. I wished he would get to the point—I wished *we* would get to the point—of why we were sitting there together eating every conceivable squash and root vegetable ever invented. I wished I could think of something—anything—to say, besides asking him if he wanted more to eat.

"No, thank you," he said. "Thank you very much."

Then I said, "You look tired." And I blushed.

"I'm dead on my feet." He also flushed, but at the word *dead*.

"Coffee?" I asked. Suddenly I remembered the clobbered mugs Dodie gave me when I first moved to Ossining, hidden in the back of my cabinet, the gold inlay shining against the cobalt-blue background. I longed to take down those mugs and carefully wipe the dust off the rims with a clean dish towel. Only then would I be able to dust off my own voice, which felt thick in my throat whenever I thought of Dodie, and tell Strauss, "My cousin gave me these"—which would be the beginning of a long story he probably did not want to hear, but would gently invite me to tell anyway.

After I thought of the cups, I remembered, to my discomfort, the first time Strauss came over to my apartment, when I tried to seduce him by luring him upstairs with the promise of a metaphorical cup of joe, and then I remembered that steaming hot cup of coffee I made for him the morning after we first made love and I found out his father had survived the war by yanking gold out of corpses' teeth. It was strange: I was sure he remembered something along the same lines. He pushed up his glasses. "Maybe a walk would do me more good," he said. "Feel like a short walk, before it gets dark?"

It already *was* dark. But maybe he, too, was thinking back toward last summer, when the sun seemed to stay high in the sky almost until the time we went to bed.

"I'll get your coat," I said.

I went back into the bedroom and took his jacket off the hanger. But something grabbed me inside—an onion-induced cramp in my stomach? Or a stitch in my soul?—and I had to sit down on the bed. I brought his jacket up to my face again, and the tweed felt like sandpaper scratching inside of me, wearing me down to pure dust, and I kept sitting there so long that when I finally looked up, I was startled and embarrassed to see him standing in the entrance of my bedroom, leaning against the doorjamb, watching me nuzzle his coat like someone with a fetish for Donegal wool.

I stood up. "Oh, why did you come here?"

He gave me a tired smile. "I wanted my tie back," he said. "But now I see you're set on keeping my jacket."

I clutched his coat against me and felt the speeding ticket crinkle in his pocket. "I'd rather keep you," I said, in a hoarse voice that seemed to come from someone else.

He blinked. To watch Strauss was like watching a child carefully consider his next move during a game of Simon Says or Red Rover. After a short silence, he dared to step forward and hold out his hand. We clasped our palms together, as if we had just been introduced.

"Lisar," he said.

"Strauss," I said. Then I grew sober. "God. Let me call you something else—"

"But what?"

Soon enough I got my chance to call him plenty of other names—many loving names, and some, I'm afraid, decidedly not. Because we never got around to taking that walk. Instead, we sat down on the bed, holding hands, each of us staring at our shoes, shy and kind of embarrassed. He finally broke the silence. "In your living room—on the floor—I noticed you've been reading *War and Peace*."

"Dodie—my cousin—was reading it. He came to visit the weekend before he died. But he got bored with the battle scenes—and the lack of romance—and he threw it on the floor." I hung my head. I started to cry. "I dared him to read it all the way through without once falling asleep—and now he'll never finish it—or go to Italy, we were going to go to Italy—and nobody he worked with even came to his funeral—and his father kept shoveling dirt onto his coffin—and he was like my twin—he sat in front of me in junior-high homeroom, and I memorized the back of his neck!—and he left me all this money—and how am I ever going to do anything good with it, I owe it to him to do something good with it, but I wish I could just throw it all into the ground, I'd throw all the money in the world into a hole if I could just bring him back—"

"Of course you would. I feel the same way about my father."

"But it's not the same thing. Your father had a chance to live—and have you—"

"It's all luck, isn't it?" Strauss paused. "Either that, or a faulty management plan." He reached into his pocket and got out his handkerchief. "This isn't completely clean, Lisar—"

"That's all right. I like your germs. I'll take it anyway. Thank you."

I blew my nose—more than once. Even for me, the sound was spectacular—loud as the orchestra horns warming up before a concert—and just as wild and strange as a mother elephant trumpeting to her young. Strauss seemed relieved when I was through.

"Listen," he said, "I'll finish *War and Peace* for him."

"You?" I asked, wiping my eyes.

"Why so surprised? I read all of *Anna Karenina*."

"Did you like it?"

"The ending was so tragic."

"I thought that might appeal to your imagination. The adulterous woman who gets creamed by a train."

"But it didn't appeal to me, it saddened me, that she wanted nothing more in life than to be loved. . . . Well, who dies in *War and Peace?*"

"In their hearts or on the battlefield?"

"Keep it," Strauss said, when I tried to return his handkerchief. He held my hand and smoothed my hair, and listened to me sniffle some more.

"I've never thought of it," he said, "but I've never been in your bedroom before." He looked longingly back toward the lace pillows fluffed against the headboard. "God, I'm exhausted."

"I'm tired too," I said. "Let's lie down."

We took off our shoes and stretched out on the bed. Then I got up, turned off the light, and snuggled into his arms, my head on his chest so the thumping of his heart began to lull me into slumber. "This room seems a bit frilly for you, Lise," he whispered, right before we fell asleep.

We fell asleep.

That, more than anything, seemed to prove we'd grown older—and wearier, if not wiser. Only when we woke, our faces crinkly and my left hand numb with pins and needles, did we use something other than words to move through the unspoken questions of whether this sort of thing was good for us? (maybe it wasn't, but too late now) and whether you could trust love that had been resurrected from grief? (well, sometimes good children came from bad parents).

I was prepared—and he also was prepared—to play it safe. But the moment he pulled it out from his wallet—I could have told him you weren't supposed to keep them there, because body heat made the latex wear thin—we got awkward and goofy as a couple of kids kissing for the first time. I didn't know how to use it. And neither, apparently, did he, because it was the devil to get it on him, and far too easy to get it off.

Oy God, Lisar, he said, when it broke. *I'm sorry.*

I wasn't sorry. At least at first. But this, I'm afraid, is the beginning of another long and sometimes sad story—which I might start writing as soon as I stop feeling so nauseous and Eben stops hovering over me worse than he fusses over his father, who finally turns toward me in his hospital bed and asks, "Baby or no baby, are you sure you want to marry this old lady?"

Rita Ciresi is the author of *Mother Rocket,* which won the Flannery O'Connor Award for Short Fiction, and the novel *Blue Italian*. She teaches at the University of South Florida and lives with her husband and daughter in Wesley Chapel, Florida.

JOURNEYS through WESTERN RAIL HISTORY

JOURNEYS through WESTERN RAIL HISTORY

Colorado Rail Annual No. 22
A Journal of Railroad History in the
Rocky Mountain West

Editors' Preface

Once upon a time, in the early 1960s, one of the editors of this volume prided himself on purchasing a copy of every new railroad book published. At that time it was reasonable to pursue such a goal, both financially and with regard to bookshelf space. It was not long, however, before interest in the fascinating business of railroading began to grow tremendously. Over three decades later, the tide of books shows no sign of ebbing. At this moment, Colorado Railroad Museum's store has nearly 1000 titles in stock, and several new ones arrive each week.

In spite of all these, there are still numerous aspects of rail history waiting to be explored. For example, many fine pictorial books have been published about the narrow gauge railroads of southwestern Colorado. But a scholarly history of those lines, which places them in the perspective of their time and place, has never been written. And when will someone write of that marvelous time in the 1930s when four rival railroads between Chicago and the Rocky Mountains competed to make the diesel-powered streamlined passenger train a success? In the process they helped to revive the spirit of the nation from the depth of the Great Depression.

Of course, we are not in a position to commission research into those topics that we would like to see covered. But we always have been fortunate, because dedicated individuals who have spent many hours doing the hard work that good research requires allow us to publish their work. *Colorado Rail Annual No. 22* continues this happy circumstance.

Jack Pfeifer is one of a handful of talented photographers who started recording the railroad scene in the 1930s. His superb 1990 book *West from Omaha: A Railroader's Odyssey* made his lifetime of color photography available for all to enjoy. We are delighted to present his account of the working part of his career, his 43 years as a Union Pacific claim agent. Railroads are admired for their locomotives and trains. But like any other organization, a railroad is a group of people. Jack tells the good and the bad, the funny and the tragic about his encounters with employees, passengers and wayward motorists.

Throughout the history of the mountains and deserts of the American West there has always been a strand of legend and intrigue associated with buried treasures and lost mines. Railroad accidents caused by the phenomenon of flash flooding in arid regions have created similar tales of "lost" locomotives. These stories usually begin with an actual incident and are embellished over the years with myth and fancy. Loyd Glasier, through meticulous research, has separated fact from fiction surrounding one such incident at Kiowa Creek, Colorado. Loyd is a retired professional engineer, residing in Parker, Colorado, not far from the site of his topic. He is actively preserving the history of his native Cherry Creek Valley, now one of the fastest growing suburban areas in the nation.

Vern Glover has a fine reputation for his many years of historical research on the railroads of northern New Mexico. His comprehensive studies for the U.S. Forest Service have been published by the Historical Society of New Mexico. He also co-authored *The Cumbres & Toltec Scenic Railroad: The Historic Preservation Study* (University of New Mexico Press, 1980). In *Short Line Through a Lonely Land*, Vern tells about the attempt of two Pittsburgh financial promoters to penetrate Santa Fe Railway's dominance of northern New Mexico transportation. In doing so, he brings to life the story of the almost forgotten New Mexico Central.

Stephen S. Hart's study of the relationship between the Moffat Tunnel and the 1921 Pueblo flood was a two-year project at the University of Colorado-Denver. His graduate work was done for a course taught by Professor Thomas J. Noel, himself a contributor to *Colorado Rail Annual No. 19*. Steve was impressed not only with the political dealing that united the tunnel and flood control projects, but also by how the outcome eventually resulted in Denver's favor. This disaster also emphasized how vital railroads were to the economy of that era.

It is a pleasant change from recounting past railroad history to cover a current event that may be seen as history in the making. The birth of Denver's new light rail line is the beginning of what will become a major element of Colorado's Front Range transportation system in the next century. Robert Rynerson is a transit professional who was a close observer of the building of the initial segment. His interest in electric railways developed while growing up in the Pacific Northwest. Prior to joining Denver's RTD his career included various phases of the Portland and Edmonton light rail projects. Bryan Bechtold carefully followed construction progress with his camera, and we are delighted that he has been so generous in making the results available here. Kenton Forrest has documented that in Denver, as elsewhere, light rail is not a new invention, but the revival and improvement of a reliable mode of urban transportation.

Finally, Matthew Young has shown that the Colorado Railroad Museum library is a useful source of historical information about a subject far removed in time and place from Rocky Mountain railroading. Yet, there is a connecting link, for among the thousands of books in our collection is an original inscribed copy of Robert F. Fairlie's *The Battle of the Gauges Renewed*. Published in London in 1872, as the steam locomotive development of which Matt writes was propelling the industrial revolution, this book advocating narrow gauge railroads includes a lengthy report on William Jackson Palmer's Denver & Rio Grande.

We think that you will learn from and enjoy the selections in this *Annual*, as we have enjoyed our editing task. We also hope that a few of you will be inspired. There is still a lot of Rocky Mountain rail history to be explored. We know that there are those who will help us to continue this series of books into the future.

Acknowledgments

In addition to those individuals cited by each author, we wish to thank the following for their assistance: Carrie Arnold, Mike Conners, James L. Ehernberger, Cornelius Hauck, Ronald C. Hill, Richard Kindig, William W. Kratville, A.D. Mastrogiuseppe, Don Snoddy and Douglas C. Wornom, as well as Robin Reid and Claudia Previn of Johnson Printing Company.

Colorado Rail Annual
No. 22

EDITORS

Charles Albi
Kenton Forrest
Richard Cooley

**Published and
distributed by**

Colorado Railroad Museum
**P.O. Box 10,
Golden, CO 80402**

ISBN 0-918654-22-X
Library of Congress Catalog Card No. 70-102682

Printed and bound in the United States of America by Johnson Printing Company, Boulder, Colorado. Layout and production by the editors

PRINTED ON ACID FREE PAPER

Table of Contents

Above: CRRM collection (Here and elsewhere this designates Colorado Railroad Museum collection)

Opposite top: Denver Public Library Western History Department

Opposite bottom: Denver Tramway 309 turns from 17th Street onto Welton on the last day of Route 28 streetcars, November 1, 1947. (Richard Kindig)

Title page: Union Pacific Challenger 3701 heads a 96-car eastbound extra at Thayer Junction, Wyoming, on October 13, 1958. (Jack A. Pfeifer)

A pile-up such as this late 1940s one at Platteville, Colorado, created reams of routine paperwork for the UP freight claim department. Jack Pfeifer soon learned that personal injury claims were equally challenging and far from routine. (Union Pacific Museum collection; 0632-4 *above*, 0632-10 *left*)

WHEN IN DOUBT, TAKE A STATEMENT:
The Reminiscences of a Union Pacific Claim Agent
by Jack A. Pfeifer

"President of the Union Pacific," was the startled reply of a shy lad in his early teens when questioned about career plans during a church study group. Though it brought a smile to the face of my teacher, the remark would not have surprised most who knew me as the youngster who rode his bicycle to the rail yards at every opportunity to record car numbers and watch trains. I had my own tinplate "empire" in the basement. I had a father and uncle working for the Union Pacific. I never passed up an opportunity, in fact I agitated for the chance, to ride a train anywhere.

Even I did not take this hasty ad lib seriously. Like most at that age, I had no idea what fate awaited me in the "real world" after graduation, still a number of years away. Besides, this was the early 1930s, when our nation was recovering from the Great Depression, and any job was a godsend. The top job on a major railroad? Nothing more than a pipe dream!

This is not the autobiography of William Jeffers, Arthur Stoddard or John Kenefick. But shed no tears for the one whose byline appears above. Soon after graduation from Abraham Lincoln High School in Council Bluffs, Iowa, and looking for *any* work in job scarce 1939, I was hired by Union Pacific as a waybill sorter at Omaha headquarters. The lofty aspiration of several years past was far from my mind when I reported for work on August 4 for my first day as a "railroader" in what was to become a career spanning nearly 43 years. In retrospect my years as a railroader were more interesting and rewarding, if not as lucrative, than the top job where I had wished myself in a spur-of- the-moment comment. After that first day there followed a series of "gofer" jobs, a mundane world to most, but tasks that sent me home each day with a smile. After all, I was working for a railroad. What more could I ask?

About six weeks later my world came crashing down. I was furloughed in the annual fall layoff. Able only to pick up an odd job here and there, I waited expectantly six long months for that call back to work. Finally it came. I was to report to work April 1, 1940. For six hours that day I was elated to be back, until notified in the afternoon that I was again furloughed. This was not some cruel April Fool's joke—just a fact of life in those days for the newcomer. On a tip I hurried to the freight claim department, where I understood there might be an opening. Smiling, I returned a short time later with the news that I was to start working there as office boy the next day. Except for 39 months in military service during World War II, I was never again off the Union Pacific payroll until my 1982 retirement.

Simple office tasks were my lot until night school classes qualified me for promotion to comptometer operator and a salary jump from $90 to $139 per month. By then Pearl Harbor was history and my friends were leaving daily. In May 1942 I made a quick trip to Colorado Springs, Colorado, to ride the homemade (from a trolley car) motorcar of the Midland Terminal Railway to Cripple Creek. A mine cave-in had closed the line between Victor and Cripple Creek, so the day's mail and I shared an ancient truck for the last four miles of the trip. A month later I enlisted in the U.S. Coast Guard, then for over three years I wrote long letters regularly to my former co-workers. Many of them responded with personal letters. Every Christmas each one of us in the military service received a small gift, and, best of all, a huge card signed by every employee in the department.

Although my day-to-day activity had changed to invading the soil of New Guinea and the Philippines, I kept in close touch with my first love, the Union Pacific, and hurried back following my discharge in the fall of 1945. My seniority had accumulated in the interim, so I returned as a claim adjuster, paying claims and distributing the payout among various railroads for the princely wage of $200 per month.

During wartime, the rail carriers had declined to pay claims resulting from delay to perishable freight, reasoning that the delay was the result of handling priority traffic for Uncle Sam. With the war over, the carriers and the perishables industry agreed all such claims would be paid at 50 percent of the actual loss if the late arrival at destination resulted in overripe produce or a decline in the market price. I was assigned to distribute the payments among the carriers. This entailed comparing each carrier's performance against its schedule to determine which bore the responsibility for the delay. Delay claims were interesting and provided an opportunity to learn more about most of the major U.S. railroads, as well as occasionally drawing me into sparring matches via the mail with adjusters on other lines. Obviously, we did not always interpret the information in front of us in the same manner. This contrasted to most other freight claim work which was a monotonous and seemingly never ending pile of claims for such occurrences as wheat missing en route, furniture marred by mishandling or glassware arriving broken in boxes showing no outward signs of mishandling.

Being raised in Council Bluffs, Iowa, was fortunate indeed. It was a major midwestern railroad terminal served by eight roads: Union Pacific, Rock Island, Milwaukee, Burlington, Wabash, Illinois Central, Chicago Great Western, and Chicago & North Western. Omaha, Nebraska, just across the river, had those plus Missouri Pacific and Chicago St.Paul Minneapolis & Omaha, the latter a part of the C&NW system, but with its own identity, equipment, motive power and separate depot. All the other railroads in Omaha used Union Station, except for the Burlington and the Chicago Great Western, which ran out of Burlington Station, just a short block away and connected to Union Station by an enclosed walkway. Omaha was the big passenger terminal, but each of the eight lines serving Council Bluffs maintained yards and engine facilities on the Iowa side of the river, and all but the Wabash had their own passenger stations in Council Bluffs.

Seven of Council Bluffs' railroads fanned out to the north, east and south, funneling much of the traffic of the East and Midwest through Council Bluffs to the West. This was much to my delight, as I haunted the local rail yards in the post-war period with a 616 Kodak in an attempt to photograph every steam engine on wheels before the dreaded diesel took over completely. Three-quarter view locomotive shots were my forte, but as more and more diesels appeared on the scene, a color camera became a necessity.

most important, milestone of the late 1940s. In September 1947, while prowling the ankle-deep cinders of Union Pacific's Cheyenne yards with a camera at the ready I met a trio of railfans, one of whom was Richard Kindig. This stroke of sheer luck was probably the most important event in my lifetime of interest in railroad photography. In subsequent correspondence, Dick encouraged my wife and me to journey to Colorado in 1949 for several of the great excursions sponsored by the Rocky Mountain Railroad Club. During these I became intimately familiar with the Rio Grande Southern, several Denver & Rio Grande Western narrow gauge lines, including the one through Black Canyon, and the Manitou & Pike's Peak cog line, among others. By the end of the year narrow gauge railroading shared that special place in my heart previously reserved for Union Pacific's massive freight power and speedy limiteds. The dedication and vitality of the members of the Rocky Mountain Railroad Club so impressed me that I became a member. Upon returning home I gathered together several railfans in the Omaha–Council Bluffs area to form the Camerail Club. While Camerail has not gained the prominence of the RMRRC, it has prospered through the

Here is an office at UP's Omaha headquarters building, where Jack went to work in 1939. (Union Pacific Museum collection 37910)

Less than a year after my return to civilian life I was married, which some find incompatible with being an unabashed railfan. It was my great fortune that, while not the least bit interested in railroads, my wife has always supported my hobby interest and upon occasion has even enjoyed a ride on the less-than-first-class accommodations of an excursion train. My mention of the increasing popularity of color photography did not fall on deaf ears. A new Retina 35mm camera appeared under our 1949 Christmas tree. Now I could do those diesels justice in color. But I soon discovered the wonderful world of steam action photography and never really "took a hankering" to the diesel, as they said in the Old West.

My introduction to color photography was not the only, nor

hard work of those who followed me at the throttle and now counts over 600 happy fans as members.

In the early 1950s, as diesels appeared in ever increasing numbers and the future of steam locomotives continued to look even more bleak, Dick and I spent many a weekend on Sherman Hill fighting the ever-present wind while photographing the waning days of steam and onset of the diesel and short-lived turbine ages. By far the most important influence on my railfan life was the time spent with Dick Kindig. I learned how and where to shoot those great action shots and, more important, how to be open and giving to other fans. In short, I learned that sharing with others brought me the greatest satisfaction from my hobby.

Midland Terminal 101, a motorized former Colorado Springs streetcar, basks under a May 1942 sun in the quiescent mining town of Victor, Colorado. Jack and the U.S. Mail finished their journey to Cripple Creek in the old truck on the platform. A month later he was in the U.S. Coast Guard. (author's photo)

As the years rolled by and the railroad industry returned to normal following World War II, perishable delay claims no longer constituted a full time job. As a result I was assigned more and more uninteresting run-of-the-mill claims. If my eight-hour workday was no longer a challenge, after work activities certainly were. Our office had a team in the Union Pacific bowling league and during the summer hiatus from bowling we had a team in the company softball league, a sport more taxing physically than bowling. I finally knew it was time for me to give up softball when the aches and pains from last week's games were not yet healed by the start of this week's game.

Lighter moments did occur to break up the humdrum routine of handling freight claims. A holdover from perhaps the earliest days of the railroad was a standard spittoon at each desk. Hardly a month went by without someone accidently

kicking over one of those little rascals, then jumping out of the way of the rush of brown water and sodden cigarette butts. This was accompanied by cheers and catcalls from those in the vicinity.

Occasionally supervisors would make their contributions to the deviation from the routine with some action that brought smiles or puzzlement to the faces of employees. One winter day there was a derailment at Laramie involving several carloads of hogs, many of which did not survive. In addition to paying for the damaged freight it was the job of our department to attempt to find buyers for the damaged merchandise. This was to salvage as much as possible financially from the situation. One of our freight claim officials in Omaha, who was known to present his wife with a new pair of hose every Christmas, whether she needed them or not, found a rendering company in Cheyenne that would pay us 50 cents for

By May 1949 the war was four years in the past, and Jack was enjoying the view of narrow gauge activity at Gunnison, Colorado, from the back end of the car *Silver Vista* on a Rocky Mountain Railroad Club excursion. (author's collection)

Jack's claim department work did not preclude him from actively participating in railfan activities on his own time. He helped to organize Omaha's Camerail Club and was aboard its first fan trip on competitor Burlington's mixed train to Prague, Nebraska, July 15, 1950. CB&Q Prairie 2219 hauled no freight that Saturday but required a heavyweight coach in addition to the regular combine in order to handle this one-day "boom" in passenger business. (William Kratville photo)

every dead hog delivered. So, instructions went out to our representative on the ground in Laramie to have the sectionmen load the dead hogs into freight cars for shipment to Cheyenne. When word got out about the great money saving venture in Wyoming, it prompted considerable snickering in our office. However, it is fairly certain that the workers loading those frozen porkers in windswept, below-zero Laramie were not snickering. In fact, they no doubt would have had ugly attitudes if they had known the whole story. In any case, it is doubtful all that effort by the Omaha official had any beneficial effect on the bottom line of Union Pacific's financial statement.

In 1951 the previously separate freight claim department (mostly union) and the general claims department (all management) were combined under one official, the general claims agent. Because of the differences in their work and personnel status, the two departments were kept separated by a long row of file cabinets. Except for loss and damage to freight, general claims handled all claims against the railroad, including personal injuries of all kinds, grade crossing accidents, "purebred" cattle struck by trains and other property damage resulting from railroad operation. Increasingly, this included traffic accidents as more and more railroaders went about their duties on rubber tired vehicles.

There were some openings in the general claims section, and I was the first of several from the freight claim section given the opportunity to transfer to more interesting and better paying jobs. It was a big step for a shy young man who

died a thousand cold-sweat deaths every time he had to give a report in school, but who was now preparing to make a living thrashing it out verbally with claimants and their attorneys.

On one of the first days at my new job, a co-worker handed me a dog eared investigation file and with a wink stated it was required reading. It was a closed case, having been settled several years before. A conductor on a through freight, disdaining the non-flush toilet in the caboose, which he claimed "worked in reverse" at high speed, answered a call of nature by standing in the doorway at the rear of the caboose. An unexpected run in of slack slammed the door shut before he could remove his anatomy entirely from the doorway. A widower, the man lived with his unmarried sister, and out of embarrassment said nothing for a couple of days, but the pain finally forced him to a doctor where a "minor" amputation was deemed necessary. Obviously, personal injury claims were not going to be boring!

Little did I realize the working atmosphere I was entering when I accepted the position in general claims, but it became evident fairly soon. The previous head of the department had reportedly "retired" by request. On the positive side, he always backed his employees and fought to see that they were well compensated for their work. Because of him, Union Pacific-trained claims personnel were in demand throughout the industry, but due to the working conditions he imposed, many had left for jobs as independent claim adjusters. His employees worked 16-hour days regularly but

Late 1930s era Yellow Coach 37-passenger highway streamliners, such as No. 1020 photographed at East Los Angeles, were the flagships of the Union Pacific Stages fleet through the 1940 decade. This was the operating entity of Interstate Transit Lines, the partly UP-owned bus company that later became Overland Greyhound. Polished boots, jodhpur breeches and Sam Brown belts were part of the standard uniform for all bus drivers in those years. (Union Pacific Museum collection 729-A)

got a break on weekends when they could leave around dinner time on Saturday and sometimes at mid-afternoon on Sunday.

In his dictatorial way this man often had employees on two or more pay scales at different times during a single day, depending upon how their performance pleased or displeased him. According to the old heads in the department, he would sometimes send claim agents from one location to another to "help out." Upon arrival they would be told that they were now assigned there permanently, leaving their family to make all of the moving arrangements. Believe me, the new eight hour days and short weekend stints brought smiles to the faces of those who had worked under the old regime.

Unfortunately, one or two of the remaining supervisors in the department were of the opinion, quite erroneously, that I had been sent over from the freight claim side of the office as a spy. Consequently, life was not pleasant for me at times, but I survived. Of course, being new in the department, I

Green River, Wyoming, was in its ninth decade as a major stop for Overland Route passenger trains when Jack worked there in the 1950s. Transportation standards of the time are reflected in the solidly-built automobiles, the streamlined Wabash coach and the Harriman standard heavyweight in the foreground—both in UP Armour yellow paint. (Union Pacific Museum collection)

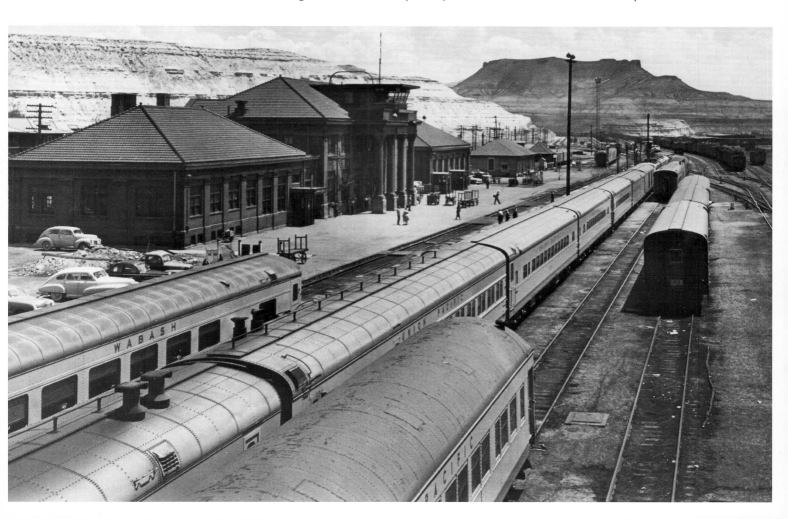

wanted to learn all that I could. On my first job there were times when I was not busy. I took advantage of such lulls to read investigation files, attempting to learn how the claim department clicked and what was eventually going to be expected of me. One supervisor noticed me one day and chewed me out. When I explained that I was just trying to learn, he very officiously pointed out that I could not learn by reading claim files during working hours but only by reading them on my own time during evenings and weekends. Alas! I was thus initiated into the world of fractured logic that seemed to pop up every now and then during my career.

On my new job I had to work a few hours every other weekend. Of course that cut into the time for railroad photography. But I made the best of it, and my trusty cameras went along each Saturday and Sunday that I worked. Since the facilities of all lines serving Council Bluffs were more or less between my home and the office, I always allowed a bit more time and went the long way.

During this time I first experienced the grim reality of being on call 24 hours a day. In the early 1950s Union Pacific was part owner of Interstate Transit Lines, a transcontinental bus line which later became Overland Greyhound; therefore, our office handled claims for the bus line as well as many other subsidiaries. One afternoon we were told a bus had caught fire in Wyoming, resulting in no injuries, but the entire load of baggage had been destroyed. The passengers would be arriving in Omaha at 2:00 am, and the office was to turn out to handle their claims during the Omaha layover. That sleepless night provided my first taste of dealing with the public as an adversary. It was an eye-opener and hinted at something I was to learn well in the years to come: in general, the American public behaves well in the face of adversity.

In 1957 I was appointed claim agent at Green River, Wyoming. It was a sudden transition from various desk jobs in the main office to having complete responsibility for han-

dling all claims on 250 miles of the mainline from Rawlins to Evanston. Many railroaders considered Green River synonymous with exile and equated time served there to Marine boot camp. I was glad to go there, or anywhere, to escape from headquarters.

Because I had little actual claim handling experience, I was assigned to work for two weeks with the more experienced Cheyenne claim agent, Tony Minardi. Tony never took short cuts and never took a two page statement when a four page one would do. He was a true workaholic but also the best instructor on the railroad, something for which I was extremely grateful the rest of my career.

I met Tony in Cheyenne. We drove to Green River, working the Cheyenne and Green River territories as we went. First item of business: two dead Navajo extra gang laborers at Medicine Bow, one having been stuck by an auto on the main street and the other by a train as he roused from an alcoholic stupor alongside the main line during the previous night. It had been payday on the gang. The Navajos were good workers, and for that reason the railroad recruited them on the reservation, but payday twice a month could be chaotic.

When approached for information during an injury investigation, a Navajo seldom admitted he could understand or speak English, making it necessary to use another laborer as an interpreter. Later, when the "interpreter" sustained an injury, it was not uncommon for him to then claim he spoke no English, necessitating the use of someone else on the gang to interpret for him! This was a humorous sidelight to working with the Navajos, but in general I liked them. They were hard workers, shyly cooperative and fair in their approach to settlements when injured.

What a revelation to arrive in Green River and overnight become a part of the operation of the railroad. I found myself in the confidence of and on good terms with the chief dispatcher, assistant division superintendent, terminal superintendent, chief mechanical officer and other officials. If a box-

Union Pacific's red brick station at Evanston, Wyoming, reflects Harriman era solidity. By the time of this photograph, however, the locomotive crew room and other offices were housed in the metal building to the right. (James L. Ehernberger photo)

Initiation of an accident report was frequently in the form of a telegram such as this one sent by the local special agent to Omaha headquarters. The information was taken from another form that had been filled in by the conductor of Cheyenne-Denver mixed train 334, which ran via the Dent branch. Prompt reporting of even minor incidents is the first line of defense in proper claims handling. (CRRM collection)

TELEGRAPHIC REPORT OF ACCIDENT
(FOR USE OF RECEIVING TELEGRAPH OPERATOR)

KEY TO SYMBOL NUMBERS

1. Date and Time.	11. Is there a Siding by which Trains can pass?	
2. Locality (Exact).	12. Will Temporary Track have to be constructed?	
3. Curve or Straight Track.	13. Help Required.	
4. Weather.	14. Is assistance needed at East or West end of Train?	
5. Cause.	15. Damage to Track.	
6. Train designation, Engine Number, Names of Conductor and Engineer.	16. Is Engine off Track?	
7. Consist of Train.	17. Damage to Engine.	
8. Speed and Direction of Train.	18. Damage to Cars and Contents, Waybill Reference, etc.	
9. Is Main Line Obstructed?	19. Detention to Trains.	
10. How long to clear Main Track?	20. Personal Injuries.	
	21. Remarks.	

Denver - Feb. 26, 1944.

JCG HHL EMP JFC LES JAC LTH - Omaha
JCG HHLEMP JAC CRK   - On line

JEW JLL - Denver

1 - Feb. 22, 1944 - 7:00PM

2 - Between Sand Creek Jct. and 36th Street Denver.

3 - Straight

4 - Cloudy, calm.

5 - Struck head against window.

6 - No. 334, Eng. 2298, Condr. J.A.Crocker, Engr. R.H.Lee.

7 - 17-11-1190

8 - Approx. 20 MPH east.

9 to 19 - Blank

20 - Richard Herbert Vecki, age 16 months, passenger, bruise on back of head.

21 - Child accompanied by parents, Mr. & Mrs. M. H. Vecki, 4030 So.Lincoln St. Englewood, Colo. traveling on revenue transportation, Cheyenne to Denver in coach UP 1241. Father of child picked him up from aisle of coach and holding him on knee, when child reared back, striking head against window glass, breaking inner pane and causing bruise on back of head. On arrival Union Station, Company Surgeon, Dr. W.M.Greig called, and gave necessary medical attention.

C-54

RAR.....900PM

car was involved in an injury, and I wanted photos of it, all I had to do was say the word. It would be cut out of a train and spotted anywhere I asked and held until I released it.

That was pretty heady stuff which I tried to take in stride. But, a railfan friend of mine exhibited wide-eyed disbelief when his perception of my influence in that area of the railroad became blown out of proportion by sheer luck. He and his wife were house guests, so I invited him along on a working trip to Bitter Creek, Wyoming. Returning on a gravel road paralleling the mainline to Point of Rocks, we stopped in a cloud of steam when my 1955 Dodge became overheated. The petcock at the bottom of the radiator had not been properly tightened when it was serviced a few days before and had worked loose on the rough road.

Traffic in that location ranged from infrequent to nonexistent, but a section crew was working about a mile away. As I started toward them to get help, a Union Pacific truck from a track extra gang pulled up to inquire about my problem. It so happened they had a barrel of drinking water on the truck. My starter would not budge the hot engine, but a push from the truck did the trick, and most of the first bucket of water

into the radiator came right back out as steam. Finally it cooled enough to accept the water. With the errant petcock tightened and thank-yous to my fellow railroaders, we were on our way in about 20 minutes. Amidst considerable head-shaking, my passenger said (several times) that if he had not seen it with his own eyes he would never have believed a company truck would come to our rescue on cue.

The primary tool of the trade for a claim agent was a portable typewriter for taking statements, the basis of any investigation. "When in doubt, take a statement" was the unofficial motto of the department. I typed statements while sitting, standing, kneeling, sweating, praying, freezing and, on rare occasions, while seated at a desk. Usually a statement was one and a half to two 8 1/2 x 14-inch single spaced pages, but in complex situations it could run to five or more pages. It soon became evident to me that typing aboard moving trains on a fixed object such as a table just would not work. The train moved one way and my body went the other, and my fingers hit the wrong keys. I became proficient at typing on my lap.

Passenger injuries constituted much of the work in the Green River territory. Four streamliners and one mail train, the former *Overland Limited*, passed through Green River in the daylight in each direction, and extra sections were the norm during the heavy summer travel period and over Christmas.

If there was an injured passenger on board, I would usually receive a phone call from Evanston or Rawlins with the information, then board the train and ride as far as necessary to make an investigation and, if possible, a settlement. Sometimes I got the word only after the train stopped at Green River, giving me all of ten minutes to be on board. Consequently, I kept a packed suitcase in my office and one file drawer was divided into "work west" and "work east," so I could grab one or the other hurriedly as I dashed out to board the train.

Handling passenger injuries usually involved an overnight stay. By the time I got off in Evanston or Rawlins all of the day's passenger trains would be gone, leaving me with the choice of losing most of a night's sleep riding the night mail train home or staying overnight and accomplishing some work. I opted for the latter as I usually had work there anyway. I never understood, however, why so many more passengers were injured on weekends and holidays than during the rest of the week. When caught away from home on the weekend, I would get back the best way possible, sometimes by Greyhound, but usually on a freight train. Dressed in a business suit, topcoat and hat and carrying typewriter and briefcase, getting on and off dirty diesel units or turbines was neither easy nor graceful, but it did provide a ride free of the slack action in the caboose.

Because our passenger trains served different areas, each had its own ethnic makeup. The *City of St. Louis*, connecting the St. Louis and southern California areas, generally had a far different passenger load than either the *City of Los Angeles* or *City of Francisco*, both of which connected Chicago and the East with the large metropolitan areas of California. The *City of Portland*, with its potpourri mix of passengers,

seemed to give us fewer problems than the other trains. When handling passenger injuries one soon learned that what seemed to work smoothly on one train did not necessarily produce the same results on another.

The dome passenger cars were an answer to advertising and traffic department prayers but were a bane in the existence of the claim department. The aisle in the dome section was lower than the floor under the seats on either side. Since there were no depressed aisles anywhere else on the train, passengers would forget they had stepped up when they took a seat in the dome. Then upon leaving the seat some time later they would fall against the seats across the aisle. I cannot tell you how many times during my three years in Green River I picked up the telephone only to have someone say, "A lady fell in the dome car on the *City of* —."

Passengers were from all walks of life, and investigating their injuries proved interesting. I recall one elderly lady who had fallen coming into Green River. I rode to Evanston and had the train held there while a doctor saw her. He diagnosed a possible knee fracture and recommended she be hospitalized. From the startled look on her face, the dear lady must have been convinced the natives were still on the warpath in Wyoming. Although in considerable pain, she made it clear she was not leaving the train in "this place," even though her daughter agreed with the doctor. She wanted to go home to southern California. I detrained there with the doctor and called our Ogden claim agent, who arranged for sleeping car space for the injured lady and her daughter to Los Angeles and had an ambulance crew come to the Ogden depot to move her from the coach to the Pullman.

During my first summer in Green River I received a call from Tony on a Saturday morning that a lady had been taken off the *City of Portland* the evening before in eastern Oregon with food poisoning from eating salmon. He said to get on and ride east, determine who among the passengers had salmon in the dining car the previous night and get statements

The troublesome depressed center aisle in the domes can be seen here. If all Union Pacific passengers had been as alert as these men and women posed by the company photographer on the loud plaid upholstery of a new domecar, a claim agent's reminiscences would have made dull reading. (Union Pacific Museum collection)

The streamliner *City of St. Louis*, parallels two-lane concrete U.S. 85 near Platteville, Colorado, behind an asymetrical A-B-A F3-E8-E8 set of diesel units. At this time No. 9 had no dome cars, but the Railway Post Office car operated between Denver and Cheyenne. Another RPO was in the consist from Kansas City to Denver. (Union Pacific Museum 90-61-A) A page reproduced from the June 20, 1954, timetable provides insight to some scheduling arrangements then in effect. (CRRM collection)

ST. LOUIS—KANSAS CITY—SAN FRANCISCO via Denver

Local No. 57 Example	69-369 17-23 Example	Pony Express-Gold Coast 37-23 Example	Portland Rose-Gold Coast 17-23 Example	Streamliner City of St. Louis-San Francisco Overland 9-27 ▲ Example	**Table E** Condensed Schedules All Trains Daily	San Francisco Overland-Streamliner City of St. Louis 28-10 Example	Gold Coast-Pony Express 24-38-18 Example		Local No. 52 Example
					Wabash				
.....	.....	.....	11.40 SUN	4.00 SUN	Lv **St. Louis** (C.S.T.).........Mo. Ar	12.29 TUE	7.35 WED	.....	.....
.....	.....	.....	7.25 MON	9.00 SUN	Ar **Kansas City**.............. " Lv	7.30 TUE	11.59 TUE	.....	.....
.....	11.30 SUN	.....	8.30 MON	9.30 SUN	Lv **Kansas City** Union Pacific..Mo. Ar	7.15 TUE	10.30 TUE	.....	.....
.....	12.30 MON	.....	◉.. "	◉.. "	" Lawrence.............Kan. Lv	◉.. "	9.30 "	.....	.....
.....	1.15 "	.....	9.38 "	10.37 "	" Topeka............... " "	5.53 "	8.55 "	.....	.....
.....	2.20 "	.....	10.33 "	11.30 "	" Manhattan............ " "	5.03 "	7.55 "	.....	.....
.....	3.10 "	.....	11.02 "	11.59 SUN	" Junction City........ " "	4.32 "	7.30 "	.....	.....
.....	3.45 "	.....	◉.. "	◉..MON	" Abilene.............. " "	◉.. "	6.55 "	.....	.....
.....	4.35 "	.....	11.54 "	12.49 "	" Salina............... " "	3.23 "	6.25 "	.....	.....
.....	6.55 "	.....	1.36 "	2.29 "	" Hays................. " "	1.34 "	4.23 "	.....	.....
.....	8.00 "	.....	2.01 "	3.00 "	Ar **Ellis** (C.S.T.).......... " Lv	1.21 "	4.05 "	.....	.....
Local No. 57 Daily Example	7.30 "	.....	1.10 "	2.09 "	Lv **Ellis** (M.S.T.)........... " Ar	12.12 TUE	2.55 "	Local No. 52 Daily Example	
	9.50 "	.....	2.23 "	3.20 "	" Oakley............... " "	11.01 MON	1.34 "		
	11.30 "	.....	3.14 "	4.09 "	" Sharon Springs.......Kan. "	10.14 "	12.40 "		
	3.12 "	.....	5.09 "	6.08 "	" Limon...............Colo. "	8.20 "	10.33 "		
	6.30 "	.....	7.00 "	7.55 "	Ar **Denver**.............. " Lv	6.50 "	9.00 "		
8.30 SUN	7.30 "	5.30 SUN	7.30 "	8.25 "	Lv **Denver**.............. " Ar	6.20 MON	8.00 "	5.20 SUN	
9.35 "	□.. "	6.25 "	□.. "	□.. "	" LaSalle ∫ *Colorado State* ∫Colo. "	□.. "	□.. "	4.15 "	
9.49 "	8.30 MON	6.37 SUN	8.30 MON	9.25 MON	" Greeley { *College of Education* }Colo. "	5.03 MON	6.26 "	4.01 "	
11.05 SUN	Via Cut-off	Via Cut-off	Via Cut-off	Ar **Cheyenne**.............Wyo. Lv		Via Cut-off	2.45 SUN	
				Lv **Cheyenne**.............. " Ar				
.....	10.50 MON	9.05 SUN	10.50 MON	11.45 MON	" Laramie.............. " Lv	2.58 MON	4.15 TUE	.....	
.....	12.58 TUE	11.30 SUN	12.58 MON	1.44 "	" Rawlins.............. " "	1.05 "	1.55 TUE	.....	
.....	□.. "	□..MON	□.. "	□.. "	" Rock Springs......... " "	□.. "	11.32 MON	.....	
.....	3.40 "	3.40 "	3.40 "	4.40 "	" Green River.......... " "	10.45 "	11.10 "	.....	
.....	5.50 "	5.50 "	5.50 "	6.45 "	" Evanston............Wyo. "	8.34 "	8.57 "	.....	
.....	7.30 TUE	7.30 MON	7.30 TUE	8.35 MON	Ar **Ogden** (M.S.T.).........Utah Lv	6.50 MON	7.10 MON	.....	
.....	5.30 TUE	5.30 MON	5.30 TUE	7.15 MON	Lv **Salt Lake City** (M.T.)...... " Ar	8.25 MON	9.45 MON	.....	
					Southern Pacific				
.....	8.10 TUE	8.10 MON	8.10 TUE	9.10 MON	Lv **Ogden** (M.S.T.).........Utah Ar	6.25 MON	6.30 MON	.....	
.....	9.45 "	9.45 "	9.45 "	6.40 TUE	" Reno (P.S.T.).........Nev. Lv	6.56 SUN	3.20 "	.....	
.....	10.50 TUE	10.50 MON	10.50 TUE	7.35 "	" Truckee..............Cal. "	5.52 "	1.58 MON	.....	
.....	3.40 WED	3.40 TUE	3.40 WED	11.37 "	" Sacramento........... " "	2.05 "	9.40 SUN	.....	
.....	5.40 "	5.40 "	5.40 "	1.24 "	Ar Berkeley............ " "	12.14 "	7.17 "	.....	
.....	5.50 "	5.50 "	5.50 "	1.37 "	" Oakland (16th St.).... " "	12.06 "	7.08 "	.....	
.....	6.00 "	6.00 "	6.00 "	1.45 "	" Oakland Pier......... " "	11.58 "	7.00 "	.....	
.....	6.35 WED	6.35 TUE	6.35 WED	2.20 TUE	Ar **San Francisco** (P.S.T.).....Cal. Lv	11.30 SUN	6.30 SUN	.....	

17

from them that they (hopefully) were feeling fine today. He would get over to Laramie and board the train there to help out. The world is full of new experiences when you are in the claim business!

I boarded the *City of Portland* in Green River and 15 miles later, during the Rock Springs stop, the operator came on board to notify me there was an injured passenger on a westbound train and I was to get off to handle it. Not knowing who had given those instructions, I got off only to learn as my train disappeared in the distance that the injury in question was minor, and the decision for me to detrain had been the operator's. Now I had a problem! The train on which I was supposed to be working was speeding east without me, a very unsettling predicament for a young claim agent in his first year on the job.

In those days the three west coast streamliners went east as a fleet about 15 minutes apart, *City of Los Angeles* first, *City of San Francisco* next, and *City of Portland* last. That day, however, the *City of San Francisco* was running last, but it was the only one of the three without a scheduled stop in Rock Springs. I hurriedly called the dispatcher and told him of my predicament. With tongue in cheek I asked if there was any possibility he could stop the *City of San Francisco* in Rock Springs long enough for me to jump on, then hold the *City of Portland* a few minutes at Rawlins so I could catch it. There was a moment of silence then, "I'll see what I can do." There was hope! If it had been out of the question, I would have been told so immediately. As the *City of San Francisco* slowed for the Rock Springs station stop I smiled—at least I had a chance.

As we rolled eastward I was not sure how I would make the transfer at Rawlins inasmuch as the eastbound trains all used the same mainline track, stopping behind one another. I could picture myself making a pretty good sprint from one train to the other laden with the usual impedimenta of the claim business—typewriter, briefcase, suitcase, etc. My anxiety was soon eased. At a lonely center siding in the Wyoming desert sat the *City of Portland* "in the hole" as we sped by. Obviously, the dispatcher's sheet that day explained putting one streamliner in the siding to let another pass without making reference to the claim agent, since I was never asked to explain. Of necessity the dispatchers were all business, but also human and cooperative to the limit of their ability when the occasion demanded. Another time the chief dispatcher stopped two passenger trains in the desert near Bitter Creek so I could ride an eastbound to handle a passenger injury and still get back that evening to present a slide program for the local Union Pacific Old Timers Club.

But, back to the fish story. Of course I detrained at Rawlins, and the *City of Portland* soon stopped there. As I walked out to board it, the conductor and head brakeman rubbed their eyes in disbelief. I had just gotten off their train in Rock Springs. We all enjoyed the joke after my explanation cleared up the mystery of the passenger train run-around in the middle of nowhere. Needless to say, I worked like a trooper, since I had already lost over two hours. From the dining car steward I determined there had been 12 salmon dinners

served the night before, and I located ten of the passengers who ate them. This allowed for the possibility that one person had detrained somewhere in Idaho, in addition to the one hospitalized in Oregon.

Only three passengers remained to be interviewed when Tony got on in Laramie. We were able to wind those up in time to enjoy a steak dinner as twilight bathed Sherman Hill. The good news was that no one we had interviewed had experienced any problem from eating salmon the night before. The bad news was to come later! All through dinner I fielded a good natured ribbing from Tony after relating the saga of my trip across Wyoming that Saturday, but he was very kind and complimented me on having the presence of mind to find a way to get back on the train.

Detraining in Cheyenne after dark, he went home and I checked into a hotel for a good night's sleep in anticipation of the next day's ride home. It would include one of my favorite pastimes—a corned beef hash and poached egg breakfast in the dome diner while charging over Sherman Hill. Ah, such sweet dreams! The spell was soon broken by the jangle of the phone. It was Tony. He had talked with someone in our Portland office, and they had just learned the sick lady removed from the train in eastern Oregon had eaten the salmon at a relative's home *before* boarding the train!

The passenger crews always were very cooperative. They appreciated our presence when they had an injury or illness on board, and I always tried to help them whenever possible. One sunny day while I was riding to Rawlins and enjoying the Wyoming scenery, the conductor came to me with a problem. A sleeping car passenger had struck her arm on something in the vestibule while detraining in Portland from another train *several days previously*, resulting in the loss of a stone from the bracelet of a matched jewelry set. However, she had sustained no injury. Most conductors would have told the lady they were sorry and let it go at that. But this one had a son working as a claim agent on another division, and I think he just wanted to see what I would do with it.

Upon being introduced to this very nice lady I followed the old claim department adage—when in doubt, take a statement. All of the details were documented: Pullman space she occupied into Portland, which end of the car she detrained from, was the train late or on time, how far from the depot crosswalk did she alight, and so forth. If nothing else, my interest in her problem would make a friend for our railroad. Besides, it would add one statement to my production report for the month. I promised to send all of the information to our Portland office, since there was an outside chance the stone had been found. I thought it very unlikely, and she agreed.

After mailing the file to Portland I gave it no more thought until a month later when I received a nice letter from the lady. She thanked me for my assistance and told how thrilled she was to have the stone back because of the sentimental value of the jewelry. By phone I learned that one of our Portland claim agents, using my statement and with the help of the stationmaster, had found the stone between the rails. Talk about a needle in a haystack!

Surprise was the order of the day when dealing with pas-

The Bitter Creek, Carter, Table Rock and Wamsutter depots illustrate Union Pacific standard plan variations. At the time it was photographed, Table Rock was being used as a section house. This 14 x 32-foot style of building was originally designed as a telegraph office. Jack had occasion to visit all of these remote locations in the course of his work. (four photos, James L. Ehernberger)

senger injuries. Normal procedure at the start of a statement was to ask to see the passenger's ticket, then incorporate the ticket number and issuing office in the statement. This was merely a formality to assure that the claimant was a fare-paying passenger, since we were not liable for injuries to pass passengers (those using free transportation). Beyond copying the required information, I paid little attention to the tickets, which came in all sizes, shapes and colors. Handling a minor injury while en route home from Rawlins, I went through the usual routine, then handed the ticket back to the lady. I was unaware that it was a clergy ticket available to "persons of the cloth" at about half fare. She looked rather sheepish, then confessed that the ticket had been purchased by her husband, a clergyman. He had become ill, so she was using it in his place to attend a church conference in California with her brother-in-law. She wanted to know if she was going to be in any trouble with the railroad.

Suppressing a raised eyebrow, I calmly took the ticket back and studied it while planning my strategy. Finally, I offered an opinion that the railroad probably would not be particularly concerned about the matter, but the sale of railroad tickets also included collection of Federal transportation tax. This raised the possibility of a problem with Uncle Sam for non-payment of the proper tax. I suggested that we go ahead and get the statement about the injury, and we could figure out something on the ticket later. Claim agents are often unjustly accused of putting words in claimants' mouths when taking statements. In this case it was not necessary. She downplayed the injury to a mere bump that needed no doctor and felt that she would be OK in a day or two. Although it had resulted from a lurch of the train, she said did not feel that the railroad was in any way at fault. I put it down exactly the way she told it and could not have dictated a report more favorable to the railroad.

By the time we finished I had a suggestion for her. I would toss off a note at Rock Springs asking the operator to alert the Green River ticket office, so that she could go into the depot during the Green River stop and upgrade her ticket to a full fare, thus avoiding the possibility of any problem as a result of using a clergy ticket to which she was not entitled. She agreed. It went off like clockwork, and as she left the ticket window clutching change from a crisp new $100 bill, she thanked me for my help. I wished her a pleasant trip. Frequently thereafter I was ribbed by other members of the department for having been the only claim agent in their memory to have *collected* money from an injured passenger.

After about a year in Green River it occurred to me that no one had told me if my work was satisfactory. I talked by phone daily with my immediate supervisor, the district claim agent in Omaha. One morning I suggested that no one had ever told me whether I was doing a good job, what I was doing right or what I was doing wrong. His straight faced reply (I heard no chuckle over the phone) was, "If we're not giving you hell, you are doing OK."

Could this be some of that fractured logic I had encountered earlier in my claim career? I will say that when I made decisions in the field he backed me up, and it was his style to calmly explain a better way if he thought something had not been handled as he would have done it. While there were no pats on the back, there also were no "chewing out" sessions. I appreciated such an attitude.

Unlike other cities where I worked, my Green River office was in the depot, affording me a ringside seat for the everyday operation of the railroad. For an avowed railroad fan this was the best of all worlds, and they paid me for it, too! It was a great learning experience in what could best be termed "Railroading 101." It soon became obvious that there was good reason for the volumes of rules under which each department worked.

One procedure not found in any rulebook did puzzle me, however. Many officials in Omaha had business cars which passed through Green River (but seldom stayed) on the rear of the various streamliners. Their arrival seemed always to be known to the local supervisors, who were usually to be found strolling nonchalantly about the station platform in close proximity to the stopped private car. Believe me, strolling nonchalantly in below zero weather and a 20 mph wind took some practice and a hearty constitution. Looking somewhat like the mating display of the green tufted grebe, this ritual apparently was designed either to be seen by the higher-up from far away Omaha or to just be available if "his nibs" desired a package of gum or bottle of aspirin from the pharmacy uptown. Whatever the reason, it occurred with predictable regularity regardless of the weather.

That I did not participate in this exercise may explain why I was never on the inside looking out when one of those cars was stopped in Green River. If, however, I had been occupying one of those plush business cars, there would have been a strong temptation to open the vestibule door and ask the strolling locals if they did not have a railroad to run. From time to time, I did receive an invitation to dine on an official car when its occupant was in town. On one such occasion the general manager's secretary invited me to lunch following a morning-long staff meeting in the depot, but we could not find the car. A brief inquiry determined it was in the roundhouse for some wheel work, so we had lunch in the car inside the roundhouse. The scenery wasn't great, but lunch was delicious.

A one-man territory had advantages and disadvantages. The work had to be kept up, and it mattered not whether it required 30, 40, or 80 hours per week to do so. As long as the work was current no one really cared if I took time out now and then to chase trains or photograph a freight derailment. In my position I could photograph anything without raising eyebrows, something not always that easy for non-railroaders. I endeavored, however, not to be seen taking photos imprudently.

For the benefit of a UP film crew, No. 5511, a 1923 veteran of many years' service on the Los Angeles & Salt Lake, "steams" westward out of Green River, Wyoming, on December 3, 1958. By lucky circumstance and some low-profile maneuvering on the part of the local staff, rather than by any management intent, the 2-10-2 eluded scrapping and in the 1990s is part of the historical collection in Cheyenne roundhouse. (author's photo)

Mainline steam became a thing of the past at Green River a month after I moved there, but from time to time one of the 3700 class Challengers still in helper service out of Ogden would pass through en route to or from Cheyenne. Following one of them east I got a couple of good action shots, but there was no smoke as it was an oil burner. While setting out a car of coal at Thayer Junction, they derailed one axle of the tender. Inasmuch as I knew only one member of the crew, I was careful to keep my camera clear of the derailed tender while they quickly rerailed it. During that time I did have an opportunity to mention the lack of smoke to the fireman. He had been introduced to me by the head brakeman, who had an injury claim pending. The fireman asked where I was going to be when they left the area. At the two locations I named there was absolutely beautiful smoke, and the fireman was looking out from behind the engineer to make sure I was there. On my next trip to Rawlins I had a handful of color prints for each member of the crew.

Being on call 24 hours a day, seven days a week was the down side of a one man territory and created some difficulty in attending parties, meetings and other functions. The westbound *City of St. Louis*, due out at 4:40 PM, was the last daytime passenger train. Once it departed I was safe. Several mail trains went through in the middle of the night, but they carried few passengers and injuries were rare. And, it did not

seem proper to board a train at 1:00 AM and start pounding a typewriter while the other passengers were asleep. When there was an injury on a night train I would arrange for someone to handle it in the morning at Cheyenne, Ogden or Pocatello.

One sure way of being home in the evening for a family gathering was to work in Rawlins the day before, stay overnight, then return home the day of the party on the last train, the *City of St. Louis*. Once it left Green River, I was free for the evening. This worked well except for one birthday when I was told my favorite dinner and a birthday cake would be on tap. Following past practice, I spent the night in Rawlins, planning to ride the *City of St. Louis* home.

The other three westbound streamliners were bunched about an hour to an hour and a half ahead of the *City of St. Louis*, and I was notified by the Laramie operator that there was an injury on the first of the three. There was work to be done, so I rode it home instead. That would have been fine, but upon arrival at Green River the stationmaster informed me there were injured passengers on the two trains following me. For a moment the birthday celebration seemed scrubbed, but a plan surfaced. The next train was the *City of Portland*. It headed northwest from the main line at Granger, 30 miles to the west but did not stop there. It always had a Pocatello crew, and I did not know them because they were on my

A few weeks earlier, a more convincing smoke exhaust had been achieved with the 1243, an 1890 product of Cooke Locomotive and Machine Works. Along with 1242, this tenwheeler saw service into the 1950s because of weight restrictions on the Saratoga & Encampment Valley branch and in 1996 was placed on exhibit at the Western Heritage Museum in Omaha. (author's photo)

Smoking past the huge coaling tower at Evanston on October 16, 1957, No. 4436 was among the last active 0-6-0 switchers on Union Pacific. Dropped from the roster the following February, it was later donated for display in Ogden, Utah. (Henry R. Griffiths, Jr. photo from James L. Ehernberger collection)

territory for such a short distance. But the conductor was sitting in the depot, so I laid my problem on him.

Ever cooperative he said, "Yes, we have to slow for the turnout at Granger, and I will stop long enough for you to get off." The dispatcher okayed the plan with a wink, and I was in business. I then wondered if there was an employee with a company vehicle working in the Granger area I could ride back with. A call to the Granger operator revealed that a sectionman there lived in Green River, and the agent would ask him to wait for me when he got off work. He did, and I arrived back at the Green River depot just as the third train with an injury on board was departing. I had had a busy day—the Ogden claim agent would have to take care of that one. Birthday cake never tasted so good!

My color camera had its assigned niche in my briefcase, and I *never* went anywhere without it. Frequently, I happened onto interesting equipment or derailments, and upon occasion I was even more fortunate. Arriving in Rawlins one day, I learned a Union Pacific film crew from Los Angeles was there and the next day planned to film 4-6-0 No. 1243 with a string of cars coming into Rawlins for the company movie *Last of the Giants.*

The 1890 vintage locomotive had been dead for some time, so no effort was made to get up steam. Instead, rubber tires were burned in the firebox to create smoke as the 1243 and ten cars were shoved down the main line into town several times by a diesel switcher, while movie cameras, and my Retina, fired away. They planned to do the same with 2-10-2 No. 5511 at Green River a month later, so I made sure to be in town that day. I thus was able to take the company film crew to a prime spot out in the sagebrush for their movies, and as a bonus I got great shots of the 5511 seemingly charging out of town with a westbound train.

In early 1959 I happened into Evanston on the day before the coal chute was to be dynamited. Steam power was rapidly becoming extinct in its last Union Pacific bastion, the Wyoming Division. The few oil-burning Challengers used in helper service out of Ogden during the previous fall were soon to be moved to Cheyenne, and the last trips for the coal burning Big Boys would be over Sherman Hill between Cheyenne and Laramie.

(continued on page 36)

Gray-painted, oil-burning 4-8-4 No. 836 eases the *San Francisco Overland* beneath the Evanston tower on a 1951 day. No. 27 was near the end of its career as a first class train and in the summer even included Chicago-West Yellowstone through cars as far as Green River. (Robert C. Myers photo, James L. Ehernberger collection)

As turbine powered Extra 4 East heads through, the tower is already charged with dynamite for its pending demolition the following morning. The blast is detonated at 11:55 AM on March 12, 1959. Oops, the division superintendent now has two problems: clearing the main line and explaining to officials in Omaha what went wrong. (three photos, author)

Jack's Photo Album

At the other end of the streetcar line which passed my home was the Council Bluffs Transfer, seen above and at right in January 1938. Here mail was exchanged between railroads and sorted for West Coast delivery. I often spent non-school days at "the transfer" fascinated by the mail activity, to say nothing of the passing parade of trains from the eight railroads serving the city.

Bicycling through the rail yards one warm July 1937 day I happened onto this spelling error, whereupon I made a dash for home and convinced my mother to drive me back to the location (with 620 box camera in hand) for a photo. In the last of her 90 years my mother was still telling friends about that incident.

A 1952 power crunch found some Illinois Central locomotives working on Union Pacific's Nebraska Division. One of them is shown above with a local freight at Columbus. Chicago & North Western streamlined 4-6-4 No. 4006 passes the brick turreted Council Bluffs, Iowa, depot (*right*) with the nine-car eastbound *Chicago Express* on July 6, 1952.

On another 1952 day the Chadron-Omaha local has discharged its passengers at the end of its run and Pacific 582 is headed for the Council Bluffs yard. The Golden Spike monument in the distance marks Union Pacific milepost 0. (*below*) Burlington 0-6-0 No. 1730 had originally been a Hannibal & St. Joseph Prairie type. It was working in the Council Bluffs yard on July 3, 1949.

Well into the 1950s Union Pacific handled most of its freight traffic with an impressive variety of steam power. Clockwise from above we see at Council Bluffs three-cylinder 4-12-2 No. 9511 bringing a 35-car train in from the west on February 10, 1952; westbound Challenger 3821 with 99 cars on February 25, 1956; and another 99-car westbound on October 7, 1956, with 2-8-2 No. 2250 helping 4-6-6-4 No. 3812.

Union Pacific's first diesel switchers were delivered in black paint but were repainted to Armour yellow within a few years. Alco S-2 No. 1142 makes an unusual double-header with 2-10-2 No. 5043 departing Council Bluffs in the mid-1940s. (*right*) Just before entering military service in the summer of 1942 I made a quick trip to Colorado Springs, Colorado, for a ride on the Midland Terminal to Cripple Creek. Here is a good side view of MT's homebuilt motor car that is also pictured on page 11.

It was a common practice to burn obsolete wooden cars in order to salvage the metal parts for scrap. Six old work motors of the Omaha & Council Bluffs Street Railway met this fate one cold February 1952 night. The following month snow sweeper 021 was still at work clearing the southbound track on Omaha's Sixteenth Street. Both these photos are a result of my habit of always carrying a camera with me.

The size, power and grime of mainline steam railroading are reflected in the faces of these Union Pacific 2-10-2 workhorses waiting for assignment at Council Bluffs. The young man in U.S. Coast Guard uniform sitting in the engineer's seat of Southern Pacific 4241 at Santa Barbara, California, on March 31, 1943, is me. During the war years a military uniform was a ticket to many places not normally accessible. (*right*, Robert McNeel photo)

In 1939, two weeks before going to work for Union Pacific, I rode the motor car to Columbus, Nebraska, on my father's annual pass, and returned home on the afternoon mail train. While there I photographed the westbound *Overland Limited* during its stop at the Columbus coal chute.

As railroads switched from steam to diesel, the two types of locomotives often worked together. A Rock Island freight heads west from Council Bluffs on November 26, 1949, behind three-unit Alco 146 and Alco 4-8-4 No. 5033. (*right*) Eleven years earlier, the original *City of Los Angeles* streamliner had been replaced by the refurbished original *City of San Francisco* trainset. While the first LA equipment was being shopped prior to going into service as the *City of Portland* the following year, its two-unit M-10002 locomotive was at Council Bluffs on October 2, 1938.

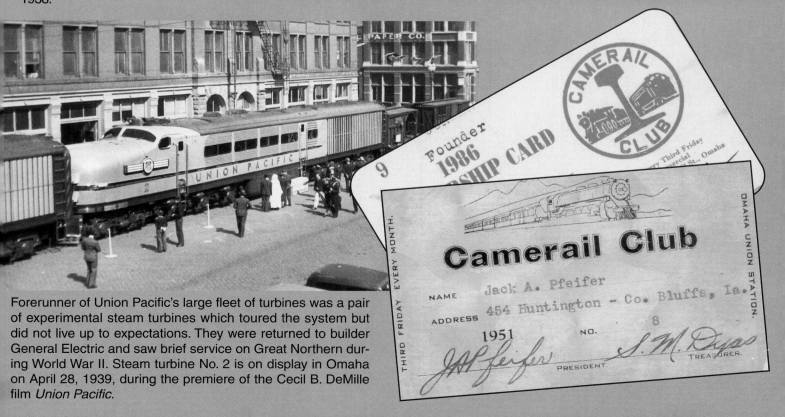

Forerunner of Union Pacific's large fleet of turbines was a pair of experimental steam turbines which toured the system but did not live up to expectations. They were returned to builder General Electric and saw brief service on Great Northern during World War II. Steam turbine No. 2 is on display in Omaha on April 28, 1939, during the premiere of the Cecil B. DeMille film *Union Pacific*.

CAMERAIL CLUB

Founder 1986

MEMBERSHIP CARD

9

Camerail Club

NAME Jack A. Pfeifer

ADDRESS 454 Huntington - Co. Bluffs, Ia.

1951 NO. 8

J. A. Pfeifer PRESIDENT.   *S. M. Dyas* TREASURER.

THIRD FRIDAY EVERY MONTH.

OMAHA UNION STATION.

Union Pacific big steam power put on a fine show right up to the end: Big Boy 4016 eastbound out of Green River with 103 cars, on October 12, 1957 (*left*); Challenger 3701 eastbound at Thayer Junction, Wyoming, with 96 cars, on October 13, 1958 (*center left*); and the 3712 with a caboose at Wahsatch, Utah, on October 17, 1958, where it was in helper service out of Ogden.

Turbine 64 was at Black Buttes, Wyoming, on June 24, 1959, after an accident at Hallville, five miles to the west. A road grader improperly secured on a flat car came loose as an opposing train met Extra 64 East, resulting in this damage, four dozen derailed cars and closure of the main line for 24 hours.

Thirty and more years ago, there were far fewer railfan photographers than there are today, and in the early post-steam years many of them were not as active as they once had been. My job as a claim agent provided opportunities to photograph scenes not recorded by others in those days.

Above, on April 29, 1958, UP GP9 No. 197 is on work train duty near Evanston, Wyoming, while to the left 143 and 192 are eastbound with the Green River wrecker near Baxter, Wyoming, on February 23, 1959.

What would today be considered a "vintage" diesel pair, F3 No. 1433 and GP7 No. 109, brings the eight cars of train 486 past the station at McCall, Idaho, on May 14, 1964.

Here is a sight to bring any claim agent to attention! After determining that all necessary precautions were being taken as this house was moved across the Kenton main line in Portland, Oregon, in April 1967, I went on my way with fingers crossed.

A turbine, Big Boy and F3 have been lined up to show the motive power transition taking place on Union Pacific in the mid-1950s. A similar photo appeared in a 1956 *Time* magazine article on the status of railroading. The castle-like Green River brewery can be seen above No. 4017's steam dome. Below, an Alco A-B-A PA set brings the westbound *City of St. Louis* through Perkins, Wyoming, on the new line completed in 1953 to reduce the grade on Sherman Hill. A few years later, dome cars have been added to the *City of St Louis*, shown eastbound (*above*) at Ragan, Wyoming, behind four EMD E8s. (Union Pacific Museum collection KDF8-11, KS-61, KS8-156)

The Ogden helpers were occasionally moved in service to and from Cheyenne. On October 13, 1958, Jack followed oil burner 3701 eastbound out of Green River and took this shot at Baxter. (author's photo)

Coaling towers (also called stations or chutes) were landmarks along any mainline railroad during the age of steam. In a state like Wyoming, they were easily the tallest structures of any type. (*opposite, top*) In October 1954 several F and GP diesels and two turbines (the roof of one is in the foreground) idle near the Green River chute. Only 4-8-8-4 No. 4003 requires its service. (Stan Kistler photo, James L. Ehernberger collection). Below is a company view of it sometime around 1940, to judge from the presence of an early 3900 series Challenger and the lettering style on the hopper car (Union Pacific Museum collection 73-172). At the top of this page is the Hanna chute in the 1920s. (*right*) The Wamsutter coaling station met a sudden demise about 1955 when a freight train derailed underneath it in a spectacular pile-up.

Straddling the main line at Evanston, a long idle concrete coal chute needed to be removed, an operation entrusted to an outside contractor and scheduled for May 12, 1959. Careful planning called for dynamite charges to be strategically placed in the supporting legs of the structure to cause it to fall toward the north and come to rest clear of the main line tracks over which it towered. In preparation the coal elevator on the north side of the chute was demolished on the previous day.

On the morning of May 12, Extra 65 West was the last train under the chute, then came final blast preparations including moving all personnel to a safe distance from the site. Most of the spectators prudently stood behind poles, trees or other objects even though they were the required distance away. I was determined to photograph the event, and that could not be done from behind such an object. Therefore, I walked the required distance east on the main line, so as to have the sun more or less behind me.

When the blast was set off at 11:55 AM, I recorded it on film. But by the time I could advance the film and aim again, I was being peppered along the ground by scores of marble sized pieces of concrete that had been impelled in my direction by the blast. Fortunately, the shower of concrete bits was mostly on or near the ground by the time it got to me. I managed to hop up out of the way of the larger pieces and continued to take photos as the coal chute fell. If anyone was watching me alternately hop up and down while taking photographs, they must surely have thought the claim agent had finally gone over the edge.

As planned, all four legs of the coal chute were severed, but instead of toppling over to the north as anticipated, the structure went straight down, then fell to the north. The stubs of the two north legs, which had dropped down next to the track, dug into the ballast and uprooted the westbound main line over which Extra 65 West had recently passed. The force of the explosion tore up the adjacent eastbound main line, which also was fouled by the stubs of the south legs of the coal chute that had not fallen as far to the north as anticipated. In short, both main lines were blocked at Evanston.

While the division superintendent paced about the area, section crews were hastily summoned from all nearby sections and worked feverishly to put the lesser damaged eastbound main back in service before dark. There were no casualties, just a few broken windows in homes north of the blast site, plus the flattened egos of the architects of the operation, who certainly had not planned to shut down Union Pacific's main line for nearly half a day.

The Green River territory had only two grade crossings of any consequence. In three years I had just one crossing accident, a fatality at a crossing near the Continental Divide on the highway south to Craig, Colorado. A husband and wife were driving separate vehicles because they were moving. She was following behind when he ignored the flasher lights and drove in front of the train. Naturally it occurred in the winter. Part of the standard investigation procedure was to measure the signal circuit from activating point to the crossing with a 50-foot tape, then obtain a statement from the signalman or section foreman who assisted in the measurement.

Have you ever tried to type after spending most of an hour measuring a half-mile signal circuit in sub-freezing cold and Wyoming wind? Typing would have been easier with splints on all fingers.

The other grade crossing on the territory was at the Carter depot. Across the road was the "town"—a filling station, post office and bar. Due to the proximity of the bar to the crossing I was always concerned that some cowboy "under the influence" and a train would try to use the crossing at the same time and that the vehicle would be hurled into the depot. Only the night mail train stopped at Carter, but the operator occasionally had to hand up orders to the other trains. It was a real experience to witness the mail thrown off, a sack of mail picked off the mail crane and three sets of orders handed up by the operator as a streamliner sped by at 70 mph. I held my breath every time I saw it. With the grade crossing so near, I prayed that no errant automobile would ever get involved.

A motor vehicle incident somewhat removed from the railroad right of way occurred just west of Green River on U.S. 30. On a long straight downgrade our maintenance of way truck caught up with an automobile towing another auto. There was no oncoming traffic so our truck started to pass the two vehicles when the driver of the lead vehicle apparently lost control, and both cars, still connected to each other, veered to the left across the highway and down into the borrow pit where they came to rest. Because our truck was starting to pass at the time, the driver had no choice but to go with the autos into the ditch while trying to brake his vehicle. Just as the truck came to a stop it struck the side of the towing vehicle resulting in a couple of minor bumps to the children in the back seat. The family was friendly and cooperative during my investigation. But when it was completed, and I contacted them with the word that there was no negligence on the part of our driver and therefore no responsibility for the accident rested with the railroad, I was met with an angry outburst from the mother. "If your damned truck hadn't been on the highway the accident wouldn't have happened," was her reply. Not only did I get fractured logic from my supervisors, but from claimants, too!

In my first summer in Green River two employees in the communications department suggested that I should start acting like a Wyoming native: i.e., get on with the hunting and fishing. I was not a hunter and had no hankering to start at that time, but the thought of all those mountain lakes teeming with trout begging to be caught was a temptation I could not resist. Early on a Sunday the three of us took off for Farson Reservoir, north of Rock Springs, with promises of success if I used the "woolly worm" lures they provided. Armed with a seldom used pole and reel I had brought from Iowa and a borrowed pair of hip waders, I was ready to do battle.

We parked and donned our gear, then with a wave of his hand toward the water the grizzled old lineman in our party started for the reservoir with the declaration, "The fish are this way." Instead of stopping at the water's edge he kept right on walking toward a spot about 75 feet from shore where he could stand in water nearly to his hips to fish. Being

On a hot July 5, 1968, the Granger operator waves at the fireman of the eastbound *City of Kansas City*. This train had recently been renamed, since it no longer ran through to St. Louis (James L. Ehernberger photo). In contrast, Wyoming winters could be brutal. Nearly 20 years earlier an unidentified Challenger had surrendered to the elements during the severe weather of early 1949.

A common sight at the time: On July 27, 1952, a 4500-horsepower turbine drifts east across the bridge over the Green River just before entering the yard. (two photos: Union Pacific Museum collection, 34699 *below*)

unable to swim I hesitated momentarily. I was there to catch the fish, not join them, but I wanted to learn. Above all, I wanted to see some of those big ones he had bragged about on the way to the reservoir, so I started to follow him. My borrowed waders were just a bit big for my feet. When I got into several inches of gooey mud at the water's edge my foot came up, but the wader did not, and I went face first into the mud. My first words were unrecorded—and unprintable! "If this is trout fishing, I don't want any part of it!" is a rough translation. The third member of the party took pity and stayed with me on the shore while the sun dried the mud on my clothing, and I tried desperately to get that woolly worm out far enough to entice a fish. Four hours later my clothing was dry, I had landed three beautiful two-pound brown trout and my whole attitude about trout fishing had turned 180 degrees. At every opportunity after that I honed my trout fishing skills, and after moving from Green River I returned often to my favorite Wyoming spots.

If the summers were great the Wyoming winters were something else. Many of the winter storms seemed to come down from Canada along the Continental Divide then peel

the road and everything on both sides was covered with several inches of new snow. It was a sea of white, and the auto's headlight beams just disappeared into the falling snow about 50 feet ahead. The reflective markers for use by highway department snowplows were the only means of telling where the highway was. As I inched along to make sure I stayed on the road a large semi-truck came up behind me, blinked his lights, then passed. He obviously could see the road so I speeded up, got behind him with just my parking lights on and followed the tail lights of the competition 15 miles to Green River. There I gave him a thank you with my lights as I turned off to go home.

I had to return to Rock Springs the following morning to continue the investigation, but I slept soundly in the knowledge that the highway department would have the road plowed off by then. However, at daybreak I found the snow had packed down into an icy surface, and a thick fog limited visibility to less than 100 feet. Due to those conditions I did not feel comfortable going more than 30 mph. Better to be a little late than not to make it at all. All went well until a pickup truck overtook me and passed. Neither of us could see

Although Green River was a major rail terminal, Union Pacific had an impressive station at Rock Springs, just 15 miles to the east. Rock Springs was a much larger town, in addition to having the only hospital in the area. At one time it had been the hub of several branch lines to nearby coal mines. (James L. Ehernberger photo)

off to the east toward Laramie and Cheyenne, but Green River was no banana belt. Every January I was there we had at least one day of minus 20 degrees temperature and enough snow every winter to give the snow tires a good workout. Add in the never-ending wind, and it certainly made one dream of summer and trout fishing.

My job required much highway driving year around. During the winter months I always carried a shovel, a parka and some candy bars just in case I got caught out in a blizzard. I never had to use the emergency equipment or supplies, but that does not mean winter driving was always a piece of cake.

One cold day a trespasser lost a leg while trying to crawl through a moving train at Rock Springs. I spent the day there, but by the time I could wrap up what I was doing and head back to Green River it was dark and snowing hard. I knew the highway well, but upon reaching the edge of Rock Springs

what was coming toward us due to the fog, and I heaved a sigh of relief when his ill-advised passing was over and he was back in the eastbound lane ahead of me.

The relief was short lived. Just then a huge westbound moving van appeared out of the fog, and I heard brakes being applied behind me. I looked into the rear view mirror and saw the side of an auto, so I maintained speed to avoid being hit from behind. As the truck passed me there was a thundering crash and I knew right away the auto had tried to follow the pickup around me and had met the truck head on. I stopped where it was safe to do so, grabbed a handful of fusees from my trunk and went back. The moving van was crosswise of the road with the cab hanging down toward a steep dropoff. The auto was still on the highway with the front demolished and an elderly couple dead in the front seat.

I gave my card to the badly shaken truck driver, then went

As passenger traffic waned, Union Pacific eliminated the *City of Denver* and routed the *City of Portland* via Denver to accommodate passengers to and from the Mile High City. The last eastbound *City of Portland* to serve Denver is shown arriving in Green River on September 23, 1967. By October 30, 1969, all *City* trains were combined into one with several connections commonly, but unofficially, known as the "City of Everywhere." (A.J. Wolff photo)

on down the fog shrouded road to the crest of a small hill where I flagged down traffic and warned them of what was ahead that they could not see. One Greyhound bus driver in particular was very grateful to find someone out in those conditions to alert him. That was one accident I did not have to investigate. The tables were turned, and I found myself answering questions instead of asking them when the insurance companies' representatives showed up a few days later to make their investigations.

Wyoming had some of the most congenial and cooperative railroaders, reminiscent of the "Howdy Pardner" of western lore. Since Green River was the away-from-home terminal for everybody, the nightly local to the Westvaco trona mine was manned by Ogden crews. They bid it for a month at a time and stayed at the Green River clubhouse. Their local was assigned a caboose specially modified with an extra stove for cooking. They went on duty about midnight, worked all night shuffling covered hoppers of soda ash at Westvaco, then prepared a big meal in the caboose before returning to Green River to tie up.

I had occasion to drive to Westvaco one morning to obtain a statement from one of the brakemen, during which time I heard some good natured complaints from the Italian conductor/cook that the rest of the crew would never buy fish for Friday morning's meal. The following Thursday morning when the crew tied up in Green River, I met them and invited the conductor to my house to select enough trout from my freezer for the next morning's meal. With a broad smile he did so and invited me to join them. It was my one and only multi-course trout breakfast, but I thoroughly enjoyed it. So did the rest of the crew, although you would never have known it by the ribbing they gave the conductor all through the meal. A few months later when the same conductor was back on the local I received another invitation. That time it was fried chicken for breakfast. Viva Wyoming!

After three years in Green River I was transferred in 1960 to Salt Lake City, where there were two claim agents plus a district claim agent who supervised all claim agents in Utah and Idaho. With a grade crossing nearly every mile in the Ogden-Salt Lake City area, crossing accidents were a way of life. Law enforcement officers in Utah were very cooperative, often issuing a ticket if the motorist survived. My crossing accident experiences in Utah would fill a book, but a couple of such tragedies remain vividly in my memory.

One involved a railroad official, apparently unable to cope with his personal problems, who waited at a crossing before, according to the engineer, deliberately driving in front of a speeding streamliner near Ogden. This was done while his good friend the Ogden claim agent was on vacation, so that someone else would have to make the investigation.

In July 1966, the long Rawlins depot was still nicely maintained and required a tow tractor (visible at the far end of the platform) to handle its fleet of baggage and express wagons. A typical Wyoming institution, the Palace Bar, may be seen across the street to the right. Nearby, but not visible, was another emporium advertising "beer, wine, liquor and general merchandise." (James L. Ehernberger photo)

The other incident was a night crossing accident at a grade crossing, protected only by crossbuck signs, in a small Utah town. It involved the wife, daughter and grandchild of a state highway patrolman, one of the nicest officers ever to wear a uniform. Law enforcement personnel almost universally sided with the railroads and against the drivers in crossing accidents. They spent most of their working hours behind the wheel and knew from experience that most crossing accidents resulted from the driver's inattention to the task at hand.

The morning after the accident, I contacted the patrolman in a small cafe to let him know we were making an investigation and how really sorry all of us on the railroad were about the accident. Although not a word was said about it, we both knew where the responsibility for the accident rested. I invited him to contact me if he had any questions about the accident or if we could be of any help to him, but he never did.

At the time of the accident there was a freight train in a passing track about a block from the crossing. All three crew members in the lead unit saw the oncoming passenger train, heard it whistle, saw the auto's headlights and knew all too well what had occurred. By the time the rear of the streamliner passed them it was in emergency, but it still required over a mile to stop.

Upon interviewing the head brakeman of the freight train, he told me that the engineer immediately headed for some nearby houses to call for an ambulance, and the fireman said he would go along to help. That left the head brakeman to walk up to the scene of the accident, a task he did not relish. To make matters worse, when he got about half way to the crossing he came upon a large object between the rails of the siding. In the stillness of the ink-black night his lantern shown upon an eerie wisp of steam curling upward from inside an automobile motor block. He knew then the situation at the crossing was tragic. At the scene he found that the baby was still alive and rushed it over to one of the nearby homes, so the occupants could care for it until the arrival of an ambulance. When I talked with the head brakeman over a week after the accident, he was still shaken by the events of that night.

On the lighter side, while working in Salt Lake City I had one of the shortest California vacations on record. The Ogden Union Railway & Depot Company switched the *City of St. Louis* at Ogden to remove Oakland cars from the Los Angeles-bound train. One winter night the switching crew slammed two portions of the train together too hard, and the two of us in Salt Lake City had to ride the train south to handle the injuries, most of which were to the Wabash dining car crew. We boarded late at night; therefore, we could do nothing until the next morning. Fortunately, there were less than a dozen injuries, none serious, and we were finished shortly before arrival in Los Angeles. We had planned to return to Salt Lake City on the *City of Los Angeles*, due out in three hours, but after lugging our briefcases, typewriters and topcoats through 75-degree weather to the Union Pacific passenger agent's office, we learned there was no space on that train. We would have to leave on the eastbound *City of St. Louis*, which was loading across the platform from the train we had just arrived on. Without leaving the confines of Los Angeles Union Station, we grabbed up all our belongings and trudged back out to the train having "enjoyed" a 15-minute sojourn in sunny southern California.

Early one morning the other Salt Lake City claim agent called me at home with the news that there had just been a crossing accident downtown, and the eastbound *City of Los Angeles*, due in about 45 minutes, had an injured passenger on board. He gave me my choice, and never being one to pass up a train ride, I opted for the passenger. It turned out to be a young black woman with a very minor injury. As I questioned her, while standing in the aisle of the coach, her small son held onto the arm rest with one hand and tugged at my trousers with the other, all of the time calling me "Daddy." Naturally, her seat was near the front of the car. Red face and all, I managed to get the information I needed and detrained at Ogden. All during the ride back to Salt Lake City I was rethinking my decision of early that morning.

To those of us in the claim department there seemed to be an inexhaustable supply of unusual incidents on or near the tracks that eventually resulted in claims against the railroad. Time was an important factor in most investigations; therefore, when on the property for any reason I tried to be alert for anything out of the ordinary. One such incident had me totally stumped, but only briefly. While passing the south end of the Salt Lake City freight house I came upon a mass exodus from the building. Bodies were streaming out of every doorway, but no smoke or flames were in evidence, and the reason for such activity was not apparent. Of course I stopped to determine if this strange behavior was going to involve our department and learned that the area had just experienced a light earthquake, which it turned out did no damage. But the employes in the old buiding were not taking any chances—they headed for the exits. Since I was in my car at the time I felt nothing, but having experienced a similar temblor during breakfast at home a few months previously, I could relate to their anxiety.

Anxiety is a state of being one lives with in the claim business, particularly upon receiving the first advice of an accident or injury that has just occurred. Details are often sketchy in the first phone call and one hurries to the scene, not knowing what carnage or surprises awaits. One incident there in Salt Lake City resulted in more than the usual amount of anxiety. It was Friday and I had gone home early to try to calm an onset of stomach flu, since it was my weekend on call. About dinner time I was advised that a transient, who had been waiting for a freight train to pass at a downtown crossing near the depot, suddenly knelt on the ground and placed his neck on the rail, resulting in decapitation. With a flu-stricken stomach already dealing me fits, the last thing I needed was a scene of that nature. As I dressed and headed for the depot, you can be sure I did not break any speed records. Anxiety I had; a yen for the task at hand, I did not. My guardian angel was on the ball that day, however, for the remains had been removed shortly before my arrival at the scene.

In 1963 I worked two major passenger train derailments. Such catastrophes usually involved a large number of injured passengers, so we gathered as many claim department representatives together as possible to work the relief trains. The first occurred in June when the eastbound *City of Los Angeles* failed to slow for some temporary track at an overpass construction site near Los Angeles and put all cars on the ground. The three of us from Salt Lake City were alerted and booked a flight to Los Angeles that evening. During the Las Vegas stop we received word to deplane because we would not make Los Angeles before the substitute streamliner left. The extra set of equipment for that train laid over in Los Angeles, and it turned out they were able to clean and turn it faster than originally anticipated.

My briefcase, extra socks and skivvies were checked through to Los Angeles and could not be retrieved, but I was assured that they would be flown back to Vegas later that night. I did not see them again until two days after I got home—my first experience with airline baggage handling. But that is another story!

After spending the night in Las Vegas and resupplying myself with forms from our Las Vegas office and a borrowed draft book, I boarded the relief train the following morning. Four claim agents from our Los Angeles office had ridden it all night. One got off to return to Los Angeles for a court appearance. The rest continued, accompanied by the three of us from Salt Lake City, one from Ogden and workaholic Tony who had driven from Cheyenne to Denver and flown to Las Vegas during the night. We worked non-stop all day, so most of us were able to detrain at Salt Lake City that night. Two stayed on to clean up the odds and ends.

Six months later, just before Christmas, the eastbound *City of Portland* piled up east of Rock Springs, Wyoming, when a westbound freight train derailed in front of it on double track. That same day the sleeping car section of the westbound *City of Los Angeles* derailed on the Milwaukee Road over in Iowa. Just what we needed during the Christmas rush!

I was at home on vacation when the district claim agent called me. He never asked me to come back to work from my vacation, but as he related the various problems to me I sensed what he was thinking. He was the best supervisor in the department, and I would have done anything for him, so I volunteered to return to work and help out on the Wyoming derailment. That afternoon he and I rode to Green River with a freight claim representative headed for the scene to handle the freight loss and damage. From Evanston to Green River, 90 miles, we drove on solid ice and through blowing snow. Weather conditions were worse by far than any I had experienced in my three years working in Wyoming. We reached Green River in late evening, and two relief trains from Ogden arrived about midnight. At that time the *City of Portland* operated via Denver and was combined with the *City of Denver* between there and Chicago. One relief train took the Denver passengers, and the other took the Omaha and Chicago passengers, operating straight through via Cheyenne. The passengers had been bused from the derailment scene back to Rock Springs and fed and made as comfortable as possible,

then brought to the depot to board the relief trains after midnight. I was assigned to the Chicago train, and of course we could not accomplish anything when everyone wanted to get some sleep. So we got berths for the night and arose early the next morning to tackle the problem.

A majority of the passengers on our train were from the Northwest, and they were a pleasure to work with. There were numerous minor injuries, but many passengers not only claimed they were not injured, but also seemed a little puzzled at all the fuss being made over them. I recall one young mother traveling with two small children. Rather than being upset and out of sorts at being dumped into the Wyoming winter by a derailment, then bused to Rock Springs to await a relief train and finally being sent on her way half a day late, she was complimenting all concerned for the way she and the other passengers had been treated. When I finished obtaining the necessary information from her, she asked who she could write to about the fine treatment she had received in this emergency. I suggested she write to the president of the railroad and, ever helpful, I wrote his name and Omaha headquarters address on the back of my card. Alas, I never found out whether she wrote the letter or not.

Late in the day, as we began to get the situation under control, I heard a rumor that our Omaha office had booked seats for the two of us from Salt Lake City to fly home that night. I did not care much for flying, particularly in the mountains during the winter. I cornered my boss and suggested that this derailment had stripped the mainline bare of claim agents between Omaha and Las Vegas; therefore, wouldn't it be a good idea if I got off at North Platte and took the first train back "just in case." He agreed, and I left the train there.

After a bite to eat at a small cafe across from the depot, I returned to find that the two derailments plus the Christmas rush had passenger service in a real mess. The operator was talking about **yesterday's** *City of Los Angeles* and **today's** *City of Los Angeles*. Nearly every train was hours, or an entire day, late. I could not determine if sleeping car space was available on any westbound train. There was one ray of hope, however. That day's mail train, which originated in Council Bluffs, and was also several hours late, carried one sleeper. When it finally arrived in North Platte I was able to get a roomette and started homeward. About noon the next day I arrived at my Salt Lake City office. There sat my boss grinning like a Cheshire cat, having flown home from Omaha during the night. He was aware of my aversion to flying, and after we parted in North Platte it dawned on him why I wanted to get off there. That incident was the source of some good-natured kidding for the rest of my time in Salt Lake City.

My assigned territory included the mainline to Milford. The Utah desert, similar to Wyoming, was an expanse of interesting country little changed over the centuries except for an occasional road, fence or pole line and, of course, the railroad. At Black Rock, Utah, surrounded in all directions by endless sand and sagebrush, the railroad had a large depot. Although not in use at the time, it was still in good condition, standing its lonely vigil as trains rattled by on the main line or an occasional auto ventured along the parallel gravel road. I wondered why there was such an imposing station at that location. Later I was told it all came about because of that precious desert commodity—water! When the railroad built through the area it required water, and the only source was on a large nearby ranch. The rancher agreed to give access to the water if a first class station was built at Black Rock. In 1931 six trains a day stopped there, and in the mid-1950s it remained a flag stop for *The Gold Coast*, the workhorse local. Black Rock had a post office until 1959, but I still wonder where the Black Rock passengers lived.

After four years in Salt Lake City events in the department pointed to the strong possibility that I would be transferred to Nampa, Idaho, a two-man territory. In May 1964, I was sent to Nampa for two weeks, primarily to train a new man just transferred there from Omaha, but also to give me a chance to get acquainted with the area. I liked what I saw, particularly the scenic New Meadows and McCall branches where photo opportunities abounded, notwithstanding ten years of dieselization. But it was not to be—a few weeks later I was transferred to Portland, where I remained until retirement.

My Portland assignment was the metropolitan area, including the Portland Traction Company, formerly an interurban line to Oregon City and Gresham, purchased jointly by Union Pacific and Southern Pacific in 1962. The PTC was like a small family, always cooperative. Its two SW1 diesels were kept in A-1 condition. When investigating crossing accidents on the Union Pacific, I would often be told by the crew about a motorist who witnessed the accident, but the crew never came up with a name or license number. The stock reply to my inquiry would be "It's not my job." Things were different on the Portland Traction Company. The crew would hand me a *list* of names and addresses of witnesses when I got to the scene. They were a joy to work with.

PTC track was not high speed. Shortly after my arrival the use of cabooses was discontinued when all assignments were bulletined as "yard runs." One night as the cabooseless train of about a dozen cars was returning from Gresham, there was a minor crossing accident on the outskirts of Portland. The train stopped with the engine several car lengths beyond the crossing. As the conductor walked back he found the hood of an auto stuck in the door locking mechanism of a boxcar, and it was not from the car they had just hit. At the crossing he determined that the accident there was minor and started up the street to a phone. He immediately met a deputy sheriff who had been trying to find the train. Some 20 blocks back an

auto had plowed into the side of the train, and the driver was being taken to the hospital. It just was not their night!

Union Pacific had two main lines from Portland east to Troutdale. The Kenton line, longer but level, was used by most of the freight trains. It had numerous grade crossings, and I got to know them well. While contacting witnesses along that line the day after an accident, I observed a freight train charge across a couple of crossings without whistling, presumably because the engineer could see there was no traffic. But, the operating rules called for whistle signals at *all* public crossings, and it was very embarrassing to have this occur while I was interviewing a witness. The incident was mentioned to the road foreman of engines, who said he would have a talk with the engineer.

Obviously he did. That engineer was involved in an accident in the same area a few months later, and there were all kinds of witnesses stating that the whistle was sounded loud and clear. This accident involved a truck which was hit on the passenger's side at a wide open crossing. The driver was killed, and I arrived while they were searching unsuccessfully for the body of the passenger. An officer finally came up out of the brush with the head of a mannequin! That explained why one eye witness to the accident told me how puzzled she was by the fact the facial expression on the passenger in the truck never changed as the train bore down on the vehicle.

"Things aren't as they appear to be" applied to other departments, too! Upon occasion the hierarchy (one or more members of the board of directors) traveled over the line, usually on a directors' special. The train's schedule was made known in advance so that each local supervisor could tidy up his area in order to create a good impression. On more than one occasion a traveling paint gang was sent out to improve the appearance of the structures along the line, only to discover that many of the buildings needed more attention than could be given in the allotted time. What to do? With a limited number of days until the passing of *the* train and more paint-starved buildings than it was possible to attend to, the ingenuity of those in charge was called into play. Where the train was scheduled during daylight hours, paint crews hastily painted one side of each building—-the side facing the tracks. Later, as the special traversed the area, the VIPs on board smilingly viewed a well-manicured property through a haze of cigar smoke. Local residents motoring along the gravel road on the opposite side of the structures could still grumble about "those grubby railroad buildings."

Not many rail photographers have visited Milford, Utah, in any era. But the renowned Dick Kindig was there on May 9, 1970, and recorded a year-old 13,200-horsepower set of DDA40X Centennials, 6907 and 6918, with a westward extra.

This fine aerial view looks northeast over the Union Pacific passenger station and freight house in Salt Lake City. While driving past the south end of the freight house one day, I witnessed a mass exodus from the building after a minor earthquake had just occurred. (Union Pacific Museum collection UP-83-B)

Here is an architect's watercolor rendition of the Union Pacific Black Rock, Utah, station circa 1925. The waiting passengers depicted at this oasis in the southern Utah desert are suitably attired for an Easter stroll down New York's Fifth Avenue. (Union Pacific Museum collection 73-12)

While the directors' specials and other trains bearing top railroad officials had the regular train crew, there almost always was another person in the cab—a road foreman of engines. He was there to see that his employes performed their jobs correctly and above all, to make certain that there was no mishandling of the train. One interesting incident occurred when the president's private car was on the rear of a streamliner. The road foreman was not only in the cab but was operating the train to make sure nothing went awry. As they approached one of the larger terminals at streamliner speed a carload of teenagers sat at the grade crossing playing "chicken," with no sign of moving off. In spite of constant vigilance by the railroad police and cooperation from other police agencies, such ill-advised conduct occurred from time to time. However, the cars always sped off the crossing as the

train bore down on them. On this night the driver of the auto was a tad tardy in moving, and the road foreman, feeling that a collision was imminent, put the train in emergency. The automobile was not hit, and the train came to a screeching halt, sending the president end over end in his car. Oh, how I would have loved to have been a mouse in the corner and have heard that road foreman's explanation to his big boss.

While working in Portland I made my first trip to prison. One of my claimants was recovering from a back injury when his wife notified me he was in the state penitentiary at Salem as a result of some inappropriate behavior involving his daughter. He had been released from further medical treatment for the injury and wanted to settle his claim inasmuch as the family needed the money. A new challenge! I could find no one in our department with experience in the "slammer." Arrangements were made with the man's counselor at the prison, and I showed up at the appointed date and time. My welcome to the prison parking lot was a large sign reading DO NOT LEAVE YOUR CAR UNLOCKED. And I had thought the crooks were all behind bars! One look at the other visitors in the waiting room brought it all into focus. Happily, the counselor appeared in short order and took me to the visitors' room as iron gates clanked shut ominously behind us. We were surrounded by inmates, friends and family all exhibiting the levity and nonchalance indicative of long standing exposure to that way of life. One inmate even drifted about taking photos of other inmates with their wives or girlfriends—for a price, of course. Although we found a quiet corner in which to transact our business, I could hardly wait for it to be finished, so that I could escape back through those noisy doors to the outside world and the sweet perfume of free air.

Being one of those very fortunate individuals whose career and avocation went hand in hand, I did not always realize how blessed I really was. They complemented each other, and I often drew upon one to benefit the other. They eventually became entwined to the point where separation was difficult, if not impossible. The years of interacting with others in the disposition of claims has largely dissipated the shyness of my youth and made me a true believer in the maxim, "You can catch more flies with honey than with vinegar." If that is not a claim agent's philosophy in the beginning, he soon becomes aware of its truth.

Most of the work in the general claims department involved on-duty injuries to employees, with whom we tried to maintain close contact. The better we knew each other, the easier it was for both to sit down and discuss a settlement at the proper time. The claims from the non-railroad public brought the most surprises, however.

One that I will never forget was a minor crossing accident involving a blonde young motorist and a slow moving switch engine. She had some bumps and bruises and was left with a tiny scar on her face that was noticeable only when pointed out. During my investigation this attractive lady and her "macho" husband were very cooperative, so much so in fact, that there were times I had that "walking on eggshells" feeling. It turned out that railroad responsibility was minor, but in view of the tiny scar and a couple of debatable facts in the investigation, it was decided to make a small offer to obtain a release. Upon meeting with the couple to discuss settlement I explained the results of our investigation and made an offer.

The lady never said a word; she just sat and smiled and let her husband carry the ball. He was pleasant and never raised his voice, but declined the small offer. During the ensuing conversation he made an exorbitant demand. As I shook my head and indicated there was no way the railroad would consider such a sum, he backed up his demand with the statement, "Because of the scar she is not as f—able now as she was before." Since no one has ever published a claim agent's handbook of snappy comebacks for such situations, I was on my own. I tried desperately to act as though I fielded such remarks daily and to come up with a response that would not get me in trouble with either of them. All the while I was attempting to keep from falling off the chair on which I was seated. My reply is long forgotten, but the situation that prompted it is not. The young woman with her frozen smile did not bat a false eyelash.

As I neared retirement the computer age was rapidly overtaking the business world, and the railroad was no exception. Those of us who had "done it the other way" for decades accepted the new challenge and some handled it better than others. One significant change in the new era was the switch from typewritten to recorded statements. With some misgivings we read instructions and attended practice sessions. Then with fingers crossed, we ventured out to take our first recorded statements. Many said that we old timers would not be able to accommodate the change, but they were soon proven wrong. Recorded statements turned out to be easier and less time consuming. They gave a better end result simply because the person's story was in his or her own words.

The microphones we used were sensitive so they could pick up everything that was said. But they also picked up all background noises, many of which we had previously been oblivious to. I recall one statement taken in a home on a quiet street, with no one else in the house. When the transcriber was typing it she called me to listen, and in the background there was a very noticeable "tick, tick, tick." I remembered that there had been a clock on the wall I was facing, but I had not been aware it was not electric. When taking recorded statements in our cars we soon learned to just stop talking when a train, truck or piece of heavy machinery went by. Our microphones had a clamp so they could be secured almost anywhere that was handy. It soon became apparent they should not be clipped onto or near a telephone. The ringing of that phone while we were taping would bring the transcriber right up out of her seat when it suddenly assaulted her eardrums. Fortunately, I was able to accommodate all the changes occurring during my last few years of claim work.

It was the "people" contact that I missed the most following my 1982 retirement, but volunteer work with several railroad oriented groups helped the transition. I particularly enjoyed a stint as personnel director for the Pacific Northwest Region of the National Railway Historical Society. I helped staff and operate many of its great Amtrak excursions to various Oregon and Washington destinations. I also worked as part of the crew when this same organization operated the famous Louisiana World's Fair Daylight behind ex-Southern Pacific 4449 in 1984. I still drive through the railroad yards en route to and from town, unable and unwilling to break the habit of a lifetime. After my retirement, the old reliable Retina was shelved in favor of a more versatile machine. My reaction to the sight and sound of a train is still akin to that of an old fire horse—-out comes the new camera while I hurry to find the best angle. But, in the diesel age it is not quite the same.

Recollections surface almost daily: of the youngster who lost both hands crawling under a train, and turned out to be the son of a witness I had interviewed a couple of years previously; of the sectionmen, the unsung heroes of the railroad—often lacking in education, but loyal in the face of tasks most of us would reject; of the waiters serving meals in dining cars flooded by ruptured pipes in the sub-zero Wyoming winter; of the emergency stop by a streamliner when the railway mail clerk hit the emergency cord with a sack of mail; of the soldier who took one long step to the ground as a passenger train unexpectedly parted at slow speed while he was walking between vestibules.

The memories never end. . . . . .

On page 25 of UP's January 1, 1970, *List of Officers, Traffic Representatives, Attorneys, Examining Physicians, Etc.*, J.A. Pfeifer's territory in the General Claims Department is shown as extending from "the west switch at Troutdale, to and including North Portland Jct." (Kenton Forrest collection)

25

TRANSPORTATION DIVISION

UNION PACIFIC RAILROAD COMPANY

NORTHWESTERN DISTRICT
OFFICERS
TRAFFIC DEPARTMENT

G. A. BROWN..........Traffic Manager..............................Portland, Ore.
R. A. Howland ....Assistant Traffic Manager...................Portland, Ore.
R. D. Toomey...........Assistant Traffic Manager...................Portland, Ore.
T. E. Tann............Assistant Traffic Manager...................Portland, Ore.
F. B. Cox............Assistant to Traffic Manager...............Portland, Ore.
R. W. McIntosh.........Assistant Freight Traffic Manager (Rates)......Portland, Ore.
A. C. Taylor..........Assistant Traffic Manager...................Seattle, Wash.
L. E. Donahue.........General Freight Agent.....................Spokane, Wash.
C. L. Chewning.........General Freight Agent (Rates)...............Portland, Ore.
K. L. Chard...........General Freight Agent (Rates)...............Portland, Ore.
D. E. Miller..........General Freight Agent (Rates)...............Portland, Ore.
R. A. Styles..........Assistant General Freight Agent...........Portland, Ore.
W. V. KEE............Traffic Manager...........................Boise, Idaho
A. H. Schipper.........Assistant General Freight Agent...........Boise, Idaho

OPERATING AND MAINTENANCE DEPARTMENTS

G. H. BAKER..........General Manager............................Portland, Ore.
R. L. Richmond........General Superintendent.....................Portland, Ore.
W. C. Krowartz.........Assistant to General Manager...............Portland, Ore.
R. B. Hardin..........Superintendent, Oregon Division..............Albina, Ore.
H. J. Bailey..........Superintendent, Idaho Division.............Pocatello, Idaho
H. L. Crawford..........Superintendent Transportation..............Portland, Ore.
R. W. Taylor..........Assistant Superintendent Transportation.......Portland, Ore.
L. G. Malzahn..........Assistant to Manager Safety and Courtesy......Portland, Ore.
A. B. Ziegler..........General Road Foreman of Engines...........Portland, Ore.
R. E. HAACKE..........District Engineer..........................Portland, Ore.
E. Schweitzer...........Assistant to District Engineer.............Portland, Ore.
R. F. Parker..........Signal Engineer..........................Salt Lake City, Utah

LAW DEPARTMENT

R. B. KESTER. ....General Solicitor......................Portland, Ore.
S. B. Stewart..........General Attorney..........................Portland, Ore.
J. F. Weisser, Jr.........General Attorney..........................Portland, Ore.
L. J. Bergmann.........General Attorney..........................Portland, Ore.
A. J. Heitkemper.........Attorney..............................Portland, Ore.
C. N. Isaak............Attorney..............................Portland, Ore.
Maguire, Kester &
  Cosgrave..............General Attorneys.....................Portland, Ore.
Skeel, McKelvy, Henke.
  Evenson & Betts.......Division Attorneys, Washington.............Seattle, Wash.
Hamblen, Gilbert &
  Brooke................Division Attorneys, Washington.............Spokane, Wash.
(For Local Attorneys see pages 12 and 13)

PURCHASING DEPARTMENT

L. W. BURNS..............Purchasing Agent.........................Portland, Ore.

STORES DEPARTMENT

J. R. Neagle..........Storekeeper...........................Pocatello, Idaho
C. C. Griffith..........Storekeeper...........................Albina. Ore.
F. D. Gilkey..........Storekeeper...........................Hinkle, Ore.
G. M. Marx............Storekeeper...........................La Grande, Ore.
H. J. Tappan..........Storekeeper...........................Spokane, Wash.
J W. Carte............Storekeeper...........................Nampa, Idaho

GENERAL CLAIMS DEPARTMENT

T. P. Minardi..........District Claim Agent...................Salt Lake City, Utah
K. L. Hubbard..........Claim Agent...........................Nampa, Idaho
  West switch at Bliss to the east switch at Huntington, including all branches.
T. L. Boyle..........Claim Agent...........................Pocatello, Idaho
E. T. Frovick..........Claim Agent...........................Pocatello, Idaho
  West switch at Granger to the west switch at Bliss, including all branches, including Butte, and to the west switch at Cache Jct., and all branches.
M. E. Hurd............District Claim Agent...................Portland, Ore.
J. A. Pfeifer..........Claim Agent...........................Portland, Ore.
  West switch at Troutdale, to and including North Portland Jct.
L. J. Ruchek..........Claim Agent...........................Portland, Ore.
  West switch at Troutdale to west switch at Hinkle and all branches.
D. A. Toman..........Claim Agent...........................Portland, Ore.
  Portland Terminal.
J. L. Olson..........Claim Agent...........................Seattle, Wash.
  East switch at Vancouver North to Seattle and all branches.
H. D. Loring..........Claim Agent...........................Spokane, Wash.
  Eastern Washington and western Idaho on Oregon Division
R. L. Jepsen ....Claim Agent...........................La Grande, Ore.
  East switch at Huntington to and including Hinkle and all branches; to but not including Wallula Jct., and Pendleton Branch in Oregon.
J. S. Olmsted..........Freight Claim Agent...................Portland, Ore.

45

One of many National Railway Historical Society excursions that Jack helped to operate after retirement was a two-day Portland-Spokane-Seattle-Portland circle trip on October 9 and 10, 1982. At Blalock, Oregon, the 11-car Amtrak special backs down Union Pacific's main line for a photo runby to be recorded by the camera laden fans lining the small finger of land jutting out into the Columbia River. (photo and passes, author's collection; opposite, CRRM collection)

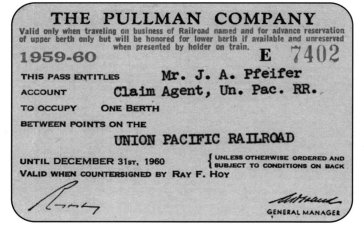

THE PULLMAN COMPANY

Valid only when traveling on business of Railroad named and for advance reservation of upper berth only but will be honored for lower berth if available and unreserved when presented by holder on train.

1959-60   E   7402

THIS PASS ENTITLES   Mr. J. A. Pfeifer
ACCOUNT   Claim Agent, Un. Pac. RR.
TO OCCUPY   ONE BERTH
BETWEEN POINTS ON THE
        UNION PACIFIC RAILROAD

UNTIL DECEMBER 31ST, 1960   { UNLESS OTHERWISE ORDERED AND SUBJECT TO CONDITIONS ON BACK
VALID WHEN COUNTERSIGNED BY RAY F. HOY

                        GENERAL MANAGER

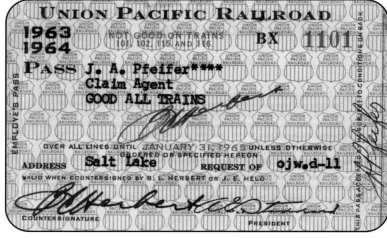

UNION PACIFIC RAILROAD

1963
1964   NOT GOOD ON TRAINS   BX 1101
            101 102 115 AND 116

PASS J. A. Pfeifer****
    Claim Agent
    GOOD ALL TRAINS

OVER ALL LINES UNTIL JANUARY 31, 1965 UNLESS OTHERWISE ORDERED OR SPECIFIED HEREON

ADDRESS   Salt Lake   REQUEST OF   ojw.d-11

VALID WHEN COUNTERSIGNED BY B. L. HERBERT OR J. E. HELD

COUNTERSIGNATURE   PRESIDENT

46

Prevention OF LOSS AND DAMAGE TO FREIGHT
...is no Puzzle!

Make '63 damage free -
Handle all freight as if it were YOUR OWN!

General Claims Dept...Union Pacific Railroad
O. J. WULLSTEIN, GENERAL CLAIMS AGENT
OMAHA, NEBRASKA

PRINTED IN U.S.A.

One of a series of bulletin-board posters currently being used in the interest of freight loss and damage prevention.

THE LOST LOCOMOTIVE OF KIOWA CREEK
by Loyd J. Glasier

Kansas Pacific No. 68 was a Baldwin 4-4-0 identical to No. 51, the locomotive lost in the Kiowa Creek flood of May 21, 1878. (DeGolyer Library, Southern Methodist University, Ag 82.86.40)

Years ago while searching for historic stagecoach trails near Bennett, Colorado, I first heard from oldtimers there the story about the lost locomotive. It was buried under many cars when a Kansas Pacific train plunged off the bridge into the raging floodwaters of Kiowa Creek about midnight on May 21, 1878. Little did I know at the time that I would eventually become deeply involved in a five-year search for the truth about that lost locomotive.

In December 1989, local and national newspapers and television stations announced that the National Underwater and Marine Agency based in Arvada, Colorado, was seeking volunteers to participate in two weekends of searching for the buried locomotive. On Saturday, January 7, 1990, I was one of more than 300 volunteers who descended on the site of the steel bridge where the present Union Pacific railroad track crosses over Kiowa Creek about a mile east of Bennett. NUMA crew chiefs were assigned large groups of eager volunteers to search specific areas below the railroad bridge. Chaos soon occurred, however. Volunteers would flock to any area where detectors had found signs of buried metal and the backhoes would start digging. It was bitterly cold weather (about 17 degrees Farenheit), and a very strong north wind was blowing. Thankfully, the senior center in Bennett served coffee and sandwiches and opened its restrooms to the shivering horde of volunteers.

Numerous pieces of scrap metal and small items of railroad origin were uncovered and collected, but no major pieces of metal were sensed by the many different types of detectors, magnetometers and ground radar units in use. Several psychics and dowsers also reported no contact. The next day, only 50 people turned out to continue the search, even though NUMA officials had predicted to the Denver newspapers that the locomotive would be found and dug up by nightfall.

On the next weekend, small crews of seasoned NUMA volunteers searched just below the west end of the present steel bridge in the area where the locomotive would most likely have gone into the floodwaters. A strong signal on the magnetometer indicated metal directly under the third span from the west end of the bridge. Excavation with a backhoe soon reached the water table about four feet below the surface, and then two portable water pumps drew down the water. Two short sections of rail were recovered and later tests showed these to be steel rail of about 53 pounds per yard. This size rail was in common use by the Kansas Pacific at the time of the wreck.

In this same excavation a cluster of old wooden pilings was uncovered directly under the center of the steel bridge span above. Some of these had broken off and others had been sawed off. We found records in our research to indicate that the bridge over Kiowa Creek had been rebuilt as a wood piling trestle at least three times after loss of the original one in 1878. Finding this cluster of old pilings under the center of the present bridge told us that this bridge is on the same location of at least two previous wooden ones. Early newspaper accounts located the original bridge several hundred feet downstream. It was 150 feet long and 30 feet high, while the 1878 replacement was about 450 feet long and 30 feet high centered over the main channel of Kiowa Creek.

Two weekends of searching with the latest high technology detection equipment did not locate any large metal objects. Particular emphasis had been devoted to a careful search of a large shallow basin in a cottonwood grove about 300 feet downstream from the west span of the bridge. Bob Richardson at the Colorado Railroad Museum suggested that we research old newspaper accounts of known past efforts to locate the sunken locomotive. We learned the following.

NUMA officials and their volunteers had searched for many years with no success, even though the agency has been very successful in locating other buried historic objects. In the early 1950s, senior class engineers from the Colorado School of Mines in Golden, Colorado, spent two weeks on the Kiowa site, mapping out a grid 400 feet square and using then state of the art locating equipment. They, too, got no sounding of any large metal object.

Kevin Mitchell and Shawn Capps, cousins and present owners of the land below the bridge, have youthful memories of an older man spending one summer camped in a trailer near the bridge. He said that he had a salvage contract with Union Pacific if he located the locomotive. Bennett citizens also remember several other search efforts, which became a nuisance. Eventually the property owner closed the area to further searches for a number of years.

We interviewed several oldtimers for their stories about the lost locomotive. Their replies are summed up very well by an account given in *Our Side of the Mountain*, a 1968 book by local historian Emma Michell, founder and longtime head of the Comanche Creek Historical Society of Strasburg. The following is quoted from her book:

> It seems scarcely feasible but none-the-less fact, that this huge steam engine has never been found. For years various people have probed the sands around this spot to no avail. Much conjecture over its possible location has been offered by all kinds of experts. Steel rods have been driven into the sand, sounding devices have been employed, and even a large magnet crowbar was once used in an attempt to locate this engine. Some theorize the churning action of the water and the quick sands washed it far upsteam. Others believe it may be found some day many miles downstream. So far it is anyone's guess where it may be. All that remains is the fact that one steam locomotive lies buried some where in Kiowa Creek these past ninety years.

Much activity followed this incident to make the stream crossable. N.H. Nicholson was in charge of this project. Cribbing was driven into the sands all around the wreck, an area about forty feet square. A small engine was set up on a platform which ran a sand pump day and night to keep sand and water out of the work area so the wreckage could be removed. The cars which had gone down were loaded with scrap iron and the rail irons were wrapped around all this metal. About two months were required to clear the wreckage and to continue the search for the locomotive. Their last attempt was to sink seventy foot long pipes into the sand and blow air into them which also failed. A temporary track was laid on the creek bottom by using local men and horses in a grading operation. Two teenage boys were among these. Henry and Gus Nordloh were working on their father's sheep ranch just a short distance up creek and they worked with their teams building the temporary bridge. Trains ran on this all summer until a new bridge could be constructed.

Gus Nordloh, Emma Michell's father, had told her that the locomotive was never recovered and not to let anyone tell her differently.

The July 1937 issue of the *Colorado Magazine* has an article entitled "The Lost Locomotive" by Alfred B. Sanford, for many years head of the Colorado State Historical Society in Denver. We quote from his article:

> . . . A few days later and after burial of the victims of the wreck, search was begun for the missing engine. Long metallic rods were driven into the sands. In some places pits were started but soon abandoned because of the heavy underflow, and the location of the $18,000 locomotive appeared hopeless, when it was estimated the bed rock formation was probably fifty feet below the channel of the Kiowa.
>
> In these days of mineral exploration certain delicate instruments are employed to locate iron deposits. These instruments respond to the magnetic influences of the salts of iron and should be more susceptible to a large mass of metallic iron, such as a locomotive would contain. Perhaps such an experiment will some time be made at this long-forgotten point on the Kiowa and someone will locate the resting place of the old Kansas Pacific locomotive.

We started library research on the train accident by viewing microfilm of the three Denver newspapers in circulation in 1878—the *Rocky Mountain News, Denver Tribune* and *Denver Times*—as well as the *Railroad Gazette* and other rail industry publications. The accounts of the accident vary some in detail, but the following is the essence of the reporting of the tragedy.

On the fateful night of May 21, 1878, Kansas Pacific freight train No. 8 was dispatched eastbound from Denver to Hugo, Colorado. The first section of the train, scheduled to leave Denver at 7:00 PM, was made up of 25 cars, mostly empties. In the locomotive cab were engineer John N. Bacon, fireman Frank Selden and George Piatt, a restaurant cook from Hugo who had hitched a ride. The second section of the train was scheduled to leave Denver at 8:30 PM. Engineer Bacon's orders that night cautioned him to run slowly and watch out for problems at bridges. Bacon had said, "I am too nervous to run on such orders and wish I did

QUEST FOR TRAIN A WASHOUT

SEARCH LEADER: Clive Cussler keeps a close eye on excavation near Bennett on Saturday.

1878 locomotive eludes Bennett throng

By Alan Gottlieb
Denver Post Staff Writer

BENNETT — More than 300 railroad buffs braved the extreme cold Saturday to spend nine hours combing a dry creek bed near this farming town for a railroad locomotive that disappeared 111 years ago.

The search, hampered by an unexpectedly large mass of disorganized humanity, was unsuccessful. But searchers found several interesting artifacts that archaeologists said may have been from the train, including a coal shovel, a chamber pot and a small coupler.

The group will resume its quest today and conclude at dusk.

Searchers hope to find the engine from a Kansas-Pacific freight train that sank in quicksand after being washed off a bridge into Kiowa Creek during a flood in 1878.

No one knows how far the swollen creek carried the engine before it was sucked into the sand. Other cars from the train were found a few hundred yards downstream shortly after the floodwaters receded. But the engine's location has remained a mystery.

What was originally planned as a low-key expedition by adventure novelist Clive Cussler's Na-

ARTIFACT? Ted Stutz holds what is believed to be a shove found during search, while ground radar crew works behind him.

tional Underwater and Marine Agency to search for the engine became a major event for thrill seekers from throughout the West.

Cussler and his chief deputy Craig Dirgo took the onslaught with good humor, even though it destroyed any real chance of finding the engine.

"To do this right you need dis-

cipline," said Cussler, as he trie unsuccessfully to line up a grou of enthusiasts wielding metal d tectors for a thorough sweep the dry bed of Kiowa Creek. "Th idea isn't to find the object; it's eliminate areas and narrow th search."

The eight-year-old group ha

Please see **SEARCH** on 2-

This coverage of Clive Cussler's search for the "lost locomotive" appeared in the January 8, 1990, *Denver Post.* The event resulted in a lot of publicity but little of substance. (author's collection)

not have the first section. It looks awfully cloudy, but if Box Elder (bridge) is all right the rest are."

Both sections of train 8 passed safely over Box Elder Creek bridge where no rain had fallen. The next bridge was nine miles east over Kiowa Creek, and no rain had fallen there either. About midnight a hobo living in a cave above the bridge on the west side of the creek was forced out by rising water. He ran up on the track embankment to warn the section crew in Kiowa that the creek was flooding. By the time the section crew got out on the track with a warning light, the headlight of the first section's locomotive appeared in the darkness and proceeded downgrade toward the bridge, about one mile ahead.

Even if Bacon had seen the warning signal, he would have been unable to stop the train before reaching the bridge. Trains of that era relied on a locomotive brake set by the engineer and brakes on each car which were set by a brakeman coming forward from the caboose. When the brakeman heard the engineer signal, he began setting each brake as he moved ahead. When the locomotive reached the bridge, the brakeman saw the headlight start to sway. He jumped off the train and warned the conductor, who jumped from the caboose to save his life.

The locomotive plunged 30 feet down into the raging waters, followed by the tender, a car loaded with rail and nine empty cars. The six rear cars were loaded with gravel and, along with the caboose, remained on the track and bridge. Newspaper accounts differ in detail here, but it appears that the bridge may still have been intact, and the train plunged off the east end where the embankment had already been washed out. We found no information as to exactly what eventually happened to the rear portion of the train, though one report said that the badly battered caboose survived. The fact that the rear cars did not immediately follow the others into the floodwaters probably indicates that the brakeman had set enough brakes to stop this portion of the train on the downgrade from Kiowa.

Engineer Bacon, fireman Selden, and hitchhiker Piatt lost their lives in the tragedy. A hobo riding in one of the box cars survived when he climbed out the top of the car after it lodged below the bridge. He said it felt like the car had rolled over at least a thousand times.

The Kiowa section workers were able to signal the second section of the train to stop before it started downgrade toward the bridge. When informed of the accident, conductor Croft of that section decided to back into Denver to alert the dispatcher, since the telegrapher there would not come on duty until 7:30 next morning. When the second section returned to the Box Elder bridge, it too was flooded and unsafe to cross. The telegraph operator at Box Elder Creek station was roused and in the morning sent news of the wreck to KP's Denver headquarters.

Superintendent C.W. Fisher quickly assembled a work train with 40 men and started toward Kiowa about 9:00 AM. They made temporary repairs to the Box Elder bridge and proceeded on to the disaster at Kiowa. The scene there was one of complete devastation. The bridge and embankments on both sides of the stream were gone, leaving a gap in the main line of about three-fourths of a mile. Five feet of water was still flowing around the huge pile of wreckage. All but seven cars were buried or washed out of sight, and the three men in the locomotive were presumed buried under the tangled wreckage.

Colonel Fisher dispatched search parties downstream to look for possible survivors or bodies. The rest of his force was put to work constructing a temporary shoofly down to the stream edge on both sides. Within 50 hours after the accident, passengers and mail could be shuttled across a foot bridge to a train on the other side. This transfer at Kiowa continued for several days until a temporary rail bridge was thrown across the creek and trains could again resume crossing the stream.

On May 23, the body of Frank Selden was found in the sand about one and a half miles below the bridge. The coroner in Denver reported that he had died from a broken neck. The body of George Piatt was recovered downstream two days later. Probable cause of his death was drowning. On the Sunday following the accident, the Kansas Pacific sent a special train out to Kiowa, offering free passage to all volunteers wishing to continue the search for the body of engineer Bacon. It was found about nightfall by a rancher ten miles below the bridge. According to the coroner, Bacon's death had been instantaneous.

Large crowds attended the funerals in Denver. Shortly after the accident, the nearby town of Kiowa was renamed Bennett in honor of Susan and Gertrude Bennett, sisters who were the widows of Bacon and Selden. Work to salvage the wrecked train and construct a new bridge was soon under way. Ranchers and farmers with their teams were hired to start rebuild-

Cussler-led group to renew search for locomotive

SEARCH from Page 1-B

searched for about 80 ships at sea and in rivers, and has found 54 of them. This wasn't the first attempt to locate an object on land — Cussler found one missing ship beneath a Galveston, Texas, parking lot, and another under an Arkansas soybean field.

Cussler and Dirgo initially publicized the search several weeks ago hoping to attract a half-dozen volunteers. "But the thing mushroomed and really got out of hand," Cussler said.

The leaders limited the number of official volunteers to 200, but nearly twice that number showed up Saturday morning. There were young children and senior citizens. Most were males.

Some wore caps with slogans custom made for the event, among them "I survived the great search" and "Where the hell is it?"

People started gathering in a field just outside town at 7:30 a.m.

'The idea isn't to find the object; it's . . . to narrow the search.'

Clive Cussler

The air was cold and clear, and a wind gusting up to 40 miles per hour easily cut through several layers of clothing.

Many participants brought along metal detectors, magnetometers, walkie-talkies and video cameras. Others took technology a step further.

Don Boothby, co-owner of Geo-Recovery Systems of Englewood, contributed a large, ground-penetrating radar system and a crew of four to operate it. Boothby printed out findings that showed irregularities in underground geology, any one of which could have been part of the engine.

Two backhoes donated for the weekend by Bennett residents then

were used to dig large craters where the radar showed promising anomalies.

The heavy equipment drew large crowds of people who were supposed to be sweeping other areas with metal detectors.

"Lean and mean is the only way to go on this type of operation," Dirgo said with a resigned shrug.

"It's hopeless," Cussler said before heading off to do some solo searching.

Kevin Mitchell, who owns the land where the search was conducted, was half hoping it would be unsuccessful. "It's been a neat little mystery around here for years. It would be OK to leave it that way."

ing the embankments at both ends, and the KP pile driver arrived from Kansas City on May 30.

Seventy years later, Elmer O. Davis played an important part in perpetuating the story about the lost locomotive. Davis was a Union Pacific civil engineer who had moved to Denver in 1909. After 40 years of service he retired and became a well-known railroad historian. His *First Five Years of Railroading in Colorado* was published in 1948. He also wrote a monthly column, "75 Years Ago Today" for the *Engineers Bulletin* of the Colorado Engineers Society in Denver. Starting in the late 1940s, he read old newspapers and journals and reported what had happened on Colorado railroads 75 years previously. Davis was thoroughly convinced that the locomotive lost in Kiowa Creek had never been recovered. We interviewed Daryl Tennal of Deckers, Colorado, who, as

May 23, 1878, *Denver Times*:
"The Kansas Pacific train, *pulled by Engine 51* consisted of 25 cars and a caboose . . ."

May 31, 1878, *Denver Times*:
"A pile driver brought down from Kansas City, started to drive pilings at the Kiowa bridge . . . *Many employees, now all deceased, who were working between Hugo and Denver at the time of the accident, have stated that great amounts of time and money were expended, trying to locate the engine but it was never found. The location is 30 miles east of Denver, a mile beyond Bennett, site of the present steel bridge.*"

DERAILMENTS, BROKEN BRIDGE.

On the 7th a trestle bridge on the Atlantic, Gulf & West India Transit road, near Waldo, Fla., gave way under a freight train, and six cars went down and were badly wrecked.

On the morning of the 11th a bridge on the Chicago, Rock Island & Pacific road, near Atlantic, Ia., gave way under a freight train and nine loaded cars went down into the water.

On the night of the 21st a freight train on the Kansas Pacific road went through a bridge over the Kiowa River near Denver, Col., the supports of which had been washed out by a freshet. The engine went down into the river with a number of cars on top of it, killing the engineer, fireman and a brakeman.

The June 21, 1878, *Railroad Gazette* gave this report of the accident which had occurred exactly 30 days before. (CRRM collection)

---

a Union Pacific employee, accompanied him to the Bennett bridge in the 1950s. They took along wrecking equipment to explore various sites below the bridge. By blowing air through long pipes, they could penetrate sand down to the sandstone which was about 24 feet below the surface at the west end of the present bridge.

In the following extracts from Davis's 1953 columns in the *Engineers Bulletin*, we have italicized those portions of his report where he has added information, changed meaning or rejected the meaning of the original newspaper account. In many hours of reading microfilm of early Denver newspapers, we found most of the events that Davis recorded and were able to determine where he had altered or edited the original.

August 7, 1878, *Rocky Mountain News:*
"All efforts to find the locomotive lost in the quicksands of Kiowa Creek in the accident on the KP last May proved fruitless until last Sunday night, when the workmen discovered the tank about thirty feet north of the old bridge and ten feet under the surface. It is believed the engine is under the tender and if so it will soon be raised and brought to Denver for repairs."

August 12, 1878, *Denver Times*:
"The lost locomotive at Kiowa, although found, has not yet been resurrected *probably the tender only*."

August 17, 1878, *Rocky Mountain News*:
"KP employees are still searching for the engine in the treacherous quicksands of the Kiowa. The workmen

sounded into the sand and struck something they supposed to be the engine but it proved to be only the tender and the mystery is as great as ever. . . A large force of men are still working away with a steam powered sand pump."

August 18, 1878, *Denver Tribune:*
"The engine in Kiowa Creek will be exhumed within a week, only about 18 inches of sand remains above the frame of the locomotive. The engine sank 17 feet below the surface."

September 2, 1878, *Denver Times:*
"The Kiowa engine is still undiscovered but the searchers are confident of finding it."

September 18, 1878, *Denver Times:*
"The work of hunting for the lost engine in Kiowa Creek has been postponed for the present."

September 21, 1878, *Rocky Mountain News:*
"The sunken engine at Kiowa Creek has been abandoned."

September 21, 1878, (newspaper not specified):
"The first train passed over the newly constructed bridge at Kiowa Creek yesterday, and the bold but dangerous, often washed out, shoofly track used since the May 21st disaster for four months is being removed."
(The new bridge was about 450 long and 30 feet high, with wooden pilings and bents 14 feet apart.)

October 10, 1878, (Davis's comment in *Engineers Bulletin*):
"*The sunken engine in Kiowa Creek is now in peace. No search is at present being made for it. It is said, however,*

it will be sought as the material is too valuable to be lost."

February 19, 1879, *Denver Daily Times:*
"*The Eastern newspapers having nearly all announced the recovery "some time since" of the KP engine lost in Kiowa Creek last May, we are again compelled to remark that such statements are incorrect. The engine has never been found and furthermore all search for it was abandoned several months ago.*"

In May 1880, the widows of engineer Bacon and fireman Selden successfully sued Union Pacific, and each was awarded $5,000 for loss of her husband. UP had acquired the Kansas Pacific from its receivers in bankruptcy on January 18, 1879. The plaintiffs argued that the bridge was too small and was not located over the main course of the stream. In addition, a watchman should have been posted at the bridge, and the train should have carried two brakemen. At the trial in Arapahoe County District Court it was stated that the locomotive had not been recovered.

We concluded that Davis, during his 40-year career as a UP civil engineer, may have interviewed oldtimers along the railroad. After he read the early newspaper accounts, he obviously felt confident that the locomotive in Kiowa Creek was still buried in Kiowa Creek. His editing and on site search efforts appear to reflect his honest opinion.

After Elmer Davis's death on March 8, 1962, his files were donated to the Western History Department of the Denver Public Library. We studied his work carefully and found nothing to indicate that he had researched any sources in

Atlantic & Pacific No. 21 was an 1870 Baldwin Tenwheeler. After being rebuilt in August 1881 to a 4-6-0, the former Kansas Pacific 51 probably was similar in appearance to this locomotive. It is not known whether or not the original wagontop boiler was retained. (DeGolyer Library, Southern Methodist University Ag 82.232.4908)

Nebraska, Kansas or Missouri for information on the lost locomotive. Our own research of newspaper microfilm in those states and at the Union Pacific Historical Museum in Omaha revealed that the engine in Kiowa Creek was indeed recovered. We found early accounts describing both the accident and events during the rebuilding of the bridge.

On June 5, 1878, just 15 days after the accident, the *Kansas City Journal* reported the following:

> Information was received yesterday at the general office of the Kansas Pacific Railway that the engine which went into the quicksand at the time of the accident has been located. It was found twenty feet below the level of the prairie and fifteen feet to the right of the track line, having been carried that distance downstream by the current. As soon as the water subsides sufficiently, the engine will be raised by use of derricks, and taken to the shop for repair.

On Friday, August 30, 1878, the *Kansas City Times* reported more news in its railroad column: "The Kansas Pacific engine which was lost in the quicksand some time ago has been recovered from its twenty-foot grave, and it passed east to Armstrong Monday night." (The main repair shops of the Kansas Pacific were in Armstrong, a western suburb of Kansas City.)

The Nebraska Historical Society library holds much information about the KP for the year 1870, including a complete description of the wrecked locomotive. No. 51 was a Baldwin 4-4-0 American type with 16 x 24-inch cylinders, 60-inch driving wheels and weighed 88,500 pounds. It carried builder's number 2162 and had cost $11,500. In the file is a book listing in detail accidents to locomotives and trains of the KP during 1870, as well as information on the insurance carried by the company on its rolling stock. Unfortunately, the library has no similar information for 1878.

Don Snoddy, of the UP museum in Omaha, has a packet of information that has been furnished to the many persons who have inquired about the lost locomotive. Included are several inventory lists of locomotives in which KP No. 51 can be traced after it had been returned to Armstrong for repair.

In 1885, Union Pacific did an inventory of all its locomotives and renumbered them that year. This inventory shows that KP 51 was rebuilt as UP 4-6-0 No. 1026 in August 1881. It had been fitted with 18 x 24-inch cylinders and 56-inch driving wheels to become a slower, more powerful freight locomotive. In his report dated October 15, 1887, United States Pacific Railway Commission inspecting engineer Richard Morgan listed No. 1026 as being in poor condition.

In 1862, Congress had passed an act to encourage private companies to build a railroad from the Missouri River to the Pacific Ocean. Government issued bonds subsidized initial construction, but the railroads were to repay the loans when the line was completed and became profitable. Several efforts to force the Pacific railroads to open their books to government auditors were unsuccessful. On June 19, 1878, the United States Pacific Railway Commission was created by Congress to force compliance with the government's demands. Five of the six railroads comprising the Union Pacific system suddenly lost or destroyed their books, and the government was again frustrated in its efforts to get repayment of the original bond money. Years later the matter was settled after long and costly litigation.

In 1973 Union Pacific demolished its old record storage building in Omaha. Previously, Nebraska Historical Society staff members selected over 800 linear feet of historical documents for the society's archives. These records were accessioned but are still in boxes waiting to be processed. Over 25,000 tons of records accumulated up to 1940 were sent to a railroad dump in California. Casey Finnell and his son Larry, of Little Rock, California, retired UP employees, witnessed the dumping of the material. Perhaps the pertinent records of the accident to the Kansas Pacific train are lost forever.

We feel that our research proves that the "lost" locomotive in Kiowa Creek was actually recovered in late August 1878. Three years later it was rebuilt by the railroad and served as a freight locomotive for many years. The last recorded trace of it was in the Union Pacific inventory of 1894. We found no record of when or where it was ultimately scrapped.

To conclude this research, we decided to delve further into the reason why the mystery about old KP 51 has persisted for over a century. Could it be that the Kansas Pacific intentionally planned to file an insurance claim for permanent loss of the wrecked locomotive? It would have been possible to recover the engine at night while local people were banned from the site, then ship the derelict under cover of night or under tarpaulins back to Armstrong, Kansas.

When reviewing the sequence of reports released to Denver newspapers from mid-August 1878 until later in the fall, it appears that the engine was almost ready to be raised on August 18. Then the news releases gradually became more negative, finally stating the engine "is at peace in its watery grave." Back at KP headquarters in Kansas City, news did leak out to the *Kansas City Times* that the engine had been recovered. This is the only newspaper article we found which gave this information.

In a final effort to solve the mystery of the lost locomotive at Bennett, Colorado, we contacted the Liverpool and London and Globe Insurance Company, Ltd. in London, the underwriter which insured Kansas Pacific's locomotives in 1870. The firm has no records dating back that far. Is the final

(continued on page 58)

Kansas Pacific's timetable in the July 1877 *Travelers' Official Guide* shows that the Denver-Kansas City eastbound express had a 27-hour 55-minute running time for the 639-mile trip with 78 potential stops, an average of nearly 23 mph. This was not bad when compared with the four to five days the same journey had taken by stagecoach only seven years earlier. Even the 61 hours 30 minutes required by the westbound emigrant train was an improvement over that. (CRRM collection)

C. S. GREELEY, } Receivers, St. Louis, Mo.
HENRY VILLARD, }
ROBERT E. CARR, Gen. Manager, St. Louis, Mo.
D. M. EDGERTON, Vice-President, "
A. H. CALEF, Cashier, "
S. T. SMITH, Auditor, Kansas City, Mo
T. F. OAKES, Gen. Superintendent, "
JOHN L. WOODS, Purchasing Agt., St. Louis, Mo.
JOHN MUIR, Gen. Freight Agt., Kansas City, Mo.

D. E. CORNELL, Gen. Pass'ger and Ticket Agt., Kansas City, Mo.
J. H. JONES, Gen. Agent, Denver, Col.
S. J. GILMORE, Land Commissioner. Lawrence, Kan.
J. T. ODELL, Supt. Kaw Valley Division and
J. C. & Ft. K. R. W., Kansas City, Mo.
J. LOOMIS, Supt. Smoky Hill Division. Ellis, Kan

C. W. FISHER, Supt. Denver Division and Arkansas Valley R. W., Denver, Col.
JOHN MACKENZIE, Supt. of Machinery, Armstrong, Kan.
FRED. KNOWLAND, Gen. Eastern Freight Agt., 287 Broadway, New York.
WM. KNOWLAND, Gen. Eastern Passenger Agt., 287 Broadway, New York.
J. D. WELSH, New England Agt., Boston, Mass.

May 20, 1877.

STANDARD OF TIME—*Jefferson City, Mo.*

WESTWARD. STATIONS.	Mls	Express.	Mix	Emg
Lve. **Kansas City**		10 55 A.M.		*7 00
" State Line	0	11 00 "	†6 00	7 20
" Armstrong	1	11 05 "	6 10	7 30
" Muncy	8	11 23 "	6 55	8 03
" Secondine	9	11 26 "	7 00	8 07
" Edwardsville	13	11 35 "	7 20	8 22
" Tiblow	16	11 45 A.M.	7 45	8 37
" Lenape	22	12 02 NO'N	8 20	9 05
" Stranger	27	12 15 "	8 45	9 30
" Fall Leaf	31	12 27 "	9 10	9 55
" Leav. Branch Junc.	36	12 39 NO'N	9 35	10 20
" **Lawrence**	38	1 05 P.M.	10 15	10 45
" Buck Creek	45	1 21 "	10 55	11 20
" Williamstown	48	1 28 "	11 15	11 35
" Perryville	51	1 36 "	11 35	11 55
" Medina	52	1 40 "	11 45	12 05
" Newman	55	1 46 "	12 01	12 15
" Grantville	60	2 00 "	12 35	12 40
" **Topeka**	67	2 25 "	1 40	1 25
" Silver Lake	77	2 52 "	3 05	2 30
" Rossville	83	3 07 "	3 45	3 00
" St. Mary's	90	3 26 "	4 35	3 40
" Belvue	97	3 42 "	5 15	4 10
" Wamego	104	4 05 "	6 00	5 10
" St. George	110	4 22 "	P. M.	5 45
" Manhattan	119	4 41 "		6 30
" Ogden	129	5 08 "		7 30
" Fort Riley	135	5 23 "		8 00
" **Junction City**	138	5 35 "		8 25
" Kansas Falls	144	5 51 "		9 05
" Chapman's	150	6 05 "		9 50
" Detroit	157	6 18 "		10 25
" Abilene	162	6 50 "		10 50
" Solomon	171	7 14 "		11 40
" Donmyer	18	7 34 "		12 25
" Salina	185	7 50 "		1 00
" Bavaria	194	8 13 "	A.M.	1 50
" **Brookville**	200	8 40 "	†7 10	2 05
" Rock Spring	205	8 50 "	7 35	3 20
" Elm Creek	210	9 05 "	8 20	4 00
" Fort Harker	218	9 25 "	9 15	4 45
" Ellsworth	223	9 37 "	9 50	5 10
" Bosland	239	10 17 "	11 30	6 35
" Bunker Hill	252	10 52 "	12 50	7 45
" Russell	262	11 17 "	1 45	8 35
" Walker	274	11 48 "	2 55	9 40
" Victoria	279	11 58 P.M.	3 20	10 00
" Hays	289	12 25 N'HT	4 20	10 50
" **Ellis**	302	1 05 A.M.	5 50	12 10
" Ogallah	312	1 30 "	6 45	1 00
" Trego	322	1 55 "	7 40	1 55
" Coyote	336	2 28 "	8 50	2 50
" Buffalo	350	3 04 "	10 05	4 15
" Grinnell	364	3 40 "	12 05	5 45
" Carlyle	376	4 10 "	1 20	6 55
" Monument	386	4 39 "	2 30	8 00
" Gopher	397	5 04 "	3 30	8 55
" Sheridan	405	5 22 "	4 15	9 35
" **Wallace**	420	6 00 "	5 50	11 30
" Eagle Tail	429	6 45 "	A.M.	12 15
" Monotony	437	7 20 "		1 10
" Arapaho	452	7 52 "		2 05
" Cheyenne Wells	462	8 20 "		2 50
" First View	472	8 50 "		3 40
" **Kit Carson**	487	9 27 "		4 50
" Wild Horse	499	9 57 "		5 54
" Aroya	511	10 24 "		6 45
" Mirage	524	10 57 "		8 05
" **Hugo**	534	11 45 A.M.		9 40
" Lake	547	12 22 NO'N		10 55
" Cedar Point	562	1 05 P.M.		12 30
" Godfrey	566	1 15 "		12 55
" Agate	572	1 27 "		1 20
" Byers	595	2 27 "		3 35
" Kiowa	608	2 54 "		4 45
" Box Elder	617	3 14 "		5 35
" Schuyler	629	3 40 "		6 40
" Denver Pacific Junc.	636	3 54 "		7 20
Arr.. **Denver**	639	4 00 P.M.		7 30

EASTWARD.	Mls	Express.	Mix
Lve. **Denver**	0	12 00 NO'N	
" Denver Pacific Junc.	3	12 06 "	
" Schuyler	10	12 20 "	
" Box Elder	22	12 47 NO'N	
" Kiowa	31	1 06 P.M.	
" Byers	44	1 33 "	
" Agate	67	2 29 "	
" Godfrey	72	2 41 "	
" Cedar Point	77	2 52 "	
" Lake	92	3 29 "	
" **Hugo**	105	4 20 "	
" Mirage	115	4 50 "	
" Aroya	128	5 25 "	
" Wild Horse	140	5 54 "	
" **Kit Carson**	152	6 22 "	
" First View	167	7 03 "	
" Cheyenne Wells	177	7 30 "	
" Arapaho	187	7 55 "	
" Monotony	202	8 27 "	
" Eagle Tail	210	8 57 "	
" **Wallace**	219	9 40 "	*6 00
" Sheridan	234	10 20 "	7 30
" Gopher	242	10 39 "	8 15
" Monument	253	11 04 "	9 10
" Carlyle	263	11 35 P.M.	10 15
" Grinnell	275	12 05 N'HT	11 25
" Buffalo	287	12 45 N'HT	12 45
" Coyote	303	1 21 A.M.	2 50
" Trego	317	1 55 "	3 55
" Ogallah	327	2 20 "	4 40
" **Ellis**	337	2 50 "	*3 15
" Hays	351	3 24 "	4 20
" Victoria	360	3 50 "	5 20
" Walker	365	4 00 "	5 40
" Russell	377	4 30 "	6 45
" Bunker Hill	387	4 50 "	7 45
" Bosland	400	5 30 "	8 55
" Ellsworth	416	6 12 "	10 45
" Fort Harker	421	6 23 "	11 15
" Elm Creek	429	6 42 "	12 05
" Rock Spring	434	6 58 "	12 45
" **Brookville**	439	7 20 "	†8 30
" Bavaria	445	7 37 "	9 10
" Salina	454	8 00 "	10 05
" Donmyer	461	8 15 "	10 45
" Solomon	468	8 37 "	11 40
" Abilene	477	9 20 "	12 25
" Detroit	482	9 34 "	12 50
" Chapman's	489	9 50 "	1 25
" Kansas Falls	495	10 06 "	1 55
" **Junction City**	501	10 30 "	2 40
" Fort Riley	504	10 37 "	2 55
" Ogden	510	10 53 "	3 30
" Manhattan	520	11 21 "	4 41
" St. George	529	11 40 A.M.	5 20
" Wamego	535	12 05 NO'N	6 00
" Belvue	542	12 22 "	P.M.
" St. Mary's	549	12 38 "	
" Rossville	556	12 58 NO'N	
" Silver Lake	562	1 13 P.M.	
" **Topeka**	572	1 45 "	
" Grantville	579	2 00 "	
" Newman	584	2 14 "	
" Medina	587	2 20 "	
" Perryville	588	2 24 "	
" Williamstown	591	2 32 "	
" Buck Creek	594	2 39 "	
" **Lawrence**	601	3 15 "	
" Leav. Branch Junc.	603	3 20 "	
" Fall Leaf	608	3 31 "	
" Stranger	612	3 42 "	
" Lenape	617	3 53 "	
" Tiblow	623	4 08 "	
" Edwardsville	626	4 18 "	
" Secondine	630	4 25 "	
" Muncy	631	4 28 "	
" Armstrong	638	4 45 "	
" State Line	639	4 50 "	
Arr.. **Kansas City**		4 55 P.M.	

(column labels: *Denver Division* / *Kaw Valley Division* / *Smoky Hill Division*)

KANSAS PACIFIC RAILWAY.

THE DIRECT LINE

To Lawrence, Topeka, Wamego, Manhattan, Fort Riley, Junction City, Abilene, Solomon, Salina, Brookville, Ellsworth, Wilson, Bunker Hill, Russell, Walker, Victoria, Hays, Ellis, Wallace, Kit Carson, Denver, Pueblo, &c.

BY
Junction City & Ft. Kearney
BRANCH,

From Junction City to Milford, Wakefield, and Clay Center, and all points in Republican and Solomon Valleys.

BY
Arkansas Valley Branch,

From Kit Carson, for Fort Lyon, Las Animas, La Junta, Trinidad, Fort Union, Santa Fé, Las Cruces, Del Norte, Silverton, San Juan City, Cucharas, Silver City, &c.

BY
Denver Pacific Railway,

From Denver, for Hughes, Platteville, Evans, Greeley, and Cheyenne.

BY
Denver & Boulder Valley
BRANCH.

From Denver to Hughes', Erie, Boulder City, Cariboo, &c.

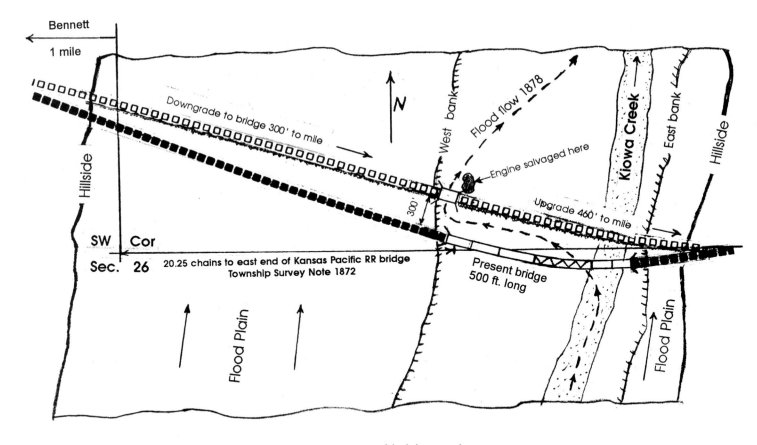

Bennett
1 mile

Downgrade to bridge 300' to mile

N

West bank

Flood flow 1878

Engine salvaged here

Kiowa Creek

East bank

Hillside

Hillside

Upgrade 460' to mile

300'

SW Cor
Sec. 26   20.25 chains to east end of Kansas Pacific RR bridge
Township Survey Note 1872

Present bridge
500 ft. long

Flood Plain

Flood Plain

Not to scale

Original and present bridge locations of railroad crossing over Kiowa Creek at Bennett, Colorado.

1870 bridge location, Kansas Pacific Railroad   □□□□□□□□□
1995 bridge location, Union Pacific Railroad   ■■■■■■■■■■

(left) This shallow basin is located about 300 feet downstream from the west end of the present steel railroad bridge over Kiowa Creek. It is roughly 100 feet long and 75 feet wide, with a center depth of eight feet. Five holes were dug down to the water table on the south side of this basin without finding any sign of cribbing that could have been used in salvaging the locomotive. (author's photo)

(opposite) Bennett and Kiowa Creek can be found east of Denver on this Union Pacific map dating from about ten years after the wreck. (CRRM collection)

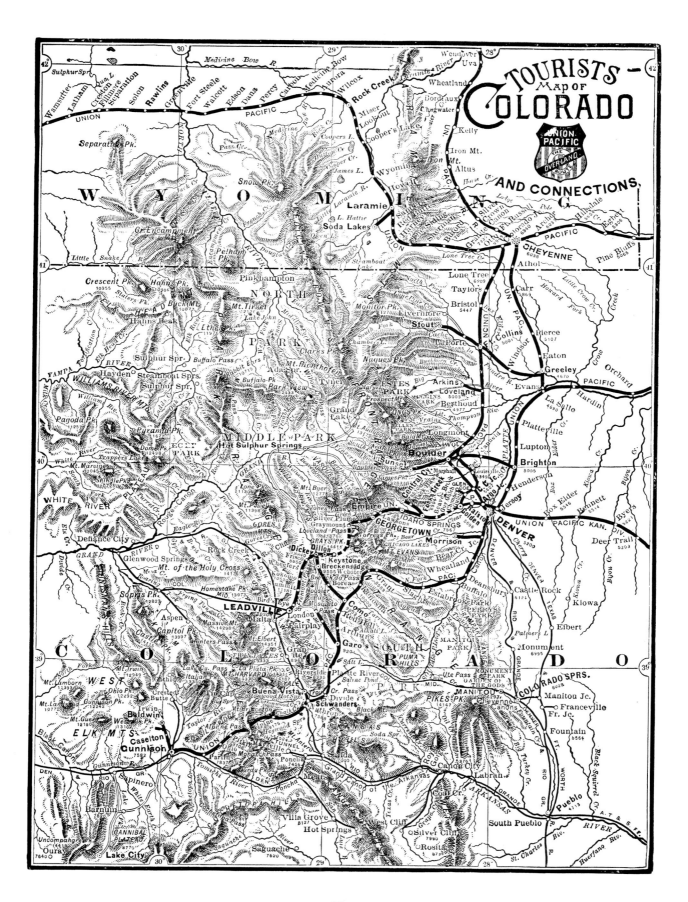

answer to a possible fraudulent insurance claim on No. 51 buried in a California desert? We understand why Elmer Davis persisted in his opinion that the locomotive was still in Kiowa Creek, and why oldtimers in Bennett have believed that, too. We hope that a 118-year-old rumor has now been buried instead of a rusty old locomotive.

---

ments, he would have given all his wagon was worth to know what the rest of that sign was. — *Burlington Hawkeye*

Fishing For an Engine

Some weeks ago a Kansas Pacific freight train went through a bridge over the Kiowa River. The river bed there was a quicksand and the engine disappeared entirely. How it was found the Denver *Tribune* tells as follows: "The locomotive which went down in the quicksand at Kiowa, has been discovered by the instrumentality of Wolfe Londoner, who visited the scene of the wreck Sunday. Wolfe went prepared for the work, and with the avowed determination of demonstrating the infallibility of a method his own ingenious brain gave birth to. He procured a metalic rod which he had heavily charged with magnetism. Armed with this he slowly passed over the ground under which, or in the vicinity of which, the engine was supposed to be buried, expecting that the mass of iron in the engine would so attract the magnet that the location of the engine would be easily indicated by the effect on the magnet above. The expectation was realized to the full. The megnet is said to have jumped around so and dived into the sand in such a frantic manner when the current first acted that Londoner and his instrument nearly perished in the quicksand. Col. Fisher was at once apprised of the discovery, and energetic digging and exploration proved that Wolfe had by this simple contrivance accomplished more than the skilled engineers employed on the work had been able to do."

Rail Cutting.

It is a very difficult thing to cut red or nearly white not rails so that they are of the same length when cold, as, if cut at different

This article describing the discovery of the "lost locomotive" is from the July 12, 1878, *Railroad Gazette*. Wolfe Londoner went on to become mayor of Denver during 1889-1891 and in 1895 was one of the principal organizers of the city's Festival of Mountain and Plain. (CRRM collection)

This photo in Union Pacific's April 1973 *Info* magazine shows how 25,000 tons of obsolete company records were removed from the annex of the Omaha headquarters building that winter. (CRRM collection)

Acknowledgments

We extend sincere thanks to all those who helped and encouraged us in this search to find out what happened to Kansas Pacific locomotive No. 51 after it disappeared into the sands of Kiowa Creek near Bennett, Colorado, in the flood of May 21, 1878.

Robert W. Richardson, Director Emeritus of the Colorado Railroad Museum in Golden gave the initial information needed to begin this research. Augie Mastrogiuseppe of the Western History Department of Denver Public Library helped us contact various museums and libraries which might have information on the "lost locomotive."

Kay Bost at the DeGolyer Library of Southern Methodist University in Dallas, Texas, provided photographs and specifications of 1870 era Baldwin locomotives from its holdings of early records of the Baldwin Locomotive Works. Colorado Historical Society in Denver, Nebraska Historical Society in Lincoln, Kansas Historical Society in Topeka, and Don Snoddy at the Union Pacific Historical Museum in Omaha, all opened their files. The Nebraska Historical Society library was especially helpful since it holds most of the surviving original records of the Kansas Pacific, donated by Union Pacific in 1975.

The "we" above includes my wife, Elaine, who did the original typing and accompanied me on our trips to Nebraska, and our daughter, Patricia Glasier of Columbia, Missouri. Pat spent many hours at the Missouri Historical Society Library reading microfilm of early St. Louis and Kansas City newspapers.

Finally, we thank Frank B. McLaughlin of Parker, Colorado, who put the report into his word processor.

> **DEDICATION**
>
> This history is dedicated to the memory of those hardy railroad pioneers who financed, built and operated the Kansas Pacific Railway across the vast treeless plains of Kansas and eastern Colorado in the 1860s and 1870s.

STORY OF VANISHING LOCOMOTIVE RECALLED AS BIG ENGINE SINKS 42 FEET IN SANDS OF THE PLATTE

History Repeats Itself as Flood Waters Loosen Piles Of Hillrose Bridge Near Brush, Causing Train to Plunge Into Stream.

(By LUTE H. JOHNSON.)   6-26-21

For nearly fifty years railroad men and laymen have listened with tongue in cheek to a legend that told of the complete disappearance of a railroad locomotive in Sand creek, where it is crossed by the tracks of the Kansas branch of the Union Pacific railroad at Bennett, in eastern Colorado.

Photograph taken from the south shore of the Platte river, showing partly submerged baggage car of Burlington train wrecked near Union, Colo., June 8. Beneath the water in the foreground lies the engine and tender, none of this part of the train being visible. Fireman Elmer C. Snedaker was drowned in this wreck.

The tale has been looked upon as one of those "tall" yarns told to illustrate the freakishness of dry creeks that course the eastern plains, rising nowhere, running nowhere and carrying their beds on their backs.

The story is told of how an engine once crossing what a few hours before had been a dry creek bed had had the bridge sink below it and how with scarcely a warning to the train crew of accident impending, it dropped into what had become in an hour a foaming torrent, sank from sight and was never seen again.

face, still sinking, and the probability of it ever being recovered are remote indeed. For the ages it too will lie there, its location shifting no doubt as did that of its Sand creek precursor, and in time it, too, will be lost. Such at least is the prospect today.

COLORADO HAS NO QUICKSANDS.

It is customary to speak of these sands as "quick." In reality there is in Colorado nothing to distinguish one sand from another. There are elsewhere sands which "rot" and merge into a clay form which has a suction quality, clinging, encompassing, soft

WATER PLAYS HAVOC WITH WORKS OF MAN.

History has a way of justifying itself. In this year 1921 the waters that fall on Colorado hills and plains have been playing havoc with the works of man as they never did since man picked them for home building. And so it happens that the tale of the Kansas Pacific engine of those days far back in the beginning of railroading on the plains has been repeated and a parallel has been provided.

Engineers of the Burlington have been sounding the water-loosened sands of the South Platte bed at the point where an engine on the Brush-Alliance branch plunged into the river two weeks ago and found it buried forty-two feet beneath the normal bed of the river. The engine, as did the one on the Kansas Pacific nearly fifty years ago, started across the Platte river bridge between Hillrose and Union with accustomed assurance of safety. To all appearances the bridge, crossed but a few hours before, was as stable as it had ever been, altho the flood was high on its piling and all but up to the ties. At a point midway of the passage the bridge melted beneath the engine and simply dropped away as tho it had not been. The engine dropped into the flood and soon was covered over. History had repeated itself, the tellers of the "tall tale" of early railroad days had been verified.

BOTH ENGINES HAVE VANISHED.

Only this difference stands between the two stories. The huge engine, one in comparison with which the early-day locomotive of the Kansas Pacific would have stood as a toy, was still visible when the train crew rushed to the scene of its dropping. It was longer going.

In the original case, even when the train crew hurried from the back end of the train to its front to see what had happened, that accident occurring in dead of night, not a trace of the engine was to be seen. In that case it had disappeared as completely as tho there had been no engine there in front drawing the train; and furthermore, all efforts thru the years to sound the creek bed for its location were fruitless. To this day no one has been able to locate a trace of that disappearing engine of times far back. It had simply been engulfed and obliterated.

The sands of the South Platte were kinder in that respect. They were longer receiving to themselves the engine of the Burlington. Furthermore, it had gone down in daylight and its sinking was seen by man. It was seen to sink lower and lower into the sands as the days went on until it was completely engulfed. Today the Burlington engineers with their sounding rods are able to tell where it rests in the sands of the river bed. But that huge engine of the modern railroad, tons heavier than the one which sank to rest in the Sand creek bed, now lies buried forty-two feet beneath the sur-

quality, clinging, encompassing, sort to the greatest depth. It is of such fiction deals in telling of heroes drawn down.

The sand of the dry creeks and running streams of the Colorado plains differ in no material way from the familiar form. When great floods of water come, these beds of sand which ordinarily have remained packed as do the sands of the sea shore, supporting on their beach-like surface the ordinary flow of water, become loosened even to their foundations and so their beds become liquid.

It is not unusual in time of summer rain for the cowboy who in the morning has ridden across such a stream as the Kiowa, the Bijou, Sand Creek or any other normally dry arroya, with scarcely the hoofs of his pony wet, returning to cross the same stream at evening to find that a cloudburst at the stream head has so loosened the sands that when his pony steps a second time onto a bar which in the morning was as firm as the beach of the sea to have it give to the horse's hoof and his mount drop in a flash to its ears, fighting and struggling for sure footing.

DAMS OFTEN GIVE WAY.

And so it is that in periods like this of exceptional rain, a reservoir dam built of sand on a harder sand foundation will give way before the repeated deluging until the bank simply melts beneath, as tho the foundations of the world had been loosened, sinking, merging as liquid sand into the primeval sand of which the plains are built. The effect is not far different from that of a tidal wave on such a sea beach as that of Galveston.

There seems no way to guard in an economic sense against these recurring periods of extraordinary rainfall. A dam to hold against such a period as this which exceeds in intensity of rainfall any within the memory of that man who has been building his home along the foothills, would need to go a hundred feet down and would be economically impossible. It is simply a case of doing the best man can and hoping that nature will be kind—that the periods of loosening the plains' foundations will be long delayed that we may for long enjoy unharrassed the fruits of irrigation and go on impounding as best we may the waters for our need.

Forty-three years after the wreck at Kiowa Creek, a similar fate overtook a Burlington passenger train at the South Platte River bridge northeast of Brush, Colorado. On June 21, 1921, *The Denver Post* carried this story comparing the two accidents. (CRRM collection)

SHORT LINE THROUGH A LONELY

by Vernon J. Glover

Introduction

Most histories of railroad development in New Mexico deal with the New Mexico Central briefly and treat it as a minor branch of the gigantic Atchison Topeka & Santa Fe Railway system. Although that was indeed the destiny of the New Mexico Central, its original goals and purposes were anything but that. Initially the railroad was to be a short but important part of at least one of the transcontinental routes being planned across New Mexico. As that opportunity faded, the railroad became a part of a land and townsite development scheme to the extent that it was impossible to determine which activity—land sales or railroad building—was the chief interest of those concerned. Once built and in operation, the railroad assumed its final form, that of a chronically impoverished agricultural hauler.

Although the railroad failed to achieve most of its goals, was frequently in the courts, and was a financial disaster, the New Mexico Central nevertheless made an important and useful cozntribution to life in the Estancia Valley. And from the vantage point of nearly a century it can be observed that many of the plans of its promoters have been fulfilled, but in ways that did not benefit the railroad. For these reasons, the New Mexico Central is worthy of study. In addition it was one of the territory's few independent short lines, and as such it was an interesting and thoroughly appealing property.

LAND: The New Mexico Central

A New Mexico Central train crew poses for the photographer about 1916. No. 8's engineer, Earl Angle, is in the center. This locomotive was purchased in well used condition from a Chicago equipment dealer during January 1912 and is said to have originally been built for the Baltimore & Ohio. (Howard Ogilvy collection)

The Santa Fe Albuquerque & Pacific Railroad

The railroad map of New Mexico in 1900 contained one significantly empty region. No tracks yet crossed the grassy high plans between the Pecos River and the Rio Grande. To be sure, this area would soon have its share of railroads. The El Paso & Northeastern was already building northward to meet the Rock Island at the Pecos River, and the Atchison Topeka & Santa Fe was investigating possible routes for a low-gradient freight line. But for the moment the region was devoid of railroads. To one group of men, this situation was an opportunity for profit, not only from the operation of a railroad but from the development of dependent properties and businesses. Even the construction of the railroad itself, if suitably organized, could be a profitable activity. And if such a railroad could be built quickly enough, there was even a chance of it becoming an essential if short link in one of the systems then forming in New Mexico.

The first move toward creating these opportunities was the incorporation on December 7, 1900, of the Santa Fe Albuquerque & Pacific Railroad. Capitalized at $2,250,000, this company intended to build a railroad of 150 miles connecting the territorial capital of Santa Fe with Albuquerque and with the El Paso & Northeastern line. The incorporators of the railroad were Willard S. Hopewell, Hillsboro, New Mexico; William H. Andrews, Pittsburgh, Pennsylvania; J. T. McGlaughlin, San Pedro, New Mexico; Joseph E. Saint, Albuquerque, New Mexico; and Charles W. Dudrow, Santa Fe, New Mexico. Two of these men were to achieve prominence in New Mexico politics using the railroad promotion as one of the stepping stones. Hopewell, later to become a power in the Democratic party, was at this time an established rancher and mining promoter in the Black Range district of southwestern New Mexico. Andrews was primarily a politician. He served in the Pennsylvania state legislature until 1902 when he moved to Sierra County, New Mexico. One of his goals, evidently, was to become a U.S. Senator when New Mexico achieved its statehood. Andrews became active in the statehood campaigns, and he ultimately served three terms as the territorial delegate to Congress. Among the others, McGlaughlin was superintendent of the San Pedro mine and smelter, and he was active in Santa Fe County politics.

The Santa Fe Albuquerque & Pacific's intended Y-shaped track provided both north-south and east-west routes across its domain, in hope of monopolizing the railroad business in that area. In theory, at least, there were many opportunities for railroad builders in this region. The mountains held deposits of gold, silver, copper, lead and zinc. There were proven coal deposits in southern Santa Fe County. Farther south lay the broad Estancia Valley, a fertile area of grass devoted to sheep and cattle ranching. In the Sandia and Manzano Mountains were commercial quantities of timber. The promotional literature of the railroad viewed all of these as potential sources of revenue. The same literature indicated that the development of farmlands in the valley would be one of the main activities of the company. Not mentioned in the literature, but carefully recorded in the county court houses, were the purchases of large areas of land by the railroad's promoters.

At the time of the railroad's organization, practically all of its industrial potential remained undeveloped. The one exception was the San Pedro mine and smelter owned by the Santa Fe Gold & Copper Company. This promising property had been incorporated in 1899 and had acquired 3,400 acres of mineral lands and 46,000 acres of other land within the old San Pedro Grant. By 1900 development of the mine had revealed the presence of substantial quantities of low-grade ore containing copper, gold and silver. In that same year a smelter was built, having a capacity of 250 tons per day. It operated during 1901 with ores having an average copper content of 4.75 percent. This type of mine could only be profitable if operated on a large scale, with cheap rail-hauled fuel and an efficient outlet to markets. As superintendent of the mine and smelter, McGlaughlin had every reason to support the projected railroad.

In spite of its evident virtues, the Santa Fe Albuquerque & Pacific did not attract the cash necessary to begin construction. For reasons that remain obscure, on July 22, 1901, the company was renamed the Santa Fe Central Railway by amending the original incorporation papers. Under this new name, the promotions continued as before and with some added features.

The Santa Fe Central Railway

On the same day the Santa Fe Central Railway was created, July 22, 1901, the same group of individuals organized another company, the Albuquerque Eastern Railway. Between them the two companies intended to build much the same railroad system as the predecessor Santa Fe Albuquerque & Pacific and for most of the same reasons. At first the new companies seemed to have no better luck than the old at attracting willing investors. It was almost a year before any beginnings were made at construction. During this period it became quite apparent that the man really sparking the enterprise was Willard S. Hopewell. Colonel Hopewell had the title of vice-president and general manager of the Santa Fe Central Railway. His offices were in the Catron Block in Santa Fe, and from this location he pushed the promotion of the railroad and affiliated business enterprises.

Hopewell superintended preliminary construction work in great detail, giving special attention to the public relations of the company. William H. Andrews, on the other hand, was apparently in charge of finance. As president of the Santa Fe Central, Andrews found the cash needed to begin construction. Two Pittsburgh businessmen, Francis J. Torrance and Arthur G. Kennedy, evidently supplied a large part of the early investment in the railroad. They remained in the background of activities in New Mexico, but their presence was always noted in reports of the company's financial dealings. Colonel Hopewell was assisted in New Mexico by J. T. McGlaughlin as treasurer and J. E. Saint as secretary of the company.

By mid-1902, when construction on the Santa Fe Central began, the railroad situation in New Mexico was changing radically. The new road's prospects were more restricted. The El Paso & Northeastern had completed its planned connection with the Rock Island lines at the new town of Santa Rosa on the Pecos River. The link was the El Paso & Rock Island Railway which opened for traffic on February 1, 1902, months before any work at all had been done on the Santa Fe Central. The Santa Fe system had located and surveyed, and would soon let contracts for a line from Belen to a connection with the existing Pecos & Northern Texas line near Amarillo. Called the Belen cutoff, this was part of a major effort to build a transcontinental freight route bypassing the severe grades of Raton Pass. Between them these two mainlines, possibly with a few short branches, could accomplish all that the Santa Fe Central and the Albuquerque Eastern ever intended. In seeming recognition of their new circumstances, the promoters quietly changed their emphasis to the development of the industries, farms and towns along the route.

The routes of the new railroads changed almost imperceptibly to pass through lands owned by Hopewell, Andrews and the others. The Santa Fe Central was to run from Santa Fe, where a connection could be made with the narrow gauge Denver & Rio Grande, south toward Galisteo. Climbing up from Galisteo Creek into the broad Estancia Valley, the line continued southward down the valley to the vicinity of the salt lakes, called the Laguna del Perro, and then curved to the southeast to connect with the El Paso & Rock Island near Corona. In addition, a branch to the San Pedro mine was planned and surveyed. An extension to Roswell was surveyed, and vague references were made to a line up toward Durango and the San Juan coal fields. The Albuquerque

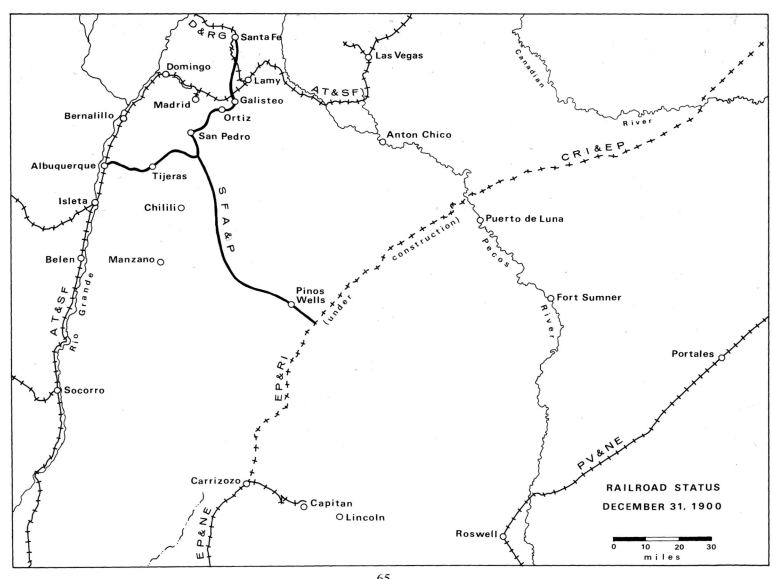

Eastern route ran west from the Estancia Valley to Albuquerque following Tijeras Canyon. An important branch was to extend north from the mainline to the Hagan and Pinavititos coal fields. This line was shown continuing beyond the mines to a connection with the Santa Fe near San Felipe.

Separate companies were incorporated to promote and build the various enterprises. The directors and officers were essentially the same as those of the Santa Fe Central. In actual practice these individuals bought and sold property and performed services for one another in a bewildering series of transactions. And, in time-honored fashion, they set up their own construction company to extract additional profits from the investors. The key corporation was the Pennsylvania Development Company, incorporated in New Jersey on August 24, 1901. Its primary function was to build both the Santa Fe Central and Albuquerque Eastern railroads. It held contracts with both roads providing for the construction company to be paid in small amounts of cash, a substantial amount of stock, and, most significantly, the entire issue of first mortgage bonds of each company. Thus, the Pennsylvania Development Company would have a first lien on the railroad and would be able to operate the line or to sell it for what it would bring, should all else fail. As if railroad construction were not enough, the Pennsylvania Development Company also operated a general merchandise business. Not only did it supply the construction camps, but it ran retail stores in all of the new towns along the route. The retail trade proved to be a little too much for the company to handle, however, and in April 1903 the business was sold to the Dunlavy Brothers of Trinidad, Colorado. At that time, stores were open at Torrance, Willard, Estancia, Moriarty, Kennedy and Hagan.

Next on the list of affiliated companies was the New Mexico Fuel & Iron Company, incorporated in New Mexico Territory on April 22, 1902. In addition to the mineral properties suggested by its name, the company acquired a lot of farm and ranch land in the Estancia Valley. Much of this land had been homesteaded in the mid-1880s, and had been subsequently purchased by Colonel Hopewell after 1900. In the typical western pattern, these lands were located on the sources of water, and were surrounded by government land still open to homestead entry. The New Mexico Fuel & Iron Company surveyed new townsites at Progresso, Willard, Estancia and Moriarty. All, of course, were on the route of the railroad. Sales of town lots and farms were enthusiastically promoted. The towns grew, and with the exception of Progresso, permanent communities resulted from their efforts. The coal and mineral lands of the New Mexico Fuel & Iron Company were located in Sandoval and Santa Fe counties. Most had been acquired through Colonel Hopewell. The most important properties were the Una de Gato and Pinavititos coal fields in Sandoval County. They were soon renamed the Hagan District after W. C. Hagan of Pittsburgh, Pennsylvania, an early investor. The chief mine and the town at its mouth were also known as Hagan. Hagan himself was to later become the secretary of the Santa Fe Central. Other properties acquired by the New Mexico Fuel & Iron Com-

pany included placer gold claims in the Dolores or Old Placers district of the Ortiz Mountains, mineral claims near San Pedro and coal mines near Tijeras. With the exception of the Hagan mines, none of these properties were of high quality, and they have been all but forgotten.

Other properties associated with the railroad were held by individuals. W. H. Andrews and some associates owned timber lands in the Manzano Mountains. These were logged in part during 1903 to provide ties for the railroad. Eugenio Romero did the work on contract. Although the Manzanos are by no means a major timber region, a small production of railroad ties, mine props and rough pine lumber continued throughout the life of the railroad. In his capacity as president of the Santa Fe Central, Andrews filed a claim for coal prospects in the vicinity of the Omera or Block mine owned by the Lewisohn Coal Company. This mine supplied the San Pedro mine and smelter when it was operating. Colonel Hopewell retained title to a number of metal mining claims at Coyote and Gallinas in Rio Arriba County, which were among the reasons for the projected extensions of the railroad to the northwest.

Although records are few, the name and location of the Kennedy iron mine strongly suggest some connection with the Santa Fe Central. This mine was located a few miles south of Glorieta in very rough country. It produced an estimated 3,500 tons of ore in the early 1900s. Most of the ore was shipped to Socorro and El Paso as smelter flux.

The financing of the Santa Fe Central Railway was accomplished through the sale of stock and of first mortgage bonds. The company had been capitalized at $2,500,000 and stock in that par value was issued. First mortgage bonds with the face value of $2,500,000 and paying five percent interest were issued and handed over to the Pennsylvania Development Company in exchange for the construction of the railroad. Most of the stock issued also found its way into the hands of the development company. The actual sale prices involved are not a matter of record. In similar fashion the $1,200,000 par value stock issue of the Albuquerque Eastern Railway became the property of the development company in exchange for the construction of that road. The Albuquerque Eastern was also authorized to issue $1,200,000 face value of first mortgage bonds. These were also to go to the development company but for some reason were never issued.

It was at this point that the financial affairs of the several companies became mysterious, at least as far as the public was concerned. In later years many of the early transactions became known as the result of seemingly endless litigation which resulted from the notable lack of profitability of the railroads.

It was not until the middle of 1902 that construction of the Santa Fe Central began in earnest. Work started at no fewer than three railheads: Torrance, Kennedy and Santa Fe. At each point the Santa Fe Central received supplies from a different connecting railroad. Grading worked south from Santa Fe, south from Kennedy and north from Torrance. At the same time bridge construction commenced at several points

A circa 1915 view of Kennedy, New Mexico, encompasses all the components of this tiny outpost of Santa Fe's empire: depot, train order signal, telegraph line, section house, water pump, fire barrel and a short string of stock cars on the house track. (Museum of New Mexico 9374)

on the north end of the line. There were 84 bridges and culverts between Santa Fe and Kennedy, and two major spans were needed just south of Kennedy. Colonel Hopewell took charge of construction from his office in Santa Fe. The detail work was carried out by superintendents in the field, while Hopewell saw to the delivery of supplies and materials. No small part of Hopewell's work was the issuing of news releases reporting the progress of the work and describing the opportunities awaiting in the area along the route.

Work moved steadily along through 1902. The telegraph line, one wire on cedar poles, was completed in September. The bridge work was finished by October except for the wood Howe truss at the Arroyo de la Jara and the crossing of the Santa Fe at Kennedy. Each of the townsites along the line received a rough building termed a "temporary station." Usu-

ally a store building and a few primitive dwellings or tents made up the initial townsite. During October 1902 work on the line reached its peak with 650 men and 250 teams of horses at work.

The Santa Fe Central received its first locomotive at Torrance on January 14, 1903. Only a few feet of track had been laid to receive it, so it stood idle for the next few weeks. Contracts for continued grading and for rails and ties were soon awarded, and the railroad began to take shape. During February new 70-pound steel rail began to arrive from Pittsburgh. It was stored at all three railheads until it was needed. By early April the grading crews from Torrance and Kennedy met at Moriarty, thus completing the entire grade. Culverts and trestlework were finished at about the same time. Neither the grading nor the bridging involved much major work, for

The NMC ran through a gap in the hogback formation a few miles south of Kennedy. This view of the abandoned right-of-way was taken on February 15, 1952. (W.O. Gibson)

the road followed the contours of the land in most places. The exceptions were at the north end and the two major crossings noted previously.

April 10, 1903, was a big day. Track laying was begun at Torrance using the imposing Harris Improved Track Laying Machine. It utilized small tram cars on tracks mounted on a string of flat cars to bring ties and rails up to a gantry crane on the leading car. The machinery worked well, and it proved to be able to lay as much as 4,000 feet of track in a day with a relatively small crew. A typical day's work, however, was closer to 2,000 feet. Once started, the track laying proceeded steadily northward. Station after station was passed, with each milestone breathlessly reported to the press by Colonel Hopewell. Directed by Chief Engineer John Harris, the track crew arrived at Moriarty, 63 miles from Torrance, on June 13, 1903. It was a Saturday afternoon, and work stopped while the crew celebrated with the simple pleasures of lighting bonfires, firing guns and consuming suitable liquid refreshment. It must have been a pretty good celebration, for work did not resume until the following Tuesday when the wye for the Albuquerque Eastern was laid down.

The completion of track to Moriarty gave Colonel Hopewell an excuse to start train service. On June 24 a mixed train began running every day from Torrance to Moriarty and return during the daylight hours. Running time was 4-1/2 hours each way in deference to the new track.

In late June construction efforts increased with the organization of two more track crews. A locomotive and a few cars were moved over the Santa Fe to the junction at Kennedy and were used by the track gang there to lay track southward. This crew handled materials by hand, and their progress was slower than the Harris machine. After some problems with hiring enough men, this crew settled down to laying about 1,500 feet of track per day. A third gang went to Santa Fe. It began working on the yards, interchange tracks and locomotive service facilities. A lot of new rail had piled up at Santa Fe after arriving on the narrow gauge Denver & Rio Grande from Alamosa, Colorado. The shipments had frequently overloaded that line's capacity, and its sidings were filled with cars of rail, many in bad order because of the heavy loading. By running doubleheaded extras on weekends, and by stationing an extra helper locomotive at Embudo, the D&RG managed to deliver the rail to Santa Fe before it was needed.

The mainline of the Santa Fe central south of Kennedy was completed on July 18, when the two track gangs met between Stanley and Clark. Within a few days the Harris track layer was moved to Santa Fe over the AT&SF, and was made ready to go to work laying track southward. For the benefit of the many people watching the construction, Colonel Hopewell brought one of his road's five brand new ten-wheelers up from Torrance. These new locomotives from American Locomotive Company's Pittsburgh Works were large and modern, and contrasted favorably with the small antique locomotives used on the construction trains. It was probably No. 54 that did the honors on this occasion. At the same time 20 new boxcars were used on lease from the Rio Grande Sierra Madre & Pacific, which was also being built during this period.

The pair of photographs above records the final rails being laid prior to driving the last spike of the New Mexico Central Railway on August 13, 1903. Perhaps the six gentlemen taking their ease atop the "Improved Harris Track Layer," not to mention the nattily attired fellow at the right, are providing moral support for the hard working crew. (Christian G. Kaadt photos, Museum of New Mexico 37171 and 14193) The art of Santa Fe jeweller S. Spitz, of Otto Mears silver pass fame, is evident in the the beautifully engraved silver spike.

As the Harris machine worked its way out of town, a great deal of other work was being finished along the entire route to make it ready for regular service. The overhead crossing was completed at Kennedy. Track crews were surfacing the new track with dirt ballast. The shops at Estancia were taking shape, although with temporary buildings in place of the permanent brick structures promised by Colonel Hopewell. Fifty-thousand gallon water tanks were finished at Estancia and at Well 425. As a finishing touch, James Spivey of Santa Fe was hired to professionally paint each of the 115 mileposts along the route, as well as signs for each station building.

Some work along the Albuquerque Eastern was accomplished during the summer, but the project was not pushed with any great vigor.

Track laying south of Santa Fe proceeded smoothly into early August. By August 13 the track was down all the way to Kennedy. This was to be another big day for the Santa Fe Central. Colonel Hopewell was in his glory making arrangements for a suitable ceremony and celebration for the completion of the railroad, as was evidenced by a flurry of press releases. An elegant touch was added with the donation of a silver "last spike" by S. Spitz, the well-known Santa Fe jeweller. (Spitz was already noted in western railroading for the manufacture of the unique silver filigree passes for Otto Mears' Silverton and Rio Grande Southern railroads.)

Early on the afternoon of the 13th, a special train left Santa Fe carrying Colonel Hopewell, Major I. Sparks, and all the local citizens and railroaders who could crowd aboard. Also riding were Frank Dibert, auditor of the railroad company, and Christian G. Kaadt, the "official photographer" of the Santa Fe Central. The two were starting a trip to photograph the railroad and its associated properties. The train consisted of the new ten-wheeler, a water tank car, a flat car with benches installed and a large caboose. Colonel Hopewell apologized for the lack of coaches and assured everyone that comfortable modern passenger cars were already on the line at Torrance, ready for the start of regular trains. The big ten-wheeler, a little heavy for the unsurfaced track, was exchanged at Vega Blanca for a smaller locomotive. The last rail was placed on the ties at 4:10 PM, and the special train arrived soon afterward. The passengers and company officials assembled along the track, and the final silver spike was driven by Major Sparks at 5:17 PM. The Santa Fe Central was complete.

The brief ceremonies were duly recorded by photographer Kaadt. After losing their way while getting down to the station at Kennedy, Kaadt and Dibert began their photographic journey to the south by wagon. They returned to Santa Fe on August 21, having taken many views of the railroad and the surrounding countryside.

Between the official laying of the last rail and the opening of the railroad for business, a lot more work remained to be done. The track was surfaced the entire length of the line, using dirt ballast. Temporary station buildings were opened at Santa Fe and other points. Sidings and small buildings were finished.

Regular service began on August 20, 1903, with the following schedule of two trains daily in each direction:

The first scheduled train was the northbound passenger, which arrived at Santa Fe dead on time. Pulled by engine No. 6, the train consisted of caboose 50 and combination baggage-passenger car 1. It was manned by Engineer W. E.

| (Read Down) | | | | (Read Up) | |
2nd Class El Paso Fast Frt. Daily	1st Class Mexico & Calif. Mail Exp. Daily		Miles	1st Class Colo. Mail & Express Daily	2nd Class Denver Fast Frt. Daily
8:00 pm	2:00 pm	Santa Fe	0.0	9:30 am	12:00 N
8:15 pm	2:20 pm	Donaciana	5.5	9:15 am	11:40 am
8:40 pm	2:55 pm	Vega Blanca	16.0	8:50 am	11:05 am
9:00 pm	3:25 pm	Kennedy	21.8	8:30 am	10:35 am
9:20 pm	3:40 pm	Clark	27.9	8:10 am	10:10 am
10:05 pm	4:43 pm	Stanley	40.8	7:25 am	9:15 am
10:35 pm	5:20 pm	Moriarty	52.4	6:55 am	8:40 am
10.55 pm	5:50 pm	McIntosh	60.6	6:35 am	8:10 am
11:15 pm	6:15 pm	Estancia	68.5	6:15 am	7:45 am
11:35 pm	6:40 pm	Spur No. 3	—	5:55 am	7:20 am
12:00 M	7:00 pm	Willard	80.8	5:10 am	6:50 am
12:30 am	7:45 pm	Progresso	91.7	5:00 am	6:15 am
12:55 am	8:15 pm	Bianca	99.2	4:35 am	5:45 am
1:30 am	9:00 pm	Torrance	115.7	4:00 am	5:00 am

B. W. Robbins
General Passenger Agent, Santa Fe

W. S. Hopewell
General Manager, Santa Fe

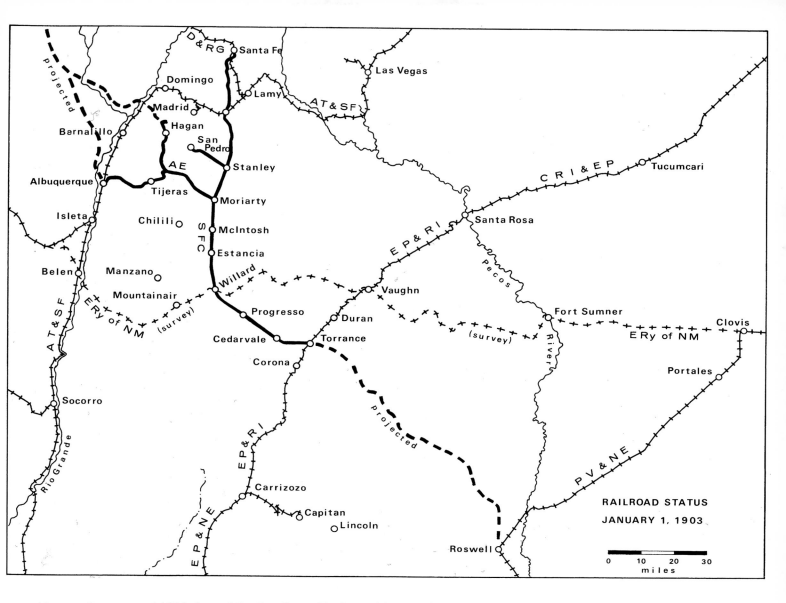

RAILROAD STATUS
JANUARY 1, 1903

0 10 20 30
miles

At some time around 1902, four of the five Santa Fe Central locomotives in series 50-54 are newly delivered and awaiting use.(Christian G. Kaadt photo, Museum of New Mexico) The map above includes the projected but never built line to Roswell.

Sowers, Fireman Booker, Conductor J. M. Whiteman and brakemen McIlee and Robb. About 20 passengers made the early morning journey.

To keep up interest in the railroad and the land office at Estancia, Colonel Hopewell ran a number of special trains during the next few weeks. One such train gained the railroad a lot of newspaper space, for the guest of honor was W. S. Burke, editor of the Albuquerque *Journal-Democrat,* the largest morning daily in the territory. Colonel Hopewell gave Burke the full treatment. At each stop the editor was shown around with special attention given to those points where the Pennsylvania Development Company was selling land. The bountiful benefits of rural life in the productive valley were fully displayed for the editor. At Moriarty the train ran westward for the few miles of Albuquerque Eastern trackage completed at that time. At Estancia, there was the rapidly growing town with its flowing spring to view. And between Estancia and Willard the editor was treated to a speed run demonstrating the high quality of the railroad's construction. Eight miles were clipped off at just over 60 miles-per-hour, a creditable showing on the fresh roadbed. The track was nearly level and nearly straight. The train consisted only of a locomotive, water tank car and a coach, so the fast run was no strain on the equipment. To top it all off, Hopewell offered to deliver the *Journal-Democrat* free of charge to valley points. Needless to say, praise for the new railroad was prominent on the front page in Albuquerque.

The brief journey of Editor Burke's special train over the Albuquerque Eastern covered most of the progress made in building that road. Roadbed had been graded to Frost and possibly beyond. A length of track had been laid, possibly as much as four miles, but more likely only the two miles that were ever to be finished with ballast and surfacing. Some 240 lineal feet of trestlework had been built, as had the necessary culverts under 18 miles of roadbed. In addition a large quantity of material was on hand, stored at Moriarty and along the route: ties, rails, bridge timbers, piling and telegraph poles. It was reported in later years that $185,000 had been spent on the Albuquerque Eastern up to this time.

Once the Santa Fe Central was operating, Colonel Hopewell announced that the construction crews would be transferred to the Albuquerque Eastern. This was not done to any great extent, and work ceased without fanfare or public notice. In the coming years the failure to complete the road to the Hagan coal mines would prove to have a profound effect on the railroad.

Following the start of regular service in August 1903, an ominous series of events began. The further development of the Santa Fe Central stopped abruptly, to the extent of leaving some important projects unfinished. The turntable at Estancia, for one thing, was not installed, and it remained in storage in the yards. (Locomotives ran up to Moriarty to be turned.) The stations along the line, opened in 1903 with a flurry of press releases, were closed and, in at least one instance, hauled off for other uses. The five proud new locomotives were never placed in service, but were stored near Estancia. By January 1904, they were leased to the El Paso

& Northeastern. A short time later they were sold to the Pere Marquette Railroad. And the ambitious schedule of trains announced in August 1903 was quickly amended to the typical short line pattern of a mixed train daily.

What had happened? The answer, although complex in its details and implications, was extremely simple. There was no more money. There was no cash to finish the Santa Fe Central line, and there was certainly no money for the expensive mountain construction needed to complete the Albuquerque Eastern. So there was no revenue from the coal mines or from connecting traffic at Albuquerque. From the day it opened the Santa Fe Central was reduced to the impoverished role of an agricultural carrier in an undeveloped arid land that was, in truth, marginal for dry farming.

It was during this early period of operation, during late 1903 and 1904, that the Santa Fe Central came to the attention of the management of the AT&SF. A letter written in late 1904 by E. P. Ripley, president of the AT&SF, tells much about the position of the SFC:

"The Santa Fe Central Railway, extending from Santa Fe to Torrance, New Mexico, had been barely put in operation before its owners discovered what everybody else knew long before, namely, that it would be impossible to make it pay operating expenses.

"The principal owner is Francis J. Torrance of Pittsburgh, Pa., who is said to have invested about $2,000,000 in the property. His representative has called on me once or twice, stating that Mr. Torrance realizes he has made a very bad investment, and wanting to know on what basis we would be willing to take it off his hands. . ."

For a time, the SFC was studied for possible use as part of a temporary link in the Belen Cutoff of the AT&SF, then under construction in Abo Canyon to the west of the SFC line. AT&SF management, very short of money, considered purchasing the SFC and using it between Willard and Torrance as part of the new mainline. Trackage rights over the El Paso & Northeastern would fill the gap between Torrance and Llano Junction (later named Vaughn). This expedient would temporarily eliminate the need to build approximately 54 miles of relatively expensive line between Willard and Llano Junction.

The temporary line would be about 8.5 miles longer than a direct line, and it would include one percent grades, heavier than the 0.6 percent grades planned for the permanent line. Nevertheless, use of the SFC was carefully examined as an alternative to construction. In July 1903, the AT&SF stopped all work on the Belen cutoff, then in progress through Abo Canyon, and discussions about purchasing the SFC ceased.

A brief description of a trip over the Santa Fe Central in its early days will serve to describe the road and to highlight some of its problems. The route began naturally enough in the territorial capital city of Santa Fe. The yards and station were located between Guadalupe Street and the AT&SF yards on the western edge of the city. The domed territorial capitol building and the plaza with its ancient Palace of the Governors were only a few blocks to the east, but the new railroad did not intrude noticeably into the old city. A track

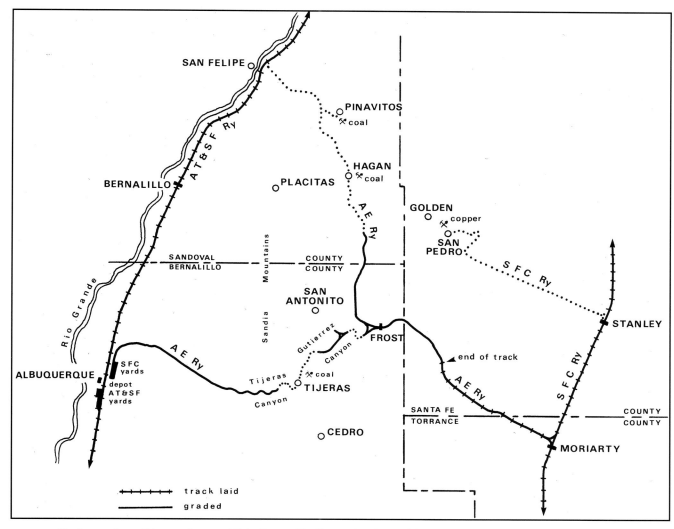

No fewer than 51 people greet this Santa Fe Central train—with an elegant combination car, a side door caboose and what looks like a former Union Pacific 4-4-0—as it pulls into "Temporary Station" somewhere in the Estancia Valley. (H.H. Dorman photo, Museum of New Mexico 11902) The map shows how little of the Albuquerque Eastern's grade ever had rail laid upon it.

of the narrow gauge D&RG had for years crossed the Santa Fe River and run down the center of Guadalupe Street past the Church of Our Lady of Guadalupe to an interchange platform at the AT&SF yards. When the Santa Fe Central was built, the narrow gauge tracks were merged into the north end of the new yards. Most of the new tracks had a narrow gauge third rail to facilitate interchange.

Santa Fe Central train No. 1 departed Santa Fe every morning. Its solitary coach, a combined baggage-mail-passenger car, waited in front of the new brick depot for passengers while the locomotive and its accompanying water tank car were prepared for the journey. The small 4-4-0 had been coaled during the night. The watchman shoveled the coal across from a gondola to the tender on the next track. Having taken water from a standpipe, the engine picked up a freight car or two and backed down to the coach. Chuffing quietly

The daily mixed passenger and freight train is headed south at Moriarty around 1916. The general poverty of the New Mexico Central is evident in the ancient locomotive, uneven track and unpainted depot. (Hal Crossley collection) The 1905 annual pass was issued to the Western Passenger Agent of the Mexican Central Railway. (CRRM collection)

out of town, the train passed a stock loading pen, and clumped across the diamond of the AT&SF crossing. The train ran almost directly southward toward Kennedy, through rolling country cut by deep arroyos draining into Galisteo Creek. The roadbed had been quickly graded resulting in an undulating profile and short gradients approaching three percent in both directions. The train speeded up going down toward the arroyos and slowed noticeably going up the other side. The trestles were approached carefully, for they could be weakened or even washed out by the summer rains. The flagstops of Crandall, Donaciana and Vega Blanca rarely offered business. The station building at Donaciana had, in fact, been removed a couple of months after the railroad's opening to become a school at Estancia.

About 16 miles out of Santa Fe, the chuffing of the little locomotive ceased abruptly, to be replaced by the metallic screech of brake shoes on wheels. The grade here was three percent as the track dropped from the high plateau to Kennedy, the junction with the AT&SF mainline. After crossing the AT&SF on a trestle and fill with a steel span over the track, the train stopped at the station. A passenger or two got on, and frequently some freight cars would be picked up. Leaving Kennedy the track curved southward once more and continued to drop down toward Galisteo Creek. This sometimes violent stream was crossed on a substantial timber trestle. The Arroyo de la Jara, a short distance farther on, was

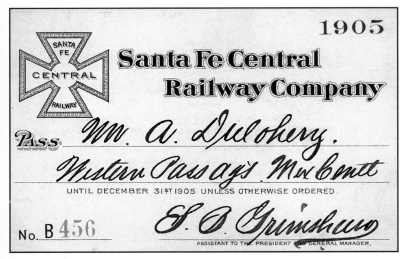

spanned with a wood Howe truss. In the next 12 miles the train climbed from the creeks to the high plains of the Estancia Valley.

The climb began easily enough as the track followed the natural waterways. Soon the little 50-ton engine was laboring mightily against an ever increasing grade. If the train was heavy enough, there would come a point at which the engine could do no more. The rear half of the train was left standing while the engine pulled what it could to the summit. After leaving the first portion of the train on a siding, the engine returned for the second part. Even though cuts and fills of 20 feet depth were built, the ruling grade here was a heartbreaking 3.2 percent. The light engines used on the Santa Fe Central were at a considerable disadvantage here, and the expense of moving a heavy train up the hill was considerable, not only in fuel and water but also in time.

Beyond the summit, the grades became easier. The train passed through broad grazing lands, green with grass and dotted with cattle and sheep. Although this was productive land, it could not be farmed in the same manner as eastern farms because of the generally arid nature of the region. Just over 40 miles from Santa Fe, the train slowed for Stanley, the first real community to be found along the route thus far. Stanley was little more than a crossroads community with a railroad station, a two-story hotel and a couple of stores. Not only did it serve the growing number of farms and ranches in the district, but it was the shipping point for the San Pedro mines and smelter. When the mines were operating, a good quantity of coal and supplies was shipped in via Stanley.

A little farther south, the train paused at Well 425, an otherwise undistinguished crossing of a shallow streambed. This place assumed importance with the drilling of a well, the installation of a windmill and pump, and the erection of a 50,000-gallon watertank. Over 44 miles from Santa Fe, this was the first water available to the railroad in the entire distance. After filling the tender and water car, the train moved on the few miles to Moriarty. Just north of the station, the train rattled over the switches of the Albuquerque Eastern wye. Here was the construction yard of the Pennsylvania Development Company, full of supplies and idle equipment.

Moriarty and the subsequent stops down the valley were all creations of the promoters. Antelope, McIntosh, Estancia, Willard and Progreso all had in common their land sales office, a general store and a cluster of new houses and shanties. Moriarty was one of the faster growing examples. The train moved quickly down the valley now, on nearly level track.

At Estancia the train stopped long enough to switch a few freight cars and to look over the locomotive. Often it would be exchanged for another of the roster of six small engines. Continuing south, the train ran through increasingly arid country. Willard was the last town of any size along the route.

Here is a mystery picture. A Southern Pacific Mogul is at Torrance Junction, New Mexico, with train No. 3, the *Golden State Limited*. The touring car reflects 1914 styling. But why was a 2-6-0 freight locomotive pulling this premier train, normally assigned a high drivered Pacific, and what was the occasion of the carefully posed photo with the automobile and the brakeman riding on the footboard? (Museum of New Mexico 11906)

At this point, the new construction of the AT&SF Belen Cut-off was prominent. The Santa Fe was building a large water system here, and a big coaling chute would guarantee that all trains stopped. At this time Willard was really two communities, the newer along the Santa Fe line and the older about a mile south, in a grove of trees. Our train moved steadily onward, unhampered by any local traffic. Progresso was marked by a siding serving a tiny and dying community that had for less than two months acted as the seat of Torrance County. This southernmost of the new towns along the railroad was located in country so dry that even irrigation was not able to make it into anything viable.

After passing several more tiny settlements, each with its short spur, the train arrived at Torrance. To the handful of passengers connecting with El Paso & Northeastern trains, it was a doubtful sort of junction. The two-story railroad station was the most prominent building for miles around. The lower floor was devoted to the business of both railroads, and the upper floor served as the agent's living quarters. Rest and sustenance for the traveler was provided by the little hotel operated by the Santa Fe Central. Most of its business came from train crews laying over. After switching out the interchange track and setting out the coach, the Santa Fe Central locomotive was placed under the sleepy care of the night watchman.

That sort of journey became routine for the Santa Fe Central. The schedules would vary considerably over the years, changing usually to make connections at Torrance. By 1906 the running time over the road had been lengthened to seven hours ten minutes southbound and to six hours 50 minutes northbound. Such a time for a run of only 115.7 miles was hardly attractive to through passengers changing from the *Golden State Limited*, but it did permit time for switching, occasionally rerailing cars off the track, and all the other chores performed by the mixed train daily. It also suggested that running speeds had been substantially reduced in comparison to the speed run made for editor Burke shortly after the railroad's opening.

In the meantime, the AT&SF had resumed construction of its Belen Cutoff and was moving along steadily toward completion of the line between Belen and Clovis. The decision was made to build a first-class mainline, and there were no more discussions of temporary routes. The SFC, nevertheless, remained a subject of interest among AT&SF executives.

During this period, the SFC was viewed as a potential competitor by AT&SF management, especially if the Albuquerque Eastern line was to be finished into Albuquerque. There was no real concern that the SFC would siphon off any significant amount of business. The AT&SF view was that the SFC would provide alternative service for Albuquerque business, and freight rates would ultimately be reduced as a result of competition.

An effort was made to negotiate a purchase of the SFC between March and December 1905. The price to be paid for the SFC became the issue of the negotiations with the AT&SF. Ripley offered $1,000,000; Torrance countered with his rock-bottom price of $1,150,000. The stalemate continued until December 1905, when Torrance withdrew his offer to sell. At this time Torrance claimed to have backing to complete the Albuquerque Eastern and to build a line between Albuquerque and Durango. That ended the discussions with AT&SF representatives, and the SFC was once more on its own.

The essential problem facing the SFC was a significant lack of revenue. Although revenues steadily increased, they barely equaled operating expenses, even in the best years.

Two cars of this Santa Fe Central passenger train have left the rails, apparently while pulling out from an unidentified station. The number of cars and their appearance suggest that possibly this is some sort of special excursion using equipment from a more prosperous connecting carrier. In any case, the two ladies protecting their Gibson Girl-era complexions from the ravages of the New Mexico sun and the other passengers forward seem resigned to a lengthy delay. (Museum of New Mexico 895)

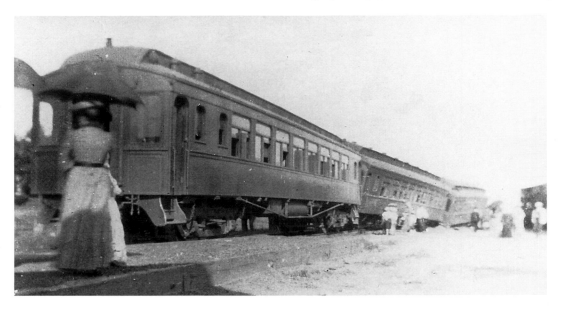

Clearly, the young communities along the line were not able to consistently support even the low level of train service offered by the SFC. The following table shows the steady but inadequate growth of revenue contrasted to the relatively stable cost of operations

Year Ending	Operating Revenues	Gross Expenses	Income
June 30, 1905	$ 43,572	$ 90,796	($47,224)
June 30, 1906	108,565	80,992	25,573
June 30, 1907	110,386	91,427	18,959
June 30, 1908	117,218	110,216	7,002

( ) indicates loss.

Ordinarily such a series of annual returns would be cause for some guarded optimism. There was, however, a serious flaw hidden away in the footnotes for each annual report. No interest was being paid on the first mortgage bonds that had been issued by the railroad to pay for the construction work. During this period the bonds remained in the hands of the Pennsylvania Development Company, whose owners also controlled the railroad. These individuals elected not to collect the interest from themselves. Had the interest been paid by the railroad, it would have amounted to $125,000 per year, i.e., five percent of the face value of the bonds. This was a sum well over the entire income of the best year the road had yet experienced. Such an expense added to its burdens would have made the situation impossible.

By 1908, of course, there was growing evidence that the Santa Fe Central was going to do little better in the future than in the past, and the management began to look for sources of additional revenue. The long idle Albuquerque Eastern project still looked good. The revenues from the potential coal traffic were still attractive, and a connection with Albuquerque could have a profound effect on revenues in the Estancia Valley. The right-of-way had been obtained, construction was partially complete and, perhaps most significantly, the original issue of first mortgage bonds remained unissued. All of these could be used to attract new investors. In his typical manner, Colonel Hopewell went east once more to Pennsylvania to see if he could find a willing investor. By the time September arrived he was ready to begin.

Derailments were not uncommon, and Section Foreman Perea's report of this one in 1907 tells management of the careful use he was making of company resources. (CRRM collection from Douglas C. Wornom)

The New Mexico Central Railroad

On the afternoon of September 3, 1908, the stockholders of the Santa Fe Central Railway met in Santa Fe to reorganize the company in accordance with Colonel Hopewell's as yet unrevealed plans. At the meeting, the stockholders voted to merge the Santa Fe Central and the Albuquerque Eastern into a single company to be called the New Mexico Central Railroad. Its capitalization was to be $5,000,000, a substantial increase over the combined capitalizations of the older companies. During the next few weeks a lot of behind-the-scenes activity took place to make it possible to put any new money invested in the project into new construction rather than old debts. It was stated publicly, of course, that the new company would assume all the debts of the old companies. The next move was the incorporation of the New Mexico Central Railroad in New Mexico Territory on September 21, 1908. The officers of the company included some new names: president, Robert Law, Denver; vice-president, Willard S. Hopewell, Santa Fe; secretary, James Arrott, Pittsburgh; treasurer, Francis J. Torrance, Pittsburgh. The directors of the company, in addition to the above, included Theodore A. Miller, Pittsburgh; E. W. Dobson, Albuquerque; and Charles F. Easley, Santa Fe.

In the press release announcing the officers and details of the new company, the name of A. L. Richmond appeared for the first time. Richmond was president of the Dominion Construction Company of Pittsburgh, and he was the man with whom Colonel Hopewell had been dealing behind the scenes. According to records that became public years later, Hopewell and Richmond had agreed verbally to the terms of a contract that provided for the construction of the Albuquerque and Hagan branches by the Dominion Construction Company. The work was to be paid for by New Mexico Central securities in these amounts: $1,000,000 face value of five percent first mortgage gold bonds, $1,200,000 face value of second mortgage gold bonds, and 22 shares of stock of par value $100. Regular monthly payments of the securities were to be made based on the amount of construction actually completed. The contract remained unsigned during 1908, but Richmond and his forces began work as agreed.

Troubles dogged the New Mexico Central literally from the very day of its creation. On that day, the district court in Santa Fe found against the railroad in a case for damages resulting from personal injuries suffered by one Harry S. Friday while performing his duties as a brakeman. The court awarded Friday a whopping $50,000, an amount equal to about half the railroad's annual revenues. There was apparently no appeal, and the New Mexico Central had to assume the debt. They began to pay Friday off on an installment plan, and the greater part of the award was actually paid during the next year. From this hardly encouraging beginning, the affairs of the New Mexico Central went from bad to worse.

The mainline from Santa Fe to Torrance continued in operation much as before. The mixed train daily came and went, powered by the collection of antique locomotives. Revenues fell noticeably in 1908 and 1909, but expenses stayed about the same, resulting in substantial deficits. Colonel Hopewell's plans to sell the New Mexico Central securities rapidly dissipated in these circumstances.

In the meantime, the Dominion Construction Company worked enthusiastically on the branch lines, especially the one to Hagan. Two construction locomotives owned by the New Mexico Central were in use, and a large steam shovel was purchased. It was of the same type and size as those then working on the Panama Canal. Many men and dozens of teams were working along the route as well. By the end of 1908 the Hagan line was almost entirely graded, lacking only the completion of some cuts just south of Hagan. The mines had been refurbished and were ready to produce as soon as rails were laid. The Albuquerque line ran into heavy work in Tijeras Canyon, and the work proceeded slowly. A few earthworks were completed, but little of the rock work seems to have started. In terms of miles, most of the line was graded, but not in connected sections.

The form of the new branches was amply clear by this time. Track laying had begun again northwest of Moriarty. At the junction of Frost, a great wye on high fills was laid out. The line to Hagan continued northward in easy country. The resultant railroad would have had reasonable grades, and the coal trains would have been easy to handle.

The route to Albuquerque was, in contrast, a very rugged affair. There was a climb from Frost to a summit in Gutierrez Canyon, and then the line dropped down into Tijeras Canyon on a steady grade varying from one to four percent all the way to Albuquerque. Some of the curves would have been quite sharp. As the route broke out of the mountains above Albuquerque, the grade continued on a steady four percent, which could have been reduced only through great sweeping curves. The line was actually graded on the shortest and steepest route across the mesa leading down to the Rio Grande. Operation of all but the lightest of trains on this line would have required helper locomotives all the way from Albuquerque to Gutierrez Canyon, a considerable expense.

By early January 1909, about 8¾ miles of track had been laid westward from Moriarty, but only about two miles had been ballasted and surfaced. This was destined to be the extent of work completed, for on January 7 proceedings of involuntary bankruptcy were filed in Pittsburgh against A. L. Richmond. Hopewell had gotten warnings of this, and he hurried to Pittsburgh to head off this disaster. The long-unsigned contract was hastily brought up to date and signed on January 6, 1909, giving Richmond a valid claim on the New Mexico Central. During January, Hopewell scrambled about trying to find still another willing investor, as well as trying to clear up the problems involved in exchanging the Santa Fe Central securities for those of the new company. Throughout January and into February Hopewell reverted to his old style of frequent and wildly optimistic press releases. According to these, the Hagan line was to be in use within 60 days, and the New Mexico Central was surveying a line from Moriarty to Tucumcari. None of this, of course, came to pass. When Richmond presented his next monthly statement for payment, the New Mexico Central could not pay. Richmond shut down the construction work immediately. Quickly, the two construction trains were returned to the New Mexico Central, and the remaining equipment, including the big steam shovel, was put into storage at Moriarty. No further work would ever be done on the Albuquerque Eastern.

A great deal of confusion has arisen over the years about the Albuquerque Eastern and its construction. Sometimes termed a "paper railroad," the it actually built quite a lot of roadbed and track, the cost of which led directly to the bankruptcy of the New Mexico Central. An authentic statement of the construction accomplished was contained in a consulting engineer's report dated August 15, 1911:

> . . . Grading was commenced and completed (from Moriarty) to Frost, 18 6/10 miles. From Frost to Hagan 11 of the 14 miles have been graded. From Frost West an additional mile was graded and from Albuquerque East 12 miles were graded—all with a 14 foot crown—a total of 31 6/10 miles of the 44 on the Albuquerque Branch and 11 of the 14 miles on the Hagan Branch. The country through which the line runs is mountainous and the part not graded on the Albuquerque Branch is through the Tijeras Canyon in the Sandia Range of mountains. The bridges in the graded portion have all been put in and are in good shape. (There is) a maximum grade of 2.1%. I would recommend that this be cut down as much as possible. About 3/4 of a mile of track from the Moriarty end was laid with old 56 lb. rails and fastenings, and 8 miles of track on the same end laid with new 70 lb. rails and fastenings, 3,000 ties to the mile. About 2 miles of track are surfaced and lined, and about 1 3/4 miles filled and ready for surfacing—the balance laid on top of the grade. Ties are fully spiked and rails spliced and fully bolted—while much of the material is on the ground.

Hopewell continued to try to sell the New Mexico Central bonds. In April 1909 an attempt was made to sell them by using the coal mines and other lands of the New Mexico Fuel & Iron Company as security. This attempt, too, failed. It was during this period that the holders of the old Santa Fe Central bonds must have started to look closely at the deteriorating situation. The railroad's traffic had dropped, the new construction was of little value, and the only visible assets were the tracks and trains of the railroad itself.

The financial returns for the year ending June 30, 1909, did not reassure anyone. To obtain revenue of $92,166, the road incurred expenses of $107,401. And, as before, no interest whatsoever was paid on the bonds. This information became public late in 1909, by which time the many creditors and the current bondholders, with the Pittsburgh Trust Company as trustee, were becoming very restless. It was only a matter of time until one party or another made a move to recover his investment from the remaining assets of the company.

Only one noteworthy change in the operating habits of the New Mexico Central occurred during 1909. Early on the morning of March 1 the old D&RG enginehouse at Santa Fe burned to the ground. The fire damaged a locomotive and destroyed a carload of coal and one nearby shed. The D&RG moved temporarily into the New Mexico Central's primitive facilities. This relationship pointed up the fact that the D&RG was the only friendly connection to the north, and that a lot of traffic was exchanged in spite of the break of gauge.

The problems of the New Mexico Central simmered along until coming to a head on January 10, 1910. On that day a suit was filed in district court in Santa Fe by the Independent Steel & Wire Company asking that the road be placed in receivership and its assets disposed of for the benefit of its

NEW MEXICO CENTRAL RAILROAD COMPANY

PASS

Mr. E. A. Hornbeck
General Manager
S. D. & C. Ry.

UNTIL DECEMBER 31 ST 1910 UNLESS OTHERWISE ORDERED

No. 178 *Halein*

GENERAL MANAGER

The SD&C was the San Diego & Cuyamaca, a predecessor of the San Diego & Arizona Eastern. (CRRM collection)

Here is the essence of the New Mexico Central: No. 6 with a single combine on dirt ballasted track during a late afternoon pause somewhere in the lonely Estancia Valley about 1915. (Anna L. Hase photo, Museum of New Mexico 14916)

creditors. Independent was a Pittsburgh firm, and the railroad owed it $12,000. This suit proved to be the opening of Pandora's box for the New Mexico Central, for there were many claimants scrambling for position in the sharing of the property. A recounting of some claims reveals something of the road's problems: Hicks Car & Locomotive Works, $5,000; Harry S. Friday, $9,000 remaining of his injury award; Robert Law (former president of the New Mexico Central), $21,000 in back salary. Law was also suing for some $50,000 in undelivered securities. This claim suggests that he had invested in the railroad. It also hints that those unissued New Mexico Central bonds had been promised to a lot of people.

Acting on the application of the Independent Steel & Wire Company, the judge placed the New Mexico Central Railroad in receivership on January 10, 1910. A receiver was appointed in the person of Charles C. Murray, former treasurer of the company. He was to operate and maintain the railroad under the direction of the court. He was to maintain the status quo, and had only limited powers to make the purchases necessary to operate the property. If authorized by the court, he could make other purchases and pay for them. If necessary and the court so authorized, he could issue "receiver's certificates" which were promises to pay at a future time. From this point on, the affairs of the New Mexico Central were very much a matter of public rather than private interest.

Through the years of the receivership, the activities of the New Mexico Central took place in two contrasting spheres. On the one hand, the railroad ran much as always. Deficits were the rule, although occasional small surpluses were reported. Only the most necessary repairs were made to the aging equipment and trackage. There was a gradual increase in small accidents and derailments, but trains were both light and slow so nothing serious occurred. On the other hand, the initial court action resulting in receivership brought forth a veritable snowstorm of foreclosure suits and countersuits, claims of all sorts and counterclaims. Each action claimed priority over the others, which revealed essentially that the securities of the several companies had been either promised or handed about rather freely. The conflicts were now up to the court to decide.

The mixed train schedule was adjusted in 1910 to require only one set of equipment. A fresh train crew left Estancia about noon and ran south to Torrance. After turning and picking up any freight cars, the train ran north to Santa Fe, with a running time for the 115.7 miles of five hours 40 minutes. The train and crew laid over for the night at Santa Fe and returned to Estancia the next morning. A second crew took over at Estancia and continued the cycle. Locomotives could be changed at Estancia as needed on either the northbound or southbound run. There was usually a spare locomotive in steam if needed. It was used on any extra trip down to Torrance to handle a freight movement.

During these years the New Mexico Central managed to run using its six old locomotives. About 25 men were employed at Estancia, ranging from one or two machinists to common laborers. The shop crew frequently went out as extra trainmen when the regular men laid off or when an extra was needed.

In early February 1911 the little Cottage Hotel at Torrance burned to the ground. It was reported that the fire left only one building remaining at the junction—the two story depot. After about three months the hotel was rebuilt, as it was necessary for the use of passengers and trainmen.

80

On Friday, June 30, 1911, the railroad earned a headline in the Estancia *News* after a bad week:

HOODOO DAY — The N.M.C. had a bad day of it Sunday, not merely because the wind blew a little, but apparently it was as bad as "Friday the 13th." The northbound train left Torrance late on account of the Rock Island being late. Arriving at Willard their engine was found in bad order, the flues leaking badly. By pushing and pulling and carrying water in pails from the water tank on the train, the crew managed to get within a few miles of Estancia before the engine died. Conductor Friday cut in on the wire and asked Estancia to send another engine. The engine brought the train in several hours late.

On the return trip at night, some place near Stanley, the rails spread, derailing the engine. Again Estancia had to be called for another engine and assistance to get back on the track. After a hard and strenuous time the train reached Estancia about two o'clock yesterday morning.

As the train pulled in from Torrance yesterday morning, the track was seen to be ablaze north of the roundhouse. The light engine ran up and using water from the engine extinguished the blaze before much damage was done, more than burning some ties. The rails were saved.

This was an unusual week, but the incidents were typical of the New Mexico Central's way of life. The trains always managed to get through, even if a few hours late.

By the end of 1911, however, the motive power situation had become serious, and receiver Murray was convinced that some "new" locomotives were necessary. During January 1912 Master Mechanic E. N. Peden went to Chicago to buy what he could. He returned in about three weeks, having found two suitable ten-wheelers. The locomotives followed, arriving at Estancia early in March. Numbered 7 and 8, they were the first new locomotives on the road since 1903. In truth they were not much younger than the locomotives they were to replace, but they were heavier and much better suited to the work on the line. As soon as they were made ready they took over practically all the work on the railroad.

Business increased substantially during late 1911 and 1912, with the road showing a surplus of $8,595 for 1912. A few of the rapidly rotting ties were replaced as one result. In mid-1912 the San Pedro mines opened after a long shutdown, increasing the traffic at Stanley. The daily train frequently hauled an extra passenger car during this period. But it was not to last, and soon the New Mexico Central returned to its deficits.

One more locomotive was purchased, allowing retirement of the six original ones. Numbered 9, this was also an antique, a small 2-6-0 dating from the 1880s. It and the two purchased in 1912 took over all the work on the railroad. All the older locomotives were stored until finally sold for scrap in January 1916. By then only a few odd parts and a tender or two remained. Most of the old wooden freight cars had become battered and worn and had been retired to company service.

During the period of receivership, trackage, stations, fuel and water facilities, and bridges remained much as originally built. The original pine and pinon ties were beginning to wear out in quantity, but only the most essential replacements were made. Bridges were treated in the same manner, with only the most needed repairs being made. As long as traffic was light, and the old locomotives were used, the situation was satis-

In about the same era as the view on the opposite page, this train crew posed by No. 8's smokebox: Earl Angle, Paul Ellis, Jim Demuir and two unidentified comrades. (Howard Ogilvy collection)

The rusting and decrepit depot at Willard is seen on December 15, 1905, only three years after its construction. With its tin sheathing, it was nearly identical to its counterparts at Moriarty and Estancia. (Hal Crossley collection)

factory if a bit shaky in places. By 1915, the Estancia shop force was only four men. The whole railroad was rapidly becoming a testimonial to just how little it took to run a railroad in dry country.

One of the continuing problems in operating the New Mexico Central was in dealing with snowdrifts each winter. Snow was infrequent, but cuts were kept filled by continual winds. The sun would partially thaw the accumulation each day, and each night it would freeze anew. The ultimate result was a cut filled with ice and hard snow. Each winter had its incidents of stalled trains, delayed mail, and hungry passengers and crew. For years the railroad had bucked snow with engine pilots and men using shovels. But late in 1915 Master Mechanic Charles Gutterman journeyed to Colorado, where he purchased a large iron snowplow which he mounted on the front end of No. 8. This helped a lot, but the cuts still gave trouble. The worst spots were the deep cut south of Moriarty, a few places south of Progresso and occasionally near Santa Fe.

Another regular problem was that of washouts. Melting snow in the spring and late summer thunderstorms caused

flash floods that could easily weaken or remove a trestle in a matter of minutes. Usually the slow moving trains stopped in time, but once in a while an engine nosed down into a deep arroyo.

While running the railroad during the years of the receivership was a matter of doing with as little as possible, the activities of the creditors and the courts arguing over the New Mexico Central's remains amounted to a circus. The civil docket of the district court at Santa Fe contains page after page listing complaints, suits, replies, decisions, appeals and more decisions from January 1910 until the final determination was ordered by the wartime United States Railroad Administration in January 1918. The following is a brief account of the progress of the railroad's affairs in the courts.

It was in January 1910 that the New Mexico Central Railroad Company was placed in receivership on the basis of a request by one of many creditors. Charles C. Murray, the road's treasurer, was appointed to operate the line as receiver. In June the Pittsburgh Trust Company filed suit as trustee, requesting that it be authorized to foreclose its mortgage on the road. It held some $2,000,000 in face value of the Santa

82

Fe Central bonds. A few days later a cross-complaint was filed by the Dominion Construction Company, which alleged a first and prior claim on the railroad property because of its contract to construct the Albuquerque and Hagan branches in return for payment in the form of specified securities. Subsequently, most of the minor claimants entered their claims with the court. These represented mostly unpaid bills and the like.

This controversy was continued in the court through the middle of 1912. In late July, having become completely inundated in conflicting claims, the court appointed a special master and referee to investigate and hold hearings to determine the facts and the law in the matter. Lorin C. Collins was the man appointed to this unenviable task. It was not an easy job.

After nearly a year of investigations and hearings, Collins released his reports during 1913. He determined that the Pittsburgh Trust Company, through ownership of the Santa Fe Central first mortgage bonds, had a first lien on the railroad. He further held that the mortgage was in default because neither the interest nor the principal had been paid as required by the bonds. The court agreed and ordered the public sale of the former Santa Fe Central property.

There were a couple of surprises hidden in the legal verbiage of the Collins reports. One was that the long forgotten Albuquerque Eastern bonds had been finally issued, and to none other than Charles C. Murray, wearing one of his many hats as receiver of the First National Bank of Allegheny. The bonds had been presented to the court as a claim in opposition to that of the Dominion Construction Company. The other surprise was the elimination of the Pennsylvania Development Company as a claimant for the Albuquerque Eastern. There was seemingly ample evidence that it had invested something, perhaps as much as $185,000, in construction of the railroad during 1902 and 1903. Nevertheless, Collins left no doubt in his findings that the contract between the New Mexico Central Railroad and the Dominion Construction Company was the prior and valid lien on the property. The court agreed with this finding, and the Albuquerque Eastern was also ordered sold at auction.

The sales took place as planned on the courthouse steps in Santa Fe, but one important participant was missing. That was a buyer. There were no bids for either property, and subsequent attempts at sales during 1914 produced the same result.

During this entire time there were continual rumors of the impending sale of the railroad—to Chicago bankers, to French capitalists and, not surprisingly, to the Santa Fe. The Chicago bankers made one inspection trip and were never heard from again. The French were understandably distracted by their country going to war. And the Santa Fe said nothing at all.

By December 31, 1914, Judge Abbott evidently had wearied of keeping track of Murray and his various receiverships and interests. On that day he appointed Ralph C. Ely to act as full time receiver of the New Mexico Central. The judge said in his ruling that the railroad had been neglected and allowed to deteriorate. That was a hard point to argue, but the blame was not all with the receiver.

An oddity of NMC's June 1916 *Official Guide* entry is the identification of the times 1215, 1240 and 1245 as "noon." Standard railroad procedure was to designate time through 1159 as "am," skip 1200 and show 1201 and later as "pm," with inverse designations around midnight. (CRRM collection)

Ely entered into his work with comparative enthusiasm, touring the railroad immediately and beginning the search for a buyer. His next move was to remove the last of the old "Santa Fe Central crowd" with the appointment of a new general counsel and a new assistant to the receiver. His campaign to find a buyer was a total failure. Aside from a couple of Dutch prospects who came over to view the property, there was little interest in the decrepit railroad. Ely had revived the idea of an extension toward the San Juan Basin, evidently to demonstrate the potential of the railroad.

In July 1916 the Pittsburgh Trust Company, still holding the Santa Fe Central bonds, began to petition the court to remove Ely as receiver. He was alleged to have neglected the railroad and to have spent too much money, among other complaints. The petitions now asked the court to permit abandoning the railroad and selling it for scrap. Ely remained in office, searching for the elusive buyer. And the railroad struggled on, with its three locomotives and its mixed train daily.

District Judge Holloman held a hearing in September 1917 on the latest petition to remove Ely. This time he replaced Ely with Ralph E. Twitchell, and he prohibited the sale of the railroad for the purpose of junking it. To allow this would leave hundreds of people in the Estancia Valley isolated, with few alternative means of transport. Roads were poor and motor vehicles were still curiosities. But agriculture was growing, with pinto beans becoming a major cash crop. Irrigation was just being tried out, and the prospects for farming looked good.

The affairs of the railroad took a sudden turn in October 1917. The old Santa Fe Central bonds had at last been sold. The new owner of the railroad was the Federal Export Company of New York. A new and improbable chapter in the story of the New Mexico Central was about to begin.

The New Mexico Central Railway

With the purchase of the valid and outstanding bonds of the Santa Fe Central Railway, the Federal Export Company acquired an enforceable first lien on the property of the New Mexico Central Railroad. This created a strong influence on the railroad, although as yet absolute control had not been established. The next move was to ask the district court to set a date for the foreclosure sale of the property. On October 4, 1917, Judge Reed Holloman did exactly the opposite, ordering Lorin C. Collins as special master to refrain from proceeding with the sale of the railroad.

It was presumed in Santa Fe that Holloman's purpose was to prevent anyone from purchasing the railroad in order to scrap it. Certainly, the times were favoring that sort of thing, with scrap steel prices high and a good market for railroad rail. The railroad remained vital to the Estancia Valley, which meant that the politics were right for continuing the operation of the railroad in spite of its losses.

The situation remained static, at least on the surface, until January 1, 1918. On that date the United States Railroad Administration (USRA) took over direct control of all railroads in the country by presidential proclamation. Almost immediately Judge Holloman reversed himself and ordered Collins to proceed with his duties in accordance with the proclamation.

During the next few weeks it became apparent that the new owners of the bonds had taken great pains to inform the USRA of the virtues of the New Mexico Central. A letter from their attorney in Albuquerque, Neill B. Field, printed in the local press revealed something of the nature of the effort. Field went on at length about the traffic in and out of the valley, and he introduced an entirely new source of revenue for the short line. He claimed that the Santa Fe could ship locomotive coal to the Belen cutoff from the northern New Mexico mines over the New Mexico Central far more cheaply than over its own lines. Not only was the net mileage less, but the journey over the short line avoided the congested yards at Albuquerque and Belen, as well as avoiding the long grade from Belen to Mountainair. (The New Mexico Central's own grade up to Williams was conveniently forgotten.) There must have been more to the argument than words and shaky logic, for in a short time it was apparent that preparations for the coal traffic were being made.

In the meantime, the date for the sale of the railroad was set for the afternoon of Tuesday, February 5, 1918. The appointed hour came, and Special Master Collins accepted the bids from the previously qualified parties. The successful bidder was the New Mexico Central Railway Company, newly organized by the Federal Export Company to operate its railroad. The bid was $300,000. The only other bid received was one for $275,000 from M. D. Radetzky of Den-

ver. Later in the same day, the Albuquerque Eastern property was auctioned for the benefit of the creditors of the Dominion Construction Company. It was obtained for $42,500 by Colonel D. B. Sellers of Albuquerque.

Even before the official sale of the New Mexico Central, orders had come down to Estancia to begin the desperately needed rehabilitation of the railroad. The trackage was the first order of business. Ties had rotted out in large numbers, cuts and fills had washed badly, and the bridges were universally old and weakened. Cleofes Romero received a contract early in February 1918 to cut and deliver 10,000 ties. Roadmaster Cunningham went to work installing the old turntable next to the shops at Estancia. The old steam shovel was ordered in from Moriarty for repairs, but these were halted when it was realized that it still belonged to the Albuquerque Eastern.

The new organization of the New Mexico Central Railway took over immediately following the sale. These were the officers and supervisory employees: president, S. C. Munoz; vice-president, A. F. Mack; treasurer, Fred L. Watson; secretary and general counsel, Franklin A. Wagner; counsel, Neill B. Field; solicitor and assistant secretary, Francis C. Wilson; general manager, C. A. Richardson; superintendent, E. E. Friday; chief surgeon, Dr. James A. Massie; cashier, J. S. Henderson; roadmaster, M. F. Cunningham; master mechanic, J. E. Brunk; storekeeper, Charles Munch.

General Manager Richardson journeyed to Denver where he purchased two badly needed locomotives. Both were eight-drivered types. A program of bridge renewal was begun, and all of the timber trestles between Kennedy and Willard were renewed and reinforced in anticipation of heavier loadings. A cistern for locomotive water was built at Williams, at the summit of the 3.2 percent grade up from Galisteo Creek. It was filled from water cars on an adjacent spur. The shop force was increased as rapidly as men could be induced to come to Estancia. By the end of February 15 men were at work.

The Albuquerque Eastern equipment and rails were sold by Colonel Sellars to the New Mexico Central during the month of March for $47,000, resulting in a neat $5,000 profit for the colonel. Included in the sale were about 15.5 track miles of rail and the big steam shovel. Once more repairs were ordered for the shovel, although it is said that it saw little if any subsequent use. The right-of-way and other real estate of the Albuquerque Eastern were sold for an undisclosed sum to Neill B. Field. Included was the choice terminal site near downtown Albuquerque as well as station sites along the route. And with these sales, the tale of the Albuquerque Eastern was ended at last.

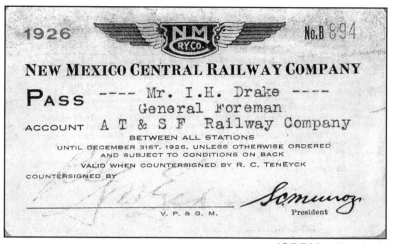

1926   No. B 894

NEW MEXICO CENTRAL RAILWAY COMPANY

PASS ---- Mr. I.H. Drake ----
General Foreman
ACCOUNT A T & S F Railway Company
BETWEEN ALL STATIONS
UNTIL DECEMBER 31ST, 1926, UNLESS OTHERWISE ORDERED
AND SUBJECT TO CONDITIONS ON BACK
VALID WHEN COUNTERSIGNED BY R. C. TENEYCK
COUNTERSIGNED BY

V. P. & G. M.   President

(CRRM collection)

Work on rebuilding the New Mexico Central slowed only briefly in August 1918 when the Estancia storehouse, shop office and water tank burned to the ground. The vital shops themselves were saved. New facilities were completed within a month. In the meantime water was obtained at Torrance from the El Paso & Southwestern's pipeline. Later in the year a work train was kept busy installing the newly cut ties.

Rolling stock received its necessary attention during 1918, too. Of the locomotives, No. 7 had been overhauled and was in good order by November 1917. No. 8 had a burned crown-sheet and was permanently removed from service in early 1918. No. 9 was in good condition and was used regularly on the lighter trains. The two new locomotives were numbered 5 and 6. The locomotives previously carrying these numbers had been junked in 1916. No. 5 was of the uncommon 4-8-0 wheel arrangement, and was a powerful locomotive with low

drivers. No. 6 was of the much more common 2-8-0 type and was equally powerful. Both of the new engines were substantially heavier than their predecessors and were considered very useful by management. The two combination baggage-mail-passenger coaches used on the daily trains were refurbished and made much more presentable as far as passengers were concerned. The third passenger car, a full coach, was retained for the times of heavy traffic. Two of the older passenger cars had by this time been removed from their wheels and refitted as dwellings at Estancia. No particular work was done on the remaining freight cars at this time. Only a few were in regular use.

The Estancia shops did not change much, although they were noticeably busier. Late in 1918, a new acetylene welder was obtained, which speeded minor repairs considerably.

The following year, 1919, brought many changes to the

By 1920, desert vegetation already seemed to be reclaiming the main line as it reached to the northern horizon near Dyke, at the Puertecito de los Salados, the "hogbacks." (Museum of New Mexico 46252)

operation of the New Mexico Central. Although the rehabilitation work was still in progress, it had reached the point where the road was in shape to accept increased traffic. Before this actually occurred, the line was struck by a series of snowstorms. The track between Willard and Torrance was badly blocked in early January. The mail was delayed and trains ran only as far as Willard or Progresso for a week. The track to Santa Fe was snowed in, opened, then closed again by snow. By the middle of January, the line was open once more, but at the cost of an immense amount of hand labor. In the meantime, Master Mechanic Peden had returned from El Paso with yet another "new" locomotive, No. 10. This was quite modern for the New Mexico Central, having been built in 1902 for the El Paso & Northeastern. It had been rebuilt and kept in fine condition by that road's successor, the El Paso & Southwestern. It was by far the most powerful and most modern locomotive on the New Mexico Central. It came to its new owner over a detour through Vaughn and Willard because of the snow blockage. Later in January, the next master mechanic, Claude A. Smith, purchased another locomotive of the same type from the EP&SW. It became New Mexico Central 11.

Once the snow blockage was broken, the New Mexico Central published a new timetable, one showing a substantial increase in train activity with a daily passenger train and a coal train supplementing the mixed train.

A major battle to break a snow blockade is taking place on February 8, 1919. El Paso & Southwestern 2-8-0 No. 256 and NMC No. 10 have come to the rescue of dead No. 8 two miles south of Moriarty. One of the engines *(right)* had an extra water tender. Blowing snow kept filling the cuts, in spite of the efforts of a large shoveling crew on the flatcars. (Herman Maxwell photos)

		New Mexico Central Railway Time Table		
Southbound			**Northbound**	
No. 72	No. 2		No. 1	No. 71
8:00 am	11:00 am	Santa Fe	9:45 am	3:20 pm
9:22 am	12:01 pm	Kennedy	8:40 am	1:50 pm
10:55 am	1:00 pm	Stanley	7:40 am	1:00 pm
11:40 am	1:30 pm	Moriarty	7:08 am	12:01 pm
11:59 am	1:52 pm	McIntosh	6:45 am	11:25 am
12:35 pm	2:15 pm	Estancia	6:25 am	11:00 am
1:10 pm	2:40 pm	Willard	5:55 am	10:05 am
1:50 pm	3:13 pm	Progresso	5:20 am	9:25 am
2:35 pm	3:50 pm	Cedarvale	4:47 am	8:38 am
3:20 pm	4:30 pm	Torrance	4:15 am	8:00 am

Passenger daily, going north No. 1, going south No. 2.

No. 71, local freight, will go north on Tuesday, Thursday, and Saturday.

No. 72, local freight, will go south on Monday, Wednesday and Friday.

The coal train will run as an extra when required, with no regular schedule, but as a rule leaves Estancia early in the morning, returning in the evening.

All trains will carry passengers.

(Estancia *News-Herald*, January 30, 1919)

The passenger train was generally made up of two cars, one of the combines and the full coach. It carried the mail, which was worked on the train by a clerk. Engines 5 and 9 shared the passenger duties equally. The local freight also accommodated passengers, carrying them in the remaining combine.

The coal train proved to be a most interesting operation. The New Mexico Central had indeed obtained a somewhat grudging contract from the AT&SF to handle coal shipments from Kennedy to Willard. This was profitable traffic, although it did require a large expense for rehabilitation, later estimated at about $100,000. The coal traffic varied from a minimum of eight cars to as many as 33 per day.

In practice, the passenger and the local freight were run about as scheduled. The coal train left Estancia almost every morning, with one or two of the heavier locomotives taking the empties north to Kennedy. There they would turn on the new wye and assemble the train of loaded coal cars. Departing on their southbound journey, the locomotives would labor up the increasing grade until they stalled. Then they would leave part of the train, taking what they could haul on the ruling 3.2 percent grade. At the summit, they would set out the loads on the Williams spur, take water from the cistern, and return for another cut of cars. Doubling the train was routine, and tripling was common enough, for even the largest locomotives, Nos. 10 and 11, were rated at only six cars each on the ruling grade. Following the climb, the trains were reassembled and moved to Willard during the afternoon and evening. At Willard, they would set out the loads and pick up the available empties. And then they would return to Estancia to tie up for the night.

The coal train was a severe test of the New Mexico Central. Constant attention to locomotives and track was necessary, and the crews put in long arduous days. Of course, any interruption would be noticed immediately by the Santa Fe. The large road was not too enthusiastic about handing over this traffic to the New Mexico Central, but they had no choice if the USRA so ordered. The Santa Fe reasoned, with justification, that their own local freights could move the coal with little added expense, since they were run anyway for other traffic.

The rehabilitation of the New Mexico Central continued through 1919. New ties were constantly being installed, and a work train was frequently out on the line. In March a new American ditcher outfit was purchased to do the heavy work on the cuts and fills. The outfit included the ditcher and two dump cars. The New Mexico Central had no flat car heavy enough to carry the ditcher, essentially a steam shovel carried on cartop rails, so a 40-foot steel car was rented from the Michigan Central. It had been the car on which the ditcher was shipped from the builder.

Three used cabooses were obtained in Colorado, possibly from the recently abandoned Colorado Midland. When the ditcher was on the line, its crew was housed in two of these cars. The third was used on the coal train.

Unfortunately the passenger train did not attract enough business to warrant the expense of its daily trip. On June 11, 1919, run was eliminated, and the road reverted to the mixed train three times a week. The train ran on a schedule designed to connect with mainline trains at Kennedy and Willard on the Santa Fe, and at Torrance on the EP&SW. Relatively few passengers went all the way to Santa Fe, and the connections were considered more important. Mail was received at Torrance, so that connection took precedence. It was announced at the same time that the coal train would continue to carry passengers, but that it might not run every day.

A coal chute was built at Estancia during 1919. This was of the old style trestle type, but it permitted rapid refueling of the passenger train and the coal train, even if coal had to be shoveled into the pockets by hand. A track scale was installed at Estancia, a great convenience for shippers.

Throughout 1919 minor derailments continued. One or two were attributed to spreading rails and soft ground in wet weather. One such incident in March took place in a cut filled with melting snow south of Moriarty. It took three days to rerail three cars of coal. In the meantime, stub trips were run from each end of the line, exchanging passengers and mail at the site of the derailment.

Occasionally the New Mexico Central would borrow rolling stock from the EP&SW. Now that the short line's track was up to a certain standard, EP&SW's two smaller 2-8-0 classes, similar to the 10 and 11 locomotives, could be safely used. The availability of additional powerful locomotives was especially helpful when one of the coal train engines was in the shop or when snow blocked the line. Passenger cars also were borrowed when heavy loads were carried. These were typically baseball excursions to Santa Fe or specials for the state fair in Albuquerque.

During 1920 and 1921, a number of service improvements were made. In mid-1920 a peddler car service was begun in conjunction with the AT&SF. The car, containing shipments of fresh meat and fruits as well as non-perishable freight, would start out at Las Vegas, New Mexico. It would travel to Lamy and Santa Fe over the AT&SF, then south over the New Mexico Central until it was empty. This eliminated the transfer at Kennedy, which sometimes involved a wait from Friday until Monday.

By 1930 automobiles dominated downtown Moriarty, and steps had been taken to accommodate them. The Estancia Valley store advertised tourist supplies, and the sign between the gasoline pumps at the Moriarty garage read "CAMP-CABINS." Wooden planks have been installed at the railroad crossing in the foreground. (Hal Crossley collection)

Between 1920 and 1926 NMC itself used a variation of automotive technology in the form of this Mack rail motor car. Alec Booth is in the doorway, with Bill Allan in a nonchallant pose, at Santa Fe prior to beginning the 116-mile southward journey. D&RGW 3316 is in a cut of narrow gauge boxcars in the background. (George Law photo, Museum of New Mexico)

A similar arrangement occurred with the EP&SW. A car loaded for New Mexico Central points was scheduled out of Kansas City three times a week. It would move directly to Torrance before being opened for local work northward on the New Mexico Central.

The lack of a daily mail train caused some criticism of the railroad in the Estancia Valley. Mail delays became common with the connection at Torrance. During 1920 the railroad began investigating means of providing daily service without the expense of a steam train with its five person crew. This was the beginning of the motor era, and it was rumored at Estancia that the railroad was looking into the possibility of running a gas car. At the same time there was talk in Albuquerque of starting a truck line between Albuquerque, Estancia and Mountainair. On October 12, the New Mexico Central's answer to criticism over the mail and motor trucks

made its first trip. The new vehicle was a Mack rail motor car, a product of the International Motor Company of Allentown, Pennsylvania, with a body built by J. G. Brill, better known as a streetcar builder. Accommodations included a passenger compartment with straight-back seats, a rear baggage room, and a tiny dry-hopper toilet compartment. A big coal stove was installed in recognition of the severe high plains winters.

Operated by a two person crew, the motor supplemented the steam mixed train. On days when the steam train ran north, the motor ran south, and vice versa. Carrying passengers, mail, express and small freight shipments, it could do anything the steam train could except move carload freight. The motor was featured prominently in advertising of the EP&SW as a through connection for Santa Fe in conjunction with the *Golden State Limited*. It is not a matter of record what impres-

Form No. I-1.

New Mexico Central Railway Company

AUTHORITY FOR EXPENDITURE

Authority for an expenditure of $ 609.28 is requested for the purpose of

Concreting Turntable Base and Pit Estancia, N. M.
(Character of change.)

to the property of New Mexico Central Railway Company
(Name of owner.)

that is now operated by New Mexico Central Railway Company
(Name of operating company.)

Santa Fe, N. M. January 1, 1919.
(Place and date.)

Sol Slayback Supt. B&B.
(Name.)   (Title.)

Location of proposed project: State New Mexico   Valuation Section NM 1

Station or M. P. _____   Division _____

Description of project: Concreting Turntable Base and Pit Estancia, N. M.

Reasons and necessity for the extension, improvement, or other change: Old Table falling in

SUMMARY OF ESTIMATE

Estimated gross cost of project	$ 609.28
Amount chargeable to operating expenses for property retired	$
Value of salvage recovered	$
Cost of property retired	$
Incidental costs chargeable to operating expenses	$
To other accounts	$
Net charge to property investment account #20	$ 609.28

Total cost to be borne by New Mexico Central Railway Company
(Name of company.)

or participated in by _____
(Name all participants and amount borne by each.)

Recommended: _J. Somes_
(Name.)   (Title.)

Recommended: _____
(Name.)   (Title.)

Expenditure and change approved and authorized:

R. E. McGwy
(Name.)   (Title.)

Recorded and registered:

Theo. Daughters _Audr_
(Name.)   (Title.)

REFERENCES				
A. F. E.				D. C. E. reference
Date	Number	State	Valuation section	
1/1/19	35	NM	NM1	15

NMC's corporate procedures were as complex as those of any major railroad. Four signatures were required to approve repair of the deteriorating turntable pit at Estancia. (CRRM collection, from Douglas C. Wornom)

sion the spartan gas car left with passengers stepping off the luxurious limited at the deserted junction of Torrance.

By the end of 1921 the New Mexico Central was in pretty good physical condition. The coal trains continued to run regularly, bringing in needed revenue. The general freight business had been good, since the pinto bean crop had greatly increased to meet the needs of the war. Although local traffic was a disappointment due to the spectacular increase in the number of automobiles, the motor car provided an answer to the problem of providing adequate train service.

During 1920 the railroads had been returned to the control of their owners, and the accounts settled. The New Mexico Central received a payment of $164,309.50 for various unreimbursed expenses incurred during government control. This payment helped considerably, but it in no way turned the railroad into a money maker. The physical property had been thoroughly rehabilitated by the end of 1921, but the account books told a different story. From 1918 through 1921, no year had shown a loss of less than $34,295. The loss in 1919 alone exceeded $200,000, and the total loss for the period was $239,879 even after the government payment.

By this time it was obvious that the owners had invested a great deal more in the railroad than they had received in revenue. They had purchased the bonds and the railroad for about $410,000. Subsequently, they had rebuilt the line for about $360,000, of which about $100,000 was estimated to be necessary for increasing the capacity of the road for the coal trains. The road was now in good condition, the coal train was running regularly and the local traffic situation, although not encouraging, was under control.

But there were difficulties and problems facing the New Mexico Central, gathering like thunderheads on the horizon. The Estancia Valley was hard hit by the drought of 1921. There was a general economic depression in the Southwest, and many formerly prosperous businesses failed. In the following years the depression was reinforced by an extended dry spell, something that can be expected in arid regions. All of this had its effect on the railroad, reducing local freight and passenger revenues nearly to the vanishing point. This was overshadowed during 1921 by the continuing coal train revenue, but that was not to last.

In 1922, facing problems of its own, the Santa Fe suddenly and substantially reduced the rate it was willing to pay for the coal haulage. The wartime peak of traffic had long passed, and the large system no doubt felt that it could handle its own coal on trains already running. It was a persuasive argument, at least to the Santa Fe, and the coal trains disappeared from the New Mexico Central. From this point on, the line reverted once more to its old role as a marginal agricultural hauler, now in a time of drought and depression.

Management did not simply accept the situation and roll along to final bankruptcy. It attacked on two fronts, one against the Santa Fe and the other to expand revenue producing capabilities. Both efforts were made, unfortunately, before the Interstate Commerce Commission, then as now a slow moving bureaucracy with sometimes hidden motives and purposes.

During July 1922, the New Mexico Central presented a complaint to the ICC alleging that the lower rate offered by the Santa Fe was in fact below the cost of hauling it on any railroad and was far below the tariff charged the public for such service. The company further alleged that, in view of the crop failures in Torrance County, it would be forced out of business unless the rate was increased. The ICC heard the complaint in July. In December its referee filed a recommendation that the suit be dismissed. The New Mexico Central counter-attacked, but it was not until January 1924, a year later, that the ICC permitted a rehearing of the matter.

During February the attack was carried directly to the Santa Fe. President Munoz met with W. C. Reid, attorney for the AT&SF, to talk over the affair. Munoz claimed that New Mexico Central could haul the coal more cheaply than the Santa Fe could and still make a profit. Santa Fe management obviously believed otherwise. Staying on the offensive, Munoz reminded Reid that the New Mexico Central had been the first railroad through Willard and had the legal right-of-way at the crossing with the busy Belen Cutoff. Munoz let it be known that he was thinking of removing the gate that protected Santa Fe trains from those of the short line. This, in effect, meant that each and every Santa Fe train would have to stop, look out for New Mexico Central trains and then flag across the diamond crossing. With four passenger trains and upward of 20 freights a day, this meant a considerable expense in stops and delays on the mainline. Late in 1924, the ICC again refused to consider the complaint, and the matter was considered closed. Munoz, of course, realized the futility of further wrangling with the Santa Fe and forgot his threat to change the crossing gate.

In the meantime, the New Mexico Central had begun the second part of its attack. It applied to the ICC in June 1923 for permission to construct an extension north of its Santa Fe terminal into the Gallinas area of Rio Arriba County, still in New Mexico. The route was to follow the Rio Grande to the Rio Chama, then follow the latter to a point where the line headed west toward Gallina. The line could then be built on into the San Juan Basin. The application was accompanied by a wildly optimistic description of the agricultural and mining potential of the district. Colonel Hopewell would have been proud of his successors!

In its fashion the ICC deliberated on the application. Months passed, and in January 1924 the examiner assigned to the case announced his decision to recommend to the commission that it refuse authority to build the extension. There was an immediate outcry from both the New Mexico Central and the state government. The ICC reopened the case.

During 1924 hearings were held at Santa Fe, and much favorable comment was heard about the extension, especially from those who were not paying for it. It was not until January 1925 that the ICC examiner once more recommended against the extension. The matter was placed before the full Commission in May 1925, and on July 7 a decision was handed down. This time the New Mexico Central won its point, and was granted permission to build. The ICC required, however, that construction begin on or before

New Mexico Central Railway Company

Time Table No. 6

TAKING EFFECT

Monday, December 3rd, 1923

AT 12:01 A. M.
"Mountain" Standard Time (105th Meridian)

DESTROY FORMER TIME TABLE

Each Train and Engine Man, while on duty, must have a copy of the Rules of the Operating Department.

For the Information and Government of Employes Only. The Company reserving the right to vary therefrom at pleasure.

Read Rules and Special Instructions Carefully. Important Changes have been made.

R. C. TEN EYCK,
Vice Pres. and Gen. Mgr.

T. C. SLAUGHTER,
Chief Train Dispatcher.

Extant NMC employee timetables are quite rare. The map on the last page of No. 6 implies, in typical short line fashion, that the 116-mile route is the key link in the transcontinental rail system. (author's collection)

BETWEEN SANTA FE AND TORRANCE

SOUTH BOUND trains have RIGHT of track over north bound trains of the same or inferior class.

Capacity of Sidings	SOUTH BOUND Second Class No. 72 Mixed Lv. Tuesday Thursday and Saturday	SOUTH BOUND First Class No. 2 Passenger Lv. Monday Wednesday and Friday	Distance From Santa Fe	Station Numbers	TIME TABLE No. 6 Tak'g Effect 12:01 A.M. December 3, 1923 STATIONS	Telegraph Signals	Distance From Torrance	NORTH BOUND First Class No. 1 Passenger Ar. Tuesday Thursday and Saturday	NORTH BOUND Second Class No. 71 Mixed Ar. Monday Wednesday and Friday	Water, Coal Wye, etc.	Altitude
	‖Lv. 9.35 AM	‖Lv. 10:45 AM	0	0	D SANTA FE	Go Z	115.7	‖Ar. 1:35 PM	‖Ar. 3:45 PM	CWT	7013
					1.1						
20	9:37	10:50	1.1	1	STOCK YARDS		114.6	1:27	3:37		
					0.5						
	f 9:41	f 10:52	1.6	2	CRANDALL STAT'N U. S. IND. SCHOOL		114.1	f 1:25	f 3:35		
					3.9						
14	f 9:50	f 11:00	5.5	5	DONACIANA		110.2	f 1:15	f 3:25		6616
					10.5						
10	f 10:20	f 11:25	16.0	16	VEGA BLANCA		99.7	f 12:45	f 2:50		6355
					5.8						
75	s‖ 10:45	s‖ 11:40	21.8	22	D KENNEDY	KY	93.9	s‖ 12:20	s‖ 2:25		6008
					6.1						
21	f 11:05	f 11:59	27.9	28	CLARK	CR	87.8	f 12:01 PM	f 2:00		6073
					5.5						
30	f 11:45	f 12:25 PM	33.4	33	WILLIAMS SPUR		82.3	f 11:45	f 1:35	W	
					7.4						
56	s‖¶ 12:10 PM 12:35	s‖¶ 12:45 1:05	40.8	41	STANLEY	BA	74.9	s‖ 11:25	s‖¶ 1:10 12:45		6317
					4.1						
6	f‖ 12:50	f 1:20	44.9	45	OTTO		70.8	f 11:10	f‖ 12:30		6204
					7.5						
48	s‖ 1:15	s‖ 1:40	52.4	52	MORIARTY	MY	63.3	s‖ 10:50	s‖ 12:10 PM		6204
					8.2						
18	f‖ 1:40	f 2:00	60.6	61	McINTOSH	MC	55.1	f 10:25	f‖ 11:35		6136
					3.5						
	f 1:50	f 2:10	64.1	64	ANTELOPE		51.6	f 10:15	f 11:25		6121
					4.4						
221	s‖ 2:40	s‖ 2:35	68.5	68	D ESTANCIA	AN	47.2	s‖ 10:05	s‖ 11:10	§ CWT	6093
					11.5						
40	s‖ 3:10	s‖ 3:05	80.0	80	D WILLARD	WD	35.7	s‖ 9:25	s‖ 9:45		6086
					11.7						
6	f‖ 3:45	f 3:35	91.7	92	PROGRESSO	PG	24.0	f 8:50	f‖ 9:05		6167
					7.5						
	f 4:05	f 3:55	99.2	99	BIANCA		16.5	f 8:30	f 8:45		6244
					5.5						
17	f‖ 4:30	s‖ 4:10	104.7	105	CEDARVALE	RO	11.0	s‖ 8:15	f‖ 8:30		
					3.9						
	f 4:40	f 4:20	108.6	109	CAMALEON		7.1	f 8:05	f 8:20		
					7.1						
45	‖Ar. 5:10 PM	‖Ar. 4:45 PM	115.7	116	D TORRANCE	X	0	‖Lv. 7:45 AM	‖Lv. 8:00 AM	CWY	6430
	Ar. Tuesday Thursday and Saturday	Ar. Monday Wednesday and Friday						Lv. Tuesday Thursday and Saturday	Lv. Monday Wednesday and Friday		
	7:35	6:00			115.7			5.50	7.45		

Texas Co. Spur Santa Fe connected at south end.
Santa Fe Stock Yards connected at north end.
Donaciana Siding connected at north end.
Vega Blanca Siding connected at north end.
Derail on south end new Passing Track at Kennedy.
Dyke Spur connected at south end.
Otto Siding connected at south end.
McIntosh Siding connected at north end.
Progresso Siding connected at south end.
Water three miles south of Stanley at Well 425.

Derail on main line 200 feet north of A. T. & S. F. crossing Santa Fe.

Wye one mile south of Kennedy.

No train will leave Santa Fe or Torrance without a clearance card.
Following signs placed opposite stations scheduled figure indicate:
"S"—Regular stop. "F"—Flag stop to receive or discharge passengers or freight. "¶"—Stop for meals. "D"—Day telegraph office. "N"—Night telegraph office only. "DN"—Day and Night telegraph office. "‖"—Trains will exchange U. S. Mail. "§"—Track Scales. "C"—Coal. "W"—Water. "Y"—Wye. "T"—Turntable

SPECIAL RULES AND REGULATIONS.

1. **Speed of Trains.** Trains must not exceed schedule time within the corporate limits of towns or cities.

Engines or trains backing up must not exceed 15 miles per hour.

Passenger Trains, when late must not exceed card time unless the conditions of track, weather, and all circumstances warrant their doing so with safety.

It is understood that Slow Orders are effective only so long as the necessity for their observance exists, but train or engine men should be particular to report at once defects observed in track or bridges.

2. **Crossing Rules.** Passenger Trains, Freight Trains, Yard or Light Engines, when approaching any railroad crossing or junction at grade, must be brought under control when passing the crossing sign 2,000 feet from the crossing (and sooner if necessary), and must invariably be brought to a full stop at the "Stop" sign, not less than 200 feet from the crossing or junction. Engineers will in no case start to cross the opposing track until the crossing is protected by Flagman, going ahead and standing on the crossing with a red flag by day and a red lamp by night to properly protect the train while using the crossing.

3. Enginemen must be particular to have the back dampers of their ash pans closed while running forward. When running backward reverse the dampers. Enginemen on work trains must watch this carefully. Enginemen must have their ash pans kept clean, carefully inspect them and have any defects remedied at once. When ash pans are cleaned, except in ash pits, fire MUST BE put out with water.

4. Engineers must know that switches are set properly before passing over them.

5. **Registering Stations.** Santa Fe, Estancia and Torrance.

6. All employes will be governed by standard rules applicable to their departments.

7. Bulletin books located at Santa Fe, Estancia and Torrance.

8. All freight for Crandall U. S. Indian School will be handled at Santa Fe Station.

9. All trains must approach Santa Fe stock yards carefully and know that switch is in proper condition before passing over.

10. North bound trains must stop at Williams and test air before descending Clark hill.

11. Crossing Gate at A. T. & S. F. Railroad crossing Willard set normally against New Mexico Central trains.

MEDICAL DEPARTMENT.

Dr. James A. Massie, Chief Surgeon_____Santa Fe, N. M.
Dr. E. L. Ward, Local Surgeon_____Santa Fe, N. M.
Dr. J. H. Wiggins, Local Surgeon_____Estancia, N. M.
Dr. W. C. Webber, Local Surgeon_____Moriarty, N. M.
Dr. Charles D. Ottosen, Local Surgeon_____Willard, N. M.
The Company Hospital (St. Vincents)_____Santa Fe, N. M.

Conductors will be held responsible for train emergency, medicine, chests and contents, and must examine same once a week and if medicines are required advise chief surgeon.

Form T. D. 37 must be made out in each instance by an authorized official when medical attention is required.

DR. JAMES A MASSIE, Chief Surgeon, Santa Fe, N. M.

GENERAL TIME AND WATCH INSPECTOR.

S. Spitz_____Santa Fe, N. M.

LOCATION OF STOCK YARDS

Clark	Santa Fe	Stanley	Moriarty	Estancia	Willard

CONNECTIONS.

At Santa Fe_____ { A. T. & S. F. Ry.
                       D. & R. G. W. R. R.
At Kennedy_____A. T. & S. F. Ry.

At Willard_____A. T. & S. F. Ry.
At Torrance_____E. P. & S. W. System

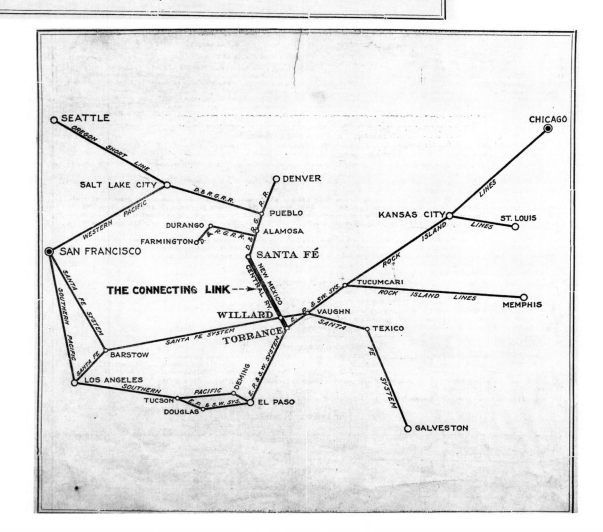

Practically all New Mexico Central facilities in Santa Fe can be seen in this early 1920s scene. The passenger station is to the rear behind the rambling wooden freight shed. The modified Ford sedan on the turntable is the general manager's inspection car. The stock cars on the left and caboose beyond the shed belong to the narrow gauge Chili Line of the Denver & Rio Grande Western. (Museum of New Mexico)

Stations and Facilities

During its construction the Santa Fe Central Railway (SFC) installed only the minimum facilities necessary to run the railroad. The ambitious and well-publicized program of construction presented by Colonel Hopewell stopped soon after the last rail was laid. A few facilities that had been built early in construction were removed and used elsewhere. Implicit in the following descriptions is a recognition of the severe limitations on operation caused by the cheap and temporary nature of almost all of the railroad's facilities.

SANTA FE, milepost 0.0, elevation 6,960
The SFC facilities were grouped around a five-track yard shared with the Denver & Rio Grande. Most of the track was laid with three rails to accommodate both standard and narrow gauge rolling stock. On the east side of the tracks were the depot, freight shed and the rudimentary engine terminal. On the west side were some narrow gauge spurs and the interchange track to the Atchison Topeka & Santa Fe yard.

The 24 x 100-foot passenger station was located at the north end of the yard between the tracks and Guadalupe Street. Although not a large structure, it included all the usual accommodations: waiting room, agent's office, telegraph operator's office and baggage room.

Bids for construction of the station were received during August 1903 and were opened on August 25. A. Winsor of Santa Fe was the low bidder at a price of $4,497.50. The contract included all the brick wall construction and interior finishing, but not the tile roof which was contracted separately. A brick platform completed the station. The total cost of building, furniture and platform was $8,500.

It was intended from the beginning that the depot be operated jointly with the D&RG, creating what was termed a "union station" for the city. There was a joint agreement dated November 1, 1906, between the SFC and D&RG regarding the depot, and references indicate that an earlier agreement established the entire terminal under joint ownership. The AT&SF, handling by far the greater traffic, ignored the whole affair and continued to maintain its own depot.

The 16 x 100-foot wood frame freight shed was south of the depot. It was set between two tracks, and the street side track was planked over to permit wagon loading as well. Next on the south was a spur track leading to a 70-foot center-bearing turntable set in a masonry pit with concrete foundations. A 36-foot, 60-ton track scale was installed nearby.

Although the SFC announced plans for a roundhouse and coaling dock, there is no evidence that they were ever built. Coaling was done by hand, the coal being shoveled from the 12x90 foot coal bunker into the locomotive tender spotted on the next track. This chore was one of the duties of the night engine watchman and any other available employee. Locomotives received water from a water column or standpipe located opposite the freight shed and between the first two yard tracks. The water was obtained from the Santa Fe city water supply, and was considered to be of good quality.

Other facilities included a tool house, a jitney shed for the roadmaster's Ford sedan rail car and an inspection pit. Off to the south were the 136 x 320-foot stock yards, which were served by three rail track.

CRANDALL, milepost 1.6
This was the station for the United States Indian School.

DONACIANA, milepost 5.5, elevation 6,658
A station building was placed here during the construction period, but by August 28, 1903, it had been moved to Estancia for use as the first school building. A few years later, it was taken to a farm and used as a barn. An eight-car spur was located at Donaciana.

VEGA BLANCA, milepost 16.0, elevation 6,370
Initially a 8,675-foot spur was built here to serve the Santa Fe Irrigation Company. This was later reduced to an eight-car capacity.

KENNEDY, milepost 21.8, elevation 6,020
A 12 x 22-foot freight shed, a box car depot and a 12 x 24-foot frame section house with 12 x 12-foot addition were built here initially. The early buildings were painted bright yellow. A 25-car capacity siding and an interchange track with the AT&SF also were built in the construction period. In 1907 a standard AT&SF 16 x 46-foot depot was built, the cost being shared by both carriers. Later additional sidings were laid down with a capacity of 75 cars. In 1919, a wye was completed some distance to the south to turn the coal train locomotives.

CLARK, milepost 27.9, elevation 6,110
A 62 x 128-foot stockyard and a 45-car capacity siding were built here. There was also a ramp to permit the dumping of wagons of coal into rail cars. The mine, called the Omara, was located a short distance to the west.

DYKE, milepost 30.3, elevation 6,240
A six-car spur was built here after the construction period, probably to provide a place for helper locomotives to wait. The name refers to the distinctive rock formation to the north, a layer of rock thrust vertically through the surface. The

tracks ran through an opening in the rock wall called Puertico de los Salados, or the hogbacks.

WILLIAMS, milepost 33.3, elevation 6,589
An 11-car siding was installed here at the crest of the steep grade from Galisteo Creek. In late 1918 or early 1919 a water cistern was dug in the ground just below the siding to serve coal train locomotives. The mainline was located in a deep cut below the cistern, allowing the tenders to be filled by gravity. The cistern itself was filled using water cars hauled in from Well 425. The short spur was extended to 30-car capacity for the water service. Between 1926 and 1931, the site was named Trahey after an AT&SF roadmaster.

STANLEY, milepost 40.8, elevation 6,334
A 56-car capacity siding, 32 x 64-foot stockyard and a 12 x 36-foot frame depot were built here. Stanley, named for a nearby rancher, was the shipping point for the San Pedro mines. A two-story hotel and a couple of stores served travelers, train crews and local residents alike. Stanley declined rapidly after the advent of good roads.

STATION 425, milepost 44.1, elevation 6,230
The only railroad facilities here were a well, a 20-foot windmill, a 50,000 gallon 24 x 16-foot wooden water tank and a standpipe. A 12 x 16-foot frame pumphouse was added later. This was the first locomotive water supply south of Santa Fe, a situation which required the use of water cars on all but the lightest trains.

OTTO, milepost 45.6, elevation 6,230
A short six-car capacity spur and a 34-foot boxcar depot were later additions to the railroad here.

MORIARTY, milepost 52.4, elevation 6,217
Initially a 30 x 51-foot frame depot with metal siding, warehouse, section house and a 48-car capacity siding served this active community. The town was named after Michael Timothy Moriarty, a well-known sheep rancher. The wye and construction yard of the Albuquerque Eastern Railway were located just north of town.

McINTOSH, milepost 60.6, elevation 6,145
Another of the promotional towns along the railroad, this site had a 30 x 51-foot frame depot with metal siding and an 18-car capacity siding. McIntosh disappeared with the coming of the automobile, but for a very brief time it rivaled Moriarty and Estancia.

ANTELOPE, milepost 64.1, elevation 6,121
Antelope was the location of the Pennsylvania Development Company's "cozy club house" and two flowing springs. There was no siding here.

ESTANCIA, milepost 68.5, elevation 6,107

Estancia was the operating headquarters of the railroad, and it grew to become the most important community along the route.

Colonel Hopewell planned an engine terminal and shop of spacious brick buildings for Estancia, including nine yard tracks, an 11-stall roundhouse with turntable, storehouse, office building and machine shop. None of these were built, although a 70-foot turntable was delivered in 1904. It was not installed until 1918.

The railroad facilities actually constructed at Estancia consisted of a number of simple frame and sheet iron buildings:

Depot, frame, 31 x 51 feet
Enginehouse, frame, 34 x 80 feet, two stalls with drop pit
Machine shop, frame, 30 x 60 feet, next to engine house
    Stationary engine, 10.5 x 16-inch cylinders
    Portable boiler and engine, 35 horsepower
    Engine lathe, 24-inch swing, 14-foot bed
    Shaper, 24-inch
    Bolt cutter, two-inch
    Drill press, 30-inch
    Pipe threading machine, one to six-inch
    Grinder, double 2.5 x 14-inch wheels
    Grindstone, 6 x 36 inch
    Forge and blower
    Air compressor, 11.5-inch locomotive type
Car shed, frame, 68 x 80 feet
Section house, frame 14 x 60 feet
Stockyards, 48 x 130 feet
Pump house, frame, 12 x 32 feet
Cistern, brick, 20-foot diameter, 16 feet deep
Water tank, wood, 24-foot diameter, 16 feet high,
    50,000 gallons capacity
Coal bins, frame, 12 x 60 feet and 25 x 28 feet
Store house, 30 x 48 feet
Sand house, frame, 16 x 16 feet

Trackage built included the main track, a long siding on either side of the depot, a house track, and spur tracks to the enginehouse and shop buildings. Total capacity was 221 cars. The turntable purchased in 1903 was finally installed in late 1918. Locomotives were coaled by hand for many years, but in 1919 a small pocket-type coal chute was installed. A nine-inch water column, located near the depot, supplied the locomotives.

The original storehouse, shop office and water tank burned to the ground during August 1918. They were quickly replaced with similar structures. By this time, two passenger cars had been retired from service and placed near the shops for use as dwellings. The station agent occupied one of them.

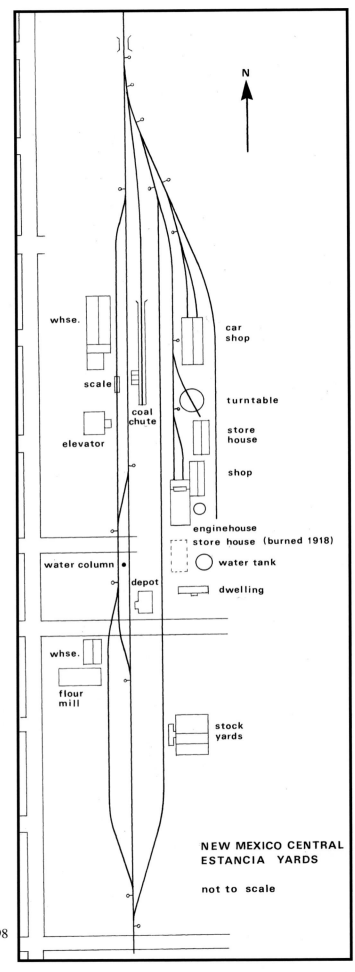

NEW MEXICO CENTRAL
ESTANCIA YARDS

not to scale

(top) Santa Fe Central was establishing its presence at Estancia about 1903. The depot is in the center, the watertank to the right and, between them, the beginnings of the shop building. (Museum of New Mexico, probably by Christian G. Kaadt) Not much had changed by the time of the September 1919 vista *(right)* looking north-northeast from an upper floor of the old flour mill. The depot is between a warehouse and the distant watertank, to the left of which sits the old Albuquerque Eastern steam shovel. (Herman Maxwell photo) Two years later *(bottom)*, looking back from the other side of the depot, we can see the enginehouse and shops. The coal chute built in 1919 is beyond the string of box cars. (Museum of New Mexico 52207)

On a September 1919 afternoon, Herman Maxwell found NMC 2-8-0 No. 11 and 4-8-0 No. 5 under steam outside the Estancia house. The flour mill is at the distant right.

On the same day, Maxwell recorded the town's somnolent main street from the top of the mill.

Over four decades later, on April 28, 1963, Henry E. Bender, Jr. photographed the Santa Fe stations at Moriarty (above), which had been converted to a store, and Estancia (right). The latter had been moved from Lucy, New Mexico, and was still active at the time of Bender's visit.

SPUR NO. 3, milepost 44.1, elevation 6,105
This point was listed in early timetables, but it soon disappeared.

WILLARD, milepost 79.7, elevation 6,096
Willard was initially located at milepost 80.8 and was moved when the AT&SF Belen Cutoff was nearing completion. The original site is marked by a cemetery and a grove of trees. Willard was named for Colonel Hopewell's son, Willard Samuel Hopewell, Jr. A 20 x 60-foot frame station, 29 x 64-foot stockyards and two sidings served the railroad here. An interchange track connected with the AT&SF.

The Santa Fe built large coal and water supply facilities at Willard, as well as a number of long sidings. Although the SFC was the first railroad at Willard, the line gave up its rights to unobstructed passage over the AT&SF crossing. A gate was installed and normally kept locked across the short line.

Willard grew during the days of the steam locomotive. The coming of the automobile and the diesel-electric locomotive removed much of its reason for existence, and it has slowly faded away.

PROGRESSO, milepost 91.7, elevation 6,167
This was the least successful of the townsite promotions. Progresso was established in 1905 as the first seat of Torrance County. It was named for Francis J. Torrance. The county itself was formed through the influence of the railroad and land companies. The newly elected county officers set up shop aboard a SFC coach set out on the siding. Within a month, the unsuitable nature of the isolated site was clear, and the county moved its government to Estancia. In the following years only a few families called Progresso home, and there was little activity there.

Railroad facilities included a 10 x 16-foot frame freight warehouse, and a 45-car capacity siding which was reduced to a six-car spur in later years. There was also a railroad-dug well here, but it was not used for locomotive water supply.

BIANCA, milepost 99.2, elevation 6,244
A 21-car capacity spur existed here for a time. It was gone by 1923.

CEDARVALE, milepost 104.8
Although not listed in early timetables, a community grew here within a few years. A 30-foot box car body was brought in to serve as a depot. There was a 17-car capacity siding with a stock chute as well.

CAMALEON, milepost 108.7
In 1903 a well was drilled here, but the water was not suitable for locomotives. There was no siding.

TORRANCE, milepost 115.7, elevation 6,430
Named for Francis J. Torrance, this point was the southern terminal of the SFC and the interchange with the El Paso & Rock Island. The SFC had a wye and sidings with a capacity of 150 cars. These were reduced to 45-car capacity over the years. The frame depot was provided by the connecting road, but it was jointly owned. Other SFC facilities included a small hotel, a 60 x 80-foot frame warehouse, a frame store building and a 12 x 28-foot frame section house.

Locomotives were serviced by a 12 x 72-foot coal bunker, a sand house and a water system. The water facilities included a 10 x 12-foot frame pump house, a 24 x 16-foot elevated water tank, and a 24 x 16-foot wood cistern. Although the El Paso & Southwestern (successor to the EP&RI) built a large water pipeline through Torrance, it did not have enough water to share with the SFC. For years the short line was forced to haul its own water in tank cars from Estancia or Willard.

There is little indication that Torrance was anything other than a railroad junction. The town of Corona, about six miles to the southwest, evidently served all the commercial needs of the district. When the original hotel burned in January 1911, the press noted that the only other building in town was the railroad depot. The replacement hotel was a one-story frame building, 30 by 40 feet with additions of 10 by 22 feet and seven by five feet.

Track and Bridges

The Santa Fe Central was originally built using Ponderosa pine ties cut in the Manzano Mountains. They were untreated and unprotected with tie plates, so their life was short. Many replacements were cut from pinon growing near the railroad. This unconventional material was characterized as lasting longer than untreated pine, but as having poor holding power for the spikes. When the AT&SF took over track maintenance in 1926, the editor of the *Estancia News-Herald* noted with surprise that they were using creosoted ties as replacement, an unheard-of luxury at Estancia.

The rail used by the Santa Fe Central was brand new 70 pound-per-yard steel of National Steel Company (Pittsburgh) section 7001 rolled in late 1902 and early 1903. The turnouts were mostly Elliot Frog & Switch Company No. 8, using Illinois Steel 70-pound rail.

Bridges, with two exceptions, were ordinary timber pile trestles. One exception was the overhead crossing of the Santa Fe mainline at Kennedy, which was a short steel deck span with fill and trestle approaches. The other was the Oregon fir Howe truss over the Arroyo de la Jara. This had been fabricated by the King Bridge Company of Cleveland. Culverts were wood boxes. In the 1919 rehabilitation, many of the trestles had some pile bents replaced with concrete piers.

Locomotives of the New Mexico Central Railroad

Number	Type	Builder Number Date	Dimensions
1	2-6-0		
2	2-6-0		
3	2-6-0		
4	4-4-0	Schenectady 2509 1888	18x26-61-101000-65100-150-17600
5	4-4-0		
6	4-4-0		
50-54	4-6-0	Alco-Pittsburgh 27179 1903 27183	20x26-61-162000-132800-200
7	4-6-0		
8	4-6-0	Richmond 2261 3/1892	19x24-57-
9	2-6-0	Rogers 3343 1883	
2nd 5	4-8-0	Schenectady	
2nd 6	2-8-0	Baldwin	
10	2-8-0	Baldwin 20077 3/1902	21x30-60-180400-155600-200-38229
11	2-8-0	Baldwin 20075 3/1902	21x30-60-180400-155600-200-38229
101	Railcar	Mack Model AB International Motor Company 70010, August 1921	

NOTES

Nos. 1-6 purchased during 1903 from F. M. Hicks and Company, Chicago.

Nos. 1-3. Of the 2-6-0 locomotives, two had 19x24 cylinders, and one had 18x24 cylinders.

No. 1. Taken out of service June 19, 1909; became stationary boiler at Estancia.

No. 2. Taken out of service August 24, 1914; sold for scrap January 1916.

No. 3. Taken out of service May 1, 1912; sold for scrap January 1916.

No. 4. was AT&SF 117, previously 212, 732; taken out of service November 2, 1914; sold for scrap January 1916.

No. 5. Taken out of service February 27, 1912; sold for scrap January 1916.

No. 6. may have been returned to Hicks circa 1904; a replacement locomotive arrived during 1905 or 1906; taken out of service January 1, 1910; sold for scrap January 1916.

No. 50-54. Purchased new. All were delivered to Santa Fe Central, but only No. 54 used. Leased to El Paso & Northeastern January 1904; sold to Pere Marquette 1904 as its nos. 187-191.

No. 7. Purchased January 1912. Rebuilt November 1917; out of service by December 1923; scrapped after 1926 lease to AT&SF.

No. 8. Purchased January 1912. Originally Chesapeake & Ohio 110. Out of service by 1918; scrapped 1919.

No. 9. Purchased November 1913. Originally Missouri-Kansas-Texas 136, 166. Scrapped after 1926 lease to AT&SF.

2nd No. 5. Purchased March 1918. Probably one of the following two locomotives, purchased from the Denver Laramie & Northwestern.

Schenectady 2422, 3/1888 20x26-51-130000.
ex-New York Central & Hudson River 3600; ex-2600; ex-Beech Creek, Clearfield & Southwestern 11.

or

Schenectady 3219, 11/1890 20x26-51-130000.
ex-New York Central & Hudson River 3607; ex-2607; ex-Beech Creek, Clearfield & Southwestern 18.

2nd No. 6. Purchased March 1918. Probably was Denver Laramie & Northwestern Ry 101. Baldwin 32132, 11/1907. Ex-Midland Valley 19.

No. 10. Purchased January 10, 1919. Originally EP&NE 73, then EP&SW 274, 205. To AT&SF 875 in 1926; scrapped November 1929.

No. 11. Purchased February 8, 1919. Originally EP&NE 71, then EP&SW 267, 198. To AT&SF 876 in 1926; scrapped November 1929.

No. 101. J. G. Brill Company carbody. Sold after 1926 lease to AT&SF. Reportedly used as a storage shed in Albuquerque, then sold to a lumber company in Arizona.

No. 9 was a former Katy engine whose bell was in an unusual location, squeezed in with the steam generator between the cab and steam dome. (Museum of New Mexico 11922)

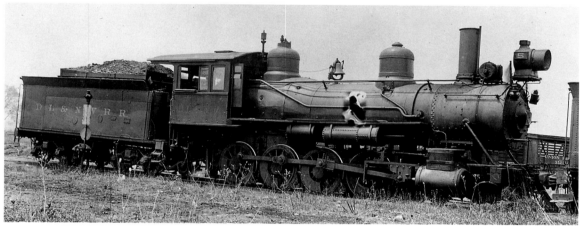

Denver Laramie & Northwestern 4-8-0 No. 5, a rare type in the Rocky Mountain West, carried the same number on New Mexico Central. What appears to be damage above the running board is a flaw in the negative. DL&NW 101 *(below)* probably became NMC second 6. (Otto Perry photos, Denver Public Library Western History Department OP-11411 and OP-11413)

Mogul No. 9 also featured the unusual bell placement, perhaps a NMC eccentricity. Its photograph was taken at Estancia in September 1919 by Herman Maxwell on the same occasion that he managed to capture most of No. 11 in two seperate shots below.

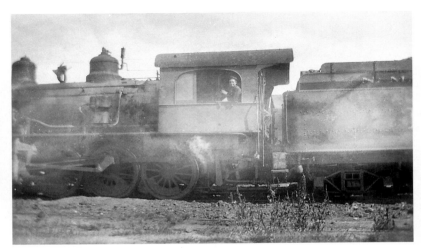

Passenger Cars

Number	Type	Notes
1	Baggage-Mail-Passenger	Purchased 1903. In service at time of 1926 lease.
2	Baggage-Mail-Passenger	Purchased 1903. Retired circa 1915; used as dwelling at Estancia
3	Baggage-Mail-Passenger	Purchased circa 1912. In service at time of 1926 lease.
10,11	Coach	Purchased 1903. One retired circa 1915 and used as dwelling at Estancia; other in service at time of 1926 lease.
	Business Car	See remarks.

Remarks:

The combination cars were used regularly on the daily mixed trains, with a coach being added when traffic warranted. Cars 1 and 3 were refurbished during the summer of 1918. The short-lived passenger train of 1919 normally had a combination car and a coach; one set of equipment sufficed for the schedule.

The Santa Fe Central was reported to have ordered a "private car" from F. M. Hicks and Company in September 1903. There was also a note that a former business car was sold, again through Hicks, circa 1910 to the Denver Laramie & Northwestern. Such a car, however, was not reflected in *Official Railway Equipment Register* listings, suggesting that it may have been purchased by one of the principals in the road rather than the railroad company itself.

Freight Cars of the New Mexico Central

DIMENSIONS

Kind of Cars	Numbers	Inside Length ft. in.	Inside Width ft. in.	Inside Height ft. in.	Outside Length ft. in.	Width at Eaves or Platform ft. in.	To Eaves ft. in.	Height from Rail to top of Platform or Running board ft. in.	To overall ft. in.	Side Doors Width ft. in.	Side Doors Height ft. in.	End Doors Width ft. in.	End Doors Height ft. in.	Cubic Feet Level Full	Pounds or Gallons	No.
Box	100 to 124	34 3	8 2	6 9	34 8		9 3 1/2	11 9	12 8 1/2	5 8	6 4			1904	40000	25
Stock, double deck	5700	34 3	8 2	6 9	34 8		9 3 1/2	11 9	12 8 1/2	5 8	6 4				40000	1
Flat	615 to 629	33 6			34	8 10		4							40000	15
Flat	630 to 639	33 6	8 10		34 8			4 1							40000	10
Flat	1000 to 1014	33 8	8 1	2 9	34 8										40000	15
Gondola	1015 to 1029	33 8	8 1	2 9	34 8			4 1	8 7					748	40000	15
Tank	A1 to A15	33													6300g.	15
Tank	A16, A17	33													6300g.	2
Dump	01, 02	25 8	9	1 11										432		2
Caboose	50, 51															2
Caboose	unknown															3

REMARKS

Most of the freight cars listed were purchased by the Santa Fe Central in 1903. Many came from the Hicks Locomotive & Car Works. The exceptions were the lone stock car S700 which appeared in 1907 or 1908, tank cars A16 and A17 obtained after 1917, dump cars 01 and 02 purchased in Colorado in mid-1919, and the three cabooses purchased in 1919. Through the years many of the cars listed were removed from the active roster through attrition or assignment to company service. The following summaries indicate these changes:

1916: 33 freight cars, 23 service cars, 1 caboose
1918: 33 freight cars, 13 service cars, no cabooses
1925: 29 freight cars, 20 service cars, 3 cabooses

Other cars known to have been used include 20 boxcars of the Rio Grande Sierra Madre & Pacific leased during 1903, and a steel Michigan Central flat car leased to carry the ditcher in 1919.

SANTA FE & TORRANCE R. R.
Santa Fe Cent. Ry.   116 m's.   Rt. 167,018.)   D.

†1a	June 9. 1907.	†2a
2 00	L..... Santa Fe, N. M .....▲	5 00
3 10	.......Kennedy, N. M	3 50
6 22	..Willard Sta.. N. M.(n.o.)..	12 41
7 50	▲..... Torrance, N. M......L	11 15

Closed Pouches.	For'd by Tr	Closed Pouches.	For'd by Tr
From Santa Fe, N. M.		From Estancia, N. M.	
aEstancia, N. M........	1	aK. C. & El Paso, tr. 4 ..	1
aK. C. & El Paso, tr 4 ..	1	aMoriarty, N. M.........	2
aK. C. & El Paso tr. 1...	1	aSanta Fe. N. M.......	2
aKennedy, N. M........	1	aTorrance, N. M........	1
aMcIntosh, N. M.......	1	aWillard, N. M.........	1
aMoriarity, N. M.......	1	From Moriarity, N. M.	
.aOtto, N. M....	1	aEstancia, N. M........	1
aRoswell, N. M........	1	aK. C. & El Paso tr. 4...	1
aWillard, N. M.........	1	aSanta Fe. N. M.......	2
aTorrance, N. M.......	1	aTorrance, N. M.......	1,
From Torrance, N. M.		From Kennedy, N. M.	
aEstacia, N. M........	2	aSanta Fe, N. M.......	2 .
aKennedy, N. M.......	2	aTorrance, N. M.......	1
aMcIntosh, N. M.......	2	From Willard, N. M.	
aMoriarity, N. M.......	2	aEstancia, N. M........	1
.aOtto, N. M.	2	aK. C. & El Paso, tr. 4...	1
aSanta Fe, N. M.......	2	aSanta Fe, N. M.......	2
aWillard, N. M........	2	aTorrance, N. M	1
From McIntosh, N. M.		From Otto, N. M.	
aK. C. & El Paso, tr. 4 ..	1	.aK. C.& El Paso tr 4 .	1
aSanta Fe, N. M.	2	.aSanta Fe, N. M......	2
aTorrance, N. M	1	.aTorrance, N. M.......	1

Railway Post Office

U.S. Mail service began on the Santa Fe Central in 1907 as the Santa Fe & Torrance Rail Route (closed pouch). This was soon changed to full RPO service, which continued until 1918. The route then reverted to closed pouch until discontinuance on April 7, 1925. Two variants of the RPO cancellation are shown here, along with the 1907 schedule from the Seventh Division of the Railway Mail Service. (James Ozment and Kenton Forrest, Mobile Post Office Society)

The AT&SF station at Moriarty was renamed Calvert in 1959 to honor F.W. Calvert, an officer at Ideal Cement Company which had built a plant at Tijeras, 16 miles east of Albuquerque. Henry E. Bender, Jr. photographed the simple structure on April 28, 1963.

Marcos Gutierrez was paid $27.15 for his work during the month of May 1910. For perspective, in that year one could mail a letter for two cents, buy a mug of beer or a Havana cigar for a nickel and a good meal in a restaurant for 75 cents. (CRRM collection)

Acknowledgments

As with most small and nearly forgotten institutions, there is no major source of New Mexico Central material. It has been broadly scattered, generally forgotten and sometimes destroyed over the years. The only collections dealing significantly with the New Mexico Central are those at the Museum of New Mexico. Special thanks are due to Stephanie Eger of the history library for permission to use the bulky back files of the *Estancia News-Herald* and to browse through the various business files that contributed a variety of letterheads as well as the all-important copy of an operating timetable. Dick Rudisill of the photo archives provided the key information on the Christian G. Kaadt photographs, and Bruce Ellis provided an old brochure showing many of the Kaadt images.

Other contributors to the story were Herman Maxwell, who remembered his youth both verbally and in the form of his own snapshots made and developed with a new Sears outfit. C. M. "Pop" Graham, too, remembered his days on the New Mexico Central. To John B. Moore, Jr. and Russell Lee Crump goes thanks for a series of documents gleaned from their researches into the Santa Fe system. And it was Ed Mahoney's big timetable collection, now in Colorado Railroad Museum's collection, that long ago showed us that the New Mexico Central did exist as an independent railroad.

SAN PETE VALLEY BRANCH

515 Mxd. dy ex Sun.	Mls.	STATIONS Jan. 13, 1918	516 Mxd. dy ex Sun.
		Northbound — Southbound	
7 45	0.	lv..........Manti..........ar	3 10
8 20	7.4	..........Ephraim..........	2 45
f 8 50	15.5	..........Chester..........	f 2 00
9 05	18.8	..........Moroni..........	1 48
f 9 25	22.8	..........Freedom..........	f 1 30
f 9 31	24.8	..........Cedar Cliffs..........	f 1 23
9 45	27.6	..........Fountain Green..........	1 15
10 07	32.3	..........Divide..........	f12 55
f10 22	36.2	..........Nebo Junction..........	f12 30
f10 37	40.8	..........Gypsum..........	f12 02
10 45	42.3	lv..........Nephi..........ar	11 55

SUNNYSIDE BRANCH

No. 138 Mixed d'ly ex. Sun.	Miles	STATIONS January 13, 1918	No. 139 Mixed d'ly ex. Sun.
10 05	0	lv..........Mounds..........ar	2 25
11 30	17	ar.....Sunnyside.....lv	1 00

THE UINTAH RAILWAY

Read down — Read up

No. 1 Daily	Miles from Mack	STATIONS	No. 2 Daily
8 15	0.0	lv..........Mack..........ar	5 00
9 05	20.0	..........Carbonero..........	4 10
9 35	28.3	..........Atchee..........	3 45
10 25	34.1	..........Baxter Pass..........	3 05
10 55	40.0	..........McAndrews..........	2 25
12 00	53.5	..........Dragon..........	1 30
12 30	62.9	ar..........Watson..........lv	1 00

THE T. B. M.

The Tired Business Man, otherwise known as the T. B. M., has often no excuse for his fatigue. Nine-tenths of it is often sheer habit and self pity. No healthy man is ever tired out by a hard day's work. That is all fudge. No normal man ever uses up all his energy in a day's work. Most men are tired because they think they are. They have lost interest in their work. They are indifferent. They don't care. Naturally, they are tired.

If hard work were hurtful, many of us would have been dead long ago. So—put this question to yourself—Am I really tired at the end of a day's work, or HAVE I LOST MY INTEREST IN MY JOB?

—The Efficiency Magazine.

COLORADO MIDLAND RAILWAY CRIPPLE CREEK AND VICTOR

Eastbound — Westbound

No. 3 Daily	Dist fr'm Colo Spg.	STATIONS	No. 4 Daily
8 15	75 0	lv.....Denver.....ar D. & R. G. R.R.	7 30
9 15	45 0	lv.....Pueblo.....ar D. & R. G. R.R.	9 25
11 50	0	lv..Colo. Springs..ar	6 35
2 15	41 0	ar.....Cameron.....lv	4 30
2 37	46 4	ar.....Victor.....lv	4 10
2 44	49 8	ar.....Elkton.....lv	4 01
2 49	49 8	ar.....Anaconda.....lv	3 55
2 55	51 7	ar..Cripple Creek..lv	3 50

BEAVER, PENROSE & NORTHERN RY.

Westward — Eastward

5 Daily	Miles	STATIONS	4 Daily
1 00	0.	..........Beaver..........	* 12 45
f 1 10	2.21	..........Fry..........	f 12 35
f 1 20	4.22	..........Dingman..........	f 12 30
1 30	6.11	..........Penrose..........	12 15

COLORADO & WYOMING RAILWAY

No 1 Dy ex Sun	Miles	STATIONS	No.2 Dy ex Sun
8 30	0	lv.....Trinidad.....ar	4 30
8 49	6	lv.....Longsdale.....ar	4 05
9 10	14	lv.....Segundo.....ar	3 46
9 22	18	ar } .....Primero..{ lv	3 30
9 25	18	lv } ....{ ar	2 17
10 40	31	ar.....Tercio.....lv	1 00

SAN LUIS SOUTHERN RAILWAY

No. 1 Daily Except Sun.	Miles from Blanca	STATIONS	No. 2 Daily Except Sun.
8 30	0	lv.....Blanca.....ar	5 10
8 50	8	lv.....Ojito.....lv	4 50
9 10	16	ar.....San Acacio.....lv	4 30
9 45	24	ar.....Mesita.....lv	4 00
10 15	31	ar.....Jaroso.....lv	3 30

SAN LUIS CENTRAL RAILROAD

N'thb'd No. 2 Mixed Dly.ex. Sun.	Miles	STATIONS	S'thb'd No. 1 Mixed Dly.ex. Sun.
9 45	0	lv....Monte Vista, U. D....ar	4 50
9 50	2	ar.....Sugar Junction.....lv	4 40
9 55	3	.....Sugar Factory.....	4 35
10 05	5	..........North Farm..........	4 23
10 30	9	..........Dunul..........	4 05
10 45	11	..........Ansel..........	3 45
11 00	15	ar..........Center..........lv	3 20

NEW MEXICO CENTRAL RAILROAD

Read Down — Read Up

No. 2 Mixed Daily	Miles	STATIONS	No. 1 Mixed Daily
10 00	0.	Lv...Santa Fe..Ar..	4 45
11 10	21.8	..........Kennedy..........	3 16
11 30	27.9	..........Clark..........	f 2 56
f2 38	40.8	..........Stanley..........	2 15
1 40	52.4	..........Moriarty..........	1 40
2 00	60.6	..........McIntosh..........	1 04
2 35	68.5	..........Estancia..........	12 41
3 10	80.8	..........Willard..........	11 42
5 00	115.7	Ar...Torrance...Lv	9 45

New Mexico Central bought this second hand caboose in Colorado in 1919. Not long afterward, a member of the crew waves from the cupola as it trails a coal train down the long lonely line through the "Land of Enchantment." (Herman Maxwell photo)

(opposite) New Mexico Central's schedule is in the lower right of this page from *The Railroad Red Book* for October 1918, a monthly publication of the Denver & Rio Grande passenger department. Eight decades later, of the railroads shown, only the San Luis Central still exists under the same name. D&RG's Sunnyside Branch in Utah now belongs to Union Pacific. It is used by unit coal trains, as well as trains hauling waste material from the West Coast to a disposal site. Most of the Colorado & Wyoming track is still in place but inactive. All the other lines are long gone. (CRRM collection)

Dreadful Flood of Pueblo, Colo 6/3-21 where most the lives lost.

THE 1921 PUEBLO FLOOD AND
THE MOFFAT TUNNEL:

by Stephen S. Hart

Economics and
Politics of a Colorado Disaster

PASSENGERS SCALE ROOF OF

PERILOUS MOMENT AS M. P. COACHES HIT DENVER CARS

SCREAMS MINGLED WITH ROAR OF SWIRLING WATER, CRASHING WOOD AND BREAKING WINDOWS

Seven Little Children Are Saved by Passenger on Denver Train—Only Five Now Believed Victims in These Wrecks.

(By BRUCE A. GUSTIN.)

Pueblo, Colo., June 6.—Three bodies have been recovered from the wrecks of D. & R. G. and Missouri Pacific trains which were overturned into the boiling floods of Friday night.

Exploration of the wrecked, mud-filled coaches was begun Sunday afternoon but was halted by the cloudbursts which sent the Arkansas on another rampage.

Five persons are believed to have perished in these wrecks instead of the hundreds originally reported. Still, the number cannot be given with any certainty until time has been allowed for a thoro search of the ruins.

The three whose bodies have been removed to the morgues are F. C. Haines, a passenger who had a ticket to Glenwood Springs; the Pullman conductor and conductor.

PASSENGERS ESCAPE BY CRAWLING THRU WINDOWS.

Most of the passengers escaped by crawling thru windows.

Spectators were kept at a distance when railroad authorities and special officers quietly began the search for victims in the demolished trains. They refused to give any details of the result of their search.

Shrieking sirens and revolver volleys gave warning of the recurrence of the flood. Thousands of persons were driven out of the danger zone. Many carried their household goods on their backs. It was hours later before the Arkansas again reached the danger stage, and as the waters poured out into the lower business section the cloudburst drenched Bessemer and swelled the flood waters west of Pueblo.

By 6 o'clock in the evening the waters were receding, but thousands of persons living in North Pueblo were marooned in South Pueblo.

A. E. Schaubel, 62 years old, of 237 Adams street, Pueblo, who is one of the flood casualties, was an uncle of A. W. Markshiffel of Colorado Springs. Schaubel and two others were trapped under the roof of a garage. One man cut his way out with a pocket knife. Schaubel said "goodby" to the man who cut the hole in the roof.

DENVER UNDERTAKERS ARRIVE ON SCENE.

Russell Law and Archie Smith, Colorado Springs embalmers, arrived Sunday to assist in preparing the dead for burial. Several undertakers are being brought from Denver.

Two men swept away by the flood are reported marooned on an island near Blendhill. The current of the Arkansas on both sides of the island is so swift rescue parties cannot reach them.

Harry Johnson, a switchman, battled with death in the flood for hours. He floated around in the yards from 11 o'clock Friday night until 8:15 o'clock Saturday morning. He was trying to get D. & R. G. train No. 3 out of the yards when the flood caught it. He said the Missouri Pacific passengers took refuge in No. 3 when their train turned over.

The railroad yards are a mass of debris, broken box cars, torn tracks and ruined freight.

A. H. Russell, 1650 California street, Denver, described vividly the destruction of the two passenger trains, probably the most spectacular incident of the flood. Collarless, his baggage lost, Russell still showed the effects of his horrifying experiences.

With scores of others he had climbed to the roofs of the coaches to escape the rising, lashing waters when his train was smashed by another string of passenger cars.

"There were about 100 passengers on the Denver & Rio Grande train, of whom I was one," said Russell. "On the Missouri Pacific train which hit us there were probably thirty passengers, mostly Mexican laborers.

"We had been surrounded by backwaters for hours and did not fully realize our danger when the river began to rise very rapidly in our vicinity. It seemed to groove out a new course aimed directly at us.

"In a few minutes we were standing on our seats. Next we took to the roofs. I think everybody got up.

"I remember there were seven little children on our train. We got them out safely.

"I think we would have escaped without much of a wetting but for the washing of huge piles of lumber against the Missouri Pacific train standing near us.

"Its passengers had likewise scrambled to the roofs. When the bulwark of timber hammered the Missouri Pacific coaches against ours I guess I thought it was all of for us. Screams mingled with the roar of crashing wood and breaking windows.

"Some men from the Nuckolls Packing plant witnessed the whole thing. They waded waist-deep to our aid.

"The coaches toppled over on their sides, making a bank along which the water momentarily swept past those of us struggling on the far side of the cars.

"I think that meant the saving of most of us. I saw a Negro porter pulling out women and children for several minutes; then a telegraph pole, undermined on the highway skirting the river, fell and hit him, crushing him into the waters.

"It's more of a nightmare than a reality to me. New trivial incidents keep coming to me all the time as my mind drags me back to its horrors."

A flash of lightning, a roar of thunder, the bellowing shriek of a siren whistle! All Pueblo knew something terrible was pending. People hurried to telephones. From "central" or from newspaper offices they learned the cause of the continuous blowing, "A FLOOD IS COMING DOWN THE ARKANSAS RIVER!"

Hundreds of persons rushed to the levees to witness the tremendous spectacle of a great wall of water rushing down the stream that most of the year is scarcely big enough to bear the title of "river." No one had any dream of the possible magnitude of the flood. While spectators were waiting for the tremendous sight, the angry waters tore a gap in the levee west of the city and the whole murky mess came pouring through. Witness John A. Martin said,

It seemed like the crack of doom, like the end of the world, like that first great flood in Genesis. I have often heard the expression, "Hell's broken loose." As I saw it from the balconies and tower of the Grand opera house, that is just what it looked like, when great burning rafts of lumber began to swirl through the streets on the fast-rushing waters. Over and over I said, "This is a historic disaster; tomorrow the name of Pueblo will be known round the world."

"3,000 ARE DEAD IN PUEBLO" screamed the two-inch headlines in the June 4, 1921, edition of Bonfils and Tammen's *The Denver Post*. The 1921 flood killed more people than the great Chicago fire of 1871, when that city had a population near 300,000. The flood probably caused as many deaths as the 1906 San Francisco earthquake, the worst natural disaster in the western United States since 1900, when San Francisco had a population exceeding 343,000.

However, the exact death toll of the flood will never be known. One 1921 estimate stated that 156 were known dead and 147 were reported missing and never found. The book *The Case of Train No. 3* stated that only 78 bodies were ever recovered—the rest were apparently washed downstream or permanently buried in the mud. A later reference quoting from Pueblo newspaper sources indicated that 132 bodies were present in makeshift morgues throughout the city on June 6, and that more than 1,500 persons were reported missing. As many as several hundred unnamed and unregistered migrant workers were known to have been lodging in rooming houses and cheap hotels in an area that became known as the "Death Lake." Whatever the actual number, as a percentage of its 1920 population of 43,000, Pueblo's death toll was

112

ENGULFED TRAIN

The Denver Post of Monday evening, June 6, 1921, provided a vivid account of the disaster in Pueblo. The "First In Everything" heading reveals that news media self-promotion has changed little in the intervening three-quarters of a century. (CRRM collection)

more than ten times that of 1871 Chicago and eight times that of 1906 San Francisco.

The 1921 flood on the Arkansas River was the most deadly natural disaster in Colorado history and one of the worst in the western United States in the 20th Century. The flood was estimated by the U.S. Army Corps of Engineers as a one time in 500-year event. This means a flood that has occurred only once since Columbus discovered the West Indies, only twice since the Normans invaded England, and only three times since the fall of the Roman Empire. Few generations, or even nations, survive long enough to witness such an event.

Immediate Relief

On the morning of June 4, 1921, hundreds were dead or missing, and thousands were homeless. Water, gas, electric power, telephones and telegraph lines were all damaged or destroyed; and both newspapers were temporarily out of business. The waterworks and the electric power plant were buried under water and mud. Puebloans were not only thirsty but were also completely cut off from communication with the rest of the world. The first public radio broadcast in the United States had occurred only eight months before the flood and only a few stations were operating nationwide. Even if Pueblo had a radio station, it had no electric power, since the riverside power plant was one of the first buildings flooded on the night of June 3. The first relief convoy left Colorado Springs at noon on June 4 but did not reach Pueblo until the next afternoon. An article in the June 6, 1921, *Denver Post* summarized the reaction of the nation:

HARDING OFFERS ASSISTANCE OF NATION TO SUFFERERS IN PUEBLO'S CATASTROPHE
Valley Forge, Pa., June 6.—The offer of public aid in the Pueblo catastrophe was extended the people of Colorado by President Harding in a wire sent Sunday afternoon to Governor Shoup. The President, who is here on a week-end visit to the home of Senator Philander C. Knox, sent the following telegram to the Colorado executive: "I am deeply distressed to read of the great misfortune which has come, with its toll of death and destruction, to the citizenship of Colorado and the valley of the Arkansas River. It is most reassuring to know how nobly your state has met the great emergency. If the federal government can be of aid to you, pray do

not hesitate to advise me, because all the people of the United States are touched by the sorrow and distress which have come to the people of Colorado. Warren G. Harding."

Although the sentiment in President Harding's message was a boost to the grieving and homeless residents of Pueblo, little help came from the Federal government. Not until ten days after the flood was $100,000 in medical supplies and military tents for temporary shelter offered for Pueblo's relief. However, even this relief was criticized by the Secretary of the Army, who was quoted in a June 17 *Rocky Mountain News* front page headline: "Pueblo Asks for Too Much, Large Funds Are Not Needed." The Colorado National Guard was mobilized in Pueblo on June 4 to oversee martial law and provide hospitals and clean water, but the state did not provide much financial relief either. Fortunately, the Red Cross quickly set up an emergency relief program that registered 11,178 persons, one-fourth of Pueblo's total population. And the widespread publicity that booster (later U.S. Congressman) John A. Martin so desperately wanted created an outpouring of monetary gifts from individuals and organizations all over the nation. An article about the flood in Pueblo appeared in the June 6, 1921, London *Times*. The newspaperman misplaced the "Pittsburg of the West," as his article called it, as being located 75 miles south of Colorado Springs. It is interesting that instead of using Denver, the largest city in the Rocky Mountain region, as his reference, he used Colorado Springs, a town with which the English were appearently better acquainted! The most poignant of these relief funds was a $2,000 donation from Johnstown, Pennsylvania.

Although the direct financial toll of the 1921 flood in Colorado exceeded $20 million 1920 dollars, the permanent economic loss to Pueblo was far greater. The city lost to Denver its perceived place as the largest railroad and industrial center in Colorado. Politically and economically, Pueblo's disaster was Denver's gain.

(text continued on page 120)

RAILROAD SERVICE CUT OFF FROM PUEBLO AND BOULDER FOR WEEK, SAY DISPATCHES

D. and R. G. Trains From South Can Get Within Five Miles of Flooded City—Repair Gangs To Rush Work.

6-6-21

Railroad officials are unable to even venture an opinion as to when service may be resumed to Pueblo. Because telegraph lines are down thruout the Pueblo district they are unable yet even to get an estimate of the damage.

It will be from three or four days to a week before tracks can be repaired and service resumed between Denver and Boulder, they say.

Dispatches from Pueblo indicate that it may be a week before the first rail communication in any direction may be established with the stricken city.

TRAINS GET TO WITHIN TWENTY-FIVE MILES.

The nearest a train from the east can get to Pueblo over the Santa Fe lines is twenty-five miles. A number of consolidated trains which have been halted near the Kansas line during the last few days because of the flood have been made up into two trains, which reached Denver at 11 and 11:30 o'clock Monday morning. They were detoured over the other lines from Salina, Kan. They were California-bound trains. All thru traffic over lines passing thru the flood area are being detoured to the north. Flood conditions in the Arkansas valley prevent the use of Santa Fe lines from La Junta to New Mexico points.

Denver & Rio Grande trains from the south of Pueblo can get within five miles of that city. The Missouri Pacific cannot get trains closer than twenty-five miles.

Trains are being operated on schedule between Denver and Colo-

rado Springs Monday, but there is no regular traffic south of the Springs.

Several bridges in the Arkansas valley east of Pueblo have been carried away, and miles of track have been washed out. The same is true of lines entering the city from the north.

Crews of laborers recruited at East Las Vegas and other northern New Mexico points are being rushed to the flooded sections to commence immediately the work of rebuilding. Rails, ties, and lumber for trestle building is being shipped in from the south and east.

A special work train left Denver Monday morning to rebuild the Colorado & Southern and Denver & Interurban tracks between Denver and Boulder.

The track between Louisville Junction and Marshall will be repaired first. Trains and cars then will be sent to Louisville via Boulder. The Louisville branch is in far worse shape than the Marshall branch, officials say. Probably ten miles of track in all will have to be rebuilt before service on these lines can be resumed. A dozen teams were at work Monday morning filling in the 1,000 feet of roadbed which had been washed away just north of Louisville Junction on the Marshall branch, where the Dry creek cloudburst passed Friday.

This newspaper story reveals that Colorado & Southern also was simultaneously having storm related problems on the Denver-Boulder line which it shared with subsidiary Denver & Interurban electric. Below, the Arkansas River downstream from Pueblo Union Depot was many times its normal placid flow. Colorado Fuel & Iron's steel plant is visible in the left distance of this scene of a section of a highway bridge mingling with several floating railroad freight cars.

After the floodwaters receded, a yard full of mostly wooden freight cars was left in disarray behind Denver & Rio Grande's Pueblo roundhouse. The aerial view to the southeast shows how the water spread through the downtown business district and the rail yards beyond. (below, Denver Public Library Western History Department F9029; others, CRRM collection)

One may speculate on how long it took to sell or rent the building visible in the upper left beyond the collapsed metal roof bearing a faded *Rocky Mountain News* sign. Below, a wrecking derrick is starting to unscramble the wrecked D&RG passenger train. Rio Grande's bridge had collapsed, while the larger and more modern Santa Fe bridge survived the flood intact. The American Smelting & Refining smelter is in the background. (Denver Public Library Western History Department F47764 and F47766)

The spindly crossing watchman's tower visible between the cottonwood tree in the center and the Santa Fe office building at the left of the above photo managed to survive the deluge. *(below)* The Nuckoll's Meat Packing Plant is beyond a pair of Rio Grande baggage cars and a Pullman. (Denver Public Library Western History Department F47765 and F47767)

Dreadful Flood of Pueblo, Colo. 6/3-21

The Santa Fe R.R. by the Nuckolls Packing Co.

Two cuts of D&RG gondolas are loaded with scrap lumber and hay bales from a destroyed warehouse, while two wreckers work in the distance. With the aid of a magnifier, freight cars belonging to Chicago Milwaukee & St. Paul, Colorado & Southern, New York Central, Frisco and Union Pacific can be spotted. (Both, Pueblo County Historical Society)

This panorama shows, from the left: Nuckoll's Packing Plant, the overturned Pullman of the D&RG train, the dislodged D&RG and intact AT&SF bridges, and the distant Union Depot tower.

Pueblo's Loss . . .

In 1921, Pueblo boasted of being the second largest city in Colorado and the largest smelting center in the nation, of having the largest steel plant west of Chicago, and of producing and moving more rail freight tonnage than any city between the Missouri River and the west coast. Pueblo's steel mill; foundries; lead, zinc and silver smelters; railroad car shops; mining machinery makers and meat packing plants employed over 20,000 workers.

The financial losses from the flood exceeded ten million dollars in the city alone. A report to the Pueblo city council stated that 510 homes had been washed away, 98 buildings wrecked, and 61 others washed from their foundations. The losses also included near total destruction of the Rio Grande, Missouri Pacific, Santa Fe and Colorado & Southern railroad main lines and freight yards; eight of the nine rail bridges across the Arkansas and Fountain Creek and 2,000 freight and passenger cars. The last included two complete, occupied passenger trains.

Local leaders in Pueblo, such as Mayor James L. Lovering and Pueblo Commercial Club President G. L. Gann, quickly realized that the only way for Pueblo to recover from the devastating effects of the flood was to roll up its sleeves and do the work itself with its own money. They also realized that to boost Pueblo's future and attract new industry, the city must be protected from future floods of this magnitude. However, the creation of a flood control district needed the approval of the state legislature and had to be signed by the governor.

Accordingly, a committee of 12 citizens was selected to plan and direct the work of reclamation until a special session of the state legislature could provide a legal framework for a permanent plan. The committee consisted of many well-known Pueblo businessmen including E. H. Weitzel of CF&I, who loaned his entire engineering staff to aid U. S. Reclamation Service engineer J. L. Savage in documenting flood extent and damage. In order to save time, the committee enlisted the Morgan Engineering Company of Dayton, Ohio, which had developed an ingenious flood control plan for the Miami River following the Dayton flood of 1911. After completing their own survey of Pueblo, Morgan engineers presented a flood control plan costing four million dollars.

Temporary Train Service
by way of
DENVER & RIO GRANDE

Beginning Today, June 10th

For Colorado Springs, Walsenburg, Trinidad and Alamosa.

Train No. 1 will leave Denver 8:15 a. m., arriving Alamosa 8:30 p. m. same day—Dining Car Service.

Trains for Monte Vista, Del Norte, Creede, Durango, Silverton and Santa Fe will operate from and to Alamosa on regular advertised schedules.

Train No. 109 for Trinidad will make connection with No. 1 at Walsenburg.

Train No. 318 will leave Alamosa for Salida at 11:50 a. m., making connection at latter point for Buena Vista, Leadville, Glenwood Springs, Grand Junction, Gunnison, Montrose, Delta, Telluride and other Western Slope points.

Train No. 15 for Colorado Springs only will leave Denver 7:10 p. m.

No person permitted to leave train in Pueblo unless holding military permit.

Frank A. Wadleigh, Passenger Traffic Manager, Denver.

6-10 1921

Emergency train schedules were quickly drawn up, such as those published in this D&RG advertisement from the June 10, 1921, *Denver Post.* (CRRM collection)

A *Post* editorial page drawing of June 6, 1921, reflects the allegorical symbolism popular with newspapers from the 1890s until the 1930s. (CRRM collection)

"WE ARE COMING, PUEBLO"

. . . Is Denver's Gain!

In 1917, Colorado's three "home-grown" standard gauge rail lines led from its major eastern slope cities across the Continental Divide. Pueblo had the "Royal Gorge Route" of the Denver & Rio Grande which crossed the divide in a tunnel below Tennessee Pass, then continued on to connections in Salt Lake City with the Western Pacific and in Ogden with the Southern Pacific. Colorado Springs had the Colorado Midland which crossed the divide through the Busk-Ivanhoe Tunnel and joined Rio Grande at Newcastle in the line to Grand Junction. Denver had the Denver & Salt Lake (Moffat Road), which crossed the divide over 11,660-foot Rollins Pass and continued to Craig, where it ended without reaching its original destination of Salt Lake City. Therefore, both Pueblo and Colorado Springs were located on east-west transcontinental routes. Rio Grande connected with the Missouri Pacific at Pueblo, and the Midland connected with the Chicago Rock Island & Pacific at Colorado Springs. Denver possessed only a dead end branch line to northwestern Colorado that connected with the Rock Island and the Chicago Burlington & Quincy at Denver. Although the Colorado cities were also served by the Atchison Topeka & Santa Fe and Union Pacific, these lines had their own transcontinental

routes that bypassed the state. They generally did not divert transcontinental traffic over the connecting lines through Colorado.

This situation was intolerable to "Queen City" boosters led by William G. Evans, son of former Colorado territorial governor and railroad builder John Evans. These included the Civic and Commercial Association, headed by Finlay L. MacFarland; the Denver Chamber of Commerce; and most Denver bankers and merchants. To these boosters, Denver had to be put on a transcontinental main line before the city lost its dominant position in Colorado business and politics. Unfortunately, not only Denver's beloved Moffat Road, but also Rio Grande and the Midland were nearing (or already in) bankruptcy in 1917. Therefore, the Colorado railroad situation appeared grim when fate, in the form of the United States government, intervened.

In the first few months of World War I, rail traffic throughout the U.S. multiplied several times as industry mobilized and war materials and troop movements intensified. By the fall of 1917, so many freight cars awaited unloading at Atlantic port cities that rail traffic nationwide was brought almost to a standstill due to a lack of empty cars. This was unconscionable to the military high command, which was trying to ship hundreds of thousands of men and millions of tons of weapons, equipment, fuel and food to France. Therefore, by executive order on December 26, 1917, President Woodrow Wilson created the United States Railroad Administration (USRA) to operate the American railroads until the end of the conflict.

Since Colorado Midland had the shorter route between Colorado Springs and Grand Junction, USRA diverted Rio Grande traffic to the Midland. Completed in 1888, the CM had been bought jointly by Rio Grande and Colorado & Southern in 1900. The Midland, however, was in no physical condition to handle such an enormous volume of traffic due to lack of capital and its run-down track and equipment. Therefore, in late May 1918, all USRA business reverted to the Rio Grande. With an 85 percent decrease in traffic and losing $10,000 each week, the Midland failed on July 1, 1918, and stopped operations on August 5. This eliminated one-half of the Moffat Road's potential competitors.

However, Rio Grande was not in much better condition than the Midland. Its financial crisis had arisen, in part, because its future had been mortgaged with railroad bonds

issued from 1904 to 1910 by New York financier George Jay Gould. Gould used the capital from D&RG bonds to construct his new Western Pacific Railroad from Salt Lake City to Oakland. His dream was to combine Western Pacific with his Rio Grande, Missouri Pacific and Wabash railroads into a true transcontinental system. As late as 1918, Western Pacific's owners were still busily involved in attaching Rio Grande's assets. Even after the USRA guaranteed an annual income of eight million dollars, Rio Grande's board of directors sought court protection from WP by going into receivership on January 25, 1918. This bankruptcy also helped protect D&RG from Western Pacific when, in May 1918, USRA gave Rio Grande a grant of nearly three million dollars to upgrade its plant and equipment. Rio Grande thus managed to profit from government takeover more than most other lines.

Denver & Salt Lake narrowly escaped the same fate as the Midland. The Moffat had been dying even before its founder, David Moffat, used the last of his personal fortune building the line. He ran out of money at Steamboat Springs, never having completed the line or constructing his real vision, a Continental Divide tunnel beneath James Peak. After Mof-

Denver & Rio Grande No. 1001 was pulling train No. 3 on the fateful day of the Pueblo flood. It came to rest at a considerable distance from the Railway Post Office car to which it had been coupled. Renumbered 801 three years later, the 4-6-2 served Rio Grande until 1953. This photograph was taken by *Rocky Mountain News* photographer Harry M. Rhoads, whose career began in 1900 and spanned an amazing 69 years. (Denver Public Library Western History Department Rh5850)

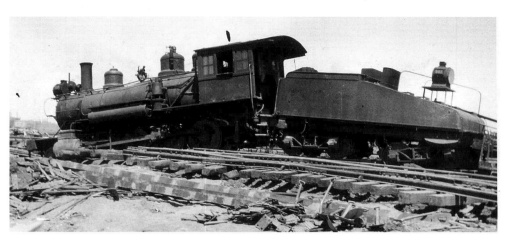

Baldwin had built No. 605 in 1890 for freight service over the standard gauge main line D&RG was then completing. Long since demoted to a switcher with a sloped tender, the small 2-8-0 was caught in the flood. Renumbered 675 three years later, it was scrapped in 1927. (CRRM collection)

fat's death, a London banker, Dr. George S. Pearson, came to Colorado to inspect the line. He was sufficiently impressed that he decided to go back to London, dispose of his Mexican Central railroad stock and complete the Moffat Road to Salt Lake City. However, the ship that Dr. Pearson chose for the trip home from new York to England in 1915 was the *Lusitania.* Denver's hopes nearly died with him.

By 1918, the Moffat's receiver had affairs in such a mess that traffic came to a complete halt in January. Denver's boosters appealed to Washington that nearly 25,000 people depended on the line, and that the vast resources of coal and oil shale in northwestern Colorado were necessary to the war effort. They were ignored by the Santa Fe-dominated USRA administration. However, when Moffat employees struck for $180,000 in unpaid wages and the road again came to a standstill, USRA took over for the duration.

Denver boosters then made an effort to induce USRA to bore a tunnel to save the $2,000 per day cost of coal required to move trains over Rollins Pass but had no more success than previously. However, USRA purchases of over a million dollars in receiver's certificates in June 1918 and the payment of a yearly rental fee did aid the harassed line.

In early 1920 President Wilson signed the Esch-Cummins Transportation Act that provided for the return of all government-operated railroads to their owners on the first day of March. In this act, federal rail experts also recommended consolidating small, financially unstable rail lines with stronger lines in order to develop a more efficient national rail system. Denver awakened to the danger of the Moffat Road being torn up or "consolidated" immediately following the war emergency. The prospect that either Santa Fe or Union Pacific might absorb the Moffat or Rio Grande was extremely alarming to Evans. The boosters were so desperate that in January 1920 they tried to induce Burlington to

complete the Moffat Road and build the tunnel. However, Burlington President Hale Holden stated at an Interstate Commerce Commission hearing that he thought other railroads were better prepared to rehabilitate the Colorado line. Without the "sugar daddy" of their choice to bail them out, the Denver boosters proposed a referendum for the November 1920 general election. This ballot issue proposed a bond issue of $18.5 million to build three rail tunnels beneath the Continental Divide. The first would be their long-planned Moffat Road tunnel; the second, a tunnel beneath Monarch Pass either for the inactive but still in place Colorado Midland, or for the Rio Grande narrow gauge between Salida and Montrose; and the third, a tunnel beneath Cumbres Pass for the Rio Grande narrow gauge between Alamosa and Durango. The idea was to defuse the objections of voters in southern Colorado, who had opposed earlier efforts to build the Moffat tunnel, by offering them two tunnels in their region. However, the ballot issue failed due to opposition from Pueblo, El Paso, Las Animas and other counties in the southern part of the state.

By April 1921 Colorado's railroad picture was truly bleak. The Midland's rails were being permanently removed in the largest railroad abandonment in the U.S. to that time. This scrapping required Rio Grande to write off its investment in the Midland, and, in spite of its war profits, D&RG soon went back into receivership. The Moffat Road again stood on the brink of a precipice, its track blocked by rock slides, and its coffers empty. Its only salvation was a tunnel but to hope for a tunnel in 1921 bordered on praying for a miracle.

The odds against miracles are nearly astronomical. But Denver got one, which shattered the last obstacle to its dream of a tunnel. The site of the miracle was Pueblo, lying exposed to the raging waters of the Arkansas River.

The Special Legislative Session of April 1922

In July 1921, with flood control uppermost in their minds, Pueblo's leaders asked Governor Oliver H. Shoup to call a special session of the legislature to consider the establishment of a flood protection district. The governor, however, waited until January 1922 to call the special session, which did not begin until April. When Pueblo lawmakers were finally told of the session, they discovered that the nature of their mission was twofold: A Pueblo Flood Conservancy bill and a Moffat Tunnel bill. Shrewdly, Denver boosters had traded on Pueblo's misfortune, using the intervening months to gain their own ends. If the "Steel City" wanted flood insurance, the "Queen City" would guarantee its passage. But what a price Pueblo would pay!

The previously prepared design and estimated cost for the flood control project were presented to the legislature at the Capitol under sponsorship of State Senator W. O. Peterson. However, the primary opposition to Pueblo's plan came, not from Denver, but from competing groups in Pueblo, led by State Senator David W. Jones of that city. A public hearing on the Peterson bill included this amazing demand by Pueblo booster, former governor, and future New Deal Senator Alva B. Adams:

> We want flood protection and we want it quick, and it is through the original conservancy measure that we plan to get it. The majority of our residents in Pueblo, in fact the leading business men, as well as various clubs and civic organizations, are behind the movement to protect the lowlands of the city against floods down the Arkansas River. (*Rocky Mountain News*, April 21, 1922)

Thereafter, the full Senate voted down the Jones-sponsored bill and backed the original flood conservancy bill.

The package plan offered Pueblo by Denver quieted its opposition to the Moffat Road tunnel, but there was still stiff opposition from El Paso, Fremont and other southern Colorado counties. Lobbying was intense. Rio Grande, Burlington, Rock Island and Union Pacific—each wanting to purchase the weakened Moffat Road to get the tunnel—endorsed the bill on April 20. On April 22, the Senate voted 24 to four in favor of a flood conservancy district, and 22 to four for a tunnel improvement district. On final reading of the two bills, the ever-consistent Senator Jones was one of the two votes against the flood bill, but switched his previous "nay" on the tunnel bill to "yea." The flood control bill passed the House on April 26, with a representative from Rifle casting the only "nay" vote. Despite numerous attempts to amend the tunnel bill to death in the House, it passed with only minor modifications, with the Pueblo representatives voting for it.

Governor Shoup signed the two bills on April 29, 1922, with the comment, "No measures passed by any other legislative session mean as much, directly and indirectly, to the state as do these two bills." William G. Evans was quoted by the *Rocky Mountain News* on April 23 as stating:

> I believe the people of the state realize the vast importance of this tunnel. Not only does it mean the building up of a section of the state that is larger than half a dozen Eastern states, and of Denver, but it means an impetus to the entire state of Colorado and to the West.

This shows the position of the stranded 605 in relation to overturned 1001, each pictured on the prior two pages. By this time train No. 3's RPO had been rerailed. (CRRM collection)

The adjacent Santa Fe and Rio Grande bridges made a popular subject for those who recorded the aftermath of the flood. Notice that while the former did remain in place, the track and roadbed was washed away from both ends. (two photos, CRRM collection)

The force of the flood waters is evident in these two scenes. Photographer C. E. Rose found SLRX 2449 nosed into the drugstore at the corner of B Street and Victoria Avenue in front of Union Depot. St. Louis Refrigerator Car Co. was a subsidiary of Anheuser-Busch Brewing Company and had a fleet of 1500 such cars at the time. It is thus reasonable to assume that No. 2449 had been spotted at the D&RG freighthouse, located behind the photographer, for unloading a shipment of "near beer" in that prohibition year. On the track side of the depot *(below)*, an overturned baggage cart is in front of a jumble of debris jammed against heavily damaged D&RG business car B-5. (Denver Public Library Western History Department F9030 and F47770)

(above) The water removed a long string of D&RG wooden gondolas from their trucks, then rolled the trucks together in a compact row. It is interesting to observe that the wooden standard gauge cars are larger versions of their narrow gauge counterparts that served the railroad well into the 1960s. (below) At 9:40 on the morning after the flood the water had receded, and several officials have gathered on the platform to decide what to do next. (Denver Public Library Western History Department F47763 and F47762)

On the opposite page, two wrecking derricks are hard at work beginning the huge task of restoring the Pueblo yards to service. The Santa Fe bridge served as focal point for many photographs of the disaster. Missouri Pacific 500002 is manuevered into place by MP 3633, a circa 1884-87 Baldwin 2-6-0 half its size. At the right margin of the top photo on this page, a huge steam ditcher works at the end of a short spur. No. 3633 appears again, this time with a small flatcar-mounted ditcher and a pile driver restoring an MP bridge. (opposite center, Denver Public Library Western History Department F47768; others, CRRM collection)

The Lingering Effects

The law creating the Pueblo Conservancy District placed it under the jurisdiction of the District Court of Pueblo County. The court selected three Pueblo businessmen—Chairman Charles W. Lee, packing plant owner G. H. Nuckolls, and Pueblo Commercial Club President R. G. Breckenridge—as the first members of the board of the Pueblo Flood Conservancy Distrct. The law also called for a bond issue of $4,509,000 and allowed four years for the completion of the project. The first steam shovel started work on the project in March 1924. The whole project—relocation of the Arkansas River one-half mile south, construction of the Rock Canyon Barrier Dam and levees, and rebuilding of the rail yards and bridges—was completed in two years. A small flood in mid-1925 was handled by the still incomplete project without any damage to the city. Many of those living in Pueblo assumed, as did author Eilene Welch in her optimistically titled *Making Pueblo Safe from Floods*, that:

Making a large city forever safe from flood—following the greatest catastrophe in its history—and moving a river in the heart of the city without disturbing industry, is the big task that is being successfully carried out by the flood conservancy board of directors in Pueblo, Colorado.

However, the four million dollars spent on the project did not prevent the immediate displacement or abandonment of many businesses in Pueblo damaged by the flood.

One of the first was the American Smelting and Refining Company's plant, a major Colorado lead and silver smelter. This plant had been built in 1882 by Mather and Geist on a site directly adjacent to the Arkansas River and east of downtown. It was permanently closed by the flood, because the owners decided that the cost of rebuilding was prohibitive. After the flood, all Pueblo employees were laid off, and the ore intended for the plant was sent to ASARCO's Globe smelter in Denver or its Arkansas Valley smelter in Leadville.

The financial loss attributed to the flood also did not include that of the Stearns-Roger Manufacturing Company. One of the firm's first large projects had been design and construction of the Globe smelter in Denver, followed by other smelters in Pueblo, Leadville and Durango. Stearns-Roger also had designed and built one of the first sugarbeet factories

in the West in 1906. Its plant was located four miles north of downtown Pueblo along the west bank of Fountain Creek. Built in 1891, it was completely destroyed by the flood. Patterns floated downstream and were found as far away as Louisiana, while some of the heavy machinery was buried in quicksand and never recovered. Immediately after the flood, Thomas Stearns decided to move his entire company to Denver.

The Pueblo Union Depot & Railroad Company was organized to build and operate a passenger terminal for the Rio Grande, Santa Fe, Rock Island, Colorado & Southern and Missouri Pacific railroads. The imposing red sandstone building, which had opened in 1890, had ten feet of water and two feet of mud in the main waiting room after the 1921 flood. At one time, the depot had boasted of 55 passenger trains each day, but by the early 1920s this number was down to 45. In part because of railyard reconstruction after the flood, Rock Island withdrew its passenger and freight service from Pueblo, the first of many departures.

Other indications of Pueblo's economic decline after the flood include property valuations and railroad jobs during the 1920s. Figure 1 shows a comparison of total property valuations for the City of Pueblo and Pueblo County from 1920 to 1924. Figure 2 compares property valuations for Pueblo (city and county) to City and County of Denver during the same time period. In both graphs, the 63 percent drop in Pueblo valuation in 1921 reflected the impact of the flood. Neither Pueblo County nor Denver showed such a sharp drop in valuations. In addition, only three-fourths of this precipitous drop had been recovered by 1923.

In 1917, the *Colorado Business Directory* indicated that "there are 4,500 men employed by the railroads doing business in Pueblo, and the tonnage is the heaviest of any western city." By 1925, the *Pueblo City Directory* reported that "the railroads employ 2,200 living in Pueblo, and there is more freight tonnage in Pueblo than any city located between the Missouri River and the Pacific Coast." In this eight-year span, railroad employment in Pueblo apparently took a 51 percent drop, in part perhaps because of the displacement of much of the city's trackage by both the flood and the subsequent yard reconstruction during the rechanneling of the Arkansas River. The Roaring Twenties were anything but roaring in Pueblo!

Figure 1.

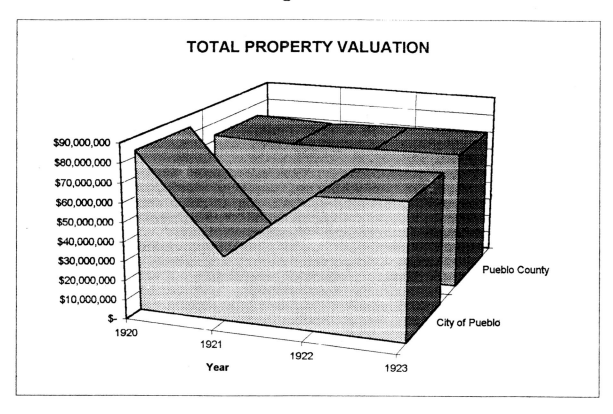

Figure 2.

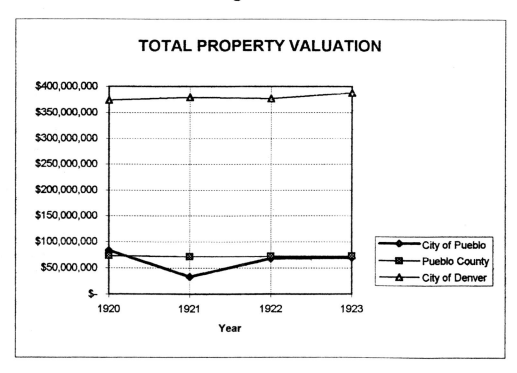

(data from *Colorado Yearbook, 1921*)

75 Years Later

The 75th anniversary of the Arkansas River flood of 1921 occurred in 1996. Most of those who witnessed the event are gone, and the terror, grief, and loss of homes and businesses are nearly forgotten. However, the long-term impact of Colorado's worst natural disaster remains in Pueblo and Denver even today.

What is Denver's status today? The Cherry Creek flood of 1935, and the South Platte flood of 1965 led to the construction dams needed to protect the city from its previously flood-prone streams. Denver is now protected from the ravages of its major drainages—Cherry Creek, Plum Creek, Bear Creek and the South Platte River—that began with the 1864 Cherry Creek flood.

By 1968 Stearns-Roger was the nation's fifth largest engineering company, and in 1975 it had a one billion dollar backlog of work. In 1985, the company's one hundredth anniversary, Stearns Catalytic had 6,000 employees, as many as Pueblo's largest employer, Colorado Fuel & Iron, had in 1920. In 1990, ASARCO's Globe smelter in Denver was still processing cadmium ore, although it was involved in a major action by the U.S. Environmental Protection Agency and the Colorado Department of Health to clean up surface soil contamination in the Globeville neighborhood.

The dreams of David Moffat and William Evans for a railroad main line through the Continental Divide directly west of Denver were realized with the opening of the Moffat Tunnel in 1928 and the completion of the Dotsero Cutoff in 1934. The Denver & Salt Lake Railway was absorbed into the Rio Grande in 1947. Forty years later Rio Grande itself was merged into Southern Pacific. The last tunnel bonds were paid off in 1982. Currently, the Moffat Tunnel Commission is under media fire as unnecessary and overly expensive. Regardless of the outcome of this conflict, the Moffat Tunnel line has been the route of Amtrak's *California Zephyr* passenger trains between Denver and Oakland since 1983. In addition, thousands of tons of low-sulphur coal and other freight travel over the route each day.

And 76 years after William G. Evans recommended that the Burlington take over the beleaguered Moffat Road, CB&Q successor Burlington Northern Santa Fe will begin using the Moffat Tunnel line. BNSF has been granted trackage rights as a condition of Union Pacific's takeover of Southern Pacific.

And what is Pueblo's status today? The bonds for the 1924 Flood Conservancy District project have been completely paid. With the exception of the replacement of the Rock Canyon barrier by Pueblo dam in 1975, the flood project continues to operate as designed. However, even after a ten million dollar flood that inundated 53 city blocks, 370 homes and 59 businesses in 1965, Pueblo is still without protection from flash flood waters raging southward along Fountain Creek!

All of Pueblo's smelters are long gone, and the steel plant has been through numerous "downsizings." Pueblo Union Depot has had no passenger service since 1971 and, although beautifully restored, is now serving as a retail and convention/banquet facility. Pueblo will no longer be on a transcontinental main line if the merged Union Pacific-Southern Pacific carries out its plan to close the Royal Gorge Route from Canon City to Dotsero.

Therefore, the economic cost of the 1921 flood to the people of Pueblo has been much greater than the combined ten million dollars in actual losses and four million cost for the Flood Conservancy District. Pueblo's temporary disaster has become permanent, and the city has been replaced by Denver as Colorado's dominant railroad and industrial center.

COMPLETE RESTORATION
of
TRAIN SERVICE
by way of
DENVER & RIO GRANDE
Effective Saturday, June 25th

BETWEEN   6-25-21

Denver, Colorado Springs, Pueblo, Trinidad, Canon City, The Royal Gorge, Salida, Buena Vista, Leadville, Glenwood Springs, Aspen, Grand Junction, Salt Lake City, Ogden, Gunnison, Montrose, Ouray, Telluride, Durango, Mesa Verde and Yellowstone National Parks; Also California and the Pacific Northwest.

NOTE—Trains 15 and 16 will not be operated between Pueblo and Grand Junction for a few days. All other train service normal.

Standard sleeper will be operated to Salida on Train No. 3, leaving Denver 3:55 p. m., to take care of passengers destined to points on the Marshall Pass-Gunnison line. Passengers may remain in sleeper at Salida.

Only 15 days after the flood, Santa Fe advertised the resumption of regular passenger service. Denver & Rio Grande followed one week later. Its notice illustrates the fact that Pueblo was the key rail point for access to almost all of Colorado west of the Front Range. (CRRM collection)

Bibliography

Athearn, Robert G., *Rebel of the Rockies, a History of the Denver and Rio Grande Western Railroad.* New Haven and London: Yale University Press, 1962.

Bollinger, Edward T. and Frederick Bauer, *The Moffat Road.* Denver: Sage Books, 1962.

Bryant, Keith L., Jr., *History of the Atchison, Topeka and Santa Fe Railway.* New York: Macmillan Publishing, 1974.

Bureau of Reclamation, *SEED Report on Pueblo Dam, Fryingpan-Arkansas Project, Colorado.* Denver: U.S. Department of Interior, Bureau of Reclamation, September 1985.

Cafky, Morris, *Colorado Midland.* Denver: Rocky Mountain Railroad Club, 1965.

Colorado State Business Directory. Denver: The Gazetteer Publishing and Printing Co., 1917.

The Denver Post, Denver, Colorado, June 4-6, 1921.

Dodds, Joanne West, *Pueblo, A Pictorial History.* Norfolk, Virginia: Donning Company, 1982.

Evans, Dannette, *Spotlight on Pueblo, Past and Present.* Lakewood, Colorado: Golden Press, 1952.

Follansbee, Robert and Edward E. Jones, *The Arkansas River Flood of June 3-5, 1921.* U.S. Geological Survey Water-Supply Paper 487, 1922.

Gratiot, Roger L., "A Medical History," St. Mary-Corwin Hospital *Pulse* (July 1980).

Hanington, C. H., "Smelting in Colorado," *The Colorado Magazine XXIII*, No. 2 (1946).

Lane, James M., Jr. *Proud Journey, The Story of Stearns-Roger: The first Ninety Years of Creative Service in Engineering, Construction and Manufacturing.* Denver: typewritten manuscript, 1976 (two volumes).

Le Massena, Robert A., *Rio Grande...To the Pacific.* Denver: Sundance, 1974.

LePak, Gregory, *Rails to the Rockies.* Littleton, Colorado: Alpine Publishing, 1976.

The London Times, June 6, 1921.

Macy, Guy E., "The Pueblo Flood of 1921," *The Colorado Magazine XVII*, No. 6 (1940).

McFarland, Edward M., *The Midland Route.* Boulder, Colorado: Pruett Publishing Company, 1980.

Martin, John A., *The Flood in Word and Picture.* Pueblo: R.C. Reeves, 1921.

Mitick, Ellsworth C. "A History of Mining Machinery Manufacture," *The Colorado Magazine XXV*, No. 2 (1948).

Morris, Ernest, "A Glimpse of Moffat Tunnel History," *The Colorado Magazine IV*, No. 2 (1927).

Parkers, Willis H., *Pueblo's Flood in Pictures and Story*. Pueblo: Dixon & Miller, 1921(?).

Pueblo City Directory, 1921. Colorado Springs: R.L. Polk Direct Co. of Colorado, 1921.

Pueblo City Directory, 1925. Colorado Springs: R.L. Polk Direct Co. of Colorado, 1925.

Pueblo Regional Planning Commission, *The Fountain River Flood Problem*. Pueblo Regional Planning Commission Comprehensive Plan, Technical Working Paper T-3, October 1965.

Pueblo Star-Journal, June 11 and 13, 1921.

Ridgway, Arthur, *The Case of Train No. 3*. Denver: Rocky Mountain Railroad Club, 1956.

Rocky Mountain News, Denver, Colorado, June 5-17, 1921, April 21-30, 1922, December 1, 1995.

Secretary of War, *Arkansas River and Its Tributaries*. 74th Congress, 1st Session, House Document No. 308, vol. 1, 1936.

Spearman, Frank H., *The Strategy of Great Railroads*. New York: Charles Scribner's Sons, 1904.

State of Colorado, *Colorado Yearbooks, 1921-1924 and 1931*. Denver: State Board of Immigration, 1921-1924 and 1931.

Stearns Catalytic, *Century of Excellence*. Denver: Stearns Catalytic World Corporation, 1985.

Stover, John F., *American Railroads*. Chicago: University of Chicago Press, 1961.

Taylor, Ralph C., *A Guide to Historic Pueblo*. Pueblo: Pueblo Metropolitan Museum, 1973.

Wagner, F. Hol, *The Colorado Road*. Denver: Intermountain Chapter, National Railway Historical Society, 1970.

Welch, Eilene, "Making Pueblo Safe from Floods," *The Santa Fe Magazine* (March 1925).

DENVER'S LIGHT RAIL LAUNCHED
by Robert W. Rynerson

After a 44-year absence, electric rail transit returned to the Mile High City in the fall of 1994. LRV 107 heads into the late afternoon sun as it leaves downtown along Stout Street.

Photography by
Bryan Bechtold

The geometry of gleaming steel and glowing copper wire returned that "big city" feeling to the Mile High City in a splashy October 7, 1994, grand opening of Regional Transportations District's first light rail line. Light rail transit, the modern child of street and interurban electric railways, was delivered on time and on budget to a populace split between enthusiastic riders and angry theorists. The opening followed two decades of studies and false starts.

Completion of the 5.3-mile starter line was the result of a chain of unlikely circumstances. Among these were: the earlier purchase of a section of Denver & Rio Grande Western main line right-of-way on speculation by RTD; passage of a state law designed to stall rail transit projects, which backfired and led to a new unity on the RTD board; a change of heart by earlier rail opponent and RTD board chairman Jack McCroskey, who came to realize that a small rail project could work as a demonstration of rail technology, without the need for bond vote on a huge system; and all the right people being in the right places at the right time.

The politics which had stopped development of rail transit in Denver over the previous two decades was still a factor after approval of the project. Driven by the knowledge that there were those who would have happily scrubbed the project at any point, even after it was built, the design and construction team oversaw completion of the entire project in 27 months from a July 6, 1992, start of construction. The rush was made easier by using a minimalist approach to "station" design; side effects were numerous minor changes in the system after its opening ceremonies. Deficiencies were cured as patrons pointed them out, a method which was either a clever way of avoiding "gold plating" with unneeded amenities or an indication of haste.

The completed line contains in essence many of the features of earlier systems in other cities, but adds some new touches. Most notably, Denver's line is the first new start to head in two directions at once from its central business district. Also of interest is the contraflow operation in the CBD, which was intended to reduce the number of accidents with motorists turning across the track. This decision proved to be a wise one, but it conflicts with traffic signal phasing. Motorists chose other locations for their collisions with light rail trains.

The northern segment of the line, which started life as part of the "MAC" (Metropolitan Area Connection) project, runs along the side of Welton Street. This line through the Five Points business district is operated with stiff speed restrictions due to station spacing, and pedestrian and auto conflicts. Thus, light rail trains run at speeds lower than parallel automobile traffic.

The conflicts are a result of a long string of compromises with neighborhood interests, compromises which have continued steadily since the line opened. Most recently and of greatest interest has been the addition of a stop at 27th Street. That corner, which has the best pedestrian access in the entire area due to its location at the namesake Five Points intersection, was preferred as a station in early plans. Community pressure against the parking and access conflicts that would result led to a decision to build two stations in the area, at 25th and 29th streets. These bracket the business district. Once the line opened, experience showed that this had been a mistake, and community groups successfully pressured RTD to open an additional station at 27th Street. Counting the northern terminal of the line, there are now four stations in a six-block stretch, closer to each other than many local bus stops. The new station at 27th Street opened on December 19, 1995.

This slow operation is even more critical because it is on single track from 24th to 29th streets. Single track construction is due to community desire to preserve storefront parking. The capacity of the line northeast of the central busines district is controlled by the time it takes trains to traverse the single track. This slow running has reduced the ability of the entire Central line to handle peak crowds and contributed to RTD's decision to order six more cars for delivery in 1996. As a temporary measure, ten express and regional peak hour bus routes were reinstated to downtown from the south terminal of the rail line, due to overcrowding on trains. Nevertheless, a rider out to enjoy a train ride or to obtain to-the-door access to a Five Points business will appreciate the stately passage of light rail cars up Welton.

Begin your first ride on Route 101-Central at *16th and California* streets. Most visitors to the city begin their rail trips at one of the 16th Street Mall stations (the southbound one is at Stout) where trains meet the free Mall shuttles. Rail-fans will find a choice of camera stores on opposite sides of the street here, and the line is photogenic (not scenic, but fascinating in details). Wait for a train displaying a "30th Avenue" destination sign. At various times of the day, alternate northbound trains turn back at 19th and California.

You must buy your ticket in advance from one of the excruciatingly slow Schlumberger fare machines. These were made by a worldwide company which won the Denver order through a court action. (If you buy two-ride or ten-ride tickets, these need to have a date/time stamp added by the adjacent validator prior to boarding for each trip.) The ticket is your proof-of-payment (POP) for fare inspections which are conducted randomly on board the trains. This fare system instead of pay-as-you-enter (PAYE), common in North American streetcar and bus systems since the disappearance of conductors, was imported from Europe by Canadians in 1980. It was introduced to the United States in San Diego the next year.

The Siemens-Duewag SD100 car approaches with little noise from the vehicle's motion but with bell ringing, lights flashing, and perhaps the horn sounding. This is to prevent pedestrian accidents. In spite of these measures, in the first six months of operation, one intoxicated pedestrian darted around the front of a light rail car to his death. Otherwise,

(left) On October 23, 1993, track work is well under way at the busy Kalamath and Speer crossings just south of the Stout Street bridge over Cherry Creek. *(below)* On the other side of downtown the tracks curve from the right on Welton around the 1999 Broadway building and down 19th Street, February 19, 1994.

This view looks southwest along Welton toward the curve shown on the previous page, and to the right is the double track curve at 29th and Downing, one block from the northern terminal.

pedestrians have proven to have more wisdom than have motorists.

Climb aboard the car, or if you are mobility-disabled, roll on via the mini-high station platform which leads to the first door on the car, immediately behind the operator. For passengers with boarding disabilities, the operator lowers a gangplank to the platform, providing an easy roll-on/roll-off arrangement without troublesome power-operated devices. Find one of the European-style facing seats or grab hold of a stanchion. The cars accelerate smoothly, with solid-state controls for their 750 DC motors eliminating controller notches. However, the fast acceleration can be surprising to riders used to conventional trains, and sudden deceleration can occur if a motorist attempts to take the right-of-way.

In the central business district, trains reach the speed of parallel traffic, but often must stop for intermediate traffic lights, since they do not have the ability to preempt signals.

At *18th and California* streets your train stops to pick up additional passengers in an area surrounded by high-rise office buildings and the Marriott Hotel. Then it proceeds to 19th Street, where routes are sorted out by the Vetag inductive signals transmitted from trains to a loop buried in the pavement between the rails. One setting sends trains to the left, and back to the south line; the other takes your train to the right, southeast on 19th Street.

From 19th Street, your train turns northeast onto Welton and stops at *20th and Welton*, then continues via the previously described stops along the southeast side of Welton to the *30th and Downing* station. There it meets four local bus routes and the skyRide service for Denver International Airport. The restaurants of Five Points, at any of the stations on the north segment, are good choices for a meal during a stopover.

On the return trip, trains pass through downtown on Stout

Car 101 was the first to arrive, on August 3, 1993, and has been spotted for unloading from Southern Pacific flatcar 620670. After clearance testing, it was returned to Siemens-Duewag for completion. *(below)* On August 24, it sits under wraps on a flatcar next to the "operations and maintenance facility," the bureaucratese translation of "car barn." The two operating tracks were ready for extension southward.

Street, making station stops at *18th, 16th* and *14th* streets. The most complex piece of rail/road traffic engineering on the line comes next, as trains cross heavily traveled Speer Boulevard with the assistance of carefully timed signals. Most of the time, all goes well, and your train will roll into the *Colfax at Auraria* higher education campus station without waiting for traffic. This is the south end of the original MAC project and the start of a whole different type of operation. Your train works its way along the southern edge of the campus before entering block-signaled private right-of-way, the east side of the former Rio Grande main line.

Reminiscent of a ride on an old time interurban line, your train rolls at 35 mph through a gated crossing at West 13th Avenue with its whistle blowing and then makes a station stop at *10th Avenue and Osage*, across from the historic Buckhorn Exchange restaurant (which has Colorado liquor license No. 1). The "wrong side of the tracks" here is the right side for railfans. Southern Pacific's integration with Denver & Rio Grande Western brought SP's major locomotive rebuild program to Burnham Shops. Cars of the Ski Train are often visible south of West 13th Avenue. At West 10th, a line of elderly or smashed-up diesels awaits the triage decision from the shop planners. In vintage railroad tradition, there is nothing explaining the great work that is going on here and which will continue after Union Pacific absorbs Southern Pacific. Thousands of riders each day get the impression that they are seeing a scrapyard.

From West 10th Avenue, your train races past RTD's Rail Division at 7th and Mariposa. Depending on the schedule, the car and the operator's experience, you then will experience a burst of 55 mph running up and over the Kalamath/Santa Fe Drive overpass. In clear weather, a 100-mile panorama of the Front Range of the Rocky Mountains appears.

The subsequent stops at *Alameda* (called South Denver on the railroad and near the site of a Santa Fe roundhouse prior to 1900) and at the *I-25 and Broadway* terminal seem anticlimatic. But these two stations provide the biggest share of the Central line's ridership. Alameda sees steady, all-day local bus activity, and I-25 and Broadway is the focal point of a big peak-hour interchange with express and regional buses. Its original 225-car park-n-ride lot has been expanded to hold 610 autos, and planning is underway to add 200 more spaces to the Alameda lot for relief. Unusual cooperation from Broadway Marketplace (between Alameda Station and Caboose Hobbies on Broadway) permits rail passengers to park free in the designated center of the shopping center's lot.

As ridership patterns emerged, February 1995 weekday trains carried about 13,000 passengers. "Normal" Saturdays accounted for about 9,800 passenger trips, and Sunday ridership was about 4,300. There are as many non-normal Saturdays as normal ones, due to the line's great access to the convention center and performing arts venues along 14th Street. Colorado Rockies baseball crowds can also fill the trains at any time of the week during the season, and numerous public festivals also add to the special event counts.

Service on the Central line continues to evolve. In addition to the 27th Street station, six more light rail vehicles were

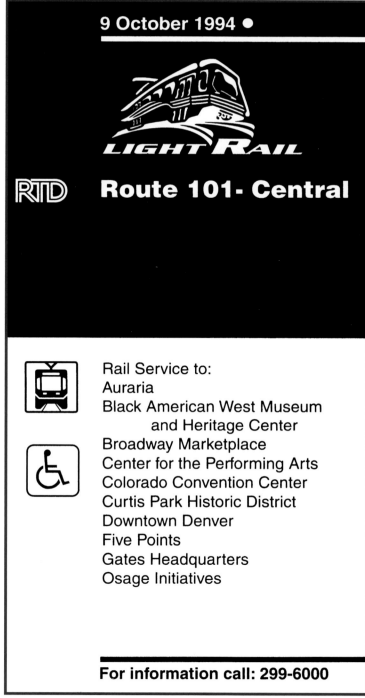

The original schedule was revised prior to the beginning of regular service on October 9. The dot following the date shows that this is the cover of the corrected version. Headways ranged from four minute rush hour to 15–20 minute base and 30-minute late-night service. A few revisions and adjustments have since been made. Operation is from 4:30 PM until 1:30 AM.

placed in service by summer of 1996. The political struggle to fund the next planned extension, southwest on the high-speed run to Mineral Avenue (south of Littleton) along the railroad main line, will continue. The projected line has

On June 18, 1994, the 107 is being pushed north along the southbound track at 24th and Welton, headed for display in the Five Points business district during the Juneteenth celebration. This had been only the second time that a car was on this portion of the line. After various experiments during the first winter of operation, a protective pilot which acts as combined "lifeguard," bumper and snowplow was added around the couplers at each end of the cars.

(left) The most unusual trip for any of the cars occurred prior to the start of regular service when 101 was towed along Southern Pacific track to Littleton for a public exhibit. That suburb's government has been a big proponent of extending light rail service south from the present end of the line. No. 101's destination sign appropriately reads "Special Service."

An historical granite marker commemorating the return of electric transit service to Denver was jointly sponsored by Colorado Railroad Museum, Denver Rail Heritage Society, Intermountain Chapter of National Railway Historical Society and Rocky Mountain Railroad Club. Retired Tramway veteran operators Leonard Lilly, Harry Ginsburg, Thomas Reeves and Walter Byers help RTD's Abe Martinez (who has Badge No. 1 on the Light Rail Division) unveil the marker, which is at the north end of the I-25/Broadway platform. This ceremony took place on September 17, 1994, at the start of a pre-opening fan trip with two three-car trains.

On Saturday and Sunday October 7 and 8, just before revenue service began, free public rides drew thousands of passengers and onlookers. Many lineside businesses, particularly in the Five Points neighborhood, were invited to participate in the festivities. Here car 106 crosses the 16th Street Mall on a northbound trip to 30th Avenue. The landmark Denver Dry Goods department store has been redeveloped into residences and retail shops, the first of many revived buildings along the route.

The 106 again, this time leading a two-car train with a standee load out of the I-25/Broadway transfer station on a short turn to 18th Street during the opening weekend.

received some federal funding to get the project rolling. This already has led to tens of thousands of additional dollars being spent on ridership counts. Although critics claim that RTD managers are making up ridership figures, new methods of counting always come up with roughly the same numbers. While angry commuters complained of being packed into trains, a "professional engineer" explained that trains were mainly carrying "curiosity riders" and that ridership "usually drops" on rail lines.

Time will determine the ultimate value and extent of the Mile High City's rail transit system. Right now, a ride on the line and visits to the attractions enroute is the best way to judge whether the initial project has been a success. Is it a useful part of the urban fabric? Does the replacement of hundreds of bus trips each day in the central business district make a difference in the flow of traffic? Are there fewer buses idling at the end of the lines in historic lower downtown? Did baseball fans use the Central line to force down season-opener prices charged by greedy parking lot operators? This writer has had the opportunity to see that the answer to each of these questions is "yes" and hopes that you will enjoy that opportunity as well.

(left) Operators have good sight lines from behind the large front cab windows of the SD100 cars. *(below)* Maintenance crews have kept car interiors clean and new-looking since service began. Although in these times all public transit vehicles suffer at the hands of the public, the light rail cars (but not the stations) seem to show less vandalism than the buses. This may be due to a combination of a public perception of rail as a quality service and the effort of RTD to maintain a good image for the system.

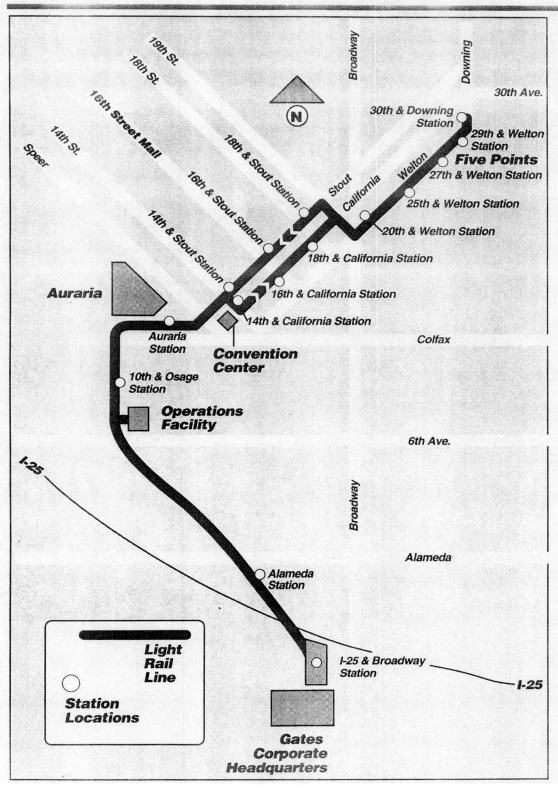

The different nature of each end of the Central light rail line can be seen from this Regional Transportation District schematic map. South of Auraria Station it is a high speed line on private right-of-way. North of Auraria it runs in designated street lanes.

Three-car trains rarely have been operated; the pre-opening railfan trip and the day of the 1996 Stanley Cup victory parade for the Colorado Avalanche hockey team were two such occasions. This test train proceeding away from the camera at 16th and California streets is over half a city block long.

(right) RT1, the Unimog road/rail truck guides car 107 around the curve at 19th and Stout during pre-startup clearance tests. This move is northbound on the southbound track. Except for his attire, the flagman is unchanged in purpose or sign from his railway predecessors of a century ago. (below) Two trains pass on the private right-of-way just south of the Colfax viaduct.

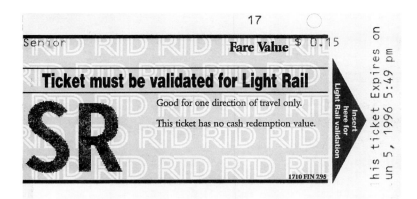

Numerous problems with the ticket machines occurred during the first week of revenue service with the immediate remedy being of benefit to riders, as evidenced by the sign at right. At the bottom of the page, car 101 heads a two-car train southwest along the single track of Welton Street during opening weekend activity in the Five Points business district. The operator has forgotten to change the destination sign from the northbound reading.

The proximity of the line to Southern (now Union) Pacific's Burnham Shops is evident in these scenes with a Rio Grande 1964 SW1200 and a Cotton Belt 1990-built GP60. Unfortunately, most commonly visible to thousands of daily riders is a long line of derelict and graffiti-smeared units awaiting sale for scrap or recycling through the locomotive rebuild program.

The opposed-to-traffic operating pattern is illustrated by a test train rounding the 19th and California turnback away from the camera and entering the track from 30th Avenue.

Colorado Rockies fans swarm aboard a two-car train at Alameda Station. Park-and-ride lots here and at I-25/Broadway have been greatly expanded since the line opened but are still full at many times. Two of the fare checking/security officers, who are contracted by a private company, are on the platform. *(below)* An inbound "train," as they are called by Denver riders, zips out of the Colfax/Auraria station past I-25-bound 105, in a night scene that should please any transit enthusiast. Students from the three campuses here use the line at all hours and many theater, opera and symphony patrons have found the service an ideal way to avoid parking congestion at Denver's Performing Arts Complex. There is time for refreshments or supper after the show, and late night trains have attracted regular riders.

LOOKING BACK: The Streetcar and Railroad Heritage of RTD's Light Rail Division

by Kenton Forrest

Denver Tramway 37 heads southeast on 11th Street at Stout after leaving downtown on the Kalamath route, February 22, 1946. This location is close to what is now the Colfax-Auraria light rail station. (R.A. Cordill photo, CRRM collection)

The construction of the new light rail line in Denver is another chapter in the public transportation story of the city. The route that it follows is very close to that of several early streetcar routes that were built before the turn of the century. This essay is a brief history of the transit routes that once were located on or near the new Regional Transportation District Light Rail Division, along with others still in operation as bus routes. Adjacent steam railroad lines also are described. Before the Denver Tramway Company was incorporated, there were various traction companies in Denver using in turn horse, steam, cable and electric equipment. Space here does not permit us to go into the complexities of their corporate histories. Even as this is being written, two large railroad mergers are occurring.

Current street names are used. The information for this history was obtained from manuscripts written by Don Robertson and Henry Couperus, and with assistance from E.J. Haley, Gene McKeever and Jim Jones.

TRANSIT ROUTES AND RAILROADS ALONG RTD'S LIGHT RAIL DIVISION

(Numbered routes are Denver Tramway lines)

Route 3   Englewood
Route 23   East 25th Avenue
Route 28   East 28th Avenue
Route 50   East 22nd Avenue-Kalamath Street
Route 62   Stout Street
Route 63   Lawrence Street
Route 64   East 34th Avenue
Route 66   Stockyards-Riverside
Route 72   Cherokee Street-Valverde
Denver Lakewood & Golden (Denver & Intermountain)
Denver Circle (Atchison Topeka & Santa Fe)
Denver & Rio Grande Western (Southern Pacific)
Colorado & Southern (Burlington Northern)

Route 3 Englewood

From downtown Denver to Alameda Avenue, this route along Broadway was a combination of horsecar and cable car tracks between 1874 and 1893. Electric operation began in 1889 from Alameda to Orchard Place (today's Englewood).

By 1900, the remainder of the route was also converted. On June 4, 1950, diesel buses took over until December 1, when electric trolley buses began. These were replaced by diesel buses again on May 26, 1955.

Route 23 East 25th Avenue

The Metropolitan Railway built this electric line from Central Loop up 15th Street to Tremont Place, then to Broadway, and via East 19th Avenue, Clarkson Street and East 25th Avenue to Humboldt Street. It opened on April 15, 1893, at a time when east Denver had car lines every few blocks. There was great competition among the early transit companies to carry people between residentail neighborhoods and downtown. Part of this line used sections of the East 19th Avenue line between Broadway and Clarkson Street. On April 1, 1903, route 23 was connected to the West 44th Avenue line via 16th Street instead of 15th Street. Part was discontinued

in 1907 when the line was rerouted from 16th Street to Welton, 26th Street and East 25th Avenue to York Street. New construction occurred on 26th Street and the extension to York. (In this area of the city *streets* and *avenues* with the same number intersect.) The Clarkson Street portion was then abandoned. The year 1910 saw the Argo line attached to the East 25th Avenue line, in place of the West 44th Avenue line. In the numbering of routes, this became route 25 but in 1917 was connected with West 23rd Avenue and became route 23. In the large route abandonments of 1930, the East 25th Avenue end was eliminated.

Route 28 East 28th Avenue

In 1874, the Denver City Railway constructed a horsecar line from downtown up 16th Street to Champa and northeast to 23rd Street, where it turned southeast running to Downing. Twenty-third Street became Park Avenue where it crossed East 20th Avenue. This was called the 23rd Street-Park Avenue line. In 1881, the cars were taken off Champa to reduce horsecar traffic on this street and moved to a new track onWelton. After 1884, when a new horsecar barn was built at 17th and Wynkoop streets, cars for the 23rd Street-Park Avenue line ran up 17th to Welton, where they turned northeast to 23rd Street, then out the original line to Downing. Two years later, the Park Avenue line was cut back to East 20th Avenue and jogged one block north to East 21st, then east to the new carbarn at Humboldt Street. When the Welton Street line was extended north to Downing, cars from both lines ran on Welton as far as 23rd Street. The Denver City Cable Railway took over operation on Welton Street in November 1889. This company had constructed a 36,850-foot cable line from West 41st Avenue and Tejon Street. The

cable ran south on Tejon to 16th Street, across the 16th Street viaduct to Welton, then northeast to 30th Street and Downing, east on East 28th Avenue to Gaylord and north to East 38th Avenue.

The Denver Tramway took over the line in 1899 and electrified it in March 1900. It then operated from Central Loop, on Arapahoe Street to 16th, Welton, 30th Street and East 28th Avenue to Josephine. The Gaylord Street portion of the line was abandoned at that time. In 1903 this route was combined with the Argo line in north Denver. In 1910 the route was again changed to East 28th Avenue-West 44th Avenue. A name change occurred on September 1, 1937, to route 44 Rocky Mountain Lake-East 28th Avenue. But on January 1, 1940, it reverted to route 28 East 28th-West 44th. On November 1, 1947, this was converted to electric trolley bus. On September 10, 1950, the West 44th Avenue portion became part of route 6 East 6th Avenue, and the remainder went to diesel bus route 28 East 28th Avenue-Berkeley.

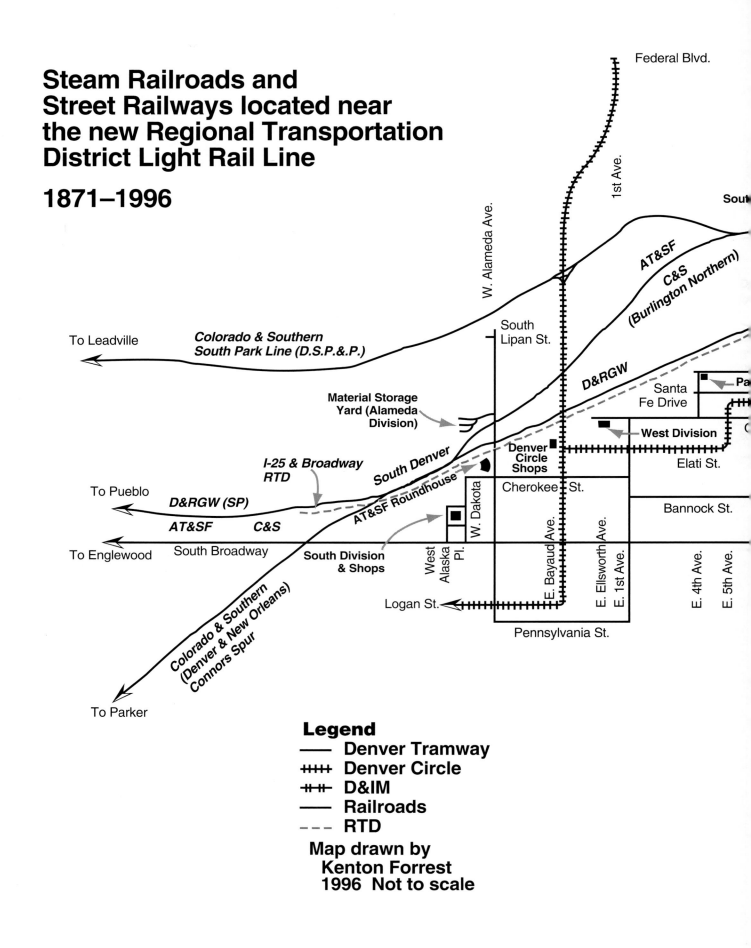

Steam Railroads and Street Railways located near the new Regional Transportation District Light Rail Line

1871–1996

Federal Blvd.

1st Ave.

W. Alameda Ave.

Sout

AT&SF

C&S
(Burlington Northern)

To Leadville

*Colorado & Southern
South Park Line (D.S.P.&.P.)*

South
Lipan St.

D&RGW

Santa
Fe Drive

Pa

Material Storage
Yard (Alameda
Division)

West Division

Denver
Circle
Shops

Elati St.

I-25 & Broadway
RTD

South Denver

Cherokee   St.

To Pueblo

D&RGW (SP)

AT&SF Roundhouse

W. Dakota

Bannock St.

AT&SF   **C&S**

South Division
& Shops

West
Alaska
Pl.

E. Bayaud Ave.

E. Ellsworth Ave.

E. 1st Ave.

E. 4th Ave.

E. 5th Ave.

To Englewood

South Broadway

Logan St.

Pennsylvania St.

*Colorado & Southern
(Denver & New Orleans)
Connors Spur*

To Parker

Legend
——	**Denver Tramway**
++++	**Denver Circle**
++-++	**D&IM**
——	**Railroads**
- - -	**RTD**

**Map drawn by
Kenton Forrest
1996 Not to scale**

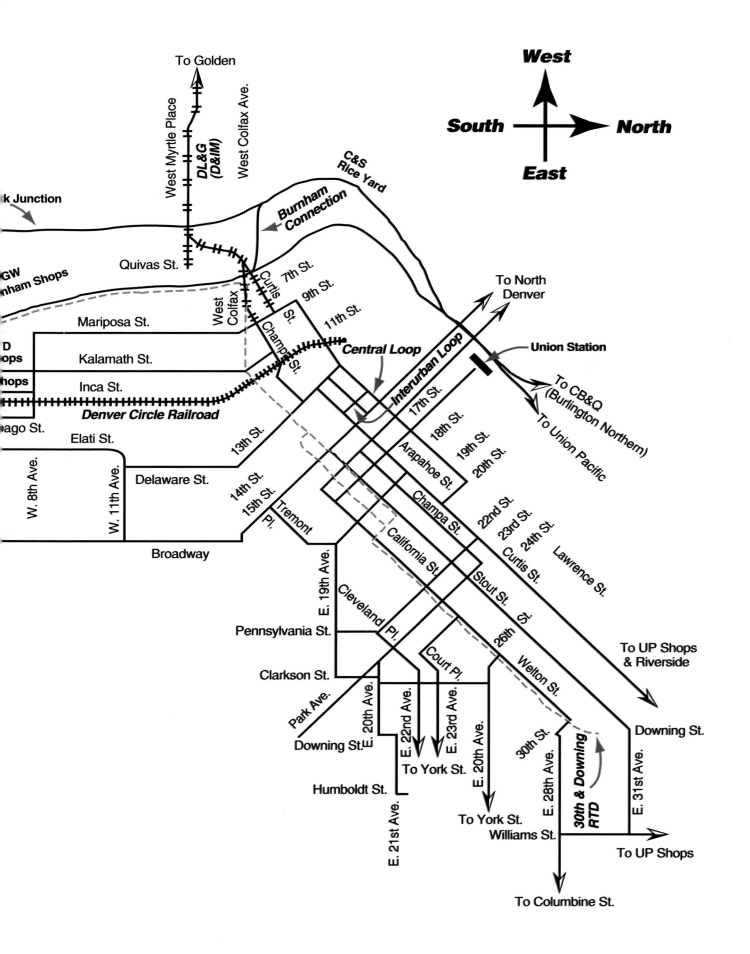

Car 362, heading northeast on Welton, is entering the intersection at 22nd Street on Sunday morning, July 6, 1947. Route 28 was converted to electric trolley buses six months later. (Bob Andrews photo, E.J. Haley collection)

Route 50 East 22nd Avenue - Kalamath Street

In 1885, the Denver City Railway Company built a horse-car line from Curtis and 17th streets to 11th Street to Kalamath, then south to West 8th Avenue, east to Santa Fe Drive and then south to West 4th. After August 1, 1889, the line was extended from West 8th Avenue along Kalamath to West 4th, with the Santa Fe Drive section being abandoned. This was a working class neighborhood, with many employed at the nearby Denver & Rio Grande Burnham Shops.

Cable cars replaced the horsecars on June 6, 1892, over the same route. A carbarn was constructed at West 4th and Kalamath. This later became the paint and construction shop for the Tramway. The building was torn down in April 1995. After the Denver Tramway purchased the Denver City Railway Company, the line was electrified on March 28, 1900. The downtown terminal was in front of Union Depot at 17th and Wynkoop. Cars ran up 17th to Curtis, then 13th Street to Champa, 11th Street and Kalamath to West 4th Avenue. In 1901 the downtown end was changed to Central Loop on

15th Street. The route was combined with the East 22nd Avenue line on April 30, 1903. With the introduction of route numbers in 1916, it was designated route 50.

The East 22nd Avenue end had been built by the Denver Tramway in 1890. The electric line opened on October 11th from 13th and Lawrence to 20th Street, Curtis, 22nd Street, Cleveland Place and East 22nd Avenue to York. Two years later the downtown end was moved to Central Loop. The line then ran up 15th Street to Curtis, 22nd Street and on to York. Somewhat parallel to this line was a short-lived horsecar route built by the Denver City Railway Company in 1881. It ran from downtown on Welton Street to 24th Street, Court Place and East 23rd Avenue to Humboldt. In 1888, it was extended to York Street but, with the electric line just one block away, was abandoned in June 1891. On December 4, 1914, the East 22nd Avenue line was routed from Curtis to 18th Street to Welton. Another minor change occurred on June 26, 1926, with the use of 17th Street instead of 18th.

Trolley bus overhead is already in place on January 22, 1946, as car 40 is heading toward downtown on Champa just south of Cherry Creek, one block downstream from the present light rail bridge. St. Elizabeth's Church remains a landmark of the Auraria campus. (R.A. Cordill photo, CRRM collection)

The Crest (left) and Astor hotels dominate the five-pointed intersection of East 20th Avenue, Broadway and Welton in this early 1900s scene. Automobile competition, including a sporty roadster at the curb, is already beginning to overwhelm the Denver Tramway car headed into downtown. (Rocky Mountain Photo Company, Denver Public Library Western History Department)

The date of this photo of the Tramway's South Water Street car house is not known. Located at what is now West Fourth Avenue and Kalamath Street, it was later converted to the system paint shop. (Intermountain Chapter, National Railway Historical Society collection)

155

A major change came on April 1, 1930, back to 18th Street, Glenarm Place and East 19th Avenue to Pennsylvania and East 22nd Avenue to York. This big adjustment was due to the discontinuance of route 39 19th Avenue, part of which was transfered to route 50. Part of route 64 also was abandoned on the same day, and the other end of route 50 was changed to include former route 64 track on Kalamath Street to West 8th Avenue, where it turned east to Galapago, to West 1st Avenue and Broadway.

The Cherry Creek flood of 1933 destroyed the Champa Street bridge, cutting the line in two. The East 22nd Avenue end continued as an electric streetcar route out of Central Loop, but the Kalamath Street end was changed to bus operation. This separation of route 50 lasted from August 4, 1933 until June 15, 1935, when a new Champa Street bridge was opened. The line was changed to electric trolley bus on May 12, 1946. Diesel buses took over on June 8, 1955.

Route 62 Stout Street

In 1890 the Denver Tramway built from the Lawrence Street line at 28th and Curtis streets to Stout and to Downing. Later the Metropolitan Railway (a subsidiary company of the Tramway) built on Stout from 13th to 28th streets to connect with this line. Operation began on January 1, 1892. Starting from the Central Loop, this line ran on 15th Street to Stout, to East 31st Avenue and Downing, east on 31st Avenue to Williams, then north to a loop at 40th Avenue. The loop was moved to 40th and High in 1921. In 1930 this line became part of route 64.

Route 63 South Water Street - Lawrence Street -East 34th Avenue

This Tramway route had a interesting beginning. The downtown section was hotly contested between the Denver City Railway and the Denver Tramway in the 1880s. Both companies wanted to build on Lawrence Street. The Tramway started first, but the Denver City Railway built an obstructing horsecar line, and the issue ended up in court. Later the Tramway wanted to build a cable line, but funds were not available.

During 1889 and 1890, a new electric line was built from the Broadway Station at Broadway and Alaska north on Broadway to Alameda, then east to Pennsylvania and north to 1st Ave. The route crossed Broadway to Galapago, then via West 8th Avenue, Mariposa, 9th Street, Lawrence, 20th Street, Curtis, Downing, East 34th Avenue, Franklin and East

40th Avenue to the Williams Street Loop, which was built in 1891 across from the Union Pacific Pullman Shops. This line was the first electric overhead streetcar line in the city of Denver. Operation began on June 3, 1890. That fall a new carhouse was built near West Ellsworth Avenue and Galapago Street. It was first called the South Water and later the West Division Carhouse.

With the 1916 numbering, this became route 63 Lawrence Street. Ten years later on May 6, 1926, the line was merged with route 64 Larimer Street. On April 1, 1930, the Mariposa Street end was abandoned, except on West 4th Avenue to Galapago Street, where a short connection was built on West 4th to the paint shop on Kalamath. The south portion of the line was combined with route 50.

Route 64 East 34th Avenue

This line originally operated on Curtis Street. Starting in 1903, it became the East 34th Avenue - Lawrence Street (see Mariposa portion of route 63). In a major route change on April 1, 1930, route 64 became East 34th Avenue. Starting from the Central Loop it ran up 15th to Stout, to Downing and East 34th Avenue to Cook. On September 4, 1949, it was converted to diesel bus service.

Car 31, displaying a dash advertisement for Ringling Brothers Barnum & Bailey, is about to turn from Stout Street down 15th to its Central Loop terminus in this late 1940s downtown street scene. Today, the two-story buildings have long been demolished, the Rio Grande headquarters building is the Rio Grande Lofts, the W. T. Grant store is also a loft building, the First National Bank Building is the Holtze Hotel and the U.S. National Bank Building yet another loft residential building. But Walgreen Drugstore is still in business! Redevelopment of these buildings has occurred since RTD's light rail line opened. (CRRM collection) Otto Perry recorded activity in front of Denver's main post office on September 3, 1949, the last day of streetcar service on route 64. The 18th Street light rail station is now in front of this imposing Colorado marble edifice, which has been converted into the Byron White Federal Courthouse. (*right*, Denver Public Library Western History Department OP-11420; *below*, E.J. Haley collection)

Route 66 Stout Street - Stockyards - Riverside

Beginning in 1892 this line ran from Central Loop, up 15th to Stout, East 31st Avenue, Williams, East 40th, Josephine, East 47th Avenue and west to the stockyards. It was extended to Riverside Cemetery in 1916, with limited service, and was discontinued on December 31, 1939.

Route 72 Valverde - Cherokee

The Cherokee line opened on April 1, 1909. From West Dakota Avenue and Bannock Street it ran west to Cherokee, then to West 1st Avenue and to Broadway. It continued via Broadway to Colfax, 15th Street, Curtis, 16th Street and Lawrence to 13th Street. On October 29, 1910, the route was changed to run from Bannock and Dakota via Broadway to downtown. The following year, a wye was built at Alameda and Cherokee, and cars started from that point. Later the route was rearranged to start at the Interurban Loop on Arapahoe Street and run via 13th Street to Delaware, 11th Avenue, Elati, West 6th Avenue, Bannock, West 1st Avenue and Cherokee to West Ellsworth. A branch also went to 1st Avenue and Broadway. In 1910, the line was extended to Cherokee and West Dakota.

On October 28, 1914, it was extended once more to Valverde via the Alameda subway (underpass) to just past South Lipan Street, near the location of the Colorado & Southern's South Park line. For a short time, Cherokee-Valverde shared track with the Myrtle Hill route from Central Loop to 11th Avenue and Delaware, where the latter turned east to Broadway and eventually to South University Boulevard and Mississippi Avenue. This line was abandoned in 1915. Valverde became route 72 the next year but was abandoned on September 30, 1929, beyond West 6th Avenue and Cherokee Street. A portion of the line became bus route 76 West Alameda. The remainder continued as route 72 Cherokee until June 3, 1950, when it became one of the last city routes converted to bus operation.

Car 152 is southbound on Bannock Street sometime between 1900 and 1909. Its destination sign reads "Pearl Street," since the Cherokee and Valverde routes were not established until 1909 and 1911 respectively. The track shown here had been built in 1891 as part of the South Tremont line of the Metropolitan Railway. The landmark brick smokestack of City Hospital still stands as part of Denver General Hospital. (Colorado Historical Society F-9815)

Having just crossed the South Platte River, Denver Tramway 365 is eastbound on West Alameda and is not far into its return trip downtown. Today's I-25 now crosses under this location. The canvas banner on No. 365's wooden safety guard advertises a play at the Tabor Grand Opera House at 16th and Curtis streets. (Charles S. Lillybridge photo, Colorado Historical Society W1986)

Denver Lakewood & Golden (Denver & Intermountain)

A suburban railroad from Denver to Golden via Lakewood was built in 1890. The Denver Lakewood & Golden Railroad started near the west bank of the South Platte River near 14th Street and went west up Dry Gulch toward Lakewood and Golden. Before electrification of the line in 1909, the company built the Gibson Street station near Decatur Street and West 14th Avenue. Here, steam trains arrived from and left for Golden, and passengers also transfered to the company's electric line to downtown. A separate electric line had been built across the South Platte River on West Myrtle Place to the Denver & Rio Grande tracks at Sixth and Curtis streets in late 1892. From there the line turned at Seventh Street to Colfax, then via Champa, to 13th Street, to Arapahoe and 15th Street. After Interurban Loop was built between 14th and 15th streets, the cars turned off 13th Street onto Curtis, entering the loop from the southeast. Later the Seventh Street portion was replaced by track on Ninth Street.

On an overcast day in the 1940s Denver & Intermountain car 25 proceeds down Ninth Street between Larimer and Champa along an unusual-for-Denver stretch of standard gauge street railway track. Elsewhere within the city standard gauge route 84 shared three-rail track with the 42-inch gauge Tramway system. Many of these houses are now part of the Ninth Street Historic District within the Auraria Campus. (CRRM collection)

Denver Tramway was narrow gauge (42 inches), but the Lakewood line was standard gauge, so there was dual gauge track from Champa Street to Interurban Loop. During 1914-1916, the West Colfax viaduct was built, and the line near the river was no longer used for passenger service. However, a jigger (shuttle) service was operated from Barnum Junction to Quivas Street until 1919. A short section of the line from Ninth and Curtis to Myrtle Place was abandoned after the viaduct was opened. The track on Myrtle Place to Quivas continued to function for interchange with the Denver & Rio Grande. The Denver Lakewood & Golden became the Denver & Intermountain Railway in 1904. D&IM operated route 84 Golden from Interurban Loop via Arapahoe, 13th Street, Champa, Ninth Street, Larimer, over the Colfax viaduct to Federal Boulevard, to Barnum Junction and on to Golden until June 3, 1950, when the line was converted to bus operation.

Denver Circle (Atchison Topeka & Santa Fe)

This narrow gauge steam line was started on January 16, 1882, on the south side of Cherry Creek at 13th and Curtis streets (later extended to Larimer). It was to be a commuter line to South Denver (then a separate community) and to the Mining Exposition grounds on South Broadway. It followed west side of Cherry Creek to Inca Street and then headed south to West 3rd Avenue, then to Elati Street and West Bayaud Avenue. There the line split, with one branch going west across the Denver & Rio Grande and Denver South Park & Pacific tracks to Federal Boulevard. The other branch went east to South Logan Street and continued on south to Evans Avenue.

Denver Circle shops and yard were located at West Bayaud Avenue and Fox Street. The entire line was abandoned in 1898. The Atchison Topeka & Santa Fe had purchased it on June 1, 1887, renamed it the Denver & Santa Fe Railway and built two branches on the south end in order to use the line as a right-of-way into Denver. This plan did not work, and Santa Fe reached Union Depot later in the same year via a different route. The AT&SF built a roundhouse at the corner of West Alameda and South Cherokee but was torn down before 1912.

Denver & Rio Grande's "Uncle Sam" commuter train is southbound out of Denver on its way to Littleton sometime in the first decade of the century. Tenwheeler No. 502, built by Baldwin in 1887, had originally been named *Pueblo*. By the time of this H. C. Edmiston photo it had been replaced on more important trains by newer and larger power. A small boy watches from the side of the track next to the switch engine. (Jackson C. Thode collection)

Denver & Rio Grande Western (Southern Pacific Lines)

Begun in 1871 as a narrow gauge line, the Denver & Rio Grande Railway started at 19th and Wynkoop streets near the Union Pacific yards. Narrow gauge was selected because of its low cost of construction. Over the next 125 years, the railroad chnged names and ownership, constructed a third rail for standard gauge, later removed the narrow gauge track, and changed motive power from steam to diesel. The original route from 19th and Wynkoop went in a southwesterly direction crossing Cherry Creek and turning south at Sixth Street toward Castle Rock and Colorado Springs.

Near West Ninth Avenue, a large shop named Machine Shop (later called Burnham, after a Baldwin Locomotive Company partner) was developed over the years to become the major repair center for the railroad. In the 1920s, the mainline tracks on the east side of the shop were moved to an easterly alignment to provide a gentle curve. The mainline remained in use until the early 1980s. Rio Grande trains were then routed via Santa Fe tracks to the west, also used by Burlington Northern, to reach a new route through the central Platte Valley. In 1989, the old right-of-way was sold to the Regional Transportation District for part of the first section of Denver's new light rail line. D&RGW had built a connecting track, called the Burnham connection, from its track at sixth Street and Curtis to the BNSF mainline so that trains did not have to backtrack to South Denver and then reverse direction to in order to reach North Yard at the other end of the city. This was due to the old mainline via Union Station being dismantled north of Sixth Street.

Passenger service along this route had been provided by such well-remembered trains as the *Colorado and New Mexico Express,* the *Colorado Eagle,* the *Scenic Limited* and its successor the *Royal Gorge,* which made its final run on July 27, 1967. There were also the "Uncle Sam" commuter trains to Englewood, Littleton and Fort Logan, starting in January 1889. These two-car locals made morning and evening roundtrips from Union Station. Burnham and South Denver were among the few regular stops for the trains. After World War I, Fort Logan was reduced in importance, and the little trains stopped running in April 1924.

In 1988, Denver & Rio Grande Western became part of Southern Pacific Lines. SP, in turn, was absorbed by Union Pacific in September 1996.

Almost 60 years after the picture on the opposite page, Rio Grande's *Royal Gorge* is on the same route as it begins its journey to Pueblo, Grand Junction and Salt Lake City. At the end of the train are through cars off the *Denver Zephyr* from Chicago that will be dropped at Colorado Springs. In 1994 Denver's light rail line began operating along the right of way seen here. (Otto C. Perry photo, Denver Public Library Western History Department OP-10918)

These three right-of-way views were taken prior to construction of the light rail line south of Colfax. The above looks north from West 13th Avenue along the old D&RGW main line in December 1988 (author); next are the West Third Avenue and Kalamath crossing tower, now beneath the long RTD elevated structure, in February 1972 (Tivis E. Wilkins, CRRM collection) and another 1988 view looking south from West Bayaud Avenue (author).

The Charles S. Lillybridge photographs above and to the right show construction of the West Alameda Avenue subway, or underpass, about 1912. The first looks north across the three-track Rio Grande bridge, the two righthand girders of which support RTD tracks over eight decades later. Looking west along Alameda, the Colorado & Southern bridge (today used by Burlington Northern Santa Fe) is beyond the D&RG structure. In the foreground, girders have not yet been placed for the AT&SF bridge. This also still exists, although the tracks have been removed. (Colorado Historical Society W1696 and W1150)

The 1988 photo below looks north from where RTD's Alameda Station now stands. (author)

Colorado & Southern
(Burlington Northern Santa Fe)

The Colorado & Southern Railway traced its route back to the Denver & New Orleans Railroad (which never even got close to the Crescent City). In 1881, the line started near Union Depot and proceeded southwest through the land now occupied by Elitch's Amusement Park. It then turned south, crossing the Denver South Park & Pacific at South Park Junction, and headed southeast to cross the Denver & Rio Grande at a new junction called South Denver. From there it continued southeasterly to Parker and Elizabeth, then on to Colorado Springs and Pueblo. D&NO went into Jay Gould's empire as a part of the Union Pacific Denver & Gulf in 1890. Eight years later the newly formed Colorado & Southern purchased UPD&G at a foreclosure sale. C&S soon began running its through trains via AT&SF trackage rights between South Denver and Pueblo. The former D&NO became a branch line and was abandoned in 1936 beyond Connors, a beet dump in the vicinity of what is today East Evans Avenue and South Holly Street. The last switching on a remnant of Connors Spur took place on November 2, 1993. Track was shortly removed to allow for light rail construction near I-25 and Broadway.

The Denver South Park & Pacific Railroad, begun in 1874, followed the D&RG to Larimer Street, from which point it wandered west to Tejon Street and headed south. From South Park Junction, the line crossed the South Platte River and continued toward Platte Canyon and eventually Leadville and Gunnison. DSP&P also became part of the Gould empire and, in 1899, the Colorado & Southern Railway. The Chicago Burlington & Quincy Railroad bought a controlling interest in the C&S in 1908. It was finally merged into Burlington Northern in 1982. BN became Burlington Northern Santa Fe in a 1995 merger with AT&SF.

Regional Transportation District
Light Rail

RTD's new line runs along former rail rights-of-way and through areas served by some of the early lines of the Denver Tramway, built a century ago. Along Welton from 28th Avenue to 19th Street and on Stout from 19th to 15th streets, it follows parts of Tramway routes 28(abandoned in 1947) and 64(abandoned in 1949). Both Welton Street and the old Rio Grande mainline have been important transportation corridors since the days of horsecars and narrow gauge steam locomotives.

This aerial view looking northwest across South Broadway, with the South Platte River to the left, was taken about 1950. (1) is South Broadway, (2) is Colorado & Southern's Connors Spur next to which the Valley Highway (I-25) was built in the mid-1950s, (3) is Denver Tramway's South Division yard and shops behind the large white Montgomery Ward Building, (4) is the AT&SF/D&RGW South Denver interlocking just to the right of which RTD's Alameda Station is now located, and (5) is the present location of the I-25/Broadway light rail/bus transfer station. (Otto Roach photo, Denver Public Library Western History Department F37633)

THE ORIGIN OF THE STEAM LOCOMOTIVE
by Matthew R. Young

Foreword

The Colorado Railroad Museum is particularly pleased to present this treatise on the birth of the steam locomotive, as the article serves as an important reminder to us all about the actual origin of the steam railway locomotive, especially when other books and articles often make major errors in that area. More importantly, however, this article was written by Matthew R. Young for a class on the history of England which he was taking at the University of Colorado in Boulder while he was also a part-time employee of the Colorado Railroad Museum. We are especially proud of the fact that Matt, who had no real interest in railroad history before he came to work at the museum, was not only motivated to write such an interesting and factual paper on the invention of the steam locomotive but also was able to locate all of the necessary research materials and sources right here in the library of the Colorado Railroad Museum. By publishing his fine article we are reminding our readers about the beginning of railroads and at the same time pointing out the tremendous assets of our library, which boasts one of the finest collections of historical railroad books and materials in the United States. We are very much indebted to Matt Young for sharing his excellent paper with us.

Ronald C. Hill, CRRM Trustee

Today the railways of England carry more freight and people than any other means of mass transportation. Considering the modern and efficient railways which now exist in England, it is difficult to imagine the humble beginnings of the steam locomotive, which originated in England. The steam locomotive helped bring the industrial revolution into "full steam." It made coal much more available for the English people who needed that valuable commodity to run their factories and to heat their homes. Eventually, it gave them something they had needed for quite some time: a reliable source of mass transportation. The steam locomotive tremendously fostered the growth of English industry as well as making England an extremely productive country in the 19th century.

The steam engine itself was probably invented in France by Denis Papin around 1690, but the initiative soon moved to England where men such as Thomas Savery (who patented a simple steam pump in 1698) and Thomas Newcomen with John Calley (who jointly made a steam engine for use in the coal mines in 1712) made remarkable progress. However, it was not until 1769 that James Watt patented the first practical steam engine, which was intended for use in mines, sawmills, rolling mills and looms. It is necessary to realize that these primitive engines were only for stationary use such as powering machinery. One very important use of the Watt engine was for pumping water out of the Cornish coal mines, where it first came to the attention of Richard Trevithick. But the joinder of steam with the wheel still remained to be accomplished.

The first efforts to combine steam with the wheel resulted in self-propelled wagons or carriages intended for use on the common roads. In 1769, Frenchman Nicholas Cugnot built a crude wagon powered by a steam engine, while soon afterward William Murdock in England used a Watt engine for the same purpose. But such lumbering monstrosities were not practical, and development of them soon stopped.

No one knows who actually invented the idea of a railway as such, but the first example of a "railway" in England consisted of rails made of smooth-trimmed tree trunks (rails) fastened to much shorter sections at right angles (ties). Wagons were pulled over these rails by horses; although the immediate problem was keeping the wagon on the rails. That was solved when the English devised a system of using a plain wheel on flanged rail, which was formed by L-shaped iron plates held in place by stones. Such a system resulted in a rough but workable railway so long as the loads were not too heavy. Obviously, a horse could only pull one wagon on a road, but that same horse could pull several wagons over rails. Thus, the railway was born.

As already observed, Richard Trevithick, a brilliant engineer from Cornwall, first came in contact with Watt's steam engine in a Cornish coal mine. He became a well-known designer and builder of dependable high-pressure pumping engines. It was Trevithick's development of a lighter, high-pressure steam engine which actually made the locomotive possible. James Watt, whose engine was far too large and heavy to be adapted to the locomotive, remained bitterly opposed to the high-pressure Trevithick design. When Trevithick conceived of the idea of combining the steam engine with a railway wagon, he became the undisputed father of the steam locomotive. In 1803 he constructed an advanced steam carriage which was exhibited in London where it attracted wide attention. Early the following year, he competed his first steam locomotive which he named *Pen-y-darran*. It had a "return flue" boiler, which meant that the cylindrical boiler contained a single large u-shaped firetube. The firebox was at one end of this tube, while the chimney was at the other end so that the firebox door was directly beside the chimney. In the tube above the firebox was a lead plug which would melt if the water in the boiler dropped dangerously low, a simple safety device which was used in most steam locomotives thereafter. A single cylinder was recessed horizontally into the boiler above the firebox door, and the cylinder drove the wheels by means of a crosshead, twin connecting rods and a train of gears. The crankshaft, which was mounted at the opposite end of the boiler, carried a huge flywheel. Trevithick already appreciated the fact that the friction between a smooth wheel and a smooth rail would be sufficient for propulsion, as his first locomotive had smooth, flangeless wheels for running over the flanged iron plateway.

Interestingly, his ideas were rushed to completion because of a wager between Samuel Homfray, the South Wales Ironmaster, and Anthony Hill of the Plymouth ironworks. Homfray bet 500 guineas that Trevithick's pioneer locomotive could haul a load of ten tons of iron on the existing "plateway" from *Pen-y-darran* (the town after which Trevithick's locomotive was named) to Abercynon Basin, a distance of almost ten miles. That auspicious trial took place on February 21, 1804, and the load consisted of ten tons of iron loaded in five wagons with 70 men riding on them. The monumental journey required four hours and five minutes, which included stops to cut down obstructing trees and remove some large rocks from the track. But the trial was a resounding success, and Homfray won his bet. Unfortunately, the locomotive proved too heavy for the track, as a large number of rails in the plateway were smashed by the weight of the locomotive. Soon after, *Pen-y-darran* suffered the ignominious fate of being converted into a stationary engine.

The following year Trevithick participated in the construction of a similar locomotive for the Wylam Colliery at Gateshead. Although it was demonstrated successfully on a short temporary track, the company refused to accept it because it was too heavy for the existing plateway. That engine was taken off its wheels and used to power bellows in the foundry.

Undaunted, Trevithick soon built another locomotive, *Catch-me-who-can*, which he demonstrated successfully in 1808 on an enclosed circular track in London. He later offered to race that locomotive against any horse which might be produced at the October, 1808, race-meeting at Newmarket, but there were no takers.

Unfortunately, in addition to being an engineer and the inventor of the steam locomotive, Richard Trevithick had other aspirations. His construction of locomotives after *Catch-me-who-can* became uninspired and sporadic. Following the locomotive, he mainly focused on other steam tools, such as drills, dredges and marine engines.

Puffing Billy was the next locomotive to come about. The man behind this one was William Hedley, who was the superintendent of a coal mine near Newcastle-on-Tyne. *Puffing Billy* was constructed in 1813 and, according to author Henry B. Comstock, ". . . triggered such a rash of locomotive building that within 16 years some 50 engines were tossing smoke, cinders and loose particles about the English countryside."

However, Hedley had nothing to do with these other locomotives: *Puffing Billy* merely inspired their production. It was left to George Stephenson to launch the first passenger railway operated with a steam locomotive: the Stockton and Darlington in 1825.

The steam locomotive established England as the most productive and advanced country in the world. The advent of this great machine was a significant milestone in the industrial progress of mankind. The locomotive has helped and is still helping further industrial progress around the world today. However, in the 19th century England was the country to benefit the most from this revolutionary machine. Extensive mining railways were constructed in South Wales and Northeastern England where coal mines were booming. Those mines produced the majority of English coal. They were also the most directly responsible for the further development of the steam locomotive, since the mines were the chief places of use of locomotives. They hauled the iron and coal to factories to be refined or converted into energy for the production of goods and materials. Such factories were the driving force of England's early dominance of the world market for manufactured products.

(County Museum, Truro - CRRM collection)